# Praise for S. M. Stirling

## *Dies the Fire*

"*Dies the Fire* kept me reading till five in the morning so I could finish at one great gulp. It's an alarmingly large speculation: How would we fare if we suddenly had the past 250 years and more of technological progress taken away from us? No more electricity. No more internal-combustion engines. No more gunpowder or other explosives. All gone, vanished in the blink of an eye. . . . Don't miss it."  —Harry Turtledove

"Gritty, realistic, apocalyptic, yet a grim hopefulness pervades it like a fog of light. The characters are multidimensional, unusual, and so very human. Buy *Dies the Fire*. Sell your house, sell your soul, get the book. You won't be sorry."
—John Ringo, author of *Into the Looking Glass*

"By ringing a clever change on his *Island in the Sea of Time*, S. M. Stirling gives himself a broad canvas on which to display his talent for action, extrapolation, and depiction of the brutal realities of life in the absence of civilized norms."
—David Drake, author of *The Far Side of the Stars*

"A stunning speculative vision of a near-future bereft of modern conveniences but filled with human hope and determination. Highly recommended."  —*Library Journal*

"The Willamette Valley of Oregon and the wilds of Idaho are depicted with loving care, each swale and tree rendered sharply. The smell of burning cities, the aftermath of carnage, the odor and sweat of horses—Stirling grounds his action in these realities with the skill of a Poul Anderson. . . . Postapocalypse novels often veer either too heavily into romantic Robinsoniads or nihilistic dead ends. But Stirling has struck the perfect balance between grit and glory."
—*Science Fiction Weekly*

"Stirling shows that while our technology influences the means by which we live, it is the myths we believe in that determine how we live. The novel's dual themes—myth and technology—should appeal to both fantasy and hard SF readers as well as to technothriller fans." —*Publishers Weekly*

"Fans of apocalyptical thrillers like Stephen King's *The Stand* will find *Dies the Fire* absolutely riveting . . . a fantastic epic work."  —*Midwest Book Review*

*continued . . .*

P9-DNL-905

"*Dies the Fire* has all the attributes of a good old tale—interesting characters, a good plot, conflict and resolution—and leaves the reader with a desire to know more. There are battles, romances, heroes, and heroines. As with the tales of old, there are lessons we can interpret with meaning to our own lives. The story gives an insight into how heroes and legends come into being. . . . In some ways, reading *Dies the Fire* is like finding out what the Witches from *The Mists of Avalon* might be like all these years later. . . . I'd recommend *Dies the Fire* for anyone who likes a good tale."

—Kate West, author of *The Real Witches'* series

"The character development is excellent. . . . I found myself devouring every page as quickly as I could. I enjoyed the thrill of a world in which so many things we take for granted are gone. . . . For fans of 'what if,' this is a must read." —SFRevu

"A fine novel that moves rapidly along and keeps you hooked until the wee hours." —Bewildering Stories

## Conquistador

"In this luscious alternative universe, sidekicks quote the Lone Ranger and Right inevitably triumphs with panache. What more could adventure-loving readers ask for?"

—*Publishers Weekly*

"A novel of complex landscapes, both moral and geographical."

—*Locus*

"Even more of a romp than Stirling's *The Peshawar Lancers*. . . . Its action scenes are state-of-the-art and its femmes wonderfully *formidables*." —*Booklist*

"The moral landscapes of this novel are intriguing, and the sight of an undeveloped West Coast is unforgettable."

—Science Fiction Weekly

## The Peshawar Lancers

"A wonderfully evocative adventure, told by an absolute master."

—Mike Resnick, award-winning author of *Soothsayer*

"[An] alternate-historical homage to a host of classic swashbucklers . . . includes the author's usual splendidly detailed world building, compelling characters, and breakneck pacing, with state-of-the-art action scenes. Nearly irresistible."

—Roland J. Green, author of *Voyage to Eneh*

"Exciting."                                    —*The Santa Fe New Mexican*

"Complex and bloodthirsty . . . superlatively drawn action scenes and breakneck pacing . . . an irresistible read."
                                               —*Booklist*

"A remarkable alternate history. Stirling's impeccable research infuses both plot and characters with depth and verisimilitude, creating a tale of high adventure, romance, and intrigue."
                                               —*Library Journal*

## Island in the Sea of Time

"A perfectly splendid story . . . endlessly fascinating . . . solidly convincing."                          —Poul Anderson

"A compelling cast of characters . . . a fine job of conveying both a sense of loss and hope."    —*Science Fiction Chronicle*

"Quite a good book . . . definitely a winner."
                                               —*Aboriginal Science Fiction*

"Utterly engaging. This is unquestionably Steve Stirling's best work to date, a page-turner that is certain to win the author legions of new readers and fans."
              —George R. R. Martin, author of *A Feast for Crows*

## Against the Tide of Years

"Fully lives up to the promises made in *Island in the Sea of Time.* It feels amazingly—often frighteningly—real. The research is impeccable, the writing excellent, the characters very strong. I can't wait to find out what happens next."
                                               —Harry Turtledove

"*Against the Tide of Years* confirms what readers of the first book already knew: S. M. Stirling is writing some of the best straight-ahead science fiction the genre has ever seen."
                                               —*Amazing*

## On the Oceans of Eternity

"Readers of this book's predecessors . . . will find the same strong characterizations, high historical scholarship, superior narrative technique, excellent battle scenes, and awareness of social and economic as well as technological factors in evidence again."                          —*Booklist*

## Other Books by S. M. Stirling

# DIES THE FIRE

## S. M. STIRLING

RoC

A ROC BOOK

ROC
Published by New American Library, a division of
Penguin Group (USA) Inc., 375 Hudson Street,
New York, New York 10014, USA
Penguin Group (Canada), 90 Eglinton Avenue East, Suit 700, Toronto,
Ontario M4P 2Y3, Canada (a division of Pearson Penguin Canada Inc.)
Penguin Books Ltd., 80 Strand, London WC2R 0RL, England
Penguin Ireland, 25 St. Stephen's Green, Dublin 2,
Ireland (a division of Penguin Books Ltd.)
Penguin Group (Australia), 250 Camberwell Road, Camberwell, Victoria 3124,
Australia (a division of Pearson Australia Group Pty. Ltd.)
Penguin Books India Pvt. Ltd., 11 Community Centre, Panchsheel Park,
New Delhi - 110 017, India
Penguin Group (NZ), cnr Airborne and Rosedale Roads, Albany,
Auckland 1310, New Zealand (a division of Pearson New Zealand Ltd.)
Penguin Books (South Africa) (Pty.) Ltd., 24 Sturdee Avenue,
Rosebank, Johannesburg 2196, South Africa

Penguin Books Ltd., Registered Offices:
80 Strand, London WC2R 0RL, England

Published by Roc, an imprint of New American Library, a division of Penguin
Group (USA) Inc. Previously published in a Roc hardcover edition.

First Roc Mass Market Printing, September 2005
10   9   8   7   6   5   4   3   2

**ROC** REGISTERED TRADEMARK—MARCA REGISTRADA

Printed in the United States of America

To Gina Taconi-Moore, and to her Andrew, currently serving the great Republic in a far-off, sandy, unpleasant place. Long life and happiness!

## Acknowledgments

Thanks to Nick Pollotta, for a neat idea; to Dana Porter of Outdoorsman, Santa Fe, for advice on cutlery and survival; to Stephen Stuebner (author of *Cool North Wind* and many wonderful books on Idaho) for his works and advice; to the folks at Saluki Bows; to Kassai Lajos, whose *Horseback Archery* is a fascinating chronicle of his reconstructions of ancient and medieval horse archery, which were invaluable; to Melinda Snodgrass, Walter Jon Williams, Emily Mah, Yvonne Coates, Daniel Abrams, Terry England, Janet Stirling and George RR Martin of Critical Mass for their analysis and criticism; to Charles de Lint for advice on music and some cracklin' good tunes; to Parris McBride for help with the Wiccan religion and the loan of helpful material; to Kiers Salmon for help with Wicca and also for going all around Oregon doing research for me; to Robin Wood, for still more help with Wicca; and to Alison Brooks for inventing the phrase "Alien Space Bats," which I stole.

Special thanks to Heather Alexander, bard and balladeer, for permission to use the lyrics from her beautiful songs "The Star of May Morning," "John Barleycorn," "The Witch of the Westmoreland," "Dance in the Circle," and "Ladyes Bring Your Flowers Fair," which can be—and should be!—ordered at www.heatherlands.com. Run, do not walk, to do so.

Far-called our navies melt away
On dune and headland sinks the fire;
Lo, all our pomp of yesterday
Is one with Nineveh and Tyre!

—Rudyard Kipling, "Recessional"

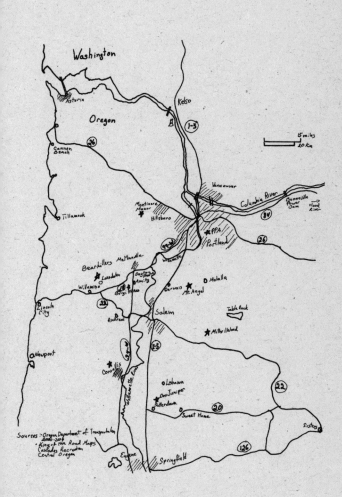

Washington

Astoria

Oregon

Kelso

B

I-5

26

Cannon
Beach

Vancouver

Columbia River

Montessor
Manor

Bonneville
Power
Dam

Hood
River

Hillsboro

PPA

84

Tillamook

Portland

26

Bearkillers

McMinnville

Lonsdale

Willamina

Dayton

Amity

Gervais

Mt. Angel

Molalla

Orez, Trans

Willamette

Table Rock

22

Lincoln
City

Salem

Richrod

Mill Hollow

99W

I-5

Newport

Corvallis

Lebanon

22

Ann Juniper

Sutterdown

20

Sweet Home

Sisters

Sources: Oregon Department of Transportation
2005-2006
* King of the Road Maps
Cascades Recreation
Central Oregon

Eugene

126

Springfield

15 miles
20 km

# CHAPTER ONE

Michael Havel pulled his battered four-by-four into the employees' parking lot, locked up and swung his just-in-case gear out of the back, the strap of the pack over one shoulder and the gun case on the other. It was a raw early-spring Idaho afternoon, with the temperature in the low fifties; the light had a cool, bleakly clear quality, as if you could cut yourself on the blue of the sky.

He walked quickly across to the door marked "Steelhead Air Taxi" and opened it with three fingers and an elbow, whistling a Kevin Welch tune under his breath. Inside he set the gear down on a couple of chairs—the all-up weight was nearly eighty pounds—and opened his heavy sheepskin jacket, stuffing his knit cap into one pocket.

That left his black hair ruffled the way it always did, and he smoothed it down with the palms of both hands. The air here smelled a bit of burned fuel and oil, which couldn't be helped around an airport.

"You said the bossman had something for me, Mellie?" he asked the secretary as he went to the pot on the table in the corner and poured himself a cup.

The coffee was Steelhead Air Taxi standard: oily, bitter and burnt, with iridescent patches of God-knew-what floating on the surface. He poured half-and-half in with a lavish hand until it looked pale brown. This was an informal outfit, family-run: Dan and Gerta Fogarty had flown themselves until a few years ago; there was Mellie Jones, who was Gerta's aunt; and six pilots, one Mike Havel being the youngest at twenty-eight, and the most recent hire.

"Yup," the white-haired woman behind the desk said. "Wants you to hop some passengers to a ranch field in the Bitterroot Valley, north of Victor. The Larssons, they're visiting their holiday place."

Havel's eyebrows went up; it was a damned odd time of year to be taking a vacation *there*. Tail end of the season for winter sports, but still plenty cold, and the weather would be lousy. Then he shrugged; if the client wanted to go, it was the firm's job to take him. Steelhead Air did a little of everything: flying tourists, fishermen and whitewater rafters into wilderness areas in summer, taking supplies to isolated ranchers in the winter with skis on the planes instead of wheels, whatever came to hand. There was a *lot* of unroaded territory around this neck of the woods. He glanced at the wall clock. It wasn't long to sunset; call it six forty-five, this time of year. Two hundred forty ground miles to the Montana border, a little more to wherever the Larssons had their country place, call it two, three hours . . .

"They've got landing lights?" he said.

Mellie snorted. "Would Dan be sending you if they didn't?"

He looked over her shoulder at the screen as he sipped the foul sour coffee, reading off the names: Kenneth Larsson, his wife, Mary, son and daughter Eric and Signe, both eighteen, and another named Astrid four years younger.

"Larsson . . . Larsson . . . from Portland, businessman?" he said. "Heard the bossman mention the name once, I think."

Mellie made an affirmative sound as she worked on her PC.

"Old money, timber and wheat—then Ken Larsson tripled it in high tech. Used to hire us regular, back before 'ninety-six, but not lately. Hasn't brought the family before."

Havel nodded again; he'd only been flying for Steelhead since the spring of '97. It was nice to know that Dan trusted him; but then, he was damned good if he said so himself, which he didn't. Not aloud, anyway.

He went through into the office. Dan Fogarty was sitting and chatting with the clients while Gerta worked behind piles of paper on the desk. There were wilderness posters and models of old bush planes and books on Idaho and the Northwest on shelves. And a faint meowing . . .

*That* was unusual.

The Larssons' youngest had a cat carrier on her lap; the beast's bulging yellow eyes shone through the bars, radiating despair and outrage. It wasn't taking the trip well; cats seldom did, being little furry Republicans with an inbuilt aversion to change. Judging from an ammonia waft, it was—literally—pissed off.

The kid was unusual as well, all huge silver-blue eyes and long white-blond hair, dressed in some sort of medieval-looking suede leather outfit, her nose in a book—an illustrated Tolkien with a tooled-leather cover. She had an honest-to-God *bow* in a case leaning against her chair, and a quiver of arrows.

She kept her face turned to the print, ignoring him. He'd been raised to consider that sort of behavior rude, but then, she was probably used to ignoring the chauffeur, and his family hadn't had many employees.

Havel grinned at the thought. His dad had worked the Iron Range mines from the day he got back from Vietnam and got over a case of shrapnel acne picked up at Khe Sanh; *his* father had done the same after getting back from a tour of Pacific beauty spots like Iwo Jima, in 1945; *his* father had done the Belleau Wood Tour de France in 1918 before settling down to feed the steel mills; and *his* father had gone straight into the mines after arriving from Finland in 1895. When the mines weren't hiring, the Havel men cut timber and worked the little farm the family had acquired around the turn of the century and did any sort of honest labor that fell their way.

Kenneth Larsson matched the grin and stood, extending a hand. It was soft but strong; the man behind it was in his fifties, which made him twice Mike Havel's age; graying blond ponytail, shoulders still massive but the beer gut straining at his expensive leather jacket, square ruddy face smiling.

"Ken Larsson," he said.

"Pleased to meet you, Mr. Larsson. Havel's the name—Mike Havel."

"Sorry to drag you out so late in the day; Dan tells me you were on vacation."

Havel shrugged. "It's no trouble. I wouldn't be bush-flying out of Boise for a living if I didn't like it."

That brought a chuckle. *You can see he's the type who likes to smile,* Havel thought. *But he hasn't been doing a lot of it just lately, and that one's a fake.*

"Midwest?" Larsson said shrewdly. That was a lot to pick up from a few words. "Minnesota? Got some Svenska in there? We're Swedes ourselves, on my side of the family."

*Not much of a surprise, with a moniker like that,* Havel thought. Aloud he went on: "Not too far off, both times. Michigan—Upper Peninsula, the Iron Range. Finn, mostly, on my father's side. Lot of Swede in Mom's father's family—and her mother was Ojibwa, so I'm one-quarter."

He ran a hand over his jet-black hair. "Purebred American mongrel!"

"Havel's an odd name for a Finn," Larsson said. "Czech, isn't it?"

"Yeah. When my great-grandfather got to the Iron Range about a hundred years ago, the mine's Bohunk pay-clerk heard 'Myllyharju' and said right then and there: 'From now on, your name is Havel!' "

That got a real laugh; Signe Larsson looked charming when she smiled.

"My wife, Mary," Larsson went on, and did the introductions.

*Her* handshake was brief and dry. Mary Larsson was about forty, champagne-colored hair probably still natural, so slim she was almost gaunt. She had the same wide-eyed look as her younger daughter, except that it came across as less like an elf and more like an overbred collie, and *her* voice was pure Back Bay Boston, so achingly genteel that she didn't unclench her teeth even for the vowels.

*That accent reminds me of Captain Stoddard,* Havel thought; the New Englander had led his Force Recon unit across the Iraqi berm back in '91. *He had that thin build, too.*

The son and eldest daughter were twins; both blue-eyed with yellow-blond hair, tall—the boy was already his father's six-two, which put him three inches up on Michael Havel, and built like a running back. Eighteen, the same age as Mike had been when he'd left the Upper Peninsula for the Corps, but looking younger, and vaguely discontented. His sister . . .

*Down boy!* Havel thought. *Jesus, though, I envy those hip-hugger jeans.*

An inch or three below his own five-eleven, short straight nose, dusting of freckles, and . . .

*Jesus what a figure . . . twenty-eight isn't that old. . . .*

"Mike's one of my best," Dan said.

"Glad to hear it," Larsson senior said.

Everyone bustled around, signing forms and collecting coats. Havel helped with the baggage—there wasn't all that much—buttoning his coat but glad to be out in the clean chill. Then he did a walk-around of the Piper Chieftain. The ground crew was good, but *they* weren't going to be taking a twin-engine puddle jumper over the biggest wilderness in the lower forty-eight.

Larsson's eyebrows went up when Mike loaded his own baggage; a waterproof oblong of high-impact synthetics with straps that made it a backpack too, and the unmistakable shape of a rifle case.

"Something I should know about?" he said.

"Nope, Mr. Larsson," Mike said. "Just routine; I'm a cautious man."

Larsson nodded. "What's the gun?"

"Remington 700," he said. That was a civilianized version of the Marine sniper rifle. "I used its first cousin in the Corps, and it makes a good deer rifle, too."

Signe Larsson sniffed and turned away ostentatiously; possibly because he was an ex-Marine, or a hunter.

*Oh, well,* he thought. *I'm dropping them off in a couple of hours, anyway.*

Eric Larsson grinned at his sister with brotherly maliciousness. "Hey, maybe he could shoot you a tofu-lope, sis, now you're back on the vegetarian wagon. Nothing like a rare tofu-lope steak, charred outside and all white and bleeding goo on the inside—"

She snorted and climbed the rear-mounted stairs into the Chieftain.

Havel admired the view that presented, waited for everyone else to get in, and followed. He made discreetly sure that everyone was buckled up—it was amazing how many people thought money could buy them exemption from the laws of nature. Then he slid into his own position at the controls and put the headphones on, while he went through the checklist and cleared things with the tower and got his mind around the flight plan.

That had the bonus effect of keeping out the Larssons' bickering, which was quiet but had an undertone like knives. It died away a little as the two piston engines roared; he taxied out and hit the throttles. There was the usual heavy feeling at the first surge of acceleration, and the ground fell away below. His feet and hands moved on the pedals and yoke; Boise spread out below him, mostly on the north side of the river and mostly hidden in trees, except for the dome of the state capitol and the scattering of tall buildings downtown.

Suburbs stretched northwest for a ways, and there was farmland to the west and south, a checkerboard between irrigation canals and ditches that glinted in quick flashes of brilliance as they threw back the setting sun.

He turned the Chieftain's nose northeast. The ground humped itself up in billowing curves, rising a couple of thousand feet in a few minutes. Then it was as if they were flying over a mouth—a tiger's mouth, reaching for the sky with serrated fangs of saw-toothed granite. Steep ridges, one after another, rising to the great white peaks of the Bitterroots on the northeastern horizon, turned ruddy pink with sunset.

Some snow still lay on the crests below and under the shade of the dense forest that covered the slopes—Douglas fir, hemlock, western cedar—great trees two hundred feet tall and spiky green. Further north and they passed the Salmon River, then the Selway, tortuous shapes far below in graven clefts that rivaled the Grand Canyon. A thousand tributaries wound through steep gorges, the beginnings of snowmelt sending them brawling and tossing around boulders; a few quiet stretches were flat and glittering with ice. The updrafts kept the air rough, and he read the turbulence through hands and feet and body as it fed back through the controls.

Larsson stuck his head through into the pilot's area.

"Mind if I come up?"

The big man wormed his way forward and collapsed into the copilot's seat.

"Pretty country," he said, waving ahead and down.

*Pretty but savage,* Havel thought.

He liked that; one of the perks of this job was that he got to go out in it himself, hunting or fishing or just backpacking . . . and you could get some of the hairiest hang gliding on earth here.

"None prettier," the pilot replied aloud.

*Poor bastard,* Havel thought to himself. *Good-looking wife, three healthy kids, big house in Portland, vineyard in the Eola Hills, ranch up in Montana—he knows he should be happy and can't quite figure out why he isn't anymore.*

He concealed any offensive stranger's sympathy, and switched the other set of headphones to a commercial station.

"Damnedest thing!" the big man said after a while, his face animated again.

"Yes?" Havel said.

"Odd news from back East," Larsson said. "Some sort of electrical storm off Cape Cod—not just lightning, a great big dome of lights over Nantucket, half a dozen different colors. The weather people say they've never seen anything like it."

Mary Larsson brightened up; she was Massachusetts-born herself.

"That *is* strange," she said. "We used to summer on Nantucket when I was a girl—"

Mike Havel grinned to himself and filtered out her running reminiscences and Larsson's occasional attempts to get a bit in edgewise; instead he turned to the news channel himself. The story had gotten her out of her mood, which would make the trip a lot less tense. Behind her the three Larsson children were rolling their eyes but keeping silent, which was a relief.

The voice of the on-the-spot reporter cruising over Nantucket Sound started to range up from awestruck to hysterical.

*They're really sounding sort of worried, there,* he thought. *I wonder what's going—*

White light flashed, stronger than lightning, lances of pain into his eyes, like red-hot spikes of ice. Havel tasted acid at the back of his throat as he jerked up his hands with a strangled shout. Vision vanished in a universe of shattered light, then returned. Returned without even afterimages, as if something had been switched off with a click. The pain was gone too, instantly.

Voices screamed behind him. He could hear them well . . .

*Because the engines are out*, he realized. *Every fucking thing is out! She's* dead. *And I'm a smear on a mountain unless I get this thing flying again.*

That brought complete calm.

"Shut up!" he snapped, working the yoke and pedals, seizing control from the threatening dive and spin. "Keep quiet and let me work!"

Sound died to somebody's low whimper and the cat's muted yowls of terror. Over that he could hear the cloven air whistling by. They had six thousand feet above ground level, and the surface below was as unforgiving as any on earth. He gave a quick glance to either side, but the ridgetops nearby were impossible, far too steep and none of them bare of trees. It was a good thing he knew where all the controls were, because the cabin lights were dead, and the nav lights too; not a single circuit working.

*Not good,* he thought. *Not good. Not . . . fucking . . . good.*

He ran through the starting procedure, one step and another and *hit* the button . . .

*Nothing,* he cursed silently, as he went through the emergency restart three times and got three identical meaningless *click* sounds.

*The engines are fucked. What the hell could knock everything out like this? What was that white flash?*

It could have been an EMP, an electromagnetic pulse; that would account for all the electrical systems being out. He sincerely hoped not, because about the only way to produce an EMP that powerful was to set off a nuke in the upper atmosphere.

The props were spinning as they feathered automatically. She still responded to the yoke—*Thank God!*—but even the instrument panel was mostly inert, everything electrical gone. The artificial horizon and altimeter were old-fashioned hydraulics and still working, and that was about it. The radio was completely dead, not even a flip of static as he worked the switches.

With a full load, the Chieftain wasn't a very good glider. They could clear the ridge ahead comfortably, but probably not the one beyond—they got higher as you went northeast. Better to put her down in this valley, with a little reserve of height to play around with.

"All right," he said, loud but calm as the plane silently floated over rocks and spots where the long straw-brown stems of last year's grass poked out through the snow.

"Listen. The engines are out and I can't restart them. I'm taking us down. The only flat surface down there is water. I'm going to pancake her on the creek at the bottom of the valley. It'll be rough, so pull your straps tight and then duck and put your heads in your arms. You, kid"—Eric Larsson was in the last seat, near the rear exit—"when we stop, get that door open and get out. Make for the shore; it's a narrow stream. Everyone else follow him. *Fast.* Now shut up."

He banked the plane, sideslipping to lose altitude. *Christ Jesus, it's dark down there.*

There was still a little light up higher, but below the crest line he had to strain his eyes to catch the course of the water. The looming walls on either side were at forty-five degrees or better, it would have been like flying inside a closet with the light out if the valley hadn't pointed east-west, and the creek was rushing water over rocks fringed with dirty ice.

*Thank God the moon's up.*

He strained his eyes . . . yes, a slightly flatter, calmer section. It ended in a boulder about the size of the mobile home he lived in, water foaming white on both sides.

*So I'll just have to stop short of that.*

In. In. Sinking into night, shadow reaching up. Gliding, the valley walls rearing higher on either hand, trees reaching out like hands out of darkness to grasp the Piper and throw it into a burning wreck. *Lightly, lightly, bleed off speed with the flaps but don't let her stall, keep control . . .*

Then he was nearly down, moving with shocking speed over the churning riffled surface silvered by moonlight. *Here goes.*

"Brace for impact!" he shouted, and pulled the nose up at the last instant, straining at the control yoke. They were past the white-water section; it should be deeper here.

"Come on, you bitch, *do* it!"

The tail struck, with a jolt that snapped his teeth together like the world's biggest mule giving him a kick in the ass. Then the belly of the Chieftain pancaked down on the water and they were sliding forward in a huge rooster tail of spray, scrubbing speed off in friction. And shaking like a car with no shocks on a *real* bad road as they hit lumps of floating ice. Another chorus of screams and shouts came from the passengers, but he ignored them in the diamond clarity of concentration.

*Too fast,* he thought.

The boulder at the end of the flat stretch was rearing up ahead of him like God's flyswatter. He snarled at death as it rushed towards him and stamped on the left rudder pedal with all his strength and twisted at the yoke—the ailerons would be in the water and should work to turn the plane. If he could—

The plane swiveled, then struck something hard below the surface. That caught the airframe for an instant, and inertia punched them all forward before the aluminum skin tore free with a scream of rending metal.

Then they were pinwheeling, spinning across the water like a top in a fog of droplets and shaved ice as they slowed. Another groan from the frame, and he shouted as an impact wrenched at them again, brutally hard. Loose gear flew across the cabin like fists. Things battered him, sharp and gouging, and his body was rattled back and forth in the belt like a dried pea in a can, nothing to see, only a sense of confused rushing speed. . . .

Then the plane was down by the nose and water was rilling in around his feet, shocking him with the cold. They were sinking *fast,* and there was almost no light now, just a gray gloaming far above.

With a gurgling rush the ice water swept over the airplane's cockpit windows.

# CHAPTER TWO

> *"On a bright Beltane morning*
> *I rise from my sleep*
> *And softly go walking*
> *Where the dark is yet deep*
> *And the tall eastern mountain*
> *With its stretch to the sky*
> *Casts a luminous shadow*
> *Where my true love doth lie—"*

Juniper Mackenzie dropped her guitar at the intolerable white spike of pain driving into her eyes, but she managed to get a foot underneath it before it hit the floor. Shouts of alarm gave way to groans of disappointment from the crowd in the Hopping Toad as the lights and amplifier stayed off.

*Whoa!* she thought. *Goddess Mother-of-All! That* hurt!

But it was gone quickly too, just the memory and no lingering ache. There was a flashlight in her guitar case; she reached in and fumbled for it, searching by touch in complete blackness, with only a fading gray gloaming towards the front of the café—the sun was just down behind the Coast Range. The batteries were fresh, but nothing happened when she thumbed the switch except a click, more felt through her thumb than heard.

*Wait a minute. There's nothing coming in the front windows from the streetlights! And they went on five minutes ago. It's as dark as a yard up a hog's butt.*

She could hear a tinkling crash, and shouts, faint with distance. *This isn't a blown fuse.* Plus every dog in Corvallis was howling, from the sound of it.

"Well, people, it must be a power failure," she said, her trained singer's voice carrying through the hubbub and helping quiet it. "And in a second, our good host, Dennis, will—"

The flick of a lighter and then candlelight broke through the darkness, looking almost painfully bright. The Toad was a long rectangle, with the musicians' dais at the rear, the bar along one side and a little anteroom at the front, where a plate-glass window gave on to Monroe Avenue. The evening outside was overcast, damp and mildly chilly; which in the Willamette Valley meant it could have been October, or Christmas.

With the streetlights out, the whole town of Corvallis, Oregon, must be dark as the proverbial porker's lower intestine. There were more crashes, a few more shouts, and more sounds of bending metal and tinkling glass, and the chorus of howls gave way to ragged barking.

Dennis at the bar was a friend of hers; he got her drinks for free, not to mention gigs like this now and then. Wearily she cursed her luck; it was a pretty good crowd for a weekday, too; mostly students from OSU, with some leftover hippies as well—most of the valley towns had some, though Corvallis wasn't swarming with them the way Eugene was—and they'd all given a good hand to the first two tunes.

She'd been on a roll, hitting the songs the way they were meant. *And* if this power-out hadn't happened, she'd have made a decent night's take for doing the thing she liked best in all the world. There were already a scattering of bills in the open guitar case at her feet for gravy.

More candles came out, and people put them in the wrought-iron holders along the scrubbed brick walls—ornamental usually, but perfectly functional, hand-made by Dennis's elder brother, John, who was a blacksmith, and even more of a leftover hippie than Dennis was. In a few minutes, the tavern was lit brightly enough that you could have read, if you didn't mind eyestrain.

The waxy scent of the candles cut through the usual patchouli-and-cooking odors of the Toad; the stoves were all gas, so food kept coming out. Juniper shrugged and grinned to herself.

"Well, you don't have to see all that well to listen," she called out. "It's the same with music as with drink: *Sé leigheas na póite ól aris.* The cure is more of the same!"

That got a laugh; she switched to her fiddle and gave them a Kevin Burke tune in six-eight time, one of the ones that had enchanted her with this music back in her early days. The jig set feet tapping and the *craic* flowing; when she'd finished she got out her seven-string and swung into her own version of "Gypsy Rover." The audience started joining in the choruses, which was always a good sign.

Maybe being in a mild emergency together gave them more fellow-feeling. Some people were leaving, though . . . and then most of them came back, looking baffled and frustrated.

"Hey, my car won't start!" one said, just as she'd finished her set. "There's a couple of cars stopped in the road, too."

Off in the distance came an enormous *whump* sound not quite like anything she'd ever heard. Half a second later the ground shook, like a mild compressed earthquake, or standing next to someone when they dropped an anvil. A shiver went through her heart, like the snapping of a thread.

"What the hell was *that*?" someone shouted.

"Looks like a big fire just started downtown, but there aren't any sirens!"

The hubbub started again, people milling around; then two young men in fleece vests came in. They were helping along an older guy; he had an arm over each shoulder, and his face was streaming with blood.

*"Whoa!"* she said, jumping down from the dais. "Hey there! Let me through—I know some first aid."

By the time she got there Dennis had the kit out and the two students had the injured man sitting down in one of the use-polished wooden chairs. One of the waitresses brought a bowl of water and a towel, and she used it to mop away the blood.

It looked worse than it was; head wounds always bled badly, and this was a simple pressure-cut over the forehead, heading a ways back up into the scalp. The man was awake enough to wince and try to pull away as she dabbed disinfectant ointment on the cut and did what she could with bandages. Dennis put a candle in her hand; she held it in front of one of the man's eyes, and then the other.

*Maybe the left is a little less responsive than the right,* she thought.

The man blinked, but he seemed to be at least minimally aware of where he was. "Thanks," he said, his voice slurred. "I was driving fine, and then there was this flash and my car *stopped*. Well, the engine did, and then I hit a streetlamp—"

"I think this guy needs to get to a hospital," she said. "He might have a concussion, and he probably ought to have a couple of stitches."

Dennis looked sad at the best of times; he was a decade and change older than her, in his late forties, and going bald on top with a ponytail behind. As if to compensate he had a bushy soup-strainer mustache and muttonchops in gray-streaked brown, and big, mournful, russet brown eyes.

He always reminded her of the Walrus in *Alice,* even more so given his pear-shaped body, big fat-over-muscle arms and shoulders and an impressive gut. Now he turned his great hands palm-up.

"Phone's out," he said. "Shit, Juney, *everything's* out."

Juniper swallowed. "Hey!" she called. "Has *anyone* got a working car? A motorbike? Hell, a bike?"

That got her some yeses; it was a safe bet, right on the edge of a university campus. "Then would you get over to the clinic and get someone to come?"

Another student went out, a girl this time. Juniper looked around at a tug on her arm. It was Eilir, her daughter— she'd be fourteen next week, scrawny right now to her mother's slimness. She had the same long, straight-featured face and the same pale freckled skin, but the promise of more height, and hair black as a raven's wing. Her eyes were bright green, wide now as her fingers flew.

Juniper had been using Sign since the doctors in the maternity ward told her Eilir would never hear; by now it was as natural as English.

*I saw a plane crash, Mom,* Eilir signed. *A big plane; a 747, I think. It came down this side of the river—right downtown.*

*Are you sure?* Juniper replied. *It's awful dark.*

*I saw bits of it after it hit,* the girl signed. *There's a fire, a really big fire.*

Dennis Martin knew Sign almost as well as Juniper did—mother and daughter had been through regularly for years, when Juniper could get a gig like this, and for the RenFaire and the Fall Festival. She knew he had a serious thing for her, but he'd never been anything but nice about its not being mutual; he was even polite to her boyfriend-cum-High Priest, Rudy, and he really liked Eilir.

Now their eyes met.

*I don't like the sound of this at all,* Dennis signed. *Let's go look.*

Juniper did, with a sinking feeling like the beginnings of nausea. If there was a fire raging in downtown Corvallis, where were the sirens? It wasn't a very big town, no more than fifty thousand or so.

The brick building that held the Hopping Toad was three stories, a restored Victorian like most of the little city's core, built more than a century ago when the town prospered on shipping produce down the Willamette to Portland.

They went up a series of narrow stairs until they were in the attic loft Dennis used for his hobbies, woodworking and tooling leather. Amid the smell of glue and hide and shavings they crowded over to the dormer window; that pointed south, and the other side of Montrose was Oregon State University campus, mostly grass and trees.

The two adults crowded into the narrow window seat; Dennis snatched up a pair of his binoculars that Eilir had left there. After a moment he began to swear; she took the glasses away from him and then began to swear too. There *was* a fire over towards downtown, a big one, flames towering into the sky higher than any of the intervening buildings. It was extremely visible because there wasn't a streetlight on, and hardly any lit windows, or a moving car.

She could see the distinctive nose of a 747 silhouetted against the flames, pointing skyward as if the plane had hit, broken its back, and then skidded into something that canted the front section into the air. She could even see the AA logo painted on its side.

"*Lady Mother-of-All!*" Juniper whispered, her finger tracing a pentagram in the air before her.

The fire was getting worse, the light ruddy on her face. She knew she ought to be running out there and trying to help, but the sight paralyzed her. It didn't seem *real*, but it was; a jumbo jet had plowed right into the center of this little university town in the middle of the Willamette Valley.

"Looks like it came down on the other side of Central Park," he said, holding out a hand for the glasses.

"Sweet Goddess, it looks like it came down around Monroe and Fourth!" she replied, drawing a map in her head. They looked at each other, appalled: that was right in the middle of downtown.

*I hope the Squirrel and the Peacock didn't get hit,* she found herself thinking, absurdly—both nightspots booked a lot of live music. Then she shook her head angrily.

"There must be hundreds hurt," she said. *Hundreds dead, more like,* her mind insisted on telling her. She swallowed, and added silently to herself: *Horned Lord of Death and Resurrection, guide the dying to the Summerlands. Merciful Lady, preserver of life, keep the living safe. So mote it be!*

Aloud she went on: "And where are the emergency people?"

"Trying to get their ambulances and fire trucks to work," Dennis said; there was a grim tone to his voice she'd seldom heard before. "Check your watch."

Juniper blinked, but did as he asked, pulling it out of her vest pocket where it waited at the end of a polished chain of fine gold links. She was wearing a sort of pseudo-Irish-cum-Highlander costume—billowy-sleeved peasant shirt and lace cravat and fawn-colored waistcoat with a long tartan skirt below and buckled shoes—what she thought of privately as her Gael-girl outfit. The watch was an old one, from her mother's father; she clicked the cover open.

"Working fine," Dennis said, as she tilted it to catch the firelight. "But mine ain't. It's digital."

He turned and switched to Sign. *How about yours, Eilir? It's an electric,* she signed. *Quartz. It's stopped.*

"And stopped at just the same time as that one on the wall over there," he said, signing as he spoke. "Six fifteen."

"What's *happening*?" Juniper said, signing it and then running her hands through her long fox-red hair.

"Damned if I know," Dennis said. "Only one thing I could think of."

At her look, he swallowed and went on: "Well, an EMP

could take out all the electrical stuff, or most of it, I think—but that would take a fusion bomb going off."

Juniper gave an appalled hiss. Who could be nuking Oregon, of all places? Last time she looked the world had been profoundly at peace, at least as far as big countries with missiles went.

"But I don't think that's it. That white flash, I don't think it was really light—it didn't *come* from anywhere, you know? Suzie at the bar, she was looking out at the street, and I was halfway into the kitchen, and we both saw pretty much the same thing."

*That's right,* Eilir signed. *It wasn't a flash, really. Everything just went white and my head hurt, and I was over by that workbench with my back to the window.*

"Well, what was it, then?" her mother said.

"I don't have fucking clue one about what it *was,*" Dennis said. "But I've got this horrible feeling about what whatever-it-was *did.*"

He swallowed and hesitated. "I think it turned the juice off. The electricity. Nothing electrical is working. That for starters."

Dennis shuddered; she'd never seen an adult do that before, but she sympathized right now. A beefy arm waved out the window.

"Think about it. No cars—spark plugs and batteries. No lights, no computers, *nothing.* And that means no water pressure in the mains pretty soon, and no sewers, and—"

"Mother-of-*All,*" Juniper blurted. "The whole town could burn down! And those poor people on the 747—"

She imagined what it must have been like at thirty thousand feet, and then her mind recoiled from it back to the here and now.

*And Rudy was flying out of Eugene tonight,* she thought, appalled. *If the same thing happened there—*

"We have to do something," she said, pushing aside the thought, and led them clattering down the stairs again.

*And we can only do it here. Think about the rest later.*

*"People!"* she said over the crowd's murmur, and waved her hands. "People, there's a plane crashed right downtown, and a fire burning out of control. And it looks like all the emergency services are out. They're going to need all the help they can get. Let's get what we can scrape up and go!"

Most of them followed her, Dennis swearing quietly, a bucket in one hand and a fire ax over the other shoulder; Juniper snatched up a kerosene lantern. Eilir carried the restaurant's first-aid kit in both arms, and others had snatched up towels and stacks of cloth napkins and bottles of booze for disinfectants.

She needed the lantern less and less as they got closer to the crash site. Buildings were burning across a swath of the town's riverside quarter, ending—she hadn't gotten her wish, and the fire covered the Squirrel's site. Heat beat at them, and towers of sparks were pouring upward from the old Victorians and warehouses.

If the plane was out of Portland, it would have been carrying a *lot* of fuel. . . .

The streets were clogged with people moving westward away from the fire, many of them hurt, and they were blocked with stopped autos and trucks and buses too. Ruddy firelight beat at her face, with heat and the sour-harsh smell of things not meant to burn.

"OK," she said, looking at the . . . *refugees,* she thought. *Refugees, right here in America!*

First aid could make the difference between life and death, stopping bleeding and stabilizing people until real doctors or at least paramedics got there.

"We're not going to do any good trying to stop *that* fire by hitting it with wet blankets. Let's help the injured."

She looked around. There was a clear stretch of sidewalk in front of a hardware store where a delivery truck had rammed into the next building down; its body slanted people out into the road like a wedge.

"We'll set up here. Dennis, see if there's any bedding anywhere around here, and a pharmacy—and anyplace selling bottled water."

He lumbered off, followed by some of his customers. The others started shouting and waving to attract attention, and then guiding the injured towards her. Juniper's stomach clenched as she saw them: this was *serious,* there were bleeding slashes from shattered glass, and people whose clothes were still smoldering. Her head turned desperately, as if help could be found. . . .

*Nobody's going to benefit if you start crying,* she thought sternly, and traced the pentacle in the air again—the Summoning form this time, all she had time for. *Brigid, Goddess of Healing, help me now!*

"You," she said aloud; a young man had pushed a bicycle along as they came. "You ride over to the hospital, and tell them what we're doing. Get help if they can spare it. Hurry!"

He did, dashing off. The first-aid kit was empty within minutes; Dennis came back, with a file of helpers carrying mattresses, sheets, blankets, and cardboard boxes full of Ozonenal, painkillers and whatever else looked useful from the plunder of a fair-sized dispensary; a pharmacist in an old-fashioned white coat came with him.

"Let's get to work," Juniper said, giving Dennis a quick hug.

The best part of an hour later, she paused and looked up in the midst of ripping up volunteered shirts for bandages. The fireman approaching was incredibly reassuring in his rubbers and boots and helmet, an ax in his hand; half a dozen others were following him, two carrying someone else on a stretcher.

"What are you doing here?" he asked, pausing; the others filed on past him.

Juniper bristled a little and waved at the injured people lying in rows on the sidewalk. "Trying to help!" she snapped. "What are you doing, mister?"

"Fuck-all," he said, but nodded approval; his face was running with sweat and soot; he was a middle-aged man with a jowly face and a thick body.

"What's wrong?"

"Our trucks won't work, our portable pumps won't work, and the pressure is off in the mains! Died down to a trickle while we manhandled a hose down here and got it hitched. The pumping stations that lift from the Taylor treatment plant on the river are down and the reservoirs've all drained. We can't even blow fire lanes—our *dynamite* won't explode! So now what we're doing is making sure everyone's out of the way of a fire we can't stop. Lady, this area's going to fry, and soon."

Juniper looked up at the flames; they were nearer now, frighteningly so—she'd lost track in the endless work.

"We've got to get these people out of here!" she said. "A lot of them can't walk any farther."

"Yeah," the fireman said. "We'll have to carry them out—the hospital's got an emergency aid station set up on the campus. We're using runners and people on bicycles to coordinate. Hey, Tony!"

A policeman stood not far away, writing on a pad; he handed it to a boy standing astride a bike, and the teenager sped off, weaving between cars and clots of people.

"Ed?" the policeman said; he looked as tired and desperate as the firefighter.

"We've got to move these injured over to the aid station."

The policeman nodded twice, once to the fireman and once to her, touching a hand to his cap. Then he turned and started shouting for volunteers; dozens came forward. The walking wounded started off westward into the darkened streets, most of them with a helper on either side.

"These mattresses will do for stretchers," Dennis said; he'd gotten them out of nearby houses and inns. "Or better still, cut off the top covers and the handles and use them that way. Hey—you, you, you—four men to a mattress. Walk careful, walk in step!"

The firefighters helped organize, then carried off the last of the worst-wounded themselves. Juniper took a long shuddering breath through a mouth dry as mummy dust. Dennis handed her a plastic bottle with a little water left in it, and she forced herself not to gulp it all down. Instead she took a single mouthful and handed it on to Eilir; the girl looked haunted, but she was steady save for a quiver in the hands now and then.

*Goddess, she's a good kid,* Juniper thought, and hugged her.

It was about time to get out themselves; the fires were burning westward despite a wind off the Coast Range— and thank the Goddess for that, because if it had been blowing from the east half the city would be gone by now, instead of just a quarter.

Shouts came from across the street, and a sound of shattering glass. The musician looked up sharply. Half a dozen young men—teens or early twenties—had thrown a trash container through a storefront window; they were scooping jewelry out of the trays within, reaching through the coarse mesh of the metal screen inside the glass.

The policeman cursed with savage weariness and drew

his pistol; Juniper's stomach clenched, but they *had* to have order or things would be even worse than they were.

*I hope he doesn't have to shoot anyone,* she thought.

Most of the looters scattered, laughing as they ran, but one of them threw something at the approaching policeman. Juniper could see the looter clearly, down to the acne scars and bristle-cut black hair and the glint of narrow blue eyes. He wore baggy black sweats and ankle-high trainers, and a broad belt that glittered—made from chain mesh. Gold hoops dangled from both ears.

"Clear out, goddamnit!" the cop shouted hoarsely, and raised the pistol to fire in the air. "I'm not kidding!"

*Click.*

Juniper blinked in surprise. A woman living alone with her daughter on the road was well advised to keep a pistol, and she'd taken a course to learn how to use it safely. Misfires were rare.

The policeman evidently thought it was odd too. He jacked the slide of the automatic back, ejecting the useless round, and fired into the air once more.

*Click.*

He worked the slide to eject the spent cartridge and tried a third time—and now he was aiming at the thin-faced youth, who was beginning to smile. Two of his fellow looters hadn't fled either. They all looked at each other, and their smiles grew into grins.

*Click.*

One of them pulled a pistol of his own from behind his back, and pointed it at the lawman; it was a snub-nosed revolver, light and cheap. He pulled the trigger.

*Click.*

He shrugged, tossed the gun aside, and pulled a tire iron from his belt instead. The youth with the chain belt unhooked it and swung it from his left hand. Something else came into his right, and he made a quick figure-eight motion of the wrist.

Metal clattered on metal and a blade shone in the firelight. She recognized the type, a Balisong folding gravity knife—if you hung around Society types like Chuck Barstow, you overheard endless talk about everything from broadswords to fighting knives, like it or not.

The banger wasn't a sporting historical reenactor like

the Society knights. He walked forward, stepping light on the balls of his feet, rolling the knife over his knuckles and back into his palm with casual ease. The other man flanking him was a hulking giant with a bandana around his head; he picked up a baseball bat from the sidewalk and smacked the head into his left palm. The full-sized Louisville Slugger looked like a kid's toy in his hand.

The policeman was backing up and looking around as he drew his nightstick. He was twenty years older than any of the three men walking towards him, and nobody else was left this close to the fires; the roaring of their approach was loud, and it was chokingly hot.

"Oh, *hell*," Dennis said. "Now I gotta do something *really* stupid."

He picked up the fire ax he'd brought from the Hopping Toad and walked out towards the policeman.

Juniper swallowed and looked around her, then at the storefront behind them. They'd broken it open for the tools they needed; she made a quick decision and dashed inside, taking the lantern with her. She hesitated at the axes and machetes and shovels . . . but she wasn't sure she could hit a human being with one, even if she had to. Instead she picked a bare ax helve out of a rack of them, giving thanks that redevelopment hadn't gotten this far yet and turned the place into a wine bar or an aromatherapy salon.

*Stay here,* she signed to Eilir. *Get out the back way if you have to.*

Then she turned and dashed out into the street; the firelight had gotten appreciably brighter in the few seconds it had taken. Dennis and the policeman were backed up against the pickup, and there was a turmoil of motion around them as the three street toughs feinted and lunged.

*No time to waste on subtlety or warnings,* she thought.

Especially not when all her potential opponents were stronger than she was, and would probably enjoy adding rape to theft and murder.

She ran forward, her steps soundless under the bellow of the fire that was only a block away now and both hands firmly clamped on the varnished wood. Dennis gave her away simply by the way his eyes went wide as he stared over his opponent's shoulder.

The man with the tire iron was turning when she hit him;

instead of the back of his head, the hardwood cracked into the side of it, over the temple. Juniper Mackenzie wasn't a large woman—five-three, and slim—but she'd split a *lot* of firewood in her thirty years, and playing guitar profession-ally needed strong hands. The unpleasant crunching feel of breaking bone shivered back up the ax handle into her hands, and she froze for a moment, knowing that she'd probably killed a man.

*Oh, Goddess, I didn't mean it!* she thought, staring as he dropped with a boneless limpness.

Dennis had different reflexes, or perhaps he'd merely had enough adrenaline pumped into his system by the brief lethal fight. He punched the head of the ax into the gut of the giant with the baseball bat, and followed up with a roundhouse swing that would have taken an arm off at the shoulder if the big man hadn't thrown himself back-ward with a speed surprising in someone that size.

The blade scored his left arm instead of chopping it, and he fled clutching it and screaming curses; he sounded more angry than hurt. His smaller friend with the Balisong ran backward away from the suddenly long odds, the flickering menace of his knife discouraging thoughts of pursuit.

He halted a dozen paces away, his eyes coldly unafraid; they were an unexpected blue, slanted in a thin amber-colored face. Juniper met them for an instant, feeling a prickle down her neck and shoulders.

"Yo, bitch!" he called, shooting out his left hand with the middle finger pointing at her. "Chico there was a friend of mine. Maybe we'll meet again, get to know each other bet-ter. My name is Eddie Liu—remember that!"

Then he looked over Juniper's shoulder, shrugged, turned and followed his bigger friend in a light, bounding run.

She turned to see Eilir coming up with an ax handle of her own, and her gaze went back to her friend and the po-liceman.

"Either of you hurt?" she said.

Dennis leaned back against the wrecked truck, shaking his head and blowing like a walrus, his heavy face turned purple-red and running sweat beyond what the gathering heat would have accounted for. The policeman had a bleeding slash across the palm of his left hand where he'd fended off the Balisong.

Juniper tossed down her ax handle, suddenly disgusted with the feel of it, and helped him bandage his wound. Out of the corner of her eye she was conscious of Dennis recovering a little, and dragging off the body of the man she'd—

*Hit. I just hit him. I had to,* she thought. *I* really *had to.*

She was still thankful he moved it, and avoided looking at the damp track the bobbing head left on the pavement.

"You folks ought to get out of here," the policeman said. "I've got to get to the station and find out what's going on. Go home if you're far enough from the fire, or head up to campus if you're not."

He walked away, limping slightly and holding his injured left hand against his chest; the nightstick was ready in his right. Juniper pulled her daughter to her and held her, shivering. She looked into Dennis's eyes; her friend wasn't quite as purple now, but he looked worse somehow.

They started up Monroe, heading back towards the Hopping Toad in silence. Dennis stopped for an instant, picked up the revolver of the looter she'd . . . hit . . . and weighed it in one big beefy hand. Then he pointed the weapon towards a building and pulled the trigger five times.

*Click. Click. Click. Click. Click.*

"Remember what the fireman said?" Juniper asked quietly. "About the *dynamite* not working? And what are the odds of that many cartridges not working?"

"You know," he said in his mild voice, "I never really liked guns. Not dead set against 'em like John, but I never liked 'em. But . . . y'know, Juney, I've got this feeling we're going to miss them. Pretty bad."

# CHAPTER THREE

*She's sinking fast,* Havel thought as he scrabbled at the restraining belts that held him into the pilot's seat.

*Got to get out! Out!*

"Mom's hurt, Mom's hurt!" a voice shouted, almost screamed; *Signe Larsson,* he thought. "She can't move!"

The interior of the plane was dark as a coffin, groaning and tilting, popping as bits of metal gave way. The gurgling inrush of water was cold enough to feel like burning when it touched skin.

*Oh, hell,* Havel thought as he reached across to the copilot's seat; Kenneth Larsson was hanging in his harness, unconscious.

A quick hand on the throat felt a pulse. *Just what we fucking needed.* Getting this limp slab of beef out in time wasn't going to be easy.

"Calm down and get the belts off her," he said as he unhitched the elder Larsson; the flexing weight slid into his arms, catching on things in the dark, and the water was up to his waist. A little more light—more of a lighter blackness—came through the rear hatch, which Eric Larsson had apparently gotten open. The cat was screeching in its box—

A thin sound cut through it, like a rabbit squealing in a trap. Havel's teeth skinned back unseen; he'd heard that sound before, from a man badly wounded.

Signe Larsson shouted: "Oh, God, Mom's hurt inside, something's broken, I can't move her—"

"Get her out now or you'll both fucking drown!" he snapped.

The floor of the plane was tilting ever steeper; probably

only the buoyancy of the wing tanks was keeping it from going straight to the bottom.

"Out, out, *out!*" he shouted. "Now!"

She must have obeyed; at least he didn't run into anyone when he scrambled into the passenger compartment himself and pulled the inert form of her father through behind him. Mary Larsson probably weighed a good bit less than her strapping tennis-and-field-hockey daughter. Kenneth Larsson's frame carried nearly a hundred pounds more than the pilot's one-seventy-five.

Contortions in the dark got Larsson's solid weight across his back, with an arm over his shoulder and clamped in his left hand to keep him from slipping back, and Havel began crawling forward with the rising water at his heels; it was more like climbing, with the plane going down by the nose.

Breath wheezed between his teeth; he'd pay for it later, but right now legs and right arm worked like pistons, pushing him up past the four seats—thank God it was a small plane.

When he got to the doorway a hand came back and felt around; he put it on Larsson's collar, and the man's son hauled away, dragging the infuriating weight off Havel's back and out into the night as Havel boosted from below. That was fortunate, because just then the inrushing water won its fight, and the Chieftain sank with its nose straight down.

"*Christ Jesus!*" Havel shouted, forcing down panic as a solid door-sized jet of icy water smashed into him, nearly tearing his hand free of its grip on the hatchway; the torrent continued for an instant, and then he was submerged and weightless—floating, as the plane sank towards the bottom.

He felt the jarring thud as the nose struck the tumbled rocks at the bottom of the mountain river.

*Don't get disoriented now or you* will *die,* he told himself grimly, hanging on to the hatch; he arched his head upward, and there was a small air bubble trapped in the tail space in back of the hatch—*above* the hatch, now. He coughed water out of his lungs and took three deep fast breaths in blackness so absolute it was like cold wet rubber pressed against his eyes.

He *thought* the tail was still pointing up—the current

would probably flip the little ship over on her back in a second or two, though.

*Get the hell out of here, gyrene,* he told himself.

It was still hard to pull his face out of the illusory safety of the bubble. He did, and then jerked himself through the hatch, pushing upward with all the wiry strength of his legs. The cold gnawed inward; water like this would kill you in ten minutes or less, and his sodden coat pulled at him. His head broke the surface with a gasp, and the moonlight was like a flare after the darkness of the sunken plane.

"Over here!" he heard; Astrid Larsson's voice, and then her sister, Signe, joining her. "Over here! Dad, Eric, over here!"

They were calling from the north bank about twenty feet away; he couldn't make much of it out, except a looming shadow, but he struck out in that direction, forcing limbs to move. The current was pulling at him too; he fought it doggedly. When he got close enough the girls held out sticks to him; he ignored them, clamped a hand on the trunk of a providential fallen pine, and levered himself up.

"Eric, Eric!" one of the Larsson girls called.

He turned his head; Eric Larsson was right behind him, sculling on his back with his father floating alongside on his back, held in an efficient-looking one-armed clamp. Havel turned to help him haul the dead weight out of the water, grunting through the chattering of his teeth.

"Good work, kid," he said, as they pulled the older man up the slope and onto a ledge a little above the water, laying him down beside his wife.

*Didn't think you had it in you,* he didn't add.

"Senior year swim team," the boy stuttered. "Signe too. God, God, what's wrong with Mom?"

"Death from hypothermia, unless we get a fire started," Havel said; his fingers had gone numb and clumsy, and it was getting hard to make them work.

The temperature wasn't all that low, a couple of degrees below freezing, but they'd all been soaked to the skin by water as cold as water could get and not turn into solid ice; and a wet body lost heat twenty-five times faster than a dry one. Plus it was going to get a lot colder before sunrise.

He had a firestarter kit in one pocket of the jacket—it was the main reason he hadn't shed it. The place they'd landed was good as anything likely to be close by, fairly dry and with a steep rise right behind it, even a bit of an overhang about twelve feet up. He gathered fir needles and leaves and twigs with hands that felt like flippers belonging to a seal a long way away, heaped them up and applied the lighter. Flames crackled, stuttered through the damp tinder, then caught solidly.

"Careful!" he said, as Signe Larsson came up with an armful of fallen branches. "One at a time. Check that they're not too damp first. Get more and stack it near the fire to dry out."

The fire grew, ruddy and infinitely comforting; he moved the two older Larssons to lie between it and the wall, where reflected heat would help a bit. As the light grew he tried to examine them as best he could; their children crowded around. The youngsters didn't have anything but scrapes and bruises, but the parents . . .

"Your dad's had a bad knock on the head," he said. "He'll be all right." *I hope,* he added to himself; a concussion was no joke.

Mrs. Larsson was a different story; semiconscious, and shivering uncontrollably. He turned her head to the light. No concussion there, thank God for small mercies.

"Her right thighbone's broken," he said; despite the lightness of his touch on the swollen, discolored flesh she started with a squeal of pain.

*Christ almighty, how did she manage that, strapped in? A major fucking fracture, joy and delight undiluted. Looks like the bone ends cut things up in there. At least nothing's poking through the skin.*

"And her shoulder's dislocated. You two hold her."

They did; he grabbed shoulder and arm, and gave a quick strong jerk. The shoulder joint went *click* as it slipped back into its socket; Mary Larsson's eyes turned up in her head, and she fainted. Which was probably all to the good, because there wasn't a thing on earth he could do about a major fracture of the thigh here and now.

"No, don't build the fire any bigger," he said, looking up as Astrid came into sight doggedly dragging a small log. For a wonder, her cat was with her—out of his box, his orange fur slicked to his body, and looking extremely unhappy.

"You get more heat out of a couple of small fires than a

big one," he explained; you couldn't get close enough to a bonfire to get the full benefit. "Start another one, there. Let's get going—"

He showed them what to do; build three medium-sized fires, and heap rocks close by on the river side of each blaze—when the stones had absorbed some heat they could be put around the injured couple, and in the meantime the rock would reflect some of the fire's warmth back towards them. For a wonder, there was plenty of fallen wood of about the right size to pile up in reserve; the only tool they had with them was his folding knife, and it wasn't much use as a woodchopper.

"Get the wet clothes off and prop them up on sticks to dry near the fires, like this," he said. "OK, cover up with these dry leaves and cuddle up close to your folks. The body heat will help. Got to get their core temperatures up or they'll go into shock."

By the time that everything was as close to finished as he could get it the numbness had faded, and he was just miserably cold. He looked at his watch—stopped at precisely 7:15—and then up at the stars, and the moon just clearing the heights to the south; maybe two hours since they'd hit. No point in delaying any further.

"Right, kid, let me have your jacket," he said with a sigh.

Eric Larsson had recovered a bit too, enough for physical misery to bring out irritation; his glare was sullen. "My name's not kid, and why do you want it?" he said.

Havel fought back an impulse to snap; it wouldn't help right now. "Because my sheepskin's too heavy," he said. "Eric. Yours is nylon and it won't get soaked, but I need it to hold some water next to my skin when I dive, I'll lose a little less body heat that way. It isn't a wetsuit but it's the best we've got."

The three youngsters stared at him. *"Dive?"* Signe Larsson said incredulously, her breath smoking out from the heap of leaves and needles where she huddled.

"Yeah, dive," he said, giving her a crooked smile, and jerked his head towards the black water that gurgled behind them. "The current could push the ship downstream overnight, and there's stuff in there we really need—the first-aid kit, and some emergency rations. We're a *long* way from anywhere, I'm afraid."

\*    \*    \*

By dawn Mary Larsson was awake enough to drink some of the hot sweet chocolate. Her husband held her head up, bringing the tin cup to her lips with infinite tenderness until she turned her head away and slid back into semi-consciousness.

The morphine had taken effect, and an inflatable pressure-bandage immobilized her thigh; they'd put one of the high-tech thin-sheet insulating waterproofs under her, over a bed of pine boughs, and slipped her into the sleeping bag of the same material. The rest of the Larssons were taking turns with the two remaining sheets, using them as cloaks while they huddled by the hearths.

Mike Havel squatted by one of the fires, concentrating on getting the last of the MRE out of the plastic pouch; then he wolfed down another chocolate bar and finished his cup of cocoa. That meant he'd put away about five thousand calories, and he'd need every one of them. It was barely forty degrees with the sun well up; the south-facing riverside cliff caught a welcome amount of the light, but it was still damned uncomfortable in their damp clothes.

Signe was finishing her pouch, too, with no more than a muttered *gross* at the meat and the amount of fat. Havel gave her a wink as he finished and rose; she turned half away, spoon busy. The rations had been designed with heavy labor in mind, and the cold counted as that.

Her father started slightly as the pilot touched him on the arm. He'd been murmuring something. It sounded like: *I'm sorry, Mary-girl, I'm so sorry.* Havel pretended not to hear, and said softly: "We have to talk, Mr. Larsson," he said, jerking his head slightly to make clear that he meant *in private.*

"Yeah," Larsson said. His face firmed a little as they walked a dozen paces upstream. "What the hell happened, Havel?"

"The engines cut out," he said. "So did every damn electrical system in the plane. I tried to restart her, but—" He shrugged.

Larsson sighed. "Water under the bridge," he said, then realized what he'd said, half chuckled, and stopped with a wince. "Signe and Eric told me how you got me out, by the way, Mike. Thanks."

He held out his hand. Havel shook it briefly, embarrassed. "Part of the job, Mr. Larsson—"

"Ken."

"Ken. Couldn't leave you there, could I?"

Larsson managed a smile. "The hell you couldn't," he said. "All right, let's get down to business. I remember a white flash . . ."

"Me too, and your kids. That's not all, though." He showed his watch; it was a rugged Sportsman's Special quartz model.

"This stopped. That might be an accident, but all your watches stopped at exactly the same time, just *before* we went down. I'd swear it was the same instant the engines died, too. The GPS unit in my survival pack is *kaput*, and I *know* that wasn't the water—everything in the pack came out of it dry—and it was secured and padded, too. The ELT in the plane is out, and those are *real* rugged. The flashlight and electric firestarter and the radio and everything else electrical in the pack are dead as well. Nothing visibly wrong, they just don't work. What's the odds on all that stuff going out *at exactly the same time*?"

Larsson's heavy face went tight. "EMP?" he said.

"I don't think so," Havel said. "I don't know what the hell it was, though, but we're in deep shit. I know pretty well where we are—"

He brought out the map of the Selway-Bitterroot Wilderness; it was printed on waterproof synthetic silk, colorfast and wrinkle-resistant.

"Hereabouts." His finger touched down. "Here, just east of Wounded Doe Ridge, near as I can figure, and north of West Moose Creek."

They knelt, putting rocks to hold down the corners of the map.

"So we're not far from the State Centennial Trail, maybe twenty miles south as the crow flies. A lot longer on foot, of course, and most of it up and down."

Larsson nodded; he was a part-time outdoorsman too. "Goddamn, but my head feels thick . . . what do you think we should do?"

"Well . . ." Havel hesitated. "Normally—if there's such a thing as a *normal* crash—I'd say you and your wife and daughters stay here, Eric and I go out on foot and get help, and we send a helicopter to lift you out. There's not likely to be anyone on the Centennial Trail in March, but there's a ranger cabin with two-way radios along it and this sure as hell justifies breaking in. Two, maybe three days on foot for fit men pushing hard."

Larsson frowned and rubbed a hand over his face, the skin of his palm rasping on the silvery-gray stubble that coated his jowls. "You don't want to do that?"

"Mr.—Ken—I checked that plane myself, and Steelhead has *good* mechanics. There wasn't something wrong with the ship; she was *knocked* out. And by the same thing that screwed our watches and the GPS in my pack. OK, so say, worst case, the radio at the cabin isn't working either."

"Ouch."

Havel nodded: "That means sixty miles on foot out to U.S. 12, *after* we get to the Centennial. Call that two days and nights and most of the next morning, carrying a stretcher; one long day and a half, again for fit men pushing real hard. Assuming we can get help *there,* that's a week or worse for you here—not much food even if we leave you all of it, and no shelter to speak of. The nights get real cold hereabouts in March and it could snow, snow hard. Plus if it gets warmer, the river could rise right to the cliff with snowmelt. If we got her out to the trail, at least there would be shelter and food."

He pushed down a whisper of cold apprehension. *Of course we can get help on U.S. 12. It's a goddamned major road, after all.*

"Mary could die in a week here," Larsson said flatly. "But she could die if we try to move her. Over country like this, carrying her—"

Havel shrugged slightly. "And it'll be a lot more than three days to the ranger cabin, with a stretcher. Call it six. It could go bad either way. That fracture is ugly. I've got antibiotics in the kit, but it needs a doctor to go in and fix things. The swelling looks bad, too. Moving will hurt, and it'll be dangerous. But staying here for a week, cold and hungry—" He spread his hands. "Your family—your call."

Larsson held out a hand. "Let me see your watch."

The older man turned it over and over; it had a thick tempered-glass casing set in stainless steel, and a set of tumblers in a row to show the day of the month.

"I know these. Good model." He sighed and handed it back. "Christ, there's no right decision here, but we can't sit around with our thumbs up our ass, either." He looked up at the streaked gray clouds. "We'll carry Mary out."

"Right," Havel said. *It'll be a lot harder this way, but I'm glad he said that.* "We'll rig a stretcher and I'll just test fire the rifle while you break this to your kids."

Ten minutes later the pilot stared at the weapon in amazed disgust. "Now, this is just—" He cut himself off, aware of the audience.

"Maybe the bullets got wet," Signe Larsson said helpfully.

Michael Havel thought there was the hint of a smile around her lips for the first time since the accident; normally, he'd have enjoyed that, even if the humor was directed at him. Now he was too sheerly disgusted.

"They're waterproof," he said tightly. "And the case was sealed and dry when I opened it. *And* I fired rounds from the same batch day before yesterday on the range."

Kenneth Larsson held out a hand. "Let me have a round," he said. "And do you have a multitool with you?"

There was an authority in his voice that reminded Havel that the older Larsson was more than a middle-aged fat man with plenty of money and bad family problems; he was also an engineer, and he'd managed a large business successfully for two decades.

Havel worked the bolt, caught the 7.62mm round as the ejector flicked it out, and flipped it to Larsson off thumb and forefinger like a tossed coin.

"This is a Leatherman," he added, handing over the multitool from his survival kit—something like a Swiss army knife on steroids, with a dozen blades and gadgets folding into the twin handles.

"Good make," Larsson replied. "I prefer the Gerber, though."

He took out his own, configured them both as pliers, and gripped one on the bullet and the other near the base of the cartridge case. Then he began to twist and pull, hands moving with precisely calculated force. When he'd finished he tossed the bullet aside and poured the propellant out on the dry surface of the rock.

"Looks OK," he said, wetting a finger and touching it to the small pile of off-white grains to taste it. "If I remember my chemistry courses . . . yeah, dry and sharp. OK, let me have a splinter from the fire."

They all stood back a little. Larsson watched in fascination as the nitro powder flamed up with a sullen reddish fizzle.

"Well, I'll be damned," he said. "Did you see that, Mike?"

Havel caught himself before he answered *Yessir*. "I did."

"Yes," Larsson said. "Whatever's happened, the stuff is slower-burning now. Not really explosive propagation at all, even if the primer had gone off, which it didn't. Hand me another, would you? One of the ones you tried to fire."

He repeated the process and returned Havel's Leatherman with an abstracted frown. "If I didn't know better, I'd *swear* this stuff wasn't nitro powder at all! It's not burning at anything like the rate it should be . . . but that's a physical constant!"

Havel felt his mouth go dry. "So's what happens inside a battery, or an electric circuit," he said.

"Wouldn't it be wonderful if all the guns everywhere have stopped working?" Signe Larsson said softly.

Michael Havel stared at her for a moment, his face carefully blank; but he was thinking so hard he could hear his own mental voice in his ears: *Girlie, if I were a bad guy and coming after you with evil intent, would you rather shoot me or fight me hand-to-hand?*

Something of the thought must have shown despite his effort at diplomatic calm; she turned a shoulder towards him and busied herself with wrapping her share of the group's load in a spare shirt before tying that across her back with the sleeves. Havel shook himself; once they got back to civilization, her opinions would mean even less than they did now. He removed the telescopic sight from the rifle and dropped it into a pocket of his sheepskin coat; it might come in useful. Then he recased the Remington and tucked it into a hollow in the rock face before covering it with stones.

*Maybe it's useless now,* he thought. He certainly wasn't going to lug an extra eleven pounds of weight through this up-and-down country. *Still . . .*

He wouldn't have admitted it aloud, but he just didn't like discarding a fine tool that had given him good service. His freezer back in Boise still had a fair bit of last fall's venison in it.

*And maybe the freezer isn't working either,* something whispered at the back of his head.

Making the stretcher wasn't too hard, now that he had the *puukko* knife and the saber saw from his survival pack. Two ash saplings nearby had the right seven-foot length; he looped the flexible toothed cable around the base of one and began pulling the handles back and forth, careful not to go too fast and risk heating the metal. It fell in a dozen strokes, and the second went as easily.

A cable saw was damned useful out in the woods and much lighter than a real saw or a hatchet, but if he had to choose he'd have taken the knife. The *puukko* was the Finnish countryman's universal tool, for everything from getting a stone out of a horse's hoof to skinning game to settling a dispute with the neighbors in the old days.

His was a copy of the one his great-grandfather had brought from Karelia a hundred years ago; eight inches in the blade, thick on the back, with a murderous point and a gently curving cutting edge on the other side; a solid tang ran through the rock-maple hilt to a brass butt-cap. There were no quillions or guard; those were for sissies.

Havel always thought of his father when he used it; one of his first toddler memories was watching him carve a toy out of white birchwood, the steel an extension of his big battered-looking hands.

He trimmed and barked the poles with the knife, and cut notches at either end for smaller sticks lashed across to keep the poles open—he had a big spool of heavy fishing line in his crash kit, light and strong. One of the ground-sheets tied in made a tolerable base.

Mary Larsson woke while they were lifting her in the bag, conscious enough to whimper a little and then bite her lip and squeeze her eyes shut.

"Take a couple of these," he said, holding up her head so that she could wash down the industrial-strength painkillers. Even then, she managed to murmur thanks.

He looked thoughtfully at the bottle when she sighed and relaxed; he wasn't looking forward to running out of them . . .

and Mary Larsson was likely to hurt worse as the days wore on. He'd had a broken leg once, and it was no joke, even when you were young and full of beans. At least she was doing her best, which was turning out to be considerable— the group's shaky morale would have been cut to ribbons by screaming and sobbing.

Then Havel sacrificed her coat to rig padded yokes at the front and rear of the stretcher, and to wrap the rough wood where the carriers' hands would go; he had good steerhide gloves with him, but the others didn't, and their palms were softer to start with. She wouldn't need the coat; the thin-film sleeping bag was excellent insulation, particularly with the hood pulled up.

*Let's see,* he thought, shrugging into his pack. *I'm worried about the twins' high-tops, but it's walk on those or their bare feet.*

Astrid's soft-sided boots had perfectly practical rough-country soles; he'd checked.

*OK, the rifle's useless, but . . .*

The four hale Larssons were standing in an awkward group, looking at him. He nodded to the youngest. Astrid swallowed and hugged her cat a little closer; the beast dug its claws into her leather jacket and climbed to her shoulder. He hoped the stuff was well tanned; wet leather was about the most uncomfortable-wearing substance known to humankind, and if it dried stiff it was even worse.

"How did that bow of yours come through? Mind if I have a look at it?"

"It's fine," she said. "Sure, here."

He examined it; he'd never taken up archery himself, but he'd flown enough bowhunters around Idaho to pick up a little knowledge of the art. The weapon was a recurve, the Cupid's-bow type with the forward-curling tips, and he could tell it had set her dad back a fair bit of change.

The centerpiece handle, the riser, had its grip shaped to the hand and an arrow-rest through the center; it was carved from some exotic striped hardwood he didn't recognize and polished to a glossy sheen. The whole weapon was about four feet long unstrung, and it had a look he recognized from other contexts—the sleek beauty of functionality.

"Nice piece of work," he said. "The limbs are fiberglass on a wood core?"

"Horn on the belly, steer-horn, hot-worked," she said, with a hint of a sneer. "And sinew on the back, with a yew core; fish-bladder glue. Cocobolo wood for the riser, leather covering for the arrow shelf and the strike plate, antelope horn for the tips. Lacquered birchbark covering."

His left eyebrow went up; that *was* Ye Ancient Style.

"It was made by Saluki Bows. I helped . . . well, I watched a lot."

"What's the draw?"

"Twenty-five pounds."

The eyebrow stayed up. Astrid was tall for fourteen; five-three, and headed higher from the look of her hands and feet—the whole family were beanpoles—but she was slender. That was a fairly heavy draw for a girl her size.

It occurred to him that she might just carry the bow for effect. She *had* spent considerable time and effort trying to dry her high-priced illustrated Tolkien by the fire, and seemed almost as upset at its ruin as at her mother's condition or the general peril they were in. Given that and her clothes . . .

"Can you use it?" he asked, and tossed it back.

He could see her flush. Instead of answering she braced the lower tip against the outer side of her left foot and pushed the back of her right knee against the riser, sliding the string up as the weapon bent until the loop on top settled into the grooves. Then she opened the cover of the quiver slung over her shoulder, nocked a shaft, and drew to the ear as she turned.

"That lodgepole pine leaning from the bank," she said. "Head-height."

The flat snap of the bowstring against the leather bracer on her left forearm sounded, echoing a little in the narrow confines of the canyon. Half a second later the arrow went *crack* into the big tree she'd called as her target, standing quivering thirty yards downstream.

"Not bad, kid," he said.

He walked over to the tree with his boots scrunching in the streamside gravel and rotted ice. When he pulled the arrow free it was with a grunt of effort; it *had* hit at head-height, and sunk inches deep in rock-hard wood. The shaft was tipped with a broadhead, not a smooth target point—

a tapering triangle shape of razor-edged steel designed to bleed an animal out.

"Ever done any actual hunting with it?"

"I shot a coney once," she said proudly. "A rabbit, that is."

Her brother grinned. "Hey, sprout, aren't you going to tell him what you did afterward?"

She flushed more darkly, and glared. Eric went on to Havel: "Princess Legolamb here puked up her guts and cried for hours, and then she buried poor Peter Rabbit. I guess they don't eat bunnies among the Faeries of the Dirtwood Realm."

"That's *elves* of the *woodland* realm, you—you—you *goblin!*"

"But she can shoot the hell out of a tree stump, and every spare pie-plate on Larsdalen rolls downhill for its life when she comes by in a shooting mood. . . ."

Havel cleared his throat. "Eric, you and your dad start with the stretcher. He and Signe can change off after twenty minutes. I'll spell you after forty, but I'd better lead the way to begin with, until we get our direction set and find a game trail."

As they lifted the injured woman he motioned Astrid aside for an instant.

"Kid, I'm glad you've got some experience shooting moving targets with that thing," he said softly.

She looked up at him, startled out of the walking reverie that seemed to take up most of her time.

"You are?" she said.

"Yeah. Look, we're going to need three days minimum to get your mother to the Centennial Trail, and then another day to make the ranger cabin, and another plus for me and your brother to get to the highway. We don't have much food. It's going to get cold every damn night and it may get wet, and carrying your mother over this country's going to be brutal. Shoot anything that moves unless it's a bear or a mountain lion. We *need* the extra food. We're all depending on you—your mother, for starters. We'll lead off, you and I, and you stay ahead afterward with whoever takes point. OK?"

He watched the girl's face firm up, and she made a decisive nod. He kept his own face grave as he returned the gesture, then looked at his compass once more and started off on a slanting line across the hillside he'd picked out earlier.

*Gunney Winters would be proud of me,* he thought.

The noncom had used exactly that we're-all-depending-on-you technique to get the best out of every guy in his squad.

# CHAPTER FOUR

"Dennis, what's everyone going to *eat,* if this goes on more than a day or two?" Juniper Mackenzie said; they were back on the third floor of the Hopping Toad, looking south. "And how can help get in from areas where things are normal?"

Her friend's smile was normally engaging. This time it was more like a snarl. "Juney, how do you know that there *is* anyplace where things are normal?"

They glanced at each other in appalled silence, and then their eyes flicked to Eilir; the girl was looking out the window through the binoculars, squirming between them to get a better view. The fire was coming closer, but slowly, and the southern rim of flame had stopped at the edge of the open campus of Oregon State.

*How do I feed my kid?* Juniper thought suddenly—something direct and primal, a thought that hit like a fist in the gut.

She'd been poor—still *was* poor, if you went by available cash—but this was different. It didn't mean living on pasta and day-olds and what she got out of the garden by the cabin, or busking for meals; it meant not having anything to eat at all.

"You still have that wagon out at Finney's place?" Dennis said.

"Yes," she replied. "He stores it for me so I can use it at the RenFaire and the festivals and meets over the summer, and he boards Cagney and Lacey for me. My pickup's out behind his barn right now. I was supposed to drive down to Eugene to meet my coven after I finished up here."

She'd have liked nothing better than to live out of the

wagon the whole summertime, ambling along behind the two Percheron mares; it was a real old-style tinker-traveler-gypsy house-on-wheels shaped like a giant barrel. Not practical, of course.

*Or it wasn't,* she thought, with an icy crawling feeling. *Now it may be high-tech. Damn, but I hate being scared like this.*

"I think we should get moving. Get out of town, find someplace real remote, and hide like hell," Dennis said. Then he hesitated: "If you want my help."

"Oh, *hell,* yes, Dennie," she said.

To herself: *I know you're trustworthy, and I can't get in touch with Rudy or anyone else in the coven and I certainly don't want me and Eilir out there alone right now. Maybe some of the others will have the same idea. Rudy certainly will.*

She went on: "The cabin up in the Cascade foothills would be perfect and I'll be glad to have you along. We'll have to cross the valley . . ."

"You think this is going to last long enough for that?" Dennis said, his voice neutral.

Her brows knotted. "You were right; we've got to act like this was all over the world, and for keeps. If we do and we're wrong, we just look stupid and scared. If we don't and it *is* like that, we could die. I'd rather look weird than be dead."

Her impish smile came back for an instant: "As if I wasn't weird enough at any time!"

"Right," her friend said, nodding vigorously. "That's *just* what I was thinking."

They clattered down the stairs again. Nobody was left but a couple of the staff, talking together in low tones.

"Boss," the cook said, coming out of the kitchen and drying his hands on his apron. "I stay and help, but my kids—"

"No, Manuel, you get home where you're needed," Dennis said. He hesitated, then went on: "You could think of getting out of town, too. And take some of the canned stuff, whatever you can carry. I think things could get, uh, hairy for a while, with this power failure and all."

He spoke a little louder: "That goes for everyone here. Take what you can carry."

The stocky Mexican gave him an odd look, then handed

the three of them a platter of sandwiches and went, grunt-ing a little at the weight of the cardboard box of food in his arms and the sack of dried beans on top of it. The rest of the staff trailed out in his wake, similarly burdened.

Juniper looked at the pastrami sandwich he'd made.

*Well, there's the farmer and his tractors, and the trucks, and the packing plant, and the refrigerators, and the power line to the flour mill, and the baker, and the factory that made the mustard . . .*

Her stomach contracted like a ball of crumpled lead sheet; she made herself eat anyway, and wash it down with a Dr Pepper.

Juniper kept her mind carefully blank as she and Dennis worked. She changed back into jeans and flannel shirt and denim jacket, then helped the manager—*ex-manager*—load their bicycles with sacks of flour and soy and dried fruit, blocks of dark chocolate and dates, blessing the Toad's organic-local cuisine all the while.

"No canned goods?" Dennis said, as she chose and sorted.

Juniper shook her head. "We'd be lugging stuff that's mostly water and container. This dried food gives you a lot more calories for the weight, when it's cooked. And throw in those spice packets, all of them. They don't weigh much, and I think they're going to be worth a lot more than gold in a while."

The garage out back held a little two-wheeled load car-rier of the type that could be towed behind a bicycle; Den-nis used that for some of his tools before piling more food on top, and she didn't object. They stowed as much as they could in the storage area of the basement; that had a stout steel door and a padlock. When that was full, they stacked boxes of cleaning supplies and old files in front of it, hiding it from a casual search at least.

"Wait here a second," Dennis said.

When he returned he had the shotgun from under the bar. He turned it on a stack of cardboard boxes and pulled the trigger.

*Click.*

It was his hopefully nonlethal backup for an emergency that had never happened—the Hopping Toad wasn't the sort of place where a barkeep needed to flourish a piece every other week.

He worked the slide twice and the second time he caught the ejected shell; then he cut off the portion that held the shot and set the base down on the concrete floor.

"Stand back," he said, and dropped a lit match into it.

There *should* have been a miniature Vesuvius, a spear of fire reaching up from the floor to waist height into the dimness of the cellar, blinding-bright for an instant. Instead there was a slow hissing, and what looked like a very anemic Roman candle, the sort that disappointed you on a damp Fourth of July.

"What's *happening*?" Juniper cried after they'd stamped out the sparks and poured water to be sure.

"Juney ... Juney, if I didn't know better, I'd say someone, or some One, just changed the laws of nature on us. As far as I can tell, explosives don't explode anymore. They just burn, sorta slow." He ran a hand over his head. "Shit, you're the one who believes in magic! But this ... it's like some sort of spell."

Juniper raised her brows. She'd always thought Dennis was a stolid sort, a dyed-in-the-wool rationalist. She started to cross herself in a deep-buried reflex from a Catholic childhood, and changed it to the sign of the Horns. The idea was preposterous ... but it had a horrible plausibility, after this day of damnation.

"Well, the sun didn't go out," Dennis said, scrubbing a palm across his face. "And humans are powered by oxidizing food, and our nerves are electrical impulses ... Maybe some quantum effect that only hits current in metallic wires, and *fast* combustion?"

Juniper snorted. "Does that mean that the dilithium crystals are fucked, Scotty?"

Dennis was startled into a brief choked-off grunt of laughter. "Yeah, that's bafflegabic bullshit, I'm no scientist— I just read *Popular Mechanics* sometimes, and *Analog*. We don't know what happened; all we know is that it *did* happen, at least locally ... but who can say *how* local? Like you said, Juney, we gotta act like it's the whole world."

He went over to another corner of the basement and dragged out a heavy metal footlocker. "I was keeping this stuff for John, he had it left over from what he sold at the last RenFaire and Westercon, and it was less trouble than taking it back home or all the way out east."

"East?" she said.

She'd met John Martin now and then and liked him, although Dennis's elder brother was also a stoner whose musical world had stopped moving about the time Janis Joplin OD'd; besides that he was a back-to-the-lander and a blacksmith. Mostly he lived in a woodsy cabin in northern California, and made the circuit of West Coast dos and conventions and collectors' get-togethers. Of course, he and Dennis worked together a fair bit, with Dennis doing the leatherwork.

"Yeah, John's in Nantucket, of all places. He's got a girlfriend there, and there are a lot of the summer home crowd who can afford his ironwork and replicas. I hope to God everything's all right in Santa Fe East. John's a gentle sort."

He unfastened the locker and threw back the lid. Reaching inside, he took out a belt wrapped around a pair of scabbards and tossed it to her.

"Put it on," he said. "Jesus, I wish John *were* here. He's a good man to have around, under all that hippy-dippy crap."

What she was holding was a palm-wide leather belt with brass studs and a heavy buckle in the form of an eagle. It carried a long Scottish dirk with a hilt of black bone carved in swirling Celtic knotwork and a broad-bladed shortsword about two feet long. She put her hand on the rawhide-wrapped hilt and drew it; the damascene patterns in the steel rippled like frozen waves in the lamplight. It was a *gladius,* the weapon the soldiers of Rome had carried from Scotland to Persia; the twenty-inch blade was leaf-shaped, tapering to a long vicious stabbing point.

Juniper took an awkward swing; the sword was knife sharp, not as heavy as she'd expected, and beautifully balanced. It was beautiful in itself, for the same reason a cat was—perfectly designed to do exactly one thing.

*Except that a cat makes little cats, as well as killing,* she thought. And went on aloud: "I can't wear this!"

"Why not?" Dennis said.

He reached into the locker and drew out an ax—nothing like the firefighting tool he'd used in the brief street fight. It was a replica of a Viking-era Danish bearded war-ax, and made with the same care that the sword had been; the haft was four feet of polished hickory.

"Why not?" he repeated. " 'Cause it'll look *silly?* I'm going to be carrying *this*, you bet. Same reason I'd have taken the shotgun, if it worked. Lot of desperate people out there right now, more tomorrow—and a lot of plain bad ones, too. We already got some confirmation of that, didn't we?"

She swallowed and unwrapped the belt, settling the broad weight of it around her waist and cinching it tight—they had to cut an extra hole through the leather for that, but Dennis had the tools and skill to do a good quick job. The down vest she pulled on over it hid the hilts and most of the blades, at least, if she wore it open.

"I don't have the faintest idea how to use swords," she complained as the three of them spent a grunting ten minutes moving a heavy metal-topped counter-table over the trapdoor to the basement.

"I just *sing* about them. And I don't know if I could actually hit someone with this."

Dennis picked up the ax and hung it over one shoulder with the blade facing backward and the beard and helve holding it in place. Eilir was frightened but excited; she took a light hatchet and long knife to hang from her own belt.

Her mother felt only a heavy dread.

"It'll still *look* intimidating as hell, if we get into any more . . . trouble. God forbid! Anyway, I used to do some of this stuff," Dennis said. "And I've got friends who do it steady—you do too, don't you?"

"Chuck Barstow," Juniper said. "You met him last Samhain, remember? His wife Judy's the Maiden of my coven."

Dennis nodded. "Hope to hell he turns up. I may remember enough to give you a few pointers. And damn, but we're better off than those poor bastards on the 747!"

"Amen," Juniper said.

She winced for a second; if this whatever-it-was *had* happened all over the world, there would be tens of thousands in the air, or down in submarines, or . . . Her mind shied away from the thought; it was simply too *big*.

"Focus on the moment," she muttered to herself as they went out into the front room of the tavern, taking a deep breath and letting it out slowly. "Ground and center, ground and center."

Then: "Dennie, what the hell are you doing? I thought money wouldn't be worth anything?"

The heavyset man had opened the till, scooping the bills into the pockets of his quilted jacket; then he ducked into the manager's office and returned with the cash box. He grinned at her.

"Yeah, Juney—it won't be worth anything *soon*. I want to look up an old friend on our way out of town."

"Friend?"

"More of a business acquaintance. He runs a sporting-goods store, and sells grass on the side. Actually, he sells pretty much anything that comes his way and isn't too risky, which is why I'm betting he'll open up special when I wave some bills at him. If he were really a friend, I'd feel guilty about this, but as it is . . ."

Chuck Barstow stopped his bicycle by the side of the road and touched his face lightly as he panted. The glass cuts weren't too bad, and the bleeding seemed to have stopped—he'd been able to dive behind the desk when the 727 plowed into the runway about a thousand yards away. Despite the chilly March night he was sweating, and it stung when it hit the cuts.

He looked over his shoulder. Highway 99 ran arrow-straight southeast from Eugene Airport. It was nearly eight o'clock, and the fires behind him had gotten worse, if anything. The streetlights were all out, but the giant pyres where the jets had dropped towered into the sky, and were dwarfed in turn where one had plowed into the tank farm where the fuel was stored. He could see the thin pencil of the control tower silhouetted against the fire, and then it seemed to waver and fall.

*I was there. Right there in that tower. Twenty minutes ago,* he thought, coughing at the heavy stink of burnt kerosene.

The highway was full of cars and trucks, both ways. Many of them had crashed, still moving at speed when engines and lights and power steering died together, and a few were burning. There were bodies laid out on the pavement, and people trying to give first aid to the hurt. More were trudging towards Eugene, but there was nothing except fire-lit darkness towards the city, either.

He could hear curses, screams, there two men slugging at

each other, here two more helping an injured third along with his arms over their shoulders. A state trooper with blood running down his face from a cut on his forehead stood by his car with the microphone in his hand, doggedly pressing the send button and giving his call sign and asking for a response that never came.

"Chuck," Andy Trethar said from behind him. "Chuck, we've got to keep going. They'll all be waiting for us at the store."

Before he could reply, a stranger spoke: a tall dark heavyset man in an expensive business suit, looking to be two decades older than Chuck's twenty-seven.

"How much for the bicycle?" he said, looking between them. "I have to get to the airport *immediately.*"

"Mister, it's not for sale," Chuck said shortly. "I need it to get back to my wife and daughter. And the airport's a giant barbeque, anyway."

"I'm prepared to give you a check for a thousand, right now," the man said.

"I said, *not for sale,*" Chuck said, preparing to get going again. "Not at any price."

"*Two* thousand."

Chuck shook his head wordlessly and got ready to step on the pedal. Judy would be worried, and Tamsin could sense moods like a cat—the girl was psychic, even at three years old.

*Powerful God, Goddess strong and gentle, they should have been at the store long before six fifteen. They'll all be there and safe. Please!*

The fist came from nowhere, and he toppled backward and hit the pavement with an *ooff!* Pain shot through him as the bicycle collapsed on top of him.

Someone tried to pull it away from him, and he clung to it in reflex. He also blinked his eyes open, forcing himself to see. Andy was pulling the heavyset man back by the neck of his jacket; the man turned and punched again, knocking Chuck's slightly built friend backward.

Some of Chuck Barstow's coreligionists were pacifists. He wasn't; in fact, he'd been a bouncer for a while, a couple of years ago when he was working his way through school. He was also a knight in the SCA, an organization that staged mock medieval combats as realistic as you could get without killing people. His daytime job as a gardener for Eugene Parks and Recreation demanded a lot of muscle too.

His hand snaked out and got a grip on the ankle of the man in the suit. One sharp yank brought him down yelling, and Chuck lashed out with a foot. That connected with the back of the man's head, and his yells died away to a mumble.

Sweating, aching, Chuck hauled himself to his feet; they pushed their bicycles back into motion and hopped on, feet pumping. The brief violence seemed to have cleared his head, though: He could watch the ghastly scenes that passed by without either blocking them out or going into a fugue.

In fact . . .

"Stop!" he said, as they reached Jefferson from Sixth.

"What for?" Andy said, looking around, but he followed his friend's lead.

"Andy, we've got to think a bit. This isn't going to get better unless . . . whatever changed changes back. And I've got this awful feeling it won't."

They were in among tall buildings now, and it was dark—a blacker dark than either of them had ever known outdoors. Occasional candle-gleams showed from windows, or the ruddier hue of open flame where someone had lit a fire in a Dumpster or trash barrel. The sounds of the city were utterly different—no underlying thrum of motors, but plenty of human voices, a distant growling brabble, and the crackle of fire. The smell of smoke was getting stronger by the minute.

"Why shouldn't it change back?"

"Why should it? Apart from us wanting it to."

Andy swallowed; even in the darkness, his face looked paler. "Goddess, Chuck, if it doesn't change back . . ."

Andy and Diana Trethar owned a restaurant that doubled as an organic food store and bakery.

"We get a delivery once a week—today, Wednesday. With no trucks—"

"—or trains, or airplanes, or motorbikes, even."

"What will happen when everything's used up?"

"We die," Chuck said. "If the food can't get to us, we die—unless we go to the food."

"Just wander out of town?" Andy said skeptically. "Chuck, most farmers need modern machinery just as much—"

"I know. But at least there would be some chance. As long as we could take enough stuff with us." Chuck nodded to himself and went on: "Which is why we're going to swing by the museum."

"What?"

"Look," he said. "Cars aren't working, right?" A nod. "Well, what's at the museum right now?"

Andy stared at him for a moment; then, for the first time since six fifteen, he began to smile.

"Blessed be. 'Oregon's Pioneer Heritage: A Living Exhibit.' "

The restaurant's window had the Closed sign in it, but the door opened at the clatter of hooves and the two men's shouts. Chuck smiled and felt his scabs pull as Judy came to the door, a candle in her hand—one thing you were *certainly* going to find at a coven gathering was plenty of candles. She gaped at the two big Conestoga wagons, but only for a moment: That was one of the things he loved about her, the way she always seemed to land on her mental feet.

"We need help," he said. "We've got to get these things out back."

His wife was short and Mediterranean-dark and full-figured to his medium-tall lankiness and sandy-blond coloring; she flung herself up onto the box of the wagon and kissed him. He winced, and she gave a sharp intake of breath as she turned his face to what light the moon gave.

"I'll get my bag," she said; her daytime occupation was registered nurse and midwife.

"Looks worse than it is," he said. "Just some superficial cuts—and a guy slugged me, which is why the lips are sore. Patch me later. How's Tamsin?"

"She's fine, just worried. Asleep, right now."

Things had already changed; yesterday his injuries would have meant a doctor. Now everyone ignored them, as they helped him get the horses down the laneway. Putting down feed and pouring water into buckets took a few moments more. The horses were massive Suffolk Punch roans that weighed a ton each; placid and docile by nature, but the noises and scents they'd endured had them nervous, eyes rolling, sweating and tossing their heads. He was glad there was a big open lot behind the loading dock; the wagons took up a lot of room, and eight of the huge draught beasts took even more.

Andy and Diana had bought this place cheap, converting a disused warehouse into MoonDance, the latest of Eugene's innumerable organic-food-store-cum-café places. The extra space in the rear of the building meant that the Coven of the Singing Moon also had a convenient location for Esbats. At least when they couldn't take the time to go up to Juniper's place; it was beautiful there, but remote, which was why they generally only went for the Sabbats—the eight great festivals of the Year's Wheel.

The familiarity was almost painful as he ducked under one of the partially raised loading doors. The back section was still all bare concrete and structural members, unlike the homey-funky decor of the café area at the front; it was even candlelit, as it usually was for the rites. The carpet covering the Circle and the Quarter Signs was down, though. Shadows flickered on the high ceiling, over crates and cartons and shrink-wrapped flats with big stacks of bagged goods on them. The air was full of a mealy, dusty, appetizing smell—flour and dried fruit and the ghost of a box of jars of scented oil someone had let crash on the floor last year, all under the morning's baking.

He counted faces. Eight adults. Children mostly asleep, off in the office room they usually occupied during the ceremonies.

"Jack? Carmen? Muriel?" he said, naming the other members.

"They didn't show up," Judy said. She was the coven's Maiden, and kept track of things. "We thought we shouldn't split up, the way things are out there."

He nodded emphatically. The adults all gathered around. Chuck took a deep breath: "Rudy's dead."

More shocked exclamations, murmured *blessed be's*, and gestures. He'd been well liked, as well as High Priest.

"All of you, it . . . His plane was only a hundred feet up. It just . . . fell. There were a dozen jets in the air, and all of them just . . . the engines quit. The whole airport went up in flames in about fifteen minutes. I was in the control tower, Wally lets me, you know? And I barely made it out. I did get a good view north—it's not just the city's blacked out, *everything* is out. As far as I could see, and you can see a good long way from there. Everything stopped at exactly the same moment."

Everyone contributed their story; Dorothy Rose had seen a man trying to use a shotgun to stop looters. That sent Diana scurrying for the Trethar household-protection revolver, and then for the separately stored ammunition, which took a while because she'd forgotten where she put it. Everyone stared in stupefaction at the results when she fired it at a bank of boxed granola.

They talked on into the night, in the fine old tradition. At last Chuck held up a hand; sitting around hashing things out until consensus was wonderful, not to mention customary, but they had to act now or not at all.

*I wish Juney was here. She was always better than anyone else at getting this herd of cats moving in the same direction; she could jolly them along and get them singing, or something.*

"Look, I really hope things will be normal tomorrow. Even though that means I'll be fired and maybe arrested, because I flashed my Parks and Recreation credentials and took all that Living History stuff from that poor custodian—he was the only one who hadn't bugged out in a panic. But if it isn't normal tomorrow, Judy and Tamsin"— he nodded towards the room where the children were sleeping—"and me, and Andy and Diana and their Greg are heading out. I'd love for you all to come with me. You mean a lot to us."

"Out where?" someone asked. "Why?"

"Why? I told you; there are a quarter of a million people in the Eugene metro area. If this goes on, in about a month, maybe less, this city's going to be eating rats—do you want your kids in that? The ones who survive are going to be the ones who don't sit around waiting for someone to come and make things better—unless they do get back to normal, but I'm not going to bet my daughter's life on it. As to where . . ."

He leaned forward. "One thing's for sure. Juniper isn't driving in tonight from Corvallis for an Esbat. I'll bet you anything you want to name she's going to get the same idea as me: head for her place in the hills."

"Oh, Goddess," Diana Trethar said. "She won't know about Rudy!"

Chuck's voice was grim. "She'll be able to guess, I think."

He pointed northeast. "We can wait things out there—live there a long time, if we have to. We'll leave a message for the people who didn't show; a hint at where we're going and what we think is happening. Look, these wagons can haul something like six tons each. . . ."

# INTERLUDE I: THE CHANGE
## Portland, Oregon
### March 31st, 1998

Emiliano knew the way to the Central Library on Tenth Street, although he wouldn't have wanted his *pandilleros* to know about it—bookworm wasn't a title a man in his position could afford. He'd still come here now and then to find out things he needed to know, though never before with his crew swaggering at his back.

Ruddy light blinked back from the spearheads of the men standing along the roadway. There was plenty—not only from the huge fires consuming the city eastward across the river and smaller ones nearby, but from wood burning in iron baskets hung from the streetlamps; the air was heavy with the acrid throat-hurting smell of both, enough to make him cough occasionally, and the flames reflected back from the heavy pall of smoke and cloud overhead.

The fighting men directing foot traffic and clumped before the library entrance got his *pandilleros'* respectful attention; his Lords were equipped with what they'd been able to cobble together since the Change, but these were a different story altogether. Half the guards had a uniform outfit of seven-foot spears, big kite-shaped shields painted black with a cat-pupiled eye in red, helmets and knee-length canvas tunics sewn with metal scales. The other half carried missile weapons, crossbows and hunting bows from sporting goods stores.

And hanging from the two big trees in front of the entrance were—

"Holy shit, man," someone said behind him, awe in the tone.

There was enough light to recognize faces; a stocky middle-aged woman with flyaway black hair, and a big burly black male.

Enough light to recognize faces even with the distortion of the cargo hooks planted under their jaws; it was the mayor and the chief of police—Cat and the Moose, as they were known on the street.

Emiliano swallowed, and Dolores clutched at his arm; he shook her off impatiently, but still licked his lips. He'd killed more than once, and gotten away with it—his time inside had been for other things—but this left him feeling a little scared, like the ground was shifting under his feet. That was nothing new since the Change, but he could sense the same fears running through his men, sapping their courage, making them feel small.

*And nobody makes the Lords feel small!* Aloud, he went on: "Hey, they got a *real* jones on for people who let their books get overdue here, chicos!"

The tension broke in laughter; even some of the guards smiled, briefly.

"And maybe now we know why nobody's heard much from that Provisional Government last couple of days."

The bodies hadn't begun to smell much; Portland was fairly cool in March, and anyway the stink from the fires burning out of control across most of the city hid a lot. The raw sewage pouring into the river didn't help, either.

*So, I'm impressed,* Emiliano thought. *But these* hijos *need us, or we wouldn't have been invited.*

The guards at the entrance carried long ax-spike-hook things like some he'd seen on TV occasionally. All of the guards had long blades at their waists, machetes or actual swords. He blinked consideringly at those, as well. His first impulse was to laugh, but his own boys were carrying fire axes and baseball bats themselves, and possibly . . .

*Yeah, I see the point,* he thought. *The points and the edges!*

"You're the *jefe* of the Lords, right?" one of the guards asked.

"*Si,*" Emiliano said.

With two dozen armed men at his back, the gang chief could afford to be confident. But not too confident. The cooking smells from inside made his stomach rumble, even with the whiff from the corpses. They'd been eating, but not well, particularly just lately. Everything in the coolers and fridges had gone bad, and he hadn't had fresh meat since last Friday.

"Pass on up, then. You and three others. The staff will bring food out to the rest of your men there."

He pointed his ax-thing . . . *halberd, that's the word* . . . towards trestle tables set out along the sidewalks. Emiliano made a brusque gesture over his shoulder, and the rest of his bangers went that way apart from Dolores and his three closest advisors; he figured that with Cat and the Moose swinging above them on hooks, nobody was going to get too macho.

He sauntered up the stairs; the light got brighter, big lanterns hanging from the entranceway arches, making up for the dead electric lights inside.

*Where did I see that guy before?* he thought, running the gate guard's face through his memory. *Yeah, he's a Russian. One of Alexi's guys.*

A blond chick met them inside the door; she was wearing bikini briefs under a long silk T-shirt effect and a dog collar, and carrying a clipboard.

*Hey, not bad,* he thought, then remembered Dolores was there. Then: *Wait a minute. She's not a* puta. *That stuff's for real.*

The greeter spoke, fright trembling under artificial cheerfulness; he recognized fear easily enough, and also the thin red lines across her back where the gauzy fabric stuck: "Lord Emiliano?"

It took him a moment to realize she was giving him a title rather than referring to the name of his gang; for a moment more he thought he was being dissed.

Then he began to smile.

"Yeah," he replied, with a grand gesture. "Lead on."

He hadn't seen a room so brightly lighted after dark since the Change; and the lobby was huge. All around it big kerosene lanterns hung at twice head-height, and a forest of lighted candles stood in branched silver holders on the tables that ringed the great space. Their snowy linen and polished cutlery glistened; so did the gray-veined white marble of the floor. All the desks and kiosks had been taken out; nothing but the head table broke the sweep of view towards the great staircase that began at the rear and divided halfway up into two sweeping curves. The flames picked out that too, black marble carved in vine-leaf patterns.

More guardsmen stood around the outer walls; in the U that the tables formed milled a crowd whose faces he mostly recognized. The Crips and Bloods, the Russians—Alexi Stavarov himself—the chink Tongs, the Koreans, the Angels, the Italians . . . and groups he thought of as whitebread suburban wannabes, but it wasn't his party and he didn't get to write the guest list, and Portland wasn't what you'd call a serious gang town anyway.

More chicks like the greeter circulated with trays of drinks and little delicacies on crackers, doing nothing but smile at pats and gropes from the hairy bearded Angels and some of the other rougher types.

Emiliano took a glass of beer—Negro Modelo—and ate thin-shaved ham off little rondels of fresh black bread, and chatted with a few of his peers. Meanwhile his eyes probed the gathering; not everyone here were his kind. Some were politicians, looking as out of place as the half-naked women; there were even a couple of *priests*. And some unmistakable university students, mostly clumped together. A few scared, some looking like rabbits on speed, some tough and relaxed.

Trumpets blared. Emiliano jumped and swore silently as an Angel with a beard like a gray Santa Claus's down his leather-clad paunch grinned at him.

A man appeared at the top of the stairs. "The Lord Protector!" he barked, and stood aside with his head bowed. "The Lady Sandra!"

The armed men around the great room slammed their weapons against their shields in near-unison, barking out:

*"The Lord Protector!"* in a crashing shout that echoed crazily from the high stone walls. Dead silence fell among the guests.

It took him a minute to recognize the man coming down the stairs with a splendidly gowned and jeweled woman on his arm. He'd never seen Norman Arminger in a knee-length coat of chain mail before, or wearing a long sword in a black-leather sheath. A follower—male, and armed—carried a helmet with a black feather crest and a kite-shaped shield. Arminger looked impressive in the armor, six-one and broad in the shoulders, with thick wrists and corded forearms. His face was long and lean, square-chinned and hook-nosed, with brown hair parted in the center and falling to his shoulders.

"Lord Emiliano, good of you to join us," Arminger said. "I believe you're the last."

"Hey—you're that guy who was writing a book on the gangs, aren't you?"

"I was," Arminger said. "As you may have noticed, things have changed."

He gestured, and spoke in a carrying voice: "Please, everyone have a seat. The place cards are for your convenience."

Emiliano sat, with Dolores and his backup men. Arminger stayed standing, leaning one hip against the head table, his arms folded against the rippling mail that covered his chest.

"Gentlemen, ladies. By now, you will all have come to the conclusion that what Changed a little while ago is going to stay Changed. This has certain implications. Before we talk, I'd like to demonstrate one of them."

Four prisoners were prodded into the broad central floor of the hall; two middle-aged policemen in rumpled uniforms, and two guys in army gear—a big shaven-headed black and an ordinary-looking white. Arminger slid the helmet over his head; his face disappeared behind the protective mask. There were three strips of steel that came to a point just below his nose, and it gave him a bird-of-prey look; the grin beneath it did too, and the nodding plume of raven feathers. He took up the shield, sliding his arm through the loops, and drew the long double-edged sword. It glittered in the firelight as he twitched it back and forth easily, making the *whisssht* sound of cloven air.

Marquez, his numbers man, leaned aside and hissed in Emiliano's ear: "This *hijo* is crazy! Four on one?"

"Shut up," Emiliano murmured back. "We'll see how crazy right now."

Arminger smiled yet more broadly at the low murmur of understanding and rustle of interest that went along the tables.

"You men," he said loudly, addressing the prisoners. His sword pointed to a trash can. "There are weapons in there. Take them and try and kill me. If you win, you go free."

"You expect us to believe that?" the black soldier said.

Arminger's grin was sardonic. "I expect you to believe I'll have you doused in gasoline and set on fire if you don't fight," he said. "And you get a chance to kill me. Don't you want to?"

"*Shit* yes," the soldier replied; he walked over to the garbage container and pulled out a machete in each hand. The others armed themselves as well—an ax, a baseball bat, another machete. The watchers stirred and rustled as the armed prisoners circled to surround the figure in the rippling, glittering mail.

Then things moved very quickly. The black soldier started to attack, and Arminger met him halfway. There was a crack as one machete glanced off the shield, and a slithering clang as the other hit the sword and slid down it to be caught on the guard. And another crack, meatier and wetter-sounding, as Arminger smashed his metal-clad head into the black man's face.

The big soldier staggered backward, his nose red ruin. Arminger's sword looped down as he turned, taking the soldier behind a knee and drawing the edge in a slicing cut. The scream of pain matched Arminger's shout as he lunged, the point punching out in a stab that left three inches of steel showing out a policeman's lower back. In the same motion the shield punched, hitting the other cop on the jaw and shattering it.

That left the smaller soldier an opening. He jumped in and slashed, and the edge raked across Arminger's back from left shoulder to right hip.

Sparks flew; Emiliano thought he heard a couple of the steel rings break with musical popping sounds. And Arminger staggered, thrown forward by the blow.

That didn't stop him whirling, striking with the edge of the shield. It hit the soldier's wrist with a crackle of breaking bone, and the machete went flying with a clatter and clang on the hardwood floor. He shrieked in pain, clutching at his right forearm with his left hand, then screamed briefly again in fear as Arminger's sword came down in a blurring-bright arc.

That ended in a hard thump at the junction of shoulder and neck. The scream broke off as if a switch had been thrown; the sword blade sliced through the neck and into the breastbone, and the killer had to brace a foot on the body to wrench it free. Then he made sure of the others—the big soldier was trying to crawl away when the point went through his kidney—and scared-looking men and women came out with wheelbarrows to take the bodies, and mops and towels and squeegees to deal with the mess. Another of the pretty girls in lingerie sprayed an aerosol scent to cover the smells.

Every eye fixed on Arminger as he turned, shield and sword raised.

"Gentlemen, power no longer grows out of the muzzle of a gun. It grows from *this*."

He thrust his sword skyward. The blood on it glistened red-black in the light of the candles and lanterns. The armored men around the walls cheered, beating their weapons or their fists on their shields. Many of the guests joined in. Emiliano clapped himself.

*Can't hurt,* he thought. *And this son of a whore is either completely crazy or a fucking genius.*

When the noise subsided, Arminger went on: "Many of you know that I was a professor of history before I dabbled in urban anthropology. Some of you may know that I was once a member of the Society of Jesus. What you probably don't know is that I was also a member of a society that meets to celebrate the Middle Ages . . . by, among other things, practicing combat with the ancient weapons. I've persuaded quite a few members of that society to throw in with me; food is a wonderful incentive. And we're recruiting and training others, many others. Some of you have already contributed manpower. As you saw out there at the front gate, we're already the most effective armed force in this city. Certainly more effective than the overweight, overaged, donut-eating legions of the former city government."

He laughed, and handed the shield and dripping sword to a servant. Quite a few of the guests joined in the laughter; this wasn't a crowd where the police had many friends.

"Making these weapons and armor requires considerable skill. Using them requires even more. But when you do have them and do know how to use them, you're like a tank to the unarmored and untrained. A hundred men so armed, acting as a disciplined unit, can rout thousands."

Emiliano nodded slowly, and saw others doing likewise. That made sense. . . .

"Now, you'll also have noticed that traditional means of exchange—money—is worthless now. Right now, there's only one real form of wealth: food."

*Yeah, and we spent a couple of days wasting our time robbing banks and hitting jewelry stores,* Emiliano thought with bitter self-accusation.

He'd been living on canned stuff for days now.

"There's enough food in this city to feed the population for about two months, if nothing was wasted. One month, more realistically, if there was a rationing system; a great deal has already been lost and destroyed. Then everyone would die. There is, however, enough for a *smaller* but substantial number of people for a year or more. And remember, gentlemen, there is no government anymore. Not here in Portland, not in Oregon, not in the United States. Or the world, probably, come to that."

That got an excited buzz.

"Yo," one of the Crips leaders said. "We thinkin' move out to the country, get the eats. With no guns, the farmers not much trouble."

Arminger shook his head again. "Not yet. In the long run, yes. Everything that's been invented in the last eight hundred years is useless now. There's only two ways to live in a time like this—farming, and living off farmers. I don't feel like pushing a plow."

Emiliano nodded; and again, he wasn't the only one. His father had been born a peon on a little farm in Sonora, and he had no desire at all to be one himself. Living off farmers, though . . .

*A haciendado,* he thought, amused. He leaned forward eagerly, hardly noticing when the banquet was brought in. He was in a golden haze from more than the wines and brandies and fine liqueurs by the end of the night.

Lord *Emiliano,* he thought. *Got a sound to it.*

# CHAPTER FIVE

"Sssst!" Michael Havel hissed, and held his left hand up with the fist clenched.

Footfalls stopped behind him as he peered into the brush and half-melted snow along the Centennial Trail, in the cold shadow of the tall red cedars.

Just being on it was a relief; all he knew of this particular stretch of country was maps and compass headings, and it was an enormous mental load off his shoulders to be able to follow a marked trail—even if it was still wet with slush, and muddy. As a fringe benefit of being here between the end of cross-country skiing season and the beginning of hiking, the animals weren't all that wary, since they didn't expect humans along.

He'd trimmed and smoothed a yard-long stick from a branch; it was as thick as Astrid Larsson's wrist, and nicely heavy. He let it fall from where he'd been carrying it under his armpit; the end smacked into his palm with a pleasant firmness. The snowshoe hare made a break for it as he moved, streaking up the slope and jinking back and forth as it went; he whipped the stick forward and it flew in a pinwheeling blur.

"Yes!" he said.

The throw had the sweet, almost surprising feel you always got when you were going to hit. The rabbit stick hit the hare somewhere in the body, and it went over in a thrashing tangle of limbs and a shrill squeal. He started forward, but Astrid's voice checked him: "There's another one!"

The second terrified-rodent streak was much farther up the slope; he waited as the girl brought the bow up, drawing in a smooth flexing of arms and shoulders as it rose.

The string snapped against her bracer, and the arrow flashed out in a long beautifully shallow curve; he followed it with an avid hope born of days of hard work and short rations.

*Damn!* he thought; the other snowshoe jinked left at just the wrong moment.

Astrid muttered something under her breath as she recovered the arrow. Then she checked it—you had to keep broadheads sharp—and smiled at him in congratulations.

"Better luck next time," he called to her.

He trotted to his kill and finished the hare off with a sharp blow of the rabbit stick; the animal was a young male, a little under two pounds, with the relatively small ears and big feet of its breed. He was crouched by the side of the trail getting ready for the gutting and skinning when the stretcher came into sight.

Eric Larsson was on one end, and his sister on the other. They both exclaimed in delight at the sight of the rabbit; even their father looked up from where he walked beside his wife and smiled.

"And *that's* why they call it a rabbit stick," Havel said, grinning and waving. "Take a rest, everyone, it's time to change off anyway."

He'd stripped off his sheepskin coat and rolled up the sleeves of his flannel shirt; it was chilly, but getting blood out of the fleece was impossible. There was a little hone in a pocket on the outside of his belt sheath; the steel went *scritch-scritch-scritch* over it as he put a finer edge on the *puukko* and began breaking the game.

Astrid drifted off ahead; she could shoot rabbits easily enough now, and was certainly willing to eat her share, but she didn't like to watch the butchering. Eric followed, probably to tease her—someone was going to have to tell the kid to lay off it, but Havel remembered what *his* brothers had been like and doubted it would happen anytime soon. The problem there would come when Eric got some food and rest and felt full enough of beans to try pushing at the older man, and hopefully this whole lot would be off Michael Havel's hands by then.

Ken stayed beside the stretcher as he always did at stops, holding Mary Larsson's hand; he and his wife talked in low tones, usually of inconsequential things back in Portland, as if this was just a frustrating interruption in their ordinary lives.

*Which means Mr. Larsson knows his wife better than I thought,* Havel told himself. *Which will teach me to try and sum someone up on short acquaintance.*

Biltis the orange cat also jumped up on the stretcher, burrowing down to curl up beside the injured woman in what Astrid insisted was affection and Havel thought was a search for somewhere warm and dry in this detested snowy wilderness. She made a pretty good heater-cat, though.

He grinned at the thought; the cat would come out for its share of the offal, right enough; it would even purr and rub against his ankles. Cats and dogs and horses were more honest than people—they really did like you when you did things for them, instead of faking it.

Signe Larsson came up; she leaned his survival pack against a tree—she carried it, when she wasn't on stretcher duty, freeing him up to forage—and squatted on her hams with her arms around her knees, watching him skin and butcher the little animal. She didn't flinch at the smell or sight of game being butchered anymore, either.

He'd roll the meat, heart, kidneys and liver in the hide, and they'd stew everything when they made camp—he still had a few packets of dried vegetables, and the invaluable titanium pot. You got more of the food value that way than roasting, particularly from the marrow, and it made one small rabbit go a lot further among six. Plus Mary Larsson found liquids easier to keep down. The antibiotics gave her a mild case of nausea on top of the pain of her leg; he was worried about the bone, although the pills were keeping fever away.

"*Who* calls it a rabbit stick?" Signe said after a moment, nodding towards the tool he'd used to kill the hare.

"The Anishinabe," he said, his hands moving with skilled precision. "Which means '*the* People,' surprise surprise—the particular bunch around where we lived are called Ojibwa, which means 'Puckered Up.' My grandmother's people; on Mom's side, that is. I used to go stay with Grannie Lauder and her relatives sometimes; she lived pretty close to our place."

"Oh," she said. "That's how you learned all this . . . woodcraft?"

She looked around at the savage wilderness and shivered a bit. "You really seem at home here. It's beautiful, but . . . hostile, not like Larsdalen—our summer farm—or even the ranch in Montana. As if all this"—she waved a hand at the great steep snow-topped slopes all around them—"hated us, and wanted us to die."

"These mountains aren't really hostile," Havel said. "They're like any wilderness, just indifferent, and . . . oh, sort of unforgiving of mistakes. If you know what you're doing, you could live here even in winter."

"Well, maybe *you* could, Mike," she said with a grin. "What would you need?"

"A nice tight cabin and a year's supply of grub, ideally," he said, chuckling in turn.

She mimed picking up the rabbit stick and hitting him over the head.

He went on: "Minimum? Well, with a rabbit stick and a knife you can survive in the bush most times of the year; and with a knife you can make a rabbit stick and whatever else you need, like a fire drill. You can even hunt deer with the knife; stand over a little green-branch fire so the smoke kills your scent, then stalk 'em slow—freeze every time they look around, then take a slow step while they're not paying attention, until you get within arm's reach."

"That's fascinating!" she said, her blue eyes going wide. "Of course, the Native Americans *did* live here."

The big blue eyes looked good that way, but . . . He gave a slight mental wince.

*I'm too fucking honest for my own good,* he told himself wryly. *Also I'm effectively in charge here, damnit, which means I can't play fast and loose. Not to mention her parents are watching . . .*

"Even the Nez Perce starved here when times were bad," he said. "Nobody lived in these mountains if they hadn't been pushed out of somewhere better. I hope you don't believe any of that mystic crap about Indians and the landscape."

"Oh, of course not," she replied, obviously lying, and equally obviously wanting to correct him to *Native American*.

"Indians have to learn this stuff just like us palefaces," he went on. "It's not genetic. But some of Grandma's relatives *were* hunters and trappers, real woodsmen, and I used to hang around them. Learned a lot from my own dad too, of course. Though I figure the Ojibwa part is why I'm so chatty and talkative. It's perverse for a Finn."

He scrubbed down his hands and forearms with some of the snow lying in the shade of a whortleberry bush, trying not to think about hot showers and soap. She passed him his coat again, and winced a bit doing it, pulling her hands back protectively and curling the fingers as he took the garment.

"Damn, let me look at that."

He took her hand in his and opened it. The palms looked worse than they were, because the strings of skin from the burst blisters had turned black. Havel drew his *puukko* again, tested the edge by shaving a patch of hair from his forearm, then began to neatly trim the stubs of dead skin; that should help a little, and reduce the chafing. There hadn't been time for her to really grow any calluses yet.

"I told you to put more of the salve on them," he scolded. "You're pushing it too hard. When something starts bleeding, say so and someone will spell you on the stretcher."

"I'm doing less than Eric is, Mike," she said.

"You're also forty pounds lighter than Eric, and most of that's on his shoulders and arms," Havel said bluntly. "I thought you had more between your ears than he does, though. You've got nothing to prove." *And you're certainly not the cream-puff airhead I thought you were,* he thought. *Massively ignorant, but not stupid.*

She learned quickly, rarely had to be told how to do something twice, and didn't stand around waiting to be found work.

*And she's no quitter or whiner. Complains less than her brother.*

"Eric may be bigger, but I'm a lot younger than Dad—I don't like the way he looks," she went on, leaning a little closer and lowering her voice. "Mike, he goes *gray* sometimes when he's been on the stretcher for twenty minutes, especially on the steep parts. The doctor's warned him about his heart. What will we do if he . . . gets sick . . . out here? Carrying him *and* Mom—"

*There she's got me,* he thought, looking over at the elder Larsson.

The flesh had melted away from him, but it didn't make

him look healthy, just sort of sagging, and his color was as bad as Signe thought. Cold and the brutal work and lack of proper sleep or enough food was grinding him down, and he wasn't a young man or in good shape.

*And this isn't the way to get into shape at his age. Much more of this and I wouldn't bet on him coming through. But I can't take him off carrying the stretcher for at least some of the time. There's too much else to do and I'm the one who knows how to do it.*

"By the way, Mike," Signe said, obviously pushing the worry aside with an effort of will. "There's something you should consider about 'mystical crap,' as you put it."

His brows went up and she continued by putting her hand out, fingers cocked like a pistol and making a *ffff-fumph* between lips and teeth, uncannily like the way his gun had sounded when he tried to fire it.

*Have to admit, you've got a point,* he thought, and was about to say it aloud when he heard Eric's voice, cracking with excitement: "A deer! She got a deer, and it's running away!"

Havel was on his feet and running forward in an instant, scooping up the rabbit stick and tumbling Signe on her backside with a squawk; she was up and following him half a heartbeat later, though.

He passed Eric, but the twins were right on his heels as he flashed into the clearing; their legs were long and their hightops were better running gear than his solid mountain boots. Astrid was a hundred yards ahead, sprinting fast with the bow pumping back and forth in her left hand; and the blood trail was clear enough for anyone to follow— bright gouts and splashes of it on snow and mud and last year's dry grass sticking through both. He pushed himself harder, knowing all too well how the tap could turn off suddenly on a trail like that, unless—

He went through a belt of lodgepole pines, like seventy-foot candlesticks; the ground beneath them was fairly clear, and the wounded animal was following the trail; that wasn't too surprising, since it was on level ground and would make for maximum speed. Massive tree boles flashed by him, and then they were out into bright sunlight with mountain ridges rippling away to the west and south like endless green-white waves on a frozen sea. Thin mountain air burned cold in his chest; Astrid's hair was like a white-silk banner as he pulled past her. Then the trail jinked a little higher.

*Good!* he thought exultantly. *Make him work at it!*

The blood trail wasn't dying off; getting thicker, if anything. Then he saw the animal in a patch of sunlight not far ahead.

*That's no by-God deer,* he thought.

It was an elk; a three-year bull still carrying his rack, a six-pointer, and he knew it must be badly wounded—a healthy elk could do thirty-five miles an hour in a sprint, and twenty all day long. As Havel neared it staggered, gave a gasping, bugling grunt of pain, and began to collapse by the rear. Blood poured out of its nose and mouth; the forelegs gave way, and it lay down and groaned, jerked, and went still with its thick tongue hanging out of its mouth.

Astrid and the twins were only a few seconds behind him. "Stand back!" he said sharply, controlling his breathing.

As if to back up his words the beast gave a final galvanic kick; it was a little thin with winter, but sill magnificent— glossy reddish brown on most of its body, with a shaggy gray mane on its thick neck and a yellowish patch on the rump around the small white tail. He could just see the fletching of the two-foot arrow against its rib cage behind the left shoulder; Astrid must have been lucky. The blade of the broadhead had struck with the edges up and down, slipping between two ribs and going through right into the lungs, probably cutting a big artery or nicking the heart too. The arrow could never have punched through the outer ribs if it had struck horizontally, not from a twenty-five pound draw.

Even so, that was a light bow and a short shaft to bring down something this size; bull elk were the size of a medium-sized horse. This one wasn't quite full-grown, but it would dress out at four hundred pounds or more of steaks, roasts, chops, ribs and organ meat, enough to feed six people for a month. The main problem would be carrying it; in this weather it would keep a long time once he'd drained it properly and dressed it out.

Astrid was dancing from one foot to another and crowing with glee: "He stepped right onto the trail! He was only twenty feet away! Go me! Go me! I got him, I got him!"

"That you did, kid," Havel said. "That makes up for a hell of a lot of lost rabbits!"

Signe hugged her sister and danced her in a circle. Even her brother gave an admiring whistle.

"I take it back, Legolamb," he said. "I'm gonna say 'sorry' with every mouthful."

Havel nodded agreement and moved in to make sure of the elk with his knife; on the one hand there was no point in letting it suffer, but on the other he didn't want a hoof through his skull or six inches of pointed antler in his crotch either.

*"Sorry, brother, but we needed it,"* he said, in an almost noiseless whisper—he never spoke that aloud, not wanting to be thought gooey or New-Agey—and passed his hand over the beast's eyes and then his own.

*Maybe we could camp for a day's rest,* he thought. *Mrs. Larsson isn't looking very good, and—*

Then what he was seeing through the stand of mountain ash penetrated.

"Eric," he said. "Come on."

"What?" the young man said.

Havel pointed and grinned. "The ranger cabin's just through there," he said. "I figure we can get your mom into a real bed and start the stove in about twenty minutes."

*Clean underwear, even,* Michael Havel exulted the next morning.

What was more, *he* was clean; it made his gamy clothes repulsive, but he pulled them on and padded out into the hallway carrying his boots and followed his nose to the kitchen, gratefully taking a cup of bad instant coffee from Astrid at the doorway.

The four-room log cabin had been built by the WPA back in the thirties, and it had a big woodstove with a water heater, plenty of stacked firewood, a meat safe and even some food in the pantry—flour in a sealed bin, canned fruit and vegetables, salt and pepper and baking soda—left for just this sort of emergency. There were blankets in a cupboard too; even in this year of grace 1998 you didn't have to assume vandals and thieves would be by, not in the middle of the Selway-Bitterroot, you didn't. That kind usually didn't have the stamina for a three-day hike through frigid mountain forest from the nearest road.

For castaways like Havel and his passengers, the Forest Service would be forgiving.

The radio was thoroughly dead, and the batteries too—not even a tickle from the tongue taste-test, which didn't surprise him although it was annoying as hell. Right now he was satisfied with something besides MREs or cold rabbit stew for breakfast.

Signe Larsson was cooking; he'd done ribs and steaks last night, and started a big pot of "perpetual stew" that still simmered on the back plate. If you brought it to a boil now and then, you could add fresh ingredients and water daily and keep it going indefinitely.

"Flapjacks," she said over her shoulder; her wheat-blond hair was loose, and still slightly damp and tousled from washing with a scrap of soap. "And canned peaches to go with them—yum!"

"Food for the gods," he said sincerely, accepting a plateful; his body craved starch, and sugar only a little less.

Eric and Astrid were concentrating on eating; like their sister, they'd bounced back with the resilience of healthy youth.

*I did too,* Havel thought. *Only the rubber's just the slightest touch less resilient at twenty-eight!*

Ken Larsson was looking less like walking death; partly due to a night on a real mattress, even if there were only blankets rather than sheets, and mostly that his wife seemed to be doing a lot better too.

"OK," Havel said, looking out the window after he'd cleared his plate the second time. It was just past dawn, with sunrise turning the snow on the peaks opposite rosy pink; if he hadn't quit soon after he'd left the Corps, this would be the perfect time for a cigarette. It was a pity tobacco was so goddamned bad for you!

"We can make it in two days if we push hard," he said to Ken Larsson. "The emergency people ought to get help back here a lot faster than that; there's a year-round crew at the Lochsa Ranger Station, and Lowell's only a ways down I-12."

"Good luck," the older man said. When Havel rose, he stuck out a hand. "And thanks, Mike."

"Hell, just doing my job," Havel said, flushing a little—and being careful not to squeeze too hard, because Larsson's hand was as mucked-up as Signe's or Eric's. "You and your family are my responsibility; I've got to see you safe."

"I won't forget it, Mike," Larsson said.

Havel grinned. "We'd better get going, before everyone gets all soppy," he said.

"Yeah," Eric said indistinctly through a last mouthful of pancakes. "Got to get Mom to a hospital."

He glanced sidelong at Signe, who was just setting down her own plate. "Though sis here is going to be *real* disappointed we're not going to Montana."

"It's amazing how repulsive you get when you're not starving," Signe said.

Eric laughed, and went on to Havel: "The ranch next to our place there uses our pasture, and pays us by doing the maintenance and looking after our horses when we're not visiting," he said. "They're *real* ranchers. And the owner's son isn't a bad guy, except that he had the bad *taste* to let my worse half here go mooning around after him making a spectacle of herself like a—hey!"

Signe Larsson held the opened salt shaker over his coffee cup. "More?" she said sweetly.

"You ruined it!"

"Salt for bacon, Eric," she said in a tone that could have cut crystal. "And you *are* a pig." She was smiling when she said it, but her eyes were dangerously narrowed.

Ken Larsson cleared his throat: "You two, can it. Remember that your mother's hurt."

They both looked abashed; Havel grinned mentally. *Not that ragging each other does their mother any harm, but guilt is the Ultimate Parental Weapon,* he thought.

The two sisters and Larsson accompanied their brother and the pilot out onto the veranda; everyone's breath showed, smoking silver in the rising light, but with warmth and food that was exhilarating, not depressing. Havel set his pack with a shrug and a grunt; they could take the remaining MRE, three bouillon cubes, and the chocolate bar; it was enough to keep them comfortable all the way there.

"See you in three days, Ken," he said. Then he looked at Astrid and Signe. "Hey, Astrid, you really did good with that elk. That was important."

The girl glowed. *Good,* he thought, and went on: "So now you'll all have plenty to eat. Do *not* go hunting,"—which she showed a natural aptitude for, now that she'd lost her inhibitions—"and in fact, I'd very much prefer it if none of you went out of sight of the cabin. It would really hurt my feelings if any of you got eaten by a bear before we got back."

He caught Signe's eye. The older girl nodded.

"I'll keep an eye on her, Mike," she said.

"Let's get going!" Eric Larsson said impatiently. "We can't stop now!"

"The hell we can't," Havel said, setting his pack down against a rock; it was two hours before sunset.

*Right on cue,* he thought wearily. *Christ Jesus, we males are predictable sometimes.*

They'd made better time than he'd expected: twenty miles at least, and they might make four more before sundown. At that speed, they could reach Highway 12 sometime around noon tomorrow.

*If* they didn't wreck themselves today.

He went on: "We'll walk fast for an hour, and then we'll rest fifteen minutes, and then we'll do it all over again. A man can walk a lot further than he can run. Right now we're at the fifteen-minutes-rest stage. We'll keep going till moonrise, eat, sleep, and get going again at dawn, and make it by lunchtime tomorrow."

"Who died and made you God?" the youth asked.

"I know what I'm doing here," Havel said shortly. "You don't."

"I think you're the hired help," Eric spat back. "And that means what I say goes."

Havel surprised him by laughing, deep and obviously genuine. "Kid, if there's anyone I work for here, it's your dad—and *he* has enough sense to listen to an expert."

"And I don't like the way you look at my sister!"

Havel laughed again: this time the sound was a little taunting. "It's 1998. If you try to play whup-ass with every guy who looks at Signe Larsson with lust in his heart, you're going to have to be a lot better at it than I think you are."

Eric came forward an inch, then jerked to a halt, looking at the rabbit stick in the older man's right hand. Havel grinned.

"That shows some sense."

He tossed it to rest by the side of his pack, then held out both hands and made a beckoning gesture with curled fingers.

"Let's get this over with, kid," he said.

Eric flushed—the disadvantage of being so blond, even with a tan—and came in with his fists up in a good guard position, moving lightly for someone his size: he was six-one, long-limbed, broad in the shoulders and narrow in the waist. Very much like his opponent, except that Havel was built in nine-tenths scale by comparison.

The young man's big fist snapped out; the blow would have broken Havel's jaw and several of Eric's fingers, except that the ex-Marine jerked his head aside just enough to let it brush by his left ear; at the same instant he stepped in and swept his shin upward with precisely controlled force, then bounced back lightly, moving on the balls of his feet and keeping his own hands open.

"Kill number one, kid," he said, as Eric bent and clutched himself for a moment. "Or at least I could have ruined you for life. And never try to hit a man in the head with your fist. You'll break your hand before you break his head."

Eric was red-faced and furious when he straightened, but he didn't make the bull-style charge that Havel had half expected. Instead he set himself and whirled into a high sweeping kick; it was well executed, except for being telegraphed, and a little off because his right foot slipped in the squishy mixture of mud and pine needles underfoot.

Havel let his knees relax, and the foot swept over his head. His hand slapped up, palm on the other's thigh, and pushed sharply.

"Shit!" Eric screamed as he landed on his back, more in frustration than in pain.

Then: *"Shit!"* as Havel's heel slammed down to within an inch of his face. The older man bounced back again, smiling crookedly as Eric rolled to his feet and backed slightly.

"Kill number two. This isn't Buffy the Dojo Ballerina. All right, let's finish up with the lesson. We haven't got time to waste."

Ninety seconds later, Eric Larsson wisely made no attempt to resist as the back of his head rang off the bark of a Douglas fir. Fingers like steel rods gripped his throat, digging in on either side of his windpipe, and he fought to drag air in through his mouth—the swelling had made his nose nonoperational.

Havel looked at him with the same crooked smile; there

was a pressure cut on his cheek, but otherwise he was infuriatingly undamaged.

"Kill number six. And you forgot one thing, kid," he said. "Never bring your fists to a knife fight."

Eric Larsson's eyes went wide as Havel stepped back; something silver flashed in his hand, and the young man looked down at a sudden cold prickle; the odd-shaped hunting knife was touching just under his ribs.

"Kill," Havel said. The knife reversed itself, lying edge-out along his forearm, then swept across Eric's throat with blurring speed. "Kill." A backhanded stab, letting the cold steel touch behind his right ear. "Kill."

Havel stepped back another pace; the younger man was chalk white and keeping himself from trembling by sheer willpower. He sheathed the knife and cocked an eyebrow, his expression cold.

"So, have we settled the 'Who's the big bull gorilla?' question?"

"Yeah. Noooo doubt about it, man."

"Good, because we've got things to do. Like saving your mother's life, saving your sisters' lives, saving your dad's life, saving *my* life, and last and way, way least important, saving *your* life. Got it, Eric?"

Eric nodded, massaging his throat. "Yeah. Definitely. *Most* definitely. All the way. One hundred percent."

Havel grinned suddenly, and extended a hand. "Actually . . . Eric . . . you're not bad at all. You're strong and you're fast and you're not scared about getting hurt. Get the right experience, and you'll be a dangerous man to meet in a fight. Are we square?"

"Square." Eric was obviously flattered by the man-to-man treatment and took his hand, starting to squeeze. Then he stopped abruptly: "Jeez, I hope I didn't break that knuckle," he said, wincing.

"*Told* you not to hit a man in the face with your fist," Havel said, wagging a finger. "Punch him in the throat or the balls, or grab any convenient rock and use *that* on his face. But don't sock him in the jaw unless you're naked and they've nailed your feet to the floor."

"Yeah, I see your point . . . actually, man, I saw too *much* of the sharp point. I wouldn't mind learning how to do that fancy knife stuff myself. Is it Ojibwa too?"

Eric picked up the bundle of gear; Havel liked that, and the absence of pouting.

"Nah, Karelian," he replied genially. "Force Recon refined my technique, but Dad taught me the basics of"—he tapped the knife—"the *puukko*."

"Karelian?" Eric asked.

"Eastern Finland, or it used to be—where the poets and shamans and knife-waving crazies came from. Farther west you get Tvastlanders, who're so dull they might as well be Swedes like you."

"I'm Yankee on Mom's side—English."

"Well, I'm sorry for you and all, but wouldn't it be better to keep that quiet?"

They both laughed. *He's not a bad kid,* Havel thought, settling his pack on his back. They started west again, side by side. *He's just high on testosterone and needed a thumping.* Aloud he went on: "Anyway, like it says in the *Kalevala,* real men use knives."

"The *Kalevala?*" Eric asked, frowning as he searched his memory for something that rang a bell, but not a very loud one.

"Finland's national epic. That great big thing that sounds like *Hiawatha,* only you can't pronounce the names?"

"Now I remember," Eric nodded. "We've got a copy at home; every line sort of repeats? Dad has it with his saga collection; he used to read us that stuff when we were little kids—that's how Astrid got started on her schtick. The illustrations were cool, but I couldn't get through it. I can't remember anything about knives, though; I thought it was all witches and monsters and Santa Claus sleigh-trips with reindeer?"

"Yeah, the Old Country version could make sex sound dull, but the one my dad taught me was sort of modified; it goes—" He began to chant as they walked west along the trail:

> *"I am driven by my knowledge,*
> *And my understanding urges,*
> *That I should commence my fighting,*
> *And begin my strong ass-whupping,*
> *With a nice sharp slashing* puukko."

Eric hadn't expected to be forced to listen to poetry, but a smile broke through his frown of puzzlement as the words sank in. Havel cleared his throat and continued, in the solemn singsong shaman-type voice purists always used for the real thing when the old farts got together at the Suomi-American Society meetings:

> "Fists are just for wussie girl-men.
> Swedes and Danes and pansy girl-men . . .
> Come and let us fight together,
> And drink potato gin forever,
> Or maybe made-from-pine-trees vodka,
> In the dreary land of Pohja.
> Let us clash our knives together,
> Let us slice and cut our fingers;
> Let us stab a cheerful measure,
> Let us use our best endeavors,
> While the young are standing round us,
> Of the rising generation."

Eric Larsson was beginning to stagger and wheeze with laughter as they walked; Havel made a grand gesture with the rabbit stick, declaiming:

> "Let them learn the way of mayhem,
> And of all our fights and drinking,
> Of the booze of Väinämöinen,
> Of the knives of Ilmarinen,
> And of Kaukomieli's pointy puukko,
> And of Joukahainen's broken bottle:
> Of the utmost bars of Pohja,
> And of Kalevala's boozing cock-hounds . . ."

He carried on through the younger man's laughter, remembering the way the sauna had run that night, he and his brothers and father howling out the verses in turn until the one reciting couldn't go on, and falling back on the scalding-hot pine benches.

# CHAPTER SIX

"Hope Luther doesn't mind us dropping in past midnight," Dennis said.

Juniper snorted wordlessly, too tired to waste breath on speech as she pedaled her heavily laden bike along the rough patched pavement of the country road. She felt every jolt, all the way up her back. The muscles of her thighs burned and cramped; the day had wrung her limp as a dishrag, even after all the miles she'd covered on a bicycle over the years. Despite the chill damp of the air she was sweating under her down coat, and the straps of her knapsack cut into her shoulders.

"Hold up!" she said suddenly, stopping and putting a foot down. It skidded through dirt and gravel along the edge of the asphalt.

They all braked and swerved. It was dark, dark in a way she'd never experienced in settled country before. Between patches of cloud the stars were a bright frosted band across the sky, and the moon was rising huge on the edge of sight; it turned the grassy fields and woodlots to silvered mystery.

*It's nearly Ostara,* she thought. That would come with the vernal equinox; also Eilir's birthday. *Night and day in perfect balance, with light on the increase. Maybe things will get better. All Gods above, I hope so!*

The tin mailbox on its post beside the turnoff was prosaic by contrast, down to the little flag in the upright position to warn the mailman there were letters waiting.

*If there's ever a postman by again,* she thought, and swallowed.

"This is Luther's drive," she said. "Another quarter mile."

Luther Finney had farmed south of Corvallis most of his

seventy-four years, like his fathers before him since they came west on the Oregon Trail the year before the California gold rush started; when the last of his children moved away, he'd rented out most of his land to neighbors and kept only the old house and a few acres around it. He still kept farmer's hours, but he'd complained to her that he slept lightly these days.

Dogs barked as the three fugitives walked their laden bicycles up the tree-lined gravel lane. The buds were out on the rock maples arching overhead—trees Luther's great-great-grandfather had planted to remind him of Massachusetts—and they turned the lane into a tunnel of shadow even darker than the open road.

*He probably* does *sleep lightly,* Juniper thought, as light blossomed in an upstairs window.

First the buttery yellow flame of a candle, and then the brighter glow of a kerosene lamp. Nothing like the hard glare of electricity, which she was already starting to miss. Luther's two Alsatians came up, excited but polite; her own nondescript black-and-white mongrel threw himself into the air around them in wriggling transports of barking joy, before making his usual nosedive for the crotch to catch up on the olfactory news.

"Quiet, Cuchulain," she said, giving him an admonitory rap on the head.

She'd named him after the Hound of Ulster, which was somewhat appropriate given the beast's mixed ancestry, though not for his entirely nonheroic nature.

He jumped up and tried to lick her face instead. She pushed him down and thumped his ribs reassuringly. The dog sensed anxiety and whined a bit, then followed them with head down and tail wagging nervously. More lights came on downstairs, and the door opened; Luther Finney came out, wrapped in a long bathrobe.

"Juney!" he cried. "And Eilir! Weren't expecting you back for another few days."

The old man's face carried a genuine smile; so did his wife Sarah's, where she stood behind him.

*Jack Sprat,* Juniper thought as she smiled back; Luther was tall and lean and wrinkled, Sarah short and round with a face like a raisin dumpling.

"Come on in," the farmer said.

He shook hands with Dennis, giving the ax over his shoulder no more than a glance; he'd met the manager of the Hopping Toad before, and even come in to hear Juniper sing a couple of times. Sarah hugged Juniper and her daughter, and shooed them forward through the hall and into the farmhouse kitchen.

*Good thing we can leave the crossbows inconspicuously with the bikes,* Juniper thought. *They might overwhelm even Luther's politeness reflex.*

They were ugly squared-off things like stubby rifles with short thick bows across the front, but light and easy to handle.

*I don't think Dennie's not-really-a-friend bought his story about a camping trip, but he wasn't asking any questions when he saw the cash. In fact, he practically drooled.*

That made her feel a bit better about the transaction; she was mournfully convinced that camping gear and high-energy trail rations and garden seeds were going to be worth a *lot* more than portraits of dead presidents by this time tomorrow, when more people had figured out what was happening.

Luther's eyebrows *did* go up when Juniper took off her down coat and the blades showed. She sighed at the warmth, and at the lingering cooking smells—those pastrami sandwiches seemed like a long time ago.

"There a reason for the cutlery, Juney?" he said. "You and Mr. Martin on your way to one of those pageant things you sing at?"

She suppressed an absurd impulse to slide the weapons around behind her; instead she unbuckled the belt and hung it on the back of a chair.

Sarah Finney didn't say anything; but then, she rarely did. Instead she started loading three plates with leftovers—cold fried chicken, beans, potato salad, string beans, and slices cut from a loaf of fresh bread. Then she put an old-fashioned percolator coffeepot on the gas range.

"Can't do filter," she said apologetically. "Power's out." She made a gesture towards the two big buckets on the counter. "Pump, too."

"Good thing the old hand pump's still working," Luther said. "Knew it would come in useful sometime."

Dennis cut in, as he leaned the handle of the war-ax against the door: "Mr. Finney, you've got a gun around, don't you?"

"'Course," Luther said, puzzled; his chin and nose looked as if they were going to meet when he frowned. "Got a shotgun, and my old deer rifle, too. Why?"

"I'd rather you see for yourself. Get one of 'em and go out back and pop off a couple of rounds into the woodpile. Either will do." He raised a hand. "I can't explain and you won't believe me until you've tried. It'll save time. This is important. Humor me."

The old man glanced at Juniper; she nodded, and he shrugged and went out. The three sat down and obeyed Sarah's smiling wave, pitching into the food. Juniper hid a smile as she bit into a drumstick; Luther affected a hard-headed practicality and a loud contempt for any "hippie nonsense," but he also kept a henhouse full of free-range Rhode Islands because they simply tasted better, and a half-acre vegetable garden for the same reason.

Dennis's eyes met hers, and she knew they shared a thought: *I hope to hell that gun works properly. . . .*

A *click* came from the backyard, followed by a muttered curse and the sound of a shotgun's slide being racked, repeated several times along with the futile-sounding metallic sounds. Juniper felt a twinge of disappointment, but not enough to make her stop eating. Luther came back with his lips moving silently. He could swear a blue streak when he wanted to, but had old-fashioned ideas about doing it in front of women or children—he'd been born in 1924, after all.

"You knew about this?" he said in a half-accusing voice, and sat—though not before he'd made sure there were no rounds left in the shotgun's magazine. He was thoroughly careful about firearms, courtesy of his father and a lifetime of hunting, plus World War II and Korea.

"Yeah," Dennis said. He glanced over at Juniper. "You want to tell 'em, Juney?"

*No,* she thought. *But I will.*

She was more articulate, anyway, as befitted a musician and storyteller. When she'd finished the old man sat and stared at her for a while.

"Craziest damned thing I ever heard, Juney," he said

after a moment. "But my equipment won't start, that's true; not the car or the pickup either. And the scattergun won't shoot worth shhh . . .shucks."

He shook his head. "There's going to be hell to pay while this lasts, too."

"How do you know it's not going to last forever?" she said grimly.

"Why . . . it *can't*," Finney said. "That'd be . . . why, that would be *terrible*."

Juniper swallowed. "Luther, it's already terrible. There are *hundreds* of people dead in Corvallis—maybe thousands. I mean that, Luther: thousands. I was down at the waterfront, helping with the people who got hurt. A 747 out of Portland crashed right there at Fourth and Monroe, and a quarter of the town was up in flames by the time we left. If it's like that in Corvallis, what's it like in Portland or Seattle? Or LA or New York?"

Sarah's face had lost its smiling composure; Luther's hand clenched, and he looked at the silent radio on the countertop by the stove.

"And nothing works, Luther. Nothing. We got into a fight—"

Luther's eyes went wide as they described it; then they went to his own shotgun, leaning against the wall by the back door, and then to Dennis's ax.

"Luther," Sarah said. "Eddie and Susan and the children!"

Juniper and Dennis winced; so did Eilir, who read lips well. Those were the Finneys' son and daughter and grandchildren . . . there were great-grandchildren too, come to think of it. They all lived in Salem.

Luther made a calming gesture in his wife's direction with one gnarled hand, a gentleness in contrast with a look more grim and intent than the musician had ever seen on his features before. Though others might have recognized it, in the bloody, frozen hills around Chosin Reservoir.

"Later, honey. Let's get things straight first." He looked back at his guests. "You figure this thing has happened all over?"

All three nodded. "I can't be sure," Juniper admitted. "But I climbed the tallest building in town and used my binoculars. It's dark out there, Luther. There isn't a single light, not a moving car, not a plane going overhead that I could see. All there are, are fires. Lots of fires. And you saw what happened with the gun—that's the way it was when we tried, too."

Luther nodded in his turn and sipped at his coffee. "So what do you three plan on doing about it?"

"Run like blazes and hide like hell," Dennis said. "I've got no family in Corvallis."

"We're going up to my great-uncle's old place in the foothills," Juniper said, leaning her head eastward for an instant. "It's nicely out of the way, and I expect some of my friends to head that way."

*And Rudy,* she thought.

The farmer frowned. "If things are all messed up this way, folks'll need to pull together," he said, a hint of disapproval in his voice.

Juniper felt herself flush—the curse of a redhead's complexion. "Luther, we've had some time to think about this. It's not just something like a barn on fire, or the river flooding."

Dennis nodded. "There's fifty, sixty thousand people in Corvallis alone," he said. "Every one of them gets their food from stores that get *theirs* from warehouses all over the country twice a week—I run a restaurant, so I should know. Mr. Finney, how many people do you think could live off the farms within a day's walk of Corvallis? Call it twenty miles, say forty on a bicycle."

Luther Finney thought for an instant, and his face went gray under the weathered tan. "Not too many. Most of the land right around Corvallis is in grass for seed, or flowers or nursery stock or specialties like mint. More'n half the farms don't even have livestock. Some orchards and truck, but not much. Take a while to plant . . . with hand tools, and getting the seed . . ."

Juniper put her elbows on the table and lowered her face into her hands, the heels over her eyes to block out the visions in her mind.

"And that's just Corvallis," she said. "The rest of the Willamette . . . there's a million plus in Portland alone, and there's Salem and Eugene and Albany . . . and no tractors or harvesters or—most *farmers* these days get their groceries from Albertsons or Smith's, just like everyone else.

No trucks, no trains, no telephones—the government's *gone*—the cops and National Guard are just guys with sticks. Pretty soon, with no fresh water or working sewage plants there'll be sickness, too, really bad."

"Holy Hannah," Luther breathed. Sarah put a hand over her mouth.

"And *that's* why we're getting out," Juniper said. "My first responsibility is to Eilir"—*though there's Rudy, and by the Cauldron I hope my coveners are all right*—"but we'd be glad to have you two along."

Luther blinked at her. "Well, thank you kindly," he said. "But surely we'd just be a burden to you? We're well fixed here if times are hard; there's the preserves, and the chickens, and the garden and the fruit trees. We're better off than we would have been back when I was doing real farming—I've had more time for puttering around putting in truck."

Dennis jerked his chin towards the shotgun leaning beside the door. "Thing is, Mr. Finney, that pretty soon a *lot* of people are going to get *real* hungry. And they're going to think that the place to get something to eat is out in the country. Then they'll come looking for dinner."

"Holy Hannah," Luther said again. Then he exchanged a look with his wife. "I see your point, you three. But we've got relatives around here, and our kids and grandkids will need a place to stay. They know where we are. No, I think we'll be staying here. And you're welcome to if you want, as well."

The floor of the Willamette Valley was mostly flat, but here towards the edge of the Cascade foothills the odd butte reared up out of the fields. Juniper Mackenzie lay on the crest of one such, training her binoculars west; the damp ground soaked into her shirt, but the temperature was heading up, finally getting springlike, and the earth had the yeasty smell of new growth. Crocus bloomed nearby, blue spears under a big Oregon oak whose leaves were a tender green.

She swallowed, her hands trembling as she watched I-5, the main interstate that ran north-south from Portland to Eugene. The litter of motionless cars and trucks hadn't changed. The first thin scatter of trudging people on foot had; most of the stranded passengers had probably dispersed quickly, and for a day or two—the day her party had crossed—it had been nearly empty.

Now it was *thronged*. Groups on foot—they probably included a lot from Salem and the first or the most determined from Portland; perhaps some walking north from Eugene in ironic counterpoint to the flood heading south away from the metropolis.

*Everyone looking for the place things are normal, and not finding it.*

A lot of the ones on bicycles were almost certainly from Portland; it was an easy three-day trip by pedal, and there were a *lot* of bicyclists there.

*From Albany, too,* she thought.

That city wasn't far away to the north; she could have seen it on a normal day. Today a thick plume of black smoke marked the location, and the faint bitter smell was an undertone to the earth scents. On the highway, a group was fighting around an eighteen-wheeler truck that had coasted into the rear of an SUV on the evening when everything Changed, carried along by momentum. Merciful distance hid the details, but there were certainly clubs and pieces of car-jack and tire-iron in use. Probably knives and shovels as well.

*Must be food inside. Oh, Goddess, there goes another bunch.*

Twenty or thirty cyclists traveling in a clump abruptly braked to a halt and drove into both groups fighting around the truck in a solid wedge. At this distance everything was doll-tiny even with the powerful binoculars, and she kept the point of aim moving so that she wouldn't catch more than an odd glimpse. There were already too many things in her head that kept coming back when she tried to sleep.

The worst of it was that she couldn't even blame them for fighting over the food. If everyone shared fairly, that would simply mean that *everyone* died of starvation. There just wasn't enough to go around, and no authority to enforce rationing if there was. Too little anywhere except in the immediate vicinity of a warehouse or a grain elevator or a packing plant—and there, too much, and no way to move it any distance before it spoiled.

*Do not think of what New York or LA is like,* she told herself. *Do not. Do not.*

That was like telling yourself not to think about the color orange, or an elephant, but she had to try if she wasn't going to curl up into a little ball and wait to die. Cuchulain thrust his nose into her armpit and whined slightly as he scented her distress.

Instead she cased the binoculars, picked up her crossbow and started to thread her way down through the tangle of trees and brush that covered the steep south face of the butte, sliding down on her butt and controlling her descent with her heels more often than not; it was better than five hundred feet of steepness. Cuchulain kept pace with her, wuffling happily as he stuck his nose into holes and snapped at long-tailed butterflies.

She felt a moment's bitter envy; as far as the dog was concerned this was a perfect spring day, out with his person in the country, and she'd even let him eat some very high carrion. The only thing wrong was that she smelled scared and sad.

Then he went quiet, stiffened, and gave a low growl. Juniper reached out and grabbed his collar, whispering *stay!* in a low emphatic tone, and pushed her way forward the last few yards.

The narrow graveled road ran along the base of the butte, with a filbert orchard on the other side. The hobbled horses were grazing there among the new spring grass and the flowers, and the barrel shape of her wagon was a little distance further from the road, mostly hidden from a casual view; Dennis had agreed that it was best to travel only at night, by the back ways, and that slowly.

Now six people on bicycles faced him and Eilir where the gate from the road went through the orchard fence. They weren't openly hostile yet, but she could hear the raised voices, and she could *see* their desperation; they looked just as dirty and tired and ragged as she felt, and thinner. She'd been eating one small meal a day since the Change after that fried-chicken feast at Luther's; they looked as if they'd had nothing for quite some time.

*Four men, two women, and a child,* she thought. *They realized they'd do best off the Interstate. Looking for "normal" means dying; better to look for food.*

The child was young, no more than four or five. A boy, and with his own miniature cyclist's helmet; his mother's bicycle had a pillion seat for him. She was Oriental, and she was dangerously well armed. Two of the others carried baseball bats, one a golf club, one a spade with a thick straight-sided blade crudely sharpened; all of them had some sort of knife, if only the kitchen variety. But the Asian woman had an honest-to-goodness bow, and a quiver clipped to the side of it with four arrows; it was a fiberglass target weapon, not even meant for hunting, but potentially deadly for all that. An arrow was nocked to the string, but she hadn't drawn it.

"Look," Dennis said, his voice tight with frustration. "Look . . ."

He had the Danish ax held slantwise across his body, one hand on the end of the haft and one halfway up. Eilir stood beside him with her crossbow cocked and loaded but not quite leveled.

"I'm sorry as can be, but there's nothing we can do for you. We don't want any trouble. You can pass on by, and nobody will be hurt."

Just then one of Luther Finney's gifts—the rooster in the wire cage on the other side of the big barrel-shaped cart—chose an unfortunate moment to crow. It took the strangers a minute to understand what they were hearing; she could tell from the once-expensive sporty look of their clothes they were all deeply urban. But *cock-a-doodle-doo!* was familiar enough to sink in.

"You've got *chicken!*" one of the bicyclists screamed; it was the sound of a beggar confronted with riches.

"No, we don't," Juniper said firmly.

Everyone jerked around to look at her as she came out of the brush at the base of the hill and onto the road.

*The stuff inside the wagon would be unimaginable wealth if you could see it,* she thought grimly, as she advanced and stood on Dennis's other side. *But it isn't. It's just barely enough to keep the three of us through until the seeds bear, if we're very lucky.*

"That's a rooster and some breeding hens and we're not parting with them to make all of you one meal," Juniper went on.

She met their eyes one by one; she could feel her

mother's accent getting a little stronger in her voice, as it did when she was angry or afraid: "They have to help feed my family from now until . . . things get better."

She knew her own eyes were steady, and the green of them cold; more to the point, the three-bladed and very pointed head of the bolt in the groove of her cocked crossbow glittered bright and sharp in the cool spring sunshine.

Several of the strangers were *literally* drooling at the thought of chicken. One shook his aluminum baseball bat.

"You've got chicken, you've got *horses,* you've got stuff inside that funny wagon!" he shouted; his face was caked with dirt, and brown-and-gray stubble showed through it. "Nobody will give us *anything!*"

He mastered himself with a visible effort. "Look, just give us what you can spare. We'll . . . look, is there any sort of work you need done? We're not thieves. We just haven't had anything to eat for a day and a half now, and that was some crackers and olives and some soup we tried to make out of grass."

The child was hugging his mother's leg where she stood beside her bicycle; he had tear-tracks through the dust on his face.

"Hungry, Mommy," he said. "I want something to *eat.*"

She looked at Juniper. "You don't know what it's like back there," she said. "Back in Portland. The whole city's burning, and nobody has anything, criminals are stealing and killing—Terry'll *die* if he doesn't get some food!"

That set them all off; they crowded closer, leaving their cycles on the kickstands or dropping them and waving their arms and shouting.

*Help!* Juniper thought, her head going back and forth, trying to keep everyone in view.

These weren't bad people; probably none of them had so much as hit anyone since junior high. But they were desperate.

*And so am I,* she thought, nerving herself. *For Eilir. For Dennis. And yes, for my own sweet life which I'm not ready to give up yet, even to get out of this hell.*

Then there was a sharp sound, a snapping *tunnnggg* of vibrating cord. Juniper's head whipped around; it was Eilir's weapon that had fired, and the Oriental woman was down on the ground screaming and writhing, clutching at a crossbow bolt through the outer part of her thigh. An arrow wobbled off from her bow and landed in the orchard not far from one of the horses, standing in the ground with the feathers up. The others' shouts turned to screams as well; Dennis took the moment to leap forward, roaring and flourishing the great ax overhead.

Eilir dropped the end of the crossbow to the ground, put her foot through the metal stirrup, and dropped the claw of the spanning device at her belt over the string. Then she hooked the other end over the butt of her weapon and whirled the crank-handle around half a dozen times. The mechanism clicked, and she put another quarrel in the groove with fumbling haste.

"Be off!" Juniper shouted at the same time, her weapon scanning back and forth.

She could shoot only one—but nobody wanted to be that one, or so she hoped from the bottom of her peaceful soul.

"Go! Now, while you can!"

They ran; not quite panicked enough to leave their bicycles, but several nearly falling in their haste as they sprang aboard them and pedaled madly westward, back towards I-5. Back towards despair and death in a ditch, most likely.

Eilir kept her crossbow to her shoulder until the last of them was out of sight. Then she dropped it and burst into clumsy racking sobs. Juniper tried to put an arm around her shoulder.

*She was going to shoot you!* Eilir cried in Sign; then the girl tore away and raced into the orchard, sitting down with her back against a tree and wrapping her arms around her knees, face pressed into the faded denim of her jeans.

Dennis leaned on his ax, taking deep whooping breaths for an instant. "Oh, fuck, that was too close," he said. "Oh, *hell.*"

Something small and hard rammed Juniper in the stomach. After an instant she realized it was the child's head, and he was trying to punch her as well.

"You don't hurt my mom!" he cried; he was sobbing too, but striking out with blind determination. "You don't hurt my mom!"

"I'm not going to hurt her!" Juniper said helplessly.

She wrapped her arms around the boy in self-defense, lifting him and handing the writhing, kicking bundle to Dennis.

"Or you either; be still, for the Goddess' sake!"

The Oriental woman was silent where she lay in the roadway, wide-eyed, clutching at her injured leg. The bolt Eilir had used had a smooth target head, and the blood trickled freely but did not have the fatal spurting flow that would mean a severed artery.

"He's just a little boy," the woman said as Juniper approached. "Please, whoever you are, he's just a little boy. He didn't hurt anyone. You've got to help him."

"And I'm not going to hurt him," the musician replied.

*And she's thinking of nothing but her child, with that through her flesh. Damn it!*

It would be so much easier just to go away and leave them if the injured woman were a ravening bandit spitting curses, or thinking of nothing but her own hurt.

"Will you let me see to the leg?" she went on aloud. A nod replied. "Toss your knife away, then. I have a daughter depending on *me*, and I'm not taking any chances."

Juniper used her own dagger to slit the tight cycling shorts up around where the shaft pierced the flesh, wincing as she looked at it. Dennis came up; he had their medicine box, and readied a bandage; the boy was standing behind him, darting looks around his legs and then turning away.

Juniper took a deep breath, gripped the bolt and pulled; it came free easily, and they occupied themselves with salve and tape for a moment.

"I'm Sally Quinn," the wounded woman said when she'd stopped panting and recovered herself somewhat. "My son's Terence, Terry."

She spoke good General American, with a very faint trace of an accent, and looked to be half a decade older than Juniper, though that might be the dirt and desperation and not having eaten much the past week.

Dennis surprised his friend by breaking into another language, fast-paced and with a nasal twang; she didn't think it was Chinese, which she could at least recognize. Sally started in surprise, smiled hesitantly through her pain and replied haltingly in the same tongue. After a moment she relapsed into English:

"But my parents came over in 'seventy-five, when I was very young," she said. "I don't remember all that much."

Juniper looked at Dennis. *Well, he's the right age, but he never said a word!*

"You were in Vietnam?" she said curiously.

"In the rear with the gear," he said, shrugging. "Supply corporal. But I did pick up some of the language, yeah, dealing with the local economy. And we better *didi mao,* you bet."

She recalled vaguely from books and movies that that meant *get out,* and it was true. She looked down at the injured woman; her son had crept close, and now he lay in the dusty grass beside the roadway with his head pillowed on her shoulder, looking at Juniper with enormous silent eyes. He had some of his mother's fine-boned comeliness, but his hair was dark brown and the features sharper.

"Was your husband with the . . . others here?" Juniper asked.

There was a wedding band on Sally's left hand, she certainly hadn't been born with the surname *Quinn,* and she had suburban respectability stamped all over her under the layer the days since the Change had left.

"No," Sally replied; her voice was tired and flat, and her face sagged with lack of sleep and food and hope. "Peter was working late at the office at HP . . . that night, you know what I mean."

They both nodded. "When things Changed," Juniper said, hearing the capital in her own voice.

"He didn't come back. I couldn't go looking for him because of Terry, and it was four days. And then there was nothing left in the apartment, and nothing worked . . . the water, the toilets . . . there was fighting in the streets! And some people I knew a little said they were going to go south to where there was food; I think they wanted me to come because I had the bow, I'm in an archery club, we meet every second Saturday. . . ."

The words trailed off. Juniper stood abruptly and paced, then turned. She left the words unsaid; Dennis was about to speak too. They met each other's eyes and Juniper shrugged angrily.

"Oh, we should not be doing this, Dennie, we really shouldn't. We *shouldn't.*"

A hand tapped her on the shoulder. *Yes, we should, Mom,* Eilir signed. *Yes, we should.* She held out a piece of cold biscuit to the boy, and he grabbed it and jammed it into his mouth.

"All right . . . Sally," Juniper said. "We can't help everyone . . . which doesn't mean we can't help anyone. You wait here, and we'll get you into the wagon when the horses are hitched." She looked at Dennis. "We'd best get a move on, before we pick up so many strays we're out of food even before we reach the cabin."

# CHAPTER SEVEN

"Well, shit," Havel said with profound disgust. "I was really hoping this wouldn't happen."

There were cars on Highway 12. The problem was that they were all stationary; he could see half a dozen, before the road curved out of sight along the steep canyon of the Lochsa. Several of them had been left with the doors open; not one was moving.

Eric halted beside him, gawking up and down the roadway. "Wait a minute," he said. "Do you mean that all the cars are stopped the way our plane's engines were?"

"And my GPS unit and the radio at the cabin," Havel said grimly.

He spat into the dirt by the side of the roadway. It seemed to be the only way to really express his feelings. *Unless I get down on the ground and sob and cry and scream and beat my fists on the pavement,* he thought wryly.

"But . . ." Eric's slightly battered-looking face went fluid with shock. "How are we going to get help for my mother?"

"You tell me," Havel said, throwing down his pack. *"Shit!"* He sighed. "All right, let's check the cars."

They did; nothing remained but a few empty plastic wrappers. *Hmmm,* Havel thought, looking through another trunk, and then casting back and forth along the road for a hundred yards either way.

"No blankets," he said.

Eric looked at him; probably big-city families as rich as his didn't think about that sort of thing.

"A lot of people out here keep spare blankets or a sleeping bag in their trunks on a long trip," Havel said. "Or emergency supplies. None of these cars have anything like that. Five gets you ten everyone's car stopped at the same moment, then they hung around for a while and eventually started walking out when they realized nobody was coming to rescue them."

He swept a hand along the road. "They were crapping by the side of the road for a couple of days too."

Eric tried a shaky smile. "I'm not much of an expert at roadside dumps," he said.

"Spoor is spoor."

Havel felt his mind struggling to refuse the implications of what he saw.

*How far does this stretch?* he thought. *How far can it stretch? All the way from coast to coast, or 'round the world?*

The two men looked at each other. It was a relief when they heard the hollow clop of shod hooves, and the harder crunch on the gravel beside the pavement. The sound came from the east, down the road that stretched in from Lolo Pass and Montana.

*Damn, it isn't the Forest Service,* was his first thought.

There were six horses. Two carried packsaddles; three bore men in outdoors dress, looking even more scruffy than Havel felt or Eric was. The lead rider had a brush of mouse-colored beard that fell halfway down his chest and . . . Havel blinked . . . an actual coonskin cap. He looked like a potato with legs, and rode like one, sawing at his horse's mouth as he pulled up; a lead rein from his saddle controlled the packhorses after a fashion.

His face was thick-featured under the matted hair, heavily pocked, with a nose like a smaller spud attached to the mass. His companions were a gangling stork and a third man much younger than the other two, pinker and fatter as well; he carried a compound hunting bow with an arrow on the string and six more in the quiver clipped to the side of the weapon.

None of them looked *quite* like it was their first time on a horse, but . . .

It was what followed that made Eric swear under his breath, and Havel's eyes narrow. There was one more rider, a middle-aged black man with his feet lashed to the stirrups and his hands cuffed before him, with the chain of the handcuffs through a ring on the horn of his saddle. Two women walked beside the packhorses, also cuffed; the older looked Hispanic, or possibly Italian; the teenage girl beside her was darker, but had a family resemblance. All three of the captives looked like they'd been roughed up, and recently, with still-wet blood running from mouths and noses; the black man looked as if he'd have trouble walking at all, though even semiconscious he rode much better than his three captors.

The saddles were Western-style, looking practical and battered enough to be real working gear, and the mounts were excellent; definitely of quarter-horse stock, but in the older style, with good thick legs and strong hooves, and big for the breed.

"Afternoon," the potato-with-legs leader said as the party drew up; he halted within talking distance, but not close.

Havel waved a greeting, unobtrusively letting the rabbit stick fall into the palm of his right hand and handing it off to the left behind his back.

"Follow my lead," he said softly to Eric.

The young man nodded; Havel could tell he was trembling-tense, but he wasn't showing it much.

"Hello there," Havel went on. "Mind telling me what the hell's going on? We crash-landed up in the woods"—he waved his left hand back towards the wilderness rearing southward—"about ten days ago, and just walked out. Is it like this all over?"

The fat rider with the bow threw back his head and yeee-hawed; Havel had heard it done a lot better. The older two laughed.

"It's the apocalypse, brother," the potato-man said, grinning. "It's the downfall of the Z-O-G, and the triumph of God's people! And yeah, it's all over. Far as we know, and we've talked with people from as far as Smithton, and over to Billings in Montana. All of 'em on bicycles, trying to get somewhere better, and not finding it. And *they'd* talked to people from farther east and west."

*Uh-oh,* Havel thought, schooling his face to polite interest. *Bad news. And probably true, even given who's peddling it.* He recognized the breed; there weren't actually all that many of them in Idaho, but they made up for it in the amount of attention they attracted and the way they gave the state a bad name.

ZOG stood for "Zionist Occupation Government." These three were obviously some variety of neo-Nazi/Christian Identity/Aryan Brotherhood types, one of the groupuscules that had set up redoubts in northern Idaho through the eighties and nineties as part of the survivalist wave—or the scum on the wave, to be more descriptive.

The redoubts usually consisted of a cluster of mobile homes and shacks on heavily mortgaged land, splitting and recombining as the quarrelsome lunatics anathematized each other over fine points of ideology and/or got arrested for credit card scams and death threats to judges and process servers, but the inhabitants could be dangerous enough when they weren't selling each other out to the FBI.

The tall thin one was riding with his jacket open over a bare chest, and the tattoos under it were pure jailhouse; all three of them looked hopped up, as if they'd done a major hit of coke or won the Powerball.

*They have,* Havel suddenly realized with a chill. *If cars and radios and guns don't work, they've just inherited as much of the earth as they can take. No laws.*

Eric bent, as if he were scratching at his leg; out of the corner of his eye Havel couldn't be sure, but he thought the younger man palmed a rock.

*Good for you,* Havel thought, and went on: "You mean everything stopping working?"

The man nodded. "Didn't we say it was coming?" he crowed. "And now we white original sovereigns are coming into our own."

"What about these folks here?" Havel said mildly, drifting a little closer.

"We got us a good husky *slave* here," the thin man said, grinning. "To look after these fine horses he brought us. He'll be real useful once we've cut his balls off to make sure he don't breed."

"Couple of nice fuck-toys too," the youth with the bow said. "I like the look of the young one."

"In your dreams, Jimmie," the thickset man said; apparently he was the leader. "But you can have her momma tonight while I break her in."

The tattooed man scowled. "They're mud people, Dan," he said, probably a long-running argument. "They're unclean, most likely full of diseases. We ought to kill them right off, like we did those Indians."

"Now, Bob, we'll find us some good pure white women for bearing children," the leader said. "When we're settled in our stronghold waiting for the dying time to pass. Meantime, a man has his needs."

The black man was sitting slumped in the saddle, resting his cuffed hands on the horn and a good deal of his weight on those. His head was down as well, but his eyes peered up at Havel, flickered to Eric. There wasn't much hope in them, but there was thought, and he was probably noticing Havel's slow, inch-by-inch drift towards the riders. He looked to be about forty, with an outdoor worker's weathered skin and squint lines beside his eyes, sinewy and strong.

*He reminds me of someone . . . Glover, the actor who plays next to Gibson in that* Lethal Weapon *series,* ran through Havel's mind at some level entirely aside from the swift calculation that filled the active part of it.

"Dying time?" he said, edging a little closer still to Dan. "Could you tell me what you mean by that?"

"Well, it figures that with all the technology gone, most everyone's going to die, except in the real backward places, bush-niggers in Africa and such. Even country folk, without their tractors and pumps, and anyway those close to the cities will get eaten out. Without guns, they can't even defend their farms from the hordes. But up here in the National Redoubt where people are thin on the ground, we can survive and expand later. Lot of cattle and a lot of grain in Idaho. Not to mention game in the forests. I figure best thing is to hide out for maybe six months, then go looking for a place to live long-term."

*Not necessarily a complete idiot because he's a total shit,* Havel thought.

The man's eyes had glazed over with lust as he spoke; partly, Havel supposed, at contemplating the death of more of humanity than a nuclear war could have managed; partly at the prospect of being a big man among the survivors, after a lifetime of total failure; and partly a more human elation that at last he'd gotten something right, even if it was only improving his chances of surviving by moving to Idaho. From his accent, he'd started out in some East Coast city, although he was trying hard to westernize it.

*You know, generally the people I've killed have just been a cost of doing business,* Havel thought. *Because they were wearing the wrong uniforms. But this bunch would be a real personal pleasure. Why is it that guys who think they're the Master Race always look like walking advertisements for retroactive abortion?*

Just a minute more to get them relaxed. . . .

"You two boys look like good original-sovereign stock," the leader of the riders said. "Why don't you—"

"Help us!" the woman walking by the packhorse cried. "For God's sake, mister, please, help us! They're crazy!"

Eric wound up like a pitcher on the mound and threw his rock; he was too close to do a really good job, but his stream-smoothed lump of granite thumped into the shoulder of the bowman.

The archer loosed, the shaft flying inches wide of the back of the neck of the thin man with the jailhouse tattoos; that one did what Havel expected—clapped his heels to his horse's sides, heading straight for Eric. He had some notion of what to do in a fight.

The younger Larsson threw himself back with a yell, landing and rolling in the roadway and then dodging around a stopped car that stood with its doors open; he came right back through it, diving over the backseat faster than the inexperienced horseman could get his mount around it.

The knife flicked into Havel's hand and the rabbit stick into the other. The thickset man's horse thundered down on him; he'd never been charged by a man on horseback before, and his stroke with the stick at the rider's knee went wide—fortunately, so did the heavy man's potentially bone-shattering kick with one cup-stirrup-bearing foot. That nearly unseated him, and he clutched at the horn of his saddle.

Havel leapt forward again, trying for a hamstringing blow, and the *puukko*'s edge parted the leather of the leading rein instead. That set the packhorses loose; they went into bucking circles, their hooves a menace to everyone.

The heavy youth with the bow tried to grab the young girl by the chain of her handcuffs with his right hand and drag her up across the saddle in front of him while slinging the bow over his shoulder at the same time; she seized the hand in both of hers and sank her teeth into his wrist.

That made him shriek in pain and start trying to shake her off instead as his horse skittered sideways; and her mother added a series of ear-splitting screams to the confusion as she came up on the other side and began beating her clenched fists on his leg.

*Who says the Three Stooges are dead?* Havel thought. Christ Jesus, *what a cluster-fuck!*

Mr. Jailhouse Bob was coming back into the fight; he had a machete out now, from a sheath strapped to his saddle. He also came straight for Havel, ignoring the rest of the milling chaos.

*This one has a hard man's instincts,* Havel thought, poising lightly on the balls of his feet, weapons ready. *OK, he's target number one.*

Fortunately Bob's time in stir hadn't included training in the equestrian arts, and he misjudged the speed of his mount. His roundhouse swing passed a foot in front of Havel's face—close enough for him to feel the ugly wind of its passage—and nearly took an ear off his own horse. Havel's return stroke with the rabbit stick cracked into his arm. The blow was glancing, but it was enough to make him drop the machete. Then he clapped his heels into his horse's flanks and circled out of the fight again, shaking the limb and cursing but looking quickly back and forth to get a sense of the action.

*Damn, he really* does *think tactically,* Havel thought— that was a gift, and not limited to good guys.

The black man made his own contribution; even without reins, he managed to get his horse moving west, probably hoping to draw the rest off from his family. He succeeded; Dan and young Jimmie turned the heads of their horses around and went after him, but Jailhouse Bob was in their path. Instead of trying to pass him the black man turned his horse up the Centennial Trail to the south, disappearing into the steep heights and the tall pines.

"Get the nigger!" Dan cried as he spurred after him.

Jimmie followed, turning in the saddle to loose an arrow

that wobbled up at a mortar-shell angle and came down with a *shhhrink* into the roof of a car. Then he disappeared up the trail, leaving his tattooed elder to face four-to-one odds.

Havel dropped his rabbit stick and scooped up the fallen machete, starting towards the last of the bandits. Eric followed, picking up a few more baseball-weight rocks; behind him the two women were getting the packhorses under control, despite the handcuffs, which argued for considerable skill.

Bob looked at the approaching men with hatred that radiated from him like heat from a banked fire, then turned and followed his companions. Havel let out a long breath and shook his head, fighting down a wave of nausea and light-headedness. It had been a long time since he'd fought in a kill-or-be-killed situation, but it was just as unpleasant as he remembered.

Eric dropped his rocks. "Damn," he said. "I'm better than that with a baseball—I should have hit that fat fuck in the teeth or at least broken his collarbone."

"Not bad for your first real fight," Havel said, punching him in the shoulder. "Which it was, right?"

Eric grinned cautiously and touched his swollen nose and split lip. "Not counting you, Mike, yeah."

Havel nodded. "Only I don't think they had education in mind."

He turned to the women. "Ma'am," he said as the older of the two began to speak. "We need your help if we're going to rescue . . . your husband?"

She nodded; a woman of about forty, full-figured and with boldly handsome mestizo-Hispanic features, wearing riding jeans with a belt of silver medallions and a blousy white shirt. The teenager nodded too; she was darker, with a mass of frizzy hair, and would be quite pretty when she wasn't bloodied and terrified.

"Will, my husband. I'm Angelica Hutton, and this is our daughter, Luanne," she said; there was a soft Tejano-Spanish accent under a Southwestern twang.

"Mike Havel. Eric Larsson," Havel said shortly; there wasn't much time for social niceties.

"What do you need?" Angelica Hutton said steadily.

"Tools, if you've got them; can't do anything until we

bust you loose of those cuffs. And knives—one of them should be the biggest you've got."

There were tools; a jumble in one of the panniers, including a short heavy pry bar and a farrier's hammer. Havel grunted in satisfaction and freed each of the women with a few short clanging blows, the chain of their handcuffs stretched across a roadside boulder.

As he worked, the woman spoke. He caught most of it: ". . . just attacked us, they came down the road on bikes to where our trucks stopped; we'd been pasturing the horses and we were about to head out ourselves, we hadn't seen anyone else and they just *attacked* us. Will's gun didn't work, and the pistol . . . They took our horses and—"

"Any more of them?" Havel asked.

"Not from what they said. I think they'd been in a fight, and they were afraid some Indians were chasing them. They just took what they could grab and made us saddle up the horses and . . . they were going to . . ."

The packsaddles bore her account out, heaped high and packed badly, with a mélange of goods and food and gear thrown on higgledy-piggledy. It was probably a very good thing for Angelica Hutton and her daughter that the Aryan Trio had been pressed for time.

*Better keep them running,* Havel thought, and looked at Eric.

"You can ride?" he said.

"Since I was six. We always had horses."

"Good. Are these saddle-broke?"

"Yes," Angelica said. "We were taking them to an outfitter in Lewiston, and the stallion, they didn't get that one. My husband and I raise and train horses. These two are the slowest of the bunch, though."

Havel nodded crisply: "Look, Mrs. Hutton, get these packsaddles off, and hide your goods up there in that thicket, behind the big rock—you can get up along the side with a little work. I'd advise you to keep extremely quiet and wait. I don't have time to argue. We'll be back when we've done what has to be done, but it could be a couple of days or longer. Are those lashings rawhide?"

They were thin and soft-surfaced.

"Wet them down for me as well, would you please? Put them in water, do that first. And get me those knives."

"Thank you, and *los santos* go with you," the woman said; she and her daughter got to work with the quick competence of people who'd handled horses and their tack all their lives.

Havel worked as well. He'd spotted suitable red cedar saplings downslope to the north and not far from the edge of the road; the wood wasn't what he'd have chosen with more time, but it worked easily, and he'd been thinking hard about their brush with the three bandits. A few strokes of the machete at their bases felled both the young trees. After trimming the first he had a straight pole five feet long and another a little taller than he was.

A single swift hard chop split the smaller end of the first down the middle, leaving a cleft twelve inches long, and he repeated the process for the second, longer one. Then he used the hammer and prybar to knock the wooden handle off the machete, and punch out the two rivets; the tang was solid except for those holes, a simple continuation of the blade. He forced it into the cleft of the shorter pole, trimming with his knife and waggling it carefully to seat it and then hammering in two horseshoe nails from a bag in the packsaddles.

Angelica brought him the rawhide thongs, which had at least been thoroughly wetted down.

"Wish there was more time to soak these," he said absently.

Eric came up and helped hold the shaft while he bound the cleft with a double layer of leather cord, using the ends of the nails as tie-points and pulling the wet leather as tightly as he could with both hands and bracing foot. Then he turned the ends of the nails down with a few swift hammer-blows; there was no wobble when he shook the improvised weapon, and in a while the drying leather would hold it on like iron. The result was a shaft about the thickness of a shovel handle, with two feet of chopping steel fixed on the end coming to just over eye level on the younger Larsson.

"Looks like a *naginata*," Eric said.

"That's the idea," Havel said. "I was stationed in Okinawa for a while back in 'eighty-nine. You ever trained with one?"

"Just a few times, and watching. Hate to have to use one and try to ride a horse, though."

"Better than nothing, and we'll get down to fight. These'll give us enough reach to get at a man on horseback; *I* ride a lot better than those clowns, and I wouldn't care to try and fight from the saddle without a lot of practice."

While he spoke he sorted through the knives; he knocked the handle off a good-sized pointed kitchen blade, and bound it into the second shaft as he had the machete. Now he had a spear as well, about seven feet long in all.

By the time the weapons were ready the horses were as well; they both had bags of food thrown across their withers.

Eric gave him a boost to mount, then sprang on with rather more agility himself; Havel was a good practical horseman, and he'd enjoyed wilderness trips in the saddle, but he hadn't grown up in a family who had a stable at a country property.

"Wait, and keep out of sight," Havel said to the two women. *They ought to be OK. Plenty of food for a week or two.* "If we're not back in seven days . . . well, do what you think best."

"God go with you," Angelica said, crossing herself.

They both pressed their thighs to their mounts and the well-trained animals moved, taking the steep section of the trail that joined Highway 12.

Havel looked up. It was about an hour to the early spring sunset; the sky was already darkening in the east, and the temperature was dropping—it might go below freezing in the dark, and they probably wouldn't dare light a fire, but the horses should help keep them warm.

"We've got problems," he said to Eric, drawing level with him. The trail was broad enough for that, and soft enough that he could read the tracks fairly easily: one horse galloping first, and then three more strung out after it. *Call it twenty miles an hour over this terrain, but they can't keep that up for long, even though these horses are pretty fresh and well-fed.*

"Tell me about it," Eric said.

The answer was probably rhetorical, but Havel took it literally: "We've got a set of problems, assuming we don't get lucky and find the Three Demon Stooges lying with their necks broken 'cause they couldn't stay on. OK, first, there's the kid with the bow."

"He didn't hit anything," Eric observed. "And we were pretty close."

"Not from a horse he didn't, no. But he might be a lot better on foot. Those hunting bows are no joke—look what your kid sister did with one, and neither of us is as tough a target as a bull elk! That means we have to get real close before he sees us. Next, there's tall skinny tattoo-man. You noticed him?"

"He's worse than the others?"

"He's a real killer, not a wannabe or a blowhard; I recognize the type. I don't know if he's got any hunting experience, or whether he's got any brains, but he won't panic or freeze up—which the other two might. That's the difference between life and death when it's for real."

Eric swallowed; he was coming down from the adrenaline high of the brief chaotic fight, and looking a bit pale. But he was a sharp kid, and he probably took the point about freezing up better than he would if Havel had stated it openly.

"What's the third problem?"

"They're heading right towards your folks . . . *stop right there!*"

The young man reined in at the snap of command.

"We come barreling down after them, they're likely to hear us coming and ambush us. Right now they're going hell for leather after Hutton—the black guy. They'll catch him, he can't get off the trail tied to his horse like that, but they won't worry about us if we're real careful."

"Why not?" Eric said.

"Because to their way of thinking, we've got the women and the stuff; plus they don't know about your family. They may know about the old cabin, though. Three on two is bad odds. This is going to be real tricky."

He paused a moment. "You realize we're going to have to kill them all?"

Eric nodded abruptly, swallowing again; he started to speak, cleared his throat, and then went on: "Yeah, Mike, I do. They'll kill my folks if we don't, won't they? And rape my sisters. And they'll torture that black guy."

"For starters," Havel said.

The sun was setting on the mountains behind them, and the beauty of it made him shiver a little as the great trees threw spears of shadow before them. He'd told Signe that the forest wasn't hostile; and that was still true. But men, now . . . men had been suddenly thrown back each on himself. The cake of law and custom had been broken; now they were all on their own, and their true natures could come out, for good or ill.

"They're fucking monsters!" Eric burst out.

Havel shook his head. "No, they're just evil," he replied. "But that's close enough for government work."

# CHAPTER EIGHT

"What the hell *is* going on?" the store owner said, under the sign that read DABLE GARDEN AND LAWN SUPPLY.

He looked at the two great horse-drawn wagons; curious children freed by the lack of school buses gathered around as well. Chuck Barstow glanced up and down the one street of the little town of Dable; houses faded into farmland not two hundred yards from where he stood, and new leaves were budding on the trees that arched overhead.

It was only nine o'clock, but there was a line outside the bakery and the little grocery store. A group of men were pushing the dead cars out of the middle of the street, clearing the way. Several of them looked speculatively at the wagons, which made him nervous.

The strong smell of the horses' sweat filled the air; getting out of Eugene had been a nightmare—if you could call this out of it, since a ribbon of suburb and strip mall extended nearly this far. Nobody had attacked them—quite—or seemed to guess what was under the canvas tilts. He still shuddered and swallowed acid at the back of his throat, thinking of the things he'd seen in the dying city.

"What do you think has happened?" Chuck said.

"Don't know," the storekeeper admitted. "Figure it's some sort of big power-out."

"What about the cars? Radios? The batteries?" Chuck said.

"Well, that could be one of those government projects—I read about it in *Popular Mechanics,* a bomb aimed at frying electronic gear. That's what must have happened; a test got out of hand."

*If that was all, I might have believed something like that myself.* Aloud he went on: "What about the guns?"

"*Guns* aren't working?" the man said, his face going fluid with shock for a second.

Then he chuckled: "I suppose that's why you folks are carrying the swords and such."

Chuck had his own Society long sword at his belt and a buckler—a little shield like a steel soup-plate—hooked over it, along with his dagger on his right hip; he'd had those over at Andy and Diana's for coven work. He shoved down a wistful thought about the gear at home in his garage; they'd decided it was too risky to go all the way south through the city for them, and that was that. The rest of the coveners had shovels, or axes, or at least long kitchen knives and baseball bats.

"What do you think really happened?" the storekeeper said.

"Well, we figure it's a global catastrophe," Chuck said. "All our technology—anything involving engines or electricity or guns—has suddenly stopped working. Planes fell out of the air. Most of humanity is going to die in the next six months, except for peasant farmers, and a lot of *them* are going to die too unless they're real lucky. It's the end of the world as we knew it, and of civilization. So we'd like to buy some things from you, if you're still foolish enough to accept money. *We're* running for our lives and honestly, I advise you to do the same damned thing."

The storekeeper was a thin balding man with thick glasses. Chuck could see his words being processed and rejected behind them.

*Weirdos,* the man thought, almost audibly. *Suckers. But well-heeled suckers.*

Chuck shivered internally. He knew he was talking to a man who would die, soon and horribly, simply because he couldn't really believe in what had happened.

It was all he could do to make *himself* believe in what had happened, despite the way everything had simply stopped working.

*Too big,* he thought. *It's just too big. For most people, at least. I'm used to believing in things everyone else doesn't, and I think it's an advantage . . . and I did* try *to tell this guy the truth.*

From what he'd seen, the vast majority of people were going to wait awhile for things to return to normal, or for the Army or the National Guard to show up. Then when they started to get hungry, or the water didn't run anymore, probably a lot of them would panic and go *looking* for a place where things were normal. The idea that the whole planet had . . . Changed . . . was simply too big to grasp; and accepting it meant looking death in the face, the death of a world.

He shivered and swallowed a bubble of nausea; it was too big to grasp thoroughly, down in the gut, and all at once. By the time most really got it into their heads, it would be too late.

*I'm among the living dead,* he thought.

There were advantages to being one of a collection of misfits who believed in magic.

"So, what would you folks like?" the thin man said.

*When the world turns weird, the weird get going,* Chuck thought. Aloud he went on, suppressing laughter—hysterical laughter that he probably couldn't stop once it started: "Do you accept personal checks?"

Sally sat beside Juniper on the driver's seat of the Traveler wagon; it was comfortable enough as they rumbled eastward along the dirt road, with a piece of artfully arranged board to support her injured leg. The Portland woman handled the reins quite well for an amateur, but the horses were experienced and knew the way as hills rose on either side.

Shadows flickered over them from tall roadside trees; between them were vistas of fields on either side, and growing patches of tall conifer forest running up creeksides and gullies towards the heights on either hand.

Juniper kept an eye cocked on Cagney and Lacey as her fingers moved on the strings of the guitar and she sang:

> *"Fly free your good gray hawk*
> *To gather the golden rod*
> *And face your horse unto the clouds*
> *Above yon gay green wood.*
> *Oh, it's weary by the Ullswater*
> *And the misty breakfern way*
> *Till through the crutch of the Kirkstane pass—"*

The slow staccato clop and crunch of the hooves beat a rhythm below the rumbling wheels, and the rattle and creak of the wagon's wooden framework. She could smell dust from the road, the strong grassy smell of the big platter-footed gray horses, and greenness from forest and field beyond; a wet breath of coolness from Artemis Butte Creek as it swung closer to the south side of the roadway.

Underneath the country smells was a tang of burning, something they hardly noticed anymore—it had been constant since the Change. The Willamette was a giant trough, and the smoke from the vast city fires would linger for a long time—until the fall rains came to clean the air, most likely.

*Not surprising. With no power, what's the first thing people will do? Make fires, for heat and light and cooking, and when one gets out of control . . .*

The music made the thoughts go away, at least for a while. When she'd finished the song, Juniper put the guitar behind her—there was a padded rack for it on her traveling wagon—and took the reins back. The road wasn't as straight and level now, as they wound up the creekside towards the mountains.

"That was nice," Sally said. "I didn't go in much for that sort of music, but . . . I've missed *music.* Any sort of music."

She'd started talking more since she'd stopped being so fearful of the strangers—a fear for which Juniper couldn't blame her, considering the circumstances of their meeting. She *could* blame her for her soft-pop tastes, but didn't, not aloud.

There were types of music Juniper liked but didn't play herself—she had a weakness for old-time blues, Americana and even some types of hip-hop—and she'd probably never hear them again.

*My entire CD collection is useless, except as coasters,* she thought. *And all the old vinyl too. No music but the live kind, from now on. Maybe I should expand my repertoire.*

"I was thinking," Sally said. "About those songs you do . . . I mean, the knights and swords and horses . . . I mean, is all that coming back?"

"All that never existed, not the way the ballads paint it," Juniper said. "I don't think what's coming will be exactly like the real past, either—but it's certainly going to have more in common with it than with the way things were right before the Change. Which is a pity; things were *real* rough back in the old days."

Sally smiled. "I suspect it's going to be a weird old world, when things settle down."

"That it will," Juniper said, musing; it was easier than thinking about the immediate future. "Well . . . buffalo on the Plains, again, perhaps?"

Sally nodded. "And not just buffalo. I took wildlife biology and ecology courses before I met Peter, and I did volunteer work at the zoo before Terry was born. Guess which country in the world has the most tigers?"

Juniper blinked in surprise. "Ah . . . India? China?"

Sally shook her head. "The United States of America. Over twenty thousand of them, mostly privately owned."

"Like that Tiger Lady in New Jersey, who turned out to have a whole pack of them?"

"Right. A lot of them are in enclosures they could get out of, with some determined effort—places out in the country. Tigers are *really* adaptable and smart and they breed fast, and without guns shooting at them they're very hard to kill. I'd be surprised if a lot of them didn't get loose. . . ."

"And there are those exotic-wildlife ranches," Juniper said thoughtfully. "Many of them well out in remote places, to be sure. And ostriches and emus and . . . why, I saw llamas in plenty the last time I was out Bend way."

Sally agreed. "If I know them, the volunteers at the zoo in Portland will probably turn the animals there loose when they can't feed them. It'll make for some interesting ecological swings, when people are . . . rare . . . again."

*Something else to worry about,* Juniper thought; it made a change from obsessively *not* thinking about what was happening to all the people right now.

The hills pushed closer to the creekside road, and fresh-painted board fences appeared to their left. She pulled in slightly on the reins, calling out a soft *whoa!* to the team, and the wagon slowed to an ambling walk as they came level with a tall log-framed gate on the north side of the road.

"Is this your place?" Sally asked.

"No, it's the Fairfax farm," Juniper said, pointing with her left hand. "They're the last house below me. It's not really a working farm, more of a hobby place for the Fairfaxes—they're retired potato-growers from Idaho."

She stood, resting one hand on the brake lever beside her and shading her eyes with the other; it was a warm day for March, and sunny, full of fresh sweet odors; they were traveling by daylight, now that they were so close to home.

The gravel-and-dirt road they were on ran east up the narrowing valley of Artemis Butte Creek; half a mile ahead it turned north to her land. It was all infinitely familiar to her, even the deep quiet, but somehow strange . . . perhaps *too* quiet, without even the distant mutter of a single engine. The Ponderosa-style gate Mr. Fairfax had put up when he bought the fifty-acre property three years ago was to her left, northward; the little stream flowed bright over the rocky bed to her right.

Hills rose ever more steeply to either side, turning into low forested mountains as they hemmed the valley in north and south; behind them the road snaked west like a yellow-brown ribbon, off towards the invisible flats of the Willamette. A cool breath came from the ridges, shaggy with Douglas fir, vine maple and Oregon oak.

"You can't see my cabin from here, but it's that way," Juniper went on, shifting her pointing arm a little east of north, up the side of the mountain.

"It's in the forest on the slope?" Sally asked.

From here, there didn't look to be any other alternative; the ground reared up from the back of the Fairfax place to the summit three thousand feet above; most of it at forty-five degrees or better, with no sign of habitation. Eastward ridges rose higher to the Cascades proper, snow peaks floating against heaven.

"No," Juniper said. "You can't see it, not from here, but there's a break in the slope—the side of the hill levels off into sort of a bench along the south side about four hundred feet up. There's a long strip more or less level, a meadow a mile long and a quarter wide. The creek crosses it from higher up, then turns west when it hits the head of this valley where the hills pinch together, and the road follows it. Right after the Civil War my ancestors arrived and spent two futile lifetimes trying to make a decent living off that patch up there. Maybe it reminded them of East Tennessee! But it stayed in the family when we moved into town in my great-granddad's time."

"Not very good land?"

"Middling, what there is of it that isn't straight up and down, but Lady and Lord, it's pretty! There's two creeks and a nice strong spring right by the cabin. All but the bench is in trees, near eight hundred acres of our woods, and more forest all around and behind it. We Mackenzies got to Oregon just a wee bit late for the share-out, you might say—story of our line since we left County Antrim for Pennsylvania in 1730, always just a little behindhand for the pickings."

"Eight hundred acres sounds fairly substantial."

"Not if you're a farmer, and the most of it's hillside! My great-uncle Earl the banker kept the farm as a summer place, and bought more of the hills about; he was a hunter, and dabbled in what they called scientific forestry. Then the good man left it to me, the unwed teenage mother, the family's shame, the sorrow and black disgrace of it; everyone said he was senile. Mind you, I'd been spending summers there all my life, and was a bit of a favorite of his, and he adored little Eilir. Well, who wouldn't?"

Sally seemed to hesitate, then spoke: "Your family has been here a long time then? I thought you sounded . . . well, a little different." She smiled. "I'm sort of sensitive to accents; I spent my teenage years trying to shed mine."

"Ah, different I am," Juniper said, grinning and dropping further into a stage-Irish brogue for an instant. "Me sainted mither was a fair Irish rose, d'ye see? From the Gaeltacht, at that—Achill Island."

In her normal voice: "She met Dad while he was in the Air Force, over in England; his side of the family are Scots-Irish with a very faint touch of Cherokee. Mom had a genuine brogue, bless her, and spoke the Gaelic to me in my cradle; and for my type of music, a hint of the Celt does no harm professionally, so I make a habit of keeping it up. Did make a habit."

"Just the opposite for me. My father was Air Force too— Vietnamese air force, of course. He flew us out in a helicopter, but I don't really remember—"

Juniper held up her left hand and pulled the horses in;

Sally fell silent at the sharp sudden movement. Then Juniper set the brake lever and stood, shading her eyes.

Terry and Eilir had been tearing along the roadside verge, playing some game; he'd even picked up a little Sign over the past few days. Cuchulain had been romping along with them when he wasn't chasing rabbits real and imaginary.

Now he stopped by the gate and looked uncertain, running back and forth a bit with his tail down.

"He smells something he doesn't like," Juniper said, handing over the reins and picking up her crossbow; Dennis was carrying his ax instead.

Dennis caught the same clue. He'd been walking by the horses' heads; now he stepped away, pushing back the brim of his cowboy hat. His right hand went back and down along the haft of the ax hooked over his shoulder, lifting and flipping it to hold slantwise across his thick chest. Short commons and hard work had started whittling down the beer belly; now he looked like a shaggy ill-kept barrel rather than a melancholy pear.

"What's wrong?" Sally said sharply.

"Nothing except the fool dog, for now," Juniper said; she spanned the spare crossbow before she handed it to Sally.

Then her own went into the crook of her arm. "But I'd better take a look."

She whistled; Terry looked up and touched Eilir's arm, and they came back to the wagon.

*Look after him, and keep an eye out,* Juniper signed—too rapidly for Terry to follow, so that the boy wouldn't take alarm; he still had nightmares.

*Be careful, Mom,* Eilir replied, getting her own weapon from the wagon and slipping a bolt into place.

"The Fairfaxes friends of yours?" Dennie said as they let themselves through the gate and started cautiously up the laneway that wove between two grassy green slopes.

"Not really friends," Juniper said, her eyes roving.

About half the Fairfax place was wooded, the steeper northern section; the merely hilly half towards the road and the creek was in pasture and fenced with white boards, apart from a bit in some bluish green grassy crop she didn't recognize and a substantial orchard. They cut kitty-corner northeast through the ancient gnarled fruit trees; it was apples mostly, with some cherries, only recently pruned and sprayed after years of neglect. Blossoms showed tender pink and frothy white, scenting the air as the two walked beneath.

The house wasn't visible from the road, being tucked into a steep south-facing hill with a pond in front of it and then more hill beyond, with grass blowing on it among the blue camas flowers.

*Too quiet,* she thought. *Doesn't feel like there are people there.*

Aloud: "Not unfriends either, for all that they're strong Mormons and went pale when they realized I was an actual living breathing Witch. Frank does me favors with his tractor now and then, and his wife gave me some jam she made last summer, but it's a nodding acquaintance."

"You afraid someone less neighborly has moved in?"

"Just fearful in general, Dennie. Hush."

They went through the last of the fruit trees, and then to their hands and knees below the crest line of the hill; Juniper could go ghost-silent that way, the fruit of months every year of her life following the ways of bird and beast in these wooded hills. Dennis had all the grace of an elephant seal hauled up on a beach, but it probably didn't matter. . . .

She uncased her bird-watching binoculars—another gift from Great-uncle Earl, who'd shared the hobby—as they lay concealed in the knee-high grass.

The Fairfax place was old, a four-square frame farmhouse built in the 1880s. It had been boarded up and derelict for years before Frank Fairfax bought it. Now the white paint shone in the sunlight; the neat lawn with its flowerbeds went down to the pond, and a tractor tire hung from the bough of a big willow, for the times his grandchildren visited. He'd added a two-car garage, repaired and repainted the barn, and put in some sheds as well. For a retired man of seventy, he drove himself hard; probably a lifelong habit he couldn't shake.

"His stock are loose," Juniper said after a moment. "Which he'd never allow."

There were a dozen sheep lying in the shade of the tree, not far from the pond, fluffy white Correidales with a collie lying close by them; it got up and barked warningly at the humans. The henhouse by the barn gaped empty and silent.

*Harder to keep chickens from being eaten,* Juniper thought with a chill.

A Jersey cow and her bull calf were hock-deep in the water, drinking; they looked up and blinked mild welcome as they scented the humans, jaws working on mouthfuls of waterweed. She scanned over to the barnyard; the gate there was open, and the fifty-horsepower tractor parked off to one side under its shelter roof. Not far from it was a truck with a seed company logo on its side. Birds flew in and out of the buildings in throngs.

"Silent as the grave," Dennis said, which made her shiver a little.

"Let's go see," she said roughly.

Dennis led with his ax at the ready, and she behind him and to one side with the crossbow held to her shoulder. Fear gave way to sadness well before they came to the veranda with its swing chair and lace-bordered cushions.

"Christ," Dennis said, lowering the ax and putting a sleeve of his dusty flannel shirt over his mouth.

Juniper tied a bandana from her hip pocket over hers as she approached the door; she could hear the buzzing of flies going in and out of a half-opened window on the second floor, over to her right—the master bedroom. A crow launched itself from the windowsill as she watched, the harsh *gruck-gruck-gruck* loud in her ears.

Juniper swallowed. *I know it's the natural cycle,* she thought. The Goddess was also the Crone, death and darkness as well as light and rebirth were Her mysteries; that was why the scald-crow was sacred to Her. *But . . .*

There was a note taped to the glass behind the screen door, and the keys dangled by a cord from the knob. Juniper read it aloud:

*"The emergency generator cut out when the main power went and I couldn't get it started, and nobody else round about seems to be better off. I put our insulin in the icebox. Joan used the last of it yesterday. It was spoiled, but there wasn't anything else, so I told her there were two doses and injected water myself. I'm sure now she'll never wake up. I'm starting to feel very sleepy and thirsty and my feet are numb; I'm sorry I can't give her proper burial, and ask anyone who finds this to try and see*

*that we're given LDS rites. Sam from the seed company left two days ago to get help and hasn't come back. I'm going to go let the stock loose so they can water themselves and set out feed while I still have some strength, but the road gate's closed so they won't wander too far.*

*"The second key is to the cellar where our emergency stores are. Anyone who needs them can use them; just don't waste anything. I think bad times are here, and that's what they're for. Whoever reads this, God keep you."*

The next part was probably written later; the strong bold hand was much shakier:

*"I can't keep awake anymore, so I'm going upstairs to be by Joan in eternity as we have been together so long in time. Tell Joseph and John and Dave and June and Kathleen and all the children that we love them. Frank Fairfax."*

Juniper turned away, clearing her throat and wiping savagely at her eyes with the back of her hand.

"Blessed be," she said softly, remembering their strained politeness, and the Christmas cookies they'd given Eilir, and the swarm of grandchildren who'd asked permission before they went up into her woods when they visited around Ostara time last year—Easter to Christians.

Silently to herself: *Dread Lord of Death and Resurrection, take Frank and Joan Fairfax into Your keeping. Lead them home, that they may find sweet rest in the Land of Summer until they return, as all things are reborn through the Cauldron of the Goddess. So merry meet, and merry part, and merry meet again.*

Dennis stood back respectfully as Juniper put a hand to her eyes; he hadn't known them, after all. Then he looked at the animals, and the open barn as she came down from the veranda; he took the keys from her hand.

"I'm sorry as can be about your neighbors, Juney. But we ought to take an inventory. Their family was in Idaho?"

"Farmers near Twin Falls," she said. "Potatoes in a large way; Frank said"—she swallowed—"that he couldn't live without putting in a patch at least."

She went into the molasses-smelling dimness of the barn; Fairfax had opened sacks of feed, and one of kibble for his sheepdog. There were more flats of pelletized alfalfa up in the loft, grain-and-molasses feed and baled hay—old-fashioned square bales, at that.

*Not only some stock, but we can feed it,* she thought, a huge weight lifting from her chest. *There's plenty of grazing here and on my place, and this will keep it over the winter.*

The milk would be good for Terry, and Eilir . . . and perhaps she could try her hand at making butter and cheese, there were descriptions in books she had. A vision of Eilir's face goblin-thin like pictures of an African famine faded from the back of her mind.

*And don't Mormons believe in keeping a lot of food on hand? Maybe that's what he meant by emergency stores. The Fairfaxes took all that seriously, I think. I'll look up some Mormons to do the rites their way when I can,* she promised herself.

Twin Falls, Idaho, might as well be on the far side of the Atlantic for all the good the Fairfaxes' family would get out of their stuff here, and they were probably better off than anyone on the western side of the Cascades anyway.

*But Eugene isn't that far away,* she thought. *Dare I go and try and find Rudy?* The place would probably be chaos and madness and stalking death by now. *But dare I not try, Goddess? Didn't You descend to Annwyn for Your consort? And there's Chuck, and Judy, and Diana . . .*

Then Dennis burst in, flourishing his ax. "Seed potatoes!" he yelled. "The sacks read 'Oregon Foundation Seed Program Certified Potatoes!' The man must have been on a delivery run when the Change hit; Juney, there's a couple of *tons* of planting spuds on the truck. And the whole basement's stuffed with canned food and preserves and flour and medicines and seeds and candles and you name it! We're saved!"

She threw herself at him, and they whirled about in an impromptu dance, whooping with glee. After a breathless moment she broke free.

*Thanks be, Mother-of-All. I see what You're telling me.*

He was still exclaiming and waving the ax when her face went sober.

"What's wrong, Juney?" he said. "We can plant enough potatoes up by your place to keep us going all next winter, if we hurry—and there's enough to feed us all until October in style, too."

"Provided nobody comes up the road with bad intent," she said. "There's an old logging track from the back of the

Fairfax place to the cabin. We'll use that up to the cabin, and get things in order. And then we'll start."

"Planting potatoes?" Dennie said curiously.

"We'll start doing what we can for the world."

"For the world?"

Juniper waved a hand at the barn. "The Mother-of-All's been good to us, Dennie. But She's giving us a message, too. We have to pay back, if we don't want the luck to leave us—threefold return for good or ill."

"Whoa," Chuck Barstow said, easing back on the reins. The other two wagons and the walking coveners halted too.

It was a bright, breezy spring day; sixty or a little more, and no sign of rain, for a wonder. The big yellow school bus ahead had swerved half off the road. That was a narrow country two-lane blacktop, fifteen miles north of Eugene and a few east of the I-5. They hadn't seen anything but a few local farmers on foot and the odd horseman for hours, which was a relief.

The wagons could carry a lot, but they couldn't do it very fast or for very long at a time, not without killing the horses. He wasn't an expert—he knew just enough to put the harness on properly—but he knew that, from Juniper's tales of her team and what he'd picked up at RenFaires and Society events.

Faces came to the windows of the bus, and two small figures ran out, jumping up and down and waving their arms at the adults.

Chuck blinked again. It was a boy and a girl, both nine or ten, both in white shirts and green blazer jackets with some crest on the breast pocket, shorts and brown shoes and knee socks. One had tow blond hair and the other dark red braids and freckles.

"Please!" the boy cried. "Sanjay's sick!"

"We're *hungry*," the girl added. "And we don't have any more water, either. Not *good* water."

Chuck's eyes flicked to the bus again; Washington plates, and they'd been heading north when things . . . Changed. Why on this side road and not I-5, the Lord and Lady alone knew.

More children came crowding out of the bus; he counted twelve, all about the same age. Diana pulled up the second wagon, and the coveners on foot gathered around—all the adults had tools over their shoulders, long-handled pruning hooks or shovels or pitchforks. The garden-supply store manager *had* been willing to accept personal checks; they'd cleaned him out of most of his seed—for plants you could eat—and the tools could double as weapons at need. He thought they might have stopped a few fights already, simply by being there.

It was a new experience, being envied for his wealth; he didn't much like it. The coveners looked at the children with troubled eyes; their own children mostly glared at the newcomers with pack-instinct suspicion.

"Sanjay's *really* sick," the boy went on.

Before Chuck could open his mouth, Judy was off the bench with her bag in hand. Chuck hesitated, ran a hand over his receding blond hair, then shrugged and followed.

"Dorothy, would you mind watering them?" he asked, in passing.

The horses stood patiently, twitching their hides occasionally or tossing a head in a jingle of harness. Chuck's own nose twitched as Judy walked up the stairs by the vacant driver's seat. Sanjay was at the back of the bus, lying on an improvised pallet of coats and covered with more of the same; the children had made a clumsy effort to clean up the vomit, but he'd obviously fouled himself as well. His clammy, sweating brown face looked at them with bewildered hope—he was South Asian, by the name and the delicate fine-boned features.

Judy knelt by his side; the boy was groaning faintly and moving, clutching at his middle. She brought out an old-fashioned mercury thermometer and her stethoscope and began an examination.

"Mister," the tow-haired boy said. "I'm supposed to give you these."

*These* were notes. The first was from a Ms. Wyzecki, teacher at St. George's, Washington, in brusque no-nonsense tones: *None of the local people know what's going on,* it finished. *I am going to contact the authorities.*

A list of addresses and phone numbers followed. The driver's note was short and to the point: *The kids are getting hungry. I'm taking the bike and going to see where the hell Ms. Wyzecki is, or where there's something to eat, or both. If I'm not back by the time you read this, look after them. They're good kids.*

The first was dated Thursday morning, the second Friday at noon, twenty hours ago.

"Chuck!"

Judy's voice was sharp, her nurse-practitioner tone. He looked up.

"This boy has a stomach bug—contaminated water. I'm going to have to rehydrate him with a drip, and then he needs to be cleaned up and kept warm. I won't use an antibiotic unless he gets worse—Goddess knows when I can get more. Bring him!"

He did; the other children gathered round him solemnly as he laid Sanjay down on a tarp and Judy began to work.

"He drank water from the ditch when the bottles ran out," the mahogany-haired girl said. "I *told* him not to."

"Oh, sweet Goddess Queen of Heaven," Chuck groaned to himself.

"Do you mean Mary, Jesus' mother?" the girl asked curiously.

"Sort of," he replied, looking around at the others.

"I'm named Mary too. My brother's Daniel. We all went to the play in Ashland, and we were supposed to be taking notes on the countryside."

"Pleased to meet you," he said, solemnly shaking hands.

Like many kids their age, these seemed to have an almost catlike concern for propriety and routine. A few were sniffling or crying with sheer relief at the arrival of adults, and accepting hugs; others were more timid. Mary and Daniel weren't crying, not out loud, but a little of the look of strain left their faces.

*I cannot leave these kids here to die,* he realized suddenly. *I simply can't.*

"Let's set up a cookfire," he said to Diana. "We'll need sterilized water."

"I'll get the water jugs," Andy said. "We could heat up some miso soup. If they haven't eaten for a day and a half, they'll need something easy to start with."

The others split apart, to get at goods packed in a hurry, or to calm their own children.

"Can you take us home?" the redheaded girl said, after

her first ecstatic gulp of water. "Our parents are going to be really worried. I mean, we couldn't phone or *anything*."

"We can't take you home just now," he said. "Where do they live?"

"Mom lives in Seattle. Dad moved to Los Angeles after they . . . well, they had a big fight."

*You'll probably never see either again, then,* he thought. Aloud: "Well, we'll just have to look after you until we can find your folks."

St. George's seemed to be an expensive private school, the sort where really rich people parked offspring they didn't have time for; the kids had been on a special excursion to the Shakespearian festival at Ashland, of all things.

Eugene had been bad enough the first night and day. What Seattle was like by now . . . not to mention LA . . .

*I don't want to think about it,* he decided. Then, looking skyward and back at the earth and over towards the children: *OK, OK, I can take a hint, You two!*

"We'll take you somewhere fun in the meantime, though," he said to Mary. "Do you like camping out?"

She nodded solemnly. "You and your brother and . . . Sanjay?" Mary nodded again. "You and your brother and Sanjay can stay with us and Tamsin until things get better."

*If they ever do,* he thought. Aloud: "OK, people, volunteers for fostering!"

"What's that?" Sally asked, pointing to a big black-walnut tree as the wagon creaked and jounced over the ruts of the logging road.

Juniper Mackenzie looked up. She'd been musing on how to get the food stores out of the Fairfax place and safely into her cabin's cellar and her barn. That was why she'd decided to take the steeper way from the back of the farm up through the belt of forest and to her land. It was quicker, and if the logger's trucks hadn't torn it up too much she might spend the rest of the day getting a first load.

*And do my shed and barn and cellar have enough room for all those seed potatoes? They need to be kept in a cool dark place until we plant. Needs must, we could bury them under straw in trenches, I suppose—*

On the path-side tree was a wheel with eight spokes. A

plank below it had letters burned into the wood: EWTWRF: AIHN,DAYW. Embracing the wheel was a huge pair of elk antlers—once the pride of her great-uncle's cabin—with a silver-painted crescent moon between them on the wheel's hub, points upward.

"That's the Wheel of the Year," Juniper said. "Crescent Moon for the Goddess; horns for the God, of course; we're the Singing Moon Coven, too. I put it up a long time ago, when I was in my new-convert, in-your-face phase."

"And the letters?"

"That's an acronym." She recited: *"Eight Words The Wiccan Rede Fulfill: An It Harm None, Do As Ye Will.* It's our basic commandment, you might say. 'Rede' is just an old word for maxim or precept or advice."

Huge Oregon white oak and Douglas fir stood tall around them; the living musty-yeasty-green smell of the spring woods was strong. The woods were second growth, but the area hadn't been clear-cut since before World War I, and they'd been carefully managed for most of the time since, not to mention widely planted with valuable hardwoods like the walnut. Their rich mast of nuts and acorns attracted game, too.

Dappled sunlight flowed over the rutted dirt of the road in a moving kaleidoscope, and Eilir and Dennis strode ahead of the horses, signing to each other. Terry was curled up asleep on a nest of sacks behind them in the wagon, and the Jersey cow walked along tethered to its rear, with her calf following of its own accord. Sally looked much more herself with a few days' rest and food; also much more ready to ask questions. She gave Juniper an odd sidelong look.

"That's . . . ah . . . a very civilized maxim," she said, glancing over her shoulder as they passed the sign.

"True. It's also bloody difficult, if you take it seriously; it includes psychological harm, and it includes harming yourself. Very different from *follow your whim.*"

"I . . . it's sort of difficult to believe you're actually a, ah . . ."

"Witch," Juniper said, grinning. She put an index finger on the tip of her nose and waggled it back and forth. "But this is broken, so I can't magic us up much in the way of goods."

At Sally's blank look, she went on: "Classical reference." *And my collection of* Bewitched *episodes on tape useless, curse it.*

"Anyway, the Craft is a religion—magic is sort of one aspect of it, not the whole thing—and anything you've heard about it is probably wrong. Or read, or seen in a movie especially."

That did get through, thankfully. *At least my charitable impulse didn't saddle me with a fanatic who doesn't believe in 'suffering a Witch to live.'* You found those in the most surprising places.

Juniper went on aloud: "My coven meets here, for the Sabbats and some Esbats; the Coven of the Singing Moon. We have a *nemed,* a sacred wood and . . . It's sort of a private faith; you won't find us knocking on doors, and we don't claim a monopoly on truth or think ourselves better than others."

Then she shrugged. "Well, being human, we actually do think we're better, but most of us try not to act like it. And . . . we *did* meet here. Goddess knows how many of my bunch are alive now."

"Is Dennie one of your . . . ah . . . coven?" Sally asked; she seemed to be having trouble making herself say certain words. "Ah . . . I'm a Buddhist myself."

"No; he's a blatant materialist, the poor man. And he's not Eilir's father, either; I know you were dying to ask. Or my lover. Eilir is living proof that you *can* get pregnant your first time: *Is minic a chealg briathra mìne cailìn crìonna,* as Mom used to say. Many a prudent girl was led astray with honeyed words. By smooth-talking football players in senior high; bad cess to *him,* but I can't regret Eilir."

Sally gave a chuckle of laughter. "She's a nice girl, even . . ."

She touched her leg where the wound from the crossbow bolt was healing nicely. Neither of them mentioned the fact that a few inches up and to the left and it would have cut her femoral artery and spilled all her life's blood on the road.

"She's a wonder, and that's the truth," Juniper said, happy for a moment. Thinking about Eilir usually made her feel that way. "Anyway, we're an eclectic Georgian group who favor Celtic symbolism; which means nothing to you, of course, but think of it as our equivalent of being Episcopalians."

"You're single, then?"

"No, handfasted." At Sally's blank look she went on: "Married, in Wiccaspeak. My man was in Eugene when things Changed. He's a systems analyst, of all things, but he loves the old music—that's how we met; and he's my High Priest. Think of it as being the vice-president of the coven." Softly: "Rudy's his name, Rudy Starn, and I'm trying not to think about him much. He'll know I've headed here, and I tell myself he'd want me to wait with Eilir until he comes, but it's hard, hard."

Then she held up a hand. Dennis had walked up to the crest of the ridge; that ought to give him a good view of the cabin, and he was using the binoculars as well. When he turned she stiffened in alarm, but he didn't seem frightened himself—just puzzled. And Eilir tore over the ridge and disappeared at a run, which she wouldn't do if there was anything to fear.

"Whoa, Cagney, Lacey," she said as she pulled in the team, set the brake lever—they couldn't be expected to lean into the traces on an upslope for long—and waited until Dennis trotted back to her, his face alight.

"What is it?" she demanded.

"There are people there," he answered. Alarm rammed through her, but he went on: "I recognize a couple of them, though, seen them with you. Chuck Barstow—I'd know that silly hat he wears anywhere. And a couple of others; come see for yourself."

A surge of hope ran through her, shocking, like a cold electric jolt. *There's no real refuge from what's happening with the world; and what refuge there is, is in other people.* An added joy: *And Rudy might be there.*

He'd been leaving on a trip down to California, to San Jose and Silicon Valley; a surprising number of Wiccans were in software.

*But maybe his flight didn't leave before the Change and he made it up here already!*

"It's the Singing Moon," she said aloud; poor Sally would be bewildered. "Or at least some of them. They'd know the way; I should have expected it; Goddess, I halfway did, as much as I dared. Chuck or Judy would have thought of coming here, at least, and we were supposed to have a meeting, the night of the Change—I was to drive in. They had farther to come, but probably had to hide less on the way."

She flicked the reins and released the brake; another bit of steep climb, a turn to the left, and they broke into the open.

A long stretch of rolling upland meadow opened out to either side, new grass rippling green and thick-streaked with early blue camas and rose-pink sorrel, dotted with big white oaks; forest-shaggy hills dark with conifers rose steep to the north. Off in the distance to the right a small waterfall went in spray down a rock face, formed a pool surrounded by willows, then lazed across the open plateau in a series of curves before vanishing from sight.

"Those people are your, umm, coven?" Sally asked, as they rattled down the rough track towards the cabin.

Eight adults and more children were running towards them, waving and shouting; Eilir was hopping up and down as she greeted them, and Cuchulain doing his usual barking wiggle at the familiar scents. Juniper scanned their faces, easy to recognize despite the distance.

"They're most of it," she said. "Chuck, Judy, Diana, Andy, Susan, Dorothy, Karl and Dave—and their kids—but all those children in the green blazers? I don't recognize *them!* Nor the wagons they all rode in on!"

Parked in front where the laneway curved by the house and trailed off to the right were . . .

Juniper blinked. *Now, that is a covered wagon, is it not?* she thought.

And strapped to its sides was a variety of historic junk, including an old-fashioned walking plow. The coveners had just begun unloading bales and sacks and boxes from inside when she arrived. Another was beside it. Eight horses grazed under a tree, big glossy roan beasts, and a dozen cattle of various breeds and . . .

"Well, Lugh love me, it's a pig!" she said to herself. A big sow, to be exact, with some half-grown piglets near it.

The cabin stood on a U-shaped rise in the center of the plateau's northern side, separated from the wooded ridge behind by a gully. It was a long low structure of Douglas fir logs squared on top and bottom, all resting on a knee-high foundation of mortared fieldstone and topped by a steep shingled roof that covered a veranda around three sides. Smoke trickled from the big central stone chimney; there were sheds and a barn of similar construction, and a gnarled and decrepit orchard on the south-facing slope below.

"That's all yours?" Sally said; she sounded impressed.

Not unreasonably, since there were three thousand square feet on the ground floor, plus the attic loft where she'd set up her loom and had a space for private Craft working.

"It is mine, and a monster that's swallowed every penny I could earn in upkeep these last ten years," Juniper answered absently. "Great-uncle Earl built it to impress his cronies in Calvin Coolidge's time. And he may have been trying to bankrupt me with his will! At least I won't have to sell off the timber to pay the taxes and keep the roof tight anymore. . . ."

She felt a huge grin break free as her coveners came closer, and she stood up on the seat of the wagon despite the lurching and jolting, holding to the curving roof with one hand.

"Welcome!" she shouted. "Oh, *Cead mile failte!* A hundred thousand welcomes!"

Hands reached up to catch her as she dove down from the seat; for a long ten minutes there was only hugging and babbling and shouts of glee.

When that died down enough, she looked around. There were Chuck and Judy Barstow, he a gardener for the city of Eugene, she a registered nurse and midwife; Diana and Andy, who ran a health food store and restaurant there . . . eight of them in all.

"Where's the others? Where's Rudy?" she said.

Her friends looked at each other, and their smiles died.

Chuck Barstow finally spoke, his voice gentle: "We couldn't find Jack or Carmen or Muriel; we left a message at MoonDance. I hope they show up later. Rudy . . . Rudy's flight was a hundred feet up at six fifteen. Andy and I were at the airport to see him off. He's dead, Juney."

She gave a sound somewhere between a moan and a grunt, feeling winded, as if something had punched her under the short ribs and made it physically impossible to breathe; somehow she'd known, but pushed the knowledge away. Dennis gave her an awkward pat on the back, and Eilir snaked through the crowd to embrace her; she'd liked the funny, skinny little man as well, even after he'd become her mother's lover.

"Blessed be," Juniper murmured after a moment. "May he rest in the Summerlands, and return to us in joy."

"So mote it be," everyone replied.

Then she took a deep breath, and wiped her hand across her eyes.

*I'll grieve later,* she thought. *Right now there's work to be done.*

"Where did you get all this *stuff?*" she said, waving at the wagons and the livestock; there were chickens and ducks and geese, as well as the quadrupeds.

"At the museum's exhibit—Living Pioneer History, where else?" Chuck grinned.

The plumed hat looked a little incongruous over the workaday denim and flannel; he usually wore it with a troubadour's costume at the RenFaires, or his knight's festival garb for Society events. He was wearing his buckler slung from his belt over his parade sword, too. . . .

*Which is perfectly good steel,* she remembered with a shiver. *Like the one I'm wearing.*

He went on: "The exhibit was mostly abandoned when we got there, right after the Change . . . all gone off to try and find their families, I suppose, poor bastards. It was chaos and old night in Eugene by then. So we just . . . liberated it, you might say, having as good a claim as anyone else. The rest of the livestock the same—some we bought, from people still taking money."

"You saved lives by doing that," Juniper said. "Ours to start with; we'll use the tools and do it in time. It'll come back to you threefold, remember. And the children? Not that I'm objecting . . . but it's going to be very tight for food before harvest."

She made a quick calculation. The Fairfaxes' stores would easily have been eighteen months' eating for three, without stinting; for . . .

*Good Goddess gentle and strong, twenty-eight including those children!*

. . . it would be about three months, carefully rationed.

Of course, they could eat the livestock if they had to, even the horses . . . the chickens would yield something. . . .

"They were on a school bus," Andy Trethar said. "All the way from Seattle to Ashland, and returning when the Change hit. And . . . well, we just couldn't leave them."

Chuck cut in: "Juney, Diana and Andy had just taken a delivery for their store, which we brought along, and we picked up everything we could along the way, and we cleaned out a garden-supply place that had a *lot* of seeds. . . . We only got here a couple of hours ago ourselves, you understand."

"Well, every mouth comes with a pair of hands," she said stoutly.

*Though many aren't very large or strong hands, in this case,* she thought. *But we'll make do—for a start.*

Rudy had always been on at Andy and Diana for carrying too much inventory at the MoonDance, tying up their scanty capital. That looked as if it was going to be a very fortunate mistake.

*Lord and Lady, we're probably better off than anyone else within a hundred miles!*

Chuck bent close: "And you don't know *how* glad I am to see you here," he half whispered. "I'd just about run out of charisma by this point. People are getting really scared. You're the High Priestess; give 'em some oomph, Goddess-on-Earth."

Juniper swallowed, then planted her hands on her hips and raised her voice to address them all. At least she had a good voice, experience with crowds, and had long ago lost all tendency to stage fright.

"Another hundred thousand welcomes, my darlings," she said. "But listen to your High Priestess now. We've got a lot of work to be done, and not much time to do it in. Here's what I think—that it's a clan we'll have to be, as it was in the old days, if we're going to live at all. . . ."

# CHAPTER NINE

Men on foot were a lot quieter than galloping horses. That was the only way Havel could justify this last-minute dash through the night to himself; he prayed with every footfall that they were going to be in time.

*Idiots,* he thought. *They're acting like idiots and it's making my job harder. Doesn't seem fair.*

The bandits had flogged their horses on all through the night, even after they'd caught up with Will Hutton, halting only when they'd run into the ranger cabin half an hour ago.

Which meant that he had to stop too, to let them have enough time to lose fear of pursuit. Fortunately he'd been able to follow them through the open patches with the telescopic sight from his old rifle. He hoped it was the right thing to do, but he could feel sand grinding in the gears of his brain; it had been nearly thirty hours of hard effort since he last slept.

"Stop!" he hissed to Eric, sinking to one knee.

He'd blackened the heads of their weapons with mud, and now he held the spear low and level to the ground. From the edge of the pines that fringed the area around the old ranger station he gave the cabin a quick once-over, looking for the men on guard. There was light from the windows, firelight and lamplight, enough to endanger his night vision; he squinted and looked aside. Four horses were hobbled in the clearing near the cabin, looking tired and discouraged and nosing at the rock and pine duff in a futile search for something to eat.

He could see two human figures there: one slumped near the steps that led to the broad front veranda, and another standing on it—a stout figure carrying a bow, but looking through the front window, with his back to the outside world.

A woman's scream probably indicated what was occupying his attention.

"Now!" Havel said, and ran forward. Eric followed.

Will Hutton was sitting on the edge of the veranda, his hands tied behind him around one of the wooden pillars that supported the roof. He'd obviously gotten another beating, but he watched the men coming across the pine needles and rocks of the space between the trail and the cabin with a hunted alertness. He raised his feet and hitched himself around the post silently as the two neared, pressing himself down flat as he did.

*Just a second more,* Havel thought. *Just a second and young Jimmie is dead meat and the odds are even.*

Eric was making a lot more noise than his companion; he wasn't used to running in the dark. Fat Boy Jimmie turned when they were still ten yards away. Havel abandoned any attempt at stealth at his strangled whinney of surprise and just ran as fast as he could, but it wasn't quite fast enough; the young man managed to draw the bow to his ear.

Havel held the rough spear underarm with both hands, like a giant rifle-and-bayonet combination, hoping that the boy would be flustered or simply miss in the shadowy light with his eyes still dazzled from looking through the firelit windows—the bow wasn't a submachine gun and he couldn't spray-and-pray.

There was no time to be afraid, but plenty to watch the archer's hands stop shaking, and steady with the three-edged blade of the arrowhead pointed directly at Havel's liver. He was using a snap-release glove, which argued for a distinctly uncomfortable degree of accuracy. Havel's snarl turned to a guttural roar of triumph as a foot lashed out and kicked the bowman behind one knee and the arrow flashed out into the night over his head, close enough to hear.

Will Hutton had just saved his life, before they'd ever really met.

Jimmie screamed and tried to dodge as Havel came up the last ten feet of rock path before the stairs to the cabin. The spearpoint took him low in his belly and he screamed again, high and shrill. The impact shocked up Havel's arms as the young man thudded back violently into the logs of the cabin and the point jammed in bone, bending back with the violence of the impact. He snarled in the ferocity of total focus, wrenched the kitchen-knife blade out of his opponent's flesh and then thrust again, with all the power of his arms and shoulders behind it and his weight as well.

It went in under the young man's breastbone and through a rib where it joined the spine and into the weathered Ponderosa-pine log behind, pinning him to it like a butterfly to a board and leaving the spear shaft stretched out like a horizontal exclamation mark.

His scream turned to a squealing babble; half a second later it cut off in a thump and gurgle as Eric's improvised *naginata* slashed down and glanced into the side of his neck before jamming for a moment in his split collarbone. Jimmie's heels drummed on the planks of the veranda, making the dry wood boom like a slack-skinned drum as Eric wrenched his weapon loose with desperate haste.

Havel felt the vibration beneath his feet as he ducked under the spear shaft. It registered, but just as data—like the rest flowing in through his skin and ears and eyes, like the spray of blood that spurted out for half a dozen feet in every direction from the huge flap of skin and flesh sliced off the dying man's neck. Havel's mouth was open too, showing his teeth. He left the spear—too big for close work—and flicked the door catch open, yanking the plank-and-iron portal towards him and bouncing back and to the side.

A chair flew through the open door, thrown from close range. The scrimmage on the veranda had been brief but noisy. Havel ducked forward again, stooping under the pole-and-rawhide chair, knife out and flashing up in the gutting stroke. The skinny tattooed bandit named Bob leapt backward in turn, hitting the floor with his shoulders and rolling erect; Havel crowded through the door quickly, before he could block it again, conscious of Eric coming in behind him.

The front room of the cabin was big, nearly thirty feet by fifteen, with chairs and a couch set in a U-shape around the fireplace; there was a blaze going in it, and a Coleman lantern on the mantelpiece over it. The thickset bandit was there, trying to stand and having difficulty with it. That was because Signe Larsson had him around the knees; he was wearing long johns with the front flap open, and she had on panties and a set of scratches and bruises. He was swinging his fists at her head and screaming curses as he tried to wrench free, but she ducked her face into the dirty gray fabric covering his legs and hung on like grim death.

That couldn't last; the bandit leader weighed two-fifty at least, and not all of it was blubber. The blade of Eric's *naginata* came up by Havel's left shoulder; blood dripped off the whole length of the steel, and off the shaft and the arms that held it. The young man's face was white but set, and heavily speckled with red drops.

"Keep him off me," Havel barked, jerking his left hand at the skinny man.

In the same instant he vaulted over the couch. The bandit chief roared and flailed his arms at Havel, kneeing Signe in the face in his heaving panic. Havel stepped in, delicate as a dancer, taking the clumsy blow on his shoulder. The *puukko* stabbed twice with vicious speed—once up under the short ribs, then up under the chin as the man doubled over like someone who'd been gut-punched. The mattresslike beard parted easily, and the front half of the bandit's tongue flew out of his open mouth in a spray of blood.

Havel knocked the dying man over backward with a grunt of effort as he shouldered past him; he fell with his head and shoulders in the fireplace and lay there with his hair burning and his blood frying and crisping and stinking on the hot iron of the log holder.

That left Eric and Jailhouse Bob on one side of the sofa and Havel on the other, moving fast towards the bandit's end to take him in the rear. The man had been on the attack, ready to take a few cuts to get in under Eric's polearm with his knife and finish him quickly before the two men could gang up on him, just exactly the right thing to do.

He hadn't quite managed it, and there was blood flowing from a shallow cut on his cheek. Now he backed again, moving fast in a straddle-legged crouching shuffle, his head swiveling between the two opponents coming at him. The knife in his hand was nearly a foot long, almost a bowie, and sharpened on the recurve; it glittered in the lantern light as he moved it in small precise arcs at the end of his long arm.

No fancy Ramboesque serrations on the blade or Klingon wings on the plain brass quillions; it was a professional's weapon, and even two-on-one Bob was likely to do some serious damage before he went down.

Behind him Astrid Larsson walked out of the hallway. She was entirely naked and spattered with blood; mostly someone else's, far too much to come from the bite-marks on her small breasts. There was an old-fashioned alarm clock in her right hand, and a collection of small heavy objects in the curve of her other—coffee mugs and paperweights.

She threw the alarm clock, hard; it jangled as it hit Bob's shoulder, and there was a look of dawning panic in his narrow hazel eyes as he flicked them back and forth, darting between the girl and the two armed men.

She followed it with a coffee cup, which missed, and a paperweight, which didn't. The skinny bandit made a sound, a scream of animal rage and fear.

*Women scare him,* Havel realized. *That's why he hurts them.*

"Kill him," Havel said to Eric, and moved in to do just that as a mug flew past Bob's head.

The bandit reversed the knife with a swift flip and threw it at Havel; then he turned and dodged Eric's thrust with the point of his *naginata* and jumped straight through the window, arms crossed in front of his face as he smashed through the glass. He was lucky—you were about as likely to cut your own intestines out doing that as not—landed flat on the veranda, and took off running towards the darkness.

Havel twisted to let the big blade go by; you could get hurt by a thrown knife, but generally only by accident. Then he put a booted foot on the windowsill to follow; he didn't look forward to chasing the stick-thin killer in the dark, but he wasn't going to have him hanging around, either.

Astrid walked to where her bow and quiver hung by the door, put a shaft to the cord, drew, and loosed through the window. Her movements had the smooth inevitability of a sleepwalker's.

The arrow made Havel jerk aside in surprise; it went by close enough that he could feel the wind of its passage, and hear the *whhhptt* of cloven air.

"He wanted to rape me but he couldn't," she said with a calm like ice on a river just before the spring surge cracked it, ignoring the savage lash of the bowstring on her forearm.

"So he took me into Mom's room and he killed her; he said he'd be able to do me after that."

Havel completed the vault and dropped down onto the broken glass that littered the veranda; it crunched and crackled under his boots.

Twenty yards away, Jailhouse Bob lay in the pathway, pulling himself along on his hands. His legs were limp, and an arrow stood in his lower back. It jerked and quivered as he tried to drag himself along, looking over his shoulder with a snarl. Havel shook himself, as if he were coming out of deep cold water.

Eric Larsson was on his knees at the edge of the veranda, puking with a violence that threatened a pulled muscle in his back, and obviously wasn't going to be much use for the immediate future. He walked over to the middle-aged black man instead, and went down on one knee to cut the rope lashings that held him.

"My family?" Will Hutton asked, working his arms and rubbing at his wrists.

"Hiding out in a thicket by the road with most of your gear," Havel said. "Should be fine."

"Lord, but that's good to hear," Hutton said, slumping in relief. He began to offer a hand, then realized Havel still had the knife in his. "Many thanks . . ."

"Mike Havel," he replied, and waved the blade slightly. "Consider this my contribution to public hygiene."

Hutton had a heavy rural-Southern accent, but sharper and more nasal than Gulf State gumbo; Havel thought it was probably Texas originally. The Corps was lousy with Texans of all varieties, and he'd heard that slurred rhythmic twang a lot in some sandy and unpleasant places.

"I'm Will Hutton," the black man replied, standing cautiously and stretching. "Nothing broke, I don't think."

He looked out into the darkness. "You going to finish off that skinny peckerwood? He's a mean one, the worst of the lot. Best be careful, like you would with a broken-back rattler."

"No hurry," Havel said. "I thought I'd let him ripen a bit; he isn't going to crawl out of reach with an arrow through his spine."

He looked at his right hand and his knife. It was dripping, and in the faint light the whole of his hand and forearm looked as if they were coated with something slick and oily and darkly gleaming.

Some distant part of his mind realized that the sight would probably come back to him for years—when he was trying to sleep or eat or make love—but right now it wasn't particularly interesting.

He could just cut Bob's throat, but Havel didn't want to get that close without a good reason; Hutton was right—the man's legs were out of commission, but his arms were still working and his teeth too for that matter. Instead he carefully wiped the blade of the *puukko* on the clothes of the dead bandit pinned to the wall by the spear, and then sheathed it before he went back into the cabin.

Astrid was still standing with her bow, staring at nothing; Signe was huddled into a ball on the floor, staring at the corpse of the bandit leader. Havel went past in silence—there was nothing he could do to help at that moment—and checked the bedrooms.

Mary Larsson lay spread-eagled on her bed; the mattress was saturated, and it dripped thick strings of blood onto the floor. Havel took one quick look and then carefully avoided letting his eyes stray that way while he found a blanket and covered her.

*I hope she died fast,* he thought, breathing through his mouth against the smell.

Unfortunately that didn't seem very likely.

Her husband was trussed to a chair in the corner of the room; alive, not too badly beaten up, but staring with the look of a man whose mind had shut down from overload, and there were vomit stains down the front of his shirt and tear-streaks through the white-gray stubble on his cheeks. Havel freed him with a few jerks of his knife, and pulled him erect.

"There's nothing you can do here," he said. "Come on, Ken." The older man's lips moved, almost silently.

Havel went on: "Astrid and Signe are fine." *Or at least alive. Technically speaking, they weren't even raped, I think.* "They need you, Ken. They need you *now*."

That seemed to get through to him; he stumbled along under his own power. Havel left him with his daughters in the living room as he hefted the dead body of the bandit chief and half carried it out to pitch over the railing of the veranda; Will Hutton watched with somber satisfaction.

Then Havel pulled the spear out of the wall. The young bandit's body came with it; the point pulled free of the wood and the heavy corpse flopped down into the pool of blood and fluids, but the square shoulders of the knife caught on something inside. Havel put a foot on the body and worked it free, careful not to loosen the bindings; then he hefted the pole into an overhand grip like a fish gig before walking out towards Jailhouse Bob.

He hadn't gotten far.

They buried Mary Larsson in the morning, and were ready to leave around noon. Her husband had come out of his shock a little by then, and none of the younger Larssons wanted to stay at the ranger cabin any longer than they had to; Hutton was anxious to get back to his wife and daughter, of course.

Astrid hadn't slept much. From the way she started screaming the moment she slipped out of consciousness that was probably just as well.

*I'll give her some of the tranquilizers tonight,* Havel thought, turning to look at her as she sat against the base of a tree, face on her knees and arms wrapped around her head. *And being away from this place will help. I hope.*

Will Hutton came up and looked in the same direction, nodding.

"Best get the horses back to the road too as fast as we can," he said, finishing his bowl of elk stew. "They need rest, but they need food a lot more, and they can't eat pine needles. I'll go take another look at the loads."

Havel waited until the Larssons had made their last farewells at the rough grave—most of it was an oblong pile of rocks. It was a bright cold day, with tatters of high cloud blowing in from the west; the long wind roared in the pines around them, carrying away most of the stink of violent death. He and Hutton and Eric had dragged the dead bandits out of sight, but nobody had been in a mood to clean up the cabin.

They *had* stripped it of everything that might be useful, from bedding and kitchenware to shovel, ax and pickax, and Hutton had improvised carrying packs for some of the horses. It was a pleasure to see him work with the animals; it always was, watching a real expert at work. He'd been a help rehafting the *naginata* and spear onto good smooth poles they'd found in the toolshed behind the cabin, too.

Signe came up to him with a brace of books in her hands. "Mike, take a look. I think these might be useful. They were on the mantelpiece, and I was reading them before . . . you know."

He did, flipping through the text and frequent illustrations. *Frontier Living*, by Edwin Tunis, plus *Colonial Living* and *Colonial Craftsmen* by the same author.

"You know, I think you're right," he said. "Pack 'em with the rest."

Astrid came out and gave him a cup of coffee; he took it, and cleared his throat as she turned silently away, slight and graceful in her stained leather outfit.

"Kid." Reluctantly, she turned back to him. "You did good. If you hadn't shot him, I'd have had to chase him down in the dark. He might have killed or crippled me and come back for the rest of you."

She nodded again; he went on: "I know you've had a real bad time, but we don't have the leisure for thinking about our hurts right now. You're the only one of us who can use a bow and we need more food, badly. We may have to fight again, too. We just can't afford you folding up on us. You've got to be functional no matter what it takes. OK?"

She nodded silently a third time; the huge silver-blue eyes seemed to be looking through to another world as much as at him.

He shook his head: "Let me hear it, Astrid. Don't go hiding in your head. We need you out here."

"I understand, Mike," she said, after taking a deep breath; he saw her blink back to being fully in the waking world.

Suddenly she spat: "They were like *orcs!*"

"Yeah, that's a fair description."

He restrained himself from tousling her hair. *You're a good kid. Let's see if we can get you going on something you care about.*

He'd never been of the talk-about-it-forever school when it came to dealing with really bad stuff; in his experience that just made you think about it more and compounded the damage. Hard work and concentrating on the future were the best way to handle trauma.

"What do you think of that bow we captured?"

It was sitting on one of the veranda chairs. Astrid looked at it and sniffed.

"It's a Bear compound," she said, with a touch of her old de-haut-en-bas tone, edged with contempt for the high-tech vulgarity of it. "Adjustable setoff, double round cams . . . with that, you might as well be using a *gun.*"

*Christ Jesus, how I wish I were able to use a gun,* Havel thought. *Guns I understand.* Aloud he asked: "Will it work?"

"Oh, it will *work,*" she said. "It's easier to use if you're not a real archer and it'll shoot hard and straight . . . until something breaks. The riser is an aluminum casting, the limbs are fiberglass-carbon laminate, and the cams on the ends are titanium, with sealed bearing races. The string's a synthetic and the arrows are carbon-composite. I could make a copy of my bow, if you gave me time to experiment and the materials I needed. I don't think anyone in the whole world can repair that one, not now, and to make a new one—forget it."

*Purist,* he thought, hiding his smile and finishing the hot drink; it was lousy, but coffee was going to be a rare treat.

He went on: "You've got a point, but we'll use it while we've got it. You can give us all instruction."

She sniffed again. "Signe can shoot. Sort of. At targets."

Then she took the cup away for washing and packing; her orange cat slunk at her heels, looking thoroughly frightened.

Havel found himself obsessively running over the inventory in his head again; particularly the food, which was about enough for everyone for four weeks, if they were very careful.

*Of course, the Huttons probably have some more back at their vehicles. And we can do some hunting. But we've got to get out to farming or ranching country, somewhere where there is food; if it's there we can get it one way or another. Now they can't ship cattle out, there ought to be plenty, for a while. And farmers store a lot of their own grain these days in those sheet-metal things.*

He'd only eat the horses if there was no other choice or the animals were dying anyway; they were too damned useful to lose. A lot of the medical kit had been expended on Mary Larsson, too. God alone knew what they'd do if anyone else got seriously ill or hurt.

*Well, yes, actually we do know. The one who gets sick will recover or die. I hope everyone has had their appendix out,* he thought grimly, hefting his spear and slipping on his pack. *Let's get going.*

Suddenly he was conscious that Signe hadn't left; she was standing by the base of the veranda stairs. The bruises on her face were purpling, and her lips were swollen, but she looked at him steadily. There was one new element to her gear; she had Jailhouse Bob's belt and blade. Unexpectedly, she drew it, looking down at the big fighting-knife with wondering distaste.

"It's a tool," Havel said quietly. "Just a tool. Anyone can use it. It's the person that matters, not the equipment."

"I know," she said. Then she looked up at him: "Teach me."

He made an enquiring sound. She went on fiercely: "Teach me how to fight. I don't ever want to be that . . . helpless . . . again. Teach me!"

Her knuckles were white on the checked hardwood of the knife hilt.

*Problem is, I can teach you dirty fighting, and how to use a knife,* he thought. *If guns still worked, I could make you into a pretty good shot in a couple of months. But damned if I can tell you how to use a bow or a sword or a spear . . . which I suspect are going to matter more from now on.*

Aloud he went on: "You bet. We've all got a lot to learn, I'm thinking."

Hutton had the horses ready and everyone was outside; decision crystallized, and Havel put his fingers to his mouth and whistled.

Everyone looked up, and he waved them over as he walked down to where the pathway to the cabin joined the Centennial Trail proper.

"Before we go, we ought to settle some things," Havel said, as they gathered around. "Mainly, what we're going to do—and if there's a *we* to do it." *Better than dwelling on our losses, at least.*

He leaned on his spear and looked at the Larssons. "I figure my obligations to Steelhead Air and its clients have about run out," he said bluntly. "All things considered."

The younger Larssons looked stricken. Ken gave him a slight smile; he recognized negotiation when he heard it, and so did Will Hutton.

Havel went on: "So if we're going to stick together, we'll have to put it on a new basis. So far we've just been reacting to things as they happened; it's time to start making things happen ourselves. If you folks don't like my notions of how to do that, we can go our separate ways once we reach the highway."

Ken Larsson was evidently relieved to have something to think about but his murdered wife. His face lost some of its stunned, blurred-at-the-edges look as he spoke.

"Something has happened and not just around here," he said. "At least over a big part of this continent, and maybe all over the world. Mike, remember just before the engines cut out, they were reporting that weird electrical storm over Nantucket? I don't think that's a coincidence—and it's also thousands of miles from here."

He shrugged. "I can't imagine what could have caused a Change like this, unless it's simply that God hates us. . . . Maybe incredibly advanced, really sadistic aliens who wanted to take our toys away? Call it Alien Space Bats. But at a guess, it started there over Nantucket—probably propagated over the earth's surface at the speed of light. It's too . . . specific . . . to be an accident, I think. If it were an accidental change in the laws of nature, we'd most likely just have collapsed into a primordial soup of particles."

Will Hutton shook his head. "Hard to get my mind around it," he said.

"We have to," Havel said bluntly. "That's the difference between living and dying, now."

Hutton nodded: "I don't know any of that science stuff, but it occurs to me this might have happened before."

They all looked at him, and he shrugged. "If it happened back in olden times, who'd have noticed? Maybe this"—he waved around—"is the way things was for a long time. That'd account for folks taking so long to get guns and such."

Havel looked at him with respect; that wasn't a bad idea, although of course there was no way to check, short of time travel. He went on: "So the question is, what does each of us want to do? Do we stick together? And if we do, what's our goal?"

Hutton scratched his head thoughtfully. "Not much use in trying to get back to Texas, for me 'n' mine," he said. "Too many hungry, angry strangers between. Got my family with me, 'cept for my boy, Luke. He's in the Army, stationed in Italy with the 173rd. All I can do for him is pray."

He winced slightly, then shook his head and rolled a cigarette, using only his right hand and offering the makings around.

"No, thanks," Havel said. "Wouldn't want to get into the habit again—not much tobacco grows around here."

Once Hutton had lit up, Havel waved towards the cabin and the congealed pool of blood still left on the veranda. "Stuff like this is probably happening all over the world. Most people aren't going to make it through the next year even out here in the boondocks, and it's going to be worse in the cities, a lot worse. I'd like to be one of the minority still living come 1999. That's going to mean teamwork. Sitting around arguing at the wrong moment could get us all killed."

Signe Larsson spoke up: "Dad, the rest of you, we should stick with Mike."

"Yup," Eric concurred. "I'm sort of fond of living myself."

Astrid nodded, silent. Her father spoke: "Money's gone, the whole modern world's gone. We'd all be dead four times over without Mike. I'm for it."

Hutton took a drag on his cigarette and spoke in his slow deep voice. "Man alone, or a family alone, they're dead or worse now. I found that out. Mike here, I've got good reason to trust him, and I misdoubt he'll get drunk with power. So if he wants to ramrod this outfit, I'm for it."

Havel held up a hand. "Let's not get ahead of ourselves," he said. A deep breath: "We have to have someplace to go, and some way of making a living and defending ourselves once we get there. That means getting land and seed and stock and tools however we can, and I sort of suspect it also means fighting to keep it. OK, that's not something a man can do alone; and we here know each other a bit."

He shifted his shoulders, a gesture he used at the beginning of a task; usually he wasn't conscious of doing it, but this time he noticed . . . and remembered his father doing the same.

"But I'm not going to take responsibility without authority. If you want to stick with me, well, I hope I'm sensible enough never to think I know everything and don't need advice, but somebody has to be in charge until things are settled. I think I'm the best candidate. We're going to have to pool everything and work together like a military unit, and a camel is a horse designed by a committee."

He caught each pair of eyes in turn: "For? Against?"

The Larssons nodded, looked at each other, and then raised their hands.

"For!" they said in ragged unison.

Hutton puffed meditatively on his cigarette again and then raised his hand in agreement. "Count me in too. Think I can speak for Angel and Luanne."

Havel nodded. "Glad you said that," he said. "I don't deny you and your horses would be very useful; and your family were pretty impressive too, on short acquaintance. You're a horse breaker, I take it?"

"No, sir, I am not," Hutton said, with dignified seriousness. "What use is a broken horse? I am a horse wrangler and trainer. Anything a horse can do, I can train into it."

Then he laughed without much humor. "And it's a trade I took up so I could work for myself. Don't see much prospect of that here. I'm a stranger, and a black one at that. Might get a bunk and eats with some rancher or farmer, yeah, but not on good terms, I reckon. Sharecropping or something like."

"We're all in that situation," Havel said. "When there just isn't enough to go around, people will look to their own kin and friends first."

He ran a thumb along the silky black stubble on his jaw. "I expect some refugees will get taken in, especially where there aren't too many, but Will pegged it. They'll be the hired help, and hire will be just their keep at that, sleeping in the barn and eating scraps. It'll be worse, some places— human life's going to be a cheap commodity."

"We could all go to our place in Montana," Eric Larsson said. "The ranch . . . we've got horses there, and there's the grazing—lots of cows around there. Or there's the summer farm in the Willamette. The ranch is a lot closer, though."

Ken shook his head. "I don't think Montana would be a good idea," he said slowly. "We'd be strangers there. That land used to belong to the Walkers . . . and with nobody to tell them no, I suspect they'll simply take back the property and the stock; the area's full of their relatives and connections. They were always polite when we did business, but I could tell they weren't too happy about needing my money."

"Yeah," Signe said. "I know I dated Will for a while, sort of, or at least hung around him, but it was me who called it quits. There's something creepy about him, and his whole family."

Her father looked at her with surprise, then shrugged. "I'd go for the farm, if it weren't for all the people in the Willamette Valley. Going on for two million . . . it'll get very ugly."

"What's it like?" Havel asked him. "A real farm, or just a vacation house?"

"My grandfather bought it for a country place back before the First World War, in the Eola hills northwest of Salem," Ken said.

For a moment he smiled, then winced. "Mary liked it . . . nice big house—Victorian, modernized—and about seven hundred acres, two-fifty of that in managed forest on the steeper parts. Gravity-flow water system, about thirty acres of pinot noir vines we've put in over the last ten years—the winery is all gravity-flow too, by the way—some old orchards, and then quite a bit of cleared land, all of it board-fenced. In grass, we ran pedigree cattle on it and raised horses, but it could grow anything. Some sheds, barns, stables . . . We know the neighbors well, too, and get along with most of them; the Larssons have been spending summers there for a long time."

*If any of the neighbors are still alive in a couple of months, that might be an asset,* Havel thought. *Unless someone's simply moved in and taken over.*

Ken went on: "Long-term, there's something else to think about." He waved a hand around them.

"There's a lot of farming and ranching here in the interior, yes. For a year or two, or four or five, it's going to be better-off than most places. The Larssons made their first pile trading wheat from Pendleton and the Palouse down the Columbia to Portland. But a hell of a lot of the crops here these days depend on things like center-pivot irrigation, or deep wells . . . and the dryland farming . . . well, it only yields really well with mechanization on a big scale, where one family can work thousands of acres. That way it doesn't matter if you get a low yield, or lose every fourth crop to drought, because you're handling so many acres."

"You mean quantity has a quality all its own," Havel said.

Ken nodded. "If you're doing it by hand and horse, it takes just as much labor to work an acre of twelve-bushel wheat land as it does one that gives you forty. With the sort of preindustrial setup we're being thrown back on, that's the basic constraint on your standard of living. And the lower the productivity, the harder the people on top have to squeeze to get a surplus."

Havel's brow furrowed. *You know, that makes an uncomfortable amount of sense,* he thought. *And Ken Larsson is no fool. Not any sort of a fighting man, but he can think, and he's got the best education of any of us here.*

"All right," he said. "Unless we see a better opportunity along the way, I'd say we head for the Willamette."

"Ummm . . ." Eric was a lot more bashful than he'd been. "What about all the people, Mike? Dad said it. The farm's only fifty miles from Portland and a lot closer to Salem."

Havel looked away for a moment, then met Ken Larsson's eyes. He gave a slight nod of agreement, and the younger man went on: "Eric, it's a long way to the Willamette on foot; and I don't intend to hurry. By the time we get there . . . overpopulation is not going to be that much of a problem."

"Ouch," Signe said with a wince. "Still . . ."

"Nothing we can do about it, I suppose," Eric said; they looked at each other in surprise at their agreement.

Silence fell as they moved out onto the trail. Ken Larsson and Will Hutton were mounted, in consideration of their years and bruises; the younger members of the party were on foot, to spare the hungry, overworked horses. The only exception was Biltis the cat, who rode perched on one of the pack loads, curled up on a pile of blankets strapped across the top and looking like a puddle of insufferable aristocratic orange smugness.

Eric and Havel carried their pole arms, and Astrid her archaic recurve bow; Signe had the bandits' high-tech compound. Hutton carried a felling ax, the top of the helve against his hip and his right hand on the end of the handle.

"Right," Havel said, swinging the spear over his shoulder at the balance-point. "Let's make a few miles before dark. Thataway!"

# CHAPTER TEN

*Fourteen days since whatever-it-was,* Mike Havel thought, looking around the clearing just off Highway 12 where the Huttons had made their camp until the bandits came.

*Christ Jesus!*

The Lochsa bawled and leapt not far to the north, gray with silt and chunks of ice. The smell somehow stung in the nostrils beneath the pine scent of the forested slopes that rose canyon-steep on either side. He looked at the sky, and blinked at a sudden thought: *I'll never fly again.*

It struck him harder than he'd have thought; never again to feel the wheels lift, or the yoke come alive in his hands as the controls bit the moving air . . .

The whole party had arrived late last night; the Huttons had slept in their tent, the Larssons in the RV and Havel in the hay of the horse trailer. Dawn had been gray and cold, but the noon sun had broken through the clouds, and it had gotten up to around fifty.

Havel shook his head and blew absently on his hands as he and Will Hutton walked around the flatbed they'd all spent the morning unloading; it had a two-wheeled bogie on either side, and Ken Larsson was underneath it, looking at the brakes. If at all possible they wanted to rig it for horse traction; that way they could take along a *lot* more gear when they headed west.

Will glanced up and smiled at his wife and daughter; he'd been doing that all morning too, and Havel didn't blame him.

He looked that way as well. They had a cookfire going and a big pot hung over it; Angelica Hutton was cutting elk meat on a folding table, and dropping the pieces and carefully measured cupfuls of dried beans and soup-barley into the bubbling water. There had been bacon and eggs for breakfast, and toast made from bread that wasn't too stale to eat, but from now on it would be the limited dry goods from the ranger cabin and the Huttons' RV, and what they could hunt or forage or barter. The remains of the elk would last them for a while, and the luckless mule deer they'd run into on the way back here. He suspected they'd all get *very* sick of game stew by then.

Angelica wore a jacket and a long skirt and a black Stetson with silver medallions around the band; her face was beautiful when she raised it from her work to smile back at Will. Then she stirred the pot, nodded, and put on the lid.

Luanne smiled in their direction fairly often too, as she sorted clothing. She even gave Eric a high-megawattage beam now and then. Havel could hear them laughing together, and then she play-punched him in the chest. He went over backward and mimed a death rattle.

Havel blinked. For a moment he saw his own hand and the knife in it, glistening red-black in the firelight as if coated in oil, and remembered spitting out salt blood to clear his mouth. Then he shook his head and focused on the problem at hand. You had to do that, the way Larsson stopped occasionally and pushed the image of his wife's death out of his head with a visible effort of will. Acts of will repeated often enough became habit, and habit carried you through.

Dwelling on the bad stuff just made it stronger, and if there was one thing in the world he despised, it was someone who let their emotions get in the way of doing their share of the job at hand.

"You can't rig something in the way of a horse collar?" he went on to the wrangler.

Will Hutton had had a lot of spare tack, leather, cord and tools; even a hollow-cast anvil, although he disavowed blacksmith status, saying he simply did farrier work and a little smithing now and then.

"Oh, I can get somethin' rigged in the way of a collar," he said. "Carve it in sections from wood, I reckon, pad it, then sew some leather over it. Problem is that the pole on this thing is too low. It's meant for a towbar."

Propped on a chunk of wood to keep the trailer's bed level, the Y-shaped pole with the towing hitch was at about knee height. Hutton held his hand palm-down in front of his body at the solar plexus.

"We need a drawshaft about *this* high, otherwise the horses can't pull good and we'll chance hurting them if we load the wagon full. Too much weight on their withers."

Ken pivoted himself on his backside, so that his face and shoulders stretched out from under the trailer. His face looked a little less doughy this morning, and he'd shaved off the silvery stubble. He looked critically at the towing bar.

"And that'll come loose; it's bolted."

His finger sketched. "We could mount it upright instead of horizontally in the same brackets, with a little file and hacksaw work, use one of the roofing struts from the horse trailer, they're already curved and about the right width."

Hutton pushed back his billed cap and rubbed his chin; the calluses on his fingers scritched on the skin as his eyes moved, tracing out the structure Larsson proposed and the lines of force that would bear on it. When he spoke, his tone was dubious: "Upright, it'll lever on them something fierce, a lot worse than a straight pull. Might be we could do it if we could weld the join, but we cain't. Those bolts'll tear through inside a day."

"You bet," Larsson said, getting to his knees and leaning over the bed of the trailer. "So we sink an eyebolt, you've got a couple in your horse trailer, *here*"—he thumped his fist on the midpoint of the decking, just forward of the axle—"through the crossbeam under the plywood, then run some rope or cable forward to the top of the A-section."

"That a damn good idea," Hutton said, grinning broadly. "Not bad at all. Won't be pretty, but pretty don't count when it works."

He looked up at the sun. "Could do it by sunset. Ain't as if we were in a hurry."

He extended a hand, and Ken Larsson used it to rise, grunting a little; he was fifteen years older than Will, and had twenty-seven on Havel.

"Right," Havel said. "Plenty everyone else can do while we're here."

*Damn,* he thought as the two older men started rooting around in Hutton's capacious toolboxes, smiling a crooked smile to himself.

*I got out of the Corps because I could see myself as Gunney Winters, with twenty years' service hammering me until I fit perfectly into a Gunnery Sergeant–shaped hole . . . and here it's going to happen anyway.*

"You need any more help with the trailer?" he asked.

Hutton shook his head, and Larsson echoed him. He looked happy to be at something that used his knowledge, and Hutton had the matter-of-fact competence of a man who'd been at home around tools and tasks since before his voice broke.

"It'd go faster if we had someone to do the fetch-and-tote work," Hutton said, modifying his gesture.

"Strong back, simple mind," Larsson said, grinning. "I know *just* who."

He looked at Havel and winked. Havel put his fingers to his lips and blew a piercing whistle.

"Yo! Eric!" he called.

The young man had been helping Angelica Hutton and her daughter carry clothes down to the water's edge, where they apparently intended to clean them by soaping and then beating the wet cloth on rocks.

It was probably a skill she'd learned from her mother as a small girl and hadn't used much since; the RV had a neat little compact washer, and from what the horse trainer had let slip the Huttons had a small ranch of their own in the hill country southwest of Austin, which they used as home base; they'd been solidly prosperous, in a hardworking, self-made, self-employed way.

Eric looked up from putting the big basket of dirty clothing down by the gravelly shore of the river. Havel gestured sharply, and he reluctantly headed their way.

"Amazin' how a little conversation can make a boy his age want to do laundry," Hutton said dryly, and all three of the men laughed.

As they watched, they heard a drumroll of hooves and turned to look west. A hundred yards away Astrid Larsson had twitched her horse into a hand gallop with an imperceptible tensing of her thighs on the saddle and shift of balance; the reins lay knotted on the horn. She flashed down the edge of the woods, her bow rising smoothly as she drew to the ear. The arrow flashed out towards a target Havel and Hutton had rigged from poles and mounted on a stout

Ponderosa pine. It missed, but not by all that much, sinking half its length into the grassy turf just short of the tree.

Astrid shouted angrily in a language that sounded liquidly pretty even then, and stopped her horse with the same smooth combination of leg-signals and shifting seat. She turned it, trotted back to the target, bent out of the saddle to snag the arrow without dismounting, then set it back on the string and cantered away down the edge of the woods.

"Lord Jesus, but that girl can *ride*," Hutton said, whistling. "About as good as my daughter, and Luanne's got prizes for barrel riding at four rodeos; she'd be up there with Sherry Potter and Charmayne Rodman if she wanted. Eric and Signe ain't bad at all, but Astrid there, she is *fine.*"

He didn't say anything about Havel's equestrian skills, which was tactful, since they were no better than competent-journeyman by his standards. Havel was grateful; from what he'd seen in the past two days, what the black man couldn't do with horses just couldn't be done.

"Not bad with that bow thing, too, nohow," Hutton went on.

He paused, adjusting a wrench and handing it to the elder Larsson before taking up a hacksaw himself. "What's that lingo she keeps mutterin' in, anyways? Ain't English or Spanish neither. French or something?"

"Elvish," Havel said, and Astrid's father laughed.

Hutton looked at Havel blankly. The younger man continued: "Elvish, Will, no shit. Girl's a Tolkien fanatic."

It turned out the Texan had only the vaguest idea of who Tolkien was; his reading ran more to books on horses and ranching, or on cavalry and other equestrian subjects, or to Western history, and fiction by Louis L'Amour and Larry McMurtry. Eric arrived while the discussion was still going on.

"Yup, Elvish," he said. "Probably something like *Curse of the Valar upon thee, crooked Orcish shaft!* That's the problem with a language invented by a professor from Oxford. No meaty, satisfying swearwords for poor Legolamb."

They *all* laughed at that, but Havel sobered as he walked away to where Signe was practicing with the captured compound bow.

*Astrid is damned good with that bow, to come anywhere near hitting something from a moving horse. She's also act-*

*ing a bit weird. Or maybe even weirder than normal would be a better way to say it. Only to be expected—*

Havel had seen what happened to people exposed to the sudden violent death of friends; it had to be worse for a teenager with a parent. He'd been keeping an eye on her, but she hadn't quite blown a gasket yet. That could be a good sign, or a bad one.

"Mike?" Signe said, lowering the bow.

"I'm a bit worried about Astrid," he said. "The problem is that I don't know her well enough, and—"

Signe smiled: "And she acts weird all the time anyway." Her face sobered; smiling hurt her, anyway, with the bruises still fresh.

"She had bad dreams again last night," Signe went on, then shrugged. "*I* just couldn't sleep at all. It . . . well, she's younger than me, and she actually *saw* what happened to Mom. And that crazy man with the tattoos—even then, he scared me worse than the others. And they all terrified me!"

"Yeah," Havel said, wincing slightly at the memory of what *he'd* seen of Mary Larsson's body—and that was just the aftermath, and she hadn't been much more than a face and a name to him.

"She and Astrid weren't all that close," Signe said, fiddling with the bow. "Mom . . . Astrid's always been moody and solitary; the sort who has one or two really close friends, you know? Just totally uninterested in boys so far, too. Mom thought kids should have an active social life; parties, and clubs, and activities, and volunteer work. All Astrid was ever interested in was those books, and her horses, and archery—Mom got worried about that, too."

"Archery isn't an activity?"

"Not if you concentrate on it too much!" Signe said. "Then it becomes an obsession. I went to archery club meetings. Astrid just walked through the woods shooting at stumps. Mom—"

She turned away, rubbing at her eyes. "God, I miss her, even the things about her that drove me crazy."

Havel put a hand on her shoulder for an instant, then removed it when she flinched and took the bow and looked down at it.

"Yeah, that's rough," he said. "My mother died of some sudden-onset cancer thing while I was in the Gulf, and I couldn't get back home. We'd fought like cats and dogs for six months before I left, too—she wanted me to go to college instead of into the Corps *real* bad. I know up here"—he tapped his forehead—"that it wasn't my fault. Nobody knew she was sick, *she* didn't know she was sick, but . . . A lot worse for you, and for Astrid."

Signe nodded jerkily. "I'm glad we've been so busy. Less time to think about . . . everything that happened. I just start feeling guilty, and then I get angry—imagining what I could have done differently, as if I could have saved her—"

"There was absolutely nothing you could have done," Havel said with flat conviction. "Apart from what you did, which probably saved Eric's life and maybe mine. Jailhouse would have gotten to him in another thirty seconds, and you saved me at least that much time.

"Sorry," he finished, as she paled and swallowed.

"No!" she said fiercely. "I've got to . . . learn to deal with it. I can't live with it clubbing me every time I get reminded."

"Which brings me back to Astrid," Havel said, looking down the meadow.

She was wheeling about, tiny with distance at the northern end of the meadow. Still shooting from the saddle, he thought, but it was hard to tell.

"Sometimes feelings bleed off, like pressure from a propane tank," he said. "That's what happens with some people, at least. Brooders, they tend to build it up and then snap. I'd read Astrid for a brooder."

Signe gave him an odd look: "You're a lot more . . . well, no offense, sensitive, than . . ."

Havel grinned at her. "Jarheads don't have feelings?" he said.

He enjoyed her blush; she probably got extreme *guilt* feelings herself when she found herself believing a genuine stereotype. That was *insensitive.*

"Actually, that's what got me thinking. You get real tight with the guys in your squad, closer than brothers—you live closer than brothers do, and you have to rely on the guy next to you to save your ass; and you have to be ready to do the same for them. Watching someone you're that tight with die . . . not easy. Some people seriously wig out after that, self-destructive stuff. I don't think Astrid will get careless with explosives—not now!—or get drunk and try and disassemble the shore patrol, but there are probably equivalents a fourteen-year-old can come up with."

Signe nodded. "I'll try and get her to talk . . . and meanwhile, shall we practice?"

"Right," he said.

He'd tried his hand at the compound; the offset pulleys at the tips made it much easier use than a traditional bow of the same draw-weight, and it had an adjustable sight. And he was strong, and had excellent eyesight, and was a crack shot with a rifle and very good at estimating distance.

Even so, he could tell it was going to be weeks or months before he gained any real skill with it, and that was frustrating—he might need it on a life-and-death level sooner than that. Given a choice, he preferred to do any fighting from a comfortable distance.

Signe had drawn a shaft to the angle of her jaw. He waited while she loosed; the arrow flashed out and thumped into the burlap-covered hay bales. It sank three-quarters of its length as well, just inside the line marking the man-shaped target.

"Not bad," he said. *You'd have lamed the guy, at least.*

"I've done target archery off and on," she said. "Nothing like Astrid, though; she's been a maniac about it for years—since she was eight or nine."

"Yeah, but you'd look silly with pointed ears," he replied, pleased when he got a snort of laughter. She'd been very withdrawn since the fight and her mother's death. Understandable, but . . .

"Right, let's take it up where we left off," she said.

They walked closer to the target; Signe had been practicing from sixty yards, and it was a bad idea to start at a distance you'd consistently miss—that way you couldn't identify your mistakes and improve. She handed over the bracer, and he strapped it to his left forearm, adjusting the Velcro-fastened straps. Hutton had rigged him an archer's finger-tab for his right hand, and he slid two fingers through it.

"We'll have to make some sort of moving target, eventually," Havel said. "And a glove fitted for this; I wouldn't want to be stuck wearing this tab thing if I had to switch weapons suddenly."

Signe moved him into proper position with touches of her fingers, which was pleasant.

"Rolling pie plates are what Astrid uses. All right, make a proper T . . . And she has things that run on wires, she had a bunch of them set up on our summer place, besides the stumps."

"Stumps you mentioned. We're not short of them, and pie plates we could probably manage too," Havel said.

Then he drew his first shot. The bow's draw-weight was eighty pounds, but with the pulleys he only had to exert that much effort at the middle of the draw. It fell away to less than forty when his right hand was back by the angle of his jaw, and he brought the sighting pin down on the middle of the man-figure's chest . . .

*Whffft!*

There was something rather satisfying about it; particularly this time, since he'd come *near* the target, at least.

*Someday I'll actually hit it.*

"You're releasing a bit rough," Signe said. "Remember to just let the string fall off the balls of your fingers—"

They worked at it for half an hour; when he stopped he worked his arms and shoulders ruefully. "This must use muscles I don't usually put much weight on," he said.

"You're making progress," Signe replied. "Any more today and you'd get shaky."

He nodded. "After a certain point you lose more than you gain," he agreed.

"And you don't mind learning from a girl; I like that."

A corner of Havel's mouth quirked up. "I'm not an eighteen-year-old boy," he said.

Their eyes went to the flatbed. Eric was standing with an air of martyred patience, holding something on the anvil with a pair of pincers while Hutton hit it two-handed with a sledgehammer; Ken Larsson observed, a measuring compass and a piece of paper in his hand.

The *ting . . . tang . . . chink!* sound echoed back from the steep slopes, fading out across the white noise of the brawling river.

"And I'm not an idiot either, if there's a difference," Havel went on.

This time Signe laughed out loud, probably for the first time in a few days.

"Knives?" he said briskly.

She nodded eagerly. They walked over towards the tree where the mule deer was hanging.

They'd wrapped it in sacking, but there weren't many flies this early in the year. He went to the tie-off on the tree trunk and lowered the carcass from bear-avoidance distance from the ground until the gutted torso was at a convenient height.

Signe watched, a little puzzled, but eagerly caught one of the wooden knives he'd whittled. She fell into the stance he'd showed her, right leg slightly advanced, left hand open and that forearm at an angle across her chest. The knife she held a bit out and low, point angled up and her thumb on the back of the blade.

Havel took an identical stance. "Now, what are we both doing wrong?" he said.

She shook her head, wincing a bit as she bit her lip in puzzlement; it was still swollen and sore.

"We're about to fight a knife duel," he said. "Which means that one of us is going to die and the other's going to get cut up real bad, get killed too or crippled or at least spend months recovering. Yeah, I'm going to teach you how to do that kind of a knife fight, eventually, but it's a last resort unless the other guy's truly clueless. I was *real* glad not to have to go mano a mano back there."

He switched the grip on his knife, holding it with the thumb on the pommel and the blade sticking out of his fist, the cutting edge outward.

"First let me show you something. Grab my knife wrist and hold me off."

She tucked the wooden blade into her belt and intercepted his slow backhand stab towards her throat. He pushed, using his weight and the strength of his arm and shoulders; Signe stumbled backward, struck the trunk of the tree and grimaced as the point came inexorably towards her throat. Suddenly her knee flashed up, but he'd been expecting that; he caught it on his thigh and pressed the wooden knife still closer.

"Halt!" he said, stepping back; he was breathing deeply, she panting. "OK, you're what . . . five-eight? Hundred and forty-five?"

"Five-eight and a half," she said. "One-forty-four, but I think I've lost some since the Change."

"Probably," he said. "Right, so you're a big girl, tall as most men, and as heavy as some; which means you've got plenty of reach, and there's no reason you can't get real fast—you've got good coordination and reflexes already, from sports."

"But?" she said.

He nodded. "But most men, even ones a bit shorter or lighter, are going to have stronger grips, and more muscle on their arms and shoulders. Speed matters, reach matters, skill and attitude matter a *lot*, but raw strength does too in any sort of close combat, especially hand-to-hand."

"So what do I do?" she said tightly.

"Don't arm wrestle 'em and don't get into pushing matches. Your brother has reach and weight on me; he's nearly as strong as I am and he'll be stronger when he's a couple of years older. I could still whup his ass one-on-one—in fact, I did. Take the same grip on your knife as I did and come at me; give it everything you've got."

She did—and stabbed a lot faster than he had, as well. He let her wrist smack into his right hand, and squeezed tightly enough to lock them together. Then he let her shove him back; she *was* strong for her size, especially in the legs.

As they neared the tree, he snapped his torso around and push-pulled on the hand that held the wooden knife, body-checking her as her own momentum drove her towards him. Then he bunched his knuckles into a ridge and punched her—lightly—right under the short ribs while she staggered off-balance.

"Oooff!" she said; but she made a recovery, coming up to guard position again.

"See, what I did there was redirect you instead of pushing back. That takes strength, but not as much as the other guy's. You just have to be strong *enough*. See the point?"

"Yes," she said slowly, nodding. "I think I do, Mike. You mean a woman needs a different fighting style?"

"Right; a woman, or a smaller man. I'll have Will do up some weights for you—and Luanne, we need to get her in on this too, and Astrid—and between that and the way we're traveling and chores, you can maximize your upper-body strength pretty quick, since you're already fit. Meanwhile, we'll work on the skill, speed and attitude. You'll practice with Eric, too, and Will. Will's got a lot of valuable brawling experience, I think."

He went over to the hanging deer carcass. "I used to use a pig carcass for this, back on my folks' place when I was a kid. They're better, because they're more like a man in size and where the organs are, but this'll do. Doesn't matter if we mess it up, since it's going into the stewpot. Go round the other side and hold on—hold it steady—put your shoulder to it."

He drew his *puukko* and took a deep breath. Then he attacked, stabbing in a blur of motion, the carcass jerking to the force of the impacts. The steel made a wet smacking sound as it clove the dead flesh, ten strikes in half as many seconds.

When he stopped, Signe's face had gone white again, shocked by the speed and power of the blows she felt thudding through the body of the deer. She swallowed and pressed her hands together for a moment before straightening up.

Havel nodded approval. "*That's* how you win a knife fight; you don't let it get started. Take him by surprise, from the back, or just get all over him before he can get set and *kill* the fucker before he realizes he's dying. OK, get your knife out and I'll hold the carcass."

He did, switching positions, although he gripped it at arm's length as she drew the bandit's long blade.

"We'll start slow. You've got to get real precise control on where the point and edge go, and get used to the feel of it hitting meat, and *feel* why it's a bad idea to turn it on a bone. He who hesitates is bossed, remember."

*Excellent focus,* he thought, twenty minutes later.

She was streaming sweat, and there were shreds of deer-flesh on her knife-hand and spattered across other bits of her, but she was boring in without flinching, eyes narrowed and seeing nothing else.

"*Jesus!*" he shouted, leaping backward.

Signe half stumbled as the deer carcass swayed unexpectedly, but pivoted with fluid balance and drove the long knife home, grunting with effort as it sliced into flesh.

Only then did she turn to see what had startled him. A

drumroll thunder of hooves announced Astrid's arrival once more, but there was a hoarse bellowing snarl underneath it.

The bear behind the horse was traveling very nearly as fast, its mouth open and foam blowing from it; an arrow twitching in the hump over its shoulders showed why.

It was a black, not a grizzly, but the point was moot—it was also a very large boar bear, four hundred pounds if it was an ounce, and moving at thirty miles an hour. Astrid turned in the saddle as her horse pounded by in a tearaway gallop, drawing her bow again and firing directly over its tail in what an earlier age had called the Parthian shot.

"No!" Havel shouted futilely.

*Well, now I know how a horsey teenage girl snaps from combat stress. She goddamn well tries to shoot a bear!*

Havel had hunted bear; he knew the vitality and sheer stubborn meanness of a wounded bruin. By some miracle, the arrow even hit—a shallow slant into the beast's rump, leaving head and feathers exposed. It halted and spun with explosive speed, throwing up a cloud of earth clods and twigs and duff, snapping for the thing that had bitten it on the backside; that let Astrid's horse open the distance between them.

Unfortunately, it also pointed the bear directly at Havel. It hesitated for an instant, as he stood motionless; then its eyes caught the sway of the mule-deer carcass, and the glint of afternoon sun on Signe's knife.

It went up on its hind legs for an instant, narrow head swaying back and forth as it gave a bawling roar and estimated distances with its little piggy eyes. Then it dropped to all fours again and came for him, as fast as a galloping horse.

"I don't fucking *believe* this!" he cried, and then, much louder: "Spear, spear, where's the goddamned spear?"

# CHAPTER ELEVEN

There was a hypnotic quality to riding the disk harrow, Juniper decided. The horses leaning into the traces ahead, their shadows falling before them, the shining disks sinking into the turned earth behind the plows and leaving a smooth seedbed behind . . .

"God*damn* it!" Dennis called from her left. "Whoa, you brainless lumps of walking hamburger! Whoa!"

His single-furrow walking plow had jammed up with bits of tangled sod again; it was one of the half-dozen copies they'd made of the museum's original. And it was scraping along on top of the turf rather than cutting it, the handles jarring at his hands. Dennis leaned back, pulling at the reins knotted around his waist; Dorothy Rose, who was walking and leading the horses, added her mite to the effort, and the team stopped.

Then they looked over their shoulders. Horses didn't have very expressive faces, but she would have sworn both of these were radiating indignation—at the unfamiliar task, and at the sheer ignorant incompetence behind the reins.

"Easy, Dennie," she said soothingly. "Remember, *bo le bata is capall le ceansact*; a stick for a cow, but a kind word for a horse."

"I'd like to use a goddamned *log* on these beasts," he said, but shrugged and smiled.

Of them all, only Juniper had any real experience at driving a horse team, and that only with a wagon; she did know how surprisingly fragile the big beasts were, though. She looked up at the sun and estimated the time since the last break. . . .

"Whoa!" she called to her own team. Then: "All right, all teams take five! Rest and water the horses!"

She hauled on the reins, wincing as they slid over fresh blisters beneath her gloves. When they'd stopped she wiped a sopping sleeve over her face, tender with sunburn despite the broad-brimmed hat and bandana—the early-April day was bright and warm. Damp reddish brown earth was soft under her feet as she jumped down. It had a scent at once sweetly green and meaty, a compound of cut grass and damp dirt and severed roots and the crushed camas flowers that starred it. That made a pleasant contrast to the smell of her own sweat, and of Cagney and Lacey's.

"Goddamn it, why does this thing keep jamming?" Dennis said. "It's not just the copies Chuck and I made, the original does it too."

There was an edge of frustration to the point of tears in his voice. He knelt and began pulling at lumps between the coulter knife that cut the furrow and the moldboard that turned it over.

Chuck Barstow and John Carson halted their teams as well; Carson turned and looked at the crooked, irregular furrows that lay behind the three plowmen.

"The plows jam because it's old meadow sod," Carson grinned.

He was a lean fortysomething man, with sun-streaks through his light brown hair, and blue eyes. He also owned the property four miles west, where Artemis Butte Creek flowed out into the valley proper and the real farmland began, and he was here as part of a complicated swap of labor, animals, and equipment.

"Hasn't been plowed in a hundred years," he went on as they unharnessed their teams. "Not even been grazed heavy these past forty or more, this bit. Lots of tangled roots, most of 'em thick as a pencil. A big tractor could just rip it all to shreds, but horses . . . Well, two hundred fifty horsepower against two-nothing, it stands to reason!"

The furrows were roughly along the contour of the sloping meadow, and *very* roughly parallel; oblong islands of unplowed grass showed between them, and the depth varied as if they'd been dug by invisible land-dolphins porpoising along.

At least there weren't very many rocks to hit around here.

"I thought I knew what hard work was," he said. "No work harder than farmin'. Now I know my *granddad* knew what hard work was, and I've been kidding myself. He farmed—I operate machinery. *Did* operate machinery."

They all unhitched their teams, leaving plows and harrow standing where they lay, and led the big animals over beneath the shade of a spreading oak to the north. They brought buckets of water from the creek rather than taking them to it—it was easier to make sure they didn't overdrink that way. The little pool below the waterfall was close there, and she gave it a longing look as she hauled the water.

The thought of stripping off her sweat-sodden clothing and diving in, then standing beneath the falling spray . . .

*Better not,* she said. *Got to keep going. And Mr. Carson might shock easily.* Presbyterians tended to be more cautious about nudity than Wiccans, in her experience.

Juniper banished the image of a whooping dive into the cold water. Instead she uncorked a big ceramic jug—until recently an ornamental sitting on the mantelpiece over the kitchen fireplace in her cabin. It held spring water, cut with cold herbal tea. When you were really thirsty, that quenched better than water alone.

After a swallow she passed it around, trying not to think about fresh lemonade. Dennis took it with a grin, wiping the neck and bowing.

"My thanks, gracious Lady Juniper, High Chief of the Clan Mackenzie, herself," he said.

"Go soak your head, Dennie," she replied, scowling. "Cut that *out.* This is a democracy. Sort of."

"If only I could!" he said, passing the jug on to John Carson. "Soak my head, that is."

Their neighbor glugged and passed it to Chuck in turn. "Time was an acre was a few minutes' work," he said. "On a tractor, that is! Even if I was towing the rototiller for a truck crop. Now I feel like I've plowed Kansas if I get an acre done in a day."

His mouth quirked: "You know, I had an old three-furrow riding plow in a shed—"

All their ears perked up; then they groaned as he went

on: "—but I sold it for scrap instead of making it into a lawn ornament like I'd planned."

The meadowland sloped gently down from the edge of the rise behind her to the lip several hundred yards south. There was the rough first-pass section nearest, the lumpy brown-green quilt of the area that had been plowed twice, then the smooth reddish brown seedbed the disk harrow left. The disks had an automatic neatness built in, chopping and mixing grass and roots and dirt into a light mixed mass. The smooth look of it was sharp contrast to work that depended on the skill of human hands, or the strength of human shoulders.

The rest of the clan were working on the finished section; adults turning over a spadeful of earth at regular intervals, the children behind them dropping in a section of seed potato and a dollop of fertilizer. Some of the children still wore green blazers, much the worse for wear and grime; most worked barefoot and in their knee-shorts.

They'd bury the cut eyes and mound up the earth on the next pass. It wasn't as heavy work as plowing, but it was monotonous; she'd done her share of that, too.

"We're getting it done," she said, almost to herself. "By the Lord and the Lady, I feel like it's aging me a year a day—not surprising, with days that feel like years—but it's getting *done.*"

*Now if the weather cooperates and the bugs and blights stay away . . . We should have an Esbat soon. There are lots of crop-magic spells.*

John Carson nodded. "By the time this field is finished, we'll all know what we're doing, a little more at least," he said. "That'll mean my fields go faster, for which I thank you. Not to mention this fall—come November, we have to start planting the winter grains."

"That harrow's yours," Juniper pointed out. "And it's saving us a lot of time. Neighbors should help each other. Not to mention that silage you're giving us. Big horses like these can't work on grass alone."

"Neighbors need to help each other more now more than ever," Carson said somberly. "I don't know what I'd have done without your plow teams, Ms. Mackenzie."

*Most of them courtesy of the museum, but let's not mention that,* she thought.

"Good of you to take in all those kids," Carson went on. "I've got my brother and his family and a cousin and *his*, besides those three the Reverend Dixon talked me into, and I had to turn away others—it hurt, but what could I do? Almost wish I'd been a Mormon instead of a Presbyterian— we'd have had more food stored. As it is I slaughtered more of my stock than I liked."

A snort. "Not that it mattered after those bastards in Salem cleaned me out, eh? It leaves the silage for the plow teams, at least."

Just then a thudding of hooves came from the streamside road. Dennis hefted his ax and lumbered over to the spot where the road emerged from the woods. Sally was there with her bow, seated behind a blind they'd rigged with every art that they could manage. She was the only adult they could spare, and that only because her leg still wasn't healed enough to let her do much work.

Juniper worried about it—it just wasn't safe not to have more people watching, given the number of hungry refugees about—but there was nothing else they could do, just yet. Not keeping careful enough watch *might* cause a disaster; not planting the crop in time would *certainly* kill them all.

A rider in blue denim overalls came through; a girl in her late teens, blond hair streaming. She halted for a moment to talk to Dennis and Sally, and then trotted her horse over to the tree.

"Dad!" she said, and then: "Lady Juniper."

*Dennis, I* am *going to kill you with your own ax for starting that* Lady Juniper *nonsense,* the musician thought, but the girl's face looked too urgent to bother with his warped sense of humor.

"There's people headed up here," she said. "We saw them pass our place—we're plowing the old south field, Dad, like you said—and they went right up the creek road. Uncle Jason said I should come right up and tell you."

"How many?" Juniper said quickly.

*Could it be a foraging party?*

The thought brought a cold chill. That was the latest bright idea of the remnant of the state government, parts of which were still hanging on in Salem. They'd started organizing bicycle-borne townfolk and refugees to go out and *requisition* food and livestock for issue as rations to the urban population, and the refugee camps—Salem hadn't quite collapsed totally, the way she heard Portland and Eugene had done.

John Carson looked equally frightened. That was how he'd lost most of the considerable herd of cattle he'd had before the Change, that and casual theft by passing scavengers, and the remaining dozen head were grazing on Mackenzie land, for safety's sake.

"Just four, on foot," Cynthia Carson said, and Juniper blew out her cheeks in relief. "They're leading a horse; one woman, three men. No bows or crossbows—just the usual."

For safety's sake, Juniper still fetched the crossbow hanging beside the seat of the disk harrow and spanned it, and strapped on her sword belt, before walking over to the guardpost. Dennis and Chuck had been talking about a simple, quick way to make body armor, and perhaps when they had the plowing and planting done . . .

Chuck brought his sword and buckler, too, his hand resting on the hilt as he peered down into the shadow of the streamside road. Then: "Alex!" he blurted, letting the long sword swing free.

Chuck's younger brother smiled and swayed, leaning against the horse he'd been leading; he had the family looks—sandy blond and leanly muscular. The girl beside him wasn't one Juniper remembered, but she'd never been much involved with Alex, since he wasn't of the Craft and didn't like her type of music—he'd been strictly a thrash-metal fan. The closest they'd come was when she'd hired him to do repairs on her barn in '95; he was a builder by trade.

The two young men behind were strangers as well—one fair and short, the other dark and tall. Polite strangers, though, since they laid down the ax and shovel they'd been carrying. All four were gaunt but not skeletal, and all carried heavy packs; the horse's load was mainly large sacks made of heavy paper, bulging with something small and homogenous, and topped by bedrolls and blankets.

"Oh, God," Alex said. "I thought we'd never make it, honestly, I did . . . And you're *here*. . ."

He was almost crying with relief, and the haunted-eyed young woman clung to him with tears streaking the grime on her face.

"I . . . this is Barbara. Vince and Steve, they saved our lives. We got caught around Lebanon by some . . ."

He swallowed. Everyone winced; they knew what he meant. Not everyone out there was starving quite yet, but enough were, the more so since everyone who *did* have food was hoarding it against the future. Some were already hungry enough to eat anything at all—and there was only one large animal still common and easily caught.

*"Eaters,"* the girl whispered.

Suddenly his eyes went wide. "Can we stay?" he blurted, looking from face to face.

Juniper caught eyes, willing acceptance; there were nods, mostly; Chuck's and Judy's were emphatic.

"Of course," she said, turning back to the younger Barstow. With a smile: "And the horse you rode in on, too."

The animal was tired-looking, but well-fed otherwise—the valley wasn't short of *its* sort of food. And it was a saddle breed, unlike Cagney and Lacey or the big Suffolks Chuck had liberated from the living-history exhibit. That would be useful.

"Welcome to the Clan Mackenzie, Alex," she said. "What's in the sacks?"

He grinned; even that was weary. "Barley," he said. "Certified seed barley. We found it yesterday in an overturned truck—the other half of the cargo was sacks of fertilizer, and they covered it up, but we saw rats digging; there's more, we hid the rest and brought what we could. And if you knew how *tempting* it was to just eat it . . ."

"Come have some Eternal Soup instead," she said, smiling. "And then we'll get a wagon ready."

*Threefold return indeed!* she thought. *Actions most definitely do have consequences.*

Not a matter of a celestial scorebook of punishments and rewards, just that everything was connected.

Then another thought struck her: *Oh, Goddess—we'll have to* plow *more!*


*There,* Juniper thought, freezing, the only motion the slow rise and fall of her chest.

*You don't see me. You don't smell me. You don't hear me. I bind your eyes, your ears, your nostrils, horned one; in the name of Herne the Wild Hunter, so mote it be.*

The mule deer hesitated, then caught Cuchulain's scent—the dog was with Dennis, two hundred yards northeast through the dense bush. The animal turned swiftly away from the smell of predator, head high and ears swiveling. The mottled clothing she wore would fade into the spring woods, and the wind was wrong for him to pick out human scent from the cool decaying-wood and damp-earth smells. Ferns and brush stood between her and it, but for a moment it poised motionless, quivering-alert.

They were up in the mountain forest, a thousand feet above the old Mackenzie land. This area had been clear-cut much more recently than hers, and there was more undergrowth. It was still cold here, the more so on a rainy day—there might be sleet or snow if they went a little further upslope. The deer had already begun to head up towards their summer pastures, though: even without guns, the hunting pressure on their herds in the foothills was much worse than usual.

She exhaled, ignoring the cold drops trickling down her neck, remembering what the book said and practice had reinforced: *stroke* the trigger gently. . . .

*Thunggg!*

The short heavy bolt flashed out, and the butt of the crossbow thumped at her shoulder. Her breath held still, as she waited for it to be deflected on some strand of second growth, but instead there was a heavy, meaty *whack*. She didn't see the strike, but nothing could hide the deer's convulsive leap.

"Dennie!" she cried, springing forward. "I got him!"

Dennis roared in triumph as he heard her voice, and he plunged towards her—she could hear Cuchulain's frenzied barking as he scented blood, and the shaking of branches as the ex-manager of the Hopping Toad pushed his way through the thickets.

Blood splashed last year's stems and the green of the new growth. She ran crouched over, sliding through the undergrowth easily. Juniper had never hunted before the Change, but she'd walked these woods on visits all her life, lived here six months in the twelve for the past decade—and all those years she'd watched the comings and goings of its dwellers, deer and fox and coyote, otter and eagle, rabbit and elk.

She half remembered the lay of the land even here, well off her great-uncle's property; she wasn't altogether bewildered when the deer disappeared in a crashing and snapping. The depth of the ravine that opened beneath her feet still shocked, and she threw herself backward and slapped a hand on a branch slimy with moss to steady herself.

"Dennie!" she called. "Careful! There's a ravine here, and it's hidden!"

"I see it!" he bellowed in return. "Wait a minute, and I'll work around the head!"

She waited, breath slowing. The path of the deer's fall was just visible, and a patch of brown hide where he lay; it was a two-year-old male, she thought, and already nicely plump—the Willamette's climate was mild and there was good grazing in the foothill woods year-round. The bottom of the ravine was full of fallen timber and thick brush; not the distinctive three-leaf mark of poison oak, thank the Goddess and Cernunnos.

A slight sadness passed through her at the thought of the deer's loveliness broken, but she'd been around enough small farmsteads to know firsthand that meat didn't come from a factory wrapped in plastic.

*And sure, my stomach is rumbling so loud I can hear it over my panting,* she thought. *Venison in the Eternal Soup, sweet richness of fat on the tongue . . . Lord and Lady, did people ever worry about* too much *fat? Little medallions of tenderloin. Grilled liver. Maybe sausages, with sage and dried onions—there's some of those left, surely? Smoked haunch . . .*

Dennis arrived, with much crackling of brush; he was a city man still, although he was learning—in coordination with the shrinking of his gut, which had gone from embarrassing to merely substantial since the Change. He also had a coil of rope around his shoulder, and his ax slung with its handle through two loops sewn to the back of his jacket.

They made the rope fast to a firmly rooted tree. Cuchulain went down the steep slope with four-footed recklessness, but the two humans were more cautious—danger to themselves aside, the clan simply couldn't spare the working time lost in an unnecessary injury. Even Sally Quinn was helping with the poultry and around the house, on a crutch. The tangled mass below was just the sort to hide a branch broken off stabbing-sharp.

The deer was freshly dead, a trickle of red running from nose and mouth.

"You'll get some, fool dog," she scolded, pushing Cuchulain aside as he lapped at the flow. "Feet and ears and offal."

Then she spoke more formally, kneeling beside the deer and stroking its muzzle: "Thank you, brother, for your gift of life. And thanks to You, Cernunnos, horn-crowned Lord of the Forest, Master of the Beasts! We take of Your bounty from need, not in wantonness; knowing that the Huntsman will come for us too in our appointed day, for we also are Yours. Take our brother's spirit home to rest in the woods of summer in the land beyond the world, and be reborn through the cauldron of the Goddess, who is Mother-of-All."

Then they ran a cord through its hind feet between tendon and bone, cast a loop of cord over a convenient branch, and hoisted it up, working quickly; she put a basin from Dennis's pack beneath it and cut the throat with two deep diagonal slashes. The carcass had to drain or the meat wouldn't keep, and the blood would go into oatmeal to make a pudding. Privately she thought that tasted awful, but she'd eat her share.

Dennis sharpened the skinning knives while she drew a sign in the air over the basin; then Cuchulain yelped, a sudden squeal of pain. Juniper looked up sharply—there were black bear and cougar in these forests as well. She caught a flash of movement in the thicket twenty yards up the gully from them, a hand holding a rock waving from beneath a pile of brush and dirt.

"That's a man!" Dennis said sharply.

"Yes," Juniper said; the patterns sprang out at her, once she knew to expect camouflaged cloth. "And a hurt one, too!"

They made their way carefully through the tangle. Closer, and she could smell human waste—the man had been trapped here long enough for that, then. She looked up, and saw slick mud and fallen dirt where the treacherous edge had crumbled beneath him. He was under an overhang of the ravine's side, jammed awkwardly up against it, and his leg had been caught between two downed saplings—the springy wood had snapped closed around the flesh again. His lips were swollen. . . .

*Dying of thirst,* she thought. *In this wet wilderness, and not ten feet from running water!*

She brought her canteen to his lips. Dennis studied the situation, pursed his mouth, and then swung the ax twice. The man's hips and legs swung down a bit as the tension was released.

"Sorry," he said, coughing, and then sipping again—which showed considerable self-control. "Thanks, mate," he went on to Dennis.

*"Don-niah iss anim dyum,"* Dennis said carefully, then winked at Juniper as he dragged brush away. "But you can call me Dennis."

"That's *Donnacadh is anim dom,* Dennie; your pronunciation would give a goat glanders," she said, propping the canteen upright and digging in her pack for some hoarded trail mix. "And speaking of which, my fake harp, *más maith leat slocháin, cairdeas, agus moladh, éist, feic, agus fan balbh.*"

The injured man smiled as he took the concentrated ration, and managed not to gulp it.

"I chucked a bit of wood at your dog because I thought it was that coyote again. One's been visiting, waiting for me to come ripe."

There was an English twang to his voice, but not Cockney or boarding school; instead a broad yokel burr that reminded her of documentaries she'd seen about places with thatched cottages and Norman churches.

Juniper nodded, examining. "He wasn't hurt, just startled. Your shoulder's dislocated," she said. "Ball right out of the socket and displaced up."

"I know, lass," he said. "Tried fixing it, but I couldn't get the leverage."

Dennis looked at him and grinned. "That's Lady Juniper of the Clan Mackenzie you're talking to, man," he said.

"You're not Scots, surely?" the Englishman said, giving her another head-to-foot glance. "Irish, I'd have said."

"My mother was born in west Ireland, my father's family came from Scotland a long time ago by way of Ulster, and Dennie here has a weird sense of humor," she said. "What else is wrong?"

"I don't think aught else's broken or torn—just sommat bruised and battered! I couldn't come at the legs with me arm out, is all."

Dennis laid down his ax and held the man steady. Juniper braced herself with a foot under his armpit and took his wrist in a strong two-handed grip; a quick jerk, and he gave a sound that was halfway between a muffled yelp and a sigh of relief.

"Dennie, you go get help," Juniper said. "Chuck, Vince, Alex, Judy if she can be spared—warn her to expect business, anyway—and a horse to the base of the trail; stretcher, tools and ropes and such."

A grin. "And tell Diana that the guest comes with a venison dinner!"

Dennis nodded, stuck the haft of the ax through its loops, and swarmed his way up the rope and the ravine's steep side, puffing like a grampus but more easily than he would have before the Change.

That done, she studied her . . . *Well, probably new clansman, if he's at all suitable,* she thought. *The unsought omen should never be disregarded. A gift from the Horned Hunter, this one.*

The man was older than her by a decade but younger than Dennis, she judged; square-faced, not tall but very broad-shouldered, with thick muscular arms and gray eyes bloodshot now; his hair was light-streaked brown, and his naturally fair skin had been tanned to the color of old beechwood by harsh suns.

She shook hands carefully; his great square paw swallowed hers. "And you're English, by the sound of you?"

"Samuel Aylward, at your service, lady," he said, then winced when he tried to give a half bow. "Samkin to his friends. Late of Crooksbury, Hampshire, late sergeant in the Special Air Service."

"You're a long way from home!"

"Not much wild land left back in old Blighty. I like wandering about in the woods; it's an old family tradition, you might say, Lady Juniper."

"That Lady Juniper is just a joke of Dennie's, Mr. Aylward. He's always teasing—well, it's a long story."

He looked at her and quirked a smile. "It's *Lady Juniper* or call you an angel from heaven, lass; I was getting fair anxious, there. What was that last bit of Erse you said to him? Stumped him, I could see."

"Roughly translated: If you want to be liked, shut up and listen. We're old friends."

"Thought so," Aylward said, then sighed and closed his eyes for a moment.

Long-held tension released his face, making it look younger despite stubble and lines and dirt. She held his head while he drank again; he knew enough to pace himself, and nibbled on some dried fruit when she gave it to him. He was wearing camper's or hunter's garb, and a pack; a long case lay not far away. She snagged it and worked it out of the tangled branches.

"What's this?"

"My bow, if it's not a broken stick," Aylward said. "I bloody well hope not. I'm no Adams, but I spent a lot of time making it, I did; it's my favorite reflexdeflex longbow."

She opened the soft waterpoof case; the stave within was yellow yew, about six feet long with a riser of some darker wood and a leather-wrapped grip; a neat little quiver held six goose-feathered arrows. The wood shone and slid satin-smooth under her touch. When she took it up by the grip it had the fluid natural feeling of handling a violin from a master craftsman's hands, despite being far too long for someone only three inches over five feet in her socks.

"It's fine, indeed. Were you poaching?" she said, teasing to distract him from his injuries—it hadn't been the deer-hunting season when the Change hit.

"There's no season on boar here," he said a little defensively; feral swine were an invasive pest, and unprotected. "And—"

She nodded encouragingly and gave him another drink of the water. *Best if he talks a little*, she thought.

"And I've the time for it these days. Call me a masochist."

He took a deep breath; she could sense he wasn't much of a man for chatting with strangers, in more normal times. *Not surprising now, when he's half-delirious and just reprieved from a very nasty death.* Juniper waited, her face calmly attentive, ready to accept words or silence.

"Is the war over?" he said, after half a minute.

"War?" she said, bewildered.

"I was looking north towards Portland from the mountainside when I saw the flash," he said. "And then everything went dark—lights out good and proper, none since, and everything electronic in my gear was buggered for fair. I was staying high, working my way south and waiting out the fallout, until I ran too hard and looked too little after a buck and landed down here."

She looked at him with pity. "Oh, you poor man!" she exclaimed. "You thought it was World War Three? It's *much* worse than that, I'm afraid!"

A day later Juniper finished adding the column of figures, wishing for one of the old mechanical crank-worked adding machines as she did, and putting it on a mental list for scavenging or swapping.

All the adults were present, including a near-silent Sam Aylward propped up on the couch with his wrenched leg and sore shoulder; Sally Quinn could sit well enough now, and move without a crutch if she was careful. The children were up in the loft with Eilir, who was the eldest, minding them—learning Sign had become a mark of status with the youngsters, since Eilir made up one hundred percent of their adolescent reference-figures. None of the other adults had teenagers, and Juniper did only because she'd started so early.

The adults of . . . she supposed she couldn't just say the Singing Moon Coven; half the people weren't coveners at all. Though to be sure they weren't exactly cowan, either.

*Well, I may have suggested we call it a clan,* she thought. *But it was Dennis who suggested* Clan Mackenzie, *the black-hearted rapparee!*

He'd been ribbing her for years about her musician's Celt-persona; she supposed this was either revenge, or a streak of buried romanticism coming out.

Most of the front of the cabin was a big living room, with the stone-built fireplace dominating the north wall. A fire crackled and spat in it now, casting a welcome warmth and filling the room with the delicate flower scent of burning applewood—she was still using the salvage from clearing out the old orchard last summer. A kerosene lantern on the plank table gave acceptable reading light—you could use gasoline, if you were extremely careful. Firelight ruddy and yellow brought out the grain of the big logs that made up the walls. Rain beat like gentle drums on the strake roof above them, and the windows looked out on the veranda like caves of night.

She'd always liked the great room; she remembered winter days, with Eilir sprawled on the rug and her schoolbooks before her, Cuchulain curled before the hearth, Juniper strumming at her guitar as she worked on a tune and listened for the whistle of her teakettle, and snow patting feather-paws against the windowpanes.

Now it had rolled-up bedding tied in neat bundles stacked around the walls; the children slept in the loft and her own former bedroom was assigned to the handfasted couples on a roster, so that they could all have a chance at some privacy.

The Hall of the Mackenzies was stuffed to the bursting point. The crowding would have been tolerable for a week or so at a pagan festival, but the prospect of living like this all her life . . .

She shook her head and got up to throw another log on the fire. Aylward spoke:

"Wait a minute, lass—Lady. That's yew, isn't it? Could I have a look?"

Everyone glanced over at the Englishman; he'd seemed a friendly enough sort, but on short acquaintance not given to inconsequential chat.

"To be sure, it is," Juniper said. "It's an understory weed tree here."

She put the billet in his big spade-shaped hands; it was four inches thick and a little over four feet long, with thin smooth purplish bark scattered with red-brown papery scales.

"Nicely seasoned," Aylward said, running a critical eye over it. "Is there any more like this?"

"A ton or so; the whole bottom half of my woodpile, out in the shed. The loggers cleared out a lot of it last year and I salvaged it for firewood; hadn't worked my way down through the applewood yet. Do you have a use for it?"

Aylward grinned. "We all do! If you let me at a drawknife and spokeshave, and a bit of hardwood for the risers, and a little glue."

Sally Quinn looked at him sharply. "You're a bowyer?"

Aylward nodded. "A hobby; I make and fletch me own shafts, too. Longbows are simple enough, even with a separate riser; I could do two or three a day, and anyone who's handy with wood could learn the trick."

Dennis grinned enormously; he *was* handy with wood, and loved learning a new way to work it. There was a pleased murmur all around the table. They had the three crossbows, which were irreplaceable once they broke down, and Sally's fiberglass target weapon, but that was it.

"Threefold return indeed!" Juniper said happily, resuming her seat and tapping the pile of figures Andy and Diana had worked up. "Now, people, we have just enough food to get everyone here"— *And how we've grown!* —"through to harvest. At a minimum diet for people working hard."

There were groans at that. Her own hands itched where the blisters never quite had time to heal. She'd had a big garden every year since she inherited this place, and now knew the difference between that and growing all your own food.

"Over to you, Chuck. Tell us what we can expect to *get,* for all the sweat we've been investing."

"Chuck, Lord of the Harvest," Judy said, grinning, leaning into his shoulder with her arm around his waist.

A laugh went around the table; it was a title of the High Priest of a coven, and Chuck had been the only candidate for *that* post, as well as farm manager. It also meant the Great Rite would be symbolic rather than actual from now on, with the High Priest not Juniper's man.

*Rudy . . .*

She squeezed her eyes shut for a moment, then forced a smile.

He took up the story, with a pad of his own. "OK, we've got all the acreage we need turned and fitted, and most of the potatoes planted—we'll keep the rest to put in between now and June, to stretch the harvesting season out, same with the veggies. Seven acres so far all up, here and down by the Fairfax place, counting what Frank Fairfax had in before the Change."

He paused to glare at Dorothy and Diana and Andy, who were organic-produce fanatics . . . or had been, before direct personal experience of hunger, which tended to make one less finicky.

"I *presume* nobody's going to object to using fungicides if we have to? 'Cause those potatoes are the margin between living and dying, and anyway, they came treated."

"If we have to, Chuck," Juniper said soothingly. "If we have to. We've got them on hand, haven't we?"

He nodded, and the three made unwilling gestures of assent as well.

*I'm Chief Soother, that's what I am!* Juniper thought. *Unruffler of Feathers! Dennis should have taken to calling me the Clan Facilitator, not the Chief.*

"The Fairfaxes had four and a half acres of fall-planted oats, which should come ripe in June; English hulled variety, good stuff. And I *think* we got that barley Alex found for us sown in time for some sort of yield. We've got a deal with the Carsons to help harvest some of their wheat on half-shares come summer; enough to really help and for seed grain of our own this autumn too. We might do the same elsewhere, but I'm not counting on it. . . ."

He took a deep breath. "Let's put it this way, Mackenzies; it'll be tight until June, and after that we're going to get awful sick of potatoes boiled and mashed and oatmeal and carrots and turnips and cabbage and beans and barley soup and whatnot, but we'll have enough to last through until the *next* crop year. *More* than enough, if we're reasonably lucky. In fact, we may not have enough people to harvest it all!"

"Of course," he went on, amid the cheers, "that brings up the question of storage. Potatoes take a *lot* of space, and we'll be storing by the *ton,* and we're going to have a fair amount of grain as well. I think more root cellars should be the first priority now that we've got *some* time to spare—"

"Oh, no you don't," Judy said. "We need a better bathhouse and laundry system for heath reasons—"

"Hey, wait a minute," Dennis cut in. "There's that old gristmill east of Lebanon, we could put it in below the waterfall with only a short sluice gate to build. Nobody's claimed it yet, and we could charge to grind other people's grain come summer—"

"And on second thought," Chuck said, glaring a little, "we ought to do a regular daily training schedule with archery and sword-and-buckler. The bandit gangs are getting—"

Juniper sighed and put her hands to her forehead. The threat of starvation had kept this collection of strong-willed individualists moving in one direction. Now she was going to have to earn *her* corn.

She looked around the table and caught several pairs of eyes—Dennis, Sally, Alex and his three friends. *Let's see, how many votes . . .* Sam wasn't comfortable enough with them to take much part yet, but she had hopes there, which was for the best.

Because some weren't going to like what *she* would suggest they do now that the most of the potatoes were planted, but the will of the Lady and Lord were plain.

*At least to me it is,* she thought.

She reached back and picked up her fiddle and bow from a table beside the couch. The first long strong note brought silence.

Then she improvised; a pompous boom for Chuck's voice, a piercing commanding shrill for Judy's, short anxious tremulos for Diana and Andy, a querulous rising inflection for Dennis's Californian accent . . .

Chuck was the first to snort. After a minute they were all laughing, and she wove the discords into a tune, one they all knew; the rollicking "Stable Boy," and moving on to "Harvest Season" and "Beltane Morning."

People missed music, with a craving almost as strong as that for food; there just wasn't any, in the Changed world, unless you made it yourself or persuaded someone in the room with you to do it. Soon everyone was singing. Eilir's head poked down through the stairs to the loft; she couldn't hear the tunes, but she loved watching the audience. Smaller heads peeked around hers.

> "Out in the wood
> There's a band of small faeries
> If you walk unwary at night;
> They're laughing and drinking
> And soon you'll be thinking—"

When she stopped the tension had gone out of the gathering. Everyone was ready to move the furniture aside and unroll their bedding; Andy and Diana were sleeping in the loft with the kids tonight, and they went up the stairs with a candle in its holder.

*And tomorrow I'll tell them about doing some outreach.*

# CHAPTER TWELVE

"*Spear, spear, where's the goddamned spear!*" Havel shouted, setting himself for a last-second dodge.

There wasn't time to be afraid. He didn't bother to draw his knife—with a bear this size, you might as well try to tickle it to death—or pay attention to the shouts and the wild neighing of the hobbled horses or to Signe dashing away.

He did when she came back seconds later, tossing the shaft of the spear in his direction. Grabbing it and whirling back to the bear gave him just enough time to set himself, with a fractional second more to be thankful he and Will had spent some time reshafting the blade firmly.

The animal would have run right over him if it hadn't paused, but bears liked to attack from an upright rear. It towered over him like a wall of cinnamon-black fur as he crouched with the spear poised; it was roaring, clawed paws raised like organic trip-hammers to smash his spine and spatter his brains across the ground.

He knew how to kill bears. You shot them from a hundred and fifty yards with a scope-sighted rifle firing hollow-point game rounds. . . .

"Yaaaaaah!" he shouted, lunging.

The impact was like ramming a pole into an oncoming truck, and it jarred every bone and tendon in his arms and shoulders and back. He shouted again, this time in alarm, as the onrushing weight drove him backward, his heels skidding in the damp grass of the meadow. The foot-long knife blade sank into the bear's middle, and part of the spear shaft after it, and the growling roar of pain and anger that followed it sprayed into his face along with saliva and a fan of blood.

The butt of the spear slid along the ground until it

jammed in a root, carrying him with it like a bundle. Then the bear screamed again as the weapon was driven deeper by its own strength and weight. It twisted frantically, trying to escape the thing that hurt it, and Havel clung with all his strength as the animal pounded him against the ground in its writhing.

Then his elbow hit ground with a jarring thump that made his hand open by sheer reflex as white agony flowed up the arm and down into his torso. The bear twisted again, and Havel felt himself thrown through the air with no more effort than a child's doll. Long training made him relax as he flew, curling loosely.

*Whump.*

The hard, hard ground still knocked the air out of his lungs and rattled his brain; he fought to breathe and collect his wits.

"Jesus!" he wheezed, scrambling backward on his butt and pushing himself with his heels.

The bear was heading for him. More slowly—the spear shaft stuck out of its middle at an angle; he'd seen before with the plump bandit that the shape of the knife blade made it difficult to withdraw once it was deep in a body. Now the long shaft kept catching on the ground and making the animal wince and stumble, and every time that happened the sharp steel was waggled about in the bear's body cavity.

But it moved, at a hunching, lurching amble, and it was coming straight for him. Blood poured from the wound in its belly, but it didn't spout with the pulsing arterial torrent that would have killed it quickly.

And he *couldn't* get up fast enough.

He tried and fell over backward; his left leg wasn't working properly yet, where he'd landed on it. The bear hunched closer, snarling in a basso growl, spit and blood drooling from its long yellow teeth. Havel fumbled at his belt for his *puukko,* snarling back at the approaching animal with an expression not much different from its own.

*If I die, you die with me, brother bear—and my people will eat you and wear your hide!*

Then it stopped and reared. Eric was there, shouting and jabbing at its face with his *naginata.*

*Nothing wrong with that boy's guts,* Havel thought. *His common sense, yes; guts, no.*

The sharp curved edge of the blade scored along the bear's shoulder. That angered it enough that it ignored everything else and swatted; it also gave Havel time to push himself backward far enough that he could lever himself erect with his hands and good leg. The other one didn't seem broken, or the joints torn; it just hurt like fire to put his weight on it. That didn't mean he wouldn't, but he'd be slowed.

"No!" he shouted, hobbling forward as he saw Eric coming back for more. "Don't get close! Just back off and let it die!"

Signe was back again too, gone no longer than it took her to run and fetch the bow. She had an arrow to the string, but her brother was far too close for her to fire. And he was too far gone in a fine fighting rage to listen, as well; he stepped in, chopping at the bear's paw as it flashed at him. Perhaps that was *his* way of showing the strain of the terrible things he'd seen and done, or maybe it was just teenage-male hormone poisoning turning off his brain's risk-management centers.

The pole gave the machete blow terrible leverage, and so did the bear's own strength. The scream it gave when the steel split its paw to the wrist was the loudest yet, and the speed of its other paw's sledgehammer blow turned the whole of that forelimb into a blur. It landed on the haft of the *naginata* rather than the man who held it, and the tough hickory snapped like a straw. That and the glancing touch of the paw was enough to send Eric's two hundred pounds spinning away like a top; he hit the ground ten feet away and bounced. He moved, but he didn't get up; his arms and legs were making vague swimming motions.

The moment he was clear Signe shot. The flat *snap* of the compound's bowstring sounded clear, and she was less than twenty feet away; the smack of the arrowhead into flesh was almost simultaneous. The eighty-pound hunting bow sent the arrow almost to its feathers under the bear's armpit. It shuddered, and the sound it made was as much a whimper as a growl, but it kept going—and straight towards Eric's fallen form.

This time nothing but death was going to stop it. In the abstract, Havel sympathized: it was doing exactly what he'd do in its place, trying to die fighting and take someone with it. In the here and now, it was trying to kill someone Michael Havel had promised to protect.

One of *his* people.

"Christ Jesus save us from heroes!" he snarled, and limped forward to seize the pole of the spear planted in the bear's gut.

Several things happened very quickly then. The bear screamed and reared as he grabbed the ashwood and hauled sideways.

Signe shot, twice, from only a few feet behind him and just to one side; two spots of bright yellow-and-green feathers blossomed against the bear's dark fur, one at the base of its throat and another just above the spear. Her sister was on his other side suddenly, panting—she must have run from as close as she could get her horse to come to the sound and smell of wounded bear. The string of Astrid's lighter bow snapped against her bracer, and an arrow sprouted from the bear's inner thigh.

Havel twisted desperately at the spear, conscious of how his bruised leg slowed him—and how the spear had sunk deeper in the bear's body, putting him close to it.

He saw Will Hutton running towards the animal from the rear, legs pounding in desperate haste, the double-bitted felling ax swinging up.

And the bear's wounded paw flashed towards him. He threw himself backward, releasing the spear, just as the tips of the claws struck.

When Havel came fully back to himself, he was chiefly conscious of a stabbing pain in his neck. Shortly after that he became aware that blood was pouring down his face, but he ignored that until he checked that he had movement in all his fingers and toes.

Then, slowly, he put a hand to his face. Light came back when he pushed back a flap of skin that was hanging over his left eye; when he had it in place, he knew there was a bad cut running from the upper peak of his left cheekbone, then beside his eye on that side—close enough to the corner to give him a cold chill—and across his forehead and into his scalp. Like all scalp wounds, it ran blood like a butchered pig hung up to drain, but he scrubbed his other arm across his eyes and the world cleared up.

The bear lay about seven feet away, very thoroughly dead; only a vet with time to do a dissection could have told what killed it, between the spear and the arrows and the ax that stood up like an italicized exclamation mark from its back, with the heavy blade buried in its spine. Blood still trickled; he couldn't have been out for more than a few seconds.

Will Hutton knelt on one side of him, Signe on the other. He let his head fall back; which was a mistake, since lights swam across his eyes.

"Eric?" he croaked.

"Fine," Hutton said, resting his hand on Havel's and moving it gently away from the younger man's wound. "Banged up. Bump on his head . . . this of yours goin' to need some stitches, though. Angelica, she kin handle it."

"Don't forget the aspirin," Havel croaked, and Hutton laughed.

"You are one tough mother, got to admit it," he said. "Cojones too. Ain't never seen a man move so fast."

"Ask the bear," Havel said. He rolled his eyes towards Signe. "Good shooting."

"It was closer than a target and bigger," she said. "Are you all right?"

"Hell, no," he said honestly. "This hurts like grim death and I'm seeing double and I'd puke if I had the strength. I'll live."

She blinked at him, frowning, then trotted away. He looked past her at Astrid, who stood beside her father and Hutton's wife and daughter, wringing her hands on her bow as if she were trying to strangle it.

"Come here," he said to her. "I can't shout—if I try, my head will fall off."

She obeyed, kneeling close to him. Signe came back on the other side with a bucket of water and a cloth; she had pills with her too, and he took them as Hutton raised his head with one strong hand. Then she began to sponge at the blood on his face. It felt so good he was reluctant to tell her to stop, but there was something to be done first.

"OK, kid," he said to Astrid, touching Signe's wrist gently for an instant to halt her.

He found he could move his arms, but only if he concentrated on it and didn't try anything difficult.

"Did that bear just light out after you, or did you shoot it unprovoked?" he asked the younger girl.

Astrid blinked, looked away, and then looked back. "I shot it," she whispered.

"What did I say?"

"Shoot anything but bears and cougars, Mike."

"Right." He put out his hand; she didn't resist when he took her bow. "This was a toy, back before things Changed. It isn't anymore. It's a weapon. You don't *play* with weapons. Understood?"

She nodded.

"And *that* was a dangerous wild animal. You don't play with them either. Understood?"

"Y-yes, Mike."

He went on: "Two inches closer and that thing would have ripped my face off. You understand *that*? And your brother and sister could have been dead too, easy. You understand *that*?"

She was crying now, but she nodded again.

"OK, you don't touch this again until I think you can use it responsibly. You want to be treated like a grown-up, you gotta earn it. A hunter doesn't take stupid chances, or shoot at all unless it's a clean kill."

He handed the bow to Hutton. "And don't let her on a horse again until I say so, either."

He let his head fall back. Signe leaned over him, sponging at the blood again; vaguely, he could see Angelica Hutton coming up with some sort of kit under her arm. The pills couldn't have been aspirin, either, or the concussion was worse than he'd thought, because he was beginning to drift away.

"This ain't fucking Middle-earth," he said—or thought he did.

Blackness.

Will Hutton looked at the electric grinding wheel, pursing his lips. It was normally bolted to a long plank; he put it on sawhorses and secured it with C-clamps when he had that kind of work to do. The motor was useless, of course, and he'd disassembled it, leaving the wheel and the driveshaft. It might not work, but he didn't have anything better to do right now; they couldn't move until Havel recovered.

"Needs a flywheel," Ken Larsson said, beating his gloved hands together—the early mornings were still chilly, and his breath showed in white puffs as he squinted at the remains of the machine.

*For a high-and-mighty executive, he makes a pretty good hands-on man,* the Texan thought.

"Right," he said. "Truck wheel, I think. Drill and mount through the hub?"

"Yup. And the fan belt from your semi would do for the drive—we take the wrecked bicycle—"

His face went blank for a moment; the bicycle had been ridden by one of the bandits who killed his wife. He swallowed, while Will looked aside to allow him a moment's privacy.

"—mount it backward—fan belt around the rear wheel once we get the tire off. Then someone pedals, and you got yourself a grinding wheel."

They both turned and looked at Eric Larsson where he sat throwing stones into the Lochsa. Not far away Astrid and Luanne were working on the bearskin staked out on the ground, scraping the last shreds of fat and flesh off the inside. Eric, on the other hand, had been starting to brood.

"Boy needs exercise," Ken said.

When Havel woke again, he felt completely drained; not in much pain—an itching stab along his scalp wound, a throb in his neck, bruises elsewhere—but weak as a kitten. Something smelled wonderful close by, though.

Gradually the picture came clear. He was lying on a bed of pine boughs, with a canvas cover over him, rigged like a tent to the side of the Huttons' RV. Blankets and the mylar sleeping bag and a low fire in a round bed of stones with a sheet-metal reflector kept things comfortably warm—warmer than he would have been inside the vehicle, with its heaters not working.

Not far away was a horse with its head down, pawing through the long dead grass for the first of this year's shoots, and then eating the natural hay when it couldn't find any.

There was a pot over the fire, and the good smell came from there.

"What's that?" he said—croaked, rather. "Christ Jesus, I'm dry."

Signe Larsson was not far away, silently practicing knife strokes against a small lodgepole; she wore clean jeans, her high-tops, and a big man's shirt of checked flannel over a T-shirt of her own, one with a whale and a circle-slash over it. When she heard his voice she stabbed the knife into the wood with a backhand flick and hurried over to him.

"About two days, right?" he said, reaching up to touch his forehead.

The long wound across forehead and scalp had been stitched in a small neat style, but he'd have a spectacular scar.

*Just like Tarzan's,* he thought to himself.

He'd been a Burroughs freak as a kid, and had spent much of the early eighties pretending the forests of the Upper Peninsula were the ape-man's jungles. He'd enjoyed the Mars books almost as much, although it put him off a bit when he realized that since Dejah Thoris laid eggs, John Carter had essentially been doing the nasty with a giant bug.

"How did you know it was two days?" Signe said, dipping a cup into a bucket that stood on a table nearby. "You came to a few times before, but you were sort of semiconscious."

"Don't remember a thing since Mr. Bear turned out to be Not Our Friend," he said, and then a long wordless *ahhhhhh!* as he drank the cold river water. "Thanks . . . no, I could tell by the state of your bruises. They're a flattering shade of yellow-green; mine are fresher. What smells so good?"

A woman was singing in Spanish in the middle distance, a husky soprano, a voice with smoke and musk and heat in it—Angelica Hutton, at a guess. He could hear the words now and then:

"*Mi amor, mi corazon—*"

Signe grinned; she *did* have a set of colors that would have done a frog proud, though the swellings had gone down, revealing the straight-nosed regularity of her face.

"It's bear broth," she said. "We're making jerky out of most of it, but the soup's good. Want some? Meal and revenge in one."

He nodded, too tired to speak much. She brought over a cup and put an arm under his shoulders to lift him so that he could sip. The contact was remarkably pleasant, in an abstract sort of way. The broth itself was delicious, mostly clear, with a little finely minced meat in it and some dried onion. He could feel the rich warmth of it spreading through his middle, and his eyelids grew heavy again.

Havel fell asleep to the sound of the Spanish song, the splashing of the river, and a distant sound like a grinding wheel on hard steel.

His next waking found him clearheaded; a day after that he was still feeling shaky but strong enough to rise and eat solid food, wash and walk. The next day he was himself again, save for a lingering stiffness.

The older men had been hard at work on the flatbed; the towing bar had been rerigged, and the gear sorted and readied for loading.

Will Hutton had set up his workbench a good ways away; near it was some contraption powered by part of a bicycle, with a transmission belt running from the skeletonized rear wheel. Not far from that was an improvised hearth of mud and rocks, with Astrid pumping on a piston-bellows setup.

"Good to see you up," Hutton said, turning from the fire; sweat ran down his stocky muscular torso.

"Good to *be* up," Havel said frankly. "Not quite good as new, but getting there."

His scalp wound itched like fire, but that meant it was healing well. For the rest he was stiff and bruised, but he'd been *there* before; with nothing torn and no damage to his joints he was ready to chalk it up to experience.

Some exercise was just what he needed.

Astrid smiled at him shyly. Havel looked at the black man; he nodded very slightly. Havel glanced back at her coolly, and then went on after he'd made greetings all around: "Maybe you should start practicing that mounted archery stuff again, kid?"

"Thanks, Mike!" she replied, and then broke into a broad sunny smile. "Mr. Hutton has the most *fascinating* book about it—mounted archery, that is!"

Surprised, Havel looked at the Texan.

"With y'all in a second," he said.

Then he took his workpiece out of the coals with a pair of pincers, gave it a quick once-over, nodded, and picked up a smoothed nine-foot pole with his other hand. The metal was a twelve-inch tapering double-edged blade shaped like a willow leaf and about as broad as two fingers, but it was mounted on a round steel tube. Using the pincers, then the anvil and a hammer, Hutton forced the tube sleeve onto the pretapered uppermost section of the pole.

The wood began to smoke almost immediately; the sleeve was heated past the red-glowing stage.

Quickly he reversed the spear and plunged the whole head and a foot of the shaft into a big bucket of water. There was a volcanic hiss and spurt of steam, dying away to a muttering and bubbling. The hot metal would shrink as it cooled, binding unbreakably to the wood.

"Saw somethin' like this in Calgary, up in Canada, when I was workin' rodeo—went for the Stampede there couple of years," Hutton said.

He took the spearhead out and wiped it dry, then wiped it again with an oiled rag, then braced the shaft between his legs with the top three feet across the anvil and touched up the edges of the head with a two-handed sharpening hone. The steel made a *scring . . . scring . . .* sound under his swift expert strokes.

"The Mounties at the Stampede used lances 'bout like this, put on quite a show."

"You were in rodeo?" Havel asked.

Astrid was beginning to fidget, then visibly controlled herself.

*Good,* he thought. *Let's introduce the concept of discipline and patience into the Elvish ranks.*

Hutton nodded. "Roughstock," he said.

That meant riding Brahma bulls, and horses deliberately picked to buck. He glanced over at his wife, who was checking the bundles and boxes of their gear against a list.

"Angel, though, she wanted more than broken bones and trophies on the wall. She was right, of course; and I'd rather work with real horses, anyhow. By then I had enough saved to get our spread and a decent herd."

He tossed the long spear over to Havel. The younger man ran his hands along the smooth length of it; the blade was sharpened right down to where the curve of the shoulders melded into the tubular socket, so it wouldn't get stuck in someone or something's body the way the knife-bladed weapon had.

"Used part of a leaf spring for that," Hutton said, waving

his hand back towards the vehicles by the side of the road. "It's good metal; forming the socket, that was the hard part. I made up a couple of 'em."

He went over to the flatbed and got something else. Havel's eyes widened a bit. It was a straight-bladed saber just under a yard long in the blade, with a three-bar brass guard. A neatly made sheath of leather-covered wood held it, with chape and mouth done in aluminum beaten to shape. Hutton handed it to him, and he examined it more closely; the hilt had wooden fillets glued to the tang, covered in layers of thin braided rawhide to shape it to a man's palm. When he drew it the weapon was heavy but well balanced, blade cross-sectioned nicely from thick back to edge; the reverse was sharpened for a foot back from the point.

It felt *right* in his hand, suited to a thrust or solid chopping cut.

"*Haakkaa paalle!*" he said, giving it a flourish. At Hutton's raised eyebrow, Havel went on: "Finnish war cry from the Old Country, way back."

"What's it mean?" Astrid asked.

"Literally? Hack them down! Freely translated: Kill! Kill! Back in the old days in Europe, the Finns fought for the kings of Sweden, who really got around—our cavalry campaigned with them all over the place. The Church had a special prayer: 'From the horrible Finns, good God deliver us!' "

He tried whipping the sword through a figure eight, and then winced slightly at how close he'd come to taking off part of his own right kneecap in his enthusiasm.

*Hope nobody else noticed that. This is going to take some work,* he thought, and went on aloud to Hutton: "I thought you said you weren't a blacksmith!"

"I ain't; and if I was, I couldn't do a sword from scratch in four days. That's not hardly blacksmith's work at all, Mike. Just mutilating a length of leaf spring. The hard part in makin' swords the old-time way was tempering, heating and quenching just right. But that, it's alloy steel and already heat-treated better than anyone could do in a forge."

"Hmmmm," Havel said.

He braced the point against a stump and leaned on it; the metal bowed, then sprang straight again. He tested the edge with his thumb. It was knife-sharp, which was practical for a weapon—a razor edge was too likely to turn on bone. A flick at the stump took out a surprisingly large chip without dulling it.

"We'll have to learn how to temper steel again by hand, eventually," he went on.

"Lord, Mike, this is *America.* You know how many tens of millions of cars are sittin' around, with every wheel hung on half a dozen sword blanks? All I had to do was be careful to keep it cool so's not to lose the temper, straighten it out with a sledgehammer, file an' cut it to shape and do the hilt 'n guard—guard's brass strip from the engine grille of the truck—then grind the blade to the right cross-section and hone on the edge. Didn't take more than a day. Astrid's pa helped a good deal, and some books on old-time cavalry I got, so I'm workin' on one for each of us."

Havel nodded, delighted, and decided to let Astrid burble before she burst: "What was that you said about Will's books, kid?"

"He has the most *wonderful* things about horses—he's sort of like a Rider of Rohan, you know? And books on cavalry, and these notes—they're called *Horseback Archery*—"

She turned in appeal to Hutton. The Texan had begun to dismantle his improvised hearth, removing the parts he'd be taking with him and stowing the tools neatly in their boxes. He gave her an indulgent chuckle and said:

"Got to exchangin' e-mail with this fellah in Hungary, name of Lajos, Kassai Lajos. They got some real horsemen there, good as any over to here, and he's been working for years on finding out how his old-timey kin used bows from the saddle, and how they made their bows and stuff. Workin' practical, with his own horses. I'd admired to see it. He's fixin' to write a book about it, and sent me a good part of his work. I printed it up an' bound it."

Hutton shook his head. "Hope he was close to home when things Changed; he's got him a little ranch and some horses out in the country there. If he was, he'll live if anyone does!"

Havel nodded. *Well, there's a change for you,* he thought. *Last month, you could chat with someone in Hungary. Now you can't talk to anyone outside shouting range.*

Out in the meadow, Luanne and Signe and Eric were

riding—galloping down a row of light sticks set in the ground, swerving in and out around each in succession in a series of S-curves, very much like the rodeo event called barrel racing.

He saw that Hutton hadn't been boasting about his daughter; Luanne was leaning in to each curve with effortless grace. Eric and Signe were very good; she made them look as if they were operating their horses by not particularly sensitive remote control systems.

*And I'm not nearly as good as either of the twins,* he thought. *Well, practice makes perfect. I suspect a lot of the rest of my life is going to be spent in the saddle.*

"Go on," he said to Astrid. "See if you can give her a run for her money."

"Luanne is *cool,*" Astrid said, and ran for a hobbled horse.

Hutton watched them for a moment; Havel went over and helped him lift his anvil into place on the trailer and lash it down.

"Mike," he said, "How were you plannin' on us making a living, while we're on the way to the promised land?"

"However we can," he said. "If we have to fight for food, we will, but I'd rather not. Overall, it depends on whether my ideas about what's going to happen are close to the mark."

Hutton looked a question at him, and Havel continued: "It's obvious what's going to happen in the big cities—and overseas, in countries that are all big city, like Japan. Remote areas like this, or the farming country . . . I think things will collapse there too, but slower. Most people will try to hang on to what they had, and the ways they did things, as close as they can. It won't work, not in the long run."

"They got along well enough with horses and such in my granddaddy's time," Hutton said. "Or at least the white folks did," he added with a grim smile.

Havel nodded; Hutton didn't have much formal education, but he was no fool—in fact, he was about the most all-round competent man Havel had ever come across, even out here in the backwoods.

"But they didn't get along without telegraphs, or steamboats, or without guns, a hundred years ago," he said. "Not for a long time before that; you'd have to go back a thousand years, nearly, I think, before it wouldn't make a difference. Someone, something wanted us knocked *way* down."

Hutton made a final tie-off and fingered the knot. "I hate to think the good Lord judged us that wicked. He promised to Noah no more water; but this time, He took away the fire."

"Could be," Havel said; he was actually an agnostic, but there was no way to disprove the Texan's idea. "Myself, I think Ken's got it right. Someone out there"—he pointed upward—"with a technology that makes ours . . . what we had . . . look like stone knives. Something so far beyond ours we can't understand it, and it's like magic. Like algebra to a monkey."

Hutton looked aside at him. "If it was some spacemen, what do you figure we can do 'bout it?"

"Nothing," Havel said bluntly. "I figure we'll just have to live with what they've done to us, and we won't even find out why unless they tell us someday. In the meantime . . . we have to find a way to live in the world they gave us. You and I, and our kids—mine when I have them, that is."

He looked at the sun. "Let's start early tomorrow. We can make Lowell in three days, taking it easy. It's all downslope."

"One step closer to Larsdalen," Hutton said, smiling.

"If that's where we end up," Havel nodded. "One step at a time. Lowell first."

"Ain't much in Lowell but about thirty people," Hutton observed.

"Right. But there'll be a fair number of other travelers stranded there. I want to look them over. We need recruits."

"We do?" Hutton said.

"We do. Anywhere we end up, if it's worth having . . . someone else will want it too."

# CHAPTER THIRTEEN

Lowell, Idaho, had a sign at the outskirts: POPULATION 24—with the 24 crossed out, and "23" written beside it.

The joke was one from before things Changed.

The tiny hamlet sat at the junction of the Lochsa and the Clearwater; in normal times it was a jumping-off point for the wilderness areas around, and for white-water rafting. Now half a dozen of its residents stood across the roadway; three of them had hunting bows, the others axes or baseball bats.

Havel reined in his horse and flung up his right hand with the fist clenched. He could hear Angelica's *whoa* to her team, and the hoof-falls of the rest behind him ceased, dying away to an occasional clop or crunch as a horse shifted in place.

"Afternoon," he said.

"Afternoon," the burly middle-aged man who seemed to be the leader said. "Lot of road people already been through."

*Road people?* Havel thought. Then: *Well, yeah, there must have been* millions *caught away from home when the Change happened. I suppose people would come up with a nickname.*

"I've got to warn you though, we don't have any food to spare. Barely enough for our own."

Havel nodded. He'd expected nothing different. This was hard country, well away from the farming and ranching areas further west and south. The locals could probably survive on hunting and fishing until winter, but not many casual passersby could.

"We're fixed, for now," he said. "Got plenty of meat."

Several of the men stiffened with suspicion. *Already?* Havel thought, and went on aloud: "Elk, venison and bear"—he touched the long wound that ran across his forehead and into his scalp—"which the bear brought on himself. We could trade some jerky for flour or rice or beans."

The little band of townsfolk relaxed. Their leader looked at the swords the travelers all carried, and the bows. Will had rigged tubular scabbards at the right rear of their saddles, and he and Luanne and Havel were using them for the long spears—lances—he'd made. He'd also done up round plywood shields, convex circles rimmed in metal and covered in elk hide; Signe and Astrid had painted the head of a snarling bear on each, quite skillfully.

"You folks are together then? Looks like you're loaded for bear!"

That brought a few chuckles from his townsmen; Havel smiled thinly—it still hurt to move his face much. "We ran into some survivalists, original-sovereign types. They seemed to think they could do anything they wanted, now that things are Changed. We're taking precautions to avoid another incident like that."

The leader's eyes took in their various bruises and contusions and spat eloquently. "Those crazy bastards? What happened?"

Havel shrugged. "Coyotes have to eat too, so we didn't bury the bodies," he said, and got another, louder chuckle. "We'd like to camp for a few days and work on our gear before we move on. We're heading towards Lewiston. If anyone wants to trade, we can do farrier work or such."

A nod, and the leader leaned on his ax. "We have a couple of horses that could use shoeing. Head on down that lane, there's a campground by the river and some cabins—use 'em if you want, but the plumbing's not working. There's some other folks who got caught on the road staying there, too."

Havel circled the small pine tree, the shield up, left foot advanced. It was starting to feel more natural, and it was what the book said you should do on foot. He had the practice sword up, point towards the tree; it had the same weight and balance as the other weapon Will had made, but it was blunt.

With a *huhhh!* of expelled breath he bounced forward off his right leg, swinging the weapon in a quick whipping cut that landed as his foot did.

*Whiiik!*

Another ragged chip flew off the trunk at neck height; he hit the tree with the shield, punching it, then stabbed under the lower rim.

*The basics are the same as a knife,* he thought. *You have to be able to put it where you want it.*

Still, he wished he had more than a couple of books to go on. He was getting better at attacking, but to learn the counters he needed a trained partner.

An *instructor* would be even better; he was afraid of drilling bad habits into his reflexes.

He backed off from the tree, broad chest heaving as sweat rolled down his taut skin, pale in contrast to the permanent tan of his face and arms.

Finding an instructor would be a fantastic stroke of luck. People who had the leisure to study swordcraft usually didn't end up in backwoods Idaho this time of year. Of course, he'd *already* had a tremendous run of luck, compared to ninety-nine in every hundred human beings alive when the Change happened; the crash, being somewhere with not too many people, surviving the deadly confused little fight at the cabin, the bear's claws within an inch of taking off his face . . .

Ken Larsson had explained it: When nearly everybody died, *any* survivor would have to be either fantastically lucky, or very able, or both. By this time next year, anyone living was going to be convinced that they could roll sixes from now until Doomsday.

Havel shivered. "The problem is," he murmured to himself, "that the dice have no memory." A run of luck could stop any instant. "And we've already *had* Doomsday."

"Boss," Will Hutton said.

Havel leaned the sword against his leg while he worked and stretched his right hand and arm. You felt every impact all the way up to your shoulder when you worked this way.

"Yeah, Will?" he said.

They'd camped in another tree-dotted meadow, well away from the river and from the other stranded wayfarers who'd ended up here. There was room for their horses, and for setting up a clothesline, and digging a latrine; they'd pitched the single big tent the Huttons had had along, too, as well as taking over a couple of the cabins. The air was wet and cold and smelled of green; in a warmer climate the whole place might be getting pretty squalid by now, but they didn't intend to stay much longer.

*Have to get another tent,* Havel thought. *We need more privacy, it's bad for morale to crowd each other too much when we're on the road—we're in each other's pockets all day as is. One tent per family, at least.*

"Got some more people interested in joinin' up," Hutton said.

He jerked his thumb towards the notional edge of their camp, where a cluster stood and waited.

"Couple of 'em look hopeful, I'd say."

"They'd be the first," Havel muttered, hanging up the practice weapon on a nail driven into the tree above head height. "OK, Will, send them in as soon as I'm ready."

It was chilly, but he'd been working stripped to the waist; sweat stung and itched in the healing wound on his forehead, and just plain itched in his new beard—one reason he'd never grown one before. The muscles of his arms burned—the shield didn't move as much as the sword, but it was heavier—and his right hand felt as if a semi had run over it. A faint line of new callus was appearing, all around the inner side of his thumb and forefinger and the web between.

Now he wiped himself down with a towel and shrugged into a shirt, buttoning it as he walked over to the table they'd set up for talking to the candidates—the similarity to a job interview seemed to reassure people. Once there he sat and laid the shield and saber across it, conscious of the position of the hilt and that of his *puukko.* You didn't take chances these days, and some of the people stuck here were visibly crazy.

The first candidate was a tall, thin, thirtyish woman with bold features and coarse abundant reddish brown hair— she'd probably been thin before the Change, too, though less so. She was dressed in moderately expensive outdoor clothes, which she'd managed to get or keep fairly clean, and hiker's boots.

"Pam Arnstein," she said, offering a hand; it was firm

and dry, and she gave a single squeeze while meeting his eyes. "I understand you're looking for people to join your group?"

He nodded: "Useful people, for mutual help here and where we intend to settle, in Oregon." He explained the rules. "Now convince me, Ms. Arnstein."

"I'm a veterinarian—worked at the San Diego Zoo. I was visiting relatives here in Idaho, then driving for recreation."

*Now that would be useful,* he thought; he liked her calm, too, and the absence of pleading. *For practical purposes, a vet can handle a lot of human illness. We need a medico.*

"Why didn't you get back to the relatives?" he said.

"They have small children. I didn't think they could afford to help me, and they would try if I asked, so I won't ask."

*Excellent,* he thought—and he was fairly sure she was telling the truth, too.

He questioned her a bit more—she hiked and did horseback trekking, rock climbing and hang gliding, was divorced and childless.

"And I do Renaissance fencing," she said. "With HACA—that's what the group is called."

At his raised eyebrow she went on: "Cut-and-thrust backsword with targe, rapier-and-targe—a targe is a small shield, rather like this one,"—she tapped the one resting on the table—"sword and buckler—a buckler is a smaller metal shield with a one-handed grip—and rapier and dagger. I got into it when I was doing amateur theatricals at UC San Diego, decided to try the real thing, and it's been one of my hobbies for years. The weapons are substantially similar to those you have on your table there."

"OK, Ms. Arnstein, you just sold me. I'm going to pass you on to our experts to check on what you said, and you can demonstrate that fencing stuff to me, but provisionally you're in."

She looked towards the cookfire and swallowed painfully.

"Perhaps you could get something to eat first. Game stew with some wild plants is all we have, but there's enough."

The next candidate was a logger, a little younger than Havel and an inch taller, a husky brown-haired, blue-eyed man. He and his young wife and their toddler daughter looked surprisingly well fed.

"You the bossman of the Bearkiller outfit?" he asked.

Havel grinned inwardly at that as he nodded and shook hands and introduced himself. He'd been thinking idly that they should have a name for the group. Apparently Signe's artistic talents had settled the matter; the bear heads on the shields were quite dramatic. That, and the boiled-down skull of the bear that had nearly killed them all resting outside the door of the tent. Perhaps he should do up a flag, and put the bear skull on top of the pole.

"I'm Josh Sanders; my wife Annie, and our Megan."

"Cornhusker?" Havel said.

Sanders had the rasping accent; he also had a grip like a vise. He wasn't trying it on, just damned strong.

"Daddy had a farm down to Booneville," Josh Sanders said.

Havel recognized the name; it was a small town in southwestern Indiana, which confirmed his guess.

"Just a little place, though; he worked construction, too. I lumberjacked some in the woods there, and then up here, up in the Panhandle, and Annie taught school for her church before the baby came; she's Montana-born, grew up on a ranch over to Missoula. I like a place where I can hunt and fish. I've been fishing here, and hunting, but only small stuff, with a slingshot—I know rifles, but not bows. Been keeping us fed since the Change, but only just. The folk in town here are sort of standoffish, not that I blame them."

*Better and better,* Havel thought.

The lumberjack's yellow-haired wife looked healthy and competent, and scared silly but hiding it well. He caught a glimpse of a tattoo under the man's sleeve, part of an anchor.

"Squid?" he said.

Josh smiled: "Guess it still shows. One hitch out of high school—Seabee. Did a fair bit of construction." The Seabees were the Navy's combat engineers. "You'd be a Jarhead, is my guess."

"Semper Fi," Havel nodded.

"Mind my asking, how did you get the—" His finger traced the place of Havel's stitched wound on his own forehead.

"Got into a close-and-personal argument with a bear, about five days ago."

"What happened?"

"Bear tastes a lot like pork, but a bit gamier. Better in a stew, or marinated in vinegar."

Josh whistled, then nodded as Havel explained the terms: strict discipline, working together, and a possible ultimate share-out in Oregon.

"All right," Havel said. "One last thing."

*Southern Indiana was white-sheet country not so long ago, settled from Kentucky and Virginia originally. Let's check.*

He pointed. "Will Hutton here is the number two man in this outfit. Got any problems taking his orders?"

"My daddy might have, but the Navy knocked out any of that horseshit left in me," Josh said. "Taking orders doesn't bother me. As long as they aren't damned stupid orders, all the time."

The last candidate was a fortysomething man with receding dirty-blond hair, long and stringy. Havel's nose wrinkled slightly at his stale sour smell; the river was right there, and the town wasn't short of soap yet, and there was plenty of firewood to heat water. He had a beaten-down-looking wife who looked older than he did and wasn't; she'd been massive before the Change, and sagged like a deflated balloon now. Their children were twelve and ten and eight, and looked as if they hadn't eaten in quite a while; unnaturally quiet, in fact.

*Loser,* Havel thought, noting the yellow nicotine stain on his fingers—he must be going through withdrawal now, a six-pack-a-day man with no tobacco at all. His hands trembled, too, and there was a tracery of broken veins in his nose and cheeks. *Alky.*

Will Hutton stood behind the man, and silently mouthed the word *trash* over his shoulder.

*And I agree with you,* Havel thought. *OK, but there's no reason to be brutal about it.*

"I'm sorry, Mr.—"

"Billy Waters, sir, and please—my children—"

"This isn't a charity, Mr. Waters. We may be able to spare a bowl for them."

*And I'd watch them eat it, to make sure you didn't.*

Well behind Havel, Eric and Signe and Luanne were practicing at a mark they'd set up, passing the hunting bow back and forth and laughing together. Waters's eyes lit on them.

"Look, sir, I worked for Red Wolf Bows in Missouri," he said desperately. "A few years back, till they laid me off. I can make you more bows, if you get me some tools! Arrows too, and do fletching."

Havel halted with his mouth open to speak the words of dismissal. Hutton's eyebrows went up.

"Get Astrid, would you, Will?" Havel said. "She'll be able to check what this gentleman says."

Bill Waters looked as if he'd like to be indignant when a girl in her early teens showed up to grill him, but his eyes went a little wide when he saw the bow she carried.

"Red Wolf?" Astrid said to Havel. "Yes, they make bows—modern-traditional, mostly, custom orders for hunting bows. Recurves. Good quality, but pricey."

Her sniff told what she thought of Mr. Waters. He sensed it, and went on: "I was on the floor two years, miss, did every step or helped with it," he said earnestly. "It's a small shop, four men, and I helped 'em all. Hunted some myself with a bow."

Havel's eyebrows went up; for a wonder, the man wasn't pretending he'd been head craftsman, rather than dogs-body and assistant. That was probably a measure of his desperation.

"You don't look like you've had much luck hunting here," he pointed out.

"Ain't got no bow here, sir."

*And couldn't get anyone to lend you one,* Havel thought. *Well, I wouldn't have lent you fifty cents, and I'd bet anything that when the Change hit you got drunk and stayed that way until you ran out of booze.*

Havel had the traditional disdain for hand-to-mouth drifters to be expected in someone who came of four generations of hard-rock miners—unionized workingmen intensely proud of their dangerous, highly skilled labor. It had been amplified in the Corps, where there was no excuse for failure. He was surprised this specimen had ever learned any sort of trade, but perhaps he'd been on the wagon more when he was younger.

Astrid asked a question, her voice sharp. Waters answered, and an incomprehensible conversation followed involving tillering and laminations, hotboxes and clamps, hand-shock and finger pinch.

"Will," Havel said, after a few sentences. "Take Astrid and Mr. Waters off, and discuss bowmaking, would you? And check him out on the target."

He waited, thinking and trying not to listen to the occasional whimpering of Waters's children, or to notice the expression of hopeless pessimism on his wife's face, born of far too many broken promises and failed hopes.

Instead he paged through a book of Will's, an illustrated *History of Cavalry,* by two Polacks named Grbasic and Vuksic—or Grabass and Youpuke, as he mentally christened them. They certainly seemed to know their field, though according to them a Pole on horseback was the next thing to an Archangel with a flaming sword.

*I wish I'd read more of this sort of thing before the Change,* he thought wistfully. *It's interesting, and now all I have time to do is mine it for the useful parts.*

He was looking at the equipment of a Polish *pancerny* horseman of the seventeenth century when the three returned; as Hutton had said, it looked simple and practical, enough so that they had some prospect of making an equivalent set of kit.

"Excuse us for a moment, please," Havel said.

Waters stood back by his wife and children as the three spoke; both the adults stared in mute desperation at the conversation they couldn't hear, and flinched when eyes went their way.

"He can shoot, Mike," Astrid said. "Better if his hands weren't shaking, but he's quite good—not as good as me, but better than Signe, on moving targets. And he really does know how to make bows. Traditional bows, not compounds— traditional forms with modern materials, that is."

Will shrugged. "He can handle woodworker's tools," he said grudgingly, and sounding faintly surprised. "I think I could pick up most of what he knows, in a couple or three months. We'll have to sort of experiment to find out how to use horn and sinew and bone glue instead of fancy wood laminates and fiberglass and epoxy anyways, but we got Astrid's bow to work from."

More quietly: "He's still trash, though, Boss. Bad news."

"Granted." Havel sighed. "We'll have to give him a try, though; long-term, it's a skill set we really need. I'll put the fear of God in him and we'll see how it works; we can always cut him loose."

Waters began babbling as soon as Havel walked towards him, and then cut it short as the younger man nodded to his wife: "Mrs. Waters, why don't you go over there to our cookfire? Angelica Hutton handles our supplies, and I think she could find you and your children something to eat, and help you get settled here."

An incredulous smile showed, just for an instant, what Jane Waters had looked like in her last year of high school, and she hustled away moving the children before her as if afraid he'd change his mind. Havel jerked his head, and walked out of hearing distance of the others with Waters beside him. Certain things had to be done in private for decency's sake.

"Sir, let me tell you how grateful—"

"Can it," Havel said.

He didn't raise his voice or gesture, but judging from the doglike grin of submission Waters at least knew a hard man when he met one. The problem with his kind was that the lessons usually didn't stick. . . .

"Waters, I know you'd say anything you thought I wanted to hear right now because you're hungry, so save it."

The older man made a pathetic attempt at dignity. "Mr. Havel, a man has to feed his children."

"That's true. And you must have been some sort of a man once; you learned a trade, at least, and held a steady job for a while. But now you're a loser and a drunk—I know the signs. So let's make things real clear. You listening?"

He waited until the man's eyes met his, and he could see that—at least for the moment—he'd stopped running through the perpetual list of excuses that were probably the background music of his life.

"I'm taking you on against my better judgment, and this is a taut outfit. I don't tolerate whining, shirking or dirt. You and your family *will* keep yourselves clean, you *will* work, and you *will* obey all the rules. You're low dog in this pack until you show you deserve better, so you'll also obey anyone I appoint to strawboss you, including that damned orange cat over there if I say so, cheerfully and without complaint. You're here on sufferance. The first time you screw up, or go on a bender and slap your wife and kids around, or any trash tricks like that, I will personally beat the living shit out of you. The second time I will beat the living shit out of you and throw you out on your ass. Is all this clear?"

"Yes, sir."

"And don't call me sir. I work for a living. Boss will do, if you have to use something besides my name. After you've eaten, you can bring your gear over. Remember what I said about the rules, because if it isn't all ready and all clean by tomorrow morning, you're not coming with us. Move!"

# CHAPTER FOURTEEN

Bemused, Michael Havel whistled as he lowered the binoculars and wiped a hand across his dust-caked face; then he made a futile attempt to scratch under the edge of his sleeveless boiled-steerhide jacket.

They were on the flats where the Middle and South Clearwater met, a half mile from the little town of Kooskia, with steep rocky slopes all around them to hold the air and reflect the bright spring sun; the smell of spray from the brawling rivers was tantalizing.

It was a hundred miles south and west from the place the Piper Chieftain had crashed, twice that as feet and hooves and wheels went; weeks of hard slow travel.

"Well, spank me rosy," Havel said, nodding westward. "Those guys look like they're out to get General Custer."

They were also just inside the Nez Perce reservation boundary.

Beyond the waiting men was a bridge over a river gray-blue with snowmelt; beyond that, the town proper—as proper as a place with less than a thousand inhabitants could be—and a high conical hill studded with tall pines; more hills reared a little beyond, green-tawny with new grass pushing up through last year's, and fingers of pine reaching up the ravines. Beyond that were rolling prairies, farming and ranching country; he'd driven through this way before the Change, and flown over it more than once.

It was hard to remember that godlike omniscience, ten thousand feet up with hundreds of horsepower at his command.

Havel wasn't surprised to see armed and mounted men strung across the valley road; every town and community they'd run across that hadn't collapsed kept a watch on the roads and checked travelers. Their scouts had probably reported the Bearkillers coming yesterday or early this morning.

The way some of them were dressed, though . . .

Several of the horsemen waiting for them a hundred yards further west along the road were in full Indian fig—feather bonnets and face paint and buckskin—stuff you usually didn't see outside a powwow and even there only on the dancers. Two of their mounts were Appaloosas, beautiful animals with dappled white rumps and bold strong lines. Sitting their horses a little apart were white men, in the usual denim-and-Stetson-or-feed-store-cap of the rural West. A lot of the Nez Perce reservation was leased to non-Indians, farmers and ranchers and a few small towns.

"It's quite a sight," Will Hutton agreed, pushing back his helmet by the nasal bar and squinting against the bright sunlight and the sweat that stung his eyes.

"On the other hand, I'm wearin' *this* stuff, Mike," he went on in a reasonable tone. The leather of his saddle creaked beneath him as the horse shifted its weight from one foot to another. "And it goes back a lot further than Custer."

The Texan had their first complete set of chain-mail armor, a knee-length split-skirt tunic with sleeves to the elbow. All you needed to make it was a wooden dowel, a pair of wire cutters, pliers, and a punch and hammer . . . plus plenty of patience, which was why they had only one suit so far. Will and his pupils could turn out a boiled-leather vest in an afternoon, and every adult had one now; a chain hauberk took weeks.

Havel took the canteen from his saddlebow and drank; the lukewarm water tasted good, and he poured a little into his hand and rubbed it over his face. Then he offered the water bottle to Hutton, who'd run through two so far today.

The Texan took it gratefully, and tilted it back until water ran out of the corners of his mouth as his Adam's apple bobbed; sweat was pouring off him in rivulets, turning the linked metal rings dark. Nights were still chilly around here in April, and days comfortable-windbreaker weather, but thirty pounds of metal rings absorbed a lot of heat. The gambeson, the long quilted jacket underneath, was even worse. Its padding soaked up greasy sweat like a sponge, too; the powerful odor combined with the scents of horse and leather and oiled metal to make a composite stink not quite like anything Havel had come across before—although it had probably been quite familiar in the army of William of Normandy.

"Yeah," Havel said, taking the canteen back. "But you're dressed up like Richard the Lionheart for a good practical reason, not just because of the way it looks."

*Although it does* look *formidable too.*

The gear and helmet added bulk and menace to the older man's lean muscular toughness. Hauberks had to be individually tailored; Havel's was nearly finished, but Angelica and Signe and Astrid were doing something confidential with it.

*I'm not looking forward to wearing that stuff myself, especially when it gets* really *hot,* he thought. *But I'd much rather be uncomfortable than dead or crippled.*

"That fancy dress may be practical too, so to speak," Hutton said, nodding his head towards the welcoming party. "These're hard times, Mike. People need somethin' to hold on to, besides the things that broke in their hands when the Change came. Might be that those old-time things are what these Indians need to get them through."

Havel thought for a moment, then nodded. "Tell me something, Will: how come you're not running this outfit?"

Hutton grinned. "Two reasons. First is, I'm the only black man in it—you might have noticed we're sort of thin on the ground here in Idaho. Simpler to tell you what needs doing and let you get folks mad at *you;* 'specially since you take advice pretty good for a dude your age."

"Well, that's honest, if not very flattering. What's the other reason?"

"You were stupid enough to want the job, Mike," Hutton said. "I ain't. 'Boss' is just another word for 'got a headache.' "

Havel snorted laughter, then stood in his stirrups to wave at the reception committee. Several of them waved back, but he waited until another rider cantered in out of the north before he moved.

Josh Sanders drew rein; he was equipped much like the Bearkillers' leader, with boiled-leather protection, sword, shield, bow and helmet.

"That's all of them, Boss," he said, pointing off towards the Nez Perce. "No ambush that I could spot."

Havel nodded; the Hoosier was a first-rate scout, mounted or on foot.

"All right. Report to Angelica"—who was camp boss and in charge when he or Will wasn't there—"and tell her I want her and Will with me while we dicker and . . . hmmm, all the Larssons. Pam to keep everyone on alert, but don't be conspicuous about it."

Sanders's eyebrows went up. Havel had never liked the blind-obedience school of discipline; when there was time, he preferred to explain things. It cut down on mistakes when people understood *why* they were doing something; he'd also never imagined he was infallible, and Sanders was smart. Letting your troops' brains lie fallow was wasteful and dangerous.

*Besides,* he thought, *this may be a small outfit now, but Josh'll need to play leader too someday when we've grown.*

"We want them to think we're tough but peaceful," he said. "Will and Eric and I can do the tough; women, kids and old people along are more likely to make 'em think we're not looking for a fight."

"That makes sense," Sanders said. "Angelica and the Larssons, pronto, Boss."

He cantered off. Will cocked an eye at Havel. "Mebbeso you're smarter than you look," he said.

Havel chuckled and turned in his saddle. The Bearkiller caravan was about a thousand yards behind him; four wagons now, and nearly fifty people in all, counting kids. They'd pulled off the narrow country road onto a fairly flat stretch of roadside sagebrush—ease of access was one reason they didn't use the Interstates much. Folk had pitched camp and were getting on with the work of the day. . . .

Signe Larsson sighed and reached for the weights as the wagons pulled off to the side of the road.

"No rest for the wicked," she said.

"If you want, I'll swap you a chores day for a weapons training day. . . ." Luanne hinted.

"That is *so* not funny, Luanne. 'Sides, the cows were such *fun* for me yesterday. It'd be *greedy* of me to snatch another day with them."

Luanne grinned, unhitched her horse and vaulted into the saddle, reaching for her lariat as soon as her boots touched the stirrups. Signe began a set of wrist curls with the fifteen-pounders. She sat on the plywood bed of the wagon, with her feet on the pavement, bracing her elbow against her thigh as she raised and lowered the leather-covered steel pipe handle of the weights. The wagon was the first they'd made, rigged up from the Huttons' trailer, and the height was convenient for the effort—the boring, miserable effort that was never *finished*.

Wrist curls on the right, on the left, stand and raise the weights to shoulder height and lower them *sloooowly*, waist-to-shoulder in front . . .

*Though the chores would be just as mindless, and the chores are never finished either. God, the good old days, they were awful. You can't even listen to music unless somebody wants to sing, and they're usually terrible.*

"How long do I have to go on doing this?" she grumbled aloud.

Her arms and shoulders ached a little, though she *did* feel a lot stronger than when she'd started this right after the Change. Pamela Arnstein was a few feet away, practicing lunges and cuts at a billiard-sized hardwood ball strung on a line and hung from a fishing pole, moving as if her legs had steel springs inside them.

"How long? For . . . the . . . rest . . . of . . . your . . . life," she said, pacing the words to her breathing.

The dulled point of the practice weapon went *tock* against the wood and knocked loose a chip. Arnstein was wearing a singlet and sweatpants; the flat muscle of her arms and shoulders stood out like straps under sweat-slick skin as she lowered the sword and stood panting, speaking again: "If you want to use a sword with any useful heft, that is. It's why I stopped doing this seriously before the Change," she went on, reaching for a towel and rubbing herself down. "It was just such a drag maintaining the upper-body strength you needed. God*damn* whoever invented testosterone—it's not *fair*, like an athlete using steroids. And if you think it's hard on *you*, try getting back into this sort of shape when you're in your thirties. You want to be on the A-list, you keep at it."

"Yes, sergeant-at-arms," Signe said, smiling.

"Swordmistress! Astrid might be listening!"

They both laughed; Astrid *loved* lurid archaic-sounding names for things, and sheer stubborn repetition had carried the day for her more than once. She sulked horribly when she lost—people had drawn the line at christening the outfit a "host" or a "free company."

"The little beast would probably have had us calling ourselves the Riders of Rohan if it hadn't been for that bear," Signe said.

She began the next set, lifting each weight back over her shoulder and down in turn. It was a rule that every Bearkiller over twelve had to train to fight, but you only *had* to do enough to make sure you wouldn't be entirely helpless if worse came to worst. If you wanted to be on the A-list, the people called on to fight in non-total-emergency situations, you had to pass some extremely practical tests. Administered in bone-bruising full-contact practice bouts by experts.

All the men and the older boys, everyone except her father and Billy Waters, tried hard to get on the list. She was damned if she wasn't going to make it too.

*Of course, I'm not going to get to lie around eating grapes whatever I do,* Signe thought ruefully.

Now that they'd stopped, the teams had been unhitched and hobbled and set to graze—not that the scanty grass and sagebrush around here would do them much good, or the little herd of cattle and sheep they'd accumulated. That was one reason they wouldn't be staying long. There was good grazing not far away.

Angelica was lifting down wire cages with chickens in them and letting the birds free to peck around, helped by Jane Waters. Billy Waters stood lounging and doing nothing, until Angelica gave him a scowl and jerked her thumb; then he picked up an ax and went looking for firewood. Ken gave her a nod and started fiddling with a lever-operated machine that was supposed to speed up riveting the rings of chain-mail armor. Annie Sanders rounded up the kids; she was the schoolteacher now, which had turned out to mean she oversaw them doing their communal chores, as well. Eric and a couple of others were unloading the heavier stuff for a one-night camp.

"Strong back, simple mind!" Signe called out to him.

The box he held wobbled, and then sent up a puff of dust as he set it down. He was working stripped to the waist, and—in an objective, grudging, sisterly fashion—she had to admit that Luanne was right; he was getting cuter.

*Lost that last trace of puppy fat,* she thought. *Major improvement in the ass. Too bad he still uses it to think with.*

He'd never been plump—more sort of beefy-jock-muscular; now he'd lost the last softness around the edges, gotten ripped and taut.

*And his face has firmed up. But he's still a jerk and a* teenager. *I don't suppose Luanne could do better, considering the meager supply of unattached young guys we've got. But much as I like her, getting enthusiastic about him shows a serious lapse in her taste.*

Eric wiped a forearm across his face, where a thin fuzz of yellow beard caught the dust and sweat. He had his old malicious teasing grin on, and hooted back: "Well, then, I suppose you're lowering your IQ weekly with those weights, hey, sis?"

Signe stuck out her tongue, then turned her back, ignoring his horselaugh.

Luanne brought in a cow she'd roped, with its calf bawling along behind. She snubbed off the lariat to a wagon, dismounted, got a bucket of hot water and soap, scrubbed the usual places and began to milk the animal into a galvanized pail. Astrid's Biltis jumped down from some soft spot now liberally dusted with cat hair; probably a basket full of clean laundry, since the animal had a tropism for freshly washed clothing and shed like a bandit whenever the weather got warm.

*Which is a lot easier to resent now that the only way to get clothes clean is to beat them on rocks and scrub 'em by hand.*

The cat sauntered over to Luanne and began cadging a drink of milk with a weave-around-the-ankles begging routine; she got the first few squirts right into her face, since you weren't supposed to drink that yourself, and then the streams went hissing into the bucket. The cow flicked its tail and did, copiously, what cows and horses were wont to do whenever and wherever they felt like it.

Signe had never minded helping muck out the stables at Larsdalen or the ranch, but . . . *I'm getting used to living in a barnyard. Jesus!*

Luanne also fended off the calf with a boot now and then, when its indignation at seeing breakfast disappearing overcame its good sense. The cow gave a plaintive moo as Luanne swore and leaned a shoulder into it to get the udder back above the pail, giving it a resounding slap on the rump when it balked.

"Madam, you permit yourself strange liberties!" Signe called, grinning.

"You're channeling cows, now?" Luanne replied.

"Beats milking them," Signe said frankly. *Although milking is good for your hand grip too. Which I now know by experience.*

The cow shifted and rolled its eyes, obviously weirded out by the whole process, despite several days' practice; at least this one didn't kick . . . much. So far their cattle were all range beef stock, Herefords and Angus, not dairy types bred for gentleness. Even when they'd become accustomed to milking and didn't need to be secured fore and aft, they didn't like it at all. The amount of work that went into getting a pint of milk out of them was daunting, but nobody they'd met had been willing to part with milch animals.

Yet. It was certainly right up there on the wish list Angelica kept, along with the barrel churn that Ken kept promising to finish.

It had been sort of cool learning how to milk a cow, with Luanne and Angelica teaching her—they were both fun to be around, and Signe had always been good with animals. Doing the milking every second day wasn't much fun at all; it made your hands cramp, not to mention getting your foot stepped on or a well-beshatted tail switched into your face.

Signe put the weights down, waved to Luanne and then went into a set of stretching exercises, head to knee, splits, touching hands diagonally behind your shoulder blades. Both Mike and Pamela insisted on that before you did any serious practice. The two of them had a lot in common, starting with a steady methodical attention to details that left her alternately enraged and awestruck.

She finished the stretches and took her practice sword

down from the rack along one side of the wagon, checked that there was no rust on the blade—Mike and Pamela insisted, even with the blunt and nearly pointless blades used for drill—and began a series of cuts, right- and left-handed, to loosen her hands and forearms.

"Good," Pamela said, tossing her a pair of leather bracers. "You're starting to dominate the weapon. Now for real."

"Who would have thought two pounds and a bit was so *heavy*?" Signe said.

She leaned the sword against her hip for a moment as she strapped the bracers around her wrists—they helped make the bruising, jarring impacts less hard on your tendons. *Somewhat* less hard; you still had to watch out for the martial equivalent of carpal tunnel.

Pamela grinned. "Anyone who's done more than a few passages with a backsword knows that a couple of pounds is of nearly infinite weight. But don't try to do it all from the shoulder. Back it up from the gut and hips. That's what the rest of your body is for."

After that Signe slipped her targe onto her left arm and began lunges at a solid plank target shaped like a man, with Pamela holding it from behind—and moving it unpredictably, along with a running commentary on her form. The impacts ran back up her wrist and arm and back, but as Pam said, you were practicing to ram the blade into someone and out the other side, not pop their zits.

She forced down memories of terror and blood and made herself spring forward, back, again . . . After a while she stopped, panting. Pamela handed her a tin cup of water and she drank, conscious of the sweat dripping down her face and flanks.

"Thanks, Pam," she said, hesitated, and then went on: "Can I ask you a sort of personal question?"

"Like we have privacy anymore? Sure."

"Tell me . . . do you think Mike *likes* me?"

The older woman gave a gurgling laugh. Signe flushed and gave her a glare. "Well, he seems to like *you* well enough!"

Pamela laughed harder. "Oh, honey, sometimes I forget you're only eighteen!"

"Nineteen in August," Signe said, and ground her teeth slightly at the smile that followed.

"I'm thirty-two," Pamela explained after a moment. "Believe me, Mike thinks of me as a cross between an older sister and one of his Marine buddies. Maybe if I was the last woman in the world, but otherwise—don't worry."

Signe felt her shoulders relax slightly. "You're closer to his age than I am," she said.

"Honey, I'm four years *older* than him. Let me tell you about another of the manifold unfairnesses of the world from our point of view—" The younger woman nodded reluctantly. Pamela went on: "Besides, if there's any man in the outfit who appeals to *me*, it's your dad."

Signe goggled at her in horror. "You're kidding! Mom—".

Pamela faced her for a second: "Signe, your mom is dead. I'm real sorry and I would never have looked at your dad if she'd lived, but she didn't."

Signe sucked in a breath. "Sorry, I didn't mean to snap at you. Things have changed so fast . . . actually, I meant, he's so *old*. Mom was old, and he's *older*."

"Well, thanks! He's also the only really interesting conversationalist we've got who isn't already taken. But don't worry about it. *We're* not teenagers, i.e., not in a hurry. Anyway, you were talking about Mike?"

"Well, he's nice, and we've had fun talking and riding together and . . . but he's never . . . you know. Tried anything."

Pamela shrugged. "I don't know why. I *do* know he thinks you're very attractive—"

"What did he say?" she cut in eagerly.

"He's never said a word, it's just obvious the way he perks up when you're there—he's not much of a smiler otherwise. You know, that stoic Finn *sisu* thing."

"Well, then why doesn't he want to talk about how he feels?" she said in frustration.

"They never do! Listen to the voice of experience. That's a major reason I ended up divorced lo these many years ago. I wanted to talk about why the relationship wasn't working. As far as *he* was concerned, if he had to talk about it . . . well, that meant it wasn't working. I insisted. He walked."

"Weird."

"Men *are* weird. Very nice in a way, sometimes, but weird. Mike . . . might actually be smart enough to play hard to get. Or he may think you're just too young for him. A strange man in some ways, very private."

"That doesn't make me very happy," Signe said, quirking a smile. "I most definitely want *him*."

"I don't think Mike's personal energy field is calibrated for *happy*. Being around him will never be dull, and it could be a lot of fun, but simple happiness isn't in the contract. Be warned." She hesitated. "Besides . . . it hasn't been very long since, ah, the incident. Are you sure you want to, mmm, get involved with anyone quite yet?"

Signe flushed. "I wasn't raped!" she snapped bluntly.

"Your call. Just a warning—if you *do* start radiating make-a-move signals and Mike does *try something,* it's not going to be a cuddle and kiss on the cheek he has in mind, you know. Not that he wouldn't take no for an answer, but he might be *really* pissed off if you got cold feet."

They both looked up at a sudden sound; Pamela blew out her cheeks in relief at the interruption. Astrid was on watch a hundred yards from the road, where a little rise gave her a view of the ground falling away to northward, mounted and with an arrow on the string of her bow. She reached down and pulled a brass bugle from her saddlebow and did her best to make it sing; what she got was a flat, sourly off-key blatting hoot instead, but it carried.

Everyone around the little caravan stopped what they were doing and grabbed for a weapon—spear, bow, ax, sword, long knife.

Then they relaxed when she repeated the call twice, paused and blew twice again, and spurred in towards the wagons.

"The all-clear," Pamela said. She slid her working sword back into the scabbard hanging from the wagon, and picked up the practice weapon she'd dropped.

"Looks like Josh's got a message from the boss," Signe replied, putting up a hand to shade her eyes.

"Good afternoon," Michael Havel said as his party drew up to the locals.

"Howdy," a squat weathered man in a billed tractor cap said.

The young Indian in buckskins beside him had a bar of white paint across his face at eye level and carried a short lance with a row of feathers on the shaft; he looked along the line of the Bearkillers and pursed his lips. "Did we interrupt a meeting of your diversity committee?" he said. "Everything except Indians, hey?"

"Unless you count me," Havel said equably.

The Nez Perce gave him a shrewd look. "Yeah, you might have some 'skin in you."

"One Anishinabe grandma, but that doesn't make me an Indian. Anyway, we're just passing through—heading for Lewiston, and then points further west."

Several of the locals glanced at each other. *Aha,* Havel thought. *Something they're not telling me about between here and Lewiston, or in Lewiston. Or both. Have to find out about that.* Aloud he went on: "Who's in charge here?"

Both the farmer in the cap and the Indian in paint started to speak. There was a pause, and the older man spoke carefully: "Sort of a committee. I'm Howard Reines, mayor around here, sort of; this is Eddie Running Horse from the reservation council. That's the highest level of government around here still working."

"Pleased to meet you," Havel said, shaking hands with both. "Mike Havel. We're—"

"The Bearkillers!" Astrid said proudly.

*Hope they didn't see me wince,* Havel thought.

Eddie Running Horse seemed impressed, though, and nobody else actually laughed.

Astrid had managed to accumulate a small library of fantasies with lurid covers, scavenged from small-town libraries and abandoned road-stop book racks. They were full of pretentious pseudobarbarian and pseudomedieval names and titles with which she played an unceasing game of pin-the-absurd-name-on-the-donkey.

Some of the books even had useful hints about how to do things, as well as quests for the Magic Identity Bracelet of the Apocalypse, and a lot of the outfit came to hear Astrid read aloud from them evenings around the fires. He had himself, now and then; there really wasn't much else to do after dark but sleep and sharpen your blades or make the night hideous with attempts at song.

*If this is what having a kid sister is like, it's a wonder any of them survive to adulthood un-strangled.*

He went on aloud: "Yeah, the Bearkillers . . . long story. I'm boss of the outfit, pretty well."

Reines nodded, face neutral. "How long do you folks plan on staying? We've already moved a lot of our townsfolk and some refugees from Lewiston out to the farms and ranches west of us and they're about full up—"

Running Horse cut in: "Frankly, we just don't have much to spare for road people, after taking care of our own."

Havel's eyes narrowed; neither leader had sounded very enthusiastic in his welcome, but Running Horse's vibes were downright hostile.

*At a guess, because outsiders are very unlikely to be Nez Perce. With thousands pouring in from the towns, they're nervous about becoming even more of a minority.*

"Good thing we aren't planning on staying, then," Havel said aloud. "We would like to trade a bit for supplies. Food, useful tools, livestock—but we're not asking for a handout."

He didn't put a hand to his sword hilt, but he *did* let the metal chape at the end of the scabbard clank against his stirrup iron.

The locals cast careful looks at the Bearkillers. Apart from Will's chain-mail armor, they all wore the steerhide jackets, and they all had bows, shields and helmets; everyone except Astrid had a sword.

That put them a substantial step up on the group facing them, and *they* probably had the best the Kooskia area could offer. Bowie knives, hunting knives, a machete, hatchets, two bows, improvised spears, ordinary chopping axes lightened for one-handed use by grinding down the pell at the rear of the blade. A few had plywood shields. Nobody had any body armor to speak of unless you counted a leather jacket with some lengths of fine chain sewn to it, and they almost certainly hadn't had the concentrated training his group had—which showed.

*They're probably figuring—rightly—that it wouldn't pay to let such well-armed people get too hungry,* Havel thought cynically. *Another couple of months, and they'd be begging us to stay to help get in the harvest and plant for next year. Probably vagrancy laws will follow after that in short order and any wanderers who don't look too formidable will end up hoeing beans whether they like it or not. Right now, looking formidable will put them in a mood to dicker.*

Aloud he went on: "We've got trade goods. Some of you

might be interested in taking a look. Also we've got some skilled people—a really good vet, some horse trainers."

*If things were a little worse, we'd have to regularly fight for food. Christ, but I'm glad I ended up in Idaho before this happened!*

The welcoming committee fell in with them and rode back to the caravan; some of them looked slightly apprehensive, despite their advantage in numbers—Pamela had everyone armed as they went about their chores, and the dozen A-list fighters in camp standing ready. Not obtrusively, threateningly ready, but she wasn't trying to hide it, either.

Havel made polite introductions; everyone dismounted, and politely declined refreshments—that *was* polite these days. Food wasn't something to take for granted. Since getting out of the woods and into farming country they'd managed to keep themselves in tortillas and beef, especially since Ken Larsson rigged up a portable horse-powered flour mill, but he was glad they'd also managed to find a crateful of multivitamin pills; scurvy might have been a problem otherwise.

It would be a while before anyone had much in the way of fresh vegetables, and canned ones were jealously guarded. Deficiency diseases snuck up on you, and they also weakened resistance to infection.

One of the wagons held their handicraft projects on the move, and some of the products. Havel led the two leaders over to it and showed them what was on offer: lance- and spearheads, arrowheads and arrows, shields, fighting-knives and swords. Those included the first ones Will had run up; with Pamela's help he'd refined the second model considerably, adding a subtle curve to the grip and a forefinger-hold, and making the blades lighter and better balanced. The originals were still superior to anything the locals had, from the way they handled them and throttled exclamations.

"Now, *these* we can really use," Reines said, eagerly fingering a little pamphlet Pamela had done up on basic sword work, with illustrations by Signe and Astrid. "We do have a fair amount of livestock we could spare, seeing's how we aren't shipping the yearlings out and we can't cut as much hay—"

"Wait a minute, Howie," Running Horse said. "The council's got first say on disposing of assets like cattle and horses for the duration of the emergency. Everyone agreed on that."

"We need weapons, and this stuff looks a hell of a lot better than anything we've been able to cobble up. When we weren't busy staying alive," Reines said. "We especially need weapons with the folks disappearing on the road up past Kamiah."

"Drifters," Running Horse said, making a dismissive gesture. "Road people. Who keeps track?"

*Well, that's fucking tactful of you,* Havel thought, keeping silent and watching the argument.

"The Smiths disappeared out of their goddamned *house,*" Reines snapped. "*And* we've had stock rustled."

"Whoa," Havel said softly, raising a hand. "You folks probably don't want to quarrel in front of outsiders."

That shut both of them up, but Reines cast him a look before going on smoothly, the anger leached out of his voice: "That's true. And why don't you folks move in closer? After we have the doc check you over, but you look cleaner than most folks around here, come to that. You could come to dinner at my place. . . ."

Havel and Reines nodded imperceptibly at each other. Running Horse scowled.

Michael Havel looked into the fire, lost in thought—though also conscious of a vague longing for a cup of coffee. They'd camped in an empty space on the outskirts of town for the past week rather than take the offer of vacant houses; it was bad for morale to scatter too much and unsafe, too. In fact, he'd had more than one inquiry about joining up, after the Bearkillers had put on a bit of a dance and BBQ and a fencing display, to repay the do Reines had gotten the town to lay on—once Mr. Running Horse was out of sight. Evidently life in post-Change Kooskia was pretty dull.

*Seen that before, too,* he thought. *Withdrawal symptoms— no TV, no radio, no Internet, no movies, no nothing except the same faces and voices. Even small-town folks were used to being part of a bigger world than you can reach in a day's walk. The way we keep moving makes it a little easier to take. Although I do admire the way Reines has kept things together.*

He must have murmured that aloud. Ken nodded from the log he sat on over on the other side of the campfire, stirring the embers with a stick.

"He wasn't mayor before the Change—some sort of real-estate man with a sideline in cattle. Everyone was rather vague on how exactly he'd acquired the office, did you notice?"

Havel shrugged. "He seemed popular enough. And he's doing a good job."

"Uh-huh. We've seen how important a good leader is. The places that just went to pieces, it was where there wasn't anyone to get people moving together in a hurry."

"Some places it just seems to happen on its own, sort of," Havel observed.

Ken snorted: "Yeah, we've seen places like that—all one of them. A committee is the only form of mammalian life with more than four legs and no brain."

"Interesting what he had to say," Havel said. "We could use that livestock and gear; we'd have somewhere near enough horses, and enough stock we'd be independent for meat. The problem is, how do we smoke out his problem? Whoever it is, they've obviously got the smarts to hide when a posse comes looking."

Ken shrugged. "Well, from Reines's point of view, that's the beauty of the deal. We don't get paid unless we get results, he doesn't risk any of his own people, they don't have to neglect vital work, and if it turns out OK he not only gets a solved problem and some powerful political mojo, but he gives Running Horse and *his* backers a thumb in the eye. I sort of suspect that they've been blocking any real effort to track down the perpetrators just so he *won't* get any of that."

"You're a cynic," Havel said.

"I've been on the fringes of politics for a long time," Ken said. "You have to be, if you're in business on the scale I am . . . was. I prefer to think of myself as a realist. On the whole, I'd put my money on Howie Reines—he's got a lot more experience than Running Horse. Of course, there may be a lot more brainpower on the tribal council. I suspect that our young friend in the feather bonnet is convinced that the Great Spirit's struck down the white-eyes' technology so the tribes can make a comeback. Which I admit is about as logical an explanation for the Change as any—though I'm sticking to the Alien Space Bats."

Havel nodded. "Notice something about Running Horse's bunch?"

"The costumes? I'm not surprised at that. Will's right— it's the sort of thing you'd expect, psychologically speaking. Though I suspect they had to read anthropology texts to get the details!"

"Nah, I agree about that. What I noticed was that more than half of them didn't look even *part* Indian, including some of the ones all gussied up like Chief Joseph on steroids. Give you odds in a couple of generations, there'll be a group here who *call* themselves Nez Perce—or Tsoop-Nit-Pa-Lu—but look a lot more like me, or even Eric."

Ken gave him a considering look. "You know, you're probably right about that. Wouldn't be surprised if the same thing didn't happen in a lot of other places, too. For that matter, long-term, we're going to see a lot of ethnogenesis going on in the next generation or so."

At Havel's look of bafflement, he went on: "Tribes, ethnic groups, call 'em what you will. Little groups forming around a community or a leader and starting to think of themselves as a people. Mayor Reines's bunch too, for that matter. Anyone who can do the job—and the first little group will sort of set the tone for those who join up. Like a saturated solution forming around a seed-crystal. It's just starting now, of course, but give it a few years, or generations."

"Yeah, I suppose a lot of these guys like Reines or like Running Horse will go down in the history books," he said aloud. "The ones who pulled things together in their own neighborhood."

Ken shook his head. "I doubt there will be any history books for a long time," he said. "I wouldn't give mass literacy more than another generation, most places—less in some—and a lot of the world's going to lose the concept of writing altogether. Too many lost skills to reinvent."

"We've found a fair number of people who know how to do things the old-fashioned way," Havel pointed out. "Hell, we've already got a blacksmith, and people who can make a saddle starting with cows or run up a house starting with trees."

Ken laughed, a little harshly. "Yup. And that's a bit of a joke, when you think about it. Pre-Change America was rich enough that people could practice black-smithing or weaving or whatnot *as hobbies*, or make a living turning out high-priced handmade goods for collectors with a lot of disposable income. Handicrafts are rarer in backward areas, apart from a few of the *most* backward. You don't go on making hand-thrown pots when you can buy cheap plastic and aluminum, not when you're living on the edge. You can't spare time or effort for aesthetics. So in the long run we may be *better* off that way than, say, Columbia or Kenya. In the short run, mass die-off, of course."

"Irony still functions post-Change," Mike said with a chuckle. There were times when gallows humor was the only type available. The problem was that those were the times you most needed a laugh.

Ken nodded, getting a faraway look. Havel recognized it; the older Larsson looked that way when he was doing the big-picture thing.

*Which is useful, within limits,* Havel thought. *Gotta make strategy drive tactics, not the other way 'round, as Captain Stoddard used to say.*

Ken went on: "When we get settled, we should look into how to make rag paper. The acid-based pulp in most modern books doesn't last more than a generation even with careful storage; anything that isn't recopied will be lost by the time your kids are my age. Books will get *almighty* expensive in the places that hang on to the notion at all. When you're talking a small-scale society that doesn't really *need* literacy to function, it just won't pay to put in the effort, not when there's cloth to weave and turnips to hoe."

"Hard to keep the history straight, then," Havel said. "That's a pity. I . . . the things we're all doing, what's going on . . . that should be preserved."

"Oh, it will be, but not as *history*. We've fallen out of history, history with a capital H."

Havel raised a brow. "How can you be outside history? Sure, maybe nobody will *record* it, but it'll still be there."

"Ever read the *Iliad* or the *Odyssey*?"

"Yeah, bits here and there. I always preferred *Ulysses;* Achilles was an undisciplined glory hound, the sort who's a nightmare to his squad leader. A good soldier needs to be ready to die, but a suicidal one just leaves you with another damned empty slot in the TOE you have to train a replacement for." He paused, then added judiciously: "Unless you need someone to play Polish Mine Detector real bad. Then a glory hound can come in *very* useful."

"Right," Ken chuckled. "But the point is that nobody *wrote* those poems. They were composed to be recited aloud and memorized, and they're full of bits from a lot earlier—half a millennium earlier, from the fall of Troy, with some chunks that may have been a thousand years old or more when Homer was singing for his supper. That's how people in that type of culture remember things—just like the sagas, only those got written down sooner. It's not history. It's folk-memory, the time of legends and heroes and myths, and anything that happens gets crammed into that framework. A sense of historical time needs a high civilization, and a particular type of one at that. Barbarians and tribes live in mythic time, legend time, not an ordered progression of centuries going from somewhere to somewhere. It might be better to say they're timeless."

"Like the *Kalevala*?"

"Yup. Or the *Nibelungenleid,* where you get Siegfried and the dragon and the cursed Rhinegold all mixed up with real figures centuries apart like Attila the Hun and Theodoric the Ostrogoth."

"And then some looney squarehead makes a *real* boring experience out of 'em," Havel said. He'd suffered through a video of the complete *Ring* cycle once, with a girl who was crazy for the stuff.

*Christ, the things I did to get laid.*

Ken went on: "Most of the Old Testament is the same sort of thing, filtered through literate scribes much later."

"So someone may make a saga out of our friend Howie someday? Or a chapter of Genesis?"

"More like Exodus. Out of a distorted what-Grandpa-told-me memory of him, yeah." Ken got up, pushing off his knees. "Or maybe a memory of *you,* Mike. You're the one who killed the bear and led his people to the promised land . . . if we make it. See you tomorrow."

*Hmmm,* Havel mused. *Ken is an interesting guy to have around.*

He poked a stick into the fire, watching the sparks fly up towards the bright frosting of stars; it was a little chilly now, with the sun well down.

*I should start thinking about the longer term, a little. Once things hit bottom, they'll have to start up again—but in a new way, or a very old way. A strong man is what's needed, leadership, and something to believe in. Someone has to build on the ruins. Ken was right; we're back in the age of legends and heroes. A dirty job, but someone's got to do it.*

Orange flames crawled over the low coals of the fire; in them he seemed to see vague pictures, visions of glory amid the fire—

"Surprise!"

He rose, pivoting smoothly and very fast, the sword coming free of the scabbard with a rasping hiss of steel on greased leather and wood. At the same time he stepped sideways so he wasn't silhouetted against the fire and cursed how it had killed his night sight for crucial seconds. He hadn't been expecting anything—

*And come to think of it, someone trying to kill me wouldn't shout "Surprise!" now, would they?*

He straightened up, blinking. People stood before him, a crowd of most of the adults in the outfit—with Signe, Luanne, Astrid, and Angelica Hutton in the forefront. Signe and Luanne had his new and all-of-a-sudden-finished hauberk slung between them on a pole run through one sleeve and out the other. Angelica had the gambeson bundled up in her arms. And Astrid . . .

Astrid was holding out a helmet.

The actual metal was the standard model they'd settled on, a round steel bowl with a leather-and-foam liner, a flat bar riveted on the front to protect the nose, and a leather skirt at the rear—the aventail—covered in chain mail to guard the neck.

This one had some additions. The tanned head of a bear was mounted on it, the top half at least, with the snarling muzzle at brow-level and enough of the fur left attached behind it to hide the helmet's neck flap. Glass eyes stared at him, and the teeth were bared in an artistic, and quite realistic, snarl. He remembered the expression vividly, from the time the beast had been about to eat him.

"Well . . ." he said, feeling suddenly inadequate. "Well, I guess that's where the bearskin went."

"Angelica and Will showed us how to do the tanning," Astrid said proudly. "Actually it was sort of gross, you use *brains.* But it looks great now. We wanted to be sure we'd got it right, so we waited and it didn't smell at all. Put it on, put it on!"

Her face was shining.

*I can't say no. It would be like . . . well, like taking candy from a kid. Hell, she is a kid, or was until the Change.*

He did spare a glower for the adults, who should have known better than to let her gussy up fighting gear with nonessentials.

The padded coat was easy, closing up the front with an overlapping flap and laces. Luanne and Signe held the mail coat over his head as he ducked, then helped him wiggle into it with a clash and clinking rustle; you *could* put it on yourself, but it was a pain.

The shifting weight dragged at his shoulders, and he quickly cinched his broadsword belt tight around his waist to stabilize it and transfer some of the burden to his hips. Will had made forearm protectors—vambraces—out of sheet steel, hammered to fit around wooden forms; he slipped on his, then buckled on shin guards, leather covered in thin steel splints, and pulled on leather gauntlets whose backs were covered in more chain mail.

*Not bad,* he thought critically, doing a few twists and deep knee bends, flexing his hands and swinging his arms, his enthusiasm growing.

*Yeah! Way lighter than the field gear I carried in the Gulf. Better distributed, too; not bad at all, once I get used to the way it affects my balance. Bitchin' uncomfortable, though, and no two ways about it. I can feel the sweat starting even after sundown, and Christ Jesus, the thought of an itch in this stuff . . . but against an unarmored man, you'd be like a tank.*

"The helmet, the helmet!" Astrid said, and a bunch of the youngsters took it up.

He took it from her and settled it on his head, fastening the chinstrap. The nasal bar bisected his view, and he found himself unconsciously shifting his head slightly back and forth to keep his peripheral vision up.

*Another thing to get used to.*

The bear head mounted on top didn't seem to make any difference, or add any real weight. It wouldn't matter in a fight, although the thing was going to look pretty tattered if a couple of edged weapons went through on their way to the metal beneath. He could always switch back to the one he already had after a couple of days.

"And we made the rest of the hide up into a cloak, for colder weather," Astrid said proudly.

At her urging he swung the heavy length of cinnamon-touched black fur around his shoulders, fastening the paws across his chest with a hammered-gold clasp—gold was easy to come by these days and a lot less valuable than food or tools. The curing was professionally done— exactly what he'd have expected of any project the Huttons oversaw—and it had only the musky-sweet new-upholstery smell of well-tanned hide. The claws clicked on his chain mail as he threw the left side back a little to free his sword hilt.

*Shit, I must look like a carnivorous Carmen Miranda,* he thought. *It's a good thing I can't see myself—*

Eric and Josh walked up with a full-length mirror from one of the houses. With a flourish they set it down beside the fire, and then he *could* see himself. For a long minute he gaped, hearing a murmur from all around him as the Bearkillers took it in, with some townies who'd been hanging around as well.

*I look like something off the cover of one of Astrid's god-damned books!* he thought. The words "no fucking way" trembled on his lips.

Astrid's face was shining. Suddenly she threw her fists in the air and cried: "All hail to Lord Bear!"

His own shout of revulsion was buried in the chorus as everyone else took it up—except for Eric, who'd actually fallen flat laughing and who lay helplessly hugging himself as he rolled on the ground.

That left Havel grinding his teeth in fury. After a moment, he realized what bothered him more: better than half the spectators weren't laughing at all. In fact, they were taking it just as seriously as Astrid.

*Christ Jesus,* he thought, stomach sinking. *The kid's making a hero-shaped hole and the entire bunch of them are shoving me into it.*

"So, does this count as a date?" Signe said. "Here we are, alone at last."

Startled, Havel looked over at her. They were side-by-side on the seat of the wagon, and he was suddenly conscious of the slight summery smell of her, clean sweat and woman.

*And she's definitely a woman,* he thought, with a wry smile. *There's* never *a bad time to stop and discuss your feelings.*

"Ummm . . . I hadn't actually thought of it that way," he said cautiously. "For one thing, your brother and Pam are under the tarp right behind us, so we're not really alone."

"Oh, don't mind *him,*" she said. "He can't see a thing."

Muffled gagging and retching sounds came from beneath the tarpaulin, then a yelp, as if someone had kicked someone in the shin. Havel felt a sudden impulse to grin enormously. He fought it down, looking around at the long empty stretch of road. They were alone; two horses drawing the wagon, and a pair hitched to the rear . . . as tempting a target as they could arrange.

*Easy pickings,* the arrangement said. *Come and get it!*

It wasn't the sort of trick he'd have pulled out in the hot-and-dirty places the Corps had sent him. Far too blatant and obvious.

*Item: Things are different now. No guns and not many good archers yet. You have to get* close *to someone to hurt them. Item: Odds are these are amateur bandits, just learning the trade, the way I'm learning how to use a sword or shoot a bow.*

For a moment he felt an enormous familiar anger at whoever or whatever had done this to his country, to his world, and then it passed away. If he ever had a chance to *do* anything about it . . . but until then, put it away.

*'Cause those who can't put it away are going to die real soon and never get a chance to do anything about it.*

Instead he spoke, his voice light: "That's flattering, Signe, but let's take a rain check. After this is over, maybe? In the meantime, we'd better concentrate on business."

She made a pout and flipped the reins over the horse's back. "Yes, O Lord Bear. Business."

"Now *that's* a low blow. And yeah, business."

*You know, this* is *business,* he realized. *Literally. We've dealt with bandits before, and this is on our way, but we've actually been hired to do it.*

They went forward at a fast walk amid the clatter and hollow clop of hooves and the creaking of the wagon's fabric. He pulled a strip of jerky from a pocket and began gnawing on it as he watched their surroundings; it tasted like salty cardboard, but it was food.

The land was tending upward, with more grass and less sagebrush as they climbed into a belt of higher rainfall, but not much cultivation yet—it would be another day's travel until they were into wheat country. Before the Change this had been ranching territory, and seasonal grazing at that—virtually nobody actually lived here. Occasionally they passed an abandoned vehicle; once they sped up as a gagging smell told them someone, or several someones, had died inside a four-door sedan flipped upside down.

They passed a few bodies beside the road as well, but birds and coyotes and insects had taken most of the flesh there, leaving only scraps of tendon and wisps of hair blowing in the warm dry wind.

"How could anyone *do* that?" Signe asked. "Just sit and die?"

Havel shrugged. "Easy," he said, and waved a hand around them at the immense silence and the great blue bowl of the sky.

"It's bigger now. Physically bigger."

"Bigger?" Signe said. "*Quieter,* yes, but bigger?"

"Yeah, for all practical purposes. I've felt it before, backpacking into real wilderness, the deep empty country. The world gets bigger. OK, now it's like that everywhere. This was pretty thinly settled country before the Change, but that was when you could do thirty miles in an hour even on bad dirt roads. Bam, the Change hits, and suddenly thirty miles, that's two, three days' walk for someone not used to hiking—if you're lucky. Suddenly every distance is fifty, sixty times bigger, or more, and the fastest way to carry a message is feet."

"That never made *us* sit down and die of fright," Signe said stubbornly.

*You know, I really like this girl,* Havel thought. *She doesn't just accept anything I say.*

He nodded. "Yeah, but I wasn't taken by surprise when I went on vacation, and I'm *used* to being on my own in remote places. Some townie type, say someone from a big city like Seattle or even Spokane, they'd be just as likely to wait a long time for someone to drive by and rescue them as to get going right away. It would even be the sensible thing to do—how could they know things were screwed up worldwide? A lot would die of exposure; it was down below freezing here at night right after the Change. And there aren't even any surface streams around here, and try going twenty-four hours without water. Wait too long and you'll be too weak to move, or you'll collapse on the way."

She shivered. When she spoke again her voice was flat with dread. "Mike . . . it's probably a lot worse than we've seen, back on the coast, anywhere with cities, isn't it?"

"Worse isn't the word. There probably aren't any words. And it'll all get worse before it gets better," he said grimly. "Your dad thinks that by this time next year, there won't be more than ten, maybe twenty million people at most left in the whole of North America, from Guatemala to Hudson's Bay."

*My, you know how to sweet-talk a girl, don't you, Havel?* he asked himself.

All the while his eyes had been moving around them; so had Signe's, come to that. The road wound and turned as it climbed, and sometimes the hillsides rose almost cliff-steep beside them. He checked his precious wind-up watch and looked behind them; a mirror-flash came at the edge of sight, just one quick blink. Impossible to tell from sunlight on a broken bottle or a bit of quartz, if you didn't know what to look for.

*That's comforting,* he thought. *Nice to know help is on hand.*

It was another five hours until sunset, and then he'd have to figure out a different trick. He wasn't going to try this in darkness, when nobody could see what was happening or rush to the rescue.

*And even in daylight, it's not all that comforting. The rest have to hang well back if they're not going to be spotted.*

"Mike!" Signe said. His head came around. "Up ahead!"

He saw only a moving dot, but Signe had unusually keen eyes. He thought for an instant, then decided to take a chance; binoculars were not something any innocuous traveler would have, but he needed to know what was going on. The road a half mile ahead sprang into sight.

*Man on a bike,* he thought. Then: *Correction. Kid on a bike. About ten, and a boy, I think. Also he's bleeding, and looking over his shoulder. I think some genuine bait got in ahead of us.*

"That's torn it," he said grimly. "All right, everyone out."

Signe pulled on the reins. Havel switched aside his broad-brimmed hat, pulled the loose shirt that concealed his armor over his head, and clapped on his helmet. Pamela and Eric were out from under the tarpaulin in less time, red-faced and sweating but fully equipped; Pam was in one-third of their current store of chain hauberks, Eric in leather like his sister. They unhitched the horses from the wagon's traces and saddled them while Havel jumped down to the pavement, grunting a little as his boots hit and the mail clashed. It wasn't that the armor was too heavy to run and leap in . . .

*. . . it's just that when I do, it's like being thirty years older.*

The boy gave a cry when he saw them waiting and tried to stop, wobbled, and went over.

"Canteen," Havel said; Pamela tossed him one, and he went over to where the slight body rested under the cycle. One wheel still spun.

Havel hooked the broken machine off with a toe, sending it clattering down the steepish slope to their left. He'd been right; it was a boy about ten, with a big shock of sun-streaked brown hair, skinny and filthy and smelling fairly high. He had a slash across one cheek, shallow but clean-edged as if done with a very sharp blade; that was just old enough for the blood to start clotting, and blackish red streaks crusted on his neck and chest on that side. He did a careful once-over to make sure the boy was unarmed—not easy to conceal a weapon when you were in shorts, a Marilyn Manson T-shirt and sneakers—and then went to one knee.

*Christ, you have to learn a whole new way of moving in this stuff.*

Pamela came up on the other side, evidently thinking the same thing from the cautious way she moved.

"Easy, kid," Havel said, as she put a hand under his head.

The adolescent wasn't really unconscious, just stunned. He sucked eagerly at the warm water, coughing and sputtering, then drinking more; his eyes widened at the sight of Havel's gear, but he didn't seem frightened of them, just terrified in general.

"They hurt my mom," he said. "They—"

"Son, calm down," Havel said, his voice firm and strong, but not shouting. "Take it from the top. I need to know what's going on, and fast."

The boy closed his eyes, took a deep breath, and then opened them again. "We—my family and our neighbors— we were traveling east, out of Lewiston, to get away from the sickness."

Havel's eyes narrowed; Pamela's hands moved with quick skill, checking for temperature and swollen glands.

"Nobody happened to mention *that* about Lewiston, did they?" she said angrily; then she shook her head, smiling a little in relief, and Havel blew out his cheeks with a *whoosh*. Medicines were getting scarce.

The boy went on:

"We don't have it! But a lot of people did. We got out a week ago, and we were traveling, going to my uncle's farm outside Kooskia. But we stopped, and they . . . they . . ." He started to shake again.

Havel gave him more water, and leaned closer to look into his eyes: "How many? Mounted, or on foot? What happened, and where did they go?"

"A lot—a dozen, maybe. I didn't see any horses. They were all around us, and I just—I saw one of them hit Mom with an ax, and I just got on my bike and went. Please, mister, you've got to help! I just ran away. I ran away from them all."

He started to cry.

"Running was the best thing you could do, kid," Havel said, giving him a quick squeeze on the shoulder. "Trying to fight out of your weight is stupid, not brave. Now how far was it, and what's the ground like?"

Havel looked up at Pamela when he had all the information they could muster; the ambush had taken place about two miles west, well uphill, and just where the road cut through the edge of the plateau. He closed his eyes for a second, calling up the terrain map of the area he'd studied.

"He's undernourished and dehydrated and he's got cooties, but otherwise fine, far as I can tell," Pamela said. "If his party had been on the road for a week, chances are they're clean."

He stood, thinking, weighing distances. "All right, this has fucked up Plan Number One to hell and gone. We've got to keep in contact or they'll get away again. Signe, light the signal and stay with the kid—that's an order!—until the rest of the A-list gets here. We'll leave sign; follow at speed. Keep an arrow on your string until the cavalry arrive and get ready to run if you have to."

He picked the boy up, laying him on the tarpaulin in the back of the wagon.

"Eric, Pam, equipment check. Then water the horses, all they'll drink. Double canteens, take nothing but water, armor and weapons."

Pam pulled out three bundled smocks. Havel groaned inwardly at the thought of putting on *another* layer, but the thin cotton surcoats were sewn with patches, camouflage-patterned in gray and brown and sage green, better disguise than even the most carefully browned metal. They pulled them on, buckled their sword belts over the cloth and swung into the saddle, giving each other's gear a quick once-over.

Signe already had the smudge pot out on the road and lit, and a column of black-orange smoke rose to the sky. That would tell Will and the rest of the mounted backup *Come at speed.*

Havel leaned down in the saddle on an impulse; Signe turned, startled, and her eyes flew wide when he gave her a brief hard kiss. He grinned and clamped his legs to his horse's barrel.

"Follow me!"

Hooves thundered, spitting gravel behind them; some of it hit the smudge pot with a sharp metallic tinking.

Havel leaned far over in the saddle to study the marks by the side of the road. *Damn, but I'm better than I was, on horseback. Well, a month of continuous practice . . .*

"Bikes and a cart with bicycle wheels," he said.

They'd seen that before, rigged up like an Asian pedicab. His eyes scanned.

"Went off upslope there. Blood trail—big splotch of blood by the side of the road, and then splashes of it; someone got cut badly."

He frowned. "Probably fatally. The splashes get smaller up the hill here, like a body bleeding out. You can track 'em by the way the ants and flies are swarming on it."

"Should we follow?" Eric said, reining his horse half around.

"Patience," Pamela said.

Havel noticed that her eyes went skyward, like his. She hadn't been a hunter until the Change, but she had spent a lot of time before that watching wildlife.

"Patience, my ass. Let's go kill something, as the vulture said," Eric began brashly, but fell silent as the others pointed upward.

"Oh. Shit."

The buzzards were circling, but as they watched one slanted downward.

"I think the killing's been taken care of," Havel said. "I also *don't* think the locals were looking very hard for the reason people were disappearing. Or maybe whoever did it was rushed this time. Slow and careful, people. If I was one of this bunch, I'd leave an ambush on my back trail. I don't expect them to, but it could happen."

He dropped the knotted reins on the saddle horn and slipped an arrow through the cutout in the riser of his bow—Waters's first really successful model. The horse picked its way obediently upslope with rocks clattering under its hooves; he kept balance without much thought, his gaze on the great bare slopes about them.

What they sought was in a narrow ravine that dead-ended not far ahead. The carrion birds hopped about, a flapping squawking carpet over flesh roughly covered with piled rocks. The long skinny necks struck downward through the gaps, and there were shreds on their beaks as they came upright to look at the intruders. Then they exploded skyward in a storm of black wings as the humans came near.

Havel grimaced, and murmured words from an old song he'd heard once:

> *"Loud and cruel were the ravens' cries*
> *As they feasted on the field."*

If anyone was watching who really knew what they were ~~doing, the buzzards and crows taking to the air would be a~~ giveaway; he'd just have to hope they *didn't* know. The pedicab lay on its side, a wheel smashed into a bent tangle; getting it over these slopes had taken a lot of effort. A few meagre bundles of clothing and possessions lay opened and scattered about, looters' leavings.

Then: "There's things we'd better check. Let's get them uncovered."

The corpses hadn't had time to stink much, but the work was grim as they tumbled rocks aside. Eric made a retching sound; for real, this time.

"Butchered" was a term you heard a lot in talk about killing people; he'd seen casualties from shellfire who really looked that way, back in the Corps.

This was the first time it had been *literally* true. There were four bodies in the ravine; they'd all been gutted, and had the major cuts—thighs, upper arms, ribs—roughly hacked free and removed. He forced himself to note details; whoever did it hadn't dressed out many carcasses.

"Yeah," Havel said, feeling a little queasy himself. "I think we can see why people would be disappearing."

"Why?" Eric burst out. "This is ranching country— there's food!"

Havel shook his head. "Not right around here this time of year. Not if you don't know how to find it; *I'd* have a tough time living off the country within easy walking distance of the road, and someone from a town, someone who thinks half a mile is too far to walk . . ."

Pamela nodded. "I'd have problems living off the land here myself, and I do—did—a lot of wilderness hiking."

"So the only animal that's big and easy to catch right after the Change would be . . . guess what? Once you'd started, you wouldn't *want* to be found."

Eric was piling the rocks back on. "Because people would *kill* you," he said fiercely.

Havel nodded, face and voice calm: "Which is exactly what we're going to do," he said. "This bunch have read themselves out of the human race. There are things you're just not entitled to do, even to survive."

Eric reached for his reins. Havel put out a hand to stop him.

"This area's too steep and rocky for horses. They'd make us slow, and give us away, and pin us down if we got into a fight. I hate leaving them, but the A-list can pick them up—we'll be leaving plenty of sign."

The horses were nervous at the smell of blood, snorting and stamping; they ran a rope between two rocks for a picket line, and spilled the oats and alfalfa pellets from their saddlebags on the ground. Then Havel did a slow three-sixty scan of their surroundings, ending with his finger pointing northwest.

"Everyone take a long drink of water before we start," he said. "They're heading that way, and it's not misdirection; that's their base."

He suited action to words and then slung his quiver over his back, stooping to make the first of a series of arrow-signs with small rocks to show their direction.

"Eric, you're point." *Because you rustle and clank less than either of us. It's not stealth armor.* "Follow the blood trail. Remember what I told you."

"Yeah, look *ahead* at the tracks, not at your toes," Eric said, with a flicker of a smile. "Look up and around every three paces. Careful where you put your feet."

"And take it slow; remember, we're watching for *your* signal. Pam, cover my left. I think they're"—he pointed again—"somewhere under that rimrock on the edge of the higher ground. They have to have water, and that's where it would be; and not more than a mile or two away, I think. Let's go."

Eric went ahead, moving surprisingly lightly over the broken ground for a young man over six feet tall and currently carrying forty pounds of gear and weapons. Havel let him get twenty feet forward and then followed, placing his feet with care on the slope of dry sparse grass, low prickly bushes and scattered gravel, careful also not to let the skirts of the armor brush stone. The metallic chinking sound of that carried annoyingly well.

The sun baked down; once they were past the dead-meat smell of the ravine, all he could smell was warm rock, sage, and his own sweat. That flowed until he felt everything inside the armor was oozing lukewarm diluted tallow, and his eyes stung fiercely as driblets squeezed out of the lining of his helmet; all the tighter spots chafed. It all seemed distant, beneath the crystalline awareness of the hunt . . . a hunt where both sides were prey as well.

Eric flung up a hand, fist clenched. They all froze, and sank quietly to the ground; they were on the upslope of a steep ridge running northwest, and the sun was low enough to be a nuisance.

Havel scanned the terrain and then made a hand signal to his left—*follow me once I'm there.*

He pulled the scabbarded sword from the sling on his belt and ran it through loops beside his quiver, leaving the hilt above his left shoulder; that was less awkward when you were doing the creep-crawl-and-run thing.

Then he went forward himself, from one cover to the next, and at the last mostly crawling, holding his bow across the crook of his elbows—it was a lot lighter than an assault rifle, but more cumbersome, and the string was delicate. More sweat ran into his face, and sharp rocks clawed at his elbows and knees. He had to move a lot more slowly, because there was no other way to make chain mail reasonably quiet.

*Well, there's one good thing about this damned iron shirt,* he thought. *Stuff doesn't gouge into you as hard while you're wearing it.*

He leopard-crawled into the slight depression where Eric lay and followed his eyes. There was a sentry on the ridgeline ahead of them. A useless sentry, standing right *on* the ridge out in plain sight of God and radar and leaning on a spear; that was reassuring, since it proved that the killers they sought really *were* amateurs.

*Unless they've got another one decently concealed, and that fool is* maskirovka, Havel thought, unshipping his binoculars. After a moment: *Nope. Unless I'm missing it completely, that's their one and only.*

Smoke drifted up, carrying the scent of roasting meat from the cannibals' camp. Havel spat to clear his mouth of a rush of cold gummy saliva, and made himself study the ground between the Bearkillers and the sentry. It was nearly a hundred yards. . . .

A faint scream came from beyond the ridge, then a series of them, shrill—a woman, or an adolescent, he thought. And the sentry was looking back over his shoulder at his own camp more than down at the approaches to it.

"I'll take him," Havel whispered, handing Pamela the binoculars. "When he goes down, both of you join me pronto."

Eric looked as if he wanted to volunteer, and Pamela looked at the younger Larsson with the wondering gaze you gave the insane; neither of them said anything aloud as Havel slipped out of the hollow and began to crawl upward.

*I'll do it because I'm the only one who's hunted men,* he added silently to himself. *It's not quite like being in a fight. Killing in cold blood's a lot harder on the nerves.*

There was a secret to stalking, and wasn't much different with deer or humans: *Don't move when they're looking at you.* Deer were harder, since their noses and ears were a lot keener, although they were a lot less likely to kill *you.*

Back before the Change in a situation like this, back when he was in Force Recon, he'd have gotten close and used a sound-suppressed pistol, or even closer and used a knife and his hands. Now there was an alternative, if he could pull it off.

Closer. Move and freeze, move and freeze—gently, gently, nothing abrupt.

*Don't stare. People can feel that. Use your peripheral vision. Think rock, think grass, think sage.*

He moved again, a swift steady crawl, completely controlled; his mind was a diamond point of concentration, but open also to every quiver of breeze and rustle of noise, as if he *was* the land he moved over. It wasn't really something you learned; you learned to stop *not* doing it. He'd gotten that in the woods from his father, and from Grandma's brothers and nephews, and from his own heart, without putting it into words until he went into the Corps and got his final polish from experts.

All you had to do was stop the part of your mind that was always telling itself stories. Humans had been predators for a very long time, after all, long before language. Just *be.*

The wind was from the target towards him; the nauseatingly good smell of meat roasting got strong, and then there was a strong whiff of sweat and human waste. It was too rank to be from one man; the campsite must be very bad to smell like this so far away, even compared to the squalor they'd often met after the Change.

Closer, a hundred feet, and he was behind a boulder half buried in the thinly grassed rocky soil. The sun was lower, and he had to squint as he checked slowly around the edge of the lump of basalt.

There.

The cannibal sentry was still standing upright, silhouetted against the evening sun as clearly as a cardboard cutout. Havel flexed his fingers before taking up the bow again. A deep breath, and a quick trained effort of will to empty his mind as he exhaled.

*Now.*

Havel rose, feet stamping down into the archer's T. The powerful recurved bow came up, stave creaking as he drew to the ear—ninety pounds draw, horn and sinew and wood of the bois d'arc tree. The triangle-shaped arrowhead touched the outer edge of the riser, and he lowered his left hand until the head met the black outline a hundred feet above him. Instinct spoke and the string rolled off his fingers . . .

*Snap.*

The string slapped against his arm guard, and the arrow blurred out in a flickering shallow curve, the razor edges of the broadhead glinting as the slight curve in the fletching made the shaft twirl like a rifle bullet. Almost instantly came the flat heavy *smack* of steel striking flesh, a thick wet sound.

Havel was moving as the shaft left the string; he could *feel* that the shot was a hit. He covered the hundred feet uphill in a near-silent panther rush, already close enough to see the sentry pivoting, eyes wide in a filthy, hairy sunscorched face, blood coughing out between his bearded lips in a bright fan of arterial red. The gray goose-feather fletching danced behind his left shoulder blade, and the point and eighteen inches of the shaft dripped red from his chest.

Havel dropped his bow and grabbed the man by the beard with his right hand, burying his left in the tangled hair at the base of his skull. A single wrenching twist, a sound like a green branch snapping, and the body jerked and went limp. He snatched up the spear—it was a sharpened shovel head on a pole—and lowered the body to the ground. Then he drew the arrow free with a single strong pull—he might need it—and hastily pushed the filthy carcass downslope behind him, wiping his gloved hands on the dirt.

The lice and fleas would be looking for a new home, and he didn't feel hospitable.

Eric and Pamela dodged the rolling body as they followed him and flattened themselves below the ridgeline. Havel stood in the sentry's place, leaning on the spear and studying the enemy camp. It wasn't far away; a little nook with a spring trickling down an almost-cliff and some cottonwoods—most cut down for firewood now. There weren't any tents, just arrangements of plastic sheeting and blankets propped on crudely tied branches, and some car seats and improvised bedrolls. A fair-sized fire was popping and flaring beneath pieces of meat on a grill that looked as if it came from a barbecue.

Even from here the stink was enough to make him gag, and he could see the swarm of flies on bits of bodies and casual heaps of human shit—one of the cannibals was squatting as he watched.

Nearby was the source of the screams. It was a half-bowshot away, but he could see that the woman—girl—was in her teens. An older man with shaggy mouse-colored hair and beard was trying to make her eat something, grabbing at her hair and pushing it towards her face; she fought with dreadful concentrated intensity, screaming when she broke free.

That never took her far, because her ankles were tied with a cord that gave her only about a foot of movement, like a horse-hobble. Several of the watchers were crowing laughter, but the man shouted angrily as she managed to rake his face with her nails. He hit her seriously then, and turned to pull an ax out of a stump as she slumped to the ground.

"Oh, I *hate* it when I have to be a hero," Havel said, tossing the spear aside. "And I'd have just as much chance of hitting her as him if I tried a shot at this distance. Here goes."

He cupped his hands to his mouth. *"Hey! You down*

*there! Yes, you, asshole! The Bearkillers are here—here to kill you all!"*

The camp below froze like a tableau behind glass . . . waxwork figures in some unimaginable future museum . . .

*Evolution of the post-Change cannibal band,* he thought crazily.

. . . then burst into activity like maggots writhing in dung.

"Oooops," Havel said in a normal conversational tone as more and more of them appeared, crawling from their nests of cloth or from under the crude sunshades. "Guess they were more numerous than I thought."

They milled about, blinking, scratching. The bushy-haired man finished pulling the ax out of the cottonwood stump and pointed up the slope with it.

"Food!" he shouted. "More food—he came to us!"

The others took it up in a second, a confused brabble of voices rising into a shrilling scream. They surged forward up the slope towards him, waving axes and tire irons and clubs and knives and a couple of improvised spears like the one he'd been holding.

"Let them get fairly close," he went on, looking down at the white faces of his companions. "I don't see any distance weapons at all, but we can't afford to waste arrows. We're none of us what you'd call crack shots with these things yet."

He picked up his bow and reached over his shoulder for a shaft.

"And I *really* hope Will gets the rest of the A-list here quickly," he said.


*"Haakkaa paalle!"*

Havel shouted the ancient battle cry as he rose and lunged. The cannibal grinned with yellow teeth, throwing himself backward and rolling downhill in a ball with the haft of his ax held across his stomach.

As he went, half a dozen others popped up from behind boulders or bushes and threw a barrage of rocks. Havel ducked down and lifted his shield, swearing, keeping his sword hilt and sword hand behind the targe as the fist-sized missiles banged and rattled painfully off his mail and shield and helmet. If he lost the use of his right arm they'd overrun the Bearkillers in minutes.

"Yuk-hei-saa-saa!" Eric shouted behind him, from where he sat—a bone-bruise on the right leg left him unable to stand. "Ho la, Odhinn!"

Gasping, Havel spared a second to grin at him. "Well, we've all got our traditions," he said. "Keep an eye out for—"

The younger man's bow sounded, a flat *snap* through the clatter and shouting. A cannibal dropped her knife and fell, trying to drag herself off with the shaft through a thigh. The rest of the band ignored her in their hurry to dive for cover, which at least made it harder for them to throw rocks accurately. A hissing shout brought his head around completely; just in time to see the tip of Pamela's backsword nick through the tip of a nose as three tried to rush her.

That brought a squeal like a pig in a slaughter chute and panicked flight. The other cannibal attacking her dodged away with a shriek of terror as she repositioned in a spurt of dust and gravel, moving with terrifying speed and grace. The third ran into her targe and fell backward as if he'd rammed a brick wall; she killed him with a neat economical downward stab.

"Watch your own side, goddamnit!" she shouted as she moved.

It was good advice. A lump of stone glanced off Havel's helmet with a dull *bongggg* sound, and he whipped his gaze back to his section, shaking his head against the jarring impact. Cannibals were bobbing up from cover to throw and then down again, and the little party had—

"How many arrows left?" he asked.

"Six," Eric said.

*Couldn't tell he's hurting from the voice,* Havel thought with approval. *He really is shaping up good.*

"Make 'em count," he said. "There are a lot more of them than I thought."

The rocks picked up again; the two mail-clad Bearkillers huddled back, protecting the more lightly armored Larsson, moving their shields to catch as many of the heavy stones as they could. After a moment Eric shot; a miss this time, but a close one, and the enemy grew cautious.

"Four left," Eric said.

"I'm surprised they haven't run," Pamela said. "We must have killed or crippled more than a third of them."

"Nowhere to go," Havel replied, keeping his eyes busy. "Wolves don't eat members of their pack who're injured. Men do, men and dogs, and I think literally here. Also that spring down there is probably the only water they know about."

The rocks slowed for a moment. "And they're probably more than half mad by now," Pamela panted, ducking low. She took a quick sip of water and carefully recorked her canteen. "Wanting to die on some level."

"Then they could obligingly try to slug it out toe-to-toe," Havel said, knocking a jagged four-pound lump of basalt out of the air with his shield, and feeling the weight all the way down his back. "We'd have killed them all if they'd kept on doing that."

"I said they were crazy, not stupid," Pamela said.

*Well, if nobody turns up soon, we're toast. In fact, we're dinner,* Havel thought.

"Here they come," he said a second later.

This time they were doing it smarter; half throwing rocks, the other half scuttling forward. Far too many . . .

*They must have been recruiting among the people they attacked,* Havel thought. *Those who refused to turn cannibal going into the stewpot.*

He saw the faces and the eyes now that they were closer; there was little human left in them. Animals, but cunning ones.

*And Pam's right too.*

"Dinner's going to be expensive," he snarled. *"Haakkaa paalle!"*

Eric shot his last four arrows, and put two more of the enemy out of action. Then they were close, three in front of Havel with blades, more behind carrying stones—one woman in the tattered remains of a business outfit clasping a rock the size of her head, ready to sling it into him at close range.

*Not good.*

He stepped forward, the downward slope giving added force to the cut. The backsword blurred down and caught the axman at the join of neck and shoulder, and the eyes in the dirt-smeared face went wide. Shock vibrated up his arm as bone parted with a greenstick snap.

He wrenched at the steel with desperate haste, beating

aside a spearhead with his shield; the blade was fastened immovably by the dead man's convulsion and the sagging weight tore the braided-leather grip out of his hand.

The time lost let a man with a hatchet too close. He dodged and the spearhead from the other side went by his face; the hatchet skimmed off his shoulder, rattling along the rings of his armor. The hatchetman stepped in, trying to grapple, and Havel lashed out with his steel-clad forearm.

The vambrace took his enemy in the face. Bone crumbled. He snapped the *puukko* into his hand and struck as he stepped in towards the spearman, the vicious edge grating on bone as he slashed it down the haft of the spear, trying to ward off a third attacker with his shield. . . .

"You didn't come!" the woman with the big rock screamed. "You left us!"

Whatever the hell that meant, she was entirely too close, raising the rock in both hands, and he couldn't dodge—not in time. Two of the cannibals were swarming over Eric, one grabbing his hair to pull his head back while the other hacked clumsily with a bread-knife . . .

Then the one with the rock looked down at the point of the sword that had appeared through her chest, dropped the big stone on her own head and collapsed forward.

Signe stood there instead, revealed like a window when the shade rattled up, leaning forward in a perfect stepping lunge, her eyes going wider and wider as she looked down at the results. Havel took a pace back and clubbed the cannibal about to stab Eric in the throat with the metal-shod edge of his shield; it clunked into the man's neck and dropped him limp on the rocky ground.

The other turned to run, and had just time to scream when he saw the line of blades coming up the ridge. One scream, before Eric's fist closed on his ankle and dragged him back towards the knife.

Havel took the time to draw three heaving breaths, straining to pull air that felt like heated vacuum into his lungs, then stepped forward to plant a foot and wrench his sword free of the body of the cannibal he'd killed.

"Thanks," he said to Signe.

"You're—" She bit back a heave. "You're welcome."

Relief was like a trickle of cool air under his gambeson.

The A-list of the Bearkillers swarmed up onto the ridge as the cannibals fled.

Then they sheathed their swords and unlimbered their bows.

"You're late for the party," he said to Will.

The Texan shot; a shriek of pain followed right on the heels of the bow-string's slap against his vambrace.

"But not for the cleanup chores," Will said.

"Well, I think we can assume *he's* innocent," Havel said.

The man lying in a cage of barbed wire stank; he was also skeletally thin, and his left foot was missing, crudely bandaged with the remnants of a T-shirt. Enormous brown eyes looked out of a stubbled hawk-nosed face. Havel mentally subtracted twenty years and put him in his thirties.

"I should *hope* so," the prisoner croaked. "Do I *look* like I've been eating well?" He waved the stump. "I've been *contributing* to the pot. Aaron Rothman's the name."

"Mike Havel," Havel said. Then: "Get him out of there."

Two of the Bearkillers went in with a stretcher. Pam knelt beside it and soaked the bandage with her canteen, edging up one end of it. When she saw what lay beneath she swore and reached into her bag for a hypodermic.

"You're a doctor too?" Rothman said. "As well as the Amazon thing?"

"Vet, actually," Pam replied. "Too? You *are* a doctor? Medical variety?"

"GP," he confirmed and weakly held up a hand. "That's the only reason they didn't kill me, dearie, when I wouldn't . . . join up."

"Thank goodness," she said. "I've got to pull you through, then. We *really* need a doc."

The wounded man looked around at the mail-and-leather clad Bearkillers, and at Howie Reines and Running Horse standing in horrified silence as the grim work of cleanup went on.

"Oh, I was *so* hoping this was all over," he sighed. "If only you'd come in helicopters!"

"It isn't over," Havel said grimly, as Pamela cleaned and rebandaged the gruesome wound. Red streaks went from it up the wasted calf. "In fact, it's probably just starting."

Rothman sighed. "It could be worse. I used to live in New York."

Havel looked around; there were half a dozen living captives, huddled under the Bearkiller blades. And about the same number of liberated prisoners getting help, counting Rothman and the girl who'd been screaming when he arrived—she huddled in a patch of shade, a blanket clutched around her shoulders and her eyes squeezed shut. A couple of young children, too—as far as he was concerned they were *all* prisoners, no questions asked.

"So, any of these innocent too?" Havel said, going down on one knee and putting an arm behind the doctor's shoulders, lifting him to a better vantage point on the presumptive cannibals.

The weight was featherlight. Rothman fumbled at his breast pocket—he was in the remains of slacks and shirt with pocket protector—and brought out a pair of glasses. He peered through them, and smiled with cracked and bleeding lips. It wasn't a particularly pleasant expression, and Havel didn't blame him one bit.

"Not a one, barring the children," he said. "And I'll testify to that in court."

"That won't be necessary, Dr. Rothman," Havel said, lowering him gently back to the stretcher. "Things have gotten a little more . . . informal, since the Change."

He looked up. There was a cottonwood growing out of the cliffside, dead and bleached but still strong; a convenient limb stretched out about ten feet up.

"Will!" he called. The Texan looked up; Havel jerked a thumb at the limb. "Get some ropes ready, would you? Three at a time ought to do."

"I can't! I'm sorry, so sorry!"

They were on a low hillside above the camp, which was the only way you could get any privacy. Havel drew his hands backward as Signe fumbled to refasten her clothes. His long fingers knotted on his knees in the cool sage-smelling darkness; herbs and long grass crackled under the blanket, adding a bruised spicy smell to the night.

"OK!" Havel said, turning his back a bit while zippers and snaps fastened. "Look, it's OK!"

*No it isn't,* he thought, and his voice probably gave his words the lie.

"I'm sorry. I thought I could—look, let's try—"

Havel made his gesture gentle. "No, we just tried to rush it, Signe," he said. "I know it isn't easy to get over the sort of thing you went through. Head on back to camp and tell them I'll be down in a while, why don't you?"

"Mike—"

"Signe, I said *head on down.*"

He waited until her footsteps had faded in the darkness before he drew his sword and looked at the twisted stump at the foot of the rock that blocked off the view to the west.

"Is it worth the risk to the blade?" he murmured. "Yes." A pause for thought. "*Hell* yes."

Then he spent twenty minutes of methodical ferocity hacking the hard sun-dried wood into matchstick splinters.

# INTERLUDE II: THE DYING TIME

"You sure this is a good idea, Eddie?" Mack said, as they walked into the built-up area of Portland from the west.

"Look, who does the thinking here?" Eddie Liu replied.

"You do, Eddie," Mack said. "But this place gives me the creeps—all those stiffs. We've been eating pretty good out of town since things Changed. A lot of places are growing stuff, too, so we can get that when it's ready. Or maybe we could go east, I hear there are plenty of cows there and not many people. So I was just asking, are you sure about this?"

Eddie Liu shrugged at the question. "No, I'm not sure. But I *am* sure wandering around the boonies looking for food isn't a good idea anymore. People are getting too organized for the two of us to just take what we need."

Too many of the little towns had gotten their shit together, with committees and local strongmen and those goddamned *Witches,* of all crazy things. He could see the thoughts slowly grinding through behind Mack's heavy-featured olive face, and then he nodded.

"We have to hook up with somebody," Eddie finished. *And Portland is where the organization is,* he thought—or at least, that was what the rumors said.

He was betting that in a big city, or what was left of it, there would be less of the no-strangers-wanted thing they'd been running into among the small towns and farms farther south.

They trudged through endless suburbs; mostly smoldering burnt-out wreckage smelling of wet ash, wholly abandoned to an eerie silence broken only by the fat, insolent rats and packs of abandoned dogs that skulked off at the edge of sight. In the unburned patches there were spots where tendrils of green vine had already grown halfway across the street, climbing over the tops of the abandoned cars.

On the roof of one SUV a coyote raised its head and watched as he went by, alert but unafraid. Half a mile later they both yelled as a great tawny-bodied cat flashed by, too fast to see details—except that it was bigger than a cougar, nearly the size of a bear.

The beast was across the street and into an empty window in three huge bounds.

"Mother of God, I don't like the idea of going to sleep with something like *that* running around loose!" Eddie said. "I know what it's been eating, too. We'd better find a place with a good strong door and a lock before we camp."

Farther east they began to reach flatter stretches where the burnt-out rubble was only patches; this road in the area north of Burnside was flanked with old warehouses and brick buildings. Some of them looked grimy and run-down, others fancied up into loft apartments and stores and coffee shops and offices, with medium-height buildings on either side, but still there was no sign of human life.

There was one encouraging sign. Someone had pushed all the cars and trucks to the sides, so that there was a clear path down the street. That had to have been done since the Change.

*No, make that* two *encouraging signs,* Eddie thought.

There weren't many bodies around, or much of the faint lingering sweetish smell he'd become used to, either; anywhere near the main roads or most of the cities they'd passed through you couldn't escape it, and the whole area just south of Portland had been like an open mass grave. It gave him the willies—not because he cared about bodies themselves, but because he knew they bred disease. And because they were an unfortunate reminder of how easy it was to join the majority of nonsurvivors.

He doubted that one in three of the people who'd been around before the Change still were.

*Food I can count on getting, as long as anyone does,* he thought. *But those fevers . . . man, you can't shiv a germ.*

"Maybe we should have kept the bitches," Mack said.

They trudged along the middle of the road—it was the safest place to be, now that guns didn't work anymore and it wasn't so easy to hurt someone out of arm's reach.

"Sandy was real pretty and she'd stopped crying all the time," the big man concluded mournfully.

"We couldn't keep 'em unless you were planning on eating 'em. Which, except as what we people who read books call a metaphor, we weren't—"

He stopped, holding up a hand for silence before he went on: "I hear something. Up that next road on the left."

The big man beside him wheeled; he was wearing a football helmet, and carrying a sledgehammer with an eight-pound head over one shoulder. His jacket had slabs they'd cut from steel-belted tires fastened over most of it, too.

Eddie had added a Home Depot machete slung over his shoulder in an improvised harness, but hadn't tried to add much protection to his pre-Change outfit—he disliked anything that restricted his speed. They both wore backpacks; Mack's held their most precious possession, what was left of a twenty-pound sack of beef jerky. He *hoped* it was beef, at least—it was what they'd traded the girls for, that and two cartons of Saltines, some peanuts and a precious surviving six-pack of Miller.

He'd considered staying with that gang, but he'd gotten a bad vibe from them all, the way they looked at him, and especially at Mack, like they were noting how much meat he had on his bones.

*I'm not really sure they wanted the bitches just to fuck 'em, either,* he thought. *Ass is cheap these days if you've got food. And they didn't look very hungry. Sorta suspicious.*

"Someone's coming," Mack said.

"Yeah. That's why we're *here,*" Eddie said reasonably. "To meet someone. Now shut up and let me think."

There were a *lot* of people coming, from the sound of it. They stepped back towards the curb, between two trucks.

The young man's eyes went wide, then narrowed appraisingly.

The first men to turn the corner were armed—a dozen with crossbows, which gave Eddie a case of pure sea-green envy; he was still kicking himself for not getting one of those right after the Change, when the sporting-goods stores and outfitters hadn't all been stripped. The other twenty or so carried polearms; murderous-looking stabbing spears seven feet long. He'd seen the like elsewhere. What really interested him was their other gear.

They all wore armor; sleeveless tunics covered in overlapping rows of U-shaped scales punched out of sheet metal somehow; they had conical steel helmets with strips at the front to protect their noses, and kite-shaped shields of plywood covered in sheet metal, painted black with a red eye in the center.

Behind them came more people; not armed, but looking businesslike, many carrying tools—sledgehammers, pry bars, saws, and dragging dollies. Behind *them* came flatbeds and improvised wagons of half a dozen types. The people drawing the vehicles were handcuffed to them, and looked a lot thinner and more ragged than the others. One of the wagons, the last, bore bodies—some fresh, many the wasted skeletons held together by gristle that littered the ground around cities elsewhere. Now he saw why the city itself was less rancid; someone was cleaning house, doing the rounds of buildings where people had dragged themselves to die.

*And I sort of suspect that these guys just pushed people out of town to get rid of them, now,* he thought. *Pushed 'em out before the food was all gone. That's why the dead're so thick south of town. Clever.*

And there was a honcho, in a rickshaw-like arrangement, sort of a giant tricycle, pedaled by another of the thin-looking men; men who worked like machines with their eyes cast permanently down. The passenger was black and solidly built and wearing a dashiki and little beaded flowerpot hat; one hand held a fly whisk, the other a clipboard.

The . . . *soldiers, I suppose; unless they're the only racially integrated street gang outside a movie* . . . stopped and leveled their weapons.

Eddie smiled broadly, raising his hands palm-out. "Hey, no problem. You guys the law around here?"

"We are the law and the prophets," the black man said, in a deep rich voice. "We are the nobody-fucks-with-us Portland Protective Association, and you'd better believe it."

"Where do we join?" Eddie asked.

Several of the spearmen looked at each other out of the corners of their eyes and grinned, not a pleasant expression. The man in the pedicab waved his fly whisk eastward.

"That way. Here."

He handed over two disks on strings; squinting at his, Eddie saw "Probationary Applicant" printed on it.

"Being an Associate of the PPA isn't all that easy, but you can try—and they'll find you something to do. Those let you go straight through to headquarters, and man, you do *not* want to be caught wandering about."

He made a lordly gesture with the fly whisk, and the two wanderers headed east. Signs of order increased; traffic on foot and on bicycles and in weird tandem arrangements hauling cargo, an occasional group of marching armored troops . . . and at what had been the green lawns of Couch Park, a huge pit.

Thick acrid black smoke poured out of it; a gas tanker stood nearby, feeding lines that spurted burning gasoline over the deep hole. Eddie watched a handcart pulled through a gap in the raw earth berm around the fire pit; it was heaped with skeletal bodies, some no more than bones held together by rotting gristle, some nauseatingly fresh and juicy, swarming with maggots or tunneled by exploring rats. Even now he gagged a little at the smell of the smoke, and of the carts lined up to feed it. He supposed the gasoline kept the fires hot enough that flesh and bone themselves would burn.

"Why're they doing that, Eddie?" Mack asked.

"Not enough room or time to bury them all," Eddie said. *This bunch doesn't fuck around,* he added silently to himself. "Rotting bodies make people sick, Mack."

The big man nodded, looking nervous. You could fight to take food or anything else you wanted, or to fend off a band after your own goods or the meat on your bones. But you couldn't fight typhus, or cholera, or the nameless fevers that had taken off nearly as many people as the great hunger, or the new sickness people whispered about, the black plague.

They went past the line of dead-carts; the guards keeping the workers to their tasks on that detail wore scarves over their mouths, and stood well back. Another civilian overseer—this time a fussy-looking middle-aged white accountant type—intercepted them. Besides his clipboard, he wore a suit and tie, the first one Eddie had seen since right after the Change.

"Doesn't anyone *listen*?" he half shrieked, looking at the disks around their necks. "South from here! See that building?"

He pointed to a tall glass-sheathed tower with beveled edges. As Eddie followed the finger, he saw a rhythmic blink of light from the roof; some sort of coded signal, worked with lights.

"That's the Fox Tower. Stop two blocks west of it and then turn south. Straight south to the Park Blocks; that's where the sorting is today. And you'd better be careful; the Protector himself is there this time!"

"The Protector?" Eddie asked. "He the man, here?"

The clerk's lips went tight. "You'll see. And you'd better be respectful."

Eddie looked at the line of spears, and the burning ground. Several other pillars of black smoke rose from the city, and now that he knew what they were he could easily tell them from the ordinary plumes from random fires.

"Oh, yeah, *duibuqi,* so sorry, *no* disrespecting, man. None at *all.*"

The streets were mostly empty; the long rectangle of park swarmed. Several of the big grassy areas had been fenced off; some held horses, others men learning to *ride* horses; one fell off and staggered to his feet clutching an arm as Eddie watched.

Much of the rest of the park had been converted to vegetable gardens; a whiff told him where the fertilizer had come from. And another line of spearmen was prodding several score men with disks around their necks towards a small baseball park with bleachers, the kind neighborhood kids would have used back before the Change. Another man with a clipboard waited there; he had a belt with tools around his waist; beside him cooks were boiling something in big pots over wood fires. It smelled like porridge of some sort, and Eddie could hear Mack's stomach rumbling.

The man with the tools shouted for silence.

"All right," he said, when the newcomers had damped down the rumble of their talk. "First thing, anyone lies to us is *really* going to regret it—but not for long. Understand?"

Eddie preempted Mack's question: "He means if you lie and they find out, they'll off you."

"Oh," Mack said, nodding thoughtfully.

"We need skilled workers," Mr. Handyman went on. "Any blacksmiths first and foremost. Farriers too."

*"Well, that lets us out,"* Eddie murmured; the closest he'd come to blacksmithing was a few hours of shop in high school, and he didn't even recognize the name for the other trade.

"Plumbers, fitters, machinists, bricklayers, carpenters," the man went on. "Doctors, dentists. Gardeners and farmers too. Line up over there at the desks and give the details. And people, do *not* lie. General laborers over here."

*Over here* had another bunch of tough guards, and a bin full of metal collars.

*No, not my thing,* Eddie thought.

There was a scattering of men and women sitting in the bleachers around the baseball field, mostly close up by home base. There were also racks of weapons near the entrance—spears and shields—and an alert-looking squad with crossbows.

Eddie nodded, unsurprised. *Yeah. An elimination event.*

Also there was a big horse-drawn carriage, the type they'd used to show tourists around town before the Change; it had four glossy black horses hitched to it, and another couple standing saddled nearby, with collared servants holding them. Plus six or seven big armored men, standing by their mounts. Eddie's status-antennae fingered them for muscle.

One more servant sat in the carriage, holding up a lacy parasol—a blond chick, and a real stunner, dressed in something out of a pervert's catalogue and a silver collar. Across from her was a woman in her twenties, a brunette—no collar, and a fancy dress. Leaning back against the side of the carriage with his arms negligently spread along the top of the door was a tall man who seemed to be clad in a rippling metal sheath.

A little closer, and Eddie could see that it was armor—

thousands of small burnished stainless-steel washers, held on to a flexible backing with little copper rivets through the holes in their center; it clad the man from neck to knees, slit up the back and front so that he could ride a horse.

Around his narrow waist he wore a leather belt carrying a long double-edged sword and a dagger; over his broad shoulders went a black silk cloak; on his feet high black boots with golden spurs on the heels. A servant nearby held his shield and a helmet, hammered steel with hinged cheek-pieces and a tall raven-feather plume.

The face above the glittering armor was narrow and aquiline; the hazel eyes that surveyed the field were the coldest the young man had ever seen. Eddie estimated his age somewhere between thirty and forty; that sort of bony look didn't show the years much.

*I think I'm in love,* he grinned to himself. *Man, this dude is bad! Look at those chicks, that carriage, that gear, all of this. I want a piece of it. Oh, sweet motherfucking Jesus, do I!*

"Hey!" he shouted aloud. "I didn't come here to shovel shit. I came here to join the Association and *fight.* I want to be with you when you move *out* of Portland."

Mack rumbled agreement, and about a dozen others among the crowd did as well; none of them had come through since the Change looking plump but they were notably less gaunt than the others.

The man in the coat of rings shifted his gaze to Eddie, coming erect with lazy grace. He walked nearer, the muscle just behind.

"And what makes you think we're leaving Portland?" he said softly; he had an educated man's voice, calm and precise.

Eddie met his eyes, forcing himself not to flinch or show the sudden rush of cold anxiety that ran from crotch up to stomach.

"Because that's where it all is, now," he said. "The farmers and the farms, that's everything. If you've got them, you've *got* everything."

A guard bristled. "You call the Protector 'sir', cocksucker, or 'Protector'."

A thin brow crooked up, and the man raised a hand for quiet. "Why did you come into town, then?"

"I figured, what with the panic and all, probably not all

the food got eaten right after the Change. Just the stuff in stores, maybe canned goods in warehouses, that sort of thing. But the bulk stuff, the wheat and like that in the silos and elevators, maybe on ships, a lot of it wouldn't get taken. Whoever got a grip on that could build up their own army—and it'll take an army to squeeze those farmers out in the valley. Freelancing don't cut it anymore. I heard some rumors about you, and I figured that was what was going on. Protector. Sir."

"Well, well, well," the lord of Portland said. "We've got one with brains. Perhaps I'll have a use for you. Any education?"

Eddie shrugged and grinned. "Two years community college," he said. "And the school of hard knocks."

"More hard knocks we can arrange," the man said. He nodded his head towards the baseball field. "It takes a special sort of man to be an Associate. We have a little contest first, a chance to show your quality. The winners are inducted into our ranks, if they're not too badly crippled."

Eddie nodded. "Figured it would be like that, from your setup," he said calmly. "One question, Protector?" At the nod he went ahead. "How come you figured things out so fast?"

The man smiled, and gestured another bristling guard back. "I was a man who realized what the Change meant," he said.

He clapped his hands sharply. "Let the play-offs begin!"

# CHAPTER FIFTEEN

"I'm surprised," Will Hutton said a week later. "Hadn't expected gratitude to last so long, but they still love us."

Havel grinned as he watched the bustle of the Bearkiller camp; the fresh morning air smelled of horses and canvas, cooking meat and baking bread and a little of dust and earth.

"I don't think they really needed those tents they gave us," he said, holding his horse's bridle beneath the jaw and stroking its nose. "And word about the cannibals spread pretty quick. The story didn't lose any in the telling, I bet, either."

Gustav tried to nuzzle his face; he pushed it away with his right palm. Horses were a bit like St. Bernards when they got affectionate, given to slobbering all over you with the drooling jaws of love. The powerful earthy-grassy scent of the big gelding was strong in his nostrils. Will Hutton had picked it for him, twelve hundred pounds of agile muscle and endurance, a descendant of Steel Dust and Shiloh on his dam's side, crossed with Hutton's Hanoverian stallion.

The tents the locals had donated were National Guard standard, meant to sleep eight men; a row of them stretched across a green meadow not far from the Clearwater. Families and groups of the unattached milled about each in the morning chill, getting ready for the day. The wagons were nearby; one of them was a ranch-style chuckwagon; Angelica had hugged the vehicle and kissed the tilt when it arrived. The horse lines lay a little beyond, and beyond that the ground sloped up towards the west; stock drifted over it, watched by mounted herders.

The cattle and sheep had been surplus to local needs too, but the extra horses were *very* welcome. So were the four precious milch cows and their calves.

Havel pushed his helmet back by the nasal, so that the padding of the lower rim rested on his scalp and he had an unobstructed view; it was becoming a gesture as natural as breathing. The long shadows of men and horses stretched before him towards the west, and the wind was gratefully cool through the steel rings of his armor. More and more of the Bearkillers drifted in, until he was ringed by faces old and new.

*So much for making a quiet exit,* he thought. *Christ, we talked about the trip long enough.*

The Larssons were there, and Pamela, and a scattering of others—Aaron leaning on his crutch, and Billy Waters too for some reason.

"I still think it's a bit risky to send you," Will grumbled. "Yeah, we *do* need a detailed scout of the way we're headed—news just plain spreads too slow and gets too garbled. It's purely foolish to keep the whole shebang pokin' ahead into the blue. So sending Eric 'n' Josh I can see. Why you, though?"

"I like to see the ground I'm going to be operating through," Havel said patiently—he'd listened to the same argument for days. "And I can bargain for us, arrange safe passage and make deals."

*Plus personal reasons,* he added to himself; Signe was hanging back, looking sheepish. *Not her fault, but . . .*

"You can run the camp well enough, Will."

The Texan grinned. "I surely can; hell, I may even get some horse wranglin' in. I'll just tell 'em if they think *I'm* tough, wait until *Lord Bear* gets back."

Havel winced slightly. "Well, whatever works. And you're needed for teaching—so are Pam and most of the others. How many newbies have we got now?"

"Twenty-seven, countin' the kids and the teenager we rescued. Eighteen grown men and women."

"Right, and they all need to know the basics," Havel said. "Half of them have never forked a horse and none of them have ever picked up a sword. We need a long stop for that anyway, and to get the bowmaking operation and the

other stuff going. Three men with a good string of remounts can travel *fast*. I should be back in about a month."

He paused. "Hey, Astrid," he called.

She started, pulling her eyes from a red-tailed hawk circling high above.

"It's your birthday next week, isn't it?"

She nodded. He turned and took a parcel out of his
saddlebag.

"Eric and I found this for you. I know you miss that
*Lord of the Rings* you had. We won't be here on the day,
so—"

The wrapping was plain brown paper, but she gave a
suppressed squeal, slung her bow over her shoulder, and
took it eagerly.

Havel hid a grin as she jumped from one foot to the
other and tried to undo the knots.

*Sort of gives you an idea of what she would be like as a
normal teenager, yakking for hours on the phone or mooning over some idiot musician,* he thought.

She gave up on the knots and drew her hunting knife to
cut the string.

"It's a *complete set*!" she burbled. The books were bound
in gray, with a golden ring and a lidless eye on the cover.

"Ohmigod! The Allen and Unwin hardcovers!" A quick
glance inside. "A *first edition* Allen and Unwin with the
foldout pocket maps intact! A—" she choked. "A *signed
first edition! Ohmigod!*"

Unexpectedly she threw herself at him and hugged him
hard; even through the mail and padding it made him give
back half a pace and go *ooof!* Usually she hated touching
anyone.

"Hey, kid, watch it—you're still holding that knife! And
Eric did a lot of the looking too."

*And the original owner is dead,* he thought, with a touch
of inner grimness. *Suicide.*

She gave her brother a perfunctory nod of thanks; he
rolled his eyes. Then there was a flurry of handshakes and
slaps on the back. Thankfully, nobody else tried to hug him.

Signe was the last. "It's my birthday soon too," she said.

"Ah . . . didn't have anything to give," he replied awkwardly.

"Yes you do," she said, and threw her arms around his neck.

The kiss went on for a long time, and grew hungry. He was dimly aware of whoops and laughter in the background; this time both Astrid and Eric were rolling their eyes, and Astrid made a theatrical gagging sound. Her brother might have made the same finger-down-throat gesture if Luanne Hutton hadn't decided to emulate her friend and caught him in a clinch; Astrid's nausea redoubled.

"I'll be waiting," Signe said, when she drew back.

"So will I," Havel answered; he had to catch his breath and clear his throat before he could finish the brief phrase.

He put his foot in the stirrup and swung into the saddle with a grunt and a rustling clink and clatter. Josh Sanders finished his good-byes to wife and child and mounted likewise.

"Eric!" Havel barked. "Tear yourself away from the tonsillectomy and get on the goddamned horse!"

The other two men fell in behind him; Eric was leading their packhorse-and-remount string. Havel took a deep breath and looked west. Running the outfit was a challenge, and worthwhile work. Getting away for a while, though . . .

"Thataway!" he said, and brought his horse up to a canter.

The crowd parted, cheering; Eric and Josh turned to wave as the hooves crunched and clattered.

Havel kept his eyes on the gravel road that stretched like a silver-gray ribbon into the green hills.

*All I've seen so far is a worm's-eye view of wilderness and a few little towns,* he thought. *It's time and past time to find out how other people are dealing with this new world we've been handed.*

*"NO!"*

Juniper Mackenzie added her voice to the chorus of a hundred others; all the adults within walking distance of this spot, in fact. The foragers approaching from the west slowed uncertainly as they heard it, a few of them ringing the bells on their bicycles as if that would clear the road. There weren't as many of them—forty or fifty, she estimated—but they all had some sort of weapon, and they had a bicycle-drawn cart behind.

"*NO! NO! NO!*"

The face-off was taking place well away from her cabin—what they'd taken to calling the Hall—down in the flatlands to the west. She could see the outskirts of the little town of Sutterdown to the north, over the tops of the pines lining a creek. Her twenty clansfolk, the neighborhood farmers and the townsmen were a collection of clumps making a rough line north and south through the shaggy overgrown pasture of the fields on either side of the road. The roadway itself was a two-lane county blacktop, and quite thoroughly blocked with a semi that had skidded across it on the day of the Change; nobody was going to move it anytime soon, since the cargo had been sacks of cement.

*Must get a wagon down here to haul some of it off,* she thought with some corner of her mind. *We can use it.*

There were so many people here, and they were so loud—but it still seemed quiet, quiet and empty: The noises were all of human voices and feet and hands, no drone or roar of engines. You noticed more without that burr of background noise. The sound of grass and twigs under feet, the smell of angry unwashed men . . .

The foragers stopped, and the shouting chorus grumbled away into a buzz of voices. That sank into near-silence as a man walked forward waving a white flag on the end of a pole. He wore a policeman's uniform, much the worse for hard use; a mousey-looking woman accompanied him, with a clipboard in her hands. He carried a much more practical hunting crossbow, with a knife and hatchet at his belt, and wore an army-style helmet.

"Listen!" he called, when he'd come close. "We're here by order of Acting Governor Johnson to requisition a quota of supplies for emergency redistribution—"

Juniper gripped her bow and bared her teeth; that was the second Acting Governor since the Change, which made an average of one about every two weeks and a bit, and nobody knew what had happened to the incumbent. In practice, what was left of the state government had no power more than two days from Salem by bicycle.

*Which unfortunately includes our land, just.*

The chorus of *NO!* erupted again; she could see Reverend Dixon of Sutterdown a ways to her left, leading the beat. Odd to be chanting at *his* direction; the man had ignored her friendly clergy-to-clergy letter before the Change, and been openly hostile since—evidently he thought Jehovah had sent the disaster as a punishment for tolerating the wrong people, of which Juniper and her friends were most certainly an example.

"Suffer not a witch to live" was a favorite of his.

The chorus died down again, and unexpectedly the mousy-looking woman shouted into the quiet: "How can you be so *selfish?* Half the people in Portland are sitting in camps around Salem and Albany now—gangsters have taken over Portland and driven them out—people are *dying*! Dying of hunger, hunger and disease—little children are starving to death!"

*Sweet Goddess gentle and strong, aid me now.* Her hand traced the Invoking sign. *Great Ogma, Lord of Eloquence, lend me your golden tongue to calm these troubled waters.*

Dixon was about to speak. Juniper opened her mouth to forestall him—the minister was definitely of the tribe who saw all problems as nails and themselves as a hammer. Or the Fist of God, in his case.

"No!" she said, and held up her bow to stop the chant when it threatened to start again. She continued into the ringing silence: "No, we will not give you our food. Not because we grudge help, but because we have little ones of our own to think of. If we gave you all that we have, you'd be starving again in a week—and so would we! Starving to *death,* before the crops came in! And we need our stock to pull plows and carts, and breed more for the years to come. You've already taken more than we can spare."

"You're as bad as those people in Corvallis," the woman said bitterly.

Juniper's ears pricked up at that, but she made her voice stern: "If you want to do something for those poor city people, get them moving," she went on, pointing over her shoulder at the distant snowpeaks of the Cascades floating against heaven. "East of the mountains, to where there's more. Or set them to work planting, find them seeds and tools. Or both. We'll help all we can with either. Don't keep them sitting until they die!"

*Something's wrong,* Juniper thought suddenly, as the woman opened her mouth again—most likely to plead for anything they could spare.

A harsh voice spoke from the ranks of the local folk; not one of her clan, probably a farmer: "Not as easy as beating people up when you outnumber them, or robbing us one by one, is it, you useless thieving bastards?"

"Wrong, wrong, wrong," Juniper said under her breath, her eyes flickering over the foragers as they bristled with anger, feeling the future shifting like tumbling rocks. "Watch out—"

Sam Aylward's thick-muscled arm brushed her aside. She staggered back, turning and waving her arms to recover balance. That let her see the crossbow bolt hit his shoulder with a flat hard *smack* sound, and a ringing under it, and to know it would have hit *her* if she hadn't moved—or been moved.

The short thick bolt hit glancingly and bounced away, because the Englishman was wearing the first of Dennie's brigandine jacks—a sleeveless shirt made from two layers of canvas with little thumb-sized metal plates riveted between. One of them peeped out through the ripped fabric now, the metal bright where the head of the bolt had scored it, then going dull red as blood leaked through.

Everything moved very slowly after that. She let the stagger turn her back westward. The Salem folk were looking at one of their own; he stood by their cart and frantically spanned his crossbow to reload. On both sides people shifted their grips on improvised weapons, some edging backward, others leaning forward like dogs against a leash.

Somehow she could hear the *whirr* of the crank as the man who'd shot at her spun it; even louder was the creak of Aylward's great yellow bow as he drew to the ear.

*Snap-wuffft!* String against bracer; whistle of cloven air.

The distance was only thirty feet; the arrow was traveling two hundred feet a second when it left the string, and to the human eye it was nothing but a bright blur in the sunlight. Then *tock* as it struck bone, smashing into the cross-bowman's face and slamming him brutally back against the cart.

*Snap-wuffft! Snap-wuffft!*

Two more of the cloth-yard shafts hit the man, bare

inches apart in his chest, the gray-goose fletching bobbing as he slumped, held up by the deep-driven heads punched through him and into the boards. Aylward had a fourth shaft on his string, half-drawn, the point shifting back and forth in deadly menace.

"Don't try it!" he roared as blood poured down the dying man's body, trickled down his own side. "Don't you bloody try it!"

Juniper felt the crystalline balance of the moment that followed, silent enough that she could hear the wind that cuffed at her hair and the scrabble of the dead man's heels as they drummed on the asphalt. She slung her bow and stepped forward into that quiet, between the two forces. The thought of hands clenching on ax hafts, fingers trembling on bowstrings and crossbow triggers was distant, remote.

*"Stop!"* she shouted, filling her lungs and pitching it to carry. *"Stop right now!"*

The moment sighed away, and people were looking at her. The trained singer's voice let her reach them all.

"There's been enough blood shed today." She spread her arms wide and up, palms towards the west. "Go back. There's nothing for you here. We don't want to hurt you, but we'll fight for our homes and our children if we must. Go! Get out!"

"Out!" Other voices took it up. *"OUT! OUT!"*

Aylward's eyes were gray and bleak and level as he waited. One by one the foragers turned and mounted their bicycles and left; Juniper let out a sigh.

"You felt it too, then?" Aylward said, as she passed a shaky hand over her face.

"Felt what?" she asked.

"The flux. We might have pulled it off without killing, if that loudmouth bugger hadn't up and told them to sod off. Nice work, Lady, the way you turned it around after that. I wasn't looking forward to a massacre."

She nodded absently, swallowing against a quick nausea.

He went on: "It's a gift, feeling the flux—situational awareness, the officers call it. Maybe you've the makings of a soldier."

"And maybe you've the makings of a Witch," she answered.

Then her giddy relief drained away, remembering the savage maul-on-wood sound of the arrowhead striking bone.

"I know you saved my life, Sam, but . . . Goddess Mother-of-All, can't we stop killing each other even *now?*"

Aylward shrugged. "Never," he said with conviction. "And especially not now. You said it—there just isn't enough to go 'round, not if it were shared ever so fair."

Juniper nodded bleakly. "Then you and Chuck have the right of it," she said.

At his questioning look, she touched her bow: "*I thought they'd* think we could all shoot like you, but that was a bluff, and bluffs get called if you go on long enough. *Ná nocht d'fhiacla go bhféadair an greim do bhreith!*"

"Which means?"

She shook herself. "Sorry. Don't bare your teeth until you can bite!"

"You'll push for more practice, then?"

"Starting tomorrow."

"Watch that!" Chuck Barstow shouted, striding over to where the older children were whacking with wooden swords at poles set in the dirt—and occasionally at each other.

"You can hurt someone with those things! Do it the way I showed you or I'll take them away."

It was an excuse to stop for a while. Juniper lowered her bow gratefully and rubbed at her left shoulder. The bright spring day caressed her face with a soft pine-scented breeze down from the mountains. It cut the haze, too, perfect for militia practice in the flower-starred meadows below her cabin.

Militia was what it was, even if a few were set on calling it the *war band* or the *spear levy*.

*You know, I thought it was just a harmless bit of speechifying to call this a clan,* she thought. *A bit of playacting to distract people from how close to death we all were—are.*

Wiccans were given to romantic archaisms and usually it was harmless enough; she'd been known to indulge in them herself, and not just for professional reasons. Now, though . . .

*I may have let a genie out of the bag. Words have power!*

Sally Quinn was in charge of the children and absolute beginners, most of them using what they'd scavenged from sporting-goods stores; she had the same fiberglass target bow she'd carried the day Juniper met her. She patiently went through the basics of stance and draw, and occasionally let them shoot a practice shaft at the board-and-dirt targets. Fortunately modern bows with their stiff risers and centerline arrow-shelves were a lot easier to learn than the ancient models.

Sam Alyward had the more advanced pupils; he'd turned out enough longbows for all, courtesy of her woodpile.

*Thank You,* she thought to the Lord of the Forest, and stepped back to watch Aylward demonstrate.

*His* stave had a hundred-pound draw. When he shot, the *snap* of the string against the bracer seemed to trip on the *smack* of the arrowhead hitting the deer-shaped target fifty yards away, and the malignant quiver of the shaft that followed. Between was only a blurred streak; she forced herself not to dwell on the hard *tock* of an arrowhead sledging into bone.

He sent three more arrows on the way at five-second intervals, all of them landing in a space a palm could have covered, then turned to her. The Englishman was sweating, but then everyone was. Sweating as hard as they had during the planting, which she almost remembered with nostalgia. The cheerful noise made it plain everyone *thought* this was more fun, though.

"Shoulder sore, Lady?" he said gravely.

"Just a bit," Juniper replied; in fact, it ached.

"Then you should knock off," he said. "Watch for a while instead. Push too hard too soon, and you're courting a long-term injury. You may be over-bowed for a beginner."

"I don't think so. Forty pounds isn't so much when you've fiddled for hours straight! But I will take a break."

She braced the lower tip of her bow against the outside of her left foot, stepped through with her right and bent it against her thigh to unstring it. She called the weapon Artemis, after the Greek archer-goddess, and although getting the trick of it was harder, she'd discovered she actually liked using it, far more than the crossbow.

When she glanced up from the task, she saw Aylward looking over at the children, and smiling with a gentle fondness you wouldn't suspect from his usual gruff manner.

*Or from the feel of his hands when he's teaching unarmed combat!* she thought, grinning. *Chucking folk about, as he calls it.*

The important thing was that with Aylward around, they had someone who really understood this business; for starters, he could *make* the bows, and their strings, and the arrows. In the long run, that would be *very* important. The machine-made fiberglass sporting toys hadn't stopped working the way guns had, but the prying roots of vine and tree had already begun their reconquest of factories and cities. In a generation those wastelands of concrete and asphalt would be home to owl and fox and badger, not men.

Dennis had made them all quivers, and waterproof waxed-leather cases for the bows that clipped alongside them; she reached back and slid hers home. She was wearing a brigandine now as well, like the one that had saved Sam Aylward from the crossbow bolt meant for her; the jack was hot even in the mild April air, and weighed twenty-five pounds. When you added in the sword and dagger and buckler—the latter was a little steel shield about the size and shape of a soup plate—it took a good deal of getting used to.

*Which is why I'm wearing it,* she thought glumly. *To get used to moving in it.*

Unlike most of the Mackenzies, she didn't see all this as a combination RenFaire and holiday, despite the moon-and-antlers design on the breast of all the jacks.

*It's not like Society gear. It's* real *and I hate the necessity. Fate throws us all into the soup, and we're still killing each other.*

She watched the shooting for a while; Aylward was a good teacher, firm but calm and endlessly patient. At last he looked up at the sun and spoke: "Break for dinner!"

Juniper suppressed a smile; the man had some old-fashioned turns of phrase. A clatter continued when all else fell quiet. Chuck Barstow was sparring with the two young men who'd come in with his brother, Vince Torelli and Steve Matucheck. Sword-and-buckler work was an active style, and they were leaping and foining in a pattern as acrobatic and pleasing to the eye as a dance. She'd never felt a desire to join in when she was busking at Society events, but it looked pretty; now that she'd done a fair bit with the other neophytes, she could even say it was fun in an active sort of way.

*If you can forget what happens when it's done with edged metal rather than padded sticks.*

Chuck jerked back from the waist to dodge a strike, then leapt to let the other sword pass beneath his boots. His buckler banged down on Vince's helmet; the blow was pulled, but it still gave a solid bonging thump that sent the younger man down clutching at his head. In the same instant he caught Steve's sword-blow with his own, locked the guards, put a foot behind his opponent's leg and threw him staggering backward with a twist of shoulder and hips. A lizard-swift thrust followed, leaving Steve white with shock as the blunt wooden point tapped him on the base of the throat.

Cheers burst out; Mary and Sanjay and Daniel rushed over and nearly knocked Chuck over himself in their enthusiasm.

"Dad's the best!" they chorused. "Dad's the best!"

Little Tamsin stumped around crowing and waving her arms, happy because her father was the center of attention. He scooped her up onto his shoulder, tucked Mary and Daniel each under an arm and let Sanjay proudly rack his equipment as he staggered over towards the trestle tables.

*Quick work,* Juniper thought.

It hadn't been long before the rescued children realized they weren't going home, or at least before most stopped talking about it; shared hunger and fear and unaccustomed hard work had probably sped up the process, and the sheer strangeness of everything.

*Now, is it a good sign of healthy resilience that some of them have started calling their foster parents Mom and Dad, or is it unhealthy denial and transference? I don't think those three in particular* had *parents before, not really, just people who paid the bills.*

"Lad knows his business as far as the moves go," Aylward said thoughtfully. "Hope he doesn't freeze up when the red wine's served for true, though."

Juniper shivered slightly and changed the subject. "You've settled in better than most, Sam," she said. "I'd have thought it would be harder for you, being so far from home."

For a moment the square, good-humored Saxon face went bleak. "It'll be worse back there," he said. "Sixty million people in one little island? It doesn't bear thinking of, and at least I don't have to watch it."

Juniper winced slightly and swallowed. *Any more than I do Los Angeles or New York,* she thought. *Or Mexico City or Tokyo or . . .*

He shook his shoulders. "Besides, I've no near kin to home, no wife or child, and even before the Change . . . it's not really the place I grew up in, not anymore it isn't— wasn't. Full of commuters, bought all the old cottages up and gussified them, they did. *And* the local farmers were all for ripping out hedges and trees and getting rid of their livestock and making the place look like bloody Canada; fat lot of good their combines and thousand-acre fields of hybrid barley will be to them now, eh?"

He shook his head. "I'd just been playing, fossicking about with this and that, since I mustered out of the SAS. Traveling, making bows, doing a little hunting."

"They must have a generous pension plan," Juniper said teasingly.

"Not bloody likely!" he said with a grin. "But my da had a bit put by—from selling the farm about the time my mother died and I went for a soldier, you see. Left it to me; fair knackered I was, when I found out, since he'd done naught but live in a cheap flat in Portsmouth and haunt the pubs. Thought he'd drunk it up years ago . . ."

Then he looked at her with his head slightly to one side: "You've a gift for getting people talking, don't you, Lady?"

Juniper grinned. "What can I say? I'm a Witch, a singer, and a storyteller—all three. So . . . the Change interrupted your life as a gentleman of leisure?"

"That it did." A shrug. "Play's all very well, but a man's life is his work; I've got a real job of work to do here."

*Well, that's more than Mr. Strong and Silent's said before,* she thought, giving him a genial slap on the shoulder; it was like hitting an oak beam. *Lord and Lady be thanked for sending him our way!*

Everyone headed for the trestle-tables and the fires with the soup cauldrons; on a day like this, it was a relief to do things out-of-doors. Juniper shed her battle gear—they had two-by-four racks set up for it—and got in line. Diana grinned at her as she ladled the Eternal Soup into bowls.

"You know, Juney, one of the things I enjoyed most about running MoonDance was looking up recipes and planning the menu?"

Juniper laughed out loud, despite the rumbling of her stomach. "And what's on the menu today, Di?"

"Eternal Soup, Eternal Soup, or today's extra-special dish: delicious *zuppa di eterno.*"

"Eternal Soup!" Juniper made her eyes go wide. "What a surprise! Still, I think I'll have something from the dessert tray instead, and some nice organic hazelnut coffee."

Diana gave a sour laugh and plopped her ladle into Juniper's bowl. Her husband, Andy, gave her a platter of wild-greens salad, half a hard-boiled egg, and one precious baking-powder biscuit.

There was also a great jug of rich Jersey milk fresh from their—single—milking cow. But that was for the children and Dorothy Rose, who was pregnant; birth control was already getting more difficult, and there would be a couple of babies before Yule.

Juniper's nose twitched as she carried the big bowl of soup over to her table. It actually smelled pretty good today, probably because they'd been getting in a little game and wild herbs—dandelion roots, fireweed shoots—plus Andy had thrown in some more of the soup barley and miso stock from their restaurant-store's inventory, plus a little pasta from the Fairfax storehouse.

They were always talking about butchering one of the steers or sheep, and always kept putting it off until absolutely necessary—everyone was worried about the gap between the preserved foods and the first harvest, with the way their numbers had grown. They had plenty of grass to keep the beasts hale, courtesy of the Willamette's mild climate and the way foragers had swept it bare of livestock.

"Mmmm," she said appreciatively as she hunted down the last barleycorn in her bowl with an eager spoon.

*I crave starch. In fact, I crave starch and fat and meat and sugar . . .*

Then she went for the salad; dandelion greens and henbit shoots and various other crunchy green things from the meadows and woods, about half of which she recognized; and some canned beets from the Fairfax stores, with the juice making do for salad dressing. It wasn't bad if you liked eating bitter lawn clippings drizzled with diluted vinegar. She saved the half-egg for last; it had a little paprika on the yolk, and a strong free-range taste. The biscuit had a chewy crust; she alternated bites with the egg, tiny nibbles to stretch out the flavor.

*In fact, I crave everything* except *dandelion greens.*

Judy Barstow licked her spoon: "You know, if there were a few more calories, this would be an ideal, healthy diet."

"Oh, shut up, you she-quack," Juniper grumbled, seconded by a few others.

Their nurse-midwife grinned unrepentantly; she'd gone from plump to merely opulent. For people doing hard physical labor every day, it was all about two-thirds of just barely enough, or at least that was what Juniper's stomach told her. Filling up on herbal tea was supposed to take away the empty feeling. It didn't; you just had to pee more often.

For a while there was only the clinking of spoons and the crunch of greenery between busy jaws. Then—

"Hamburgers," Diana said hollowly, looking at her own empty bowl.

"Shut up, Di," her husband said. *"Please."*

"Cheeseburgers with sautéed onions and maple-cured bacon. French fries—big, greasy home-fries with lots of salt. Pork chops, with the fat brown and crispy at the edge and collard greens on the side. Thai shrimp curry with basmati rice. Steamed snow peas. Fried eggplant with grated cheese. Barbecued ribs. Pasta with homemade tomato sauce and Parmesan melting on top. Mashed garlic potatoes with butter and chives. Bacon-lettuce-and-tomato sandwiches, the tomatoes just out of the garden and still sun-warm, dripping with mayo."

*"Shut up!"* It was several voices together now.

"Slabs of MoonDance fresh whole-wheat bread, brown and crusty, still steaming when you cut it, with organic butter melting into the surface. And jam, wild blueberry jam, and honey. German chocolate cake with coconut sprinkles on the frosting. Good Costa Rican coffee in a big mug with thick cream, while you eat a cinnamon-apple Danish and—"

*"Shut up!"* they all screamed in chorus; the children giggled, but nobody else was laughing.

Someone broke down and started that sort of drooling food-porn every second meal on average. It drove everyone else crazy; they would have thrown food if there had been any to spare.

Juniper used a dandelion leaf to wipe out the inside of her soup bowl, then sighed as her inner circle headed her way with rolled-up plans in their hands; Dennis had what looked like a big cake covered in a cloth . . .

*. . . and there I go thinking about food again!*

It turned out to be a scale model. Juniper looked at it in bemusement as Dennis whipped away the towel; then she looked at *him* and raised a brow as her glance dropped downward.

"Is that a *kilt* you're wearing, Dennie?"

He grinned at her. It was; the sewn, pleated skirtlike variety invented in the eighteenth century, not the true wrap-around Great Kilt of the ancient Gaels. The cloth was even tartan, of a sort, mostly green and brown with stripes of very dark blue.

"Isn't that made from one of that load of blankets we salvaged?" she said, pursing her lips as she struggled not to laugh.

*The ribbing* does *pass the time.*

"There's plenty," he said. "Nice strong wool, too. And it's quick and easy to make—Andy's got that sewing machine working off a treadle—and it wears longer than jeans."

"It's not even the Mackenzie tartan!"

"It is now," he said cheerfully. "Didn't you say the Victorians made up that stuff about clans having special tartans after the fact anyway? This is what we've got—we're the Mackenzies around here—it's the Mackenzie tartan if we say it is. QED."

She threw up her hands. *"Cuir sioa ar ghabhar agus is gabhar I gcónai é."*

"You calling me a goat?" he said, mock-frowning.

"No, just a Sassenach. A goat's a goat even in a silk coat, if you want a translation. But I suppose if you want to wear a pleated skirt, you can wear a pleated skirt. It's a harmless eccentricity."

She pointed at the wooden model his cunning wood-worker's fingers had put together. It showed the Hall built up to two stories, a duplicate not far away, more barns and sheds, and a high log wall around the whole irregular oblong of high ground on which the buildings rested.

"Now that—*that* is a menace! We've a limited amount of time and work, in case you hadn't noticed, and an infinity of things to do with both."

He grinned, but it was Alex Barstow who spoke up: "Actually, Juney, it's not crazy—we wouldn't build it all at once, of course, but we *do* need more room and we *do* need a defensive wall."

That put her brows up again. Alex was a housebuilder by trade, and he knew his business—she'd hired him for repairs before the Change, and knew others he'd done more ambitious work for.

Dennis spoke: "It's courtesy of Cascade Timber Inc. I remembered how you bitched and moaned back in 'ninety-six about having to sell them trees to pay taxes on this place, and then again when they went bankrupt and left it all on your hands. So I've been checking while I was out hunting—"

She heard a subdued snort, possibly from Sam Aylward; the only use Dennis had on a hunt was to scare the game into an ambush set by someone else.

"—and yeah, you have a *lot* of stacked logs in the woods here. Nicely seasoned by now, too. More than enough."

Alex nodded. "Log construction is fast and simple, and strong and warm if you do it right—square the top and bottom so they fit snug, deep-notch the ends—it just needs lots and lots of big high-quality logs. Back before the Change that was expensive, but we've *got* the logs, great big thirty-foot monsters."

He pointed to the middle of the model: "See, we've already started on the bathhouse. Now, the next thing we do is double the space in the Hall—your cabin. It's just a log box; the foundation's the difficult part, and that's already done. All we have to do is take off the roof, put on an extra story of log wall minus cutouts for windows, then put the same roof back on. This lean-to extension out back is the new kitchen, with those woodstoves we salvaged."

Diana nodded. "That'll save a lot of cooking time."

"And bingo, we have another three thousand square feet of living space," Alex enthused; his blond ponytail bobbed as he spoke.

"All right," Juniper said dubiously. "Much as I love every darling one of you, my treasures, I've grown fair weary of hearing you all snore, and that's the truth. But this Fort Apache arrangement—"

She pointed at the palisade that surrounded the buildings.

"Nah, that's not all that hard either," Alex said. "Actually, Chuck gave me the idea, something about how the ancient Gauls did it, plus some bits I remembered from a book on the frontier stations, you know, Kentucky in Daniel Boone's day. Look, the Hall's on an oblong rise, right? The sides slope back at about forty-five degrees and then it's flat on top, pretty well, except where the spring bubbles up and flows off the edge."

He pointed to the north. "Twenty-five, thirty feet above the level of the meadow here. So what we do is just dig a ditch halfway up the slope, say seven or eight feet deep. We stand a log upright, pour concrete around the base, then use that and some block and tackle to set the next log upright—next four or five—spiking them together and then pouring the base—and eventually we have a complete oblong log palisade. Really not too complicated, good and strong, and it'll last if we do the drainage right."

"Hmmm."

*Those poles are thirty feet tall. Fifteen feet of steep hill, then twenty feet of yard-thick logs above the surface. We would sleep better of a night.*

"Why not at the *top* of the slope, where it would be that much taller?" she said. "If we start the wall further down the slope, here will be a big notch between the inside of the wall and the flat top of the rise the Hall's on."

Alex's smile had a crackling enthusiasm that was hard to resist. "*That's* the good part! We do a little cutting and filling, and we've got a twelve-foot-deep ditch all around on the inside. Or a fieldstone-and-concrete-lined cellar, with a little more work. Good drainage, too."

"More than enough storage space for all our crops," Chuck cut in.

His brother burbled on: "Then we run more logs out from the flat to the wall, and plank 'em over, and we've got the floors above the cellars, and we plant the cabins—or workshops or whatever—overtop of that. Fighting platform for the wall goes above the roofs; and we pipe all the rainwater to cisterns, to help out the spring. We can get windows, doors, roofing shingle and plumbing fixtures from half a dozen abandoned places not far away, and sawn timber from that mill south of Lebanon—there's a couple of hundred thousand finished board feet sitting in their covered yard."

"Floors? Roofs?" Juniper said; she didn't have a painter's imagination, or a draughtsman's. Then: "Oh, of course!"

Alex nodded. "We use the palisade as the outside wall for the cabins, give every family their own bedroom and hearth. Sort of like log row housing—"

"And we *can* spare the people and horse teams, until harvest and fall plowing, so—"

Juniper sat back, smiling and nodding as the enthusiasm spread and the clan convinced itself.

*This will get a majority vote, no matter that it'll keep everyone working,* she thought. *It's good to have the Chief overridden now and then.* And *it's no bad thing to be busy, and tired at night. It keeps you from thinking about what you've lost, and* who *you've lost, and what the world is like right now outside our little enclave.*

She let herself cry for Rudy now and then, mostly at night. Sleep came quickly, a gift of the Mother-of-All, and her dreams of him had been good.

After a while most of the adults and half the children were crowded around the table, adding suggestions. Judy gave her own:

"And that'll give us a regular place to hold school lessons."

A subdued groan, but not much of one—after pulling weeds all day, even a ten-year-old could contemplate sitting still at a desk for a while.

"And a place for Esbats and Sabbats when it's too wet to use the *nemed*. The barn's smelly and it leaks."

Juniper nodded; her Sacred Wood with its eerie circle of oaks and stone-slab altar had made the Singing Moon Coven the envy of pagan Oregon, but when it settled into rain, come September or October here in the foothills, it *rained*. Sometimes the sky wept chill drizzle for weeks at a time.

"We'll have space for a Moon School as well," Judy said. "And for private Craft workings."

As Maiden, she was responsible for training; the children enjoyed it, too, a lot more than the conventional schoolwork.

"Right," Judy said, looking around. "All in favor?"

For a wonder, the vote was unanimous; that saved the effort of talking a holdout around. She preferred to work by consensus . . .

*Which the next bit will not be getting,* she thought. *Not without a lot of work.*

"Two more things we should be doing," she said. "And that's sending out . . . scouts. Emissaries, perhaps." A few frowns, more wonder.

She pointed eastward; the peaks of the Cascades stood there, long dark-green ridges rising to saw-toothed silhouettes against the afternoon sky.

"There's that old trail, the foot trail—it should be open by now. The main roads over the passes are far too dangerous, but nobody lives up there. You could ride over to the Bend country."

Andy and Diana both perked up. They'd owned a store-cum-restaurant before the Change, of the type that was always looking for a new source of fresh produce, and they'd gone on trips combing the backcountry for sources.

"Lot of ranching country over there," Andy said. "No big cities. They're probably in better shape than we are, at least for food."

Chuck mused thoughtfully, scratching in his new orange-yellow beard: "I remember from the museum—that exhibition, 'Cowboys in Legend and Reality'? Ranchers sell off about a third of their herds every year, the yearlings. They just keep the breeding heifers and some replacements. Bet they'd be willing to trade; cattle, sheep, maybe even horses. We could *really* use more horses and most of the livestock around here got eaten, so we've got lots of pasture that's going to waste. And if we had more cattle than we could use ourselves, the Horned Lord knows there are people who'd be glad to trade with us for them."

"What would we trade for *cattle?*" someone said; visions of barbecue danced in everyone's head at the thought—and a stomach rumbled, loudly, bringing a general chuckle.

"Oh, Sam's bows. Arrows," Juniper said.

She pointed to another table. It held boxes of stainless steel spoons, plus hammers and files and a section of railroad iron to use as an anvil. Spoons turned out to be the best possible starting-blank for a broadhead. Sam's outdoor workbench under its tarpaulin held stacks of wood—walnut blocks for the risers of new bows, and roughly shaped yew limbs amid a litter of shavings, and chisels and gouges and clamps. Dennis and a few others were learning the art of the bowyer from him.

"Maybe lessons from Chuck and Sam as well. And ... oh, you know that hopfield just this side of Lebanon? I bet we could scavenge or swap a *lot* of hops there. Over the mountains, they'll be wanting to make beer, come later this year when there's never a six-pack to be found. Hops don't grow well there."

"*I* could make beer, come to that," Dennis said. "I worked in a microbrewery once; there's a good one at Brannigan's, over in Sutterdown, at that." He smacked his lips. "Or we could make mead, if we had honey; don't the Carsons have some hives?"

Voices babbled, ideas treading on each other's toes. "That's the happy part," Juniper said. Into the silence that fell: "We've also got to find out what's going on in the Willamette. Before it rises up and hits us unawares. And from what that forager said, Corvallis is still holding out. I've connections there, friends, and they could be a help to us all."

The babble *was* a lot less happy this time; all they had were rumors, but they were ghastly. Juniper settled down to argue with a sigh; it was a perfect spring afternoon for a walk with Cuchulain, or maybe getting out her fiddle ...

*Well, by the Lord and the Lady, if you want to call me Chief, you'll* listen *to me. And if I make it a point to show you that you can do without me for a while, you'll listen to that too!*

# CHAPTER SIXTEEN

"Whoa," Michael Havel said, lowering his binoculars. Then: "Someone's been a *busy* little bee."

The roadway along the south bank of the Columbia Gorge was blocked; cinderblock to chest height, making a retaining wall to hold the dirt and rocks heaped above, with a palisade that looked like it was made of utility poles atop the massive earthwork. Working parties were driving in long angle-iron fence-posts in a checkerboard pattern over the earth berm and fastening barbed wire to them.

Sunlight winked off spearheads along the palisade; in the center was a solid blockhouse-like structure, with a gate whose lower edge ran on truck wheels.

A tall flagpost rose from the blockhouse, and high above it floated a hot air balloon, tethered by a cable that stretched up in an arc like a mathematical diagram. As he watched a bright light flickered from the basket, a Morse-coded heliograph signal.

The rest hadn't changed, not the bones of the earth and its growth. It was hot down here near the Columbia even this early in the year, and a constant gusty wind made the horses stamp and toss their heads. Basalt cliffs reared southward, black or red where stands of pine hadn't hidden the rock with green; and beyond that loomed the cone of Mt. Hood, dreaming blue and white and perfect against heaven.

"Not much like the last time my family drove out the Banfield," Eric Larsson said.

Dry understatement hid an edge of nervousness; probably shock at seeing what the Change had done to something *familiar*.

"And he picked a pretty spot—most places the south-bank hills hide Mount Hood from the road."

"Most places the south-bank hills would overlook that berm and blockhouse," Havel said.

Closer were thickets of willow tender green with new growth, and the shimmer of black-cottonwood leaves, green above and silver below, trembling in the wind; beneath them were sheets of yellow bells, maroon-colored clusters of prairie stars, grass widows and blue penstemon.

The great river stretched lake-broad to their north, glimmering silver under the noonday sun, mostly empty all the way to the steep northern shore. It was quiet, save for the huge murmur of the water, birdsong, the distant sound of voices, oars and footfalls.

*The river's* mostly *empty,* he thought, turning his glasses that way.

There were sailboats on it, and what looked like cut-down yachts with wooden superstructures holding rowers pulling on great sweeps. Some of those were hauling barges, and other barges had been fitted with basic lug-sail rigs.

The older men's silence gnawed Eric's nerves, and he waved towards the wall and burst out: "Fuck, how did anyone get all this done so *fast?* There aren't any bulldozers or backhoes working! Even if this Protector guy started right away—"

Josh Sanders clicked his tongue against the top of his mouth. "Oh, you could do the berm, no problem. Material from that hill over there. Say a thousand people with hand tools and wheelbarrows; eight cubic yards a day each, that's no big deal; take you about a week, less if you used more labor and worked shifts around the clock. Put it on in layers, ram it down, repeat."

"It's not just a heap of dirt," Havel pointed out. "There's the cinderblock work, and the palisade, and the gate."

Josh nodded: "I couldn't say about the gate, but the retaining wall, that's easy, and the palisade? Just utility poles. Shiftfire, give me the materials, the tools, ten guys who know what they're doing and a whole big bunch of people to do the gruntwork, and I could have put this up my own self in a couple-three days. You could bring the materials in on the railroad."

*Can I pick them, or can I pick them?* Havel thought proudly. That was the biggest part of leadership.

Eric was frowning. "But the railroad isn't working," he said.

*Keep talking; you're helping me organize my thoughts. And that balloon is a good idea. I should have thought of that. We'll have to get one. Christ Jesus, hang gliders and sailplanes would still fly too, wouldn't they? Maybe I was a little premature, hanging up my wings.*

"Sure, the railroad's working," the ex-Seabee said to Eric. "It's the locomotives aren't working, bro. You can pull a hell of a lot more on welded rail than you can on a road, with a horse or with men. Fifteen, twenty times as much. So you get some work gangs out levering the dead locos off to clear the tracks. Use a hand-cranked windlass for that, off a boat, maybe . . ."

"Even this time of year, you'd have a couple of big lines of grain hopper-cars between here and Portland," Havel put in. "Probably they hauled those in, then got the idea of using the rails long-term."

Josh nodded. "From the look of the dirt, that berm's just finished. Last couple of days. I'd put topsoil on and then turf, to keep it from melting away in the winter rains."

"Yeah," Havel said, then pointed as the wind fluttered a banner out over the gatehouse. It was black. He peered a little closer: black, with a red catpupiled eye in the center.

"That tells us something too," Havel said. "The folks back at Hood River weren't shitting us; this Protector guy really is a maniac. Loopy. He's not for real; he's playing games."

"Why?" Eric asked curiously, shifting in a creak of leather and chime of ringmail. "Astrid's always using stuff out of those books. So, I grant you she's a flake—a big-time, fresh-from-the-flake-box flake—but not a maniac."

"She uses the good-guy stuff, Eric," Havel said. "If *I* were running Portland and surroundings, I'd be using the Stars and Stripes—no matter how much of a dictator I was, and how much of a lie the flag was. You don't put up a sign that reads 'HEY, I'M EVIL! GEN-U-WINE SADISTIC LOONEY! REALLY, REALLY BAD!' Particularly not if you *are* evil."

"Why not?" Eric said curiously. "If you're a bad guy, that is."

"'Cause most people don't think that way, even if they are rotten. How many are going to stick with you when things go wrong, if you *advertise* you're a shit?"

"Hey, it's cool to be baaaad."

"Not the same thing." Havel grinned for an instant. "Hell, *I'm* bad, in *that* sense. *This* jerkoff's coming right out and saying he'll screw you over in a minute; guys like that have a short half-life. Maybe you can run a cocaine cartel that way, but not a country or an army—or if you do, the results are what a lieutenant I knew used to call suboptimal. Probably the only reason he got any traction at all was that Portland was a complete madhouse right after the Change."

"He's a fruitloop with a lot of troops, right now," Josh said. "That makes me nervous, Mike. You see the heads over the gateway? Those look too fucking real for this ol' boy's taste."

"Well, we *are* here to find things out. If Mr. Me So Bad has a lock on the Willamette, our people need to know so we can pick another destination. And they *did* say he didn't usually molest travelers who toed his line. Let's go. And mouths shut, ears open. This isn't risk-free, either."

Havel rode in at an easy fast walk; there wasn't much traffic, mostly improvised wagons drawn by men, or people on foot—thin and frightened-looking and mostly very, very dirty. He wrinkled his nose; the three Bearkillers were fairly ripe in their armor and gambesons, but they tried to keep the bodies underneath as clean as possible.

The guards were another story; all equipped in scale-mail, and all looking reasonably well fed. The heads spiked to the timber of the gate above their spearheads were all fairly fresh too. Above them, some sort of machine moved to cover them behind a slit in a sheet-metal shield; he'd have bet that was some sort of giant crossbow or dart-caster . . . or possibly a flamethrower.

"Hi," Havel said to their leader. "I'm here to see your Protector."

"Not just nails—twelve-inch spikes!" Alex Barstow crowed from inside the truck. "Crates of nice big bolts. And half-inch cable, by God, a whole hundred-yard spool. Fan-fucking-tastic!"

Outside his brother Chuck quirked a smile. "That's Alex. Do you know, even when we were little kids he could build the most fantastic castles out of matchsticks?"

A deep breath: "Do you really have to do this, Judy?"

"Chuck, I need to know what's going on out there epidemic-wise if I'm going to do my job helping keep this bunch healthy. We've been over this. I love you."

"I love you too," he said; they embraced. "Merry meet, and merry part."

"And merry meet again," Judy said; they both had tears in their eyes. "See you before Beltane."

Juniper had made her good-byes back at the Hall; she looked away, swallowing, as her friends made theirs, letting her fingers busy themselves checking her gear.

Then she waved and put her foot to the bicycle's pedal as Judy broke free. They were well past the Carson place, due west of Mackenzie territory; everyone around here knew them by now, and more to the point was familiar with their wagons and the way they sent them out to scavenge supplies from stranded trucks and abandoned stores.

Plus farms that looked to Sutterdown for guidance tended to shun the Mackenzies—Reverend Dixon's influence, she supposed. The Carsons and a few other cowan friends passed on news from there. Nobody would notice four Mackenzies on bicycles heading out from the wagon.

Steve scooted ahead of her, taking point as Sam Aylward called it; Vince dropped behind, and Judy pedaled beside her. The spring sun beat down on a world of green around them as their wheels scrunched, and on the quiet dirt country lane it might almost have been before the Change . . . save for the occasional car or tractor they passed, frozen since that evening; save for a farmhouse abandoned, or crowded with refugees.

And save for the ever-present faint acrid tang of smoke from cities burning.

"Keep your eyes open," she told herself.

They were going to loop up north, then cross the river and see what was going on near Corvallis.

"Time to come out of the cocoon and learn."


"You do yourself nicely here," Havel said.

He sipped at the single malt, savoring the smoky, peaty taste as he looked around the big high-ceilinged room and the glowing Oriental rugs on the floor; evidently if you had unlimited labor, it didn't take long to turn a library built in

1903 into a fair approximation of a palace. The wall that cut off this corner of the former Government Documents Room looked like professional work; the faint smell of fresh plaster confirmed it. Shelves had vanished, replaced by hangings and pictures that had the indefinable something that screamed *money* even to an art-infidel like Havel, or at least hinted at foraging parties with handcarts and sledgehammers backed up by swords and spearheads.

Dinner smells lingered a little too; skillet-roasted mussels in a coconut curry broth, a salad of pickled vegetables, garlic-crusted rack of lamb and fresh bread, finished off with a noble Dutch-style apple pie and cheeses, and accompanied by wines finer than Havel knew he had the palette or experience to appreciate.

Portland might be just getting by, uncounted millions were starving to death around the world, but the Protector and his friends certainly weren't on a ration book. There wasn't any point in not enjoying the dinner, either.

The smell of the kerosene lamps was a little incongruous— but the light was welcome. You *missed* electricity after dark.

Norman Arminger and his wife lounged on a black-leather sofa; Havel was surprised she was with him. The scantily clad servants had given him the impression of a man with serious harem fantasies. The Protector leaned back with a shot of the whiskey in his hand; his dark-haired wife had a glass of white wine.

Then Arminger spoke; he had a deep voice with an edge of humor to it. He'd been doing most of the talking, at that, but he was never boring.

"Well, it is the City that Works," Arminger said. "I'm doing my best to transform it into the Kingdom that Works. If people are to survive above the level of cannibal bands or isolated farms, there has to be organization, leadership . . . and it has to be based on realistic principles. Post-industrial democracy was wonderful, but it's not possible now. The foundations of that way of life have been knocked out from beneath us. We have to turn to older models."

"That sounds reasonable," Havel said. "Similar things had occurred to me, actually."

Arminger lifted his glass with a smile. "Meanwhile, I'm impressed with the equipment you had," he said. "Much,

much better than the usual improvisations. Did you have any SCA people in your group?"

"No," Havel said. "A lot of people expert around horses, good handymen, some books on cavalry warfare and gear, and someone who was involved with a Renaissance fencing club. HACA, I think it used to be called, or ARMA—not sure which."

"Ah, surprising and very fortunate for you—the Association of Those Who Like Hitting Things with Sharp Pointy Things," Arminger said. "I attended a few of their gatherings. Very focused, very practical—in the sense of recreating effective sword styles, which in those days wasn't of much *practical* use at all. The Society was deplorably eclectic, although the Pensic War was always entertaining. And a surprising number of its members proved to be excessively sentimental and had to be . . . removed from the equation."

"Things *have* Changed," Havel said. "We also found a bowmaker, and we had one very good and one pretty good archer to teach the rest of us. That wasn't so odd; hell, there were a couple million bow-hunting licenses issued last year."

Sandra Arminger snorted. "We prefer crossbows. Easier to make, and easier to learn."

"And in the long run, less problem to armored horsemen," the Protector said. "Wouldn't want the tenants to get too uppity."

"Less useful than a bow from horseback, though," Havel pointed out.

"You're aiming at doing things Mongol-style?" Arminger said, raising his brows. "Ambitious!"

"I always liked that saying of Genghis Khan's that a year after he sacked a city you could gallop a horse across the site without stumbling. Say what you like about Genghis, he got things done," Havel observed.

Arminger grinned, a charming expression. "I think you may be a man after my own heart, Lord Bear."

*Christ Jesus, I hope not,* Havel thought, with an imperturbable shrug.

"I understand you came through Pendleton," Arminger said. That was a logical deduction; it was the major city of northeastern Oregon. "Have they started their civil war yet?"

"There was some tension between the reservation and

the city, but on the whole they seemed to be doing pretty well," Havel said. "They've moved most of their urban population out to the ranches and farms. In fact, they're wondering why they didn't see a lot more refugees from Portland than they got. They've got a lot more wheat than they can harvest with the hands available; it'll all go to waste, since they can't transport it—or plant nearly as much this fall."

"Pendleton only had, what, eighteen thousand people in the city limits?" the Protector observed. "Seattle tried moving people east en masse, and it didn't work very well, even before the final collapse there. Mostly it just overburdened the rural areas close by. I, ah, encouraged the surplus population here to move out southward. Mainly by setting more fires and cutting off the water supply. It's gravity-flow here, and should last for generations with some upkeep. We've had some success with using water-power to run machinery; for stamping out armor scales, for instance."

Havel sipped at his whiskey, keeping his face neutral. "I noticed a lot of damage to the city," he said.

"The big jets coming down hard set most of the area east of the Willamette on fire," the Protector replied. "Giant bombs full of fuel, you see—surprisingly effective. And we did more around the fringes. Nothing essential lost, though."

He snorted. "And in *this* climate, the ruins will all be overgrown in a single summer—we have to cut back vines on the roads that grow two inches a day! The burned-out areas will be scrub in a year and forest in ten."

He paused, considering. "Why did you decide to come this far west? I've had scouts of my own as far east as Montana and as far upriver as Lewiston, and the situation *is* a bit less dire out there. So far."

"So far, like you say. I'm just in charge of this scouting party," Havel said. He'd been careful to give that impression here. He wasn't altogether sure how much Arminger had been taken in. "Like when I was back in Force Recon."

*Surprising how many educated people think a Marine noncom must be a no-neck dullard. Useful misconception, though.*

"The consensus is that the land's better here, and that by the time our whole party reaches the area it'll be near-enough empty, more so than anything good east of the Cascades where the initial die-off isn't so bad. There's a lot of people on the move there, and not just townsfolk; places that depended on pump-irrigation, for instance. The best spots are already held and the farmers and ranchers have most of the labor they need and all they can feed until the harvest. We didn't want to settle for being sharecroppers or hired hands anyway."

"Logical," Arminger said. "I think this generation's sharecroppers and hired hands will be the serfs and slaves of the next. And you're not sentimental; I like that. But by the end of this year, or next at most, I intend to control the Willamette. It's the natural core for a . . . kingdom, state, whatever . . . ruling the Northwest; nearly ten thousand square miles of the best rain-fed farmland in the world. You . . . Bearkillers . . . would be well-advised not to try to fight me for it."

*Now we get down to it,* Havel thought.

"We didn't intend on making a bid for the whole thing. You'd prefer we go somewhere else?"

"Oh, on the contrary. I can always use a group of . . . sensible . . . fighting men. Centralized government isn't possible anymore, without powered machinery or fast communications. Or without cannon for that matter. I would grant you lands, and authority over those living on them—provide you with labor, if necessary, farm tools, seed, livestock. In return, you acknowledge me as ultimate overlord, furnish armed men when I call for them, plus labor for public works like roads, and give me a reasonable share of the yearly profits from your . . . demesne, shall we call it. In return, you get the help of the whole Portland Protective Association when you need it."

The word *demesne* tickled Havel's memory, a vague recollection of something Ken Larsson and Pamela had mentioned in one of their campfire conversations. So did the whole setup Arminger was outlining.

"Exactly what period of history were you a professor of, Lord Protector?"

Arminger looked at him with narrowed eyes; the expression on Sandra's face was identical. Havel cursed himself behind an impassive mask.

*You should be consistent when you try and get someone to underestimate you. Bad Lord Bear. No biscuit for you!*

"Ninth through twelfth centuries," the Protector said. "Early feudal Europe, specializing in Normandy and the Norman principalities—England, Wales, Ireland, Sicily."

"Sicily?" Havel said, trying to sound idly curious.

"Indeed, Sicily and southern Italy; conquered by Norman religious pilgrims on their way to the Holy Land. They went to do good, and in fact did very well . . . rather as I plan to do."

Havel raised a brow and smiled crookedly. He didn't want Arminger to think he was a patsy, either.

"But you *don't,* as of now, control the Willamette? Sir."

"No," the Protector said. "Right now, it's Portland, and part of the lower Columbia. Our current southern and western border is roughly a semicircle from Oregon City to Tualtin. Does that mean your group won't consider my offer?"

"No, sir. We will most definitely consider it—when and if we get here."

*Leaving you to assume that here means Portland, and that we'll come up I-84. Assume makes an ass of you and me.*

Aloud he went on: "And depending on our appreciation of the situation then in the light of our own interests. I'll certainly recommend that we take your offer under advisement and send further scouts later in the year, when we're closer. The Pendleton committee offered us land; it just wasn't very *good* land when you don't have modern equipment to work it. Plus the politics there look unstable, as you said."

Slowly, Arminger nodded; then he made a gesture of dismissal, with grudging respect in it.

"You can start on your way back tomorrow then. Ask the steward for anything you need in the way of amusements tonight, or supplies tomorrow."

"Thank you kindly, sir."

Havel stood, nodded his head in an almost-bow, and led his companions out the carved-teak door, moving easily, but conscious of the sweat that trickled down his flanks despite the coolness of the air. They were billeted in a yellow-brick apartment building half a block away, and he'd be *very* glad to get there.

"Mike!" Eric hissed, after they passed the guards with their halberds and crossbows. "What the *hell* were you—"

He gave a muffled *oofff!* as Josh took his arm and elbowed him in the ribs as he did it. Havel draped a comradely arm around his shoulders for an instant, and said loudly: "Yeah, sounded like a pretty reasonable proposition."

Josh nodded. "Certainly the best offer we've had so far."

Eric missed a step and then nodded vigorously; he was young and still had a bit of the sense of entitlement produced by being brought up rich, but he wasn't stupid. They passed through the corridor, then into a vast open area where the reconstruction work was still under way. From the looks of it, this was going to be a barracks or readyroom.

Havel stopped, looked around, and went on: "Thank God we don't have to worry about electronic bugs anymore ... anyway, didn't it occur to you that he has a vigorous zero-fault tolerance program for those who tell him 'no' to his face? Like, nailing their heads up over the door?"

Eric nodded. Havel thought for a moment: "You ever do any of that role-playing stuff?"

"D and D? A little. I wouldn't have figured you for the type, Mike."

Havel gave a rare grin. Eric wore a lot better now than he had when they'd first met; he suspected it was mostly a matter of having real work and real responsibilities.

*When you're in it, you grow up fast.* Aloud he went on: "I wasn't into D and D; working on my Harley and deer hunting and track and field were more my style, when I could duck out of chores at home. I even read the odd book."

Eric mimed staggering in surprise, and Havel gave him a playful punch on the shoulder.

"But there was this girl I knew in high school in 'eightyseven who was a fanatic about it; Shirley, real cute, and by rumor a demented mink in the sack—"

"—and you thought you could make a saving-roll into her pants?"

"Hey, I was a teenager, all dick and no brains, like some people around here right now. Thing is, she liked the Chaotic Evil types and I couldn't compete." Seriously: "The Protector and the way he operates remind me of the guy she dumped me for—dressed in black a lot, had this little scraggly peach-fuzz goatee like a landing strip on his chin, lot of attitude, thought he was seriously bad. And he was smart, but not as smart as he thought he was—for example, he thought all those little needling jabs were going right over my thick jock head. *And* he thought he could fight 'cause he'd pranced around a dojo a little, in a black *gi*, of course."

A reminiscent smile, and he rubbed the knuckles of his right fist into his left palm. "About the time I finally gave up on Shirley, I broke the little pissant's nose out behind the school gym—caught hell from the principal, but it was worth it, and I planned on enlisting anyway."

Soberly: "Anyway, give you odds the Protector was his clone when *he* was a kid and always played a, what the hell was the name . . . yeah, a dwerg or a draug or a Dark Elf or magical assassin or something."

"Now he's trying to do it for real?"

"Yeah, and it won't work in the end, I'd bet. We may have had a change in the laws of nature, but I don't think even the Change could make the world that much like a D and D game. Plus I think he's got this thing about the history he used to study, the feudalism thing, and *that* won't work either, at least not right away, although it's a better bet long-term than the Evil Overlord stuff. We may have had all our toys taken away, but the people he's dealing with weren't born back then."

"I don't know, Mike," Eric said. "He has taken over around here, and he looks like he's getting things organized. People will put up with a lot, for that and for food."

"Yeah," Josh said. "And he's also operating on a pretty big scale. What was that Russian saying Eric's dad quoted?"

"Quantity has a quality all its own," Havel said. "Yup. I'm not saying the Protector would be a pushover. Even if he goes down, he could do a lot of damage first; in fact, he certainly *will* do a lot of damage whether he wins or loses."

A glance over his shoulder, and he continued meditatively: "If he weren't such a looney-tooner, I'd actually give that proposition of his serious consideration. Even though he is . . ."

Eric made a disgusted noise. Havel went on: "I said *if,*

kid. The other problem is that he's got big eyes. I think it's going to be a join-him-or-fight-him thing everywhere in the Columbia basin, eventually. Damn."

Eric nodded. "We're still not committed," he pointed out. "I mean, we could head southeast, try the Snake River country, or even get out across the Rockies over the summer. Try the High Plains, or find somewhere to winter and then a chunk of good farming country we could claim."

Josh tapped the fingers of his left hand on his sword hilt; the brass strips of the guard rang a little.

"Problem with that is, first, good country isn't going to be all that easy to find without we drive off someone else. And second, we could walk straight into something just as bad as this Protector guy. I got this ugly feelin' ambitious men are going to be right common for a good long while now."

"We'll see," Havel said. A grin: "I mean, hell, *I'm* ambitious. And tomorrow, we ride out of here—south. He admitted he doesn't control the Willamette. I'd like to see if anyone does, and what the prospects are, before we go back and start making decisions."

Kenneth Larsson wept with the jerking sobs of a man unaccustomed to tears.

"Shhh," Pamela said, holding his head against her shoulder in the cool canvas-smelling dimness of the tent. "Shhh. It's all *right*, Ken."

The tears subsided. "I'm so fucking *useless*," he said. "I'm sorry, Pam."

"For what?" she said. "Hey, Ken, *I've* been having a fine old time tonight. Young men don't make love to a woman; they use the woman to make love to Mr. Dickie. Give it time."

He relaxed, probably amazed she didn't want to kick him out of her bedroll and never see him again. Pamela's lips quirked in the darkness.

*I meant what I said,* she thought. *And besides, Ken—we can't walk out on each other, not anymore. We're all stuck with each other unless we want to leave the outfit.*

Ken took a shuddering breath. "I haven't been much use to any woman, since Mary . . . died. I couldn't protect her or my daughters—*yeeeeow!*"

Pamela poised her fingers to give his chest hair another painful tweak.

"What was *that* for?" he gasped.

"For being *stupid,* is what. It isn't like you. Will Hutton couldn't protect his family, and he's as tough as anyone in the outfit. And Mike couldn't have alone, either—what's the old saying, even Hercules can't fight two?"

"He rescued us."

"With Eric and Will helping! *We protect each other.* You didn't protect your family before the Change, either: the law did, and the police did, and the military did, and the State of Oregon did, and the U-S of A did. Now the outfit does. And you're our engineer, and you know a hell of a lot of history. You're at least as useful to everyone as I am, or Will is."

Softly: "I *played* at Renaissance fencing because it was fun, Ken; I'm a middle-class Jewish veterinarian from southern California! I never thought I'd have to *kill* with it. Hold me, will you?"

A few minutes later: "*Yeeeow!* What was *that* for!"

"To drive the lesson home." Her hand strayed.

"Thanks, but—"

"Hey, I'm doing that 'cause *I* like it, buddy! Doesn't feel bad, does it?"

"No, but—"

"There's no prize for making the finish line here," she said. "Just two codgers having fun. . . ."

A moment later: "Well, well!" She rolled over and straddled him. "That *does* feel nice!"

# CHAPTER SEVENTEEN

"Lord and Lady, I don't think I can stand this much longer," Judy Barstow said, her olive Mediterranean skin gray.

Juniper nodded. They were ten miles north of Salem, and . . .

She wiped at the flies crawling over her face, spat, and pulled the bandana up over her face again, which let her breathe through her mouth without inhaling any of them— even after many days' exposure, she hadn't gotten used to the stink. Her eyes skipped over the bodies lying by the road, and the rats that crawled bloated and insolent among them. Rags and tatters of flesh were left; the crows were at them too, but the rats were so numerous that they could drive the birds off in chittering hordes. Inside an SUV windows pullulated with heaving gray bodies. . . .

"It's almost as bad here as it was along I-5," she said. "I don't think we should try to get any closer to Portland."

"No," Judy said. "I don't either. My grandfather got out of Lithuania in World War Two . . . I never really understood what he was talking about before."

Almost compulsively she opened the economy-sized bottle of sanitizer again, and handed it around. Juniper's face and hands were already raw and chapped from the desiccating effect of the alcohol-based solution, but she obediently scrubbed down all the exposed parts of her body. Steve and Vince followed suit.

None of them had much skin exposed, despite the mild heat. When you thought of where the flies had been . . .

"No, we shouldn't be here," the nurse-midwife went on. "We're endangering the whole clan as well as ourselves. I never thought it could be as bad as this! If someone *designed* an environment to spread disease, this would be it."

She swallowed and went on: "How . . . how can They let this happen?"

Juniper pushed her bicycle over beside her friend's and put her arm around her shoulders; that was more symbolic than anything, when the person you hugged was wearing an armored jack, but symbols counted.

"How could They let the Holocaust happen, or the Black Death, or the Burning Times? We're not People of the Book; everything's connected, but we don't have to imagine that everything happens according to a Divine Plan. It could be *our* fault, something humans did through carelessness or malice. It could be aliens doing the same. Or . . . it could be something the Otherworld did for our own good."

"Our *good?*" Judy asked, looking around.

"We might have killed the planet, if this hadn't happened. Killed the whole human race, and the plants and the animals too. I don't know, but it's possible."

Judy drew a breath, coughed, and nodded. "All right. Thanks. But let's get *out* of here!"

Juniper nodded and pulled out the map. "All right," she said. "We had to know . . . but oh, how I wish we didn't!" Her finger traced a road west and then south. "We'll cross here, near Wheatland, and turn south towards Corvallis, then slant across to home the way I did right after the Change."

Vince Torelli had put an arrow to his bow as soon as they stopped. He left it there as he put the weapon back in its frame across the handlebars, held by the nock's grip on the string and the angle of the arrow-shelf. Then he stepped on the pedals and darted out ahead of them, keeping a careful hundred yards in advance. The two women followed; it took them a little more time to build up speed, as their bicycles were towing little baggage carts that held their modest supplies. Steve Matucheck followed behind, looking over his shoulder regularly.

The stink died down as they moved west—away from the produce truck that had probably attracted the group of people who stayed around it and died, and into open country. They wove down the two-lane blacktop, eyes busy keeping watch on the empty fields to either side—and not ignoring the abandoned cars and trucks that sat as they had since 6:15 P.M., March 17th.

Back at her cabin, she could go hours without thinking about the Change; days, sometimes, in the scramble to get the fields planted. Out here, not a minute went by when you could forget.

Once they were out from strip-mall development the fields were eerily silent; grass tall and shaggy, but not a cow to be seen; now and then a field of beets gone tangled with weeds, or wheat beginning to head out, or an orchard with fruits or nuts starting to swell. There were still occasional bodies by the road—people had stuck to those lines of travel, mostly trudging back and forth until they dropped, as far as she could see. The sun was cruelly bright, and she swallowed as a brace of crows launched themselves off a telephone wire.

Another hour, and they stopped for a drink from their canteens; Judy restrained herself from checking the water, since she'd made sure they brought it to a rolling boil for twenty minutes that morning.

"Anyone seen those dogs?" Juniper asked; a feral pack had shadowed them.

"Not since about ten," Steve Matucheck said.

"Odd. We haven't seen a living soul since yesterday, and yet so many stayed by the roads until they died," Juniper said.

Surprisingly, Vince Torelli spoke up. "Lady Juniper, I think it's part of the same thing. The ones that stayed at home, or walked back and forth on the roads, they died. The ones with sense enough to get away, they stood a better chance—but we won't be seeing them, much. Not around here."

Juniper nodded, trying not to let the young man see how much being called *Lady Juniper* annoyed her. Yes, you called a High Priestess *Lady* in the Circle, but it didn't apply in day-to-day life and Vince wasn't even a member of the coven. Dennis had started doing it, and she suspected it was as much to irritate her as anything else; his sense of humor had been easier to take when she only had to do it occasionally, instead of 24/7.

*But I'll be glad to get back to it; and Eilir; and the others . . . even Cuchulain.*

A little of that eagerness was sheer hunger. There hadn't been much to spare for them to take along on this trip; the Eternal Soup was a fond memory.

Judy nodded. "Just being away from a big city is the biggest survival factor," she said. "But a close second would be sense enough to realize that the Change was here to stay, and not sit around waiting for rescue or go wandering aimlessly. Chuck and I managed to talk our people into getting right out. You made for the hills right away too."

*Some truth in that,* Juniper thought, bending to massage a kink out of one calf. Judy had a core of hard common sense, probably from her years as a nurse.

*On the other hand, how could anyone* know *that the Change was here to stay, or that it was everywhere?*

For that matter, she still didn't *know* that the Change was worldwide. She was morally certain, but that wasn't proof. If you were a garden-variety common-sense sort of person, staying put probably looked better . . . until it was too late.

"Plus we're just too close to Salem," she said, looking back a little east of south. "The requisitioning parties probably got everything around here."

They could still see the black columns of smoke around the city as a smudge on the horizon; luckily the wind was from the west, and bent them towards the distant line of the Cascades—she could still see the peaks of the Three Sisters from here.

"Are you sure?" she asked Judy.

The other woman nodded. "I'd never seen it before, but the black patches of skin and the swellings in the armpits and groin are unmistakable."

A long breath. "It's been three days now. We'd be showing symptoms, if we'd caught it, but my skin still crawls."

*And mine, at the memory,* Juniper thought. *Those pits, where the bodies still smouldered . . .*

The truck stop a little way up the road had a gas station with attached convenience store, and a long low-slung board building advertising the fact that Bill's BBQ had the best dry ribs in the Willamette; a graveled country lane crossed the blacktop there, and the parking lot was dirt. They swerved in, coming to rest in a rough line and looking the windows over.

Quite often there was something useful in places like that. Not food, of course, but aspirin, sterile bandages, condoms, toilet paper—newspaper left stains, they'd discovered, and twists of grass could leave you itching for days. Sometimes there was even instant coffee or diet sweetener, occasionally salt. Nothing with any calories, but it made bland boring food taste better, and they were all worth the effort of lugging along. Sometimes they spotted something useful enough and bulky enough that it was worth marking down for a foraging party to come fetch with a wagon and escort, although they were getting too far from home for that.

"Wait a second," Juniper said, as she heeled down the kickstand of her bicycle. "I smell something cooking!"

*It's meat, too.* Her mouth watered and her swallow was painful. *Meat and a trace of woodsmoke, or charcoal. Could someone have found a last strayed cow in this wilderness of death? Could they be talked or traded out of some?*

Something moved behind a Subaru a few yards away. Juniper tensed slightly, then relaxed as she saw it was a girl in a stained white dress; about twelve, she thought, with stringy brown hair.

The girl waved and walked over towards them, smiling; a couple of her teeth were missing. As she got closer, Juniper wrinkled her nose.

*I'm not a blooming rose myself, but that's awful,* she thought.

The girl *looked* bad, too. Not emaciated like so many they'd seen; if anything, a little overweight, which was something she *hadn't* seen much lately. But her hair was thin on top, showing patches of scalp, and there were odd-looking lumps on her arms; she walked like someone much younger, holding her hands behind her back and half skipping. There was a small sore beside her left eye, trailing yellow matter.

"You're sick!" Juniper said, and looked over at her friend.

"Not the plague," Judy muttered. "Where have I seen—must have been a textbook—"

"It's all right!" Juniper called. "We don't want any of your food. Maybe we can help, if you're ill."

The girl giggled, coming closer. "It's all right," she said

back, her tone singsong. "We've got plenty to eat. You can come for dinner!"

*We?* Juniper thought.

Perhaps that was what made Juniper start to jerk backward as the hand came out from behind the girl's back with a glint of steel. The long kitchen knife missed her throat; it would still have killed her as it stabbed into her chest, but the plates of her jack turned it, breaking the point.

"*Oooof!*" Juniper said, struggling for wind.

The girl screeched, puffing the smell of rotten meat in Juniper's face, stabbing again and again with the sharp broken stump of the knife. She'd probably never met body armor before. Long detested hours of instruction from Chuck and Aylward took over; made Juniper duck a shoulder forward to body-check and knock the enemy back on her heels, reach down and grab the hilt with the right hand, rip it out and *swing* with the same motion.

The point scored across the girl's body, and the cloth parted—skin beneath, too, blood leaking as she turned and fled clutching at herself and screaming in shrill squeals.

Juniper fought shock. *I just cut at a child!* she thought.

More figures popped up from among the cars and trucks and poured out of the buildings. One burst right out of the rear doors of a van not fifteen feet away, roaring and holding an ax above his head in both hands. He was naked to the waist, his torso covered in boils. Vince drew to the ear and waited until the axman was five feet away before shooting; the arrow struck full in the throat, splitting the neckbone with an audible *crack*. The shouting cut off with knife finality, and the man toppled backward like a cut-through tree.

A woman with a butcher's cleaver ran at Matucheck. "Night of the fucking living dead!" he screamed, eyes wild.

He punched the blow aside with his buckler in an iron clang of metal on metal and stabbed, as much in revulsion as anger. The point slid home.

Judy was grappling with a teenage boy who tried to gnaw at her face as they danced in clumsy circles. Juniper bared her own teeth and struck with her buckler, using it like a two-pound set of brass knuckles. The crumbling feeling as the steel disk struck just below the base of his skull made the hair bristle up along her spine even then.

"It's a nest of Eaters!" Juniper shouted.

Most people would rather die than turn cannibal, but when you were talking about millions, a small minority was far too large. And they were starting to get hungry, as their food became scarce in turn.

"Get back in here!" she called. "Stand them off!"

Three cars made a loose triangle; too loose, but the Eaters were all around them. The Mackenzies retreated, Vince shooting as fast as he could knock and draw, then turned at bay. But the gaps between the cars were too big, and the Eaters swarmed over the hoods and trunks as well. For a minute the four of them pushed and shoved, hit and stabbed and chopped; their jacks were a huge advantage, and health and sanity and real weapons they had some idea of how to use.

But there *were* too many; it was like trying to fight in a nightmare where nothing worked and more and more came at you. Juniper knew with some dim distant part of her mind that the horror would come back to her if she lived, but most of her was a reflex that shouted and swung and struck.

Then something hit her across the shoulders, sending her reeling forward into the press. Two Eaters grabbed at her buckler and dragged it down. Another hugged her sword arm, and a third raised a baseball bat in both hands—

*Thock!*

A broad arrowhead stuck out from the Eater's chest, barely to the left of the breastbone. Blood gouted from his mouth, and he had just enough time to look surprised before he collapsed, kicking.

Behind him was a mounted giant with the head of a bear.

Juniper had only the blurred glimpse; then she was too busy getting her right arm free from the momentarily slackened grip. She hadn't lost her sword—the sword Dennie's gentle brother had made for show and play and the beauty of it, before the Change.

It was still the weapon of Rome's legions, the most dreadfully efficient tool of slaughter humankind had invented until Hiram Maxim's time. A short punching stab in the throat sent the Eater backward gobbling and clutching his throat.

"Let me *go!*" she shouted, chopping at the other two as if she were jointing a chicken. "Let me *go!*"

They did, running in squalling panic, grabbing at terrible slash-wounds, and then there were no more of their kind left within the space marked out with the three cars; none living, at least. Juniper gasped and leaned her fists on her knees as she tried to suck air in through a mouth gone paper-dry.

All the rest of her people seemed to be on their feet too, with nothing worse than cuts and scrapes and bruises; she squeezed out a brief, heartfelt wordless thanks. Outside the Eaters were running about the graveled parking lot, squealing and screaming. Three mounted men loped their horses after them, shooting methodically at close range with short powerful recurve bows, turning their mounts as nimbly as rodeo cowboys.

*It's a headdress on top of a helmet, not a bear's head,* Juniper thought. *Gave me a start there!*

Animal-headed god-men were very much a part of her faith, but she hadn't expected to run into one in the light of common day. It was almost as frightening as the prospect he'd rescued her from, of grisly death and dreadful feasting.

After a moment the cannibals gathered, clustering around a leader—one with a louder voice, at least. The three armored men dismounted, tied their horses to the chain-link fence, drew long swords. The round shields on their left arms bore a uniform mark, the stylized outline of a snarling bear's head, red on dark brown.

The noon sun blazed on the edged metal of their swords, and the man with the bear helmet shouted: "You in there! The party's not over and the mosh pit is sort of crowded. Pitch in if you can!"

The shout carried easily across the twenty yards, through the brabble of the Eaters' lunatic malice; a voice trained to carry, but not a musician's like hers—more of a crashing bark. Juniper looked with disgust at the blood on her blade and arm and side.

"Let's go," she said. "Come on, Mackenzies!"

The three strangers formed up with their leader as the point of a blunt wedge and charged in a pounding rush with the skirts of their mail hauberks flapping around their knees, armored from shin to helmet. Their great straight-bladed sabers went up in glittering menace.

*"Haakkaa paalle!"* they shouted in unison; the words weren't English or any language she knew, but they prompted a flicker of memory. *"Haakkaa paalle!"*

Then they struck the loose crowd of their foemen, and the mass seemed to explode in a spray of blood and screams and swords swinging in arcs that slung trails of red droplets yards into the air. Juniper gritted her teeth and made herself move forward with blade and buckler.

The Eaters stood and fought—mostly, just died—for a brief moment, then spattered screaming across the parking lot and out into the fields around, running for the shelter of the woods. Steve and Vince retrieved their longbows and shot while any targets were still in range; Juniper stood shuddering and blinking as the tall strangers made sure of the enemy dead.

Then there was no sound except their own panting and a series of quick are *you all right* queries. And the sickening knowledge that a single minute's delay would have seen them all dead and dismembered.

"Oh, Goddess gentle and strong, I want to go *home*," Judy whispered, then straightened. "We ought to check out the buildings. There might be things that . . . need doing."

"Damn right," one of the strangers said.

Juniper looked around. She had been controlling the churning in her stomach by main force of will; the movement distracted her, and she swayed backward against a car, sliding sideways. The world swam, narrowing and graying at the edges, and her mouth filled with spit.

Judy reached for her, but the stranger was quicker, holding her upright until she recovered a little. His grip was firm but not painful, although she could feel the remorseless strength in it, but she swallowed again at the sight and smell of the blood and matter that clotted the mail on the back of his leather gauntlet.

"Easy," he said. "Your first sight of combat?"

He held a water bottle to her lips. She filled her mouth and turned her head to spit, then drank.

"Not . . . not quite," she said, looking around at the bodies.

*And every one of these a child of the Goddess and the God.* Hard to remember that, but she must. *May they find rest and peace in the Summerlands, and come to forgive themselves!*

Aloud she continued: "But nothing before the Change, and nothing since like . . . like this."

He nodded and stepped back as he felt her strengthen; his friends came up behind him and followed his lead as he took off his helmet.

Their eyes met. For an instant that stretched green gaze locked with gray; Juniper felt a sudden shock, like a bucket of cold water and a jolt of electricity and all the chakras—power points—of her body flaring at once. She could see very clearly; clearly enough to notice the sudden widening of his pupils as he stared at her with the same fierce focus.

Then the moment passed, so quickly she wasn't sure if it had been more than her wooziness; it did blow the horror out of her for a while. Instead she was chiefly conscious of another reaction: *My, but he's pretty.*

Almost beautiful, in a hard masculine way: square-chinned, with high cheekbones and short straight nose and slanted gray eyes, the long chiseled line of his jaw emphasized by the close-cropped black beard. Only a scar running across his forehead and up into the bowl-cut raven hair marred it.

*Oh, my, yes,* Juniper thought, surprised she could notice at a moment like this; and even then she thought she caught a flicker of kindred interest on his face.

Then: *They're not giants, either.*

She'd had a confused impression that they were all huge men; but on second glance the leader, the one with the bear's head . . . *let's mentally subtract all that gear* . . . was tall but not towering, and not even thick-built; broad-shouldered and long-limbed, rather, narrow in the waist and hips. He moved easily under the weight of cloth and leather and metal, light and graceful as a leopard.

The youngest *was* an inch or two over six feet, a fresh-faced freckled blond no more than twenty at the most, already heavy in the shoulders and thick-armed. The other was about halfway between his two companions in build.

"No disgrace to feel a bit woozy after something like this," the gray-eyed leader said. "I was, first time. You get used to it."

"Goddess, I hope not," she said.

He raised a brow at that—*observant of him*—and looked at the four Mackenzies, quickly taking note of their gear and the antlers-and-moon blazon on the breast of their jacks.

"Well, your Goddess must have been looking after you; we've met bunches like this before and decided to pile in and help on general principles. Ah . . . I'm—"

The blond boy grinned. "Lord Bear, war chief of the Bearkillers! At least according to my sister, Princess Astrid Legolamb."

The older man—*about my age, give or take a year*—grimaced at him, and the other one smiled.

"I'm Mike Havel." He jerked a thumb at the youngster. "This is Eric Larsson, and his family are all humorists—in their own opinion, if nobody else's. The sensible one here is named Josh Sanders."

The other man had brown hair and blue eyes and a narrow planes-and-angles Scots-Irish face that reminded Juniper of her own father; he pulled off a gauntlet and extended his hand.

"Pleased to meet you, ma'am," he said. "Mike is the bossman of our outfit, right enough."

Eric went on: "The rest of us are a long ways east of here; we're scouting," and the other two scowled at him.

She noticed with amusement how Vince and Steve bristled just a little as she made her own introductions; and her trained ears pricked up at the strangers' accents. The mix was odd, and she could usually tag someone within a hundred miles of their birthplace.

*The blond boy, Eric, he's a native Oregonian,* she thought. *From west of the Cascades, at that, like me, but probably raised in metro Portland rather than the valley. Hmmm . . . is that just a wee tinge of New England? Mr. Sanders . . . Midwestern flat vowels for sure; but there's something harsher there too, hill-country Southern; born not far north of the Ohio and on a farm, or some little crossroads town. Our Lord Bear is interesting; Midwestern too, I'd say, but from a lot farther north. And there's just a hint underneath of something else, not English. Singsong, but very faint.*

"Your friend was right," Havel said. "We should check out those buildings—together, and cautiously."

"You think there might be more Eaters?" she said.

"Eaters? That's what you call them around here? Possibly, or more likely prisoners, alive so they'd stay fresh. Like I said, we've done this before."

He looked down at one of the dead; his expression was clinical, and the other two looked matter-of-fact as well; the youngest was a little green around the gills, but only slightly.

Havel and Sanders were calmer still; not exhilarated or excited either, their breath slowing gradually from the brutal exertion of fighting in armor far heavier than hers, but calm. The bodies seemed to disturb them no more than the blood that clotted on their mail, the way a farmer would ignore muck-covered boots when he shoveled out a stall.

*Hard men,* she thought, with a tinge of distaste and then a rush of shame; they'd saved her life and that of her friends at the risk of their own, doing the deeds for nothing but the deeds' own sake.

*Not wicked, I don't think they're* bad, *but hard. This Havel, he probably was that way before the Change, too.*

She'd always trusted her first impressions of people, and had rarely been disappointed. Havel would make an excellent friend and a very bad enemy; provoke or threaten him or his and you could look for a sudden frightful blow, without warning, like a thunderbolt from a clear sky.

"A lot of this bunch look sick, too," he said. "I've noticed that before as well."

Judy spoke: "They were probably undercooking their . . . food," she said. "You can safely eat fish or even beef rare, most times. Pork you have to cook thoroughly. Human flesh . . ."

"Right. Josh, cover us. You two"—he nodded to Vince and Steve—"keep an arrow on the string and an eye out behind us. One of you stay at the entrance when we go in, and watch the horses. Don't want them creeping back to corncob us. Ms. Mackenzie, if you and Ms. Barstow could back me and Eric up directly?"

They all moved towards the BBQ place; that was where the smoke came from, trickling out of a sheet-metal chimney. The big picture window was unbroken; the lower half was frosted as well. Nobody felt like trapping themselves in the revolving door.

Havel looked at Eric; they nodded without words, laid their swords down carefully, and picked up a big motorcycle between them; then they pivoted and threw it—six feet and through the glass. The crash and tinkle sounded loud across the corpse-littered parking lot.

Juniper noted that the two young Mackenzies looked impressed; she snorted slightly to herself.

*A horse is even stronger, but those two don't get that me-am-awestruck-junior-dog look when one hauls a ton of logs out of the woods. Men!*

Havel looked through the shattered glass, blade and shield up. Then he turned his head aside, grimacing slightly.

"Christ Jesus!" he said, spat, then turned back to whatever was within.

Judy looked as well, then turned and began vomiting. When Juniper stepped forward in alarm, Judy waved her back as she spat to clear her mouth. Mike Havel held up a palm to stop his own men likewise.

"No point in letting this inside your heads unless you have to."

"They were . . . cooking," Judy said. "They had a—" Another heave took her. "I wish I hadn't seen it."

Havel nodded, sheathed his sword and drew the long broad-bladed knife he wore across the small of his back.

"I'll handle this," he said with calm, flat authority.

He went inside; they could hear wood scraping and crunching, and then his voice, speaking loudly as if to someone deaf or ill:

*"Do . . . you . . . want . . . to . . . die?"*

A rasping mumble, suddenly cut off; Juniper made the Invoking sign, as did Judy—and to her surprise, so did the two young men. Then Havel called an all-clear, and they stepped cautiously into the big dining area; the stench was stunning, even to noses grown far less squeamish since the Change. Even with the front window smashed in it was dim, which she was thankful for, and she let her eyes slide a little out of focus as well. Havel had spread some of the filthy crusted tablecloths over . . . things . . . lying beside the big fireplace hearth that stood in the center of the room, radiating heat from a bed of coals.

That had a copper hood, and firewood heaped nearby; the Eaters had been burning bits of planking and broken-up furniture . . . complete with the varnishes and stains in the wood.

*No wonder they were all mad! From the chemicals, as well as guilt and horror.*

The table beside it was scored with cuts, soaked with old blood and littered with knives, saws and choppers, a moving coat of flies buzzing around them.

"I . . . don't think there's anything here," Juniper said, lifting her eyes and focusing on the PLEASE WAIT TO BE SEATED sign still standing near the door. "If they're holding prisoners, it'll be out back. We ought to shout and then listen first; it might save poking around."

They did; in the ringing silence that followed she heard a muffled calling and pounding. She led the way back through the kitchen—empty, save for a few boxes of spices and salt and a severed blackened hand kicked into a corner and lying with its fingers clawed up as if reaching for something.

She moved on grimly, down a near-lightless corridor, to a metal door that had probably been a cold-store for meats. Even in the dimness she could see long scratches in the paint on the walls, as if someone had tried to cling to the smooth surface while being dragged. Voices and thumping came from behind the metal door, muffled by the insulation.

"We've come to get you out safe!" she called. "Hold on!"

The voices redoubled, but the door looked strong, and the padlock was a heavy model with a stainless-steel loop as thick as her middle finger. Her heart revolted at the thought of rooting through the clothes of the dead Eaters outside, or among the grotesque filth in the room around the hearth of abominations; both would be dangerous. And the one with the key might have been among those who fled, anyway. She began to look around for a tool.

"Just a second," Mike Havel spoke, surprising her. "Josh, check the packtrain. I don't think any of those maniacs would stop running that close, but no need to take a chance. And get some torches ready; we'll want to burn the place down when we've checked things over. Ms. Mackenzie, I'll be right back."

They squeezed past the knot of people in the corridor; Havel *was* back in a few seconds. Oddly, he was carrying a rifle.

"Thought I saw this on a rack in the main room," he said. "Over by the cash register."

"But . . . that won't *work*," Juniper said.

Havel grinned, a flash of white teeth in the darkness. "It won't *shoot*, but it'll work fine as a pry bar," he said. "An ax or a sledge would be awkward, the way the door jamb is right against the end wall. This is a Schultz & Larsen 68DL hunting rifle, of all unlikely things, always wanted one myself. Hell of a thing to do with a fine piece of gunsmith's work. . . . Stand back, please."

He slid the barrel through the padlock between hasp and body, tested the position once or twice, set his hands on the underside of the stock and put a booted foot against the further wall. That made the skirt of his hauberk and gambeson fall back; he wore copper-riveted Levi's beneath, and the incongruity of it made her blink for a second. Then he took a deep breath, emptied his lungs, filled them again . . .

*"Isssssaaaaa!"* he shouted, teeth bared in a rictus of effort.

The lock parted and flew apart with a sharp *ping* of steel striking concrete. Havel threw the gun aside too, panting; the barrel had a perceptible kink in it now.

"Show-off," the blond youth said, but he smiled as he did.

Juniper ignored them, pulling the latch open and then working the handle of the door; she had to dodge as the heavy portal swung open.

A woman with matted hair and a face covered in bruises and crusted scabs ran out, bounced off Havel's armored form with a shriek, then stopped and stared at Juniper's face. The dim light in the corridor must seem bright to her; the inside of the cold-storage locker would have been stygian-black. And Juniper's molten-copper hair was hard to miss.

"Juney?" the prisoner said. *"Juney?"*

"You know me—*Carmen?*" Her eyes went to the other captives. *"Muriel? Jack?"*

The slight dark woman threw her arms around the High

Priestess of the Coven of the Singing Moon; then the others were around her as well.

"Juney, they wuh, wuh, were going to—"

"Shhh, I know. You're safe now. We cast the Circle and made the rite, and She brought us to you."

# CHAPTER EIGHTEEN

*"Oh, ladies bring your flowers fair*
*Fresh as the morning dew*
*In virgin white and through the night*
*I will make sweet love to you;*
*Your petals soon grow soft and fall*
*Upon which we may rest;*
*With gentle sigh I'll softly lie*
*My head upon your breast . . ."*

Juniper finished the tune, and laid her guitar aside. Their campfires were in a hollow where the hills began west of Salem, cut off from the flatlands, overlooked by little except the Coast Range forests. A huge oak leaned above the little hollow, and the low coals of the fires lit its great gnarled branches and the delicate new leaves, turning them brown-gold and green-gold. The sky above was clear, frosted with stars and a waxing moon that hung huge and yellow above the mountains; sparks drifted up to join them now and then, when a stick broke with a sharp *snap* amid the coals.

She was feeling pleasantly not-quite-full, although closer to it than she had been in weeks. The kettle had held three big rabbits, as well as some wild onion, arrowhead tubers, herbs, and bits and pieces from both parties' stores; noodles and sun-dried tomatoes and two cans of lima beans they'd found in an abandoned camper.

The smell of it still scented the air, along with the fresh green grass and camas lilies. She'd contributed the makings for herbal tea, and she picked up a cup of it now.

"Good of you to slow down and keep us company for a

while," she said across the coals. "It's been a nice couple of days; a chance to let clean air blow the grue out."

It was a joy to be able to chat with someone new, as well, the pleasant meandering talk you had when people struck a spark of friendship and got to know each other. Beyond essentials, they'd mostly talked about times before the Change, as if to raise a barrier against the grisliness of their meeting. He'd found her ex-surburban, only-child, déclassé-boho life as a wandering minstrel intriguing; just as she had his hard-grit blue-collar rural upbringing with swarms of siblings and relatives; and they shared a love of the woods and mountains, the trees and beasts.

"No problem, we were heading this way anyhow," Mike Havel said. "It's been fun, and fun's thin on the ground these days."

They were a quarter-circle away from each other; Judy was a little farther from the fire, and the second hearth held most of the rest—she could hear Muriel's voice. A dear lady, but given to babbling at the best of times, and more so now; Eric and Josh were going to get an earful of Wiccan herbalism, whether they wanted to or not; at least that was happier than the bursts of tears in the first day and night.

*They've been surprisingly patient and gentle with the captives, that they have, with strangers they owe nothing,* Juniper thought. *Good hearts under those iron shirts.*

Mike Havel sat with his back against his saddle; his hands worked on a rabbit trap without needing to look at the task, long fingers fashioning the bent willow-withe and nylon cord with effortless strength. In boots and jeans and T-shirt under a battered-looking sheepskin jacket he appeared a good deal less exotic than he had in hauberk and bear-crowned helmet, but just as good.

*I'm not one to need a Big Strong Man at every moment,* she thought. *But I'm fair thankful this one came along when he did. Nor is he hard on the eyes, by Macha! Not stupid either, and strong of will without being a macho jerk; the women of the Bearkillers must be fair blind! Nice pawky sense of humor, too.*

Tactful questions had revealed he was single so far. There was wistfulness in the thought; they must part, and soon.

"Figured your friends needed some recovery time," he said. "Cutting our way through that hell-on-earth south of Portland wasn't any fun for us three, either, and hard on our horses—we took it as quick as we could and not founder them. Slowing up for a bit makes sense."

He grinned: "And besides, while your style isn't what I usually put on the CD player, it's good—and Lord, but I've missed music! The only people in our outfit who can sing at all do cowboy songs. Mind you, it could be worse—one of my father's sisters was always trying to make me and my brothers listen to Sibelius."

"Cowboy songs? You don't like country?" she said, surprised.

"Oh, I like country a lot. I meant *real* cowboy songs: cows, dust, horses—the old stuff actual trail riders sang to the dogies. Not bad, but sort of monotonous. My tastes run to Fred Eaglesmith, say, or Kevin Welch."

"Kevin Welch, is it?" Juniper said with a smile; she picked up her guitar and struck the strings, whistling for a second to establish the beat, tapping her foot and then putting a down-home rasp into her voice:

> *"My woman's a fire-eater,*
> *My woman's 'bout six feet tall . . ."*

Havel exclaimed in delight when she'd finished, leading a round of applause.

" 'Hill Country Girl'! My favorite tune—never thought I'd hear it done right again!"

Juniper laughed. "We have *céili* all the time; well, all the time we're not working or too cursed tired."

"Kailies?" Havel said, which was roughly the way it was pronounced.

"Singsongs, really; the word's Gaelic. Music and dancing; I was a professional, of course, and I can handle several instruments—not badly, either, if I say so myself—but Chuck's a good hand on the mandolin and Judy can do wonders with a bodhran drum, and Dorothy is a piper, and plays a mean tenor banjo as well, and most of my old coveners can carry a tune. There's a lot of sheet music at my cabin, of course; it was my base and as much of a home as I had. I specialized in Celtic music and folk and my own stuff, but it's not all we do."

Havel whistled. "Sounds better than a CD player!"

"More fun, truly. What do your people like to entertain themselves with of an evening, then?"

"Well, we *try* to sing something else, now and then," Havel said. "Angelica knows some Spanish folk songs. Astrid—Eric's younger sister—does readings from her favorite books, or just tells stories; she and Signe both draw and sketch, and they've been teaching some others; and we have games, play cards . . . I do wish we'd had a good musician, though. Maybe we'll get one."

"You don't have a bad voice, Mike," she said. "It just needs training."

"Haven't had the time," Havel replied. He hesitated, and went on: "Is Juniper your real name?"

"It is now," she said cheerfully, putting the tea down and strumming a little to accompany her words. "And has been these fourteen years; it's my outer Craft name. I was sort of militant about it then; put it down to being sweet sixteen and at outs with my parents."

"Er . . ." Havel said. "I'm sort of a lapsed Lutheran myself. I haven't known many Wiccans."

Juniper laughed: "And the ones you did see tended to the impractical? Endless discussions of anything under the sun? A preoccupation with dressing up? Sort of flaky, overall?"

She watched his embarrassment with a slight smile; he was about the most relentlessly practical man she'd ever met, on first impressions. He was probably trying desperately to avoid saying words on the order of *some of my best friends are flakes.*

"Well, that's not entirely mistaken," she said, taking pity on him. "But there are all types in the Craft, from herbalists to dental hygienists, some varieties more flamboyant than others; not to mention the different traditions, which are as distinct as Baptists and Catholics. My coven, the Singing Moon . . . well, we're a straightforward bunch. A musician—myself—a city gardener, a nurse, a couple who owned a restaurant . . ."

"Certainly sounds like you've been doing well," he said

with relief. "Anyone who's alive and not starving and has a crop planted is!"

They looked at each other for a moment while she let a tune trickle out through her fingers. Then Havel cleared his throat and gestured at the piled rabbit-traps he'd wrapped in a blanket for carrying.

"Guess I should get these set," he said, then coughed into one hand. "Ah . . . care to come along?"

"I'd be delighted," Juniper said gravely, suppressing her smile—men had fragile egos and big clumsy emotional feet. "It's a useful skill, setting snares for rabbits. Learned it from your grandmother, did you say?"

"Her younger brother, Ben."

They both picked up their sword belts and buckled them on. As she rose and turned to slide her guitar into its battered case she saw Judy smiling at her from across the flame-lit darkness, raising her hand in the gesture of blessing.

Juniper stuck out her tongue briefly, and turned to follow Havel into the darkness. They both stopped for an instant beyond the reach of the firelight, staring outward to let their eyes adjust; she noticed Havel noticing what she'd done, and his nod of respect.

The moon was a week past full, still huge and yellow, shining ghostly through tatters of cloud, and the stars were very bright—even now she wasn't quite used to seeing them so many and so clear in this part of the country. Together they made it easy enough to find your way, if you were accustomed to nighted wilderness.

After a moment they moved off the trail, through long grass thick with weeds, where a spiderweb shone like silver with beads of dew. Havel moved quietly—very quietly for a big man, and in unfamiliar country. Juniper followed him up the slope, through overgrown pasture towards a line of brush and trees behind a wire fence.

"Good spot," she said in an almost-whisper, when she saw where he was heading.

She pointed, and they could both see the tracks and the slight beaten trail. "Creature of habit, your average rabbit, likely to come through here again."

"You a hunter?" he asked softly with a chuckle in the tone.

"No," she said. "I didn't hunt, not until the Change. But I liked watching the birds and animals, when I got the chance."

They both ducked through the wires of the fence, holding it for each other—his long saber was more of a nuisance than her gladius—and moved to where a fallen tree trunk made good shelter for a small animal low on the food chain to scan the meadow before venturing out. He rubbed grass and herbs between his hands before he planted the trap, and baited it with a handful of evening primrose roots. The next few went further up along the brush-grown verge, natural stopping-places for an animal attracted to the varied food that grew in edge habitats.

They moved into the woods; mixed fir and oak, old enough to have a canopy over their heads. The cool green smell was different from the open meadow, more spicy and varied. It was much darker here, just enough to see their way.

"There," she said, pointing.

The spot showed close-cropped grass, beneath a high bank that cut off the wind; it also broke the roof of branches above, and let in a little starlight and moonlight.

"Good spot," he repeated. "Wouldn't be surprised if there were some burrows there."

"You men are unromantic beasts," she said, laughing. "I had a bit of a stop in mind, Mike."

He had a crooked smile, but an oddly charming one. "You know, I was hoping you'd say something like that." He hesitated. "I can't stay. I've got my people to look after—commitments elsewhere."

"Me too, but you're a gentleman to say so." She put her arms around his neck. "Now shut up, will you?"

*My, my, my,* Juniper thought.

She stretched luxuriously and then hugged the sheepskin jacket around her shoulders against the chill, watching as Mike Havel lit a fire a yard away. He had an old-fashioned liquid-fueled cigarette lighter to do it with, and the wick caught the second time his thumb worked the wheel in a little shower of sparks. The light showed for a moment through the teepee of twigs and duff he'd laid as tinder.

"It's not that cold," she said. "Besides, it's fun to cuddle, and we've got this blanket you so *accidentally* wrapped those traps in."

He looked over his shoulder. Squatting naked wasn't usually a flattering position for a man, but he was as unselfconscious about his body as a wolf. *Odd that he got a bear-name dropped on him.* He wasn't furry, less body hair than most, but a wolf was what he reminded her of, or a cat; something lean and perfectly shaped.

*Except for the scars,* she thought, with a quick surge of compassion; she'd noticed, of course, but things had been too . . . urgent . . . to ask before.

"How did that happen?" she asked gently.

He glanced down at the white seamed mark on his leg as he carefully added deadwood to the little blaze.

"Slipped cutting down a dead pine," he said. "Christ Jesus, did my dad give me hell about it!"

She nodded, but went on: "No, I meant *that*."

*That* was a curious radial pattern on his ribs; the muscle and tendon moved easily beneath it, but the flickering underlight of the fire brought out the tracery of damaged skin.

He glanced up at her quickly, his eyes cold and withdrawn for a moment, then thawing.

"No," he said. "You're not the sort of girl who'd get off on scars, hey?"

"I'm not any sort of a girl," she said tartly. "And not that sort of woman, either. I like you, Mike. I just wanted to know about you."

He grinned and finished building the fire. "OK, point taken, and I like you too, Juney. It was an RPG."

"Role-playing game?" she asked, bewildered, and saw him laugh aloud, his head thrown back—for the first time since they met, she realized.

"Rocket Propelled Grenade," he said. "Freak thing—should have killed me, it hit the rocks just to my left and then shit was flying everywhere."

He looked down at his hands; they slowly closed. "Next thing I knew I was crawling and pulling what was left of Ronnie Thibodeaux out and yelling for a corpsman. You would have liked Ronnie—Cajun kid from the bayous, turned me on to zydeco music."

The flames cast shadows on the bank of earth behind, moving like ruddy ghost-shapes in the darkness.

"I may be a beast, but not an unromantic one; a fire always makes things nicer, right?"

Juniper threw back the coat and opened her arms.

Mike Havel always found partings awkward; he'd expected this to be worse than most, after the holiday feeling—like three days spent out of time, without the sensation of knotted tension he'd had most days since the Change and every day since he saw the Protector's outposts. He'd always gotten good-byes over with as fast as he could, keeping his eyes fixed ahead.

Oddly enough, *this* good-bye was easier than most; not less for regrets, but . . .

*But then, she's . . . comfortable to be around. Cuter than hell, but not at all the pixie you'd think from her looks. There's steel underneath. Damn, I wish life wasn't so complicated.*

At that he had to chuckle; since the Change, it had gotten complicated beyond belief—but apparently the personal stuff didn't stop. Juniper looked up at him from her bicycle, smiling in her turn. The young sun flamed on her hair, falling in loose curls to the shoulders of her jack; she had her bow over her shoulder, and her bowl helmet slung from the handlebars—as if this was a carefree day before the Change, and she someone heading out on a mountain bike. The air had a cool bite to it, a wind out of the west that hinted at rain, but for now the clouds were white billows sailing through haze-blue sky.

"What's the joke, Mike?" she asked; her voice still had that hint of a lilt and burble to it.

"That this doesn't really feel like good-bye," he said.

"Well, maybe it isn't, then?" she said, grinning at him. "I have a strong premonition we'll all meet again—and I'm a Witch, you know."

She looked past him to Eric. "I've a present for your sister," she said.

"Signe?" he blurted, then looked as if he wished his lips would seal shut.

"No, Astrid," she said; then glanced at Havel.

He could read that glance: *I'm already sending Signe something.*

"From what I heard, your Astrid and my Eilir would get on like a house on fire—tell her that from me."

She unsnapped the dagger from her belt. It was a Scottish-style dirk, ten inches of tapering double-edged blade, guardless, with a hilt of bone carved in interwoven Celtic ribbon-work, and a pommel in the form of the Green Man's face. More of the swirling patterns worked their way down the sheath, tooled into the dark leather.

She tossed it up to him, and then turned her bicycle; the rest of her people were straddling their machines in a clump—the nest of Eaters had had half a dozen workable trail bikes.

"Merry meet and merry part," she said, waving to the three Bearkillers; her eyes met Havel's, and he felt a little of that shock again. "And merry meet again!"

Havel waved, then leaned his hands on the pommel of his saddle as the knot of . . . Well, "Mackenzies," he thought. *Makes as much sense as "Bearkillers," doesn't it?* . . . coasted off southward, freewheeling down the slope that took the two-lane road weaving among trees and fields.

"Damn. That is quite a woman," he said quietly to himself. "One hell of a woman, in fact."

Eric was looking over the dagger; he drew it and whistled at the damascene blade. "Legolamb will love it," he said. "Looks Elvish to a fault."

"Scottish," Havel corrected.

"Whatever." Then his glance turned sly: "Shall I tell Signe about the circumstances?"

Havel shook himself slightly, touching the rein to his horse's neck and turning the big gelding westward, up the gravel road that intersected the county highway.

"No, I'll tell her."

"Why shouldn't I do it first?" Eric said, grinning.

"You over that constipation, kid?" he said.

"Well . . . yeah," Eric replied, frowning in puzzlement.

Josh Sanders was chuckling on Havel's other side as the three horses moved off, the pack-string following.

"Then if your bowels are moving regular, you really shouldn't tell Signe a word," Havel went on seriously.

"What's that got to do with it?" Eric said.

"It's *real* difficult to wipe your ass when you've got two broken arms," Havel said.

Sanders barked laughter; Eric followed after a moment. "Want me to take point?" he said.

"Let Josh do it first," Havel said.

Sanders nodded and brought his horse up to a canter, pulling ahead of the other two riders and the remount string. The road they followed wound west into the Eola Hills; the slope was gently downward through a peach orchard for a long bowshot, and Havel lost himself in it for a moment as petals drifted downward and settled in pink drifts on the shoulders of his hauberk and Gustav's mane. There had been enough ugly moments since the Change that it was a good idea to make the most of the other kind.

The thought made him smile. Morning's chill and dew brought out the scent; it reminded him of the smell of Juniper's hair for some reason, and the almost translucent paleness of her skin where the sun hadn't reached.

The road broke out of the little manicured trees and crossed a stretch of green grassland that rose and fell like a smooth swell at sea; from here they could just see how it turned a little north of east to head for a notch between two low hills shaggy with forest; there were more clumps of trees across it, and along the line of the roadway. Beyond all rose the steep heights of the Coast Range, lower than the Cascades behind them and forested to their crests.

Beyond that . . .

*The coast, about which nobody seems to know much. Beyond that, ocean and Asia . . .*

Would ships sail there in his lifetime? Perhaps not, but maybe in his son's, or grandson's; windjammers, like the Aland Island square-rigger that had brought his great-grandfather to America. He shook his head, and Gustav snorted, sensing that his attention was elsewhere.

*Back to practicalities.*

Salem lay to their rear across the Willamette; Corvallis was two days' walk southward. The closest town was the tiny hamlet of Rickreall, miles off to the left and over ridges. The hills ahead were an island in the flat Willamette, steep on their western faces, open and inviting when you came in from the east.

The only human habitation in sight was a farmhouse and barn off to the right about half a mile away, and it felt abandoned—probably cleaned out by foraging parties from the state capital right after the Change.

"Mike . . ." Eric began.

Havel turned his head. "Thought you had something to say."

"Are you and Signe . . . well, together?"

"Yes and no," Havel said. A corner of his mouth turned up. "Or yes, but not really, not quite yet. Want to have another go about the way I look at your sister? Or did you think I was cheating on her?"

"Well . . ."

"You and Luanne have a commitment, right?" Eric nodded. "Well, Signe and I don't, yet."

Eric flushed, and went on: "Just wanted to know. I mean . . . are you two going to get married, or something?"

"Probably," Havel said. "Very probably; depends on what she decides. But I haven't made any promises, yet."

*Although that's probably not the way a woman would look at it,* he acknowledged to himself.

Eric nodded; he *was* a male, after all, and a teenager at that.

"She'd have to be pretty dumb to pass you up, Mike," he said. Then he went on, in a lower tone: "Thing is, if you two get married, that'll sort of make us brothers, won't it? I've never had a brother."

Havel gave one of his rare laughs and leaned over in the saddle to thump his gauntleted hand on the younger man's armored shoulder.

"I could do worse. What's that old saying? 'Bare is back without brother to guard it'? We've watched each other's backs in enough fights by now that we're sort of brothers already. Now let's see this home of yours."

"Yours too, Mike," Eric said.

*Hero worship's natural at his age,* Havel thought indulgently.

They moved along smoothly, keeping the horses to a fast walk and occasional canter. From what Juniper had told him, this area had been swept clear by those idiots in Salem, and they were well south and west of the refugee hordes along the main roads now. There was still no sense in taking chances—a flood tide that big would throw spray and wrack a long way.

"Might be some people left further up and in," Havel said. "More places to hide."

Ahead the broad meadow narrowed, rising to low, forested heights coastward, shaggy with Douglas fir and oak. Once past the place where the hills almost pinched together the land opened out again in a wedge with its narrow part to the west. The rolling lands were silent, grass waist-high in the pastures, shaggy in the blocks of orchard and vineyard too—the south-facing side of the valley was all in vines—and the neglect was a disquieting contrast with the still-neat fences of white painted board. Willows dropped their tresses into ponds, and ducks swam.

The big house on its hill was yellowish-red brick, mellow with ivy growing up the south-facing wall, bowered in its trees and in gardens that looked lovely even at this distance. Barns and stables stood off at a little distance, and a smaller cottage-style house.

"Don't get your hopes up," Havel warned as he unshipped his binoculars for a brief scan. "I can't see any movement."

"Well, it didn't burn down, either," Eric said, smiling. "That's something."

They rode up the graveled road, hooves crunching in the loose rock; that turned to white crushed shell as they entered the gardens and lawns proper, in a long looping curve leading up to the white-pillared entrance to the main house. Velvety grass dreamed amid banks of early flowers—the Willamette was prime gardening country—clipped hedges, huge copper beeches, oaks, walnuts, espaliered fruit trees blossoming against a brick ha-ha.

*Old money indeed,* Havel thought.

He scanned the windows carefully; some of the dormers that broke the hipped roofline were open, and he saw a gauzy curtain flutter free.

*Just the thing to hide someone looking down at us,* he thought.

Aloud: "Eric." The younger man looked at him. "This place has good memories for you. You're probably feeling happy and relaxed to be here, down deep. Bad idea. Keep alert."

Josh Sanders was looking around, fingering his bowstring.

"Someone's been doing maintenance here since the Change," he said. "The grass isn't as long as it would be otherwise, and there's been some weeding. And that's horse dung, there, and hoofprints. Not more than a day old."

*"Throw down the weapons!"* a voice barked from an upper window. *"Give it the flick, yer bastards, or come a guster!"*

The thunking twang of a crossbow followed on the heels of the command; a shaft whipped by and went *tock* into the smooth gray trunk of a beech, quivering with a malignant wasp-whine.

# CHAPTER NINETEEN

Juniper kissed the vine leaf and dropped the thanks-offering into Rickreall Creek, chanting softly:

> *"Water departing*
> *Sky endless blue*
> *Both forever;*
> *Lord and Lady*
> *My love to you always flowing*
> *As rain and river to the sea*
> *Blessed be."*

Water took it and whirled it downstream, quick with the cold mountain waters of spring, past the pilings of the bridge and on towards the Willamette River to their east. Highway 99 stretched southward through open fields.

Then she and Judy leaned in to the pedals of their bicycles. They were on point today; she'd decided that the freed prisoners needed Steve and Vince by them, being unarmed save for belt knives and still feeling shaky, for which she couldn't blame them. They *could* haul the cargo carriers; she hoped some food would be available in Corvallis. The rabbits wouldn't last long.

"Well, you're looking like the cat that got the canary," Judy said after a while when the singing *humm* of tires on asphalt was the only sound to rival the birds.

"Mmmmmm," Juniper said wordlessly, and laughed at Judy's scowl.

"It's not like you to do the whirlwind romance thing and get swept off your feet," her friend said.

"Other way 'round," she said. "He's a nice guy, but I sort

of had to prod him into action." A giggle. "If you'll pardon the expression."

"Not your usual style," Judy repeated.

She frowned. "It wasn't, though, was it?" A shrug. "Things have, you may have noticed, changed. We didn't have all that much time."

Judy's thoughts had moved on. "I wonder why they didn't want to come on to Corvallis?"

"I think I can guess that. When I asked him about it, he just smiled and said that it was usually easier to get forgiveness than permission. Which I take to mean the Bearkillers don't want to attract attention to the place they're thinking of settling until they *are* settled and it's a done deal. And pre-Change title deeds don't mean much anymore. It's a lot closer to Corvallis than it is to our land, of course."

"To the Mackenzie clachan," Judy said, smiling; it lit up her full dark features.

"Oh, don't *you* start in on that stuff! Leave it to Dennie and his mispronounced bits of Gaelic."

Judy gave a broad shrug and flipped up one hand: "*Nu*, I should know from Gaelic? I'm just a simple Jewitch girl, after all."

They both laughed, and Juniper said more seriously: "*Giorraionn beirt bothar;* two people shorten a road. Glad you're along, Judy."

She smiled back. "You do have one for every occasion!"

"Mom was fond of 'em." She frowned. "I'm not sure it's a good idea now."

"What's the harm? For that matter, all this clan-Celtic business *is* more suited to the world we're living in now."

"That's what worries me," Juniper said. At her friend's glance, she went on: "Look, *we* know all this high-Celtic Deirdre-of-the-Sorrows sort of thing is a bit of a joke, and we don't take the old-country stories too literally either. But now we're pushing on an open door—there's no TV, no . . . no *world* to push back. What about our children's children? It was my father's people who gave the words 'blood feud' to the English language; not to mention 'blackmail' and 'reiver' and 'unhallowed hand.' "

Judy shrugged again, normally this time. "Right now, shouldn't we be more concerned about getting through to harvest? And whatever works."

"I suppose so," Juniper said with a sigh.

Her eyes had been moving as they spoke. "Look!" she said suddenly.

"It's a microwave relay tower," Judy said.

"But there's someone *in* it. Right up near the top, that looks like a platform added recently. Perfect spot for a lookout. Sort of ironic, isn't it?"

She halted and got out her own birding glasses. "And he's signaling someone, using a mirror. Clever." She paused to take a deep breath. "I can smell turned earth, not too far away."

It hadn't been a main road before the Change, but someone since had taken the trouble to push the occasional cars aside and bury the bodies—she could see fresh graves in the fields to either side. And that wasn't all. . . .

"Bunch up," she called back over her shoulder. "We're getting closer to town and I think they've got a lookout system set up."

This part of the Willamette was fairly flat. That cut visibility, but . . .

"We weren't the only ones to scare up some seed potatoes," Juniper said, looking left and right. "And is that barley?"

"Barley in this field, oats in the next, I think," Judy said. "Hard to tell when it's just showing. Spring planted—not too late, I hope."

Every day past the optimum cut the yield and increased the chances of running into the fall rains at harvest time.

Then: "Oooops!"

They cleared a slight rise; someone was waiting beyond. Everyone grabbed the brake levers, and the Mackenzies halted.

*About sixty someones,* Juniper thought.

Most of them were puffing and blowing, as if they'd arrived quickly . . . which the rows of bicycles hinted at, too. All the people waiting for them were in chain mail shirts that came to their thighs, like metallic extra-large T-shirts, with shortswords and bucklers hung from heavy belts.

Half of them carried long spears, made up of two sections that fitted together; a few were still getting the joint locked.

*That was quick,* Juniper thought, looking at the armor;

she had a vague memory that chain mail was expensive in the old days. *I'll have to ask Chuck.* The SCA had gone in for re-creating that sort of thing.

At a guess, someone from the Society had been advising this bunch as well.

"Pikes actually, not spears," she murmured. "Sixteen-foot pikes."

While she watched, they hurried into a four-deep line. Someone called out: "Pikepoints—*down!*"

The great spears came down with a shout, presenting a quadruple rank of sharp blades. The rest of the welcoming party were on either side, aiming crossbows. They all looked the more intimidating because their helmets came down in a triangular mask over the eyes, and flared out behind.

Their leader had a different weapon: a five-foot shaft with a head like a giant single-edged knife, curved on the cutting edge and thick and straight on the back, tapering to a murderous point. *A glaive,* she thought—the word came to her from some Society get-together where she'd played.

"Halt where you are!" the man with the glaive called when they were about twenty feet from the line of points. "In the name of the University Council!"

*And the Continental Congress and the Great Jehovah,* she thought irreverently, but she obeyed.

Those pikes looked unpleasantly, seriously sharp; so did the heads of the crossbow bolts.

"This area is under quarantine," the young man with the glaive went on. "I'm Lieutenant Peter Jones, Committee militia. Anyone found to be infectious will be put in isolation; turn back now if you are."

He pushed up on the mask. That turned out to be a jointed visor, and the face below was disconcertingly young; he also wore sports glasses with an elastic strap at the rear.

"We're peaceful travelers from a community on the east side of the valley," Juniper said, and gave their names. "Just out scouting, trying to find out what's going on. We have a registered nurse with us, and as far as we know we're healthy."

The word "registered" brought a bristling. "Not working for the state government, I hope," Jones snapped.

"They tried to take away our *livestock!* Until we taught them better."

"Our area had the same problem, but I don't think there is a state government anymore," she said, jerking a thumb northeast in the direction of Salem.

"Why not?"

"Plague. We got near enough to see the pits where they tried to burn the bodies, but from the looks of it the last survivors just lit out for everywhere else."

Jones cleared his throat and barked an order with self-conscious sternness; she put him down as a teaching assistant before the Change, possibly in one of the more practical departments, like agriculture or engineering. The pikemen—or in a few cases, pikewomen—swung their weapons upright again, and the crossbows went to port arms.

"We'd heard about that," Jones said. "The plague, that is."

His eyes flicked to Carmen, Muriel and Jack, all of who still had ripening bruises from their brief captivity.

"These are friends of ours," Juniper said in haste, and they nodded enthusiastically. "We rescued them from a nest of Eaters north of Salem, then looped around west of the river and came down Highway 99."

"You see we have to be careful about checking . . . ah, good."

More bicyclists had come up, from the direction of town. Two of them had white boxes marked with the Red Cross strapped to the carriers of their bikes, and they immediately came forward.

"Blood samples," one said.

"And customs inspection," the other added.

Juniper bristled slightly—she'd thought the Change had eliminated bureaucracy, at least—but the pikes and crossbows were a powerful argument. Plus they *needed* to contact any surviving nuclei of civilization out here. She'd been beginning to doubt there were any, beyond the three-families-and-some-friends level.

*It would be truly alarming if Clan Mackenzie and Reverend Dixon's flock were it as far as rebuilding goes!*

Judy chatted in medspeak with the doctor taking the blood samples; he had an optical microscope ready on a table by the side of the road, and could evidently identify most diseases from the shape of the bacteria in their blood. She recognized about one word in eight; and *Yersinia pestis* only because Judy had been using the technical term for bubonic plague rather frequently of late.

Jones examined their weapons. He sniffed at the jacks—"kludge" was the expression he used—and the swords were much like the ones the Corvallan militia carried, cut and ground out of leaf springs. The longbows brought his eyebrows up, and the dozen staves they had in the baggage carriers made him lick his lips, an expression she doubted he was conscious of. The bundled arrows brought nearly the same light of lust to his eyes.

"Wait a minute!" the customs inspector said. "They've got meat here!"

*Everyone* bristled at that, and some of the weapons started to swing in her direction.

"Venison jerky!" Juniper exclaimed, keeping her voice from panic. "Just venison jerky. There are a lot of deer up in the Cascades."

The doctor took a moment to confirm her claim, and everyone relaxed. Jones had the grace to look apologetic.

"You understand . . ." he said.

"Yes." Juniper winced slightly at her memories, and Judy put a hand to her mouth. "We've had . . . experience with . . . Eaters."

"Eaters. I suppose we needed a euphemism," Jones said. "You can follow me. The Committee will want to speak to you."

He had a bicycle of his own, waiting; if it was one thing every town between Eugene and Portland was plentifully equipped with, it was bikes—Corvallis had had scores of miles of bike path. Jones was full of pride as they cruised down Highway 99, pointing out the signs of recovery; they were still some ways out of town.

". . . and after the riots, we—"

"*We* meaning who, precisely?" Juniper asked.

She *was* impressed by the scale of planting on either side of the road; everything including former suburban lawns right up to the big Hewlett-Packard plant was in potatoes or vegetables, or spring grain. People stopped working for a moment to wave, or shout question to Peter Jones, then went back to weeding and hoeing.

*And I'm almost as impressed by the lack of stink,* she thought; there was a heavy scent of manure and turned earth, but none of the sickly smell of sewage or decay. Although she did catch the heavy ashy taint of burnt-out buildings as an undertone.

"Well, the agriculture faculty, mostly, and then the engineers and the history department, and some others. We were the ones who realized what had to be done—the ones who saw that letting Salem take all our food wouldn't mean anything but *everyone* starving. We got things organized. West to the Coast Range, now, and we're expanding."

Judy and Juniper looked at each other. *This is promising,* ran through her.

"Do you know Luther Finney?" she said. "Is he . . . still there?"

"The farmer?" Jones asked in surprise. "Why, yes—he's a member *of* the Committee, and not the least important one, either. He and his family helped get their neighborhood organized."

Juniper smiled, heart-glad to hear her friend was still alive, and only somewhat surprised; Luther was a tough old bird, and nobody's fool. *And . . . it never hurts to have references.*

A good deal of that happiness evaporated when they stopped at 99W and Polk. Someone had gone to the trouble of knocking down the ruins that stretched along the riverfront—she saw a wagon of cleaned-up bricks go by, pulled by a dozen sweating townsfolk—but the sheer extent of it shocked her. She could see all the way to the waterfront from here. A sour ashy smell clung to the fallen buildings. Broad streaks of destruction reached north and westward, too, looking more recent. There were a fair number of people about, but nothing like the numbers before the Change; about a tenth as many, at a quick estimate, but probably a lot more had moved out of town to work the land.

"I was here the night of the Change . . . presumably a lot of other people had the same idea, and headed out?"

Jones cleared his throat. "A lot happened that first *week*—the fires burned for days, and we had to tear down firebreaks to stop them. Then there were the food riots . . . we had outbreaks of cholera and typhus . . . a fair number of people moved off to Salem when the state government said they should. . . . We've got about six thousand in the area the Committee controls."

She nodded, but suspected that "food riots" covered a lot of internal conflict; better to blame everything on outsiders, once order was restored once more.

She took a deep breath. It had been silly, expecting anything but devastation here, too. This *was* a hopeful sight.

*I should be glad so much was saved,* she thought. *It's a good sign that they're already salvaging building materials.*

Jones made another throat-clearing noise: "So you'll realize . . . well, probably you can't stay very long. We're still *extremely* short of food, just barely enough to get ourselves through to harvest, and except in special circumstances we just can't feed outsiders."

Juniper looked at the rubble that covered the site of the Hopping Toad. Odds were nobody had tried to search the basement.

"Oh, I think we may have some things that would interest your Committee," she said with a smile. "Besides our trade goods, that is."

Luther Finney nodded: "Figure you made a good choice, Juney," he said. "Most places, it was just as bad as you thought it would be, from what I hear. Salem and Albany, for sure, and there aren't any words for what we've heard of Portland. H— heck, it was bad here! If it hadn't been for you and your friend warning me, I might not have done near as well myself."

The big farmhouse kitchen was a lot more crowded than it had been that night of the Change; brighter, too, with three gasoline lanterns hanging from the ceiling. Juniper's presence required a lot of shuffling and pushing about of tables and chairs; and the meal wasn't anything like the fried-chicken feast she remembered so fondly, either. There were a round dozen sitting down to dinner, counting children, and more out in what had been the rarely used formal dining room.

She got a bowl of porridge, some anonymous mixture of grains with husks in it, and the dried beans she'd contributed from the basement cache of the Hopping Toad were served with obvious reverence. Everyone got one hardboiled egg, as well. For the main meal of the day among people doing horse-heavy manual labor, it wasn't much.

*At least the porridge is fairly good. Smells nice, too, like fresh-baked bread, and it tastes a little sweet. Maybe molasses-and-rolled-oats livestock feed?*

"We got to work right away, because of that. And we were lucky," Finney said, after they'd bowed their heads for grace. "*Real* lucky," he went on, beaming at his son and daughter and their spouses and his grandchildren and one wiggling pink great-grandchild.

Edward Finney shrugged; he was a square-built man in his forties, a compromise between his mother's stocky frame and his father's lean height. The erect brace of his shoulders showed the legacy of twenty years in the Air Force.

"We were lucky to get out of Salem before everything went completely to hell," he said. A grin. "Looks like I'm going to be a farmer after all, like Dad wanted. And *my* kids after me."

"Not just farming," Luther said grimly.

His eyes went to the door. Outside in the hallway chain mail shirts hung on the wall, with swords and crossbows racked near them, and pikes slung from brackets screwed into the ceiling.

"Well," he went on to Juniper. "Things are looking up, provided we can keep this sickness away; the doctors have some medicine left, but not much. The first of the garden truck looks set to yield well—I give those people at the University that, they busted their . . . butts getting seed out to everyone and into the ground, and we've laid claim to a fair piece of fall-seeded wheat. Lord, though, doing everything by hand is hard work! If we could get some more harness stock, that would be grand—that team of yours would have been real useful around here."

"Cagney and Lacey are useful around our place too, Luther."

He nodded. "I expect they were, but if you can spare any . . . We stopped using horses when I was about twelve, but I remember how."

"We could use more stock too," she said happily. "But my people were going to try scouting east for them." Then: "About this committee running things here, Luther—"

\*   \*   \*

"Back!" Havel shouted as the crossbow bolt buzzed past his ears.

All three men spun their mounts and went crashing through greenery and lawn until they were out of range—a hundred yards was plenty, unless the crossbowman was a crack shot. He blessed Will Hutton's liking for nimble quarter horses and his training of man and beast; and the wide sweep of Larsdalen's lawn made it next to impossible for anyone to sneak up on them.

One nice thing about horses was that for the first ten miles or so they were a lot faster than men on foot.

*"Christ Jesus, what the fuck do you people think you're doing?"* Havel shouted, rising in his stirrups to shake a fist at the window.

"They weren't trying to kill us, Boss," Josh said.

"I know that, or I wouldn't be trying to talk," Havel snarled. "But anyone who got in the way of that bolt would be just as dead, accidentally or not. What sort of idiot fires a warning shot that close without a parlay?"

Eric was flushed with anger too. He pushed his helmet back by the nasal and called out: "What are you doing in my family's house?"

A voice came from the same upper window, thin and faint with distance: "Who the hell are you, mate?"

Havel blinked at the harsh almost-British accent . . . *An Aussie, by God. What in the* hell?

"Mr. Zeppelt?" Eric said, still loud but with the anger running out of his voice. "What are *you* doing here?"

"Eric? Your pa bloody well hired me, didn't he, sport? I've been looking after the place and the staff."

"Wait a minute," Havel said, baffled. "You know him?"

"Well, bloody hell," the voice from the house said, dying away.

A few moments later the doors opened and a short stout man with a crossbow in his arms came out; he was balding, with a big glossy-brown beard falling down the front of his stained khakis. A tall horse-faced blond woman with an ax followed him. Several other figures crowded behind her.

"That you in the Ned Kelly suit, Eric-me-lad?" the man called. "Who're your cobbers? S'truth, it's good to see yer! C'mon in and have a heart starter—we're a bit short of tucker, but there's some neck oil left."

# CHAPTER TWENTY

*"For the road is wide—and the sky is tall*
*And before I die, I will see it all!"*

Juniper Mackenzie broke off at the chorus as three armed figures stepped into the roadway. She stopped her bicycle and leaned one foot on the dirt road and called a greeting, putting a hand up to shade her eyes against the bright spring sun. Judy Barstow stopped likewise, and Vince and Steve waved hellos of their own; the rest of their party stopped as well, uncertain.

They'd all relaxed now that they were well into the clan's land—past the Fairfax place, and just where the county road turned north along Artemis Butte Creek—and they'd been singing from sheer thankfulness, despite the bone-deep ache of exhaustion.

Homecoming was sweet almost beyond bearing.

"Hi, Alex, Sam," Juniper shouted, returning their waves of greeting as she swung her other foot down and started pushing the bicycle towards them. "Merry meet again!"

Alex had his bow over his back, a buckler in one hand and a spear in the other; six feet of ashwood, with a foot-long head made from a piece of automobile leaf spring. He leaned the spear against a tree to put a horn to his lips—it was the genuine article, formerly gracing the head of a cow—and blew one long blast and three short ones, a blatting *huuuu* noise not like any sound metal had ever made.

Then he grinned and waved it overhead as the bicyclists approached. The other two slipped their arrows back into their quivers—which meant poking a razor blade on a stick past your ear, so you had to be careful—and tapped their longbows on their helmets in salute. One was stocky and broad-shouldered, unmistakable even in green jack and helmet and . . .

*And a kilt, by Cernunnos! Dennie's got them all doing it, the black-hearted spalpeen!*

"Glad to see you've got them alert, Sam," she said to the Englishman. "That's the second time I've been stopped!"

*Because one guard post at the border isn't enough, curse the expense and lost work of it!*

The other archer was a lanky blond girl in her late teens, and definitely *not* a member of coven or clan that Juniper remembered, despite the Mackenzie sigil on her jack—the crescent moon between elk antlers.

"Cynthia?" Juniper said. *What's a Carson doing on sentry-go for us?* "Does your family know you're here?"

"My folks are up at the Hall, Lady Juniper; it's Cynthia Carson Mackenzie now," the girl replied with self-conscious dignity.

Juniper felt herself flush slightly, and Alex gave her a wink as he leaned on his spear, grinning.

*Goddess, it's embarrassing when people call me that!*

So was the growing practice of calling her cabin the Chief's Hall. *Dennie's fault again,* she thought. *And he's* enjoying *doing it to me!*

"Dennie and Chuck can give you the whole story about the Carsons and the Smiths," Alex said. "Hey, fancy armor—where'd you get it? Who are the new folks?"

Juniper wasn't in a jack herself. She wore a thigh-length, short-sleeved tunic of gray-brown chain mail.

"Corvallis; and these are three of my coveners—made it out of Eugene after the Change and were on their way here, and a couple of—but you'll all get the full tale of our travels at dinner in the Hall," she said, retaliating a little for frustrated curiosity.

"Pass then, Lady Juniper," Alex said formally, rapping his spear on his buckler and stepping aside; Cynthia and Aylward tapped their helmets again.

The travelers pushed their bicycles upslope. Judy Barstow leaned over and whispered in her ear: "Maybe you should have taken a horse anyway, *Lady* Juniper," she said. "More dignified, for the exalted chieftain of the Clan Mackenzie. . . ."

"Oh, go soak your head, you she-quack," Juniper grumbled, sweating as they pushed their bicycles up the slope.

"*Just* what I was hoping to do," Judy said. "I hope they're stoking the boiler in the bathhouse right now." Then her smile faded. "And we need to do it, just in case. I'm pretty sure we're all still clean of infection and that the fleabane worked and that we scrubbed down enough, but . . ."

Juniper shrugged, lightening her mood with an effort of will: "And horses are far too conspicuous and edible to take into the valley. *And* too valuable."

The creekside road wasn't very steep, but the chain mail shirt and the padding beneath were *hot* on the fine late-spring afternoon, besides weighing a good quarter of her body weight. She had her quiver, buckler, helmet and other gear slung to racks behind the seat, and the bow across her handlebars, but she still had to push the weight uphill; and none of them had eaten much for the past full day, or very well over the last ten.

She could smell her own sweat, strong under the green growing scents; the faint cool spray from the stream tumbling down the hillside in its bed of polished rocks was very welcome. They were deep in shade now too, big oaks meeting overhead, and flowers showing white and crimson and blue through the grass and reeds and shoulder-high sword ferns. The other side of the water was a steep hillside, covered in tall Douglas fir.

"It's the Mackenzie!" someone shouted as they came out of the woods into the meadowland. "The Mackenzie herself!"

A crowd of adults and more children were waving and running onto the rough dirt road ahead of her, alerted by the horn or by a runner from the outer sentries. Dennis's bulky form led them.

And yes . . . every third adult was in a kilt now, and half the children.

"It's herself herself!" he caroled, waving on the cheers as more people ran in from the fields.

"Will you stop *doing* that, you loon!" Juniper called, laughing. "You'll have them all clog dancing and painting their faces blue next!"

"There can be only One," he said, making his voice solemn and portentous.

"How about the One throttles you with your fake kilt?" she said. Then louder to the crowd, holding up her hands: "*Sláinte chulg na fir agus go maire na mná go deo!*" she said, laughing: "Health to the men and may the women live forever! I said I'd be back by Beltane, didn't I?"

That was the spring quarter-day festival, not long off now, a time of new beginnings.

*And my, things have been happening here, too!*

There was more than one face she didn't recognize; evidently her lectures about sharing when you could had born fruit. She *did* know Dorothy Rose, who was not only in a kilt but wore a plaid improvised out of one of the same batch of blankets and a flat Scots bonnet with a feather on the side.

She pumped up the bellows of her bagpipes and then lead off the procession, stepping out with a fine swirl and squeal, not spoiled in the least by half a dozen dogs going into hysterics around her—Cuchulain was throwing himself into the air like a hairy porpoise breaching, wiggling in ecstasy. The rest of the people crowded around her and her companions, taking their baggage . . . and then suddenly seizing her and carrying her along behind the pipes, whooping and laughing as they tossed her overhead on a sea of hands.

"Put me down!" she cried, laughing herself. "Is this how you treat your Chief, returned from a quest?"

"Damn right it is!" Dennis bellowed.

She felt a huge load lift from her chest at the cheerful expressions; obviously nothing too dreadful could have happened while she was gone—dreadful by the standards of the first year of the Change, that was. Dennis was looking good himself; the kilt flattered him, and it was perfectly practical in this climate, and he had the additional excuse that none of his old clothes came close to fitting anymore.

*But mostly it's playacting. Well, people need play and dreams. In bad times more than good, and there are no badder times than these, surely?*

Jack and Muriel and Carmen were weeping openly as their fellow coveners danced them around in circles; Juniper finally struggled back to her feet and called Diana aside and gave instructions; the three were still too weak for her taste, and it would be better to get them fed and rested before the stress of meetings and explanations.

Dennis was tanned dark and wet with sweat from whatever work he'd been at; carpentry, going by the sawdust and wood shavings in the curly, grizzled brown hair on his barrel chest. With just barely enough food and more hard work than they'd ever dreamed of doing every adult in the clan had lost weight, but it looked much better on him than most. The sagging paunch had shrunk away, and the heavy muscle stood out on his tanned arms and shoulders like cables. He'd gone for a close-trimmed beard rather than the distinctly unflattering muttonchops, and overall he looked ten years younger than he had that night in Corvallis.

Sally Quinn evidently thought he was good enough to eat; she was beside him, hanging on to one arm, unconsciously curving towards him as they walked despite her mud-stained working clothes. Her delicate amber-skinned looks made a vivid contrast to his hairy massiveness; her son, Terry, walked on the other side, with Dennis's arm around his shoulders.

*Now, that's only a surprise in that it took so long,* Juniper thought happily. *I saw that coming the day they met, I did.*

She finally persuaded the mob to set her down, and even reclaimed her bicycle.

"Good thing we cleaned up yesterday," Judy grumbled. "This bunch have *no* idea what it's like out there."

"That's why we went on our journey," Juniper said. "To find out. But I would like a hot-water bath very, very much."

She raised her voice: "Is the bathhouse finished? And if something to eat could be arranged, that would be very welcome. We're tired and dirty and hungry, Mackenzies."

Most of the crowd went back to their work, save for Dorothy marching before; everyone had gotten used to the fact that there were never enough hours in the day to get everything done that needed doing.

*And everyone's been very busy,* Juniper thought, as she pushed her bicycle back westward along the dirt track that led to the Hall; the dust and ruts were worse than they'd been, with the wagon and sledge traffic.

*Mental note three thousand and sixty-three: Get someone to run a scraper over the bumps and maybe pitch gravel in*

*the holes, in our copious spare time. Or this will turn to a
river of mud come autumn.*

She'd left on the meet-and-survey trip because the main
crop was planted. It all looked much neater now, turned
earth showing green shoots and tips in orderly rows.
Adults and children were at work, hoeing or kneeling to
weed with trowels; Juniper almost drooled at the thought
of harvest.

*I crave fresh greens in an* astonishing *way,* she thought.
*Not to mention food in general.*

Others were laboring with pick and shovel, horse-drawn
cart and wheelbarrow on the contour ditch that Chuck
Barstow had laid out from the pool below the waterfall to
water the garden. It was another blessing that they had a
year-round stream tumbling down from the steeper hills
northeastward.

*Which reminds me . . .*

She craned her head over her right shoulder for a second. The twenty-foot wheel of the mill was actually *turning*
now; they'd been arguing over how to mount it when she
departed. Dennis deserved a lot of credit for it, even if they
*had* simply carried off most of the works from a tourist
trap near Lebanon.

Nobody had been around to object—another opportunity that had been worth the risk and effort to get done before someone else had the same idea.

Ahead to westward the open land had been left in grass,
a rippling green expanse starred with hyacinth-blue cam-
mas flowers, better than knee-high already; grass never really stopped growing in the Willamette, and in spring it
took off as if someone was pushing hard from below. Some
of it was being mown by a team swinging their scythes together in a staggered row, followed by another with rakes
gathering it into rows. The wild sweet smell lifted her spirits further as they passed the swaths of drying hay.

*Not to mention the fact that nobody's digging the point
into the ground every second stroke, or the blade into their
neighbors' ankles. I nearly cut off my own foot on my first
try,* she remembered. *Chuck's lessons have sunk in, at last.*

The haymakers stopped to wave and shout greetings,
and the travelers replied in kind; so did a brace of archers
practicing at the butts. Improvised railand-wire fences

made corrals for the precious horses and the livestock on the rest of the open land; there were moveable pens for the poultry and pigs. They had about twenty sheep now, with a ram among them, along with half a dozen lambs; and as many cattle.

*Or more,* she thought with keen interest; there were white-faced, red-coated Herefords among the cows that she didn't recognize, skinny yearling beasts that grazed with concentrated zeal as if they'd been on short rations. New horses, too . . .

*Aha! The* other *emissaries' trip bore fruit as well.*

The higher plateau that held the old cabin stuck out into the benchland like a steep-sided U; she was surprised at the amount the clan had gotten done there while she was away. The roof was off the main cabin, and poles stretched down to ground level to make ramps for the logs of the second story. What was really surprising was the progress on the palisade; the first log hadn't yet gone in when she left. Now a hundred feet of the defensive wall was complete.

*Thank You, Goddess Mother-of-All, and You, Lord Cernunnos of the Forest,* she thought. *We take these trees from Your woods that our clan may live.*

The better her group did at feeding itself, the more likely it was that some gang of killers would come and try to take it all away.

She puffed a bit as they went up the last section. The area around her half-dismantled cabin was nearly unrecognizable; half a dozen other structures in stages of construction ranging from sticks and string outlining their foundations to cellars nearly complete; dirt and rocks and ruts and horse dung in the open spaces between, sawhorses and frames and people cutting with everything from hatchets to two-man whipsaws, the clatter of hammers . . .

Nothing of the serenity she'd known here before the Change when it was her refuge from the world, a well of deep peace broken only when her coven arrived for the Sabbats and Esbats or by a rare guest. And yet—

*And yet I don't feel the least saddened at how it's changed,* she thought, waving and shouting greetings as Eilir came out of the cabin door with a book in one hand—she was helping teach school, with younger children crowding behind her.

*Perhaps because now it's my home—a refuge from horror and death. Home isn't a place. Home is people.*

From the rear of the cabin there came an intoxicating odor along with the woodsmoke. Juniper's nose twitched involuntarily at the unmistakable smell of barbecue; if they had meat enough to actually roast and grill, rather than throwing it into the Eternal Soup cauldrons, then things *were* looking up. She felt slightly guilty at the waste, but her stomach rumbled disagreement. Soup got *boring*.

"Now give me some peace!" she called, putting her hands on her hips and facing those who'd followed her all the way to the bathhouse door, grinning. "Let me wash, at least, and put on some clean clothes!"

They stripped to the skin before the door of the bathhouse; smoke was pouring out of its sheet-metal chimney, and Juniper's skin itched in pleased anticipation. Stripping took a little doing, when you were wearing a mail shirt; first taking off the sword belt, then bunching up the skirts as much as you could, then bending over with your hands on the ground and wriggling until it fell in a rustling, clinking heap.

"What a relief!" she wheezed—the contortions required were rather active. *Like a rich armor worn in the heat of day, that scalds with safety.*

The padded tunic underneath came off more easily, and soon the clean wind was telling her exactly how much rancid sweat had stuck to her skin.

*It's like wearing winter clothes in summer, and then lifting weights, and not being able to change into clean. How Mike and his friends bore those hauberks, I can't imagine.*

She hopped on one foot and then the other to get the hiking boots off, and scrambled out of jeans and T-shirt and underwear even faster.

"Take all the cloth and boil it in the laundry," Judy said, dumping the party's clothing in a hamper. "Boil it for fifteen minutes at least, with the special soap. Move!"

The helpers moved. Despite being tired to the bone, Juniper practically skipped up the steps and into the washing room with its flagstone floor. They'd set things up Japanese-style, that being simplest. The boiler they'd made from a big propane tank was hissing; water from that and the cold taps got splashed everywhere in glorious abandon, as the returned travelers sluiced each other down with bucketsful, soaped, rinsed again, massaged suds into their hair. The gray water ran out a drain and down a pipe into the orchard and herb garden below the plateau, so nothing was wasted.

Juniper groaned with pleasure even when her loofa hit spots that had chafed raw and the strong soap stung her eyes and the blistered bits. Eventually Judy was satisfied, and they trooped through into the next room to sink into the tub—*that* was a big sheet-steel grain bin, one of a series lined with planks and sunk halfway into the ground, separated by board partitions. They settled into the water, scented by herbs and the sauna smell of hot damp pinewood.

"Hey, you folks noninfectious now?" came a deep voice from the doorway. "Mind if we join you?"

"Yeah, Dennie," she said. "But don't get between me and the kitchen, or I may trample you!"

He stood dripping in the doorway; Sally was with him, and Eilir, and Chuck Barstow. Everyone tried to speak at once, and Eilir's hands flew, her slim coltish body dancing accompaniment to the signing.

*Thanks to the Lady you're back, Mom. I was so worried, I've got* pages *of new protective spells in my Book of Shadows!*

*And the same back to you, my child of spring,* she replied. *I could feel your well-wishes every moment of night and day.*

Meanwhile Dennis brought one thick hand out from behind his back. He had a bowl, a huge turned-wood thing; her eyes went wide as she saw it was heaped with vegetables: snow peas, green peas, carrots, deep-green broccoli florets, pieces of snow-white cauliflower . . .

Her mouth actually cramped in longing for a moment.

"Blessed be the fruits of the Lady's womb, and hand 'em over, Dennie! Don't tell me you've found some way to make veggies grow *that* fast!"

"Nah, we came across a big winter garden, well-mulched," he said, complying.

You could grow hardy vegetables over the Willamette's mild winters, with luck and a lot of work. Few had bothered, back when you could just drive down to the supermarket.

"Where?" she cried. "Frank Fairfax didn't have one!"

"Believe it or not, it's from the Smiths."

Juniper made a wordless sound as she popped pieces into her mouth, trying to decide whether the carrots really were as sweet as apricots, or if it just felt that way because they were the first fresh food she'd had since the Change.

*And here I thought the Smiths disliked us,* she thought; they were strong followers of the Evangelical minister in Sutterdown. *Maybe Dixon's mellowed!*

"You won't believe what dinner is," he said, as the four sank into the tub.

Eilir crowded under her mother's arm and laid her sleek dark head on her shoulder. The bowl was thick wood and floated easily, which let them push it around the circle like a food-bearing boat.

"We're having something besides Eternal Soup, from the blessed smell of it?" Juniper said, lying back with a sigh of contentment. "And fresh veggies ..."

He nodded, smiling smugly. "Our hunters must be in right with Herne, or Sam the Silent's finally learning how to teach as well as he stalks. We've been getting a mule deer or whitetail every couple of days for the last ten, and then yesterday I got a young boar. All two hundred pounds of whom is over the coals as we speak. Ribs, loin, crackling, gravy, liver ..."

She threw a splash of water at him as her stomach rumbled and saliva spurted into her mouth. There were plenty of feral swine in the Cascades, crossed with European wild boar introduced by hunters; they'd been regarded as pests before the Change. A lot of them hung around this section, because the hardwoods her great-uncle planted left mast for them to eat, and there was camas-root in the mountain meadows. The problem was that they were fierce and wary, and hard for mostly inexperienced hunters to take without guns. Which prompted a thought ...

"Wait a minute! *You* got it, Dennie? As in, actually shot it yourself?"

"I found a *much* better method than sneaking around in the woods. I just waited up late by the gardens." He smiled smugly. "If you grow it, they will come."

A groan went around the tub.

"There aren't all that many veggies, I'm afraid, but eat,

eat—it's a special occasion, after all! Oh, and Di is sacrificing some of her flour to make buns to go with the pork-and-sage sausages...."

The two younger members of the traveling party excused themselves with exquisite good manners, grabbed towels and bolted ...

*Or perhaps they've just got enough energy to pester the cooks,* she thought. She felt her friend's description right in her stomach, but the hot water was soothing away her aches so pleasantly that she could wait. Particularly with each piece of garden truck a sweet explosion of pleasure in her mouth.

*Or maybe the youngsters are off to their girlfriends. Certainly Chuck and Judy are devouring each other with their eyes, and perhaps playing touch-toes.*

The brief meeting with Mike Havel already seemed like a dream; an ache went through her....

*Ah, Rudy, Rudy, I miss you! You'd bless me from the Summerlands if I found a man, but who could take your place?*

"So," Chuck Barstow said, tearing his gaze away from his wife's eyes, and other parts of her. "Obviously you *did* have luck. I couldn't believe you got Jack and the others back!"

"We had help, and until then it was a very sticky situation indeed...." Juniper began, and gave a quick rundown. A murmur of *blessed be* ran through the coveners.

"Who says the Lord and Lady don't look after Their folk?" Chuck said.

*He was always keen, but we're all turning more to the Goddess and the God,* Juniper thought. *Perhaps because there's so little else to hold on to.*

When she mentioned that Luther Finney had survived, Dennis swore in delight, and Eilir clapped her hands.

"Who says you don't have the Goddess looking out for *you,* special?" Dennis grinned. "Little stuff *and* big? There were those yew logs seasoning at the bottom of your woodpile that you never got around to burning, just waiting to be made into bows...."

"That would be the God looking out for me, as Cernunnos Lord of the Forest, Dennie. But I make allowances for the ignorance of a mere cowan."

He splashed water back at her; "cowan" was Wiccaspeak for a non-Witch, and not entirely polite.

"Hey, you're playing confuse-the-unbeliever again. I have *never* been able to get a straight answer on whether you guys have two deities or dozens, taken from any pantheon you feel like mugging in a theological dark alley. Which is it? Number one or number two?"

"Yes," Juniper said, with all the other coven members joining in to make a ragged chorus; Eilir concurred in Sign.

Dennis groaned, and there was a minute of chaotic water-fighting. Juniper rescued the bowl and held it over her head to keep it from sinking until things quieted down again. That exposed more of her, but if everybody felt like throwing hot water at her aching, overworked, underfed body, she wasn't going to object.

"Or maybe it's just that *somebody* had to be lucky," he went on. "Anthropic principle—anyone still around to talk about it nowadays *has* to have had a string of lucky coincidences helping them, and more so every day that passes. If someone's breathing, they're a lottery winner. You, Juney, you're the Powerball grand-prizer."

Juniper's chuckle was a bit harsh; after her trip through the valley that bit a little closer to the bone than she liked. But when gallows humor was the only kind available . . . well, that was when you needed to laugh more than ever.

"Scoffer," she said, and continued: "Anyway, I spent time with the Committee running things in what's left of Corvallis; mostly the aggie and engineering faculties and some other folk—Luther's on it himself. They're talking about a meeting of the honest communities sometime this autumn or early winter to discuss mutual aid—especially about the bandit problem."

"Well, blessed be Moo U," Chuck said. "That could be *really* useful."

Juniper nodded. "Good people, though a bit suspicious. They can offer a lot of varieties of seeds and grafts, and stud services from their rams and bulls and stallions, and farming and building help in general. They've got real experts there; I've got forty pages of notes, advice they gave me on our problems. The difficulty is that what they want most besides bowstaves is livestock; heifers and mares and ewes particularly, to breed upgrade herds from their pedigree stock."

Chuck Barstow breathed on his nails and polished them on an imaginary lapel; Dennis grinned like a happy bear.

"Those Herefords?" Juniper asked.

"Yup. We got a small party through there about five days after you left. They got back day before yesterday, driving their flocks before them—twenty-five head of cattle, twenty sheep, six horses. Mostly breeding females."

Juniper made a delighted tip-of-the-hat gesture to the two grinning men. That solved their unused-pasture problem, with a vengeance! They could get a good crop of calves, lambs and foals too. And they could slaughter a steer every couple of weeks. . . .

*Or if we can trade for more, maybe we can spare some for Corvallis . . . have to arrange escorts across the valley, though . . . if only Highway 20 were open . . .*

It wasn't; by all they could tell, it was a gauntlet of horrors, everything from plain old-style robbers to Eaters. Aloud she went on: "What's it like over there in the Bend country?"

Chuck went on: "The Change hit them about like us, just not so much. Bend and Madras and the other bigger towns have pretty well collapsed, but a lot of their people got out to the farms and ranches, since there weren't millions of them to start with; if anything, they're short of working hands."

*That* sounded familiar. It just took so much effort to get anything done without machinery, particularly since nobody really knew *how* to do a lot of the necessary things by hand. There were descriptions in books, but they always turned out to be maddeningly incomplete and/or no substitute for the knowledge experience built into your muscles and nerves.

"And they've got local governments functioning in a shadowy sort of way—they're calling it the Central Oregon Ranchers' Association. They've got more livestock than they can feed, too, without the irrigated pastures . . . this year, at least; next year's going to be tighter for them too. We traded them bows and shafts and jacks for the stock, and for jerky and rawhides. They've got bandits of their own and the ranchers who're running things over there want weapons bad. They *really* miss their rifles."

"Congratulations," Juniper said sincerely.

The night when she'd nearly had a fit over hitting a man in the head seemed a long way away, except when the bad dreams came. She wasn't happy about becoming case-hardened, but it was part of the price of personal sanity and collective survival.

"Congratulations!" she said again. "It sounds like the eastern slope is a lot better off, at least for now."

"What was it like out there in the valley?" Dennis said. "I *still* say it was a crazy risk, you going out."

"Worth it," Juniper said. "Rumor isn't reliable and we have to know what to expect. The way the world's closed down to walking distance, you don't know until you go there and see or it comes to you. I'm not absolutely indispensable, either."

"The hell you aren't," Dennis and Chuck said together.

"I may be the High Priestess, but I'm not the Lady come in human form, you know, except symbolically and in the Circle."

Chuck snorted; he tended to pessimism, as befitted a gardener-turned-farmer.

"You're here and you're Chief. We're alive where most aren't," he pointed out. "*And* we're doing much better than most who *are* still alive. The two things are probably connected. Anyway, to repeat the question . . ."

Juniper shrugged, stroking her daughter's hair. "As to what it was like . . . some of it was very bad. Most of it was worse. And a few things like Corvallis were encouraging, which is what I'll make the most of when we have everyone together."

"You're turning into a politician, Juney," Dennis said, grinning.

"Now you're getting *nasty*," she said.

Then her smile died. "Hope is as essential as food. We have some here, of both. Out there . . ."

Judy went on grimly: "The bad news there is what broke up those refugee camps around Salem and Albany, apart from plain old-fashioned starvation."

She looked around the circle of faces; Juniper put her hand over Eilir's eyes; the girl stirred restively, and she sighed and removed the fingers. This wasn't a world where you could shelter children much; not anymore.

"Plague."

There were murmured invocations, and some old-fashioned blaspheming of the Christian deity.

"What sort of plague?" Dennis asked.

Judy snorted, and her husband chuckled, being more accustomed to the fact that she said exactly what she meant when medical matters came up. She scowled at him as she replied: "I'm not joking and it's *not* funny at all."

"Sorry—"

"It's *Yersinia pestis. The* Plague. The Black Death. Those camps were filthy and swarming with rats, and plague's a species-jumper endemic among ground squirrels here in the West. Then it got into someone's lungs and changed to the pneumonic form—which is standard in a big outbreak—and *that* spreads from person to person, no fleas needed. Spreads very easily. Plus pneumonic plague'll kill you *fast,* sometimes in a day. It's been a long time since our ancestors were exposed, much. Mortality rate of over ninety percent, like a virgin-field epidemic, and they ran out of antibiotics quickly."

That shocked Dennis into silence, not something easy to accomplish.

"I identified cholera morbus and typhus, too . . . and half a dozen other diseases . . . but the plague's worst of all. They tried to burn the bodies, but that broke down. We could see the smoke from the death-pits still rising around Salem."

"And we could smell it," Juniper said quietly. "We might think of setting out parties to burn down abandoned sections and clear out the rats."

Judy shook her head. "We're going to have to pull in our horns—set up a quarantine. And we shouldn't send anyone into the valley until the first hard frost unless it's life or death for the clan. With the plague and the cholera and typhus piled on top of sheer hunger . . . this time next year . . . a hundred thousand left between Eugene and Portland? Fifty thousand? Less?"

A cry from the heart: "If only we had some antibiotics! There probably *are* some left, but we can't find or ship them."

"Shit," her husband said quietly.

"Yes."

"And you haven't heard about what's happening *in* Portland," Juniper said. "We met a group that had come through the city—come all the way from Idaho—and ..."

When she'd finished the silence went on until Juniper reached out and took the last of the cauliflower.

"Well, we don't have to think about this Protector person for a while. The sickness will shut the valley down until autumn."

There were some things you simply *couldn't* think about too much, or you'd lose the will to live. She suspected that many had sat down and died for just that reason.

"What did we trade the Smiths for this stuff?" she said in a lighter tone. "I'd have said they wouldn't spit on us if we were dying of thirst, for fear it would give us the strength to crawl to water."

The stay-at-homes looked at each other before turning back to her; she recognized the gesture as one showing more bad news was on the way. There had been an awful lot of that, since the Change.

"Bandits hit the Smith farm," Dennis said. "Took them by surprise. No survivors except for Mark."

That was the Smith's youngest, about seven. She winced; she hadn't liked the family, they'd been rude to her and Eilir before the Change and downright nasty to the Mackenzies since, but ... And their children had been just children, and they'd taken in as many relatives from town and plain refugees as they could and not starve right away. *And* treated them fairly, which was more than you could say for some.

"Mark got out and ran to the Carsons', and they got a message to us; Cynthia galloped up on their horse. We called out everyone and trapped the bandits, there were about a dozen of them—took them by surprise, nobody on our side hurt much. None got away."

"Blessed be," Juniper said sadly. "I wondered what Cynthia Carson was doing, on guard duty here and calling herself a Mackenzie. Her whole family moved in, then?"

"Joined the clan formally the next day, them and all their dependents," Chuck Barstow said. "Not to mention the Georges, the Mercers, and the Brogies. They weren't happy with the way the Sutterdown militia showed up a day late and a dollar short, as usual."

She blinked, a snow pea pod halfway to her lips. That was an *awful* lot of people. He went on:

"The whole thing scared them all several different shades of green, and I don't blame them; it was damned ugly at the Smith place, and they saw it—the bandits had the whole bunch hung up by their heels and . . . well, I don't know if they were Eaters or just vicious. The problem is . . ."

"Oh," Juniper said. "Let me guess. Cynthia wants to join the coven, not just the clan—I remember her asking questions—and her folks aren't enthusiastic about it?"

"Worse. She *and* her mother *and* her brother want to join, and her *father* isn't too enthusiastic. Not that he's a bigot, he just thinks we're weird."

"We're Witches, Chuck," she said reasonably. "We *are* weird."

"Could be worse, from his point of view," he said. "We could be strict Gardnerians, and do *everything* nekkid."

"Wait a minute," Sally said, looking down at herself as the Wiccans laughed. "I hadn't noticed you guys got upset about skin, much. For example, right now we *are* naked."

"Well, yeah," Chuck replied. "But that's because right now we're in a *bathtub*."

That time everyone laughed; Sally joined in, then went on: "Who's Gardner? I've heard you coveners mention him."

Chuck grinned. He'd always enjoyed the early history of the modern Craft.

"Gardner was this early Wiccan dude over in England, back in the forties, fifties," he said. "In our particular Tradition, we sort of save skyclad work for special ceremonies or solitary rituals and use robes most of the time, but he thought you should do pretty well *all* the rituals skyclad, which is Wiccaspeak for bare-assed."

Juniper popped another piece of carrot into her mouth, savoring the earthy sweetness.

"There are two schools of thought on that," she said around it. "One is that the Goddess revealed to Gardner that you ought to always be skyclad in the Circle so you could conduct energy better, and it had nothing to do with sex. Then there's the other school, to which I subscribe."

"What's that?" Dennis asked.

"That's the school which says that Gardner was a lecherous, voyeuristic, horny old he-goat who loved to prance through the woods with nekkid women, but since he was also an Englishman born in 1884, he had to come up with a religious justification for it."

She sighed. "Of course, he *did* do a lot for the Craft; he's one of our modern founders. He just had ... problems. And mind you, Gardnerians *don't* have his problems; they simply end up taking off their clothes an awful lot, even in *really* cold weather ... chilblains, head colds ..."

"Purists," Chuck said, and grinned. "Say, how many Gardnerians does it take to change a light bulb? Twelve: consisting of evenly matched male-female pairs to balance the Divine energy with a leader as number thirteen to—"

The Wiccans all chuckled, and then Juniper went on: "Back to business: I'll talk to John Carson and his family. Cynthia's a bit young for such a major decision. . . ."

*Older than you were, Mom,* Eilir signed. *I've talked to her too, she signs a bit, and she's real sincere about it. I think the Goddess has spoken to her heart.*

"We can't very well turn clan members away, but all these new candidates, and then the Carsons . . ."

Dennis and Sally were looking at her with odd smiles. "Oh, no, not you two as well! I thought life was all a dance of atoms, Dennie!"

"Let's say my faithless faith was shaken by the Change, OK?" Dennis said. "I'm not the only one to have that experience. And if I started believing in Jehovah, I'd have to blame *Him* for all this since there's only one address for complaints in that system."

"And Sally, you're a Buddhist!"

Sally shrugged. "*Was* a Buddhist," she said quietly. "I *already* believed in karma-dharma and reincarnation and multiple spiritual guides—the difference is more in the terminology than the theology. Plus Terry wants to go to Moon School with his friends; it's important to belong at that age. Plus Dennie and me want you to handfast us, too. And soon. I'm pregnant, and"—she raised a hand out of the water, all fingers folded except the index, which she trained on Dennis—" guess who's daddy."

Juniper stared at her for a moment. *Oh, Lady and Lord,*

*I wish we had more contraceptives.* Condoms were already scarce, and pills worth their weight in . . . not gold, in *food,* even with the way the low-fat diet cut down on fertility.

"Congratulations," she said weakly.

Then she turned her head to Chuck and Judy: "Do you two feel the truly bizarre irony of someone wanting to become a Witch so they can *fit in*?"

Judy nodded; then, uncharacteristically, she giggled—it *was* funny, if you'd spent time in that subculture of misfits.

"When can you swear us in?" Dennis said. "Sooner the better; I've talked with some of the others, and they think so too."

"Now, wait a minute, Dennie," Juniper said warningly. "This isn't something to rush into. You can become a Dedicant right away, but Initiation isn't like Christian baptism; it's more like finding a vocation to the priesthood. You have to study a year and a day, and you have to really *mean* it."

Chuck cupped his hand full of steaming water and scrubbed it across his bearded face.

"Well, yeah," he said, hesitation in his voice. "But Juney . . . there has to be some reason why the Lord and Lady have set things up this way."

She conceded the point with a gesture—there were no coincidences—and turned back to Dennis and Sally: "Look, this is no joke. This is our faith you're talking about. It's a serious commitment; people have died for the Craft."

More soberly they linked hands and nodded. Juniper sighed again, troubled. Covens in her Tradition were quite picky about who they accepted as Dedicants, and how many . . .

*Of course, traditionally we were a self-selected microscopic minority. All of a sudden we're an Established Church in this little hilltop world, with people beating at the door, and I'm not sure I altogether like it.*

Things were a little different outside, too: Wiccans were doing a bit better than the general populace, from what Carmen and the others said.

*Which means just a large majority of us have died, rather than an overwhelming majority. Still . . .*

After a moment's thought she threw up her hands: "Oh, all right, let's assume the Lady and the Lord *are* telling us something; we can see what our coveners think over the next couple of days."

She raised a brow at Chuck, who was High Priest; traditionally somewhat secondary to the High Priestess, but to be consulted on any important manner. Rudy had been her High Priest before the Change . . . she put the thought out of her mind. Chuck was nodding reluctantly; he shared her reservations, but there really didn't seem to be any alternative that wouldn't leave people feeling hurt and excluded.

"I think it'll be good for the clan," he said. "We can't have resentments and factions and quarrels—Goddess spare us!"

Judy nodded in her turn. One thing they'd all learned, living in each other's laps like this, depending on each other in matters of life and death, with no escape—not even any music that they didn't make together—was that you *had* to keep consensus. Public opinion had a frightening power in a community this small and tight-knit; and divisions were likewise a deadly threat.

Juniper threw up her hands in surrender and went on: "Then we can do the Dedications at Beltane, which is to say, right now; so Dennie and Sally, you can start spinning a white cord, if you're serious—pass the word. The handfastings we'll have at Lughnassadh, after the First Harvest, you certainly don't have to be Initiates for that and we'll be able to afford decent feasts then, and the Initiations we'll have at Yule, at the turning of the year."

"Not Samhain?" Dennis asked.

"*No!* First, it's too soon even if we're going to hurry things; second, that's the festival for the *dead,* Dennie. We have an awful lot of people to remember, this year. Not appropriate. By then, I expect you to know *why* it's inappropriate, too."

She turned back to Judy: "As my Maiden, I expect you to run a turbocharged Training Circle to the max—fast but nothing skipped; I don't care how tired people are in the evenings. Let them show whether they're committed or not. That includes you, Dennie."

She paused to glare at Dennis and Sally. "We'll have a bunch of Giant Monster Combined Sabbats, OK? Initiations, handfastings, square dancing, bobbing for bloody apples. There. Is everyone satisfied?"

It was good to laugh with friends; good to have *some* problems that looked solvable, as well. And sometimes the Goddess just gave you a bonus. Keening over the Smiths wouldn't bring them back before their next rebirth—that was between them and the Guardians. And in the meantime . . .

She looked at Chuck: "I presume we're taking over the Smith place?"

The Carson farm went without saying, and the others who were coming in; if you joined the clan, you pooled everything but your most personal belongings and you pitched in as the clan decided. Life alone post-Change was nasty and brutish and for most, short; particularly for a single household isolated in a violence-ridden countryside where once again a mile was a long way to call for help.

Chuck shrugged and raised his hands in a what-can-you-do gesture he'd picked up from Judy. The Smith farm and the others were good alluvial terrace land as well, much of it planted before the Change and needing only tending and harvest this year.

She went on, musing aloud: "On the one hand, I hate to profit from the misfortunes of neighbors; on the other, the Smiths were a bunch of paranoid bigots, and the Carsons and the others will be a real asset; on the third hand, that land is going to be a gift of the Goddess . . . *if* we can hang on to it; and work it properly."

"Hell, the Smiths even had beehives," Dennis said, smacking his lips. "Which means *we* now have beehives. Mead . . . And the Georges planted a vineyard three years back."

"We can work all those farms from here, with bicycles, or sending people out in a wagon," Chuck said, giving him a quelling glance. "Thank the Lord and Lady you can't run off with a field of wheat!"

"But," Juniper said.

"But," Chuck answered. "*Guarding* that land's going to be the hard part. If we pull everyone back here every night . . . and you thought we were shorthanded before? Get ready for everyone to make like an electron—we'll all have to be in two places at once from now to Samhain! Not to mention housing; Dennie's crew are running up bunk beds for here and the Fairfax place."

Juniper made a mental tally: "With the Carsons and the others that gives us ... what, sixty adults sworn to the clan, now? Blessed be, but we've been growing!"

"Fifty-nine, counting Cynthia Carson but not her brother Ray—he's seventeen come Lughnassadh. Forty-two children, half of them old enough to do useful chores or mind the toddlers. We've got more people, but a *lot* more land to work. It wouldn't be so bad, if we didn't have to spend so much time on guarding and sentry-go and battle training, but we *do*."

"Truly, by the Morrigu Herself," Juniper said, closing her eyes and juggling factors. They'd taken in as many as they could, from the beginning ...

*Just one year,* she thought, and prayed at the same time. *Just one year and one good harvest and enough seed corn, Lady Gaia, Mother-of-All. Then we can start the spiral of energy going up instead of down.*

Chuck went on, as if echoing her thought: "But the food we got from the Smith place put us ahead of the game in reserves; they had a lot of oats and root vegetables in store, and all the farms had quite a bit of truck planted and some just coming ripe, besides the fruit. John Carson's a first-rate livestock man, too, which is something I'm no expert at and Sam doesn't have the time for. John was wasted without a herd to look after, I've been working off his advice since the start."

"How much grain?"

"Between the new farms and what we planted in spring, counting wheat and barley and oats together—call it eight thousand bushels all up, less fifteen percent for wastage and seed if we want to double the acreage for the fall planting, yields will be way down next year without brought-in seed. ... We were counting on exchanging the labor of our people and the use of our hauling teams for some of the crops anyway, but this way we get it all."

Juniper nodded. "Enough to put our diet this winter from 'just barely' to 'rude plenty,' with more to come next year, despite the way we've grown."

She did a piece of quick mental arithmetic: sixty pounds to a bushel, so ... "That's multiple *tons* of grain; we'll need to start thinking bulk storage."

"If we can harvest it all," Dennis said. "The grain's going

to come ripe real soon now—the first oats in a month, the rest from mid-July on."

"Maybe we could take in a few more refugees, then," Juniper said. "Since we're going to have a surplus. That group at the schoolhouse near Tallmar? We know they're healthy, they were grateful enough for the rose hips"—which had halted a nasty case of scurvy. "A couple of them know useful stuff like cooperage, and they'll not make it through till winter by themselves. And we could loan some seed-grain later to . . . Hmmm. Maybe we could throw up a mound and palisade around one of the farmhouses too, and settle some of our people there at least part-time? That way—"

The water had cooled from hot to lukewarm before they thrashed out the details to put to the clan as a whole, and it was nearly sunset outside; they all heaved themselves out, pulled the plug and began to towel down. Diana and Andy Trethar stuck their heads in.

"That pig is incredibly ready, and we're putting the sausages on, so anyone who feels like dinner had better come," she said. "The only leftovers are going to be bones for the Eternal Soup Stock."

"Yum," Juniper said, pulling a robe over her head from the stock kept ready for bathers. "Yummy yum—"

Then a disquieting thought struck her, and she turned to the others as she knotted her belt.

"Wait a minute, though—I suppose all the cowan within a day's walk of the Smiths are hopping around frothing about our taking over their land? Not to mention the sheriff! And Reverend Dixon . . . The Wicked Witches strike again? It's all a Satanic plot?"

"Right," Chuck and Dennis said, in chorus, as they sidled towards the door.

Dennis went on in a reasonable tone: "But we told them Lady Juniper could explain it all when she got back."

Juniper gave a wordless howl of wrath as they both ducked out—you had to be careful about spoken curses, when you knew they could stick.

She dashed after them with the skirts of the robe hiked up in her hands so she could kick both backsides; symbolically, but with feeling.

A cheer went up as she appeared in the door, and she dropped the fabric hastily; flashing the crowd wasn't exactly appropriate behavior for the head of the clan. Nearly everyone was gathered, minus the first watch of the night guard and some of those doing kitchen duty—and those were loading the trestle tables in the Hall and on the veranda and the scrap of lawn preserved before it.

Someone came up and put a wreath of wildflowers on her head, red and yellow columbine laced with lavender vetch and white daisies; everyone else was wearing one too.

*I'm home,* she thought. *And I'm going to see my people safe; I can't save the world, but what I can save, I will.*

She set her hands on her hips. "All right, then—let's eat!"

*That* could always be relied on to get a positive reaction, these days.

> *"Come away, human child*
> *To the woods and waters wild*
> *Weaving olden dances*
> *Mingling hands and mingling glances*
> *Till the Moon has taken flight . . ."*

The voices and the strings of the small harp went plangent through the soft cool spring night, full of the green sap-scent of trees, and of the flowers along the way; there was a hint of woodsmoke and cooking from the Hall below, a breath of cooler air from the great forests of the mountains whose snowpeaks were lit by moonlight far above. The quiet rustle of many feet and the hems of their robes through the grass blended with the creaking of the forest and the night sounds of its dwellers.

Juniper had always loved this part of her great-uncle's land, even on brief visits as a little girl, frightened of the intimidating, solitary old man but bewitched by the place. Having it for her own had brought incredulous joy, and so had sharing it. The path wound up eastward from the cabin, through stands of huge Douglas firs and groves of pine and big-leaf maple, past openings and glades; sometimes the candles and lanterns of the coveners caught the eyes of an animal for a fleeting moment of green-yellow communion.

She led the procession, the hood of her robe thrown back, the silver moon on her brows, her belt woven from cords white and red and black and carrying her scabbarded athame. Behind her walked Chuck—Dragonstar in the Craft—with the elk mask and horns of the High Priest on his head, and Judy—Evenstar, the coven's Maiden—at his side; then the rest, two by two, cradling their candles and the tools of the ceremony.

The dew-wet stems of the grass seemed to caress her ankles. At last they came to the place, high on the mountain's slope, where a knee of its bones made a level space jutting out into emptiness.

Why her great-uncle had planted a circle of trees here she'd never known; but that had been nearly ninety years ago, and the oaks rose straight and tall all about it. Their boughs creaked over her, a patient sound, waiting as they had through all those decades for their destined use.

Just outside the circle to the west was the spring that was the source of Artemis Creek—how fitting the name! It flowed clear and pure among rocks and reeds, trickling away down the slope and making a constant plashing murmur between banks glowing with the pale golds of glacier lilies and stream violets. She could feel the care and trouble melting away as they approached, the gentle familiarity of the ritual and the place soothing like cool fingers on a hot brow.

Within the enclosure was close-cropped grass, soft as a lawn but shot through with the small purple flowers of wild ginger; in its very center a shallow fire pit lined with stones. At the four quarters, brackets of wrought iron reached out from the trees. Against the northern side of the ring was a roughly shaped altar, made from a single boulder.

They halted at the northeast quadrant of the great circle. With the sword in her hand she traced the perimeter deosil, sunwise, past the great candles flickering at the quarters in their iron-and-glass holders:

*"I conjure you, O Circle of Power, that you may be a meeting-place of love and joy and truth; a shield against all wickedness and evil; a boundary between the world of humankind and the realms of the Mighty Ones . . ."*

Stars arched above, like the glowing hearths of an endless village; the moon hung over the mountaintops, white splendor, bright enough to dazzle her eyes. When she was finished she admitted the coven and sealed the circle behind them; the Maiden lit the censer and took it up, casting a blue trail of incense and sweetness behind her to mingle with the spicy smell of the wild-ginger leaves bruised beneath their feet. Two more followed with their bowls of salt and water. . . .

*"I bless you, oh creature of Water; I bless you, oh creature of Earth; come together you power of Water, power of Earth. Cleanse all that must be clean, that this space be made sacred for our rites."*

The words and movements flowed on:

*"Guardians of the Watchtowers of the East, ye Lords of Air . . ."*

Her athame's blade traced the Invoking pentagram in the air; in the eye of the mind it hung there, blue and glowing against the yellow flicker of candle flame.

*"Guardians of the Watchtowers of the South, ye Lords of Fire . . ."*

*"Guardians of the Watchtowers of the West, ye Lords of Water and of Sunset . . ."*

Facing the altar at last:

*"Ye Guardians of the Watchtowers of the North! Oh, Lady of Earth, Gaia! Boreas, North Wind and Khione of the Snows, Guardians of the Northern Portals, you powerful God, you strong and gentle Goddess . . ."*

At last all had been cleansed and purified: with Water and Earth, Air and Fire. She stood with the Wand and Scourge in her hands, facing the coven as the High Priest called:

*"Hear you the words of the Star Goddess, the dust of whose feet are the hosts of heaven, and whose body encircles the universe!"*

Juniper's eyes rose, beyond the heads of the coven and the rustling dark secrecy of the trees, to where the stars made the Belt of the Goddess across the night sky, frosted silver against velvet black. Her lips moved, but she was hardly conscious of the words that rang out:

*"I who am the beauty of the green earth and the white moon among the stars and the mysteries of the waters, I call upon your soul to arise and come unto Me. From Me all things come and unto Me all must return. . . . Let there be beauty and strength, power and compassion, honor and humility, mirth and reverence within you. And you who seek to know Me, know that your seeking and yearning will avail you*

*not, unless you know the Mystery: for if that which you seek,
you find not within yourself, you will never find it without."*

Her voice rose triumphantly:

*"For behold, I have been with you from the beginning,
and I am that which is attained at the end of desire!"*

The stars seemed to open above Juniper, rushing towards her as if she were falling upward or they into her, through galaxies and the veils of nebulae whose cloak was worlds beyond counting. But that infinity was not cold or black, not empty or indifferent. Instead it was filled from edge to edge with a singing light, from unknown Beginning to unimaginable End radiant with an awareness vast beyond all understanding. So great, yet that greatness looked on her, at her, into her, the atom of being that was Juniper Mackenzie.

As if all that was lifted her in warm strong arms, and smiled down at her with an infinite tenderness.

Sight and sound returned; she was conscious of tears streaming down her cheeks, and of the High Priest's tenor singing:

> *"We all come from the Dark Lord*
> *And to Him we shall return*
> *Like a leaf unfolding*
> *Opening to new life . . ."*

And the Maiden's alto weaving through it, the words mingling without clashing:

> *"We all come from the Goddess*
> *And to Her we shall return*
> *Like a drop of rain*
> *Flowing to the ocean . . ."*

Higher and higher until the song became one note and broke on the last great shout of power like a wave thundering on a beach. . . .

With that she was herself once more, among her own in the Circle; yet still glowing with thankfulness. Only a handful of times had she felt this so utterly, but that too was good—some joys could only be had rarely, or you would break beneath them. . . .

When the working was done and the Circle unmade, the coven making its way down the nighted trace, Chuck drew her aside.

"Something special happened, didn't it? I could feel it. I think most of us did."

She nodded solemnly. "I think . . . I think the Goddess promised me something, Chuck. I just don't know what."

# CHAPTER TWENTY-ONE

Michael Havel leaned back against his saddle and gnawed a last bite off the rib; he took a quick drink of water afterward, and a mouthful of bread as well. Angelica's homemade BBQ sauce had *real* authority, as well as lots of garlic.

*I can just about handle it now,* he thought. *After years of pouring Tabasco over MREs to hide the taste. It would have killed me when I was Eric's age.*

Most of the people in his neck of the woods clung to Old Country cooking habits, and Finns thought *highly seasoned* meant putting dill in the sour cream.

The eating part of the Bearkillers' homecoming celebration was about over; mainly variations on meat and bread, but well done; the grateful smell lingered, along with woodsmoke and livestock. It was full dark now, with a bit of a chill in the air and only an enormous darkness around their fires. Somewhere in the distance a song-dog howled at the stars, and he could hear horses shifting their weight and snorting in the corral behind the wagons.

He flipped the bone into the fire, watching as it crackled and hissed and then burned when the marrow caught. Not far away a hound pup followed the arc with wistful eyes, but she was lying on a pile of them already, stomach stretched out like a drum. Havel was thinking of naming her *Louhi,* after the Old Country sorceress who could eat anything.

*And Christ Jesus, it's good to be home.*

Will Hutton wailed a note or two on his new harmonica and set it down again.

"You really ready to get back on the road?" he said.

"You haven't been back but half a week, and busy as hell that whole damned time."

Havel nodded. "We've about outstayed our welcome in the Kooskia area if we aren't here for good," he said. "We'll start south tomorrow. Josh and Eric and I were doing fifty, sixty miles a day most of the way back."

A smile. "Tiring him out was the only way to keep Zeppelt from playing that goddamned accordion. Christ Jesus, if you knew the hours I'd suffered listening to those things as a kid, and watching the old farts lumber around dancing to it! And the kraut version is even worse."

"He 'n' his lady did seem a mite sore when they got in," Hutton grinned. "Fact is, though, he's not bad on that squeeze-box at all."

Havel shrugged; he didn't want to argue a point of musical tastes. "So five or six miles a day with the whole outfit will be a rest-cure."

"That slow?" the Bearkillers' trail boss said.

Havel nodded: "I don't want to travel too fast; Pendleton or the Walla Walla country by July or August—we can hire out to help with the harvest, or just pick some out-of-the-way wheatfields nobody's working on and help ourselves—and Larsdalen in say October, November. By then the sickness ought to be burned out, and until then we don't go near cities."

"Bit late for plantin' surely?"

"Not in the Willamette. You only get occasional winter frosts there; you can put in fall grains right into December, and graze stock outside all year 'round."

Will frowned, turning the mouth organ over in his battered, callused hands. "Don't like what you told about this Protector mofo," he said. "Don't much like it at all."

Havel grinned like a wolf. "The guy seriously torqued me off, yeah, I admit it, but I'm not just looking for a fight. The Willamette's still the best place going, and I don't think Mr. Protector is going to stay satisfied with what's west of the Columbia Gorge, either. From what he said, he already had his eye on the waterways inland, too—and you can sail all the way up to Lewiston, if you hold the locks. That's cheap transport nowadays."

Hutton's lips pursed in thought. "Bit far to reach, things bein' the way they are."

"Not him directly. But remember that deal I told you he offered *me*? One gets you five that's his boilerplate—and every would-be little warlord within reach of Portland gets the offer. No shortage of *them*; they're like cockroaches already. Give them some organization and backup, and things will get nasty all over this neck of the woods."

Ken Larsson nodded. He and Pamela Arnstein were sitting close with their hands linked; that had surprised Havel and flabbergasted Eric when he got back, but even Signe and Astrid seemed to be taking it in stride.

Ken spoke slowly, deep in thought: "Not surprising, given what you told me about his academic background. I think he's jumping the gun a little—it's a bit early to try for full-blown feudalism. But it's certainly more workable than trying to keep the old ways going."

"Like, we've got to learn how to crawl before we walk," Havel said; a corner of his mouth turned up. "Get tribes and chiefs right, before we can have barons and emperors."

"More or less."

Hutton had been thinking as well: "Mike," he said after a moment, "Does it strike you as a mite strange that the plague, the Death, got as far as Lewiston so fast?"

"Hmmm. The Columbia-Snake-Clearwater *is* an easy travel route, and refugees from the coast *did* get that far . . . You suggesting Professor Arminger helped it along? Let's not make him the universal boogeyman."

"Could be; or not," Hutton said. "For sure it's helpful to him that way, keeping the interior all messed up while he gets himself set. Anyway, I see what you're drivin' at. Stay here, go there, we're still gonna end up fightin' the man. Unless we move far south or east, and that's damn risky too. Could be worse there and we'd be committed. Only so many months in the year and we need to find somewhere we can put in a crop. The Willamette . . ."

Havel nodded. "It's best because things are worse; no organized groups to stop us settling . . . well, not in parts of it, at least. There's that bunch of monks around Mt. Angel, and Juniper Mackenzie and her neighbors, and Corvallis, and a bunch of small holdouts around Eugene, but that chunk around Larsdalen's clear. Most of the central valley is empty."

"Thought you said there were families holdin' out 'round the Larsson spread."

"By hiding. Nothing organized—and if they don't get someone *to* organize them, none of them will last out this winter. You need some security to farm. I think we could provide it."

Just then Signe came back to their campfire with a basket, followed by Angelica with a bottle and tray of glasses, and Astrid staggering under a collection of wooden struts and a large rectangular object. The basket held little chewy pastries done with honey and nuts; the bottle was part of the town's gratitude, good Kentucky bourbon—priceless now, and usually jealously hoarded. Havel poured himself a finger of it, and splashed in some water.

"What've you got there, kid?" he asked the younger Larsson girl indulgently; she had that epic-seriousness expression on her huge-eyed face.

He'd noticed some smudges on her fingers lately, Magic Marker and paints. Signe had real talent when it came to drawing, but Astrid was better-than-competent herself. Apparently Mary Larsson had thought it was something suitable for her girls to learn.

She gave him a smile, and went to work. The struts turned out to be an artist's tripod and easel; the strange object she put on it was about the size and shape of a painting, or a very large coffee-table book.

"Dad helped me find the paper," she said, one hand on the cloth that wrapped it. "At the Office Max where we got all that stuff, you remember? Art supply section—non-acid-pulp drawing paper. And Will did the covers."

"We weren't doin' anything with that piece of elk hide," Hutton said, a little defensively. "I like to keep my hand in at tooling and tanning leather. It'll be right useful, one day."

"Signe helped with the drawings. And I took notes from *everyone* about *everything*!"

Havel felt a sinking in the pit of his stomach; Astrid's pale eyes had taken on that dangerous, joyous glint they had when she came up with something truly horrifying.

She used her new dagger—which she wore every waking moment—to slit the string binding, then whipped off the cloth. Beneath lay a book—leatherbound board covers, rather, with an extensible steel-post clamp at the hinge for holding the paper.

Across the front, tooled into the elk hide, was: THE CHRONICLES OF LORD BEAR AND HIS FOLK: THE RED BOOK OF LARSDALEN.

The letters were archaic-looking in a sloping, graceful fashion, carefully picked out in gold paint.

Havel felt his throat squeeze shut and his eyes narrow. Signe sank down beside him, elaborately casual, and leaned towards him on one elbow.

*"She needs to do this, Mike. It's like therapy. Go with it? Please?"*

He forced himself to relax. A crowd had gathered, standing behind him. It was the usual suspects—everyone who didn't have something urgent to do. There wasn't much in the way of entertainment on a typical evening, and this made a delicious change.

Astrid threw back the cover. The pages inside were large in proportion, big sketch-pad size. Across the top something was written in spiky letters; between the odd shapes and the flickering firelight it took him a moment to read:

The Change came upon us like a sword of light!

*The Change came upon us like a monumental pain in the ass,* Havel thought; but the drawing below was interesting enough—complete with him wrestling with the Piper Chieftain's controls and Biltis yeowling inside her carrier box—the actual cat was sniffing around people's feet and hissing at the hound pup.

Astrid began to read the text. It was written in the Roman alphabet, cunningly disguised to look runic. Her high clear voice made the mock-archaic diction sound less ridiculous; absolute faith could do that. He *almost* rebelled when he got to the appearance of the Three Aryan Brotherhood Stooges, and she faltered a little.

"You *said* they were like orcs, Mike!"

"Ahh . . . Yeah, kid, I did say that. Go on, you're doing great!"

*I didn't say they had fucking fangs, girl, or arms that reached down to their knees, or little squinty yellow eyes and scimitars!*

Signe murmured in his ear again: "It's sort of metaphorical. Showing them outwardly the way they were inwardly."

Havel smiled and nodded. It probably *was* theraputic for Astrid to do this; and looking around he found amusement and fondness on a lot of the adults' faces. The problem was that the youngsters were just plain fascinated, and God alone knew what stories they'd be repeating when they were parents themselves. He kept smiling and nodding when the Eaters became a nest of goblins, his meeting with Arminger turned out to be a confrontation before a huge iron throne, with the Protector ten feet high and graced with a single slit-pupiled red eye in the center of his forehead. . . .

And Juniper Mackenzie was evidently a sorceress Amazon with a glowing nimbus of power around her, a wand trailing sparks, and guarded by Scottish-elf longbowmen.

"More whiskey," Havel said hoarsely, holding his glass out without looking around. *"Please."*

"Was she really like that?" Signe said. "Beautiful and mysterious?" A smile: "I sort of resent it when you go fighting cannibals with anyone but me, you know."

*Tell the truth,* Havel told himself.

"Beautiful? Nah," he said. "Cute, in a . . . cute sort of way, sort of like a scruffy hobo pixie. About five-three, redheaded, thirtyish—looked like she'd been spending a lot of time out of doors. Skinny. Nice singing voice, though."

Astrid finished up: "And to Larsdalen and home, he showed the way!"

There was a moment of silence, and then a burst of whooping cheers; he wasn't quite sure whether they were for him, as the subject of the epic, or for Astrid's treatment of it. It certainly came out more colorful than the dirty, boring, often nauseating reality. Eventually they dispersed towards the open space in front of the wagons; there had been talk of dancing. Of course, that meant the Bearkiller analogue of music . . .

"Got the storyteller's gift, that girl," Will Hutton said. "Tells things the way they *should* have been." He popped one of the pastries into his mouth.

"Married this woman for her cookin'," he went on contentedly.

Havel grinned at the smoldering look Angelica gave her husband; the fire that slipped down his throat as he sipped the bourbon was no more pungent-sweet.

"My cooking? *De veras?* And here I thought it was because my brothers were going to kill me *and* the worthless *mallate* cowboy I'd taken up with!"

"Now, honeybunch, you know it was your momma I was frightened of," he said, mock-penitent.

Then he looked over at the cleared area, brightly lit with half a dozen big lanterns. "Oh, sweet Jesus, no, no! Spare us, Lord!"

Havel glanced that way himself, and snorted. Eric Larsson had a feed-store cap on backward, and a broomstick in his hand, evidently meant to be a mike stand; he was prancing around—

"Christ," his father said. "A capella karaoke rap! How could it come to this? How did I fail him?"

"That boy may be able to jump some," Hutton said dourly. "But Lord, Lord, please don't let him try to sing!"

Luanne Hutton leaned against the wagon behind Eric, holding her ribs and gasping feebly with laughter. A few of the other young Bearkillers were making stabs at dancing hip-hop style, and doing about as well as you'd expect of Idaho farm kids with no musical assist.

Hutton surged upright. "C'mon, Angel. We got to put things right; let's find Zeppelt and his squeeze-box."

Havel looked at Ken Larsson. "What gives with you gettting your vineyard guy from *Oz* of all places?"

"Australia has a lot of fine winemakers," Larsson said defensively. "Hugo Zeppelt is first-rate. Smart enough to hide out in that old fallout shelter my father built, too, *and* get our horses into the woods when the foragers from Salem came by."

The chubby little Australian and his tall gangling blond wife had pushed Eric out of position with the Huttons' help, and they were warming up on their instruments— accordion and tuba. *Oom-pa-oom-pa* split the night, already familiar from the trip back; Josh and Annie Sanders started organizing the dance—they had no musical talent to speak of, but she'd helped at church socials a good deal in her very rural Montana neighborhood.

"Do-si-do, turn your partner," Havel said. "Not only an Aussie with an accordion, but an Aussie who's obsessed with *polkas*?"

"He's from the Barossa valley in South Australia, and it

was settled by Germans," Larsson said defensively. "And Angelica likes it."

"She's Tejano," Havel said. "San Antonio and the Hill Country used to be lousy with krauts. The oom-pa-pa beat spread like the clap. Put Zeppelt and Astrid together, and in a generation we'll all be wearing lederhosen to go with the pointed ears . . . the Tubas of Elfland, going oom-pa, oom-pa."

"C'mon," Pamela said; she'd been quiet that evening. "Let's dance, oh fiancé. Mike's in one of his grumbling moods. Signe and the dog have to listen but we don't."

They wandered over to where couples were prancing to the lively beat. Signe sipped at her own whiskey; her cheeks were a little flushed. For a moment they leaned shoulder-to-shoulder; then Louhi crawled between them, licking at hands and faces.

"All right, that settles it. I christen thee *Louhi,* and you can start learning manners. Been ten years since I had a dog."

Signe smiled, tousling the young hound's ears. "I'd have figured you for a dog sort of guy, Mike."

He shrugged. "I was, when I was a kid. Had this German shepherd called Max—very original, hey? From the time I was eight until just before I graduated high school."

He smiled, looking into the flames: "He used to sleep on the foot of my bed, bad breath and gas and all, and I even took him hunting."

"It's odd to take a dog hunting?"

"Max? Yeah, sort of like taking along a brass band. He saved a *lot* of deer from death. My dad couldn't stand it— the mines were always laying people off with about a week's warning, and there were four of us kids, so a lot of the time we *needed* that venison. But Max, he'd howl something awful if you tied him up when you got in the canoe."

"Canoe?"

"Yeah, we had this creek that went by our place, and ran through some marshland—man, when I remember what my mom could do with wild rice and duck—then into a little lake with some pretty good hunting woods. Even better if you took a day or two and portaged a bit. White pine country before the loggers got there; lots of silver birch, and maple. We had a good sugarbush on our land, in the back of the woodlot."

"It sounds lovely," she said. "In fact, it sounds like Sweden—we visited there a couple of times, Smaland, where our family came from originally."

Havel's mouth turned up. "Yeah, the Iron Range country is the grimmer parts of Scandahoofia come again—it's even more like Finland. Makes you wonder if our ancestors had any brains at all—those of present company excepted, of course."

"*Que?*" Signe said.

That was one of Angelica's verbal ticks, and a lot of people had picked it up while he was gone.

Havel mimed wonder: "Like, did they say to themselves: *Ooooh, rocks and swamps, crappy soil, mosquitoes bigger than pigeons, blackflies like crows, and nine months of frozen winter blackness! Just like what we left. To hell with pushing on to golden, mellow California—let's settle here!*"

Signe laughed and wrinkled her nose: "I saw the Larsson home in Smaland, and you could grow a *great* crop of rocks around it. Oregon probably looked *really* good by comparison. I mean, Sweden's a pretty nice place to live now—or was before the Change, you know what I mean—but back in the old days, you could starve to *death* there."

"And in 1895 the Upper Peninsula of Michigan *didn't* have a lot of Russians trying to draft you into fighting for the Czar, yeah, point taken. Anyway, Max, he would have starved to death if he'd had to hunt on his own—what the shrinks call poor impulse control. He got his nose frostbit a couple of times trying to track down field mice in winter; he'd go galloping across the fields with his muzzle making like a snowplow. I was too young myself to train him properly when he was a pup."

Louhi crawled further up, stuck her nose into Mike's armpit and promptly went to sleep.

"I'll do better with Louhi here. Hounds scent-hunt anyway."

Signe considered him for a while, head on one side: "What happened to Max?"

"Besides scaring the bejayzus out of deer and squirrel, getting into pissing matches with skunks, and shoving his face into a porcupine's quills once a year? He used to get into the maple-sap buckets in the spring, too, pretty regular. Ever tried to get that stuff out of the fur of a hundred and ten pounds of reluctant Alsatian?"

"In the end, I meant."

"In the end? Got run over a little while before I graduated high school," Havel said. "Broke his back; I found him trying to crawl home. I had to put him down."

*And he kept expecting me to make it better,* Havel remembered. *Right up to the second I pulled the trigger.*

"That must have been terrible," Signe said, laying a hand on his.

He turned his over, and they linked fingers. "Yeah, I missed him."

To himself: *I couldn't have proven in a court who did it, but then, I didn't have to.*

A flicker of grim pleasure at a memory of cartilage crumbling under his knuckles: *Beating me out with Shirley was one thing, but killing my dog . . .*

"Is that why you didn't get another dog?"

"Nah, didn't have the time, and it's not fair on the animal if you don't—they're not like cats," Havel said. "Now things are different."

Signe nodded, and looked over to the open space; it was square-dancing now.

"That fiancé thing seems to be breaking out all over," she said. A pause: "You . . . you've been sort of quiet since you got back, Mike. I . . . there wasn't anything with this Juniper woman, was there? Eric won't talk about it at all."

"Just giving things a rest," he said, sitting up and resting his free arm on his knees. "And yeah, I won't deny there was a sort of mutual attraction, pretty strong for short acquaintance. She had a lot of character."

Signe froze, her hand clenching on his, and he went on: "But we decided we both had commitments elsewhere; she had her kid to look after, and her people. I do have commitments here, don't I?"

Signe nodded, flushing redder. "Ummm . . . I hope so. Nice night for a walk out?"

Havel uncoiled to his feet, pulling her up. "Walking's nice, but we can do that any night. Right now, why don't we dance?"

She smiled, a brilliant grin that made her eyes like turquoise in the firelight.

"I'll dance your feet right off, mister!" she said.

A room on the new second floor of the Chief's Hall held

the clinic. Juniper Mackenzie swung her feet down from the stirrups and over the edge of the table; her voice was almost a squeak: "I'm *what?*" she said.

"Pregnant."

"Are you sure?"

The room was still a bit bare; glass-fronted cabinets, rows of medicines and instruments and herbal simples, anatomical diagrams, and a well-laden bookshelf. It smelled of antiseptic and musky dried wildflowers and fresh sappy pine. Judy finished washing her hands—the stainless-steel sinks had come from the kitchen of a Howard Johnson's ten miles northwest—and turned, leaning back against the counter as she dried her hands on a towel and spoke tartly: "Look, Juney, I'm not a doctor and I've felt inadequate often enough trying to do a doctor's job here, but I *am* a trained midwife and I can recognize a pregnancy when I see one!"

"I simply can't believe I'm . . ." Juniper said, letting the sentence trail off weakly.

"Pregnant," Judy said with sardonic patience. "Preggers. Knocked up. Expecting. *Enceinte.* In the family way. Have a bun in the oven. Providing a home for someone back from the Summerlands—"

"I'm familiar with the concept! I thought I was just missing a period because I'd lost weight—how could this have happened?"

Judy's voice dropped into a sugary singsong she never actually used with children: "Sometimes, little girl, when the Goddess and the God fill a man and woman's hearts, so that they love each other very much, they show their love by—"

"Oh, shut up, you she-quack! What am I going to *do* about it?"

"You want a D and C? Pretty straightforward at this stage."

"No," she said, firmly and at once, surprising herself a little; her mind had apparently made itself up without telling her. "No, I'm definitely keeping it."

She looked around the room. It was bright and cheery, morning sun bright on fresh-sawn wood and paint, but the only personal touch so far was a watercolor Eilir had done for Judy back before the Change. It showed the Goddess as the Maiden of Stars; the features were done in a naïf schoolgirl style, but held an enormous benevolence.

*I never thought there would be any child but Eilir,* she thought. *But it seems You had other ideas. . . .*

"Not much doubt about who the father is," Judy said. "Not unless there's been a miracle—and you're not a virgin, not Jewish, and that legend's from the wrong mythos anyway."

"No," Juniper said. "No doubt at all. But let's not be spreading the parentage abroad, shall we? It could be . . . awkward down the line."

"Well," Judy said, briskly practical, starting a new page in the file on the table. "It isn't your first time; that's good. How did Eilir go—apart from the measles, that is?"

"She was premature, eight months and a bit, but otherwise fine; seven pounds and no problems, no anesthesia and no epidural, three hour delivery. No morning sickness, even. I was just sixteen, and didn't realize what was happening until about three months in."

Judy's brows went up. "Well, that's an old-fashioned Catholic upbringing for you."

"Speaking of my mother, now that I think back on it, I remember her saying that I was easy, but a bit early, too."

"Likely to be a genetic factor with the premature birth, then," she said. "Have to check carefully later."

"I'll just have to make him feel welcome, I suppose," Juniper said, smiling a little and putting a hand on her stomach.

"He?"

"Suddenly . . . I've got a feeling."

Judy wrote again: "Now, we'll put you on the special diet and the supplements—thank the Mother-of-All and the Harvest Lord we aren't quite as short of food as we were! Apart from that, pregnancy isn't an illness and a first-trimester fetus is *extremely* well cushioned, so there probably won't be any problems; you won't have to start being really careful until the fourth, fifth month unless something unusual happens. Report any spotting, excessive nausea—"

Juniper nodded, listening . . . but half her mind was drifting over the mountains eastward.

*Mike, Mike, we didn't plan on this! How are you faring?*

# CHAPTER TWENTY-TWO

"Something's happened here," Michael Havel said thoughtfully, lowering the binoculars and looking at the rising smoke in the distance.

The June wind stroked his face; it was that perfect early-summer temperature that caresses the skin the way a newly laundered pillowcase does at night.

*Even better if I didn't have to wear this damned iron-mongery and padding,* he mused absently—in truth, he'd gotten so used to it that he only noticed it when he consciously thought about it.

"Pretty country otherwise," Signe said. "Lovely colors."

He nodded. Acres of blue flowers nodded among the rippling tall grass along the fringe where hills gave way to flatland, sprinkled with yellow field-daisies; this area of upland plain in western Idaho had been called the Camas Prairie once, when it was the hunting ground of the Nez Perce bands.

His horse shifted its weight from hoof to hoof, tossing its head and jingling the metal bits of its bridle, eager to be off and doing.

"Quiet, Gustav," he murmured, stroking a gauntlet down the arch of muscle that made its neck.

Most of the rolling lands southwestward were green with wheat or barley rippling in the breeze, with field peas or clover, save where a patch of fallow showed the rich black soil. Distant blue mountains surrounded the plain on all sides, giving it the feel of a valley; small blue lakes and little farm reservoirs added to the impression, but there were occasional gullies or creekbeds below the general level. He couldn't see any cattle from here, but a herd of pronghorns ran through a wheatfield, bounding along at better than fifty miles an hour with their white rumps fluffed—something had spooked them.

He handed the glasses to Signe and leaned his hands on the saddle horn, cocking his head slightly to one side. There was a rustling chink of chain mail as his helmet's rear aventail slid across the shoulders of his hauberk. He had good distance sight, but hers was about the best he'd ever run across. To the naked eye the pillar of smoke was distant, and the cluster of buildings at its base barely visible where they nestled under a south-facing hill.

"I can't see anyone moving either," Signe said at last. "I'm not sure I can see people at all. They should be out fighting the fire, if there's anyone there at all. But . . . I don't like those crows and buzzards. See the clumps?"

*That could mean plague,* he thought. *Trying to burn the bodies, and then the last survivors crawling away to die . . . but I doubt it. That's a farm, not a town; they wouldn't have enough people for that.*

"We'd better scout it, cautiously," Havel said.

With people so afraid of sickness, news spread even more slowly than it had right after the Change. It was doubly difficult to keep informed, and doubly needful.

"Luanne and Astrid?" he asked.

They were still the best riders, bar Will, and they rode light; it was unlikely anyone could catch them. Plus Astrid was still their nearest approach to a good mounted archer . . . and it was his observation that when girls were told to go take a look at something and come back, they were less likely to get themselves into unnecessary trouble by pushing on regardless.

"I wouldn't send them together," Signe said.

There was a smile in her voice. Havel looked over at her, and there it was, framed by the round helmet with its barnasal in front and curtain of chain mail to the rear.

"I thought Astrid thought Luanne was, ah, radical cool," he said.

"She did," Signe said; now she was grinning. "But not anymore."

*"Que?"*

"Astrid caught her making out with Eric behind the chuckwagon two nights ago, which was disgusting—and I see her point, you know? The thought of someone making out with *Eric* . . . that *is* disgusting. Anyway, then Luanne told her how she'd understand when she was older and her figure developed—a real low blow. So now Astrid's not *talking* to her anymore."

Havel made a strangled sound. "I don't know if she's worse when she's pretending to be an elf, or when she's relapsed into being a real human teenager. I do know—"

The young woman finished his sentence for him: "—that Gunney Winters never had to face this sort of problem in the Corps. They wouldn't have taken Astrid at Parris Island, though, Mike."

"We'll do the scout ourselves, then. Get Will."

"You're the bossman."

She reined around and cantered off. Havel looked after her briefly; the rest of the outfit were waiting a quarter mile back, wagons—there were a lot more of them now—stopped on alternate sides of the narrow ribbon of road, with outriders on the edge of sight, others working at the horse and cattle herds to keep them bunched, and some folk on foot by the vehicles.

*Half old-style cattle drive, half gypsy caravan, half small-scale Mongol migration,* he thought wryly.

Then he turned back to look at the long country ahead, thinking. He was uneasy, and he'd never liked that when he didn't know precisely why. Presently hooves thudded behind him, and he nodded over his shoulder.

"Will."

"Mike?" Will Hutton said. "You called?"

"Well, first thing, Luanne and Astrid have decided to spend the afternoon together making armor links, to teach them to enjoy each other's company more."

Hutton grinned. Making the rings was about the most unpopular chore in the Bearkillers: not particularly hard, just tedious, frustrating, finicky detail work with dowel and pliers, wire cutters, a little hammer and punch, and roll after roll of galvanized fence wire.

"What do you think of that place just behind the ridgeline for a camp?" Havel went on, pointing.

"Fine, if you want to stop this early."

They all looked up to estimate the time; it was about two o'clock. Pre-digital mechanical watches had become a valuable type of trade goods, along with tobacco and binoculars and bows.

Hutton went on: "Flat enough, good water and firewood, good grass, good view. You don't want to try and make Craigswood today?"

Havel shook his head. "I'm not easy about what I can see from here," he said. "I want to find out more before we're committed."

"Nice if we could do some trading here, at Craigswood or Grangeville, or just pick up stuff," Hutton observed. "There's a lot of things we could use, or are gettin' short of, not to mention more remounts. Some training we could do easier if we stopped for a week or two, as well."

"That all depends," Havel said. "See that line of smoke there? Looks like a farm or a ranch house where something got torched, and nobody's moving, but you can see it's been worked since the Change—fresh-plowed land, and spring plantings. We're going down to check. Have Josh and a squad keep an eye out from here, out of sight on the reverse slope. If things have gone completely to hell in this neighborhood, we may have to take another detour."

Will nodded and reined his horse about, gliding away at a smooth trot.

*Christ Jesus, I was lucky there,* Havel thought; he didn't think he could be as good a chief-of-staff and strong-right-arm, if their positions were reversed.

"Equipment check," he said to Signe, and each gave the other's gear a quick once-over.

They were both in full armor. That was Bearkiller practice anywhere not guaranteed safe, now that they had enough chain hauberks for the whole A-list. He looked at the bear's head mounted on his helmet for an instant before he put it back on and buckled the chin cup.

*Well, it doesn't smell, and it makes good shade on a sunny day,* he thought.

He'd gotten used to the way the nasal bar bisected his vision, too.

*Plus bear fur won't make the helmet work any worse if someone tries to hit me on the head.*

He told himself that fairly often; it beat admitting that he just didn't want to deal with one of Astrid's sulks. They both pulled their bows out of the leather cases and fitted arrow to string.

*We're mounted infantry with cavalry tastes,* he thought to himself. *But if we keep working at it harder than anyone else, then we're going to have a real advantage.*

They put their horses down the slope, slowly until they were in the flat, then up to a walk-canter-trot-reverse rhythm, their eyes busy to all sides. The horses were fresh, and the day was pretty; at least until they came to the dead cattle.

"Very dead," Havel muttered.

Hacked apart, and the bodies rubbed with filth, and a chemical smell under the stink made him suspect poison, which a couple of dead crows confirmed. He looked beyond them to the fields. The wheat was a little over knee-high on a horse, with the heads showing—harvest would be in another five weeks or so—but great swaths of it were wilted and dying.

"Roundup," he said. Signe looked a question at him.

"See how the wheat's wilted in strips? Someone went through spraying weed killer on it, Roundup or something like it. The stuff's available in bulk anywhere there's much farming and it acts fast."

Her face had gotten leaner and acquired a darker honey-tan, but it still went a little pale. Havel nodded. Wasting food like this was the next thing to blasphemy.

The dirt road joined a larger one, and they slowed down as the drifts of dirty-brown smoke rose ahead. From the clumps of squabbling crows, he knew there were bodies of men or beasts in the fields to his right. Men probably, given what had been done to the cattle; the way they didn't fly away also told him that the feast hadn't been disturbed.

So did the coyote that sat looking at him with insolent familiarity, and then trotted off unconcerned. Havel suppressed an impulse to shoot an arrow at the beast. It had already learned that men weren't to be feared as much as formerly. . . .

*But if men are less the wolves will be back soon, you clever little son of a bitch,* he thought grimly. *Try pulling tricks like that with* them, *trickster, and you'll regret it.*

When they came to the sign and gate they were coughing occasionally whenever the wind blew a gust their way, but the smoke smelled rankly of ash, not the hot stink of a new fire.

"*Clarke Century Farms,*" Havel read. "*Homesteaded 1898.*"

The first body close enough to identify was just inside, tumbled in the undignified sprawl of violent death; a fan of black blood sprayed out from the great fly-swarming wound hacked into his back with a broad-bladed ax, where the stubs of ribs showed in the drying flesh. There was already a faint but definite smell of spoiled meat.

Someone had taken his boots, and there was a hole in the heel of one sock.

A dog lay not far beyond him, head hanging by a shred of flesh, its teeth still fixed in a snarl. The bodies hadn't bloated much, although lips and eyes were shrunken, but that could mean one day or two, in this weather; the ravens had been at them, too. In the field to the left was a three-furrow plow that looked as if it came from a museum and probably did. A stretch of turned earth ended where it stood.

One dead horse was still in the traces before it, and a dead man about four paces beyond, lying curled around a belly-wound that might have taken half a day to kill him. Two of the big black birds kaw-kawed and jumped heavily off the corpse when Havel turned his horse to take a closer look.

"Crossbow bolt," he said, when he'd returned to his companion. "Looks like it was made after the Change, but well done."

They passed another pair of bodies as they rode at a walk up the farm lane to the steading, near tumbled wheelbarrows.

The main house hadn't been burned; it stood intact in its oasis of lawn and flower bed and tree; a tractor-tire swing still swayed in the wind beneath a big oak, and a body next to it by the neck. There was laundry on a line out behind it. The smoldering came from the farmyard proper, from the ashes of a long series of old hay-rolls, the giant grass cylinders of modern farming, and from where grain had been roughly scattered out of sheet-metal storage sheds, doused in gasoline and set on fire.

The oily canola seed still flickered and gave off a dense acrid smoke. There was a wooden barn as well, gray and weathered; a naked man had been nailed to the door by spikes through wrist and ankle. He was dead, but much more recently than the rest, and he was older as well, with sparse white hair.

Written above his head in blood was: *Bow to the Iron Rod!* There was a stylized image underneath it, of a penis and testes.

Signe was hair-trigger tense as they rode up to the veranda; she started when the windmill pump clattered into the breeze. Water spilled from the tank underneath it, which looked to be recent—probably the windmill was an heirloom, only brought back into use since the Change.

"Wait here," he said, returning bow to case and arrow to quiver.

He swung down and looped his reins over the railing of the veranda. His horse bent its head to crop at the longer grass near the foundation.

"From the look, whoever did it is long gone. But stay alert."

Havel drew his backsword and lifted his shield off the saddlebow, sliding his left forearm into the loops. There was a scrawled paper pinned to the door with a knife—inside the screen, so it hadn't blown free. Printed on it in big block letters with a felt-tip pen was: FOR REBELLION AGAINST DUKE IRON ROD!

Underneath it was a logo, a winged skull, human but with long fangs.

"And I suppose the Lord Humungous *rules* the desert, too," he muttered; it didn't seem like simple banditry. "What the hell is going on here?"

Then he nudged the door open with his toe—it was swinging free, banging occasionally against the frame, and went through with blade ready and shield up.

There was no need for it. He blinked at what he saw on the floor of the living room, glad he hadn't sent Signe in—she'd toughened up amazingly, but he just didn't want this inside the head of someone he liked. He made himself do a quick count as he went through the rooms of the big frame farmhouse; there was no way to be precise, without reassembling everyone. Nothing moved but some rats, although he saw coyote tracks; probably one of the scavengers had gotten in through a window.

"That's where the women and children were," he said grimly as he came out.

Signe swallowed and nodded; she didn't bother to ask what had happened to them.

Havel went on: "I make it at least twelve adults, and quite a few kids. Say six families, give or take."

He looked around at the steading. This had been a large, prosperous mixed farm; probably the owners had called it a ranch, Western-fashion. Judging from the stock corrals and massive equipment that stood forelorn and silent in its sheds, it was something on the order of three square-mile sections or more—six hundred and forty acres each. That was typical for this area, which grew winter wheat and barley and canola and other field crops and ran cattle.

Before the Change, that would have meant one family and occasional hired contract work, but . . .

"Probably the farmer's family took in a lot of townspeople," Signe observed. "Relatives, and refugees."

They'd seen that pattern elsewhere, once the nature of the Change had sunk in.

"Yesterday?" Signe went on. "Day before?"

"Dawn yesterday," Havel agreed, narrowing it down a little more. "They had food cooking on a wood range and the kids were mostly in PJs."

Signe winced. "The bandits ran off most of the stock, looks like. I suppose we should look for anything useful, but—"

"But I'm not going into the buzzard business, until these folks are buried," Havel said for both of them.

Signe's head came up, looking back the way they'd come. A light blinked from the ridgeline there, angled from a hand mirror. They both read the Morse message. Not for the first time, Havel blessed the fact that Eric had been an Eagle Scout; he'd been full of useful tricks like that. He even knew how to do smoke signals.

*Twenty-plus riders bound your way approaching from southeast on section road.*

Signe took a mirror out of a pouch on her sword belt and replied, then looked a question at Havel.

"We'll meet them out by the gate," he said. "If they look hostile, we can run—tell Will to have everyone ready. I don't think we'll have to fight; whoever did this wasn't planning on coming back anytime soon, in my opinion."

When they halted at the junction of lane and dirt road, she said quietly: "I hate this kind of thing, Mike. I hate seeing it and I hate smelling it and I hate having to think about it later."

He leaned over in the saddle and gave her mailed shoulders a brief squeeze; like hugging a statue, but as so often with human beings it was the symbolism that counted.

"Me too," he said. "But I hate something else worse— the sort of people who do this shit."

"Yes!"

He glared around. There was no *reason* why people here had to die. It was far away from the cities and their hopeless hordes, and for the first year or so there would be more food than people could handle—plenty of cattle, more grain than they could harvest by hand from last year's planting. They weren't short of horses, either, and with some thought and effort they'd be able to get in hay and sow a good grain crop come fall; nothing like as much as they usually planted by tractor, but more than enough to feed themselves and a fair number of livestock.

It was security that was the problem: without swift transport, or more than improvised hand weapons, without phones and radios to call for help . . .

Light winked off metal in the distance where the road came over a rise, revealing movement.

*Which is why I had all our gear done in brown or matte green,* he thought, with pardonable pride.

He unshipped his binoculars and focused; two dozen, all right, all men and riding as if they knew how. The one in the forefront had a U.S. Army Fritz helmet, and a couple of the others did as well, or crash-helmet types. Several wore swords, Civil War sabers probably out of the same sort of museum that had yielded the three-furrow plow; the others had axes or baseball bats, and two had hunting bows.

Mr. Fritz also had a county sheriff's uniform, and a badge . . . as they drew closer, he saw that several others had badges as well, probably new-minted deputies. The sheriff was in his thirties, the other men mostly older—no surprise there, either. The average American farmer had been fifty-three before the Change.

"They look righteous," Havel said. "Signe, take your helmet off, but keep alert."

She did, and shook back her long wheat-colored braids; that tended to make people less suspicious, for some reason. He turned his horse's head slightly to the left, and kept his bow down on that side with an arrow on the string, not trying to hide it but not drawing attention to it, either.

"Afternoon," he said, holding up his empty right hand when the riders came near.

The sheriff looked at them, giving their horses and gear and faces a quick, thorough once-over; he was a lean hard man with tired blue eyes and light-brown hair going gray at the temples.

"You're no bikers," he said; his men relaxed a little too.

"Jesus Christ!" one of the riders muttered to a companion. "It's King Arthur and Xena the Warrior Princess."

"Shut the hell up, Burt," the sheriff said. "What's going on here?"

Havel pointed up the laneway, then back over his shoulder.

"Our outfit's passing through. We saw the smoke from that ridge back there, and thought we'd take a look. Someone killed everyone at this farm, burned their grain stores and canola and hay, killed some of their stock and ran off the rest, and I think sprayed Roundup on their standing grain. It's real ugly in there. Signed by Duke Iron Rod, whoever or whatever he is."

Several of the men cursed; one turned aside, hiding tears. The sheriff's long face seemed to acquire some more lines.

"We're too late," he said. "Henry, you go check."

A fist hit the pommel of the sheriff's saddle, making the horse sidestep. "They hit three farms this time, and led us by the nose from one to the other! Now they're headed back."

He shook himself and looked at Havel. "You're passing through? You look a lot better fed and armed than most of the road people we see."

"Thought we might stop and feed our beasts up a bit, if you can spare the grazing. And we can trade," Havel said. "We've got a farrier and smith, a first-class horse man, an engineer, couple of construction experts, a leatherworker, a doctor and a really good vet. Plus some weapons— swords, arrows, shields, armor."

He held up his recurve, twanging the string after he dropped the arrow back in its quiver.

"Plus the ones who made this, and our armor." That raised some eyebrows. "So we won't be begging."

"Say!" one of the posse said, nodding towards the image on their shields. "Aren't you the Bearkillers?"

As Havel nodded, he turned to the sheriff. "Bob Twofeather told me about 'em, remember? They were up on the Nez Perce rez for a bit. They helped with those guys who'd gone crazy and started cutting people up."

Havel nodded. "That was us. We went over to Lewiston, nearly. Once we heard what was happening there we decided to turn back and try crossing into Oregon a little further south."

Everyone flinched a little at that; the Black Death scared even the bravest. Havel took off his own helmet.

"Yeah, you're the Bearkiller *jefe*," the man said. "They call you Lord Bear, right? Got the scar killing a bear with your knife, was what I heard."

Havel shrugged, mouth twisting a bit in irritation at the fruits of Astrid's imagination. And it was worse than futile to go around correcting every urban legend, like the one about the bear . . .

*It's a rural legend, actually,* he thought with mordant humor. *Amazing how they spread with no TV. And anyway, it's helpful psyops.*

Aloud he went on to the sheriff: "I could bring down some of my people, help you with cleaning up. We don't have the sickness. And you're welcome to share our fire tonight. We should talk."

The sheriff thought for a moment and then nodded decisively. The man he'd sent to the house returned, pale-faced and scrubbing at his mouth with the back of his hand.

"Kate Clarke's missing," he said, which brought more curses and clenched fists. "The rest of them are all there."

"Right," their leader said. "Louie, you go get the doc and tell him I need a bunch of people checked over to make sure they're clean."

He turned to Havel as his rider galloped off southwestward. "No offense."

"None taken. We're careful too."

"I'm Robert Woburn, county sheriff. Since the Change."

"Mike Havel," he replied. "Boss of the Bearkillers."

They moved their horses shoulder-to-shoulder, and he

stripped off his right-hand glove for a quick hard shake. The back of the glove was covered with more ringmail, leaving only the palm and the inner surface of the fingers plain leather.

The sheriff turned to his men: "We'll get these people buried, and then the rest of you can get back to town and tell everyone what's happened. No use in trying to catch them now. I'll stay here and bring these folks in tomorrow; it'll take all day with wagons and a herd. Henry, you tell Martha I'll be late, but I'll have some guests tomorrow. Jump!"

# CHAPTER TWENTY-THREE

Duke Iron Rod—even he seldom thought of himself as Dave Mondarian anymore—rolled off the woman. She was the new one, taken in the latest raid, but she'd stopped screaming and fighting by now. Pretty, though, and young—eighteen or thereabouts, healthy farm-girl type.

"Get out," he said, yawning and stretching and scratching. "Go do some work."

She'd rolled over onto her side; his broad hand gave a gunshot slap on her butt and she rose obediently, stepping into the briefs and belting on the short bathrobe that was standard wear for the new captures. It made them feel more fearful and obedient; and besides, it was convenient.

"Wait," he said, and stood to piss in the chamber pot. "Take that, too."

"Yes, Duke Iron Rod," she said, and scurried out.

*I don't care what the Protector says,* Iron Rod thought. *Duke's fine, but* nobody *is going to call me* grace.

He heard a smack and yelp from the next room; that was Martha, his old lady from before the Change. She liked to keep the new bitches in line.

"Don't make her spill it!" he shouted, pulling on his black leather pants. "You'll clean it up yourself if she does!"

*Gotta get the plumbing working,* he thought, as he stamped his feet into the heavy steel-shod boots. *Pots smell and they're a pain in the ass.*

The problem there was that this place was on top of a hill—it was a lot easier to defend from a height, but without power-driven pumps it was also hard to get water up here. The hand pumps on the first floor worked well enough for drinking and washing water, but not to run the toilets on the upper stories, according to the plumbers. Since they didn't change their tune after he hung one of them off the walls, they were probably telling the truth.

The rooms he'd chosen for his own were in the west corner of St. Hilda's, on the fourth floor; this one still had a window, although there was a pair of heavy steel shutters ready to swing across it and leave only a narrow slit. One of the new crossbows was racked beside it, and bundles of bolts, and a half-dozen short spears for throwing.

He liked standing there, or even better up in one of the bell towers, and looking out over the land that he was making his. A white grin split his face as he thought of that: *Even fucking wheat-country looks better when it's your very own private Idaho!*

Today he went out into the outer room of this suite; it was fixed up with tables and sofas, as well as more weapons racked on the walls and his armor on a stand. It was full of the good smells of food, too, and his stomach rumbled. Martha had breakfast waiting; a big beefsteak with fried eggs on top, and hash browns and coffee. It all still tasted a little funny, except for the coffee, and the cream in that was different too. He supposed it was because it was all fresh country stuff, right from the farms or the cows.

When he'd wiped his mouth he looked at Martha; she was a tall rawboned woman with faded bleach-blond hair, a couple of years younger than his thirty-eight.

"You gotta get the girls working on keeping this place cleaned up. The doc says we'll all get sick, otherwise, especially the kids."

"Then stop the boys crapping and pissing in corners 'cause they're too lazy to go downstairs or look for a pot!" she said. "Or tell 'em to go live in the stable with the fucking horses!"

He liked the way she stood up to him—had in the old days, too, even after a beating; she'd stabbed him in the foot, once, when he knocked her down, put him on crutches for weeks.

"Yeah, I'll work on that," he said mildly.

It was a warm day, and he didn't bother with a shirt. He did pick up his great sword in its silver-chased leather sheath, buckling it across his back on a harness that left the hilt jutting over his right shoulder ready to his hand. The weapon was a favorite of his, a present from the Protector like a lot of their new gear; it had a winged skull as a pommel, and the two-handed grip and long double-edged blade suited his style. The knife he tucked into its sheath along his boot was an old friend from before the Change, though.

Then he went out into the corridor. "Moose, Hitter," he said to the men on guard, slapping their armored shoulders in passing. "Go get some eats, bros."

They were old-timers from the Devil Dogs; not too bright, but *loyal* as dogs. Pleased grins lit their faces as they clanked away.

The place did smell a little gamy as he walked down to the staircase. On the floor below, big arched windows looked down from the corridor onto the courtyard. Iron Rod threw one of them open—the air outside was fresher.

The block off to the east had been the church; it had the two towers, and big doors gave in onto it. From the rear, two wings ran back to enclose the court, ending in a smooth curtain wall.

They used the church as the main dining hall these days; his followers were spilling out of it right now, except the ones nursing hangovers. The big hairy men were loud and happy this morning, after a successful raid; he'd have to give them a couple of days off, before he got them working on weapons practice again, and riding. They were good guys, tough and reliable, but most of them weren't what you'd call long on planning.

Iron Rod was; he'd made the Devil Dogs a force to be reckoned with in Seattle's underworld over the last ten years, made those washed-up old geezers in the Angels back off, and the gooks and greasers and niggers respect him. The drug trade was competitive; you didn't stay in business long—or stay breathing—if you couldn't think ahead and figure the angles. He'd come through the automatic-weapons anarchy of the crack epidemic still standing because he thought with something else besides his fists and his balls.

Another man approached along the gallery, and Iron Rod watched him with the same instinctive wariness he would have a brightly patterned snake.

Baron Eddie Liu wasn't one of Duke Iron Rod's

gangers. Neither was the huge figure that followed him, dressed in rippling armor made from stainless steel washers on leather, faceless behind a helmet with only a T-slit for vision and carrying a heavy war-hammer over his shoulder. Even among the Devil Dogs he was impressive.

Those two were the ambassadors from Portland, the Protector's men . . . from what he'd heard, Liu was one of the Protector's roving troubleshooters.

*And he's smart, too,* he thought, watching the slender figure in the dark silk shirt, black pants and polished boots and fancy chain belt.

*But this ain't Portland,* Iron Rod thought. *This is my turf now.*

Then he turned to the archway, raised his fists and bellowed, a guttural lion roar of dominance and aggression. All eyes in the court turned to him. He knew he cut a striking figure; as huge as any of his followers, with thick curly black hair falling down on massive shaggy shoulders and a dense beard spilling down the pelt of his chest.

Unlike most of his men he was flat-bellied, though—had been before the Change, too. Muscle ran over his shoulders and arms like great snakes wrestling with each other; every thick finger bore a heavy gold ring, and two gold hoops dangled from his ears. The face between was high-cheeked, hook-nosed, the eyes brooding and dark.

"Devil Dogs!" he shouted. "Dog-brothers!" That brought a chorus of howls and barks and yipping.

"Devil Dogs *rule!* We beat these sorry-ass farmers *again!* We took their food and their cattle and their horses, we burned their barns, we fucked their bitches!"

A roaring cheer went up and echoed off the high stone walls of the courtyard.

"Pretty soon, we'll have Sheriff Woburn hanging from a hook!"

There were half a dozen set in the walls now, between the towers and over the old church doors, taken from a slaughterhouse and mounted in the stone. All were occupied at present, but he'd clear one for Woburn, when they caught him. A wordless howl of hate went up at the sheriff's name, hoarse and strong.

*I got a serious jones for Woburn,* the Devil Dog chieftain

thought. *Worst I've had since those pissants ran us out of the Sturgis meet back in '94.*

"The prairie is mine! All bow to the Iron Rod!"

A chant went up, falling into a pattern: "Iron Rod! Iron Rod! Duke! Duke! Duke!"

Most of them hadn't known a Duke from a Duchess and thought both were country and western stars, back before the Change. He'd been fuzzy on it himself until the Protector's people explained, but he liked the sound now.

When he turned from the window, Liu and his troll were there, which he liked rather less; so was Feitman, the Devil Dogs' own numbers man, a skinny little dude in black leathers with a shaven head and receding chin. He also carried two knives, and he was as fast with them as anyone Iron Rod had ever seen. The boys respected him, despite the time he spent with ledgers and books, and with computers before the Change.

"We just wanted to say good-bye," Liu said.

He was skinny too; some sort of gook, although he had bright blue eyes. You didn't want to underestimate him, though.

"The Protector's going to be real pleased with the progress you guys are making," he said. "And with the horses, provided we can get them down the river and past the locks."

Iron Rod grunted. Then he spoke: "Something I've been wanting to ask."

Liu made a graceful gesture.

*Fag,* Iron Rod thought, then shook his head. *Nah.* He'd made quite an impression on the girls here. *And even if he was a fag, he'd still be dangerous as a snake. Watch him careful.*

"What I'd like to know is why the Protector is giving us all this help over the past couple of months," Iron Rod went on.

And it had been a *lot* of help; weapons, armor, some skilled workers and a couple of instructors. Surprisingly, those had been even more useful than the swords and scale shirts; disconcertingly, they'd stayed more afraid of the Protector than of Iron Rod, even behind his walls and among his men.

Most useful of all had been the advice on how to take over this turf, and how to run it afterward.

"He's not exactly *giving* it all away," Liu said, his left

hand on the hilt of his long curved sword—a *bao,* he'd called it.

"We're getting the cattle and horses—those'll be real useful, and they're sort of scarce west of the Cascades right now. When you're set up here, you'll send men to fight for the Protector on call, like we agreed. And you'll want to buy lots of stuff from Portland; we'll take a rake-off on that."

Iron Rod nodded. "Yeah, yeah, but that's all sort of, what's the word, theoretical. And does the Protector trust me that much?"

The blue eyes went chilly. "Nobody stiffs the Protector, man," he said, in a flat voice the more menacing for the absence of bluster. "Nobody. Not twice, you hear what I'm saying?"

Iron Rod wasn't afraid of Liu, or his master; he wasn't afraid of much. He *was* good at calculating the odds, and he blinked as he thought.

"Maybe," he said. "My word's good on a deal, anyway. It's the Protector's angle I'm trying to figure."

Liu looked at him with respect—he'd always been polite, but Iron Rod knew that his appearance made people underestimate his brains. That was useful, but it was still pleasant to see the gook's opinion of him revise itself.

"It's what the Protector calls strategy," he said. "We want to get rid of all the old farts anywhere we can—the sheriffs, the mayors, army commanders, all the types who think they can run things like they did before the Change. Those wussies in Pendleton, they look like they might cause us a lot of trouble in times to come. With you strong here, and you being the Protector's man, we'll have their balls in a vise."

Iron Rod nodded somberly, looking westward. He wasn't worried about Lewiston or Boise; the plague was finishing off what the Change had left. Craigswood and Grangeville he could take care of himself; if he left anything standing there, it would be because it was useful to him. Pendleton—the main center of eastern Oregon's farming and ranching country—hadn't been hit nearly so hard; they were getting their shit together, and it might be a real problem later.

"Yeah," he said. "I can see that. Tell the Protector, anytime he wants to take them on, once we've settled our accounts here—"

He put out a massive hand and slowly clenched it into a fist, as if squeezing a throat.

"First things first," Liu said. "You gotta take care of Woburn, and then build the rest of those little forts, like the Protector said, and get men to put in 'em and keep the farmers working. You know what the Protector says. There are only two ways to live now; farming, and running the farmers. We're working on that back west of the mountains right now."

"Yeah, yeah," Iron Rod said; it was a good idea and he was going to do it, but he didn't like being hectored. "Don't get your balls in a twist, bro. Woburn'll be hanging from a hook pretty soon, and I'll pickle his deputies' heads in vodka before the snow flies."

Liu shuddered. "One good thing about Portland, it doesn't snow much," he said.

The great steel-clad figure behind him rumbled agreement.

"Pansies," Iron Rod said, grinning. He'd been from upstate New York, back when. "Say, one thing—you're Chinese, right?"

"Right. Born in New York, father from Guangzhou—Canton to you round-eyes."

"How come the *blue* eyes, then?"

Liu grinned back. "Hey, my momma was a Polack. Ain't you never seen *West Side Story*?"

*Oooof,* Juniper thought, straightening up for a second and rubbing at her back. Then: "Oooof!" as it twinged her, reminding her she was thirty—thirty-one at next Yule—not eighteen, and that she'd been working from before dawn to after sunup since the grain started coming ripe two weeks ago.

*Harvest* would *come just before I'd be off the heavy-labor list,* she thought.

So far all pregnancy had done for her was give her a glow and an extra half-inch on the bust.

It was a hot day; July was turning out to be warm and dry this year in the Willamette, a trial for the gardens but perfect for harvesting fruit and grain. The cool of dawn seemed a long time ago, although they were still two hours short of noon.

Ahead of her the wheat rippled bronze-gold to the fence and its line of trees. Cutting into it was a staggered line of harvesters, each swinging a cradle—a scythe with a set of curving wooden fingers parallel to the blade.

*Skriiitch* as the steel went forward, and the cut wheat stalks toppled back onto the fingers, four or five times repeated until the cradle was full; *shhhhkkkk* as the harvester tipped it back and spilled them in a neat bunch on the ground; then over and over again . . . A dry dusty smell, the sharp rankness of weeds cut along with the stalks, sweat, the slightly mealy scent that was the wheat itself.

Birds burst out of the grain as the blades cut, and insects, and now and then a rabbit or some other small scuttling animal. Cuchulain and a couple of other dogs went for them with a ferocity so intent they didn't even bark; they'd all grasped the fact that they had to supply more of their own food by now, as well as working to guard or hunt.

Each of the dozen harvesters had a gatherer behind him; Chuck Barstow was the first, over on the left-hand end of the line, with Judy following behind him, and Juniper was binding for Sam Aylward at the far right-hand position; those were their two best scythesmen, and it helped to pace the others.

*Not to mention pacing the binders,* she thought, wheezing a little; the thick-bodied ex-soldier cut like a machine, muscle rippling like living metal beneath skin tanned to the same old-oak color as his hair.

*Planted by tractors, cut by hand. The last wheat planted with a tractor this world will see in a long, long time.*

The thought went through idly as she scratched and stretched again, feeling the sweat running down her face and flanks and legs.

Aylward also worked in hat, boots, a kilt and nothing else, and looked disgustingly comfortable, relatively speaking. Juniper was running with sweat too, but she wore loose pants, a long-sleeved shirt, and a bandana under her broad-brimmed hat; the sun would flay a redhead like her alive if she didn't. Every bit of cloth in contact with her skin was sodden, and it chafed. Unlike some, she didn't find the Willamette's rainy, cloudy winters a trial.

*So I bundle up, Lord Sun, despite the heat and the awns sticking to me and itching in every place imaginable including some I'm still shy about scratching in public,* she thought. *It's very unreasonable of You.*

The damned little bits that broke off the heads and floated to stick on your wet skin and work their way under your clothes were called awns, according to Chuck. They were a confounded nuisance any way you took it.

She rubbed at her back again, and looked over her shoulder, mostly to stretch—something went *click* in her spine, with a slight feeling of relief. Much more of this twenty-acre stretch was reaped than wasn't, and it was the last field—two ox-drawn carts were already traveling across it, with workers pitching up sheaves. The Willamette had surprisingly rainless summers, and you didn't have to leave the sheaves stooked in the field to dry except for the seed grain.

The sight was a little bizarre; the carts themselves were flatbeds, each with two wheels taken from cars and vans, drawn by converted steers under hand-whittled wood yokes.

Juniper shook her head; you had to get used to that sort of contrast, in the first year of the Change. She took a swig of lukewarm water from her canteen, moved her bow and quiver and sword belt forward a dozen paces and Aylward's likewise, and bent to work again.

Grab an armful-sized bundle of stalks as the cradle had left them, move them forward, grab and move, grab and move, until you had enough for a sheaf—a bundle as thick as you could comfortably span with both arms. Then you held it in front of you, grabbed a handful just below the grain ears, bent the straw around the whole bundle at the middle, twisted and tucked the end underneath to hold it . . . and then you did it all over again, and again.

*So this was what the phrase* mind-numbing toil *was invented for,* she thought. *I wonder how many others are making that discovery!*

At that, most of them were doing about half what the books said an experienced worker could finish in a day. She tried not to think again, mentally humming a song instead. It was easier if you could get into a semitrance state, where time ceased to flow minute-by-minute. Gradually her hands and legs and back seemed to move of their own volition.

A heartbreaking share of the grain in the valley wasn't being harvested at all, going to waste from plague and fear and lawlessness, something that made her stomach twist to think of.

Then someone called out; she stopped in midreach and looked up, shocked to see the sun past the noon mark.

"Blessed be!" she said, and many more voices took it up; there were shouts of sheer joy, and some of the younger harvesters managed an impromptu bit of dancing.

They weren't *nearly* finished anymore; they *were* finished. Everyone grouped around her in a circle; she wiped a sleeve over her face and gathered up the last of the wheat. First she tied it off as she had the others; then she went to work shaping it, with legs and arms and a twist of straw for a mouth.

"Hail to the Goddess of the ripened corn!" she said, laughing and exhausted, bowing before the sheaf. "We thank You, Mother-of-All, and the Harvest King who is Your consort."

Later they'd take the dolly back to the Hall; and then there were the rites of Lughnassadh next week, when the Oak King gave way to the Holly. But for now they all admired the Queen Sheaf as it was carried across the field towards the southeast corner and shade on the end of a scythe-shaft.

"Go us!" someone yelled, and everyone took it up for a moment, pumping their fists in the air. "Go us! Mackenzies rule!"

"Do you realize," someone else said reverently, when the chant had died down, "That from now on we can eat bread *every day*?"

"In the sweat of our brows," Juniper said, grinning and wiping hers.

That got a chorus of groans. *But it's true,* she thought. *And the bread is very, very welcome.*

They all picked up their tools and weapons and followed the Sheaf to the southeast corner of the field where an oak and a group of Douglas firs cast a grateful shade. There were four big aluminum or plastic kegs of water on two-by-four X-trestles as well; she drank, washed face and hands, peeled off bandana and shirt, poured several cupfuls over her head, drank again . . . Heat seemed to radiate away from her, like a red-hot poker cooling, as if her hair was flame in truth.

"Dinner!" someone cried.

Eilir drove the delivery cart, which was one of her chores; two-wheeled, with a single ex-cow-pony between the shafts. The soup came in two cauldrons, one double-walled aluminum, the other thick pottery; both types held the heat well. After they ate, they could help the loaders get as much of the cut wheat as possible out of the fields today.

*Congratulations!* Eilir signed, as eager hands unloaded. *What a beautiful Queen Sheaf! Now we can get back to work on the palisade!*

Bits of straw and grass and twigs flew in her direction; she giggled and held her buckler up in front of her face to protect herself from the mock attack before she turned the cart with a deft twitch of the reins and trotted off.

Juniper ambled over and raised the lid on the pottery container, full of Eternal Soup—but a considerably richer variety than spring's.

"Well, blessed be," she said. "Onions, carrots, peas, all still recognizable. Wild mushrooms. Turnips. Potatoes."

There were chunks of mutton, too, not yet boiled down to stock; she addressed them in a tone dripping with sympathy: "Blessed be—is that the G-L-L I see? Greetings, Goddamn Little Lamb! You've gone completely to pieces. I'm so sorry . . . actually, I'm sort of happy to see you like this!"

*Everyone* laughed at that; even Sam Aylward smiled, though it looked as if it hurt.

Goddamn Little Lamb was—had been, until day before yesterday—the stupidest of the ewes in the clan's painfully acquired little flock; which was saying something, since they'd discovered that the hardest part of raising sheep was keeping them from killing themselves. They might be near-as-no-matter brainless in every other respect, too stupid to walk through an open gate, but in self-immolation they showed boundless ingenuity.

GLL had come close to taking several inexperienced

shepherds with her while she threw herself off high places, nearly hung herself on low-lying branch forks, tried to poison herself on unsuitable vegetation, and finally succeeded in drowning herself as she attempted to reach some floating weeds in the millpond, got bogged in the mud, and sank nearly out of sight. Eilir had gone in with a rope to pull the carcass out . . .

The good part in herding sheep was that you usually didn't have to slaughter them yourself; all you had to worry about was getting to the body before the coyotes did.

Besides the soup there were baskets of—

"Oh, smell that smell!" Chuck said, reaching in for the bread under the towel.

The loaves were round, mushroom-shaped as if they'd been raised and baked in flowerpots—mostly because Diana and Andy had found that clay flowerpots *did* make excellent containers for baking, and there were a lot of them available. The loaves had an eight-spoked pattern cut into their dark-brown tops; the sides and bottoms were honey-brown, with just the right hollow sound when flicked, and the coarse bread made from stone-ground flour was fresh enough that it steamed gently when torn open by eager fingers.

*Every bit as good as they baked at MoonDance,* Juniper thought happily. *A bit crumbly*—they were using soft white winter wheat—*but very, very tasty!*

There was butter too, now that they'd gotten more milkers; creamy yellow butter in Tupperware containers, strong-tasting and rich—the mill turned a big barrel-churn as well as grindstones. The first cheeses were already curing in the damp chill of the springhouse beside it. Juniper anointed her chunk of loaf with a lavish hand, watching it melt into the coarse brown bread.

People settled down to concentrated munching; it seemed like a long time since this morning's oatmeal and fruit. Juniper felt an inner glow when she went back for a second bowl and realized that there was enough for everyone to eat until they were *full,* at an ordinary field supper rather than a special occasion.

That hadn't happened much until the last few weeks.

*How many times did I get up from a meal with my stomach still clenching, and have to go right back to work?* she thought. *Far too many. Being that hungry* hurts. *Goddess Mother-of-All, Lord of the ripened grain, thank You for the gifts of Your bounty!*

There was even a basket of fruit, Elberta peaches, their skins blushing red amid the deeper crimson of Bing cherries. She snaffled two of the peaches and a double handful of the cherries; most of the fruit crop was being dried and pressed into blocks or turned into jam or otherwise preserved, but they were so good *fresh* from the tree. The juice dripped from her chin onto her throat and breasts, but there was no point in being dainty; the bathhouse awaited anyway, and the harvesting crews got first turn.

Chuck looked over at her. "Got one of those deep-wisdom Celtic sayings to lay on us, your Ladyship?" he grinned.

She threw a peach pit back at him. "Indeed and I do. *Níl anon tóin tinn mar do thóin tinn féin.*"

"There's no hearth like your own hearth?" he said. "Hey, no fair, that's not relevant!"

"Close but no cigar," she said, waggling her eyebrows and leering. "This one sounds a lot like that, but it actually means: There's no sore ass like your own sore ass."

That got a universal, rueful chuckle. "Hey, what about a song?" Judy asked.

"Well, I'm not playing today," Juniper said, with a pang. "Not until my hands are in better shape." That brought groans of disappointment, and they sounded heartfelt.

*It's different, in a world where all music has to be live,* she thought. *I'm good, but am I* as good *as everyone says, these days? Or is it just that there's no competition?*

Although Chuck and a few others were gifted amateurs, come to that.

Surprisingly, Sam Aylward produced a wooden flute and began to pipe; Chuck grinned and started to tap a stone on the back of his scythe-blade for accompaniment; someone else beat a little tambourine-shaped hand drum they'd brought along this morning—songs were a lot more usual on the way to work than afterward.

She recognized the tune at once, cleared her throat and began, her strong alto ringing out in the slow, cadenced measure of the song's first verse:

> *"Let me tell the tale of my father's kin*
> *For his blood runs through my veins—*
> *No man's been born*
> *Who could best John Barleycorn*
> *For he's suffered many pains!"*

Then a little faster:

> *"They've buried him well beneath the ground*
> *And covered over his head*
> *And these men from the West*
> *Did solemnly attest*
> *That John Barleycorn was dead!*
> *John Barleycorn was dead!*
> *But the warm spring rains*
> *Came a'pouring down*
> *And John Barleycorn arose—"*

It was a very old tune, and popular:

> *"And upon that ground he stood without a sound*
> *Until he began to grow!*
> *And they've hired a man with a knife so sharp*
> *For to cut him through the knees—"*

More and more joined her, but then the voices jarred to a sudden halt.

A dunting *huu-huu-huu* from the west brought heads around; that was the alarm from the mounted sentries, blowing on horns donated by slaughtered cattle. Everyone felt uncomfortably exposed here; the valley floor was dead flat and the road net was still in good shape; with bicycles raiders could strike from anywhere. Horses were faster in a sprint, but men on bicycles could run horses to death over a day or two.

Aylward laid down his flute and rose as smoothly as if he hadn't spent the hours since dawn swinging a twenty-pound cradle scythe, usually with half a sheaf of wheat on it. He picked up his great yellow longbow and strung it the quick, dirty and dangerous medieval way—right foot between string and stave, the horn tip braced against the instep from behind the anklebone, hip against the riser, flex the body back and push the right arm forward and slide the cord up into the nock at the upper tip.

Juniper used the more conservative thigh-over-riser method for her lighter weapon, and then relaxed slightly at the next horn call.

All around her people paused as they reached for jacks and bucklers and spears and quivers.

*Huu-huu-huu, huuuuu-huuuuu,* repeated twice. Three short and two long meant *friendly visitors,* not attacking bandits, in the current code.

The sentry rode over the ditch and into the field from the western edge, raising Juniper's brows again; it was Cynthia Carson Mackenzie, with ends of blond hair leaking past the metal-and-leather cheekpieces of her bowl helmet. She was in jack and full fig—longbow and quiver across her back, buckler hooked over the scabbard of the shortsword at her belt, and spear in her right hand. That also held the reins of a second horse.

"Where's Ray?" Juniper asked as she pulled up.

Sentries never operated in groups of less than two, and it was her brother's mount the blond girl was leading, with the stirrups tied up to the saddle. The usual patrol was three, and three threes to make a squad; mystically appropriate, and solidly practical.

"He's with the others," Cynthia said. "We thought you'd better come quick, Lady Juniper. It's Sutterdown—they're here, by our . . . by the old Carson place."

"Someone from Sutterdown?" she replied.

She took a moment to put her shirt back on; Sutterdown was a straitlaced community these days. Then she slung her quiver over her back on its baldric and thrust her strung bow through the carrying loops beside it before she buckled on her sword and dirk.

"We *told* them no visitors until the sickness passes out there."

"No, not just visitors. The whole town, and a lot of others. Lady, you'd better come."

"Coming, coming," Juniper said, alarmed. "Sam, get the word out."

Anything out of the ordinary was likely to be a threat. *Not while we're getting the grain in, please!* she thought, as she put a foot in the stirrup, swung aboard, and took the reins.

*Have they gotten hit by the plague, Goddess forfend?*

That wouldn't make them up stakes and head for Mackenzie land, though. Nobody let in anyone who might be infected; and anyway, from what she'd heard, Sutterdown had been singularly fortunate—which in turn was fortunate for Clan Mackenzie, since Sutterdown and its associated area neatly blocked off the rest of the Willamette and made a buffer against the Death.

They cut across the laneway opposite, through a field in shaggy pasture with a couple of dozen recently acquired and painfully thin ranch-country Herefords gorging themselves in it, and then along a dirt-surfaced, tree-lined farm lane in grateful shade to the old Carson place.

The laneway from *that* gave out onto a paved local road; the house was on a slight rise, brick-built, a hundred and twenty years old, and until recently it had been bowered in century-old maples and oaks and ash trees.

Those had been cut down and a square was pegged out about the farmstead, where the ditch, mound and palisade would go when they had time after the harvest. Juniper regretted the trees—they'd been beautiful, and had stood so long—but you couldn't leave cover near someplace you intended to live. In the meantime it was their border post and base for the frontier patrols.

Juniper's eyes widened as she saw the crowd filling the road beyond the house. There were at least a hundred people there, both sexes and all ages, and a round dozen vehicles, horse- or hand-drawn; all of the men and a lot of the women were armed, mostly with improvised weapons of various sorts, spears made from fitting knives to the ends of poles, pruning hooks, axes, machetes, a scattering of bows and crossbows—and Aylward-style longbows they'd bought in the past few months. Few had any body armor, or worthwhile shields.

They also looked thinner and dirtier and more ragged than her clan on average, and a few were bandaged; some of the bandages seeped blood. She recognized individuals from Sutterdown, and the farms about that centered on it.

*If they've run into a bandit attack they can't handle, that's bad. That's very bad.*

The area between her lands and Sutterdown had been tranquil—by post-Change standards—not least because both communities were fairly well organized, and acted together against reivers and Eaters.

Most of them rested quietly, except for the crying of children. There were five armed Mackenzies strung across the road, spears or bows in their hands. Three of the Sutterdown folk stood arguing with the guards, trying to come closer and then flinching back at shouts of warning. It didn't look like a fight brewing—they wouldn't have brought their families along if they were going to try and run the clan off the disputed Smith land—but she didn't like it at all. They *knew* about the quarantine regulations; and had their own, for that matter.

"Stand back there, and we'll talk," she called as she reined in; the horse's hooves rang hollow on the asphalt.

Juniper dismounted; no sense in towering over the men waiting for her and putting their backs up even more. Men were strange about things like that, even the best of them—which these weren't.

"Sheriff Laughton," she said, nodding in greeting as polite as you could make without coming close enough to shake hands; he was a middling man of about her own age, in a long leather coat covered with links of light chain sewn on with steel wire.

"Dr. Gianelli." Slight and dark and balding, glaring at her.

"Reverend Dixon." Heavyset before the Change, sagging now, and glaring twice as hard as the doctor, in a black business suit and tie that fit him like a flopping sack. There was a mottled purple look to his face that might be anger, or might be ill health, or both. Judy would have prescribed a regimen of herbs and meditation to control choler, and willow bark to thin the blood.

"We need to talk to you, privately," the preacher said abruptly, stepping forward; he had a Bible in his hand, with a golden cross gleaming on the cover and his finger inside it marking a place.

One of the Mackenzies leveled his spear and prodded the air six feet in front of the Sutterdown man with a growl. The bright whetted steel and the tone stopped the cleric as if the point had been at his chest. The spearman spoke: "That's *Lady Juniper,* to you! The Mackenzie gave you your titles! Show some manners, cowan. You're on our land."

Juniper held out her hand soothingly, making a patting motion at the air. "Ray, let's be tactful. Manners work both ways."

Then she turned back to the Sutterdown leadership; as she did so she stripped the glove off her right hand. One of the flaps from a burst blister had been bothering her. She bit it off and spat it aside, then caught the odd looks directed at her.

"We're just finishing up our harvest?" she explained, puzzled. The Sutterdown folk would be too.

"*You're* harvesting, personally?" Sheriff Laughton said. "Lady Juniper," he added hastily as the guards scowled.

"I'm the clan's leader by the clan's choice," she said shortly. *And to Anwyn with your stupid rumors about the Witch Queen.*

Aloud she went on: "I'm not their master. Everyone takes a turn at the hard work here. And what brings you here on this fine day, with all your people?"

Dixon took a deep breath. From what she'd heard, he was the driving force who'd held Sutterdown together, persuaded and shamed and tongue-lashed and sometimes outright forced people into cooperating and doing what was necessary; a strong man, if not a good one, and very shrewd. The fact that he was here asking for help showed that.

"We were attacked," he said bluntly. "Not by the ordinary sort of trash, road people and Eaters—we could deal with *them*. By about a hundred men, organized, with good weapons—much better than ours."

All three flicked their eyes to the improvised militia among the crowd on the road, and then to the near-uniform, purpose-made equipment the Mackenzie warriors carried.

Dixon cleared his throat and continued: "They hit us just before dawn, killed six of our people who tried to resist, ran us out of town. They claim—their leaders claim—to be from Portland and say they've come to settle and govern the area, and they made demands."

"Demanded that we give them a third of our crops, and every family send someone to work for them one day in three!" Sheriff Laughton said indignantly.

The doctor took up the tale: "Said they'll burn the town and all the farms if we don't obey! They say they work for . . . what was it, the Portland Protective Association? And said their leader is the *baron* of this area."

"The Protector, that was who they talked about mostly," Dixon said. "Perhaps . . . ah, we should have taken your warnings about this Protector more seriously. But we didn't expect anything this early in the year."

*Neither did I,* Juniper thought, feeling an inner chill. *But farmers are most vulnerable when the crops are ripe. A band of Eaters would be* less *of a threat.*

Eaters tended to be self-destructive and usually more than half mad, and they also died of disease faster than anyone else, naturally enough—a case of catching whatever you ate had. They were like wildfire: hideously dangerous, but inclined to burn itself out quickly.

"We need your help . . . Lady Juniper," Dixon said.

The last came out as if he had to force it; for herself, she didn't care, but she couldn't let an outsider scorn or disrespect the clan. Reputation *mattered* these days; it might be the margin between being left in peace and attacked.

"I'll need to talk this over with my advisors, and put it to the clan's vote," she said. "I'd be inclined to help you, gentlemen; it's what neighbors do, and these people are likely to be a threat to us, too. But the plague . . . you understand why we've been very isolated since the outbreak."

The doctor spoke: "None of our people have the plague," he said, and the others nodded vigorously. "I swear it."

He looked around. "I can . . . I can reassure you on that, Lady Juniper. If we could talk privately."

Decision firmed. "That's as it may be. I'll have to ask you to scrub down and change clothing at least, before we can go up to the Hall. Ray, show them where."

They'd got the bathrooms in the old Carson place functioning, if you didn't mind hand-pumping and toting wood for heating.

"It shouldn't take long."

"Yes, Lady Juniper," he said, scowling and signaling them towards the farmhouse with the point of his spear.

"And Ray?"

He looked at her, then flushed and hung his head when

she shook an admonishing finger; his face looked very young then.

"Be polite. And see that drinking water's brought out for all these folk and their beasts; they're our neighbors and friends, not our enemies. *Aithnitear car í gcruatán;* a friend is known in hardship. Threefold, remember?"

When the Sutterdown men had gone, Juniper turned to her escort; Cynthia had the best horse and was the best rider besides.

"I want . . . Judy, Chuck, Dennis, Diana, your father, and Sam, ready for a private conference at the Hall, and fast," she said.

She looked out at the fresh refugees. *Curse it, these are people who were doing all right until today! They had crops harvested, they were going to* make *it!*

"And tell Diana to throw together what ready food we can spare, load a wagon and have it brought down here— we can push it out to them. Eternal Soup ought to do, and maybe some bread and dried fruit. Git, girl!"

Cynthia left in a thunder of hooves. Juniper spent the time pacing and thinking, and once sent out a rider with more orders. Other members of the clan trickled in to take over making sure that the people of Sutterdown didn't surge past the notional line that marked the boundary, and the scouts went back about their business. One emergency didn't mean that another might not pop up.

When the three Sutterdown leaders came out they were in plain dark sweatsuits, though Dixon still grasped his Bible. The wagon arrived promptly at about the same time; Diana had probably diverted something meant for the harvesters, or a party of herd-watchers.

Juniper turned to the men: "We'd like to leave the food on the road, and then have your people share it out. It's not much, but . . ."

"Thank you very kindly," Laughton said, sincerely.

After the spring and summer past, giving away food was something people took *seriously.* Even Dixon nodded. He'd been accused of many things, but never of taking more than his share, or letting anyone under his authority do so either.

"And if you'll follow me?"

They perched in the buckboard, one of the ones her

clansfolk had *liberated* from a tourist attraction; it was odd how long that idea had taken to spread. Juniper took the reins and flicked them on the backs of the team. She took the long way round—the fewer people who knew about the other way up from the back of the old Fairfax place, the better.

She could feel them gawking as she drove past the mill, working now and roofed, although the walls were still going up; past the truck plots and potato fields and watering furrow; past haystacks, past archers practicing on deer-shaped targets and others who used sword and buckler on posts or wooden blades on each other; past a hunter, coming in with a brace of deer slung across the packhorse that walked behind her jaunty bow-crossed shoulder.

*The Mackenzie clachan,* she thought wryly. *I wonder what Great-uncle Earl would think of it now—that respectable small-town banker, who left the place to* me, *of all people? Or any of the other Mackenzies?*

Such a trail of their generations, in the Old Country and the long drift westward over mountain and forest, prairie and river. Bad and wicked, a few, feud-carriers and cattle-lifters. Some heroes—her favorites were the two sisters who'd been lynched in North Carolina for helping the Underground Railroad. A scattering of backwoods granny-witches and cunning-men, as well. Plain dirt farmers, the most of them, down all their patient plowing centuries—living in the homes they built and eating from the fields they tilled, until they laid their toil-worn bodies to rest in earth's embrace.

She glanced over her shoulder at the three men from Sutterdown, and felt all those ancestors behind her.

*They didn't often walk away from a neighbor's need—and* never *backed down from bullies!*

When they came to the Hall with its half-completed palisade, Laughton burst out:

"How did you get all this done? There aren't that many of you, and I *swear* nobody could have worked harder than we have!"

The curiosity seemed genuine. Because of that, Juniper answered frankly: "Apart from the favor of Brigid and Cernunnos? Well, mutual help. You people are trying to live mostly with each family on its own, like they did before the

Change, but without the machinery and exchange that made that possible."

"We get by," Laughton growled, then flushed and waved a hand around. "Sorry. You obviously do better than 'getting by.' "

Juniper nodded. "Our clan work together and live close, so we can take turns on sentry-go, or support people doing one thing most of the time . . . or throw nearly everybody at a job that needs doing, like the harvest, with only a few to cook or keep an eye on the children."

"Sounds like communism," Dixon growled.

"It's more like tribalism, Reverend, with a bit of kibbutz thrown in," she said, keeping her voice neutral. "Call it common sense, for now. Things may be different in a few years . . . or not. And if you'll excuse me a moment, I need to freshen up while my advisors arrive."

She pulled in before the Hall, finished just before the wheat came ripe; Dennis had already started stenciling the designs he wanted to carve into a lot of it, particularly the tall pillars that supported the wraparound second-story gallery and the new roof.

Eilir came out and took the horses.

*It's all ready, Mom,* she signed, looking at the three men in the wagon with a mixture of curiosity and distaste. *Want me to lay out some ceremonial stuff for you? Scare them* green, *that would!*

*Thanks, but I'm trying to get them in a mood to cooperate!* she replied. *A plain brown around-the-house robe . . . oh, and just for swank, that moon pendant Dennie and Sally made for me.*

She dropped to the ground, and winced a little as that jarred into the small of her abused back. It was almost a pity in some ways that they'd reverted to peasant attitudes about early pregnancy. There wouldn't be time for anything but a quick sluice-down, either.

*And they're going to make me miss my soak, too,* she signed. *We old ladies are wont to get irritable and cranky when we miss our soak . . . Show them up to the room and get 'em the refreshments, my child of spring.*

The loft bedroom-office-sanctum was one luxury she'd allowed herself when the Hall was put back together. It still brought her a surge of slightly guilty pleasure as she climbed up the steep staircase from the second-story corridor to join the waiting Sutterdown men.

The attic space under the steep-pitched roof was brightly lit by the dormer windows on two sides and the bigger one in the eaves. Dennis had pitched in to furnish it; there were hanging bookcases, a long trestle table for conferences or paperwork that could be folded out of the way, shelves for her Craft tools and for the neatly rolled futons and bedding that she and Eilir used, and a little iron woodstove for winter. Her old loom was set up at the far end.

A big desk held a mechanical adding machine they'd salvaged, and a manual typewriter. There were filing cabinets as well, map boards, all the necessities of administration, which she loathed even as she did her share. And a cradle Dennis had made for her, ready for later in the year, carved all over with knotwork and intertwining beasts.

She was amused to see that the Reverend had a reflex Juniper shared, whenever she went into a new house: checking the bookshelves. You could tell from the slight tilt of his head.

The bulging eyes were probably because of the selection, though. Here, besides books like Langer's *Grow It!*, Livingston's *Guide to Edible Plants and Animals,* Emery's *Encyclopedia of Country Living* and of course Seymour's *Forgotten Arts and Crafts*—their most valuable single work—the shelves held references useful to a High Priestess.

*Eight Sabbats for Witches*—a slightly outdated classic— and the more modern *Spellworking for Covens,* just for starters. Dixon's face was getting mottled again.

She tried to see the room through the eyes of the Sutterdown men. Judy's cat had managed to get in, for one thing. It was a big black beast with yellow eyes, and it was glaring at Reverend Dixon, who stared back in what he probably didn't know a cat would regard as an insult and challenge.

"Out, Pywackett!" she said, and slung the protesting beast down the stairs, closing the doorway after her.

Then there was a lectern, the top covered with a black cloth that had a golden pentacle-and-circle on it; Dixon would probably guess, rightly, that the square shape beneath was her Book of Shadows. Her personal altar stood below the north-facing window in the eaves, with candlesticks and chalice and ritual tools and small statues of the Lady and Lord. A few prints were pinned up on the log walls, and a ceramic tile she'd bought back in 1986 that showed elk-headed Cernunnos playing on a flute as he skipped through an oakwood surrounded by skyclad dancers. . . .

*Well, by the Cauldron and the Wand, if they want to beg our help they're just going to have to take us as we are,* she thought, and sat at the head of the table.

Eilir had set out plates of fresh-cut bread, butter, cherry jam and small glasses of mead—they didn't have much yet—along with a big pot of rose-hip tea; she was glad to see that even Dixon had sampled the refreshments.

*Because now he's a guest and I* can't *lose my temper with him.*

The food scents went well with the beeswax-paint-and-fresh-wood smell of the building; rather less well with the sweat-and-cows aroma of several of the clansfolk, who'd come straight from the fields without bothering to hit the bathhouse. She *hoped* they'd remembered to use the wooden boot-scraper at the front door. Keeping clean was hard work these days.

"Let's get going," she said when the last person was seated and the strained attempt at chat ended. "This is one of those no-time-to-waste things, so we'll have to put aside our cherished tradition of talking everything to rags. You're all up to speed on what our neighbors have told me?"

She looked around, checking the nods. "Subject to the voice of the clan assembled, is everyone agreed that if the information proves to be true, we can't tolerate a big bandit gang making its headquarters next to us? Worse, one that tries to set itself up as overlords, and has ties to the Protector in Portland."

Another chorus of nods; everyone had heard a little of what was happening there, and even by the standards of the fifth month after the Change, the stories were gruesome.

"Then the first order of business is what Dr. Gianelli said about guaranteeing against exposure to the plague."

Everyone's ears perked up at that; the silence grew taut.

Gianelli licked his lips. "I said that would have to be in *private*, Lady Juniper."

She looked at him, her green eyes level under the hood of her robe, which she'd drawn up to cover her damp hair.

"This *is* private," she said. "These are my advisors. And I'm not a dictator here, unlike some places I could name. Something that important can't stay between the two of us; my people expect to be informed, and listened to, when decisions are made. And I'm not going to expose my clan to the Death on just a hint from you, Doctor."

Gianelli looked down at his hands, then clenched them into fists. He was an olive-skinned man in his thirties; when he went pale the blue-black stubble stood out vividly.

"Streptomycin," he said, still staring at his hands and spitting the word out as if it were a blow.

Judy Barstow gasped. The other Mackenzies looked at each other uncertainly.

"That's an antibiotic, isn't it?" Juniper said.

Judy nodded, a quick hard jerk of the chin. "It's a specific against *Yersinia pestis,* if it's administered early," she said. "A good prophylactic at low doses, if you take it a couple of days before possible exposure, but it can damage your kidneys if you continue for more than a month. It's also valuable against a lot of other bacteria, and it keeps indefinitely in powdered form at room temperature. We ran out of it two months ago—I could never locate more than a couple of doses."

Her calm broke. "How much have you got!"

Gianelli went on in a monotone: "Bulk powder from my hospital in Albany in sealed packages. Twelve thousand adult doses."

*Crack!*

Her palm slammed the doctor's head to one side; the arm rose again for a backhand as she leaned far across the table. Sam Aylward had Judy by the shoulders before the second blow could fall, forcing her back into the chair.

"Bastard!" she spat at the Sutterdown doctor, fighting against the great callused hands; there were two red spots on her cheeks, as bright as the print of her palm on his.

"Bastard! I lost one of my patients, one of our *children,* and you had—you weren't even *using* it!"

Gianelli looked up again, ignoring the imprint of the

hand on his cheek. "It was all I had! It's like food—I can't give it to everyone who needs it, or it'll all be gone in a week, and then everyone will be as bad off as before! The other antibiotics, most of them need refrigeration. I had to save it!"

He buried his head in his hands, and the rigid brace went out of his shoulders. "The hospital . . . there were so *many* . . . so many, and I couldn't *do* anything, we didn't have any *food,* and the head of administration killed himself and I took the box and I ran, I ran . . ."

"Quiet," Juniper said.

She heard what Judy was muttering under her breath— in this context, there was only one reason for calling on Three-Fold Hecate—and reached aside to lay a finger across her lips.

"Don't say that, Maiden," she said, in her High Priestess voice.

That seemed to startle Judy out of her anger somewhat, or at least back to control. "Don't think it, either. Not if you want to stay under my rooftree."

Her eyes flicked across the three men. "As I said, neighbors help each other. We'd all be better off now if we'd co-operated more before. It has to be mutual, though. So if we're going to help you, you have to help us."

"We're willing to share the medicine," Dixon put in.

"Excellent. We'll want enough to protect any of our people who go out to fight, and then half the remainder." Her tone made it clear that the statement wasn't a question or a request.

All three of them nodded; not that they had much choice. Inwardly, she felt a single cold knot relax for the first time since she smelled the death pits outside Salem; with five or six thousand doses, they could stop any plague outbreak among the Mackenzies cold—and possibly protect some other communities she knew of, combined with preventative measures.

"And if we're going to fight and win where you lost, we insist on being in command of our joint muster," she said.

More nods, a bit slower this time, and glances at Aylward and Chuck.

"And good neighbors don't preach hatred against each other."

Now Dixon sat rigid, glaring at her, and the doctor and the sheriff exchanged worried glances. Juniper went on: "We don't cast spells of bane and ruin against you. I'd appreciate it if you'd stop doing so against us, Reverend. Times are difficult enough as it is without wasting effort on counterspells."

Dixon's face went still more blotchy. "I cast no spells!" he spat. "I pray to the living God!"

Juniper took a deep breath. "Let's put it another way: We both believe in the power of prayer. If a group of people get together to chant and ill-wish someone, it has a way of working regardless of the details of the ritual . . . and then of bouncing back on the ill-wishers, which has already happened to your town, no?"

She raised a hand. "Or let's discuss it in purely secular terms. You're an influential man, ruler as well as priest— and believe me, I've come to understand what that means, however much I didn't want to. If you go on inciting people to regard us as evil Satanists worthy of death, and quoting Exodus 22:18 or Galatians 5:19 as if they applied to us—"

"It is the Word of God—"

Judy slapped the table with a crack like timber breaking and barked: "They're *mistranslations*, you nitwit, as anyone who knew more Hebrew or Greek than King James's so-called scholars could have told you. *M'khasephah* means someone who malevolently uses spoken curses to hurt people, which we're *specifically* forbidden to do by the Wiccan Rede, and *pharmakia* means a *poisoner*. If you want to preach against suffering a poisoner to live, go right ahead!"

"Spiritual poison—"

"*Shut* up!" Juniper said. Then, more calmly: "Whatever the origins of the phrases, keep repeating them and eventually you'll produce a community which hates us and attacks us physically. In which case, why should we fight for one enemy against another?"

Laughton cut in: "We have freedom of religion in Sutterdown, Ms. . . . Lady Juniper."

"And we Mackenzies do too," she said, nodding towards John Carson. "Our livestock boss here is a Presbyterian. Some of our clan are Witches, some are unbelievers, some are Christians of various sorts."

*The latter two a rapidly diminishing proportion, I admit,* she didn't say aloud. *That would diminish the force of my point.*

"We don't call anyone evil because of their faith. There are many roads to the Divine. We'd just like you to promise to reciprocate, as a demonstration of goodwill."

Dixon looked out the windows, then back at her.

"You'll take my promise?" he said, sounding surprised.

"I don't like you," Juniper said bluntly, meeting his eyes. "But I've never heard that your word isn't good."

The silence stretched; then he nodded. Juniper returned the gesture with an inclination of her head.

"Chuck, rumors are probably flying. Tell everyone we'll have a clan meeting after supper to thrash things out, and an Esbat tomorrow night to call for the Lord and Lady's aid, and would welcome any other variety of prayers as well. We'll need all the help we can get."

The moon wouldn't be full or dark for the Esbat, but that wasn't absolutely required, just customary and preferred.

"We'll also send out scouts to get our own information. Sam, handle it, and get us ready." He nodded silently. "John, we'll need pretty well all the saddle-broke horses."

"Not bicycles?" he said.

"No. Horses are faster over the distances we're talking. And a wagon team at least. Diana, Andy, supplies. And whatever we can spare for the Sutterdown folk, until this is over; slaughter some stock if you have to. Judy, as far as getting our people protected against the plague, and for casualty care . . ."

When she was finished, she leaned over the table to shake hands with the town's three leaders. Dr. Gianelli looked drained, as if he'd had some noxious cyst lanced; Sheriff Laughton was relieved, like a man drowning who'd been thrown a spar. And Dixon, as usual, looked full of suppressed fury.

*You did help neighbors. It wasn't necessary to like all of them.*

# CHAPTER TWENTY-FOUR

"Lord Jesus, Mike, these were a bad bunch did this," Will Hutton said quietly; his face was grayish.

They bore the last of the bodies out of the Clarke farmhouse wrapped in blankets. They could each carry one easily; neither corpse weighed more than fifty pounds. They'd found these in an upstairs bedroom. It looked as if they'd tried to hide under a bed, and been dragged out by the ankles—a small leg had been severed at the knee.

One still had a stuffed toy bear in a cowboy outfit in his hands when they found him; Havel had wrapped it with the body.

"Bad as I've ever seen," the Texan went on as they carried them out to where the gravediggers labored. "Bad as those crazy men north of Kooskia."

"Worse, Will," Havel said. "More of them, and better organized."

He didn't add: *And dead is dead; it doesn't matter much what happens to the body.* Hutton was a more conventional man than he, and Havel wouldn't willingly offend him.

And the skin between his shoulders crawled a little at the memory, anyway. It reminded him a little too much of stories he'd heard Grannie Lauder tell, stories of *wendigo* and *mischepesu.* Only those had been stories, something for a kid to shiver over while he sat on the floor in front of the fire. This had been unpleasantly real . . . and in the Changed world, who could tell what was real, anyway? Maybe there *were* man-eating spirits in the winter woods, now.

He didn't want to talk about that, either.

"Glad it's still coolish weather," he said instead.

The Clarkes had a family graveyard, in a patch bordered

by pines and willows near the crest of the low hill to the west of the homestead. The first headstones marked Clarke were dated before 1914, but these would be the last of that line, he supposed.

More than twenty fresh graves doubled its size, and spadefuls of the wet black earth were still flying up; two Bearkillers helped stand guard, and another six helped Sheriff Woburn's posse dig, their armor and weapons draped across their saddles. The horses all grazed nearby, hobbled, rolling now and then. There was no point in keeping them out of the wheat.

Woburn called one of his men over, turning his back when he drew up a corner of each blanket so that only the two of them need see the faces.

"That's little Mort Williams, all right," the man said. "And Judy Clarke, old man Clarke's great-granddaughter, her parents came back from Lewiston right after the Change. Jesus wept."

"I don't doubt Mary did," Hutton said quietly, crossing himself; he'd become a Catholic to make peace with his wife's relatives, but it had taken.

"This the Devil Dogs' work, all right," Woburn said with frustrated anger leaking through the iron calm of his voice. "Worse than ever."

"Devil Dogs?" Havel said.

They stood back from the graves. He'd kept the gruesome work of wrapping the bodies for himself and Hutton while the younger Bearkillers dug. Sheriff Woburn had done the same, pitching in with the disgusting task, which put him up a notch in Havel's view. He'd always respected an officer who was willing to share the unpleasant bits.

"Devil Dogs, the bikers," the lawman went on. "It's the gang's name. They broke away from the Hell's Angels years ago—thought the Angels had gone soft. Bunch of them were holding a meet at a motel south of Lewiston when the Change came. Iron Rod's their leader, I don't know his real name."

"Duke Iron Rod?" Havel enquired.

Woburn's face went crimson. "That's new the last little while. He's trying to extort protection money, I mean payments in food and supplies, from the ranchers and towns. Bastard's claiming to be Duke of the Camas Prairie!"

Havel's brows went up. *Have to get the details on this,* he thought. *Doesn't sound right. Or . . . if it's our good friend Arminger prompting, it* does *sound right.*

They'd seen plenty of petty theft and one-on-one violence in the first weeks after the Change, and hit-and-run banditry on an increasing scale since, plus what Ken Larsson and Pam Arnstein and Aaron Rothman called incipient feudalism—strong-arm rule. That was mostly by local bossmen, though, and the more unscrupulous ranchers taking advantage of homeless, desperate city-dwellers and travelers as cheap labor.

This didn't quite make sense, not on a purely local basis.

He stood back respectfully and bowed his head with his followers when Woburn pulled a Bible from his saddlebags and began reading a service. He'd fallen away from the Lutheran faith of his ancestors himself, but he'd been raised among believers.

When the rest of Sheriff Woburn's little posse had ridden off towards their homes, Havel gave a short sharp whistle.

The two Bearkillers who'd been riding sentry turned and moved the horses back towards the others. Those got each other into their gear—you could wiggle into a hauberk alone, but it went faster with help—saddled their mounts, and formed up in a column of twos. One at the rear led a packhorse with their picks and shovels.

"Got 'em well trained," Woburn remarked. "How many men—"

Signe Larsson looked at him in the act of putting on her helmet, then settled it and clipped on the chin cup. Gloria Stevens, the other woman present, snickered.

"—well, troopers, do you have?"

"We've got around a hundred adults now," Havel said. "Carefully picked. Not all of them have the heft or the inclination for a stand-up fight or to go along when we ride out like this, but things being the way they are, I try to give everyone some weapons training."

*Including even utterly hopeless cases like Jane Waters and Rothman,* he thought. *But let's not talk about that now.* Aloud he went on: "You may not plan on having the fight at home, but . . ."

Woburn nodded. "Yeah, the other guy sometimes has

plans of his own, the dirty dog. I can see why you'd want all your people to know how."

"Your Kate Clarke would probably have wanted to know how, yesterday morning, for example," Signe said, then dropped back into the column.

Woburn winced a little and looked at the horses, changing the subject: "All well-mounted, too."

"We've done this and that here and there, helping people out with jobs or problems," Havel said neutrally.

*And liberated some stock left wandering, or plain looted it from people who tried to attack or cheat us. Plus there's no better judge of horseflesh in the world than Will, with Angelica a close second.*

"We take payment in tools, food and animals, mostly. Lucky this part of the country isn't short of livestock. And as I said, we've got a really good horse trainer."

Woburn didn't seem concerned to be alone among armed strangers; that made him stupid, suicidal or brave, and Havel thought he was probably the last. He was also keeping his eyes open.

"All this weird old-time knights-in-armor gear still looks funny to me," he said. "I mean, I have problems taking it seriously."

Havel shrugged and drew his *puukko*. He handed it to Woburn, who tested the edge automatically, raised his brows in respect, and handed it back. Havel pressed the blade to his mail-clad body and then ripped it down from shoulder to waist, just beside the diagonal line of the bandolier that held his quiver. The steel cut a bright line along the little interlinked rings with a rattling click.

"Point taken," Woburn said.

On a man in cloth, that would have worked like a chain saw on wood. Not for the first time, Havel thought how much of a survival advantage it was to be mentally flexible in this Changed world.

Woburn sighed. "I know up in my head that guns don't work anymore, but there are times when"—he patted the vintage saber at his saddlebow—"this doesn't seem real. Plus there's no time to learn how to use it properly. Some of our people have been sewing washers or pieces of metal on coats and dusters. Or making jackets of boiled steerhide."

A scowl: "A lot of Iron Rod's men use scales fastened to canvas backing, too, recently."

"I've seen gear like that," Havel said. *A lot of it in Portland, to be precise.* "It's heavier and less flexible than chain mail, though. We can sell you some armor, and more importantly we can take some of your people through the whole process of making it."

It was past four o'clock when they passed the Bearkiller sentries; some of them were carrying lances as well as swords and bows, which impressed Woburn. Havel hid a smile as he returned their fist-to-chest salutes; so far, only the unanimous verdict of Will's cavalry manuals kept him trying with the damned bargepoles. They were as hard to manage on horseback as archery!

The Bearkillers' camp was in a clearing just back of the ridge where the lane led down to the prairie; the grassland there covered several acres, interrupted by scraggly lodgepole pines and some aspens. The afternoon sun gilded the tall grass, and cast blue shadows towards the east. A scent of woodsmoke and cooking came from the hearths, and the cheerful sound of children playing, the *tink . . . tink . . .* of metal on metal, the rhythmic *tock* of axes splitting firewood.

More of the wagons' loads had been taken down than was usual for a one-night stopover; Havel wanted Sheriff Woburn impressed, and it had been easy enough to send orders back from the sacked farmstead.

The tents were pitched in neat rows, one per family with more for the single men, single women and outfit purposes; each had a fire in front of it and a Coleman lantern hung from the peak. A latrine trench was behind a grove of aspens, and a canvas enclosure for bathing stood beside a wheeled metal water-tank, another Ken-and-Will joint project; it was built so that a heating fire could be kindled in a hearth at one end. A woman was tossing chunks of pine into the fire, and a valve hissed on top as the water came to a boil.

"Helps avoid giardia," Havel said.

Woburn nodded; the nasty little parasites were endemic in Idaho streams, including the "purest" mountain brooks.

"Pretty piece of work," he said.

Havel nodded gravely, grinning to himself. He wasn't

quite running a Potomekin village setup for the good sheriff, but he *was* putting the best foot forward.

"Lord Bear," one of their more recent recruits said, taking the reins as Havel and his guest swung down out of the saddle.

Havel felt his teeth gritting. Breaking people of calling him that was probably more trouble than it was worth, and most seemed to like it better than "Boss." Giving Astrid a sound spanking for coming up with the idea was almost certainly more trouble than it would be worth ... but it was so *tempting,* sometimes!

He steered Woburn past the portable smithy—they had a real blacksmith now, freeing up a lot of Will's time—the arrow-making operation, the armor-assembly area from which Astrid and Luanne had been reprieved for awe-the-locals purposes, and on to the bowmaking benches.

*Interesting,* Havel thought. *When he's actually working, our Bill looks almost trustworthy. The problem is you have to stand over him to keep him working.*

Right now he was opening the insulated hotbox and checking a bow-limb curing there, the half-S shape secured between plywood forms with metal screw-clamps; the box reduced the time needed for the glue to set hard from a year to weeks, at the cost of a slight loss in durability. An assistant had a hardwood block clamped in a vise; he was shaping the riser into which the limbs would be pegged and glued, roughing out the shape of the pistol grip and arrow-shelf with a chisel. Shavings of pale myrtlewood curled away from the tap-tap-tap.

Havel nodded towards the pots of glue, planks of osage-orange wood, bundles of dried sinew, pieces of antler, and a box of translucent lozenges sawn from cow horns.

"We'll always have *those* materials."

"You've been thinking ahead," Woburn said respectfully.

They passed the school, taught open-air by Annie Sanders when there was time, with a folding blackboard and students from six to twelve. Reuben Waters, Billy's eldest, made his typical entry—Annie dragged him in by one ear, with occasional swats to his backside along the way. She thought the Waters kids were salvageable, and they did seem a bit brighter than their parents.

Astrid galloped her horse past a deer-shaped target—

and the arrow flickered out to go thump behind the shoulder. Others were on foot, shooting at Frisbee-sized wooden disks rolled downhill, or at stationary man-shapes; the shooters were crouched, kneeling, walking, as well as standing in the classic archer's T.

Luanne was on horseback too, picking wooden tent pegs out of the ground with a lance as she galloped. It made a dramatic backdrop for Will's horsemanship class with its jumps and obstacles.

*Hope she doesn't dig in and knock herself out of the saddle while our guest is watching,* Havel thought. *She's the only one we've got yet who doesn't do that all the time!*

Those just starting with the sword were hacking at pells—posts set in the ground, or convenient trees—or slicing pinecones tossed at them. He didn't have anyone riding the wooden hobbyhorse just now, learning to swing a blade from the saddle without decapitating his mount—it was essential, but he had to admit it looked so . . .

*Dorky,* he thought. *There's no other word that fits.*

Except for Astrid and a few other fast-growing teenagers, all those at weapons practice were working in chain mail, to get used to the weight and constriction and sweat-sodden heat of it. That was only marginally more popular than the regular exercise sessions wearing the stuff, jumping and running and tumbling and climbing ladders.

*My sympathy is underwhelming, you poor little darlings,* Havel thought. *Try humping an eighty-pound pack through fucking Iraq.*

Pam Arnstein had one of her fencing classes going for the better students, with Signe as her assistant.

"The targe"—she insisted on using the fancy term for *small round shield*—"is not there for you to wave in the air! Keep it in front of you. Remember it's a weapon like your sword—weapons are kept face to the enemy. Pivot the rear foot as you move—heel down, Johnson! Passing thrust—passing thrust—cut—cut—forehand—backhand—at the man, not at the shield! Stay in line, in line!"

Impatiently, she called Josh Sanders out from the double line of pupils. Havel watched with interest as she drove the brawny young man down the field in a clatter and bang of mock combat.

"Right, try it again . . . better. Now free-form! I deflect your cut with my blade sloped behind my back, and make a crossing attack, stepping forward to cut in turn to the hamstring . . . so."

"Ouch!" He stumbled and recovered.

"I knock your shield out of line . . . so. The body follows the sword, remember. Swords first, foot just a fraction of a second behind. Then I thrust to the face . . . cut to the neck—no, don't block with the edge of your targe, you'll get it sliced off. With the surface—that's why it's covered in rawhide. Good parry, now I'm vulnerable, hit me with it—"

*Crack!* as leather met leather.

"Sorry!" he blurted, as he knocked her off her feet and onto her back.

The sixteenth-century European blade styles featured a lot of bodychecking, throws, kicks and short punching blows with the pommel of the sword or the edge of the shield, too. The brutal whatever-works pragmatism was precisely to Havel's taste.

"That's the first completely correct move you've made today," Pamela said as she rolled erect again. "You've got the advantage of weight—so use it. There aren't any bronze or silver medals in this sort of fencing. Win or die!"

Havel inclined his helmeted head towards the practice field. "Like you said, Sheriff, it's not just finding or making the weapons, it's learning how to use them."

"Doesn't look like what I remember of fencing," he said, shading his eyes. "Watched the Olympics once."

Havel nodded. The motions were much broader and fuller, with all the body's coordinated strength and weight behind them. He went on aloud: "One of these cut-and-thrust swords will blast right through an épée parry and skewer you front to back, or gut you like a trout. We were real lucky to find Pam Arnstein—that's our instructor there."

Ken Larsson was working on a drawing pinned to a folding draughtsman's table nearby, looking up occasionally at the sword practice; Aaron Rothman rested his peg leg in a canvas recliner nearby.

Havel introduced them, and the elder Larsson went on: "Pam was a stroke of luck. She's our vet too, and doubled as our medico until we found Aaron here."

He grinned and jerked a thumb at the doctor, who was starting to look just skinny again.

"Lord Bear's Luck, some call it," Rothman said. "And *believe* me, I was glad to get a share of it!"

*I really* wish people wouldn't say that, Havel thought. *The dice have no memory. You've got to earn your luck again every morning.*

Four Bearkillers were passing by with a quartered beef carcass in wheelbarrows, heading for the cooking fires and the chuck wagon. Arnstein looked at Havel, who nodded. She halted them, and had the hindquarters hung on hooks hoof-up beneath a tree while she laid down the practice lath, unhooked the wire-mesh screen from the front of her helmet and took up her battle sword.

A whistle brought the novices' practice to a halt; Signe flashed Havel a smile as she helped chivvy them into place, sheepdog style.

"This part's popular, for some reason," Havel said, as they walked over; Sheriff Woburn was looking puzzled. "But it has to wait for a butchering day. I've got to admit, it's sort of cool to do."

He raised his voice. "Gather 'round, those who haven't seen this demonstration. And those who want to see it again."

A few of the neophytes looked as puzzled as Woburn. The rest grinned and nudged each other as they shoved the others closer to the hanging meat.

"Now, watch closely. And keep in mind that this"— Havel drew his sword, and tapped one of the hanging quarters lightly—"is the ass-end of a nice big cow. Range heifer, about seven hundred pounds. Bone and muscle and tendon, just like us, except thicker and more of it. Pam, do the honors on Cheek Number One."

Pamela poised motionless, then attacked with a running thrust, right foot skimming forward and knee bending into a long lunge. The point of her saber hardly appeared to move; it was presented at the beginning of the motion, and then six inches of it were out the other side of the haunch of beef. She withdrew, twisting the blade.

"Examine that, please," she said.

The novices did, one of them gulping audibly as he put a finger in the long tunnel-like wound. The tall wiry woman grinned as she went on:

"While not so deep as a well, nor so wide as a church door, it's more than sufficient to let out a *lot* of blood. And now if you'll back off slightly—"

She reversed to her original left-foot-forward stance, poised for a second with targe and point advanced, then attacked again; this time she cut backhand with a high wordless shout, foot and edge slamming down together as if connected by invisible rods and hips twisting to put a whipping snap into the strike.

The blade slanted into the meat with a wet *thwack!* and a great slab of flesh slumped down; they could all see where her saber had cut a deep pinkish-white nick into the surface of the butchered steer's legbone. Flecks of meat spattered into the faces of the closest onlookers.

"And that, ladies and gentlemen, could be you," she said, panting slightly. "Which is why there's no prize for second place." There were a few more shocked faces among the grins.

Pamela went on: "Lord Bear will now demonstrate what happens when someone hits you *hard* with a backsword, instead of a light cut like that."

Havel slipped the shield off his back and onto his arm, standing with left foot and arm advanced. Then he screamed and pounced and struck in the same motion, steel whirling in a blur of speed, long blade at the end of a long arm in a looping overarm cut.

*"Haakkaa paalle!"*

A wet cleaving sound sounded under the shout, and a crackling beneath that. When the beef haunch swayed back, they could all see that the steel had sliced through eight inches of hide and meat to make a canyon gape several feet long, and split the heavy legbone beneath— lengthwise. Chips and dust lay in the marrow at the bottom of the cut, shattered out of the bone by the violence of the impact.

A chorus of whistles and murmurs went through the ranks of the novices, along with a dabbing at faces.

Havel spoke: "And that, ladies and gentlemen, is why we don't bitch and moan about how *hot* and *heavy* and *uncomfortable* the armor is."

*I may have to grind away to get good at archery, but it seems I've got a natural talent for this.*

"Supper's at seven," Havel said; Woburn was looking

suitably impressed. "Why don't you look around for a little while? Ken can answer any questions you have. I've got to get out of this ironmongery and there's some business to attend to."

As he turned away, a thought struck him: *If this Duke Iron Rod really* is *in with Arminger, how many other people are fighting the Protector right now?*

Angelica Hutton was just putting a Dutch oven full of biscuits into the embers in one of the fires behind the chuck wagon when Havel arrived, his hair still damp from the bath. There were a dozen working there, amid a cheerful clatter and chatter that didn't disguise the size of the task or the efficiency with which it got done.

"Jane, remember to get the tortillas into that warmer the minute they're done," she said, her voice friendly but a little loud and slow; then she wiped her hands on the apron she wore over her Levi's and shirt.

The smile died as she and the Bearkiller leader walked aside: "Mike, that woman!" she continued; speaking under her breath, but clenching her fists beneath her chin and making a throttled sound of wordless exasperation.

"Specific problem?" he said.

"She is . . . no, she is good-hearted, and not even lazy if you tell her everything she is to do, but I have met mesquite stumps with more brains! She speaks of nothing but TV shows and the days when she was a cheerleader."

You could believe that more easily these days; Jane Waters didn't look shapeless anymore—she was even pretty, in a blowsy, faded-rose way.

"And she is a natural . . . what is the old English word . . . I saw it in a schoolbook of Luanne's . . . no, not slut, that means *puta*, right?"

Havel nodded, and the Tejano woman went on: "Slattern, that is the word. She cannot even *cook;* not at all, I do not mean fancy things. Before the Change her children ate from McDonald's and Taco Bell every day! Or from cans and frozen pizza."

"Not everyone can meet your high standards, Angelica," Havel said, grinning. *And oh, for the days when even poor people could get* too much *of the wrong sort of food!* "I wanted to check on supplies."

"*Y bien,*" she said, pulling a list out of a pocket. "We've got enough meat, I ordered a steer butchered this afternoon—it arrived a little worn, no?"

He smiled and made a placating gesture.

"If we stop anytime soon, I want to try to make dried and smoked sausage; there is plenty of jerky, but it is boring even in a stew. So we must have spices—sage, garlic. For the rest, we need some sacks of salt, badly. We are short of flour, and potatoes, and down to the last of our beans, rice, and oatmeal. We need vegetables very badly, dried or canned, also fruit—it is not healthy, to live so much on meat and bread, even with the vitamin pills. Shortly we will need clothing, particularly boots and shoes, and especially for the little ones . . ."

Angelica went through her list; then she darted back to make sure her assistants weren't spoiling anything.

After a quick check she began beating on a triangle. Everyone gathered 'round their mess hearths by squads and families, as youngsters carried the food around; tables were too much of a bother to drag along on the move, but they had good groundsheets so you could sit down dry and reasonably comfortable around a fire—most were leaning against their saddles, cowboy fashion. Shadows closed in around the fires and the first stars appeared in the east.

Woburn bit into his burrito, then looked down at it with surprised pleasure as the tangy carne asada hit his palate, cooled with sour cream.

"All right," he said to the Bearkillers' leader. "You've got a real slick operation here, Mr. Havel. Now, you were hinting that you could do something about the Devil Dogs."

"That depends," he said. "They've got some sort of base, right? A hideout you can't come at, or more likely they've forted up someplace you can't take."

"They're at St. Hilda's," Woburn said, respect in his voice.

Havel's ears perked up at that; he saw that Ken Larsson's did, too. It was one of the big Idaho tourist attractions; you couldn't live in the state and not know about it.

He held up a hand for a moment, and turned his head to Will Hutton; the various bosses-of-sections were eating around Havel's fire tonight, as usual when there was serious business to discuss.

"Will, St. Hilda's is a Benedictine abbey over by that butte. Near the top of it, in fact."

He pointed southwest. A wide cone with gentle slopes dominated the rolling plain, visible many miles away; right now it was silhouetted against the westering sun as the long July evening drew to a close.

"Built like a fort," he added. "I saw it a couple of times before the Change."

"Me too," Ken said. "Literally like a fort, Romanesque Revival. Nineteen-twenties construction; ashlar stone blocks, a hard blue porphyry, and walls over three feet thick at the base. Four stories in a block around a courtyard, with two towers on the front—both nearly a hundred feet high. Interior water source, too. Not surprised some bandits took it over. It's the closest thing to a castle in the state, after the old penitentiary in Boise."

Woburn nodded. "When the Change hit, the Devil Dogs stole real bikes, mountain bikes, and then horses, and looted a bunch of wilderness outfitters; after that they started raiding for supplies. That was bad enough. Then in May, they changed their operations. Got a lot of good weapons from somewhere, and then they hit St. Hilda's."

"What happened to the Sisters?" Hutton said, concern in his voice.

"They killed some of them and threw out most of the rest; Mother Superior Gertrude is staying with me. And since then they've been using it as a base. They've been giving us hell—well, you saw it."

Havel looked at Signe, and she opened a plastic Office Max filing box. It was filled with neatly labeled maps in hanging files; she pulled out the west-central Idaho one, tacked it to a corkboard, and propped it up where the command staff could see it.

"How many?" Havel said. "Organization? Leaders? What's Iron Rod like? What weapons, and what's their objective, if it isn't just loot?"

Woburn looked at the map. "There were about fifty to start with," he said. "Twice that now—they've been recruiting from the—no offense—road people."

Havel smiled thinly; road people was what settled folk around here had taken to calling the wanderers, those stranded on highways by the Change and others who scoured about looking for food. They were a natural breeding-ground for brigandage, not to mention for transmitting disease, and neither well-regarded nor very welcome.

"None taken. We're going somewhere, not just wandering around aimlessly looking for a handout or what we can steal."

"I can see that," Woburn said, looking at the map, and then the purposeful activity about him.

He tapped his finger on the map: "Anyway, there's near a hundred fighting men, plus . . . well, they had some women with them to start with. There are more now—some kidnapped. Some men they've taken and are using as slave labor, too."

Havel nodded; he'd seen similar things in embryo elsewhere, but not on this scale . . . yet.

"I presume you've tried smoking them out," Havel said. It wasn't a question.

Woburn flushed in embarrassment. "Yeah. You understand, things were total chaos right after the Change, and then we were all working as hard as we could to salvage bits and pieces. People around here are real spread out, and without trucks or phones it took us weeks to get any organization going at all. First we knew was when they started hitting farms—or hitting them up for tribute and ransom."

"Then you got a big posse together, and they handed you your heads," Havel guesstimated.

Woburn looked aside a bit. "Yeah. Two hundred men, and we had an I-beam for a battering ram, and some extension ladders."

Havel winced slightly, picturing how he'd have managed the defense.

Woburn nodded: "Thing is, they've made the place into a real fort. They filled all the windows on the lower two stories with rebar grates and then bolted steel plates over the inside and outside and filled the holes with concrete—the Sisters were doing a construction project and there was plenty of material. Steel shutters with arrow-slits in the upper windows. They'd cut down all the trees around, so there wasn't any cover for us, and they poured boiling canola oil down on us from the top . . . we lost twenty dead, and six times that number injured, a lot of them real bad."

"And that was the last time you could get that many together," Havel said.

"Well . . . yeah."

This time Woburn's look had an element of a glare in it. Havel looked at Ken Larsson, and the older man spoke thoughtfully, tugging at his short silvery beard.

"Either they've got someone very shrewd in charge, or they have an implausible number of construction workers in their ranks. Something odd there. Starving them out, perhaps? Or catching parties of them on the move?"

Woburn snorted. "There's no communications! What men I can scrape together end up running from one place that's been raided to another. If we get a big bunch together, they just retreat into the fort and laugh at us until we go away—we can't keep up a siege, everyone's needed on the farms. That place is stuffed with stolen food."

Havel nodded. "And they can see you coming, since they hold the high ground. And they probably hit the farms of your supporters, and probably some farmers and ranchers are already paying them off or slipping them information and don't get attacked."

"I don't blame them," Ken Larsson said, wincing at the memory of what he'd helped bury.

"I do!" Woburn said; his face flushed with anger. "The Devil Dog honcho, Iron Rod—he's started calling himself Duke of the Camas Prairie, the bastard! You saw what his scum did!"

Havel nodded politely. Behind the mask of his face he thought: *And they're getting stronger, while you get weaker. If things go on the way they are, you'll all be on your knees to Duke Iron Rod by this time next year. Or on your backs, depending on your gender and his tastes.*

"I suppose you tried to get some help from Boise," Havel said.

He didn't bother making it a question. Woburn spat into the fire.

"There's plague in Boise, too. Really bad, and typhus; we haven't had but one outbreak here, thank God. That was in Grangeville, and we managed to damp it down quick with quarantine. Iron Rod's been careful not to attack the Nez Perce . . . yet. He'll be their business if he finishes us off!"

"That's too bad about Boise," Havel said. "There's a lot

of good land west of the city with gravity-flow irrigation; they might have made it."

*And I've got friends there,* he thought. *I hope Eileen's OK, even if she did dump me, and the folks at Steelhead.*

The thought was oddly abstract. Things had closed in since the Change; people and places beyond a day's ride were . . . remote. The world felt a whole lot bigger.

"Could be worse," Signe said unexpectedly. "It could be like the coast . . . or like St. Louis."

Everyone shivered slightly. A spray of bicycle-born fugitives had made it from the big cities of the Midwest, and from the Pacific coast. A lot of people didn't believe the stories. Nobody wanted to believe them.

"OK," Havel said. "Here's your problem. They've got an impregnable base. You've got more men"—although not a lot more; there were probably only about five thousand people left within three or four days' travel—"but yours have to stay split up most of the time, and his are concentrated. He can strike any ranch or farm with superior numbers, then retreat behind his walls if you get together. And he doesn't have to worry about getting a crop in. It'll be worse at harvest time, which is soon. It's always easier to stop other people doing something than it is to do it. The grain'll be dry enough to burn then, too. If you don't get rid of them in the next month or so, they'll wreck you. You'll have to surrender, or move far enough away he can't reach you."

"The filth destroy what they can't steal," Woburn said bitterly. "We can't farm if we have to stand guard twenty-four hours a day! But if we leave, get out of range, we're homeless, we're road people ourselves."

Ken Larsson nodded. "You're spread out too much," he said. "Even resettling townsfolk on the farms, the properties are too big and too widely scattered, which means every household's on its own and impossibly far away from help. What you should do is group together, village-style, with settlements of . . . oh, say fifty to a hundred people, minimum, in places with good water and land. Then they could defend themselves—run up earth walls and palisades, too, maybe. And have specialists where they need them. We're all going to run out of pre-Change tools and clothing eventually."

"I can't make people give up their land!" Woburn said, scandalized.

Ken shrugged. "They don't need most of it," he pointed out. "This area"—his hand took in the Camas Prairie—"produced wheat and canola and beef for hundreds of thousands of people. Now it only has to feed the few thousand people who live on it; and that's going to take only a fraction of the area, which is lucky since you won't have the labor to work more anyway. What would be the point in growing more when you can't ship it out? To watch it rot?"

Woburn looked sandbagged. "Hadn't thought about it in quite that way," he said. "Haven't had time, I suppose."

Havel cut in: "Essentially, what Iron Rod's trying to do is charge you rent for living here, by making life impossible for people who won't knuckle under. You have to winkle him out of his fort. And you also need a standing force; full-time fighters, well equipped and trained."

Woburn's eyes narrowed. "You asking for the job?" he said softly.

The obvious drawback was that a standing force would be functionally equivalent to Iron Rod and his merry band, and might well end up with similar ambitions.

Havel laughed and shook his head. "Emphatically, no!" he said. "We've got a destination further west. But you ought to think about raising some rangers or soldiers or whatever you want to call them. And if you can't afford it . . . well, think about whether you can afford Duke Iron Rod."

Woburn took a deep breath; he looked relieved. "Thing is, Mr. Havel, I was wondering—"

"Whether we could get rid of Iron Rod for you," Havel said. He looked at Ken Larsson, who nodded imperceptibly.

"I'd heard that you did some work like that elsewhere," Woburn said.

"Not on this scale, we didn't. I've got forty people I'd be willing to put into a fight," Havel said. "Forty-five if I stretch it and include some damned young teenagers. Getting into a stand-up toe-to-toe slugging match with the Devil Dogs by ourselves isn't on. I'd like to see the people who did that"—he pointed towards the sacked farmstead, invisible in the gathering dusk—"in hell where they belong, but I'm not going to get half my people killed to do it. And frankly, Sheriff, this is your fight and not ours."

Woburn's face dropped. Larsson went on: "There are things we could do, though, as . . . ah, contractors."

*Condottieri,* Havel thought silently. *Which means, literally, "contractors."*

He nodded, as if reluctant. Ken Larsson took up the thread smoothly: "When I was studying engineering, back in the 1960s, I had a professor who taught us the history of the field. And until a couple of hundred years ago, what engineers mainly did was build forts and engines to knock 'em down. Now . . ."

# CHAPTER TWENTY-FIVE

The warriors of Clan Mackenzie arrived on horseback for the joint muster with Sutterdown in the cool just after dawn, with a horse-drawn wagon behind them. Each wore jack and helmet, had spear in hand, bow and quiver slung across their back, sword and buckler and long knife at their waists; each carried three days' worth of jerky and crackerlike waybread and cakes of dried fruit in their saddlebags.

The birds were waking as the stars faded, and the stubble-fields to either side were silvered for a moment with dew. Many flew up from tree and field at the rumbling clatter of hooves.

At their head Juniper Mackenzie rode, in her rippling shirt of mail. Her helmet had a silver crescent on the brows, and the standard-bearer beside her carried a green banner with the horns-and-moon.

The refugees from Sutterdown and its farms looked on—the ragged fighters grouped together, listening to a sermon from Reverend Dixon, and the families camped on either side of the road; she could smell the woodsmoke of their cooking fires and the boiling porridge—one thing the Mackenzies had in reasonable quantity right now and could spare for gifts was oatmeal.

A loud *Amen* came from the Sutterdown men as the Mackenzies reached the encampment—and it was all men in the armed ranks, she noticed.

*Well, we had our ritual,* Juniper thought. *They have a right to theirs. People need faith in a time like this; if not one Way, then another. There are many roads to the same goal.*

She felt far calmer than she'd feared; increasingly so,

with every hoofbeat that carried her away from home. Calm in an almost trancelike way, but her mind was keenly alert, and she felt as nimble as a cat. That was one thing she'd asked for at the ceremony last night, but she'd never led a war-Esbat before—against whaling and nuclear power stations, yes; for help in battle, no. She wasn't sure how it worked. There were certainly enough crows around today, bird of the Morrigan.

The Sutterdown leaders waited to greet her, beside a table set by the side of the road. She threw up her hand and the column clattered to a halt; then she dismounted and walked towards them, leading her horse. Cuchulain padded beside her.

"Whoa!" she said suddenly.

She pushed back on the bridle to halt the animal as a small form darted out from the crowd; the mare snorted and danced in place, hooves ringing on the asphalt, trying to toss its head and failing as her grip on the reins just below the jaw calmed it.

The child was a girl, about six, her face smudged and long tow-colored hair falling over her grubby T-shirt. She wore jeans and sneakers, and she stood belligerently in Juniper's path with her chubby arms crossed on her chest; there was a shocked gasp from the onlookers as she spoke up in a clear carrying treble: "Are you the Wicked Witch?"

Juniper laughed, and went down on one knee. That brought her head about level with the girl's; she'd long ago found that children generally didn't like being loomed over. Particularly by mysterious strangers, she supposed.

"You're half right, little one," she said, looking into the cerulean blue gaze.

It was like and unlike Eilir's at the same age; just as fearless but solid and direct, without the fey quality she remembered.

"What's your name?"

"Tamar."

"That's an ancient and wonderful name, Tamar; a princess of long ago was called that. My name's Juniper, like the tree," she replied.

Her other hand went out for a moment to calm the mother who was hovering, waiting to snatch her daughter back.

"And I am a Witch, yes. But I'm a *good* Witch."

"Then will you make the bad men go away?"

"Yes, darling, I will do that. I promise."

Tamar glanced to either side, then leaned closer.

"Can you really do magic?" she whispered.

"Why, yes I can!" Juniper replied, keeping her face serious. "In fact—"

She'd been palming the half-eaten Snickers bar while she spoke; not without a pang, because they really didn't have many left. Now she produced it with a flourish, and the girl's eyes went wide.

"—I can make *chocolate* appear."

Tamar's eyes went wide as she recognized the silver-foil wrapping; she probably hadn't had any candy since right after the Change. But she restrained herself nobly; Juniper held the bar forward.

"For you."

Tamar took it eagerly. "Thank you," she said politely. Then her face fell a little: "But that wasn't *real* magic, was it?"

"No," Juniper said, laughing. "That was just a trick. But I can do real magic, too. Real magic doesn't make rabbits disappear in hats or chocolate bars appear out of pockets. It does great and wonderful things, but they're secret."

Tamar nodded gravely. "I hope you make those bad men disappear," she said. "They're really *really* bad. They chased us out of our house and they took my Mr. Rabbit and they hurt people and scared my mom and made her cry."

"Then by spell and sword we'll make them go away, and get you back Mr. Rabbit, and your house," she said. "And none of them will make your mom cry again."

Then she looked to either side as the child had, and lowered her voice: "Do you want to know a secret?"

Tamar nodded eagerly, leaning forward herself and turning her head so that Juniper could whisper in her ear.

"I can do real magic. *And so can you.*"

Tamar gave a squeal of delight, and Juniper rose, putting a hand on the small hard head to steer her back to her waiting mother; the woman snatched her up, but Tamar waved gleefully with the hand that held the chocolate bar.

Juniper was still smiling slightly when she reached the Sutterdown triumvirate.

"Sorry," she said. "But I couldn't resist."

Sheriff Laughton nodded. "Tamar's my sister's daughter," he said. "Her dad was in Washington—D.C.—on the day of the Change. Thanks."

Then he took a deep breath. "We're ready," he went on. "But an awful lot depends on you."

"And I'm laying the life of my people on the line," she said. "This is all of us, bar the children, the *very* pregnant, the nursing mothers and the sick. Our lives are riding on this, and the lives of our children."

He nodded jerkily, and traced two roads on the map. "We'll draw them back to here." His face went distant for an instant, as if at some memory, and not a good one. "It's not easy, getting men to stop running—even if they know they're supposed to run in the first place."

"As agreed, here," Juniper said, taking the meaning if not the reference, tapping the map in her turn. "And it's our best chance, Sheriff. We'll just have to hope the enemy are as arrogant and overconfident as they seem."

There was a grassy hill not far east of Craigswood. As the sun set, Michael Havel and Signe Larsson walked to the crest. The lights of the town showed below them, soft with firelight and lantern light; the smaller cluster of the Bear-killers' camp was directly below, distant enough that the sound of voices singing in chorus was faded to a blur. Within their own scouts' perimeter, they could dress as they pleased; Havel found himself reveling in the light feel of the T-shirt, Levi's, and Stetson.

Signe was dressed similarly, except that she wore a flannel shirt over her "No Whaling" T-shirt, with the tails tied at her midriff.

They both carried their backswords and shields, of course; by now that was as instinctive as putting on shoes. They leaned them against a lone pine that marked the crest, spread their blanket and sat, elbows on knees, watching the sky change from salmon pink and hot gold to green shading into blue as the sun dropped below the jagged horizon.

"Pretty," he said.

Signe turned her head and grinned at him; at close range, he noticed how the down-fine gold hairs on her skin stood out against the golden brown of her tan, like very faint peach fuzz.

"You're supposed to say *but not as pretty as you,*" she said.

"I suppose that's one reason I'm still single, not saying silly stuff like that," Havel said, smiling back. "I mean, you are pretty; you're beautiful, in fact. But you aren't a sunset."

"So, is *this* our first date?"

"Well, if you don't count fighting cannibals together—"

They shared a chuckle, then sat in companionable silence for a while.

"They seem like nice people," Signe said. "The Woburns, I mean."

Havel nodded; dinner had been pleasant. "Nice to eat at a table again, too."

"Yeah!" A pause. "You know, this is a very pretty area, too. Looks like very good land, as well."

He turned and looked at her; she'd laid her head on her knees, and the last sunlight gilded her hair. He replied to her unspoken question.

"No, I don't think settling down here after"—he nodded towards the outline of Cottonwood Butte where Duke Iron Rod laired in his monastery-cum-fortress—"we take care of him would be a good idea. Doable, perhaps . . . but not a good idea."

"There's a lot of vacant land, *good* land, with good houses and fencing already in place. And they'll be grateful; we could help them set up their defenses."

He nodded. "Gratitude is worth its weight in gold."

She thought about that for a moment and then made a growling sound and hit him on the shoulder.

"You are the most cynical man I've ever met!"

"I was a blue-collar kid," he grinned. "And then a grunt. Dirty end of the stick all the way. Cynical I can do in my sleep. No, the main reason is up there."

He nodded north. "This was all Nez Perce land once. They haven't forgotten—Running Horse told me more than he intended, I think. What's more, you're right, it's good land and well watered, about the best farming country in Idaho that doesn't need to be irrigated. Much better than anything the tribe have left. Give it a generation or so . . . well, I wouldn't want to leave my kids that sort of war as an inheritance."

"Oh," she said. "And I suppose the Protector would be after us too, if we knocked off his local boy. And Sheriff Woburn might cause problems."

"Bingo, *askling,*" Havel said. "You're not just a pretty face, you know?"

She hesitated. "Mike, do you like me?" At his raised brow, she went on: "I mean, I think you do—we get on better than I ever have with a guy . . . but then . . ."

He leaned back on his elbows, plucking a grass stem and chewing on the end; it was sweet as honey.

"Didn't think you'd want to be bothered with men hitting on you for a while, judging by our last try."

She looked down at his face. "Better not let anyone else hear that," she teased. "It might spoil the great, ruthless Lord Bear's reputation."

"Hmmphf." He hesitated in his turn. "Well, if you want to know the absolute truth . . . The other problem's been that while I do like you, I'm in charge here. Had to be really sure you reciprocated, you know?"

"You're a gentleman, and a gentle man, in your way, Mike."

"Within limits," he grinned; his arms came up and encircled her.

"Lord Bear! Lord Bear! Lord—oh, shit, I'm sorry!"

The messenger turned and dashed back down the hill, standing looking ostentatiously away thirty feet downslope.

Mike Havel looked down into Signe's face. A little of the glaze went out of her eyes; then she wrapped arms and legs around him.

"If you stop now, I'll . . . I'll make sure you never can again!"

"Come back in ten minutes!" Havel shouted.

Signe giggled again and bit him on the shoulder; Havel gave an involuntary yelp, loud enough for the messenger to hear. *They* could hear his floundering retreat.

"Ten minutes! You unromantic *beast!*" Signe said, running her heels up the backs of his thighs. "Where were we?"

*       *       *

Signe paused as she began to tie her bootlaces, looking at Havel out of the corners of her eyes.

"Well, that sort of rushed things, didn't it?"

"Yeah, it *did* sort of rush things. Goddamned embarrassing interruption, too."

"You're an old-fashioned guy in some ways, Mike."

"Backwoods upbringing," he said, buckling on his sword and jamming the hat on his head. "This had better be important."

"Wait a minute," Signe said, fingers plucking. "Grass in your beard . . . there, got it."

"Your hair is full of the stuff . . . *hey, kid! The message!*"

She was running a comb through the dense yellow mane when the adolescent returned.

"Mr. Hutton says to tell you there's a bad discipline problem with Waters, and you're needed pronto," the boy said, still facing away.

"Tell him I'll be right there," Havel said.

*And in no very good mood. Billy boy, you have the worst timing of any man I've ever met.*

The crowd parted at the sound of hooves; Havel reined in, hearing murmurs of "the bossman" and "Lord Bear." He slid from the saddle and someone took the reins; possibly Signe, but he wasn't looking around right now.

Several of the lanterns that hung before the family tents were lit; that and the fires gave plenty of light, but the people crowding around were flickers at the edge of sight, their faces uneasy.

Billy Waters stood, looking sullen and flushed, two men holding him by the arms—both his neighbors. Jane Waters sat by the front flap of their tent in a boneless slump, her face covered with the red flush of incipient bruises, tears leaking down her face; her two younger children huddled near her, torn between fear and need for their mother's closeness.

Reuben Waters was not far away, lying on his back while Pamela Arnstein worked on him. Her hawk-featured face was incandescent with fury; Havel felt it through his own anger as he knelt beside Waters's twelve-year-old son.

"He was just woozy," she said. "I gave him something to make him sleep."

She touched the boy's face gently, turning it towards the brightest firelight. Relaxation made the narrow foxy hillbilly-Scots-Irish face look younger than its twelve years.

"See here? He's going to have a shiner, and this tooth is loose. Punched twice, I'd say. Those are a grown man's knuckle marks. All he needs now is cold compresses and rest. And a different father!"

Havel nodded, walked over to Jane Waters, and crouched on his heels so that their eyes were level. He touched her chin with a finger, turning her left cheek to the light and studied the swelling marks of a man's hand.

"Jane," he said. "Why don't you help Pam get your son to the infirmary tent?" She looked at him with dumb fear. "Jane, whatever happens, you've still got a place here—and your kids. Understand?"

He helped her rise, and composed his face when he realized it was frightening some of the onlookers. The stretcher-bearers took Reuben off, with his mother walking beside him.

"Angelica," he went on. "You've got some of those cookies left, don't you?" At her nod, he went on: "I think it would be a good idea if you and Annie took the kids—everyone younger than Astrid—and fed them some cookies over by the chuck wagon, and tell 'em stories. Tell 'em about Larsdalen."

Their destination was assuming mythic proportions; he hoped the reality didn't disappoint too much.

She nodded: "I'll get Sam to check Rueben over just in case and help with the kids."

Rounding up the children wasn't hard; they all thought cookies and a tale by the camp's best storytellers was far more interesting than a frightening confrontation among the grownups.

"Get all the adults here, except the sentries," Havel went on.

That took a few minutes. He ducked into the Waterses' tent—normally something never done without invitation—and rummaged. The bottle he'd expected was still three-quarters full. It was Maker's Mark, first-class Kentucky bourbon, expensive as hell even before the Change. There was another just like it, empty.

"All right," he went on, when he brought the bottles out

and held them up for the company to see. "Everyone here? Good. Now you, Fred Naysmith, you give me the details."

The man holding Waters's left arm gulped, and stuttered. The Bearkillers' judicial proceedings were refreshingly simple, so far; a trial by a quorum of the adults, presided over by Lord Bear. Punishments were simple too. With fines and imprisonment impractical, they went quickly from "extra duties" through a mass kicking around that Pam called "the gauntlet" to "expulsion," which was equivalent to a death sentence.

Naysmith licked his lips and spoke out: "I heard the Waterses arguing—sounded like Billy was yelling at Nancy." That was the bowyer's eight-year-old. "Then she started crying and screaming at him to stop, and . . . well, we hadn't been listening too hard before, you know, Boss?"

He nodded understanding. There wasn't much privacy in camp; the tents were set far enough apart that ordinary conversation didn't carry, but shouts certainly did. A convention had grown up of pretending you didn't hear family arguments—one of the little forbearances that made the tight-knit group's life tolerable.

"But it got sort of scary. And I could hear Jane screaming at him to stop, too. Then he started hitting her—hitting Jane, that is—and then Reuben tried to make him leave her alone, and he started hitting the kid, real hard, yelling bad stuff, really bad. So Jake and I went over and dragged him out. He tried to slug us too, and he smelled and acted drunk, and we sent someone for you, Lord Bear."

Havel looked around the circle of firelit faces; most of the men had close-cropped beards like his, and most of the women braids. Underlit from the flames, they all had a hard feral look, new since the Change. He held up the whiskey bottles again. There were resentful murmurs; pre-Change liquor was already extremely valuable as trade goods, like tobacco.

"This isn't from our stores. I think we can all guess how Billy got it from the townies over there."

He uncorked it and took a slug, baring his teeth and exhaling as the smooth fire burned its way down his gullet.

"That's the real goods, and no mistake. The man who took Bearkiller equipment for this didn't cheat Billy the way Billy did the rest of us."

More formally: "Anyone want to speak for this man? Anyone have a different version of what came down here tonight? Anyone know another way he could have gotten this liquor?"

There was an echoing silence; Waters didn't have many friends, and since he was obviously guilty as sin the few he did have weren't going to court unpopularity by swimming upstream. Being severely unpopular in a small community like this was unpleasant to the point of being dangerous, when you had to rely on your fellows for your life in a world turned hostile and strange.

Havel tossed the empty aside and handed the full bottle to someone, and it passed from hand to hand, with a little pawing and cursing and elbowing if anyone kept it tilted up too long—there was just enough for a sip for everyone who wanted one.

"One last time, does anyone want to speak for Billy Waters? It's any member's right to speak freely at a trial."

More silence, and Havel nodded. "Hands up for not guilty. Hands up for guilty . . . anyone want to propose a punishment? Or shall I handle it?"

There was a rumble of *you're the boss* and *let Lord Bear decide.*

He sighed. "Let him go," he said. The two men stepped aside, and Havel moved forward.

"Waters, you sad and sorry sack of shit," he said in a conversational tone, and then his open hand moved with blurring speed.

*Crack!*

Waters went down as if he'd been hit across the face with the flat side of an oak board, but nothing was broken; Havel had calculated the blow with precision.

Waters cringed and tried to scramble back as the Bearkillers' leader stepped forward, moving with the delicate ease of a great cat.

"On your feet! Christ, you're getting the beating whatever you do. Take it like a man, Waters, not a yellow dog!"

Havel raised his voice a little after the older man crawled upright, holding a hand to the side of his face.

"Do you remember what I said to you when you joined the Bearkillers, Billy?"

The man nodded quickly. "Said I shouldn't go on no benders, Lord Bear. Look, Boss, I've been making the bows good, haven't I? I'm real sorry and it won't—"

"What I said was that if you went on a bender and slapped your wife and kids around, I would beat the living shit out of you the first time, and beat the living shit out of you and throw you out on your worthless ass the second time. Didn't I?"

Waters's mouth moved. The second time he got the *yes* out audibly. Then he licked his lips and spoke:

"I was just giving Nancy a spanking, Lord Bear—she back-talked me. A man's got a right to do that."

Havel nodded. "Yeah, sometimes you have to give a kid a swat on the butt to get their attention, like using a rolled-up newspaper when you're housebreaking a puppy."

He held up his right hand; his index finger rose to make a point. Billy Waters watched it with fascinated dread as it approached his face.

"Since you are such a *stupid* sack of shit, I will now demonstrate, using visual aids, that there is a big fat fucking difference in kind between a spanking and a punch in the face."

Then he closed the hand into a fist and struck with a short chopping overarm blow. This time the sound was more like a maul striking wood.

Havel rubbed his right fist into the palm of his left as Waters rolled on the ground, moaning and clutching his face. Havel's knuckles hurt—the move wasn't one he'd have used in a fight, but the purpose here was punishment . . . and education, if possible.

Waters staggered up without an order this time, for example, which showed some capacity to learn.

"That's what it's like to be punched in the face by someone a lot stronger than you are, Billy. Did *you* like it?"

Waters swallowed and lowered a hand from his right eye; the flesh around it was already puffing up. He shook his head wordlessly.

"I'll bet punching Reuben out made you feel like a real man, didn't it, Billy?"

*Crack.*

Havel struck again, with his left palm this time. The man spun to the ground and hugged it, rising only when Havel encouraged him with the toe of his boot.

"Now, where were we?" Havel said, when the bowmaker was back on his feet, swaying a little. He went on, his voice flatly cold: "Yeah, we were talking about how a real man acts. Reuben, now, he tried to defend his mother against long odds, which is a pretty good example. God knows where he learned it, since he didn't get the idea from *you!* I think we've established that a real man doesn't punch little kids in the face, though. Haven't we? I'm waiting for an answer, Billy."

"Yes, Lord Bear."

"Now let's move on to the subject of how a real man treats his wife. A real man doesn't slap even a ten-dollar hooker around, if he's got any self-respect, much less hurt his own woman. Much less ten times over the mother of his kids. A *real* man busts his ass to feed his family, fights for them if he has to, dies for them if he has to. And he treats his wife with *respect* every day of his life, treats her like a queen—the queen of the home she makes for their children."

*Crack. Crack.*

Havel struck again with both sides of his open hand, forehand and back. Waters slumped to his knees, blood pouring from his nose and the corners of his mouth where the lips had cut on his teeth.

"Chuck that bucket of water on him," Havel said, without looking around.

Someone did, and awareness came into Waters's eyes once more. Havel bent, forearm on thigh, so that he could speak close to the man's face, more quietly this time.

"By now, you probably feel a bit hard-done-by, Billy. Just remember this: anytime you want, you can be treated with respect by me and everyone in the outfit. All you have to do is *earn* it! Now get out of my sight. Go puke out the booze and clean yourself up. I'm giving you this one last chance, for your kids' sake."

Havel turned to the assembly as Waters scuttled away. His voice was hard and pitched to carry, but calm: "I cannot abide trash behavior. I will not tolerate it in the Bear-killers. Remember, we're supposed to look out for each other; so don't let this sort of thing get started. Lights-out in an hour, people. We'd all better get ready to turn in."

The crowd dispersed, murmuring, as he walked back towards the command tent; most of the murmurs were approval. More than a few slapped him on the back; he answered with polite nods, but stayed wordless. Signe followed, leading their horses.

"Mike—" she said.

He turned with a wry smile. "Sorry, *askling,* but I'm not fit company for man or beast right now."

The smile turned into a grimace. "I feel like I need a bath—and a strong drink, to get the taste of that out of my mouth."

She smiled and leaned forward, kissing him with brief gentleness. "Well," she said, "It's not as if either of us is going to fly off to the Côte d'Azur tomorrow, right? What say we make a date for the next nice sunset?"

He grinned suddenly. "I'll look forward to it."

"And you'll treat me like a queen, hey?" she asked, smiling impishly.

He swept an elaborate courtly bow. "And so will everyone else," he said. "If I have anything to say about it."

When she'd left, he stood smiling his crooked smile for a moment.

"And maybe, just maybe, I will," he murmured to himself.

For Ken Larsson was right; he had been very damned lucky indeed, so far. And . . .

"How did your dad put it, Signe? Yeah. People live by myths, but myths change . . . the Change threw 'em all up for grabs. *And the first king was a lucky soldier.*"

# CHAPTER TWENTY-SIX

"Complicated plan," Sam Aylward whispered. "Depends on the enemy doing what we want."

Juniper nodded. "It also allows a good chance for us to run away if things go bad," she replied softly, concentrating on the view through her binoculars.

"It also depends on the Sutterdown folk doing what they promised."

"*Ní neart go cur le chéile*," she said. "There's no strength without unity. We can't do this by ourselves."

She lay at the edge of a patch of woods that covered a low rise in the valley floor. Beyond that was a narrow strip of plowed land grown with weeds, earth turned before the Change but never seeded. Beyond that was a wire fence, now down and derelict, and a narrow two-lane road; beyond that was a fair-sized wheatfield, reaped but with the grain still lying in windrows, and beyond that a line of trees along the irregular course of a small creek.

The sight of the grain lying out disturbed her, even though the land was well beyond the clan's borders and into Sutterdown territory. Every night it lay out was one more for the birds and animals to eat more, and the risk of it spoiling was unbearable. In fact, she could see jays at it now, and crows, and a rabbit hopping through looking for good bits.

*The waste of war,* she thought. *Bad enough before the Change. Worse now.*

She laid the glasses down and turned her head, looking through a fringe of cloth. The long hooded poncho they'd christened a war cloak was light fabric, splotched in gray-green-brown, and sewn over with loops that held twigs or served to break her outline; Sam called it a ghillie suit. All the Mackenzie fighters wore one, and even though she knew where they were, she could see no more than a few—Dennis, lying with the ax blade beside his head, and John Carson beyond him.

The Englishman had taught them that trick; he was willing to give advice, or train, or fight, or even lead a small group, but not to command overall, though they'd offered him that. What had he said?

*Hasn't been an Aylward ranked higher than sergeant in seven centuries, Lady. I wouldn't want to break the tradition.*

She didn't look behind herself. The horses were safely on the other, eastern side of the woodlot; Eilir and half a dozen other kids too young to fight but old enough to be trusted held them, ready for retreat. If worse came to worst, most of her people could probably flee . . . but she didn't expect that.

*I've never felt like this outside the Circle,* she thought, but the musing was distant. It wasn't that she was brimming with confidence; she just . . . waited.

The first Sutterdown men to come by were running, and for real; weaponless, some leaking blood, but not too badly to keep them from making good speed. They came down the road and vanished around the corner as it curved eastward, to her left. The rest came in a clump; many more wounded or limping, some lying in a cart drawn by a single horse. She knew that meant others were dead; that a rear guard was spending their lives buying time for the rest to retreat and make their stand.

Even wondering if they'd stop didn't make her feel anxious—just a slight tension, like a tight string on a guitar.

They did stop. Reverend Dixon was there, the only man on horseback, but sharing his parishioners' danger. She could hear his voice, though not make out the words: harsh, hectoring, shaming the men into halting and turning to face the foe once more. But she could feel the power in it, as he gestured with the Bible in his hand.

*I'll never like him, and we may be enemies someday, but respect him I must, however reluctantly. He's no hypocrite.*

There were a hundred or so of the Sutterdown militia, working with frantic speed to make an improvised barricade where the road turned east, hauling fence posts with a tangle of wire and shoving a couple of abandoned cars into place before rocking them over on their sides; forty of her Mackenzies waited along the edge of the woods. Silence fell again, more or less; birds sang with cruel indifference, and insects burrowed and bit.

And the braying sound of a trumpet came from the northwest, towards Sutterdown, faint but menacing. A man on a bicycle came from that direction too, stopped on a straight section of the road just beyond bowshot of the militia's barricade and looked about with binoculars of his own.

She lowered her own lest the reflection give her away and waited; he seemed to give only perfunctory attention to the side of the road. The barricade got a close going-over, and the scout wrote in a spiral-bound notebook. Then he extended a fist with all but one finger clenched into a fist, pumped it in an unmistakable gesture, and pedaled off towards Sutterdown again.

When he returned, the whole band was with him. Only two of them were on horseback, one who seemed to be the leader—he had a tall feather plume on his helmet—and a standard-bearer beside him. The flag that hung from the crossbar on the pole was black, with a cat-pupiled red eye on it; her mouth quirked slightly, at the evidence that someone—perhaps this Protector—had a nasty sense of humor.

*Or as Mike said, a weak grasp on reality; possibly both.*

The rest were on bicycles. Her lips moved again, in a silent curse. With bicycles and good roads, raiders could travel fifty miles in a day and strike without warning; and in the short run bicycles required neither the skilled care nor the expensive feeding of horses. That alone made things different—and worse—than in any of the history everyone was mining for clues on how to live in the Changed world.

*Take bandits, add bicycles and shake, and what do you get? Instant Mongol!*

Now someone seemed to have figured out how to apply the same advantage on a large scale. You couldn't fight from the saddle of a bicycle, but then, nobody around here could fight from the back of a horse either. Not yet.

*Sixty-three,* she counted; that didn't include the banner man. *Thirty with crossbows.*

Pre-Change crossbows, or made well since; they also wore short sleeveless tunics covered with metal scales, helmets, and had small shields slung across their backs; and they all seemed to have long knives or shortswords at their belts. Many carried hatchets as well.

The remaining dozen had knee-length hauberks of rings or scales; their armor had sleeves, and they wore steel-splint protection on their forearms and shins. Their shields were thick and broad, strapped with metal, and they were armed with heavy spears, long swords or axes. The mounted commander halted them along the eastern side of the road, and Juniper felt a stab of anxiety—had they seen her folk?

*No,* she decided. *He's just holding them there ready to charge.*

She could see them laughing as they dismounted from their bicycles, leaving them on their kickstands, forming up in a column shield to shield; a few paused to piss by the side of the road, holding the skirts of their armor aside.

The invaders had a supply wagon with them as well. It wasn't horse drawn, though: men powered it, seated on six bicycles bolted into a frame. Scrawny men clothed in rags, whose feet were chained to the pedals of their machines.

*Now, are these the Good Guys, or the Bad Guys?* she thought grimly. *Nice to know your first impression isn't mistaken. Cernunnos, Lord of the Gates of the Underworld, make ready!*

The crossbowmen formed up in a double line and began walking towards the Sutterdown position; they moved in open order, leaving gaps for the second rank to shoot through. Archers and crossbows opened up on them as they came within a hundred yards, but they ignored them—and ignored the man of theirs who fell kicking with a bolt in his thigh, except that they shuffled their ranks to close up the empty space.

At eighty yards they stopped with a single long shout. The first rank leveled their crossbows and fired, a harsh unmusical snapping of strings and whistle of bolts; then they dropped the forward ends of their weapons to the ground, unshipped the cranks at their belt, hooked them to cord and butt and rewound.

The second rank fired as they reloaded; then the first raised their weapons again, steady and methodical . . .

*They'll keep shooting until the militia are badly shaken,* she thought.

Behind them the full-armored fighters were shouting and slapping their weapons on their shields, waiting their turn.

*Then the heavies will go in. Morrigan witness, nobody really knows how to fight this way. A hundred Romans or Normans could wipe the floor with the lot of us. But the Protector's bunch are a little less ignorant than most.*

"But perhaps not so wise as they supposed," she murmured to herself, and whistled softly in signal.

*BOOM!*

The deep throbbing note of the drum echoed out across the empty fields, seeming to quiver in the hot still air, fading into distance. The noise from the road dropped away; the crossbowmen halted their mechanical rhythm of aiming and firing, looking over their shoulders. So did the heavy infantry preparing to charge.

*BOOM!*

It was the sound of a four-foot Lamberg drum, beaten two-handed with split canes; the instrument her Scots ancestors had employed to shatter the spirit of their enemies. She had only one here, rather than massed ranks, but the sound rippled up her spine and seemed to jolt in her skull.

*BOOM. BOOM. BOOM—*

"And now for the second great instrument of Celtic psychological warfare," she muttered.

Her voice sounded distant and muffled in her own ears, as if the part of her mind that dealt with rational thought and speech was withdrawing from the waking world.

Dorothy's bagpipes started then. It wasn't the mannered, cultured version you could hear on most CDs before the Change, or at a festival in Edinburgh. This was a raw eerie wailing; the same music the old Gaels had used to lash themselves into frenzy, until they ran heedless into battle, stark naked and shrieking and sheerly mad.

That too played along her skin; yet the anger that followed was not hot, but cold: as if a wind blew through her from a place of ice and bones, sweeping away all that was human and leaving only incarnate Purpose.

Six months ago, what had these men before her been? Criminals? Perhaps; or perhaps auto mechanics and computer salesmen and clerks.

*But now they come to kill, to rape and steal and destroy, to starve our children and take the works of our hands and the Goddess' blessings and drive us out on the road to die or turn cannibal.*

Her voice was a whisper; cold and small in her own ears:

*"In the name of the babe beneath my heart, I curse you. And Your curse upon them: you Dread Lord, wild huntsman; you Dark Goddess, raven-winged and strong! Come to me, in power and in wrath! May Anwyn take them, and ill may be the house to which You lead them!"*

The rage was enormous, beyond all bearing; her hand scrabbled at the catch of her cloak as if it choked her. She cast it off and rose, ignoring Sam Aylward's cry—this wasn't in the plan. She ignored his second cry, as well, of stark terror when he saw her face: turned bone-white, white as the rim all about her staring eyes. The pupils expanded to swallow all else, depthless pools of night. Teeth showed bright beneath lips drawn back in a she-wolf's killing grin.

When she shouted the sound was huge, loud enough to strain even her trained singer's throat, loud enough to shock the drummer and piper into silence for a moment:

*"Scathach!"*

Even her coveners recoiled in horror, as she invoked the Dark Goddess in Her most terrible form.

Scathach, the Devouring Shadow.

She Who Brings Fear.

Shrieking it, standing with feet planted wide apart, her red hair bristling like the crest of a fox at bay, bow in one hand and arrow in the other as her spread arms reached skyward and completed the double V.

*"Scathach!"*

Eyes turned in her direction from all across the battlefield-in-the-making.

*"Scathach! As they have wrought, so it shall be returned to them, threefold!"*

She put the arrow through the ledge of her bow's riser and drew, drew until the stave creaked and the kiss-ring on the string touched her lips. When she released it was into the air without aiming, but she knew where the shaft would fall.

It came whistling down out of the sun, and the banner-bearer of the enemy had barely time to look up before the chisel-headed bodkin point sank into his face and he fell, the black flag toppling to cover him as he struck the pavement.

"*SCATHACH!* They are Yours!"

Her hand stripped another arrow from her quiver; and all along the woodland edge the Mackenzies shed their war cloaks and stood, longbows in their hands.

Few of them were really masters of their weapons as yet, but the target was massed and stationary and nowhere more than fifty yards away. They had all shot at marks further than that for an hour or more most days since the Change, under Sam Aylward's merciless tuition, and everyone here could draw a bow of fifty pounds weight or better.

Now the strings began to snap against the bracers, and the gray-feathered arrows flickered across the weed-grown field. Cloven air whistled under a hail of steel points and cedarwood. Juniper's was among the lightest bowstaves, but it seemed she could not miss and that two more shafts were in the air before her first had struck.

Then she reached over her right shoulder and her hand grasped at emptiness. There had been forty-five arrows in the leather cylinder on her back, and as many in every other quiver. Near two thousand shafts had flown, in the brief minutes while the Protector's soldiers wavered between the Sutterdown men before them and the clan's warriors to their left. Those who tried to charge the line of archers along the woods simply made better targets of themselves, attracting the eye as they came running into the teeth of the Mackenzie arrow-storm.

Many of those shafts had missed, and stood upright in earth or broken on asphalt; many were turned by shields or armor. Still horror wailed and crawled and writhed across the ground, and death lay still with the arrows still quivering.

"*At them!*" Juniper screamed, dropping her bow and ripping out her short-sword. "*At them, Mackenzies!*"

She snatched up her buckler and ran forward, keening a

wordless saw-edged ululation. The armor seemed no more than a cotton shirt on her back, and the rough ground merely gave strength to her feet as she bounded forward like a deer.

Dennis ran beside her on the right, bellowing and flourishing his great ax; Chuck was to her left, snarling and intent behind the point of his spear; Aylward came behind, with an extra quiver slung over his shoulder and a shaft nocked to his terrible hundred-pound bow.

Chaos greeted her, as the Sutterdown men came out from their barricade in a roaring wave. Most of the invaders threw away their weapons and ran. It did them little good. The armor which had guarded them also slowed them, and vengeful spears and axes ran behind in the hands of those whose homes they'd seized.

Some remained to fight, but they seemed to be moving as if encased in amber honey. An armored man swung a jointed iron flail from a pre-Change martial-arts store at her; she ducked beneath it and smashed the edge of her buckler across his instep. Then she came erect like a jack-in-the-box as he doubled over in pain, driving the point of her shortsword up under his chin. Chuck's spear drove into a belly, hard enough to snap scales loose from their leather backing; wet ruin spun away from the edge of Dennis's bearded ax.

A man came at her with a spear, but she didn't bother to guard; a flash drawn across her vision was Aylward's arrow, and it went through his throat in a red splash and spray, hardly slowing . . .

It seemed only seconds later when the only living enemy were a handful who fled, wailing as they ran across the reaped wheat towards the tree-lined creek beyond. Juniper laid her sword in front of Aylward's bow.

"No," she said, conscious of the same cold wind still blowing through her.

Others were shooting, but they missed. Aylward wouldn't.

"We want a few to spread the word that this is no place for reivers to come."

Quiet had fallen, save for a broken whimpering and the wheezing breath of the enemy commander's horse, dying slowly with three shafts through its ribs. Sutterdown men and Mackenzies alike hesitated for an instant of ringing silence, their eyes on her.

Of themselves, Juniper's arms reached up again, holding her buckler and dripping blade this time, spread over the field of battle. Wings beat at the corners of her consciousness, vast and black-feathered.

"*O you of humankind!*" she cried. "*Make peace with your mortality. For when you call on Me in such wise, then this too is God!*"

Then she staggered, knees buckling and eyes turning back up into her head for an instant. The world turned gray and light shrank to a point. Hands grabbed her under the arms, supporting her as she wheezed and fought for breath.

"Anyone got any candy left?" she croaked.

Someone did, giving it up without question; she stuffed it into her mouth despite the salt blood on her hands, washed it down with water and felt the dizziness recede, and the grayness fade from the edges of her sight.

"I'm all right," she husked. "I'm all right."

The men supporting her stepped back. One of them was Dennis; his ax was bloody, and more was splashed across his face and body, but the fear in his eyes was directed at her.

She shook herself. "I feel . . . I feel like a flute that Someone was playing on."

"Jesu— I mean, God and Goddess, Juney, that was the scariest fucking thing I've ever seen!"

He shook his head, leaning on his ax and panting like a great wheezing bellows for a second.

"What happened? First it was like you were screaming right in my ear—or inside my head—and then you were like the original whirling Dervish, you were a *blur*. I didn't even think about anything else except following you and hacking these guys up."

She felt her everyday self return, and with it a sharp twist of nausea at the sights and smells about her, and held up a hand palm out while she struggled back to self-command.

*Before the Change, this would have sent me catatonic,* she thought. *Now it just sickens me. Goddess, let me never see such things without sorrow. Let me never see such things again, please.*

Dennis was still staring at her. She answered his question: "Well, there's a rational explanation for what happened, Dennie."

"Shit, I hope so, Juney."

She nodded: "Hysterical strength, amok, berserkergang; it's all a well-known phenomenon, right there in the textbooks. There weren't any miracles, were there? I didn't glow red, or levitate, or cast thunderbolts, after all. Although . . . this is the sort of thing that gets legends and myths started."

"Ah," he said, looking relieved. His face relaxed. "You think that's what happened? Your subconscious took over?"

"Oh, no, Dennie, you don't get off that easy—and neither do I," she said, looking into his eyes.

He retreated a little as she went on: "What I think—know—is that I called on the Dark Goddess . . . and She came to me. It isn't all light and love and laughter, my friend. There's blood and fear and death and wickedness in the world, and the Mighty Ones act through *us.*"

She reached out and touched the pentagram-and-circle amulet he'd taken to wearing. "And if this is more than a piece of jewelry, you've picked which explanation you want to believe, haven't you?"

"Yeah," he said soberly. "I suppose I have."

Chuck came up to her. "One dead of ours," he said, his eyes avoiding hers a little. "John Carson. A couple of wounded, but . . . mostly it was over by the time we reached the road. Judy and Dr. Gianelli are getting to work. They think the clan won't lose anyone else."

"Blessed be," she said sadly. "But it could have been worse." She looked around, letting her eyes fall out of focus a little to miss detail. "Was worse, for them."

Aylward paused in recovering arrows and spoke with a surgeon's calmness: "It's like that, with surprise. Especially if the side surprised just gets the wind up and sods off regardless. They can't run and fight, but you can chase and kill at the same time."

She nodded. "Find out how the Sutterdown people did, Chuck," she said. "Get me Sheriff Laughton, if he's alive and fit to move."

When he showed up a few minutes later Laughton had a bandage covering half his face, but he seemed to be coherent enough; a dozen of his townsmen came with him, some of them bandaged or limping.

"Lady Juniper," he said. This time there was no awkwardness to the title. "Thank you. Thank you all from the bottom of our hearts. We'll get our homes back, now."

"You will," Juniper said. "And you'll be able to feed your children through the winter."

*Which are the only reasons good enough for this vileness,* she thought.

"We had thirty wounded and . . . nine dead," Laughton went on. He swallowed. "Including Reverend Dixon."

Her brows went up. "Dixon?" she said. "How?"

"He just . . . died. He just dropped down and died," Laughton said.

*Well, he* was *a coronary waiting to happen,* Juniper thought. *Plenty of stress today to set it off.*

"He'll be missed," she said soberly, and fought not to think: *But not by many.*

Then she saw the eyes of his men on her, all wide and fearful and a few of them full of the beginnings of adoration. The echo of a cold wind seemed to blow up her back, despite the hot sun and the sweat-dripping weight of mail and padding.

*This is how legends and myths start,* she reminded herself, and shivered ever so slightly. *Goddess gentle and strong, powerful God, what is it that You want of me?*

"Well, we'll have to see to the wounded," she said, dragging herself back to practicalities.

Her voice gained strength. "And to getting your families back to your homes, and we Mackenzies will pitch in to help get the rest of your crops in safe—we don't have anything to waste. And then we'll talk about making sure we're not caught by surprise like this again, and with all the other communities around here about defense. The man who set this on us, the one who calls himself Protector . . ."

"Yes, Lady," Laughton said.

Ray and Cynthia were kneeling by their father's body when she found them. A crossbow bolt had struck him just left of the breastbone, sinking in through the armor until only the fletching showed. There was a spray of blood beside his mouth, but the wide eyes looked surprised, as if it had been very quick. The flies were already coming, but they had plenty to feed on today.

Cynthia started to rise. Juniper sank down on her knees on the hot pavement between them, pressing a hand gently on the girl's shoulder and on her brother's. He looked stunned, unbelieving, his face much younger than the body beneath his warrior's gear, blinking his eyes at his father as the bloody work of cleanup went on around them. A seeping bandage marked where the little finger of his left hand had been, but he ignored that too.

"S-sorry, Lady Juniper," Cynthia said. "We should help—"

"You should both stay here and mourn your father," Juniper said quietly. "There's hands enough to do what needs doing."

The girl's face crumpled, turning red. "He . . . he shouldn't have died like this!" she cried.

"No," Juniper agreed. "He shouldn't. He was a good man, who only wanted to tend his fields and do right by his family and neighbors. There were years yet of work and joy ahead for him. He should have died old and tired and ready for the Summerlands, with you and your brother and *your* children around him to bid him farewell. He gave all that up, for us."

"I'm sorry," Cynthia said, putting the heels of her hands to her forehead. "Can . . . can we have a rite for him?"

"Certainly we can among ourselves, honey," Juniper said gently. "But he respected your choice; you have to respect his. We'll get the ritual he'd have wanted for his burial. Just let it go, for now. Mourn him, girl, and you too, Ray. Cry. Scream if it helps. There's no way around the pain, you have to go through it to the end and beyond. Blessed be."

She left them sobbing in each other's arms; Eilir was coming, riding a horse and leading another for her mother, her eyes wide with horror as she looked about.

When Juniper Mackenzie stood it was as if the weight of the world pressed down on her shoulders.

# CHAPTER TWENTY-SEVEN

*Problems,* Mike Havel thought.

*I didn't have enough of my own, so I took on a hundred other people's. Then we all decide to make a living solving problems for strangers . . .*

Mother Superior Gertrude was a horse-faced woman in her early sixties. She wasn't quite what Havel had expected in a nun; she did wear a headdress, but the rest of her clothing was overalls and a checked shirt and heavy shoes of the sort once called sensible.

Now she finished making corrections on the graph paper that Ken Larsson had pinned to a corkboard supported by a tripod. They were in Sheriff Woburn's house, a painfully ordinary suburban living room—except for the lampholders screwed into the walls, and the smoke marks above them; the whole house smelled not-so-faintly of woodsmoke from the kitchen, ashes from fireplace, and burnt gasoline from the lanterns.

There were improvised stables out back, too, and you could smell the horses as well, and their by-products. Flies buzzed about, despite the screens on windows and doors. There was too much manure around, and it made an ideal breeding ground; so did the broad—and heavily fertilized—truck gardens the residents of Craigswood had put in.

*Well, hello, Good Old Days,* Havel thought absently. *Eau de Horseshit and all. At least wandering about we can escape from our own crap.*

Woburn caught the drift of Havel's thoughts as he glanced about. "Not lookin' forward to an Idaho winter with only the fireplace and the woodstove," he said.

"Damnit, we should be laying in wood now, but we don't have time."

Havel nodded. *It would be even worse in a tent,* he thought.

Eric and a couple of others had suggested that they take up the wandering life full-time, herding cattle and sheep and horses for a living and trading for what else they needed. Then Ken Larsson had given a brief but colorful description of a north-plains winter in a teepee or equivalent, which had been enough to put paid to that. Plus the bit about their grandchildren being—literally—louse-eating nomads.

Susan Woburn came out with two big plates of bacon-lettuce-and-tomato sandwiches in her hands; Havel took one eagerly, with a word of thanks. They didn't eat bacon very often—pigs really weren't very practical to drive along for long distances—and they got fresh greens less often than that. There was even mayonnaise, and just eating light risen bread was a treat—on the move it kept falling and rising again, and ended up . . . *chewy* was the most charitable way to describe it.

Woburn nodded to his wife. "Thanks, honey . . . At least we haven't been short of food, praise God," he said. "And we shouldn't be next year, even with all the damage the Devil Dogs have done. If we can get things in order soon."

Ken Larsson leaned back from his sketch. "This is best we can do. Combination of the original plans and the latest intelligence."

Havel brought his sandwich over. "Damn, that does look like a fort," he said. "All right, what about doorknockers?"

Ken fanned out a selection of diagrams. "This is what I think we can make, given the materials available."

Havel nodded, impressed. He noted that Woburn looked a lot less happy.

"The problem is . . . well, to tell the truth, the problem is that . . ."

"You can't get enough men together to surround the place," Havel said. "Not after getting whipped last time. Lots of people finding excuses for not showing up."

Woburn nodded, mouth drawn in a bitter line. "What I need is a big win," he said. "Beating the crap out of a bunch of them. I could get the support I need after that."

His hand—the one not holding a sandwich—clenched into a fist and came down on his knee. "And then there'd be some changes around here! We're not doing half the things we should. Too much talk, not enough action."

*I detect a certain amount of bitterness,* Havel thought.

It occurred to him that if Woburn did come out on top, things might get quite uncomfortable for temporizers and those who'd tried to play both sides against the middle.

*Hereditary Sheriff Woburn the First? Not my business how things turn out here,* he thought. *I'm just passing through . . . and they could do worse. Duke Iron Rod is a chancre that needs cauterizing. Not unlike his big-city patron.*

"What we need," he said aloud, "is to cut up a couple of their raiding parties. For that we need recon. How big a gang do they send out?"

"Two dozen on a serious raid, give or take," Woburn said. "Enough to swarm any resistance on a single farm and get away fast. Usually they set out around dawn. They probably won't try again for a while after the most recent lot. But I don't see how you can intercept them any better than we can. It's not as if we could sneak someone up onto Cottonwood Butte with a radio!"

"What we need," Havel went on, "is aerial recon."

Woburn snorted. "That's not funny. Why not wish for a couple of working tanks?"

Havel grinned, and saw a frown of puzzlement growing on Woburn's face.

He went on: "You're forgetting something, Sheriff; truth is, I hadn't thought of it until my last trip down the Columbia Gorge. Electricity doesn't work anymore, and guns neither. But hot air still rises. Got much propane left around here?"

Billy Waters sat on the curb and watched men and a few women going in and out of the tavern. It had been one before the Change, one of three in Craigswood; it was the only one left now. A sort of sour half-spoiled smell came from the buildings to its rear, and he recognized the scent—mash getting ready for the still, with an undertone of beer fermenting. The thought made him smile a bit, and he hummed a few bars of "Copperhead Road"; then the pain in his lips brought reality crashing back.

The day was bright and warm, but he shivered. Memories tormented him; the smooth heat of the whiskey going down his throat, and the sweet hiss of the cap coming off the beer bottle, the first cool draught chasing the fire all the way to his belly. . . .

*Just one,* he thought. *Havel wouldn't mind if it was just one. He never told anyone not to take one drink. Hellfire, he likes his beer, and a whiskey now and then.*

A horse-drawn wagon made from a cut-down truck went past while he was thinking, and nursing the bruises. He touched his face gingerly, trying to summon up enough anger to get him across the street and into the tavern.

The problem was that he couldn't; all he could feel was fear.

He could feel anger at Jane, for making him hit her, and at that deceitful little bitch Nancy, and at Reuben for trying to hit his own father, but when he thought about Havel it was as if a white light filled his head, like it had the day of the Change.

All he could feel was the pain and the fear.

*I can stand up to him!* he thought. *I can—*

"Excuse me," someone said.

Waters looked up. The man standing over him on the sidewalk looked nondescript; not young, not middle-aged, dressed in a T-shirt and jeans, cowboy boots and Budweiser billed cap.

"Yeah?" he said.

"You're the guy who can make bows, aren't you? Name of Billy Waters?"

"Yeah," Waters said.

"I heard how you got beat up just because you spanked your kid. That doesn't sound right."

Waters levered himself stiffly to his feet, squinting at the unremarkable man. That also wasn't how he'd heard that people in Craigswood had gotten the story, either. Most of them who'd heard anything at all had been treating him like something nasty they scraped off their shoes on a hot day. And Craigswood was small, about a thousand people before the Change, half that now. He knew how news spread in a setting like that, having spent most of his life in one small town or another; the largest place he'd ever lived was Little Rock, and that only for a few months.

"Smith," the man said, offering his hand. "Jeb Smith. Thought I might like to talk to you about bows, and other things. Care for a beer?"

Waters's eyes flicked to the tavern, with its neon sign that probably hadn't worked before the Change and certainly didn't now. He shook the man's hand, but the white explosion of light seemed to fill his head again. Someone would talk . . .

"Ah . . ." he began.

Jeb laughed. "Not that horse piss. It's overpriced anyway, you have to trade half an hour's work for a glass, or something pretty fancy in the way of hard goods. No, I've got some home brew that isn't doing anything but filling up a crock."

He released Waters's hand, but steered him along for a moment by the elbow. "Seems to me a man who knows how to make bows should have a better position," he said. "And be able to sit down and have a beer when he feels like it."

"Damned right," Waters said. "*Damned* right. It's like being in the fucking Marines!"

They entered a nondescript ranch-style bungalow; the two on either side were abandoned; all the lawns had been plowed up for vegetables.

Jeb waved a hand at the houses on either side: "Stupid bastards are out somewhere shoveling cowshit for a rancher," he said. "There are easier ways of making a living, even these days."

"Yeah," Billy Waters said again.

"Me, I swap things and, ummm, sort of arrange deals," Smith said as they seated themselves in the dim coolness of the living room. "You need something, like say an old hand pump, or parts for a windmill, and you come to Jeb. Jeb can find it, or put you in touch with someone who has it or can make it. All for a very reasonable commission."

A woman came out with a pitcher of beer; it wasn't refrigerated, but drops of condensation slid down the sides of the glass, and Billy licked his lips. He had time to notice how good-looking she was before she handed him the tumbler.

"Ahhh," he said as the first glorious swallow slid down. It wasn't like anything he'd tasted before the Change, but it was undoubtedly beer. For a wonder, he didn't feel like gulping it and going right for another, either. Maybe it was because, for the first time in months, he wasn't bored.

"Your daughter, Jeb?"

"Naw, girlfriend," the other man said, giving her a casual slap on the butt as she went past. "Sort of. A man with connections has got more, oh, call it bargaining power, these days."

Waters looked around. The house was well furnished; it had an iron heating-stove in one corner of the living room, with its sheet-metal chimney already installed, and he could see through an archway that the kitchen had a wood cooking range. That was wealth, these days. Waters grinned; it reminded him of the one his mother had had, and she'd grown up no-doubt-about-it *poor*.

There was also a good hunting crossbow racked beside the door, and a belt with a bowie and hatchet scabbarded on it, with a steel helmet—an old pre-Kevlar Army model—and a plywood shield faced in sheet metal.

"So, you one of the sheriff's posse?" he asked.

"Nope. Not interested in getting myself killed for Woburn's benefit," Smith said. "Any more than busting my ass playing farmer."

He smiled and leaned forward. "Let's talk."

*And I thought that things would get easier after the harvest,* Juniper thought bitterly. *And surely after we beat the Protector's men back from Sutterdown.*

Aloud she spoke to Laughton with patient gentleness: "Sheriff, I really *can't* turn the McFarlanes down if they want to join us. Even though it's inconvenient for all concerned."

He was looking mulish again. Juniper fought an impulse to bury her face in her hands, and an even stronger one to grab her fiddle and head out into the woods with Cuchulain and lean against a tree and play until her nerves unknotted and she floated away on a tide of music.

Instead she took another sip of chilled herbal tea and looked out the north-facing window of her loft-bedroom-office for an instant and sighed. August was hot this year and there was a little smoke haze in the air over the mountains from the big burn further northeast, towards the Three Sisters; she worried about it spreading, too.

*At least I'm not huge yet. Showing, but not huge. That will be later, when it's cool and there's nothing much to do.*

She turned back to Laughton, looking over his shoulder through the west-facing dormer. She could see a squared timber swinging up on its rope, running from the two-horse team through the big block-and-tackle on the ground to the log tripod at the top of the half-completed gatehouse tower. Dennis's voice rang out, calling to Sally at the horses' heads; she halted the team and then backed them step by careful step, and hands on the scaffolding around the gatehouse guided the timber down.

"I know it makes things awkward, Sheriff," she said.

The gatehouse and nearly finished palisade were reassuring. So was Sally, with her tummy starting to bulge out over her chinos. Life went on; children got born, crops got planted, things got built. They'd get through somehow, Lady and Lord helping.

"You think it doesn't make it awkward for us, too?" she asked, tapping the map on the table between them.

That was of the Artemis Creek area, from the high hills north and east of Dun Juniper, down through the spreading V-shaped swale that held the old Fairfax place and out into the flats around Sutterdown, with the Butte beyond.

"Even out of Dun Carson"—the old Carson homestead, now well on its way to being a fortified steading—"getting our people up to work this farm will be a nightmare of time wasted traveling back and forth. What we might talk about is a swap for something closer, if any of your folk are interested."

"Hey, wait!" Rodger McFarlane said.

"Well, if you *don't* want to join and put the land at the clan's disposal . . ."

Maisie McFarlane stamped on her husband's foot under the table; at least that was what Juniper assumed, from the way her shoulders moved slightly and her tight smile and the way he smothered a yelp. She'd probably heard the sudden hope Juniper tried to conceal.

The farmer went on: "We certainly do want to join, Lady Juniper. It's not that everyone in Sutterdown doesn't do their best, but we're scared spitless out on the edge the way we are, never getting a good night's sleep. And we want school for our kids and stuff—we're just too far out and on our own we can't spare them from work. It's just . . . it's good land, two hundred and eighty acres."

"I thought we'd be moving in here," Maisie McFarlane said.

*I would really like to find that tree and my fiddle,* Juniper thought. Instead she made her voice kind and went on: "The palisade around Dun Carson is going up very quickly, and it'll be as safe as this."

*Or nearly. Maybe I* am *turning into a politician,* she thought, and made a sign of aversion under the table.

And the McFarlanes had brought in a good harvest—the fighting hadn't touched them much, though it had scared them green when the Protector's men marched past.

*I must not just see them as a nuisance, or an opportunity,* she told herself sternly. *They're people and terrified. For their children and kin and the people they've taken in, as well as themselves. And they're right to be terrified. Mother-of-All, help me be wise!*

"There's still a problem," Laughton said. "Look, we're all grateful for the help you gave us, in the fight and afterward. But the fact is the people who've joined you since—the Hunters, the Dowlingtons, the Johnsons, now the McFarlanes—they're not only putting islands of your territory in ours, they're the ones with the biggest grain reserves—and everyone in town pitched in to help get that grain harvested. We've got a system for sharing things around, but it's . . . Lady Juniper, it's all just falling apart without Reverend Dixon. Reverend Jennings . . . it's just not the same."

"I can't say that I liked Dixon," Juniper conceded. "But he was a strong man and he could get people to do the needful."

She sighed. "Sheriff, you can tell your townspeople that nobody's going to starve this coming winter because someone else has joined us. We'll see about the . . . swapping."

Laughton smiled as he rose and shook her hand, but he had that odd look in his eyes again—the one she'd seen on the day of the battle.

"Lady Juniper, you may find that there's a simple solution to that problem; everyone in Sutterdown joining up. Barring the Reverend Jennings and a few dozen others."

*Urk!* She hoped she didn't look as sandbagged as she felt.

*   *   *

When Laughton and the McFarlanes were gone, Juniper did drop her head into her hands and groan. Chuck let her alone as a few others filtered in: his wife, Judy, Dennis and Sally, Andy and Diana, and Sam Aylward.

Eilir went out and came back with lunch—bread and butter, cheese and fruit; the Sunrise apples on the old Fairfax place were ripe, and the dairy's output was going up fast.

*Eat, Mom,* she signed.

One of the advantages of using Sign was that you could talk with your mouth full. She had a crisp red-yellow Sunrise held in her mouth while she spoke.

*I'm not hungry,* Juniper replied.

*You'll be hungry once you start eating. Then all you reverend elders can yell at each other and wave your arms in the air. I'm going off with the book scavenging detail.*

*And I envy you that,* Juniper signed. *It's that mall place today, right?*

*Right. A lot of useful handicraft stuff there, and I'm hoping for a copy of* Arrows of the Queen *or* Somewhere to Be Flying.

*Be careful.*

*Always. Bye, everyone!*

Juniper watched her bounce out of the room with boundless fourteen-year-old energy, and lifted a slice of the bread without enthusiasm. Her stomach was knotted with tension, but the smell of the fresh bread and the half-melted butter on it made the organ in question rumble instead and she bit in. After that, the digestive system quit complaining and started to do its job.

*Would that everyone else did the same!*

"There are just too many people here now."

Judy shrugged. "What we've been doing is working. Everyone loves a—what's that saying?"

"*An té atá thuas óltar deoch air; an té atá thíos buailter cos air.* He who succeeds is toasted, who fails gets kicked. I feel toasted, all right—over an open fire!"

"You've done a wonderful job," Chuck said soothingly. "We're alive, aren't we? Everyone's got enough to eat, don't they? That's *why* we're flooded with people. After what's happened, they're desperate for something that looks secure."

Juniper sighed. "When we started, it was like a big family and everyone agreed on most things, but you can't do that when there are . . ."

Someone handed her a list.

". . . Goddess gentle and strong, a hundred and fifty not counting kids!"

She waved the paper over her head. "I can't keep people straight without a *list,* for sweet Brigid's sake; I'm turning into a *bureaucrat.* Even when I was sleeping in my car, I didn't sink that low! And we're spending more and more time talking. What are we going to do about it? I want everyone to have their say, but it takes forever!"

Chuck rubbed at his sun-faded sandy beard. "Well, let's stick with the model we picked—it's worked so far. Scottish clans got a lot bigger than this," he said. "How did they manage it?"

"By bashing heads, a good deal," Juniper said. "If the songs are to be trusted. And the Chief, the head of the Name and Ilk, what he said went, unless he got so crazy they arranged for him to accidentally get shot in the back while out hunting. Of course, he didn't have everyone living at his Hall, either, though he kept open house and any clansfolk could come sit at his table."

"Lucky him," Diana said, looking as frazzled as Juniper felt. "Do you have any idea how cumbersome it's getting to be, cooking three meals a day for a hundred and fifty people at three locations? I mean, when Andy and me ran MoonDance back before the Change at least people had a choice. Now everyone eats the same thing—I'd be complaining about it myself, if I didn't know I couldn't do anything about it. But whenever anyone else bitches about the food, I feel like throwing a cleaver at them! At least there's *enough* now."

"Crime," Dennis said. They all looked at him, and he went on: "Eventually, someone's going to commit a crime—I don't expect it ever to be a big deal, but eventually we're going to have to have some equivalent of judges and courts."

Juniper groaned again and buried her hands in her hair,

suppressing another urge—this time, it was pulling out handfuls.

"I kept wishing we weren't in a desperate scramble to grow enough food to get us through the winter," she said. "Ah, how fine things will be, I thought, when the grain's in and we have a few months before the fall plowing when we only have to work hard, and not fall into bed like a cut tree every evening. And now, I'm almost nostalgic for the fear of starving. At least it kept people focused!"

A sigh. "And Laughton was hinting that everyone in Sutterdown wants to join *us*—Judy, you do it for me!"

"Gevalt!" she said.

Everyone else made sympathetic noises. It was the songs that gave her the idea eventually; she ran through a half-dozen ballads in her head, searching the lyrics for clues.

"Look, as I remember it, the way the old Gaels did it, the Chief of the Name handled the big things—perpetual feuding, large-scale cattle theft, and how to keep others from stealing *their* cattle, and which doomed rebellion to support and get everyone killed in—and the . . . hmmm, I think they were called septs—sub-clans, I'm not sure whether it was an Irish word or Scottish—did the local work. Under a tacksman—usually a relative of the Chief. Probably it wasn't as neat as that, and the Victorians tidied it all up the way they did the tartans, but that's the bones of it."

Chuck rubbed his beard again. "You know, splitting up the land we've got—and are getting—into a bunch more separate farms would save a lot of time and effort. *My* time and effort, to start with. We've got enough farmers, and they've all had experience in the new methods—well, old methods—by now. There's no real need for me to go around saying 'hoe this row' anymore. We could draw up a general plan and let each . . . well, call it each sept . . . manage the day-to-day stuff on their own. We could still get together for big jobs."

Aylward nodded. "No reason our militia couldn't work that way too," he said. "Easy enough for someone like me"—he grinned a sergeant's grin—"to go around checking that nobody's slacking off or playing silly buggers. Say ten to twenty families in each settlement, and a palisade like we're putting in at the Carson place. That would be enough to stand off a gang of bandits or Eaters long enough for help to gather."

Sally had been quiet. Now she spoke up: "We could have the library and high school here, and an all-grades primary at each dun."

"Hey, and we could call the septs after a totem animal," Andy Trethar said; he'd always liked shamanistic stuff like that. "You know, wolf, raven—"

Juniper sat back with relief and let them go at it. *Of course, I'll have to persuade people in general, and get their ideas, and . . .*

*At least we're not fighting a war anymore.*

# CHAPTER TWENTY-EIGHT

"Confirm . . . enemy . . . position," Havel read, binoculars to his eyes.

The Bearkiller column and Woburn's posse were down at the bottom of a swale. That cut visibility to a thousand yards in any direction, but it meant nobody could see them either, except from a height.

A height like that of the hot-air balloon floating over the Bearkiller camp in Craigswood, for example; the three Bearkillers in the basket hanging two thousand feet above ground level had an excellent view. He could make out the semaphore signal quite clearly through the field glasses, and they'd be able to pick up his mirror-flash of light even more easily.

"Damn, I wish I'd thought of that," Woburn muttered awkwardly. "We might not be in this mess, if we'd had a balloon."

"Everyone tends to think engines when they think aircraft," Havel said. "I certainly did; but the Protector over in Portland didn't."

Woburn rubbed his lantern jaw. "Sort of hard to think of Portland having much to do with our problems. These days, it seems a long ways off."

"Believe it," Havel said grimly. "I doubt Iron Rod would have been more than a major nuisance without someone giving him help and ideas. Hell, the Protector gave *me* ideas, unintentionally."

He looked at the balloon again. It had taken a bit of finding . . . but there were a surprising number of hot-air balloon enthusiasts in Idaho—had been, before the Change.

It was still an hour before noon, and the sun wouldn't be getting into anyone's eyes for a couple of hours, no matter which way the fight turned.

*God, I hope this isn't too expensive when the butcher's bill is totaled up,* he thought.

Partly that was the simple desire to keep his people from harm; he'd selected every one, and a lot of them were friends by now, and all of them were *his*. Partly it was a desire to conserve the Bearkillers' capital assets.

*Condottieri,* he thought. The word simply meant "contractor" in Renaissance Italian. *That's what we've ended up as.*

It turned out that Pam and Rothman and Ken all knew a lot of stories about Renaissance Italy, and they were a lot less dull that what he remembered of high school history classes; if Woburn had heard some of them, he might have been more cautious about hiring his fighting done.

Particularly the ones about condottieri leaders deciding they'd rather be Duke of Milan or something of that order. Havel intended to keep scrupulously to the terms, but how could the sheriff know that?

*On the other hand, Florence got taken over by a family of* bankers, *of all things,* he thought with a taut grin. *Now, there's a real gang of mercenary pirates for you.*

At least he had the consolation that he was fighting people who needed killing, on the whole.

He leaned forward and slapped his big bay gelding affectionately on the neck; it tossed its head and snorted, shifting its weight from foot to foot, making its harness jingle and his armor rustle and clank.

"Work to do, Gustav," he said. Then, louder, he turned in the saddle and called to his Bearkillers: "Time to do good, and earn our pay!"

That brought a cheer; Signe grinned at him and tossed her helmeted head. She had an old-style cavalry trumpet slung from her saddlebow, a relic of the last Indian wars a century and more ago, salvaged from a museum up in the Nez Perce reservation.

*Damn, but I wish she weren't here,* he thought. *Nothing to be done about that, though, except win this fight as quick as we can.*

His eyes made one last check of equipment, although he would have been astonished had anything been less than perfect. Also present, through unavoidable political necessity, were twenty of Woburn's posse members, which made him a little less than happy. They were equipped with anything that came to hand, and about half of them were pushing into middle age.

Sixty-odd horsemen took up a lot of room. The strong musky-grassy smell of the horses and their sweat filled the hollow, and the scents of human sweat soaked into leather and cloth, of steel rings wiped down with canola oil, of fear and excitement, and of earth torn open by ironshod hooves.

"Will, you get going on your part of it," Havel said.

The horsemaster nodded and reined his mount around; rather more than half the Bearkillers followed him, and all Woburn's men except the sheriff himself.

"Let's go, Gustav," Havel added to his mount, and gave the big gelding a leg signal; the horse broke into an obedient canter. A file of twenty followed him, and Woburn—but he didn't expect the sheriff to do much fighting. He pulled his bow from the case that slanted back from his left knee under the saddle flap and reached over his shoulder for an arrow, conscious of everyone doing likewise behind him . . . except Woburn, of course.

"I'm really starting to think we can run this raiding party off," the local man said.

"No!" Havel answered sharply, without looking around. "We are not going to chase them away. We're going to kill every last one of the filth, for starters."

The horses crested the top of the hill without pausing; the land to the south was flatter, rolling so gently it would have seemed level without the wind ruffling waves through the knee-high wheat that covered it and showing the long low swellings. The hooves were a drumroll under the soughing breeze.

"There!" Signe called, pointing southwest.

There was a dark clot against the green, one that swiftly turned into a group of armed men on horseback. Twenty or so of them, all in scale-mail tunics and steel helmets; one of them even had bulls' horns on his, bad-movie–Viking style. With them were half a dozen captives, four women and two men, with their feet lashed into the stirrups of their horses and their hands tied behind their backs, and a biggish herd of cattle and horses being driven along. Many of the horses had bags of plunder thrown over their backs to make rough packsaddles.

He could hear the outlaws' yells and whoops as they caught sight of the Bearkillers; one or two stayed to guard prisoners and plunder, but the rest hammered their heels into their mounts and thundered forward. Havel's eyes narrowed as the distance closed; the Devil Dogs were in no particular order, but they didn't appear to be shy of a fight. Their bellowing cries were full of blood-lust; and worse, of confidence.

*Not very good riders,* he thought; none better than he'd been at the Change, most worse. Big men mostly, with beards spilling down their chests. Well-armed.

They all had decent body armor, and they all had a crossbow slung like a rifle at their saddlbows. For the rest they carried swords—double-edged swords with long hilts, what they'd called a bastard sword in Europe in the old days—or axes ground down so they were light enough to be used single-handed. And they all carried shields slung over their backs, kite-shaped models bigger than the Bear-killer targe, and heavier too from the looks.

"Let's give them their first surprise!" he shouted over his shoulder. "Signe, *Shooting circle* and *At the gallop.*"

She put the trumpet to her lips and sounded the calls, the bugle high and sweet in the warm still air. Havel dropped the knotted reins on his saddle horn and leaned forward, signaling his horse up to a gallop. Distance closed with shocking speed; he could see the leader of the Devil Dogs shouting and gesturing frantically to his men.

Havel's lips skinned back from his teeth in a carnivore grin as the Devil Dogs began to pull up and dismount; they weren't going to fight on horseback, and he'd confirmed with Woburn that nobody else around here had tried it more than once or twice.

*Not that we're very good at it yet,* he thought. *But we have trained for it. And they're expecting us to get down to fight too.*

He waited until the distance closed further; one pre-Change military skill that still had value was being able to do a quick accurate assessment of how far away something was. The Devil Dogs had all gotten off their horses, and they were bending to span their crossbows—the weapons shot hard and straight at close range. They were expecting to catch his people dismounting and shoot them up before they could reply.

"Yo!" he shouted, and turned his horse with balance and knees—skills Will and Luanne had taught them all.

Gustav pivoted neatly, like a rodeo mount in a barrel race. The dozen riders behind him did likewise, at well-timed intervals; suddenly they were galloping from left to right across the line of the Devil Dogs' formation. Black soil flew up in divots; the horses' heads pounded up and down like pistons, and he felt a sensation of rushing speed no machine could quite match as the great muscles flexed and bunched between his legs.

Havel clamped his thighs to his mount and raised his bow, drawing to the angle of his jaw with the chisel point slanting up at a thirty-five-degree angle. Horn and wood and sinew creaked as the string pulled the recurved stave into a smooth half-circle; he breathed out in a controlled *hooosh* as he pushed and pulled and twisted his torso to put the muscles of gut and back and shoulders into the effort.

It wasn't just a matter of raw arm strength. You had to know how to apply it.

He waited for the high point of the gallop and let the string fall off the balls of his fingers. *Crack-whipppt!* as the string lashed his steel-clad forearm and the arrow flicked out, blurring with speed. The bow surged against his left arm with the recoil; his right hand was already reaching back, plucking another shaft out of his quiver: knock, draw, loose—

He had two in the air before the first one struck—struck and stood in the ground ten yards in front of the nearest Devil Dog.

*Congratulations, Genghis!* he thought acidly.

The next one banged off the curved surface of a helmet, making the bandit spin and then stagger; he felt a little better after that.

*And I'm not aiming at one man. I'm aiming at twenty, and their horses, all nicely bunched up.*

Behind him the other Bearkillers were shooting as well. He leaned to the right, and Gustav pivoted, turning. The others followed, and the line became a loose oval like a racetrack. The arrows had come as a complete surprise to the enemy; the problem was that not many of them had hit.

A horse ran plunging across the wheatfields, with an arrow buried half its length in the beast's rump. A bandit was down on the ground, screaming shrill bubbling shrieks as he rolled about and clutched at a shaft that had slanted down through one cheek and out the side of his jaw, slicing his tongue and shattering half a dozen teeth as it went.

Most of the Devil Dogs had dropped their crossbows and swung their shields around, holding them up against the sleet of steel-tipped wood.

He saw two arrows strike one shield, and the man take a step backward as the points punched *crack-crack* through the sheet-metal covering and buried themselves in the ply-wood beneath. Then he was curving around again himself, his left side towards the enemy once more. Some of them were shooting; a crossbow belt went by a few feet ahead of Gustav's nose, with an unpleasant *vwup!* of cloven air. Another struck a horse, and it went down with a scream to lie thrashing; two more riders halted for an instant and bore the rider off to the remount string before they returned to the shooting circle.

None of the bolts had struck a Bearkiller yet, which wasn't surprising, with moving targets that shot back.

Havel smiled an unpleasant smile as he shot again, and again, and again, and then wheeled his horse around once more. The Devil Dog leader was trying to get more of his men out from behind their shields to return fire at the elusive riders, without much success.

He was discovering some very nasty facts about being a stationary target; the ones that had let horse-archers grind infantry armies into dust from China to Poland before gunpowder came along.

*More useful hints from Will's books on cavalry.*

An arrow struck a Devil Dog, and the shaft sank halfway to its flight-feathers after it knocked a steel scale away spinning and twinkling in the sunlight. The man went down and writhed, clawing at the trampled wheat, trying to shriek as he coughed out bits of lung and gouts of blood.

The fourth time he finished the circuit Havel found his quiver empty. He cased his bow and took the reins in his left hand again, cantering away to where Astrid waited, with Reuben Waters helping. Each was leading packhorses, and a saddled remount string to replace losses.

The youngest Larsson turned and grabbed a bundle of arrows from the racks on the back of a packhorse.

"Thirty-inchers, and when are you going to let me into the line, Lord Bear? I'm a better shot than you are!"

"Thirty-inchers," Havel confirmed, bending so that she could untie the bundle and slide them loose into his quiver.

He reined around: "And you can ride in the line when you can pull a fifty-pound bow twelve times a minute and do the assault course in a full-weight hauberk."

*My opposite number must be getting pretty desperate,* Havel thought, as he trotted back towards the action.

*Once he realizes we can keep this up all day, whittle them down one by one no matter that we're lousy shots. If they scatter, we can bunch up and ride each one down separately. And any time now he's going to look west and see—*

A screaming shout went up from the Devil Dogs. A lot of them were pointing west. Several thousand yards in that direction were Will Hutton and the rest of the Bearkillers, with Woburn's men behind them. Neatly blocking the direct route to St. Hilda's and the Devil Dog base; as an added bonus the distance made it impossible to tell who was who, so they'd probably think that all the mounted men there were armored Bearkiller horse-archers.

"Shouldn't get your attention so set on one thing that you forget to look around you," Havel called out to the enemy, grinning like a wolf. Then, louder: "Fall in here, out of crossbow range! Everyone make sure your quivers are full and your mounts sound!"

The Bearkillers did, one of them swearing white-faced at a crossbow bolt standing buried deep in the cantle of his saddle, sunk through layers of leather and wood. Three inches closer, and it would have nailed his thigh to the saddle, or buried itself in his groin.

Havel ignored that, after checking that it hadn't injured the horse. Instead he uncased his binoculars. The Devil Dogs were doing the only thing possible; the man in the pseudo-Viking helmet seemed to be in charge, and he was getting them mounted again, abandoning the prisoners and cattle and heading south of west, to loop around the blocking force and get back to their base. Havel stood in the stirrups and waved to Hutton; the second-in-command waved back, and began to trot his band towards the commander's.

"What's horns-on-head trying to do, Mike?" Signe asked, jerking her head after the departing enemy.

Havel cased the binoculars again and took a sip from his canteen—not too much, since taking a leak while wearing the armor required contortions.

"The one with a crap-brown beard? He's trying to disengage," he said. "He's still not thinking in terms of mounted combat. If he only had Woburn's men to worry about he'd be home free. All they could do was follow him until he got back to St. Hilda's. Mounted infantry can't force each other to fight, because the other side can just trot off. But we *can* make him fight, because we don't have to stop and get off our horses to shoot."

"Not just a rat, but a stupid rat," Signe said. Her expression was grimmer than his, if anything. "I hope those farmers, the Clarkes, can watch from wherever they are."

"What goes around, comes around," Havel replied, nodding. "Sound: *pursuit at the canter.* Let's go!"

The Devil Dogs were galloping off, but they couldn't keep that up for long—not without more remounts than they had along. Carrying a heavy man in armor was hard work for a horse, the more so if he rode badly. Havel set a loping pace, letting the enemy draw ahead. Any chase was going to be from behind, here; the land was open and the Devil Dogs had been cutting fences all over the place precisely so they could move without running up against one.

*Don't want to catch up to them too soon anyway,* he thought. *Not until Will rejoins. Let brown-beard-horns-on-head relax in his illusions for a while.*

Then the Devil Dogs stopped, milled around, turned further south; they had to, if they wanted to keep from being caught between the two Bearkiller forces. Havel gave Will a high thumbs-up sign, and got a wave in return.

*So far, so good. We've cut them off from home. Now for the hard part.*

The muffled thunder of hooves seemed to drum inside his head and chest, beating like his heart. Even forty or fifty horsemen gave you a surprising sense of power, of irresistible momentum, as if so many hooves and so many tons of muscle and bone could ride down anything.

*This is why so many brave idiots were in the cavalry,* he thought.

He looked around carefully—the helmet and neck guard cut down on your peripheral vision—and waved a hand in summons. Woburn turned his horse until he was cantering knee-to-knee with the Bearkiller leader.

"Slick!" he said, grinning. "I dropped off a couple of men to look after the prisoners we got back—and all that stock."

"Thanks," Havel replied—by the terms of the contract, most of it went to his folk.

To himself: *Slick? We shot three hundred-odd arrows at them and knocked out three men and one horse!*

He went on aloud: "What I'd like you to do, Sheriff, is push them, since most of your people are riding lighter than mine."

Havel waved ahead towards the fleeing enemy. "Don't try to engage them, just get their horses lathered and blown, and stay on their right hands so they've got to keep heading south instead of right for St. Hilda's."

Woburn settled the Bearkiller-style helmet he'd bought. "That we can do," he said.

Whooping, he rode over to his men and shouted to them. They spurred their horses, pulling ahead of the double column of armored fighters, closing rapidly. The Devil Dogs flailed at their own mounts with their heels and the loose ends of their reins, pulling ahead again.

The whole clot of horses and men disappeared over one of the long low swellings; there wasn't much dust, but the rumble sounded loud through the warm air. A canter made enough wind to dry some of the sweat that runneled down his body, but not enough to get through most of the quilted padding under the armor.

Time crept by at a walk-trot-canter rhythm; he started to wonder whether he should step up the pace himself.

*No. Remember the horses. They're not Humvees and ours are carrying a lot of weight.*

Over the next rise, and a black clump showed in the distance. Down another shallow dip in the prairie, through fields of clover that smelled candy-sweet when crushed underhoof—that required a little discipline, because the horses saw no pressing reason not to stop and eat—and through a shallow creek fringed by pines, and then up another swale. The tracks of the Bearkillers and Woburn's men showed clearly, black against the poplin-green of wheat and the crimson-starred clover. This time they could see both parties; the Devil Dogs had slowed to a jog-trot.

Closer still, and he could see the streaks of foam on the necks and flanks of their horses, hear the wheezing bellows panting. They were tiring quickly; not in as good condition as the Bearkiller mounts to begin with, and badly ridden. Havel slowed, dropping down the column.

"Be careful when we catch up," he repeated over and over. "Remember, we don't want to let them close in too soon. Listen for the signals and keep alert."

"Yes, Mother," Eric muttered.

Havel rang the knuckles of his armored glove off the younger man's helmet.

"Hey!"

"Shut up!" Havel said. The white noise of the hooves would cover the words. "People are going to start dying right about now."

*That won't work,* he thought. *This kid's still eighteen. He's seen people die since the Change but he still doesn't really believe it could be* him, *not down in the gut.*

Inspiration struck: "Luanne there could die."

That got through; he saw Eric flush and then go pale.

"So let's all keep fucking focused, shall we?" he concluded grimly.

Havel tightened his thighs and shifted his balance, bringing Gustav up to a hand gallop. Woburn came alongside when he came back to the head of the line.

"What now?" he asked.

Havel cocked an eye at the sheriff's horse, and those of his posse. Not bad. *About as worn down as ours, much less than the bad guys' nags.* Woburn's men weren't wearing much armor, and they were a lot easier on their horses than the Devil Dogs.

"Hang back," he said. "You can't help with the next part. Stay in range—get ready to pile in if you have to, or chase 'em for real if they scatter."

"They're going to scatter?" Woburn asked.

"Well, if they don't there won't be any problem," Havel

said. "Because then they'll all be dead. It'll take a while, though."

The sheriff peeled off to the loose array of his posse. Havel reached over his shoulder for a shaft and slid it through the arrow-shelf in his bow's riser, thinking hard.

The Devil Dogs weren't riding in any particular order; more like a loose mass that anything resembling his staggered column of twos. Havel waved his right arm and chopped it forward, brought the Bearkillers up level with their opponents and to their right, no more than forty yards away.

A few of the Devil Dogs had loaded their crossbows, and tried to shoot them one-handed like huge pistols; mostly they ended up sinking shafts into the ground at their horses' feet, or in wild arcs up into the air.

That bought a few derisive shouts from the Bearkillers, and elevated-finger salutes. Then they drew their bows. The sound that went up from the Devil Dogs as the first slashing volley of forty arrows arched out towards them was as much frustration as fear, but there was a lot of terror in it too. Two men went down when their horses were struck; the range was much closer this time, and more of the horse-archers were in the firing line.

Havel looked behind. One of the enemy fighters was down under his thrashing horse; the other was crawling on hands and knees, stunned, as Woburn's posse trotted towards him.

*Hope he remembers we could use some prisoners,* Havel thought. Then he shouted aloud: "Aim at the horses! Dismounting one is as good as killing him!"

Though that had the disadvantage that the horses didn't deserve it and their masters most certainly did—but the world wasn't fair. The Change certainly proved that, if there was any doubt.

The Devil Dog leader in the horned helmet screamed out an order and turned his horse, waving his long sword overhead as he charged. Havel didn't bother to give Signe a verbal command, just jerked a hand in the opposite direction; she put the trumpet to her lips and sounded: *Parthian retreat* and *Form line abreast on the commander.*

They all turned their horses right, a unified surge of motion at ninety degrees to their previous course; that gave him a fierce satisfaction. A lot of hard work was paying off. The Devil Dogs rode in a dense clump as they pursued the neatly spaced Bearkiller line; they were roaring again, gaining on their tormentors . . .

. . . and then the Bearkillers turned in the saddle and began to shoot again, back over the horses' rumps.

Forty bows snapped. This time the range was close. Close enough to see men shout, close enough to see blood fly in sun-bright drops when an arrow punched into flesh. Close enough to hear the high shrill screams of wounded horses, unbearably loud.

Half a dozen Devil Dog mounts went down as if they had run into an invisible wall, throwing riders or rolling over them. Even then, Havel winced inwardly. He hated having to hurt the horses, but there really wasn't any alternative.

And then the enemy broke; one moment attacking, the next spurring off in every direction, like spatters of butter dropping on a hot skillet. For once, panic was making people do the less-bad thing—stop being a big clumped-up target at point-blank range.

"Sound *Pursuit by squads,* and *Rally in one hour,*" Havel said, and Signe gave the call.

Woburn's men led, whooping with bloodthirsty glee; Havel's followed more sedately. He drew rein himself, turning his head to make sure all the Bearkillers were sticking to their four-fighter squads rather than hairing off individually. Unconsciously he made a slight shrug with his shoulders and a *hunff* sound as he looked back over the battlefield.

They were the same gestures his father had used back on the Havel homeplace when he shifted a big rock from a field drain, or got a tree down just the way he wanted. Hard dangerous work, done right.

Eric was part of the headquarters squad, along with Luanne and Signe.

"Well, that was easier than I expected," he said, flexing his right hand with a creak of leather and rustle of chain mail; pulling a bow to full draw over and over again was hard work.

"It's not over yet," Havel replied. "But yeah, so far. We surprised them badly. That always makes things a lot easier. Get inside someone's decision loop, and he's always re-acting to what you do—usually badly—instead of doing something himself and making *you* react."

Luanne spoke: "*Was* there anything they could do?"

"Couple of things," Havel said. "Scatter right away; a fair number of them would have escaped. Fort up on a rise until dark—maybe kill their horses for barricades. Once the sun went down, we couldn't find most of them, and it's only about six hours' walk to their base. Or . . . well, they didn't have the leisure to think about it, and they got spooked when we showed 'em we could hit them without their being able to hit back. Plus I suspect their honcho just wasn't very bright. Anyone stupid enough to put horns on their helmet, where they'd catch a blade . . ."

"Ooopsie, speak of the devil," Signe said, pointing. "I think that's their command group, and they've stopped."

"No rest for the wicked," Havel said, turning Gustav forward.

They spread out into a loose line abreast. The wind was from Havel's right hand, hot and full of grassy smells.

That also made it possible for Signe to speak to him without the others hearing:

"*Are* we the wicked, Mike?" she said; he could hear a shiver in her voice below the steady beat of the hooves. "I'm . . . I couldn't have *imagined* doing . . . this . . . before the Change."

He looked at her with a crooked smile. "Nah, *askling,* we're not the wicked. We're the people who keep guys like Duke Iron Rod—who really *is* wicked—away from people like . . . oh, Jane Waters and her kids."

His smile grew to a grin: "Like Aragorn son of Arathorn, in those books of Astrid's. Or those two guys in the *Iliad.*"

"You read the *Iliad?*" she said, surprised.

"Some of it, a long while ago. And your dad and I were talking about it just the other day. There's this bit, where two guys—soldiers—are talking, and one of them says something like . . ."

He paused to think: "*Why is it, my friend, that our people give us the best they have, the vineyard and the good land down by the river, and honor us next to the immortal Gods? Because we put our bodies between our homeland and the war's desolation.*"

"Speaking of which," he said in his ordinary voice.

Five of the enemy had halted—one because his horse had keeled over, with arrow-feathers showing against its side behind the girth; as they looked it gave a final kick, voided and died.

A horse took a surprising amount of time to bleed out, if you didn't hit something immediately vital.

The rider looked to have come off unexpectedly and hard. Two others were trying to get him up, and nearly succeeding. Another two were riding double, seemingly arguing with each other.

All of them were too busy to keep lookout. When they saw what was approaching, the man on the double-ridden horse struck backward with his head, throwing his partner half-off, then pushing and shoving and beating at him with one fist as the horse swung in circles, rolling its eyes and getting ready to buck.

It *did* buck once as the second man came loose, and then starfished and crow-hopped sideways across the knee-high wheat; that spooked the mounts of the two trying to lift their fallen commander. They let him drop for a second to snatch for their reins, while the Devil Dog who'd shed his friend hammered at his mount with his heels until it lumbered back into a weary gallop.

Havel snorted. "Hope to God I never have to depend on a buddy like *that*," he said. "Eric, Luanne, take him. Be careful."

"You said it," Eric said grimly. "*Haakkaa paalle!* Let's go!"

He drew his backsword; Luanne reached behind and lifted the lance from its tubular scabbard at the right rear of her saddle, hefting it with a toss to grab it by the rawhide-wound grip section. Their horses rocked into a lope after the diminishing dot of the fleeing outlaw.

Havel squinted against the sun, shading his eyes with one hand and considering the three Devil Dogs grouped around the enemy commander. *He* was on his feet again, if a little shaky, and he'd kept one of the big kite-shaped shields his gang favored, decorated with the winged skull and twin runic thunderbolts. The other two had only their swords; one had lost his helmet.

"How are you doing for arrows?" Havel asked.

"Twelve left," Signe said, reaching over her shoulder to check with her fingers; you couldn't see them, of course.

"I've got eight," Havel said.

He looked around; nobody close—in fact, nobody in sight, except for the balloon. A cavalry battle in open country was a lot like one at sea; distances could open out *fast*.

"Ummmm ... Mike, shouldn't we offer them a chance to surrender?" Signe said, nodding towards the three men a hundred yards away.

"I wish they *would* surrender," Havel said. "We could get some useful intelligence. But they won't."

"Why not?"

"Woburn, for starters. Remember that gallows he's building, in front of the county courthouse?"

"Yeah," she said, wincing slightly. "You know, before the Change, I was big against capital punishment."

"Well, we've all had to give up luxuries," he chuckled. "And considering these guys' records in the armed robbery, murder, arson and rape department ..."

"Yeah," she said, her face hardening. "There is that."

They were two hundred yards away now. *Worth a try,* Havel thought. *It really would be useful to get one for interrogation before we try conclusions with Duke Iron Rod. Is he really going to sit still while we trundle the doorknockers up to his front porch?*

"Give up!" he shouted. "Give up, or your ass is grass!"

The reply came back thin across the distance: "Fuck you!" and the three men waved their swords and shook fists.

"You guys called it," Havel said with a shrug, pulling out an arrow. "Geeup, Gustav."

The horse was tired, but not worn out. He could feel it gathering itself as he leg-signaled it; it was getting so he was as comfortable riding with the reins knotted on the saddlebow as with them in his hands. And the Devil Dogs hadn't tried to skewer him with a crossbow bolt, which meant they probably didn't have an intact weapon between the three of them.

The horse went trot-canter-gallop. He went close this time, watching carefully and picking his target. The two shieldless men tried to duck under the cover of the dead horse ...

\*   \*   \*

"I don't fucking *believe* it," Ken Larsson said, staring at the steam engine.

Randy Sacket darted a triumphant glance at his father, who was about Ken's age; the younger man was in his twenties, with dark hair slicked back into a ponytail and tattoos on his forearms. His hands were big and battered as he traced the water and steam lines on the miniature traction engine—it stood about four feet high at the top of its boiler, with a disproportionately large seat.

"You're *sure* it's not some sort of mechanical failure?" Pete Sacket said.

The older Sacket ran a garage-cum-machine-shop on the edge of Craigswood, or had before the Change—it wasn't far from the spot the Bearkillers had picked to camp. Now he and his son and daughter-in-law cultivated a big truck garden and helped improvise plows and cultivators that could be drawn by horses or newly broken oxen. The steam engine stood in the dirt parking lot behind the sheet-metal buildings, along with a good deal of other abandoned equipment . . . much of it valuable for the heavy springs it contained.

You could throw things with springs and gears; he'd fired up the steam engine for curiosity's sake, and to keep his mind off the fact that his children were out fighting, and him not there.

Its boiler was hissing merrily, and wisps of steam escaped as more and more fuel oil was fed to the boilers—the machine was meant for tourists, and shoveling in coal would have been more authenticity than most at the county fair wanted.

*What's happening is that the goddamned pressure isn't going up like it should,* Larsson thought, wiping his hands on an oily rag.

He looked up at the setting sun, feeling a little guilty; there was a working day gone.

"No, it's in perfect working order," he said. "It's just that no matter how much fuel you put through, the pressure doesn't get high enough to do more than—"

He pointed to the flywheel, which spun—very, very slowly—in its mount on the top right of the boiler. Suddenly he threw the rag down and stamped on it, startling both of them; he wasn't a demonstrative man, and they'd both picked up on that even on short acquaintance.

"I *told* you, Dad," Randy said. "It's something to do with the Change!"

All three of them glared at the big toy. "How the *hell* could anything make steam engines stop?" the older mechanic said.

"How the hell could anything make radios and gasoline engines stop? All we can do is guess," Larsson said bitterly. "We're like King Arthur trying to make sense of a cell phone. This tears it, though—I'm morally certain it's some intelligent action. Alien Space Bats *are* stealing our toys. Someone or some-thing's *sucking* energy out of anything that meets certain parameters. And they're doing it selectively—just on the surface of the earth."

He shook a fist at the sky. "If we ever get a chance at payback, you sick sadistic bastards, you'll regret this!"

"I regret it already," Randy Sacket said mournfully. He pulled a package of cigarettes from the pocket of his denim vest. "These are my last smokes. And man, I miss my Harley *real* bad."

All three men sighed. Peter Sacket snapped off the feed to the little engine's firebox, and the hissing died. The flywheel took another few turns and stopped, and the pressure gauge dropped down from its pathetic figure towards zero.

"You know," Ken said thoughtfully, "you *could* build a steam engine to operate at the pressures we got here."

"You could?" both the mechanics said.

"Yeah. Sort of like the first ones ever built, we studied them in our history of engineering courses. The problem is that they'd weigh about half a ton per horsepower with cylinders ten feet long and they'd gobble fuel so fast you could only use them where it was pretty well free—that's why the first ones were used to pump out coal mines. For doing any useful work, and *particularly* for pushing a locomotive or a boat or a road vehicle . . . *forget* it. You'd be better off with an exercise wheel full of gerbils."

He nearly asked for one of the younger man's cigarettes, but restrained himself. Getting readdicted to a drug about to disappear for good from this part of the world would be extremely stupid.

"So much for the Chinese being better off than the rest of us," he said.

"Why *should* the Chinese be better off?"

"They still use a lot of coal-fired steam locomotives . . . or did, before the Change. Apparently whoever did this to the human race was quite thorough."

He sighed and turned back to the weapons he and the mechanics had been working on; gas cutting and welding sets still worked, and would as long as the acetylene held out. They'd already done the frames, wheels and parts to his specifications.

"This is the catapult," he. said, pointing to the first. One of the Sackets lit a gasoline lantern and hung it on a pole. "It'll shoot great big steel spears. This is going to be the trebuchet."

"Tree bucket?" Peter Sacket asked.

"Tray-boo-shet. It's just a big lever with a weight on the short end and a throwing sling on the long one," Larsson said. "It'll throw rocks; rocks weighing hundreds of pounds, and throw them half a mile, *hard*. Then this thing is going to be a covered ram, with a sloping steel roof and a big I-beam for the ram. Last but not least, this'll be a pump with a long nozzle controlled by the gantry I showed you the drawings for."

"Might be useful for firefighting," Sacket said.

Behind him, his son rolled his eyes.

Larsson grinned. "No, what'll be pumping is a mixture of chopped up tires dissolved in gasoline, then thickened further with detergent—soap flakes."

"Napalm!" the older Sacket cried in delight. "Christ, I was an armorer's mate in 'Nam and we loaded that stuff all the time. Those sorry-ass bikers will get out of town *fast* when that comes calling!"

"Yup," Larsson said. *Guess I'd better not mention being an antiwar protester back then.* "Then there are these metal shields on wheels, to push up to the wall—"

He stopped. Neither of the other men were listening to him anymore. Both were staring over his shoulder. He wheeled himself . . .

"That's torn it," Havel said grimly.

"What?"

Luanne Hutton looked up; she'd been scrubbing blood from the foot-long steel head of her lance with a handful of grass.

Everyone else was doing the chores; piling up enemy weapons and armor, getting the wounded onto their horse-drawn ambulance and headed back to camp with Astrid and her teenagers; the battle had looped around quite close to Craigswood in the course of pursuit and maneuver. And making sure the enemy dead really were. Piling up the bodies and taking tally, too—the Bearkillers were being paid a per-confirmed-kill bonus.

They had taken a couple of prisoners, both wounded, and Pam was patching those up too. The sun was low in the west now, making Cottonwood Butte a black outline across the rolling prairie.

"Signe!" Havel called, cursing himself behind an impassive face. "*Signe!*"

The girl was a few yards away, helping with the captured horses and not looking at the gruesome clean-up work.

"Sound *Fall in!*"

She gave him a startled glance and then scrabbled for the bugle slung across her shoulder. The first try was a startled blat; then it rang out hard and clear. Everyone was tired, but they moved fast; horses were resaddled and everyone ready to go within a few minutes.

"Look yonder," he said grimly, as Signe fell in by his side.

The balloon had been winched down. Now it was rising again, rising high and paying out southward as fast as the cable could come off the windlass. The propane flame lit the white-and-red envelope from within, turning it into a Chinese lantern of improbable beauty with each flare as it rose against the darkening horizon to the east.

Havel rose in the stirrups and raised his voice: "Possibly I'm being too nervous, but I'm going to assume that means an attack on our camp. We're going home—as fast as the horses can carry us. *Now.*"

He pulled Gustav's head around and clapped the spurs home.

"Buttercup," Billy Waters said.

The teenager standing guard at the Bearkillers' notional

perimeter nodded and replied: "Bluebonnet—advance and be recognized."

There was a sneer in the words as he gave the counter-sign, and Waters felt his teeth grind at it.

*You'll be laughing out of the other side soon, you little fuck,* he thought.

The twilight was deepening, but the youth's eyes widened at the sight of the men coming up behind the bowyer. A dozen big hairy shaggy men, carrying wrapped bundles in their hands.

"Hey, you guys aren't locals!" the teenager said. He raised his bow. "You stop right there!"

He raised his voice, a warbling yell with a break right in the middle of it: "Camp boss! We got a problem here!"

One of the Devil Dogs shoved Waters aside with a curse; that saved his life, that and Jeb Smith's hand on his ankle pulling him to the ground.

The Devil Dog swept his war-hammer free of the con-cealing rags and charged roaring, flourishing the massive weapon overhead. The boy on guard fired by instinct, with the same reflex he would have used if he'd suddenly found a scorpion in his bedroll.

The bowstring went *snap* against his leather bracer, and the Devil Dog's roar turned into a scream of pain as the arrow sank to its feathers in his thigh; the sweep of the war-hammer buried itself in the hillside turf.

Smith went *tsk* between his teeth and leveled his cross-bow from where he lay. The short weapon gave a *tung!* and the heavy bolt hammered into the boy's body just below the breastbone, and he dropped like a puppet with its strings cut. Waters stared at the figure that jerked and then lay still . . .

"Thought you wanted 'em all dead," Smith observed, kneeling to drop the spanning claw over his crossbow's string and hook the crank to the butt.

"Uh . . . yeah," Waters said, licking his lips. *Too late to back out now. Christ, what have I gotten myself into?*

"Too late to back out now," Smith said, and Waters started at the words. "Well, get his bow, man. We've got work to do, and you wanted to see to your family, didn't you?"

Waters nodded dumbly and took the weapon and quiver; he already had a sword and knife at his waist, but he'd never pretended to be a blade man. The bow he could use; it had a lighter pull than his regular one, but just as heavy as the models he'd used to hunt deer. Together they ran on through the growing chaos of the camp; he could see fires and hear screams from the darkened town beyond as well.

*I'm gonna be a big man here,* he told himself. *The Duke knows he needs me.*

The dark was getting deeper, but only a few of the lanterns had been lit; what light there was came mostly from the hearths and cooking fires, red and glimmering. Figures ran past him amid a rising brabble of voices and the sudden scrap-metal clamor of edged metal striking its kin. Suddenly Smith was cursing beside him; he grabbed the lighter man by the sleeve and yanked him around.

"Jesus!" Smith said. "They're going to see that and Lord fucking Bear's only a couple of miles away. Come *on!*"

Waters's head jerked around. The balloon was rising again, with a booming roar of propane and a flare of light. He ran in Smith's wake, fumbling out an arrow for the bow.

"We're killing the horses!" Luanne cried.

"We can replace them," Havel snarled over the thunder of hooves.

"Shut up and ride, girl," her father gasped.

The Bearkillers came over the last crest. Craigswood lay below them, T-shaped—one main street, a crossbar and some laneways beyond. There were a couple of houses burning already, and more fires in the Bearkiller camp beyond.

*No time to blame yourself,* he thought. *Just do what you can.*

"Will!" he said, dropping back beside him. "We'll punch through Craigswood, and then clear the camp out. When we've finished there, we'll punch *back* and do the same in town."

"Yeah," the other man said. "How'd you know something was happening when you saw the balloon?"

"It occurred to me that if Duke Iron Rod was smart and had spies in Craigswood, he'd know that sitting and waiting for a siege where we had Ken's doorknockers was a bad idea. Looks like he threw double or nothing. Infiltrated most of his men in small parties, hid them out in

ravines or something, and then launched that raid in broad
daylight to draw us out."

"I'll take the rear," Hutton said, nodding. "Chance to finish *him* off, too."

He dropped back along the column of twos, pausing to
brief the fighters. Everyone was grimly anxious—they
could see their families and moving home under attack in
front of them—but nobody broke ranks. Riding fast in the
dark was risky enough as it was . . .

They passed the first house, dark and shuttered; then
there were a line of men across the road, barring their way.
Light gleamed red on the blades of their swords and axes.

Havel drew his sword, leaning forward with the point
advanced and feet planted firmly in the stirrups.

"*Haakkaa paalle!*" he shouted.

"*Haakkaa paalle!*" the Bearkillers roared behind him,
louder than the thunder of hooves on asphalt.

Waters raised the bow uncertainly.

In and around the balloon wagon were a knot of Bearkillers; a couple of armored fighters, and a tangle of women
and children. Not *his* children, except for Reuben . . . and
then he saw the faces of the others peering over the edge of
the balloon's basket; them and half a dozen others and a
twelve-year-old to keep them in order, and the weight must
be why the rise was so slow. But there were Devil Dogs
about, too, and he saw a brief bright glitter from the head of
a crossbow bolt as it arched up towards the gondola.

"No!" he shouted.

"Oh, we are *so* fucked," Smith said conversationally. "I
think a move's in order. Portland, maybe."

The other man's head swiveled back and forth; then he
shrugged, sheathed his weapons and faded into the darkness. Waters felt an overwhelming urge to follow him . . .
but walked forward instead.

His wife, Jane, was beside Reuben and Angelica Hutton,
clutching a spear in an uncertain grip and prodding gingerly at dark figures that dodged about. Astrid Larsson
sprang up from behind the massive winch that controlled
the balloon and shot, the arrow a flickering streak in the
semidarkness; someone shouted in pain amid the scrimmage beyond.

A huge bass voice bellowed: "Out of my way, you pussies!"

Iron Rod's great sword spun in the firelight, a pinwheel of light. The ash-wood of the spear shaft cracked, and the head flew off into the night. Iron Rod bellowed and strode forward, an iron-clad giant, swung again. Jane Waters flew sprawling; the merciful darkness hid what fell. The long sword rose again, over Reuben and Angelica where she stood by the wagon wheel, knife and hatchet in hand, spitting defiance.

Waters shot. The arrow punched into Iron Rod's heavy shield and stood quivering, humming a malignant note under the shrieks and clatter. He dragged his own sword free and ran forward, trying to remember the detested lessons, threw himself forward in a lunge. The point struck something hard and slipped, and he dropped the hilt and pinwheeled his arms as he staggered on the wet ground trying to regain his balance.

Something hit him, and he was lying on the ground. Thunder drummed in the earth beneath his ear, and then faded into a warm darkness. A sharp pain came with it, and then seeped away in weariness.

"Haakkaa paalle! *Haakkaa paalle!*"

Signe was screeching it as they thundered down the laneways between the tents, sheerly mad.

"Oh, *shit!*" Mike Havel shouted; he couldn't keep Gustav abreast of her—the gelding had been carrying more weight all day.

A huge figure in armor turned, throwing aside his broken shield. Ken Larsson toppled away as he turned; his face was a mask of blood, but he was clutching at his left wrist with his good hand as his sledgehammer dropped.

Havel could see the Devil Dog—surely Iron Rod himself—grin tautly as he poised ready, the bastard sword in a two-handed grip with the point up and back. The big man moved with astonishing grace as the horse thundered down on him, pivoting, the sword lashing out in the same motion. It cut the left foreleg in two just above the cannon bone, with a sound like a giant ax striking home in hardwood.

The horse's scream was enormous even among the clamor of battle. Iron Rod spun with the impact, laughing in his dense mat of beard, and Signe flew from the saddle to land with a bruising impact. Even then she managed to get her shield up, but the targe splintered under the stroke that glanced off it and into the nasal bar of her helmet.

He could hear her scream through the snap of breaking metal.

*"Haakkaa paalle!"* Havel shouted, as he slugged Gustav back on his haunches.

The big gelding reared, his hooves steelshod clubs flailing in the darkness. Iron Rod skipped backward, but that gave Havel the time to kick his feet free of the stirrups and slide cat-agile to the ground. The horse ran free, wild-eyed; Signe rolled in the dirt, both hands clutched to her face, screaming through her fingers.

Iron Rod roared and charged, his great blade whirling and scattering red drops. Havel landed with his knees bent and shield and blade forward, poised and ready.

The bastard sword swung down from left to right, a blow that would have lopped through a four-inch sapling. Havel moved *into* the stroke, hilt up and blade angled down behind him.

Iron Rod's sword struck his; there was a long *skr-rinnnngg* as the steel slanted away, redirected by the angle of impact. Even then, the weight of it nearly tore the hilt from his hand.

"My turn," Havel snarled.

The stepping lunge had taken him past Iron Rod, and the Devil Dog was twisted to his own right, locked for a moment by the momentum of his two-handed blow; not even a man that strong could stop a heavy sword instantly after putting everything he had into a strike.

Havel cut, backhand, the saber whistling with the speed of it. Then there was a heavy wet *thunk* as it struck behind Iron Rod's right knee below the skirt of his scale hauberk— the hamstring parting like a tense cable as Havel twisted and pivoted.

Iron Rod tried to pivot as well, and the leg buckled under him. He struck the earth with a bellow that was more rage than pain. The Bearkiller leader pounced again, smashing one heel down onto the hand that still gripped the heavy sword. Bones crunched, and Iron Rod shrieked;

Havel lashed out with one foot and the metal-shod tip of his boot struck his foeman's skull.

Iron Rod went limp. Havel sheathed his sword and took three paces before he knelt, holding Signe by the shoulders.

"He cut off my nose!" she cried in a thin shriek.

"No!" Havel said sharply.

She quieted; he forced her hands down and washed away some of the blood with his canteen.

"No, it's just a cut. It'll heal—not even much of a scar. The shield and the nasal bar broke the force." He pulled a bandage from the first-aid pouch at his belt. "Hold this to it."

Then he rose, looking around him; Pam had a tourniquet whipped around Ken Larsson's left forearm, he had his good hand pressed to one eye socket . . . and there was still fighting in the dark. Most of the attackers wouldn't know their leader was down. They'd have to do it the hard way, hunt them down through the night like the huge cunning sewer rats they were.

*"Rally to me, Bearkillers!"* he shouted.

To himself: "Let's get this cluster-fuck under control."

Sheriff Woburn nodded. "Let's give him his last wish!" he called up to his men. "He wanted to be hung here, and here he'll swing. Prod the bastard out!"

Michael Havel leaned on the pommel of his saddle as the Duke of the Devil Dogs stepped from the window of St. Hilda's tower; there were spearheads behind him, but he moved before they touched him.

*Plus I think Sheriff Woburn has decided that* his *HQ should be here too. Smart man.*

The heavy body fell four feet and jerked to a halt as the noose went tight; Iron Rod kicked for a moment and then hung still, his eyes looking out over the fair land of his duchy.

# CHAPTER TWENTY-NINE

"Didn't know you played country!" Sheriff Laughton called, as he whirled by in the line of dancers.

The late September night was cool, but his face glittered a little with sweat in the red light of the great bonfires. Every now and then someone stumbled on the sheep-cropped grass, but enthusiasm made up for want of grace and a smooth floor.

Juniper grinned as she fiddled; the tune was actually "The Green Fields of Rossbeigh," and Celtic as all get-out even if it did start out with banjo and spoons. At least you *could* play country or traditional styles all-acoustic. People devoted to rap or metal were just shit out of luck.

The expression on the Laughton's face changed a little as Judy and Diana came in on the flute and the bohdran drum, standing behind her beneath the great oak. Suspended from a branch was the twelve-foot shape of the Green Man, a human form made from wicker and laced with leafy vines and twigs.

But "Rossbeigh" made an excellent toe-tapping hoe-down tune, and her free foot—she was sitting on the green mound with one leg tucked under—started tapping on its own. Her developing stomach wasn't getting in the way, quite, but she couldn't see the tapping toe, either. Luckily, a kilt and plaid made good maternity clothes. She'd hated the Mother Hubbards that were all she could wear when she was bearing Eilir.

The fiddle sang on. *American country music started with the Scots-Irish, anyway,* she thought. *This is where it all came from.*

The big trestle tables with the food were off to the side,

including heaps of honey-sweetened pastries and fruit-and-nut scones to honor the occasion and—strictly rationed—some homemade ice cream with bits of dried cherries and filberts in it; sugar was the bottleneck there, since they'd used just about every scrap for putting up jams and jellies. Fruit-flavored yogurts were plentiful as all get-out.

People moved from dance to the food tables and back ... or sometimes out into the darkness, hand-in-hand; it was an eat-dance-and-eat occasion.

*Not to mention a drink-and-dance occasion,* she thought. *Well, Wine Harvest is another name for Mabon, after all.*

There were also a couple of barrels of Dennis's beer and mead, besides what they'd salvaged from a winery. He thought that would be better in a year or two, but it was certainly drinkable now; he wanted to put in a winepress of their own next year.

She finished the tune with a flourish, and everyone came to a halt as the bohdran gave a long final rattle; someone put a mug of the home-brewed in her hand. She drank it down with another flourish to whoops and cheers, and wiped the foam from her lips; nicely hopped, with a nutty undertaste.

"*Brigid linn is deoch is ni ráibh tu riamh bocht!*" she cried to the assembly. "Brigid with us, and a drink, and may you never lack!"

Judy held up an index finger: *one only.*

A little did no harm, but she nodded *no seconds*—and besides that, beer went through you even faster when you were pregnant. A buzz of voices rose above the cheerful crackle of the bonfires, sparks flying up into the dark star-rich sky.

The dance was in the open meadow below the gatehouse; the palisade and the tower reared black and jagged northward, the hills forest-shaggy beyond. The bright paint and carving on the great posts to either side of the gate stood out more clearly for that: the God as Lugh of the Sun on the right, the Goddess on the left as Brigid, carrying the sheaf and surrounded by the flames of wisdom.

*Dennis has gone berserk, and it's catching,* she thought ruefully. *All that seasoned wood just waiting to be carved ...*

The fires gave off a clean hot scent, mingling with the

sappy-tarry odor of the big logs in the structures above and the farm smells that had become the background of her life, and the cool *aliveness* that poured down from the forests. Children ran around outside the line of dancers; only the infants and toddlers were off sleeping yet. Juniper made an inconspicuous signal.

*Best to gather them up now, before they get overtired and cranky,* she thought. *Besides, there's grown-up business to attend to.*

She shivered at the thought, then managed to push it away for the moment. Chuck and Judy caught the eye of Daniel and Sanjay and Mary; they herded the preteens together and brought them over to the little hillock where the musicians had sat.

None of the children were shy around her anymore; certainly not Chuck and Judy's Mary, who had brass enough for three and a real feeling for music.

"Can we sing the hymn now?" she said eagerly. "Dad said we could."

*She's calling Chuck Dad so natural now,* Juniper thought behind her smile. *Now, is that a sad thing, or happy, or both at once? At that, she and Daniel didn't have much of a father or mother before the Change, as far as I can tell. Why bother to have children at all if you don't want to spend time with them?*

"That you can," she said aloud. "But first, since Mabon's the Wine Harvest, you should all have a wee glass—it's a special occasion, to be sure."

The children were eager; chances were they wouldn't actually like it much—dry red Pinot Noir was an acquired taste—but it was a chance to play grown-up. Small cups clutched in small hands, they filed past the big wickerwork, vine-woven figure behind her dressed in their Mabon best with ribbons of red, orange, russet, maroon and gold, each pouring a libation for the Green Man and the tree before drinking down the rest themselves.

*Which will make them sleepier,* she thought. *And it's a cunning High Priestess you are, Juniper Mackenzie.*

Mary cleared her throat impatiently and Juniper gave them the note, the fiddle singing long and pure. Judy tapped her bohdran. They'd all practiced hard, and everyone came in on the beat, although there were a few wobbles to be corrected with desperate speed:

> *"Autumn colors of red and gold*
> *As I close my eyes tonight*
> *Such a wonder to behold*
> *I feel the Goddess hold me tight*
> *Watch leaves turning one by one*
> *Though it grows dark, I shall not fear*
> *Captured bits of Autumn Sun*
> *For Divine Love protects all here*
> *Soon they'll fall and blow away*
> *Through the night, until the morn*
> *The golden treasures of today*
> *When the shining Sun's reborn*
> *When the trees are bare*
> *Time to sleep, time to dream*
> *And the ground grows cold*
> *Till warm gold rays upon me stream*
> *These warm memories*
> *I'll still hold . . ."*

The adults behind broke into a chorus of claps and cheers as they finished; dogs ran about; it was another twenty minutes before the children were all through the gatehouse and abed, or led off to the tents that housed the visitors and the clansfolk from the outlying duns. While that was going on Juniper headed for the tables and loaded a plate, resisting temptation and making herself take some potato salad despite how sick she'd gotten of the spud in general.

"Which isn't surprising, considering how often we all meet Mr. Spud when it *isn't* a festival day," she muttered to herself. "Mashed, boiled, roasted . . ."

At least there was plenty in the way of fresh greens and tomatoes, which her mouth still craved, and Diana had managed to make plenty of wine vinegar. Most of it had gone into pickling and preserving, but there was enough for dressing, another taste everyone had sorely missed. Everyone with inclinations to cooking had contributed something; Dennis had produced a lovely baked-bean dish too, smokey and rich with bits of bacon and onion.

The bread was excellent, though less of a novelty now that a two-pound loaf was the basis of everyone's daily diet; but for today there was cheese-bread as well, and some with caramelized onions in the crust, and varieties done with honey and nuts . . .

*A good old-fashioned Wiccan potluck . . . but blessed be, no tofu!*

It would have been a valuable source of protein, but fortunately the soybean didn't grow around here. She'd always loathed the bland custard-like dish, no matter what people claimed they could do with seasoning. Eating seasoned tofu was like licking a rubber snail dipped into garlic butter and calling it escargot.

*And hard it was to escape tofu, at our gatherings before the Change; you'd think it was sacred.*

Full of virtue, she added a single slice of ham and one of roast venison. Another month and they'd be slaughtering more—getting the necessary salt for laying down salt pork was proving difficult—but for now pig meat was short, and they always had to be careful with the deer for fear of hunting out the vicinity. Being cautious with the gifts of the Goddess was more than a principle now, it was *necessary.*

The second set of fiddlers came on with "Bully of the Bayou"; they were from Sweet Home, refugeed out a month ago when that town broke up in internal fighting. When she got back to the oak tree and the table beside it, she found Sheriff Laughton waiting, along with several of the other guests—ranchers from across the Cascades. They'd come over the mountains in a body, with armed guards from them . . . *Well, I suppose you could call it their retainers,* she thought. *Anyway, their cowboys and all those people from the towns they've taken in.*

All the bigger ranches on the eastern slopes were like hamlets themselves now, she'd heard, or at least the ones that didn't absolutely need power-driven pumps to survive.

*And the ranchers like little lords on their properties, getting used to having their own way,* she thought. *It'll be a good long while before we know all the things the Change has brought on us.*

They were influential men, most in their thirties and forties—the half-year since the Change had not been kind to the elderly anywhere, even in favored areas like theirs.

Mostly lean—looking as if they'd always been lean—and weathered; and not a few were looking distinctly nervous at the tall bushy figure of the Green Man beneath the tree, and the Horns of Plenty and ribbons hung from the branches.

They were all impressed by the feast, though, and by the tall log walls of Dun Juniper, and by the exhibition of massed archery the clan had put on earlier that afternoon.

*Everyone can shoot in the general direction of the enemy, and then we have a few like Aylward and Chuck who do marksmanship, and they think* all *of us can shoot like that. Would that it were so!*

"Ah, Lady Juniper, I didn't want to intrude on your, well—" Laughton began.

*Being polite,* she thought. *Actually, he's frightened.*

"Don't worry," she said soothingly; Laughton was still a little uncertain about what being a member of the clan meant. "This isn't a religious ceremony, not really. We've already had that."

Searching for a comparison: "It's just like, oh, having a turkey dinner and giving presents and singing carols at Christmas. Not something secret or barred to outsiders."

Dennis winked at her. She knew what *he* was thinking: *And it's good for the mystique of the Witch Queen.* Her lips quirked. *Scoffer,* she thought with affectionate exasperation. *Though technically, I* am *a Witch Queen.*

Any High Priestess was automatically, if your coven split off more than a couple of daughters, which hers had— several times over. That didn't mean all that much, besides prestige and people asking for your advice; the Craft didn't have popes or ayatollahs or anything resembling them. And of course, you got to put some doodads on your garter . . .

*Or at least it didn't mean much before the Change,* she thought uneasily.

Dennis left and came back with a keg of his beer over one thick shoulder; there were appreciative murmurs from the ranchers, since there hadn't been much worthy of the name east of the mountains in some time. Eilir bustled about with mugs and glasses, and set up a little spirit-lamp with a big pot of chamomile tea near Juniper's place.

There were also a number of visitors from little clusters

of coveners who'd survived in the mountainous backwoods south of Eugene and some other out-of-the-way spots. They were respectful to a degree that made her blink; granted, the Mackenzies had been able to spare some much needed help there, the difference between life and death in some cases. And her clan were much better off than any of theirs, and for that matter the Singing Moon had had a good reputation for years, still . . .

Luther Finney grinned at her as he detached himself from the dancing and came over to the table. "Nice spread, Juney. Haven't had a good barn dance like this in ages, neither."

"Good to see you can still cut a rug, Luther." She nodded at him, and his younger companion, before turning to the other guests: "Luther Finney, a member of the University Committee, and Captain Peter Jones, of their militia."

Handshakes went around; Juniper made small talk—mostly about crops and weather—until the food was finished. Some of the people on kitchen duty came and took away the empties; and *at last* Sam Aylward gave her a thumbs-up signal from the edge of sight . . .

"I think the other guests have arrived," she said, leaning forward to turn up the knob of the table lamp.

Heads came around at a uniform tramp of feet and clash of metal. There were a few gasps when five Bearkillers marched into sight, looking like giants in their long mail hauberks, vambraces, shin guards and armored gauntlets; they had their shields on their arms, and their bowcases and quivers slung over their backs. The sixth was in civil garb, dark cargo-pocket pants and duster and broad-brimmed hat, but he had the red snarling-bear outline embroidered on the left shoulder of his jacket. He also had one of the long straight-bladed, basket-hilted swords at his waist.

"Ma'am," he said, taking off his hat. "Will Hutton, at your service. Ladies, gentlemen."

*You know, it's been weeks since I saw a black person,* she thought suddenly.

That brought a momentary pang for the thronging many-threaded tapestry of life before the Change; even his accent was nostalgic, a twanging drawl from off the southern plains, Oklahoma or Texas.

"Mr. Hutton," she said, rising and extending a hand. "Mike Havel told me a great deal about you."

"Likewise, Lady Juniper," he said.

His grip had the careful gentleness of a very strong man. And his hand was callused in a way that spoke of hard work long before the Change, battered and a little gnarled—the hands of someone who labored outside in all weathers. Otherwise he was unremarkable, middle-aged and wiry save for broad shoulders . . . and a steady shrewdness about the eyes.

One of the ranchers blurted: "*You're* this Lord Bear we've heard about?"

"No, sir, I am not," Hutton said with dignified politeness, unbuckling his sword belt and handing it to one of the troopers before he sat. "I'm ramrod and second-in-command of our outfit, and I have full authority to negotiate for the Bearkillers."

"Wait a minute," another rancher said. "Hutton . . . didn't you used to ride roughstock? Saw you at the Pendleton Round-Up back in 'seventy-five, 'seventy-six—that was one *mean* bull."

Hutton smiled whitely; it made his rather stern, weathered brown face charming.

"Long time ago," he said. "Been wranglin' horses since 1977, until the Change."

"I've talked to men who bought horses from you."

That seemed to break the ice. Hutton made a motion with his hand, and one of the armored men took off his helmet. It was the blond young man she'd met with Havel that spring; looking older and tougher now, his beard a little less fuzzy and a recently healed scar on his chin.

"This here is my aide-de-camp"—Hutton pronounced the words as if he'd learned them from a French speaker—"Eric Larsson; our bossman's going to be married to his elder sister, Signe. We're headed for the old Larsson place west of the Willamette. He's engaged to my daughter Luanne."

The ranchers nodded; they understood blood ties, and that Hutton had made good his claim to be high in the Bearkiller hierarchy. Now that the elaborate panoply of bureaucracy and cities and civilization was gone, such things were beginning to take on their old importance.

Juniper sighed to herself. *Oddly sweet, those few days. But not lasting . . . she set a hand on her stomach . . . except for the consequences!*

"And this is his *younger* sister, Astrid, who's here 'cause she sketches good; she's got drawings that'll interest you gentlemen."

A coltish teenager; you could see Eric's chiseled Nordic looks in her face, but finer-boned, almost ethereal; and the eyes were remarkable, huge and pale, blue rimmed and streaked with an almost silver color. Her outfit looked a little like something you'd have seen at a RenFaire before the Change, or a Society meeting—Robin Hood gear, but in good-quality leather, and showing signs of hard use. Juniper's dirk stood at her waist, and a beautifully crafted bow and quiver over her shoulder.

Eric was standing near Juniper. She could hear his sotto voce murmur:

"*And with luck, she won't have put in any unicorns or trolls.*"

The girl glared at him, but silently. Her fingers moved in patterns Juniper recognized.

So did Eilir, and she leaned forward from her position behind her mother's chair and replied: *You know the Sign for* abortion *and* bad odor *and* completely unnecessary person?

Astrid's white-blond mane tossed as she nodded: *I've been studying Sign all summer.*

*From a book, I bet,* Eilir replied. *You need to know some stuff they don't print—the Sign for* creep *and* jerk *and* moron. *How come you were studying, though?*

*Ever since I got this utterly* rad *dagger from your mom and heard about you guys. Are you really Witches? This is* so *interesting!*

Juniper ignored the byplay—one of the convenient things about a Sign conversation was that you didn't *have* to overhear it—and spoke aloud:

"I don't think your people need to stand there being uncomfortable, Mr. Hutton. There's plenty to eat and the dancing will go on for hours."

He nodded to her, and then to Eric. The younger man spoke: "Stand easy—friendly country protocol."

Hutton relaxed and turned for a moment to put his mug

under the spigot: she noticed that he hadn't eaten or drunk before his men could. The menacing iron statues turned human as they came out from behind the nasal-bars of their helmets, grinning and nudging each other as they moved off to shed their armor; then they headed for the food tables, and any interesting conversations they could strike up—being figures of strangeness and glamour, that ought not to be very difficult.

Eric disarmed too, but came back quickly.

"Sorry we're a bit late," Hutton said easily, then took a draught. "My oh my, I've missed a good beer! Yeah, we had a little bandit trouble gettin' over the pass."

"Serious?" Sam Aylward asked.

"Not for us," Hutton said with a grim smile.

Chuckles ran around most of the men at the table. Juniper winced inwardly, then spoke herself: "Now, you've all heard of the Bearkillers?"

The ranchers nodded; so did Luther Finney and Jones, though their information all came through her. One of the ranchers spoke: "Yeah, we're in touch with Pendleton, and they've done some good work there—honest crowd, from what we hear. Helped keep trouble off their necks while they got the harvest in, was what we heard."

Another nodded: "And I know Hank Woburn up Grangeville way, in Idaho. Couple of messages passed through with travelin' folk."

He looked around. "Remember, I told everyone about it? That thing with the guy who called himself Iron Rod. These Bearkillers, they cleared that up."

Hutton nodded. "We didn't plan it that way, not at first, but it turned out that about all we've done since the Change is fight, train to fight, and work on our gear. Now we've got near two hundred first-rate cavalry, about the only ones around . . . and war-engines, too; also about the only ones around, outside Portland. Quite a few folks have tried to tangle with us, and a few of 'em have regretted it ever since."

"Only some? What about the others?"

"Dead, mostly."

That got a real chuckle. "But one thing we've noticed, comin' west. After the Change, the worst problems people had were the work of this Protector fella, over to Portland.

Iron Rod, he was gettin' help from there direct, and he wasn't the only one. Things've been bad enough, with someone stirring the stewpot."

Juniper nodded. "We had a fight with a group of his men too, back around Lughnassadh, late July. They tried to move in and build a fort and start demanding taxes and labor from everyone around here. They *have* moved into a lot of the northern and eastern side of the Willamette—and the Columbia Gorge, you'll have heard about that."

She turned to the ranchers. "We've been able to help each other a good deal, but you know what a handicap it's been not to be able to use Highway 20 regularly."

The man who seemed to be the ranchers' main spokesman nodded thoughtfully, reaching into the breast pocket of his shirt for tobacco and papers. When she nodded he rolled himself a cigarette and spoke through the smoke:

"Eaters and rustlers and plain old-fashioned bandits. Figured winter'd take care of them, though. Next year we could clear the road of what's left."

*Ouch*, Juniper thought. *He means people starving, freezing, dying of typhus, and eating each other.*

"Well, you won't have to worry about them anymore," Juniper said grimly. "About three weeks ago, nearly a thousand of the Protector's men came down I-5, turned east and destroyed Lebanon. Destroyed most of it, took over what was left. You can hear firsthand accounts of what they did then."

"A *thousand?*"

"Yes. All armored, all well-armed, and with abundant supplies. And—"

She gave a few details of what had happened in Lebanon, and even the tough cattlemen winced.

Hutton nodded: "That's the type he hires on. We've all done some killin' since the Change when we had to—"

Everyone nodded, matter-of-factly or regretfully.

"—but the Protector, this Arminger, he likes to kill for fun. Figures the Change means he can act like a weasel in a henhouse, and we have to swallow it."

Several men swore; the one with the cigarette just narrowed his eyes.

Juniper went on: "We and our neighbors got a fair number of refugees from there. The reason you didn't hear about it was that the Protector's men sent a big gang east on bicycles, up Route 20, what you might call a bicycle blitzkrieg. They went right through Sweet Home—not much left of it, anyway, between the fighting and the fires—and up the highway across the pass. They pushed as far as east as Echo Creek, not a day's travel from Springs."

A rancher stirred. "We heard about *that*, but not the details. Couldn't make head nor tail of what we did hear. Figured we'd look into it when things were less busy."

Juniper nodded to Hutton, and he gestured Astrid forward; he had to add a sharp word before she noticed.

"Now, we've been sending scouts through the Cascades since spring, talked with Ms. Juniper's folks here now and then. She asked us to see what we could see. Here's what the Protector's boys have put up at Echo Creek."

Astrid came forward with an artist's portfolio book, unzipping it and taking out a thick sheaf of drawings, done with pencil and charcoal. There were more amazed oaths.

"What *is* that?" the rancher asked.

Aylward and Chuck Barstow looked at each other, and Chuck made a gesture; the Englishman answered:

"It's a castle. Early type, Norman motte-and-bailey; there's one near where I was born, or at least the mound's still there if you look. You dig a moat, use the dirt for an earth wall, put a palisade on top of that, and you've a bailey. Then do the same thing inside the bailey—only a smaller, much higher mound, with a great tall timber tower on top as well as a palisade; that's the motte. You can do it fast, with a couple of hundred men working; the Normans used them to tie down territory they'd taken. Each one's more than a fort—it's a base for raiding parties, or for collecting tribute and taxes and tolls."

He pointed to two of the drawings. "The buggers got clever there with the location. See, the eastern one is at the western end of a bridge—so it commands the bridge, and they've got this section here that they can take up, like a drawbridge. Same thing mirror image over on the western end of the pass. And they've got some refinements added—metal cladding on the tower."

Hutton nodded: "We could get by easy enough, sneaky-like, but you couldn't take wagons or big parties that way.

Most of the old-fashioned bandits in between, they got chopped or ran, 'part from a few we met."

Juniper let them pass the drawings around and talk out their first fright and indignation.

"We Mackenzies have sources inside Portland—our co-religionists who got trapped there."

She nodded to another guest, a square-faced blond woman with a teenage daughter; they'd both been quiet, and concentrated on eating.

"This is the Protector's opening move for what he has planned next year; he wants to cut off the Willamette from the eastern part of the state."

Luther Finney spoke for the first time: "Arminger took over a lot of food in Portland; it's a major shipping port, even off-season. He drove out most of the people to die; but he's got enough to feed what's left for a year—feed an *army*. After that he's going to need farmers; only he's calling them serfs, and guess who's he's got in mind? And I *hope* none of you Bend folks think he'll stop this side of the mountains."

"What can we do?" one of the ranchers asked, alarmed.

"We'll have to get the CORA"—the Central Oregon Ranchers' Association, the nearest thing the eastern slope had to a government nowadays—"to hold a plenary meeting . . ."

Hutton snorted. "What we've got to do, is work fast. It's going to get mighty cold up there and soon."

Juniper sighed, and the fiddles in the background swung into "Jolie Blon." The dancers' feet skipped over the close-cropped turf . . .

*And how many of them will lie stark and sightless soon, with the ravens quarreling over their eyes?*

The "Twa Corbies" had always been one of her favorite tunes. She didn't know if she could ever play or sing it in quite the same way again.

When the talking was done for the night and she took the guests up to the Hall, Hutton fell into step beside her.

"By the way, Mike wants to ask you a favor."

Juniper's eyebrows went up. "Yes?"

"He'd like Astrid to stay here until this problem with the highway's solved."

Juniper looked behind her. The other Bearkillers were leading their horses up; Astrid had two, lovely dapple-gray mares with wedge-shaped heads and dark intelligent eyes, their tails arched and manes dressed with ribbons, with silver-chased *charro*-style saddles and tack. As she watched, the girl handed the reins of one to Eilir. Her daughter went blank for a moment, then gave Astrid a spontaneous hug, and another to the horse. The animal nuzzled at her, and accepted an apple with regal politeness.

"You'll be looking after it yourself, remember!" Juniper signed, smiling at her daughter's delight.

"That's Astrid for you," Hutton said dryly.

"Generous?"

"Sort of, if you don't mind it goin' off 'round corners. That there horse and saddle was supposed to be a diplomatic gift from the outfit for *you*."

Juniper laughed. "In that case, I'd have to put it in the common pool. But Eilir will enjoy it more; she's entranced with horses. Myself, I like them well enough, but . . ."

"But you ain't a teenager," Hutton said dryly.

"I don't think having Astrid around for a month or so will be any great hardship," Juniper said. "But why exactly does Lord Bear want it so? Doesn't he like the girl?"

"He likes her fine—says he always wanted a sister," Hutton said. "And I do too, like she was my own. But . . . well, the girl's a handful, and we've got somethin' comin' up where she might . . . let's say she had a hobby befo' the Change that would sort of expose her to danger."

*Aha, a mystery!* Juniper thought; she recognized a don't-ask-me-now as well as the next person. *And an opportunity . . . it would be well in years to come to have a good friend of the Mackenzies among the Bearkillers, I think.*

"I'd be delighted to put her up," she said aloud. "We can say she's an envoy; she'll like that . . . at least, Eilir would if the positions were reversed . . . Didn't Mike say Astrid's prone to whimsy and romantical gestures?"

"Lady, you got no *idea*." He hesitated. "Thing my Angel wanted to ask?"

"You have a personal angel?" Juniper replied, interested. "That talks to you?"

Hutton grinned wearily; he'd had a very long ride, cold and wet and dangerous.

"Don't we all, ma'am? Sorry; I forgot we'd just met, y'all were so friendly-like. I mean Angelica, my wife. When she heard you folk were Witches, she wanted to know if you're a hexer or a healer—she comes from down around San Antonio way."

Juniper nodded. "Ah, you mean whether I'm a *bruja* or a *curandera,* then, in her terms. Definitely a healer, Mr. Hutton. Definitely."

*But sometimes a healer has to cut.*

Mike Havel whistled softly as he looked through the binoculars up the route of Highway 20, where it wound upward into the eastern slopes of the Cascades.

"Oh, my, they do like digging, don't they?"

A cluster of Bearkiller fighters kept watch, but he rode among the commanders of the allied force; the Bearkillers, the Mackenzies, and the CORA.

Sam Aylward grunted and passed *his* glasses to John Brown, the CORA delegate. The road was at three thousand feet just east of Echo Creek, and November was getting definitely chilly. Now Havel was glad of the warmth of his padded gambeson, and of the horse between his thighs; he'd added good wool hiking pants. When it started raining— or snowing—they were all going to be very, very miserable in tents. A while after that, people would start getting sick.

*While the Protector's men sit fat and happy in nice warm barracks. We can't even really besiege the place because we can't get* around *it. Christ Jesus, did these ranchers have to go take a poll of all their cows before they could do what was fucking obviously the one possible thing to do? The only result being that we lost a month of passable weather to do it in.*

"We aren't going to get into that by walking up and pissing on the gate, that's for sure," Brown said.

The fort—*castle,* Havel told himself—was mostly reddish brown dirt, and then light-brown log palisade above that, stout ponderosa logs with their bases set deep amid rock and poured concrete; the whole of the earthwork was covered in a dense net of barbed wire secured by angle-iron posts driven deep into the soil. The mound that bore the tower was just behind the wall, northward from the east gate; starting high, the thick-walled timber structure had a hundred feet of vantage over the bridge that spanned Echo Creek.

About twenty feet of the bridge's pavement had been removed from the western edge, leaving the steel stringers exposed. A notch in the earth wall held the fort's gate, a massive steel-sheathed timber structure with a blockhouse over it; a drawbridge winched up by woven-wire cables covered the gap in the bridge when it was down, and reinforced the gate when it wasn't.

Right now it wasn't, and he could see the tiny figures of men walking on the parapet above, behind the heavy timbers. The morning light glinted on edged metal as they moved.

The wind down from the heights had a tang of iron and ice in it, along with the cold scent of pine and damp earth. He looked from the steep heights of Echo Summit to the north, across the little valley's flatlands to Browder ridge five thousand feet above to the south; both were timbered, but not densely—stands of Ponderosa and lodgepole pine for the most part, interspersed with scrub and open meadow. The creek tumbled down from the north, crossed the prairie—making a little U-shape with the bridge at its apex—and then joined another, larger stream that flowed at the foot of the southern hills; both had water now, though they were dry most of the summer. The U gave the castle what amounted to a natural moat over nearly half its circumference to supplement the one its builders had dug themselves.

The valley floor was sere autumn grassland; it had been called Lost Prairie once.

Aylward snapped his fingers. "Bugger! The location looked wrong, but of course that's why they put it there!" he said, evidently continuing an internal argument. "No mortars! I've ruddy well *got* to get my reflexes adjusted to the way things are now!"

Brown looked puzzled. Ken Larsson spoke without looking up from where he balanced a map board across his saddlebow.

"My son-in-law will enlighten you."

Havel nodded: "Before the Change, you wouldn't put a firebase—a fort—down on a low spot like that, not with high hills so close to either side. Death trap. Anyone could have put a mortar on the hills and hammered them there. We have to get a lot closer, a trebuchet is sort of bulky—and what we throw isn't explosive."

The CORA leader's name fitted his appearance—his hair, eyes, and skin were all shades of that brown, and so were his rough outdoors clothing and wide-brimmed hat, and the horse he rode.

"And they've got that wall and tower an' about two hundred men with crossbows," he said, and spat aside in disgust. "Got dart-throwers there, and something inside the walls that lobs rocks, and containers of gasoline; they can hit all the way from the south hills to the north. Our local council of the Association tried havin' a run at them before you fellahs arrived—didn't like the thought of 'em settin' up shop here—and they stopped us before we got started, so we yelled for CORA."

*And CORA insisted on talking about things for most of a month,* Havel thought. *God knows how long it'd have gone on without the Mackenzies. Though to be fair, with the way they're spread out meetings aren't easy.*

"Siege?" he asked. He suspected the answer, but . . .

"Nope." Brown pointed south at the low gnarled mountains. "That's bad country, all wrinkled like an ol' lady's . . . ass."

Then north. "That's worse. Oh, you could get around on foot, even take a horse, we got people who know the country real good . . . but it wouldn't be no damn use at all. This is the perfect place for a cork on Highway 20. And according to Ellie Strang, they've got plenty of food in there anyway. Enough to last to spring if they aren't picky."

"Ellie Strang?"

"She, ah, sort of works there. Local gal, not what you'd call respectable, but patriotic."

"Be a right butcher's bill, trying to storm it, even if it weren't for that riverbed between," Aylward said.

Will Hutton cantered up along the roadside verge; avoiding the pavement was easier on the horse's hooves, when you could.

"Everything's ready, boss," he said to Havel. "Ken's people are champin' to get set up."

The Bearkiller leader grinned at the others. "You know what Arminger's problem is?" he said.

"He's a bloody maniac?" the Englishman replied.

"No, that's *our* problem. *His* problem is that he thinks it's 1066 come again."

The Englishman touched the bow slung over his shoulder, and looked at the Bearkillers' hauberks. "It isn't?" he said.

"Let my father-in-law-to-be tell it. He's the intellectual."

Ken Larsson made a rude gesture with his hook before he spoke. "Look, Alien Space Bats may have stolen our toys—"

Several men snorted laughter.

"—but we're not eleventh-century *people*. We know how to do things they couldn't, *including* things that don't require powered equipment or electronics or explosives. Someone's done something to . . ."

"Mucked about with," Aylward said helpfully. "Buggered for fair."

". . . those parts of natural law, somehow. But all the *other* parts seem to be working as usual."

He held up his hook. "I lost this hand because someone cut it mostly off with a sword. But I didn't get gangrene; we had a doctor who didn't rely on eye of newt and dust from a saint's tomb. You expecting to lose many men to dysentery?"

"Of course not," Aylward said, indignation in his tone. Then: "Oh. Well, bugger me blind. I see what you're driving at."

"Yes. We can keep a camp clean, if not a city, just because we *know* why clean water is important. And the same thing applies to other tricks."

Havel took up the thread: "Which I sort of suspect Arminger doesn't know much about. His interest in history stops about the time of Richard the Lionheart. I think *he* thinks it's been all downhill since then."

Larsson grinned. "Why do guys like that always imagine they'll be the king and not the man pushing a plow?"

"Plus his men are mostly frighteners," Aylward said thoughtfully. "Hmmm."

"Yes, and frighteners aren't Norman knights, either; different motivations. Meanwhile, let's go have breakfast," Larsson said.

The command group turned and cantered eastward down the verge of the road, eyes slitted against the rising sun; it got a bit warmer as the orange globe rose. The valley got wider as well; they turned off 20 and onto a local road that wound southward around a butte that hid them from the Protector's castle.

There were over a thousand people camped on a long sloping shoulder of that rise. You could tell who was who easily enough. The Bearkillers' encampment was laid out in neat rows of tents and wagons—not too many of the latter, since this was an A-list expeditionary force, not the whole outfit. Surrounding it were coils of barbed wire, and mounted sentries rode the perimeter. The Mackenzie camp was further upslope, among the pines; less geometric, but taking advantage of the ground for shelter from the keen wind and prying eyes as well, tents in circles around central hearthfires.

They'd brought their supplies on packhorses—the enemy controlled all the roads across the mountains—but they didn't look as if they lacked for much.

And as for the CORA men . . .

*Well, I've never really seen a gypsy camp,* Havel thought. *But I think that's how they were supposed to do it, pretty much.*

Every rancher-member of the Association had arrived as he—or in a couple of instances, she—pleased, and with what followers they could muster; and that ranged from four mounted men with their bedrolls to thirty or forty with a chuck wagon and a big pavilion tent for the boss-man and his family. They'd come *with* what they pleased too, which often meant as much of the comforts of home as they could carry. They'd also scattered themselves across a huge sweep of hill and down the tree-clad banks of Hackleman Creek towards the blue of Fish Lake, just visible now. Herds of horses and cattle moved in that direction as well.

The smoke of their campfires wafted towards the riders, along with the sounds—a farrier's hammer shaping a horseshoe, the shouts of playing children . . .

Havel's eyes met Aylward's. They'd only met the day before, but they'd already discovered a great deal in common.

*Shambolic,* Aylward's lips shaped soundlessly.

*What a cluster-fuck,* Havel's eyes replied.

Brown seemed to catch some of the byplay. "Well, you've got some womenfolk with you too," he said defensively.

"The only ones in our camp are in our support echelon,

medicos and such, and some who're wearing a hauberk," Havel said bluntly. "And *those* all passed the same tests as everyone else on our A-list. The noncombatants and kids are all back where we've got our base set up."

Brown flushed a little. "We're providing most of the men for this fight," he said. "And the supplies. We've got plenty of veterans, too."

*But no single one with enough authority to get you all organized,* Havel thought. He didn't say it aloud, or let it show on his face; they weren't here to quarrel with the locals. Instead he went on: "Granted. And you've provided first-rate intelligence—"

*Or at least Ellie Strang has.*

"—that drawing of the gate and drawbridge is going to be extremely useful, I think. See you at the noon conference."

One corner of Havel's mouth drew up as the mollified rancher smiled and turned aside with his men. Aylward laid his rein on his mount's neck and came closer.

"Not telling him exactly what you have planned for that information, are you, Lord Bear? Perhaps a little worried intel might be flowing into the castle as well as out?"

"Does the Pope shit in the woods?" Havel said. He hesitated: "How's your boss, by the way?"

"Lady Juniper?" Aylward said. "Coming along fine, if you mean her condition."

"More a matter of 'What's she like.' We only met for three days and a bit; I was impressed on brief acquaintance, but you've been at Dun Juniper for most of the time since the Change."

Aylward nodded. "She's strange. And lucky, and it rubs off."

"Rubs off?"

"Well, take me—when she found me, I was trapped in a gully, dying of thirst four feet from water, and like to be eaten alive by coyotes. And that's gospel."

"That would have been a waste," Havel said.

He looked at the square tough weathered face; it would indeed, to lose this man of formidable strengths and so many skills.

"Lucky for her you were there," he said. "But even luckier for you."

"That's exactly what I mean, mate," Aylward said. "But

it was lucky for *me* because I was in the ruddy ravine *in the first place*. Think about it for a bit. Here's me, traveling about doing as I please, South America, Africa, Canada, and I get an impulse to go fossick about the Cascades in bleedin' *March*—might as well be Wales, that time of year. Then I take the Change for a nuclear war—well, that's not so hard to believe—so I *stay* up in the mountains afterward. Then that fuckin' ravine crumbles in just the right spot, I put me shoulder out an' get me legs caught in a scissors by two saplings, and *she* 'appens by, before I'm too far gone."

He touched the horns-and-moon symbol on his jack. "It's enough to get you thinkin' serious about this Goddess of hers, innit? Not that I'm not grateful to her and hers, mind." A shake of the head. "She's got the flux. Daft things happen around her."

"Flux?" Havel asked.

"Chap I knew used the word—when I met him I was in the SAS and he was runnin' a pub called The Treadmill. Did everything in his day, Foreign Legion an' all, right tough old bastard. He thought some people had it, sort of like a magnetic field that pulled in odd happenings. Willie was always on about some bint he'd known in the old days, and if half what he said was true . . . anyway, Lady Juniper has it in great job lots."

"When I think of the times *I* almost died before the Change and after . . . maybe I do too."

"Nar, I figure you were just born to hang, mate."

They both laughed; after a moment the clansman went on: "But she's not *just* lucky. She's fly." At Havel's raised eyebrow he went on: "Clever at outguessing you. *Dead* fly."

# Chapter Thirty

"Are you sure you're up to this?" Judy asked, turning and needlessly arranging some instruments in one of the clinic's cupboards.

"No," Juniper said frankly to her tense back. "But I think I've got a better chance of bringing it off than anyone else. What's your medical advice?"

Her friend swallowed. "Well, you're a day or two short of eight months," she said. "But it's been as smooth a pregnancy as I've seen, right out of a textbook. As long as you don't try leaping about or riding a horse—"

"Come on, Judy, we've known each other since we were teenagers."

"That's why I specified," she said dourly. "It's a wonder you're not east over the mountains with Sam and the others, waving your sword and waddling into battle like a pregnant duck."

"*Is maith an scáthán súil charad!*" Juniper replied ruefully. "A friend's eye is a good mirror!"

"Then delegate," Judy said.

"I can't. There are others to fight for us, but this I honestly think I'm best for—and I *don't* need to be all that mobile, just able to talk."

Judy shook her head and bit her lip; Juniper gave her an impulsive hug and left the little clinic. The corridor of the Hall's second story was dark, lit only by the windows at either end that gave out on a cloudy, foggy morning; the staircase was in the center of the hallway, and it was steep.

*And I* am *waddling,* she thought. *You two should not make me come up and get you.*

She sighed and waddled up the steps; it didn't occur to

her to call instead until she was nearly at the top—you lost the habit, when your daughter was deaf.

"You two were supposed to be packed by now and—what *are* you doing?"

She choked the words off. Eilir and Astrid were kneeling on the floor facing each other, across three taper candles with a chalice and two cups, and a pinch of incense burning in that, and ritual tools scattered about. Eilir's Book of Shadows was open on a folding rest nearby, and they had the backs of their right wrists pressed together as they chanted.

You didn't interrupt a ritual.

". . . all my wisdom and all my secrets I share with you for as long as this life endures. Until we meet in *Tir na m Ban*," they finished. "So mote it be!"

Juniper frowned as they put down their wrists, and a bright bead of blood showed on each—the loft office-bedroom got a lot more light, which was one reason she'd snaffled it off for her own.

"Now, *what* on earth are you two doing?"

"Swearing blood-br—well, blood-sisterhood!" Astrid said brightly. "Like, we're going to be friends and comrades forever! And be Paladins who fight evil and right wrongs and, oh, all that sort of stuff."

Eilir wiped off the bead of blood with a piece of cotton swab and handed Astrid another.

*Like she said, Mom,* she signed. *You know, like Roland and Oliver. Anamchara.*

"Or Gimli and Legolas," Astrid said helpfully. "Only we're both . . . well, Eilir's not a dwarf."

*Tolkein and the others have a great deal to answer for,* Juniper thought. *Do they think those white horses are magical totems, somehow? As I recall, at their age my best friend and I were mostly concerned with music and TV shows and talking about boys. Of course, things* have *Changed . . .*

Silently, she held out her hand and looked a question. She didn't order. Eilir's Book was her own; she generally didn't mind her mother reading it, but Juniper never did so without permission.

*Oh, my,* she thought, looking through the ritual that her daughter had come up with.

The girl had a natural gift for it, probably someday she'd

be a great High Priestess and leave a lasting mark on the coven's own Book of Shadows, but . . .

*Oh, my. No sense of proportion at all. Well, neither did I at that age—but I wasn't raised in the Craft, with magic sung over my cradle.*

She spoke, signing at the same time: "And on the strength of a two-week acquaintance, you're promising to . . . let's see. Defend each other to the death and always answer the other's call. Be guardians of the weak and helpless. Be Goddess-mothers to each other's kids; that's all right . . . Goddess gentle and *strong,* you've each given the other a veto on choice of boyfriends and spouses!"

*Well, we couldn't be Paladins together if the other fell for someone yucky, could we?*

"That's something you have to get *right,*" Astrid said forcefully.

Juniper stifled a small moan. *"Ni thagann ciall roimh aois,"* she said, and didn't translate: Sense does not come before age.

Eilir recognized it anyway, and gave her a stare and a sniff.

Juniper held on to silence with both hands: *Oh, won't that turn adolescence into a total paradise! Did your best friend ever think a boyfriend was worthy of you, any more than a father did? Unless your best friend wants him herself . . .*

Aloud, she went on: "At least you didn't make vows of celibacy or promise to always wear the same outfits and do each other's hair and eternally help each other with dishes and homework!"

Both gave her hurt looks. She sighed. "Eilir, Astrid is cowan . . ."

*. . . though I suspect not for long,* she added to herself, as she continued aloud with voice and hands: ". . . but I suppose *you* did remember that a ceremony like this is a promise to the Mighty Ones? That you've *asked* Them to bind you to a purpose? And that They are likely to hold you to it?"

Her daughter nodded solemnly, and so did Astrid.

Juniper sighed. "Parenthood! All right, done is done. If you're coming, come along, Oh Blood-sworn fourteen-year-old Paladins."

The girls picked up their saddlebags, shouldered their bows and followed as Juniper turned and walked cautiously down the stairs.

The open space before the Hall was crowded, horses milling, kilted archers saying good-bye to children and spouses and friends; Dennis and Sally were in a desperate clinch made awkward by a stomach the size of Juniper's, with Terry sobbing and clutching at their legs. The climb down the stairs to the ground floor left Juniper puffing a bit, and lagging behind the youngsters who tumbled out the door and sprang into the saddles of their Arabs.

Before she stepped into the waiting buggy—another bit of useful museum plunder, well-sprung comfort for her currently cumbersome self—she turned and looked at the Hall. The great house loomed dark above her in the morning gloom, hints of color and shape and drifting fog. Then a break in the lowering sky let the morning sunlight in, and the shapes blazed out at her, curling up out of the mist that lay along the ground and drifted amid the tall wet forest that rose north and east, breaking like surf over the teeth of the palisade.

The great tree-trunk pillars that ran from veranda to second-story gallery and supported the roof above had been shaped smooth, then carved with intertwined running designs like something out of the Book of Kells, stained and painted in rich browns and greens with gold hints and then covered with varnish. Where the support beams for the gallery crossed the pillars their ends jutted a yard further out, worked into the shapes of beasts real and mythical, the newly chosen totems of the Mackenzie septs— snarling wolf and horned elk, hawk and raven, dragon and tiger.

At each end of the house the two timbers of the roof had been extended up past the peak, curling around into spirals— one deosil, the other widdershins—and between them the antlers and crescent moon.

"It's like Edoras, and the Golden Hall of Medusel!" Astrid said behind her, her voice soft with awe.

*It's like a cross between an Irish museum and a very gaudy backwoods Chinese restaurant,* Juniper jibed to herself. *Dennie and his apprentices went bloody well* berserk.

All the same, she shivered a little. If she'd seen something like this before the Change, she would have laughed until she cried. Now . . .

*We need myths,* she thought. *We live* by *them. But can we live* in *them?*

"Now, when this pin has been pulled free, Mr. Trebuchet is *no longer our friend.* Understand?" Ken Larsson said.

He ignored an impulse to beat his hands together against the chill of the mountain valley and the cold wind that blew down from the heights. That really wasn't very productive when one hand was off at the wrist, and you had a leather sheath tipped with a hand-sized steel hook strapped over the forearm. It still hurt a little too, even a quarter-year after Iron Rod's sword hacked through, and he could still wake up remembering the ugly grinding sensation of steel cracking through bones. Rothman and Pam had done a good job with it.

*She never said it didn't make any difference to her; just showed it by the way she acted,* he thought, with a brief stab of amazed pleasure even now. *Christ, I'm lucky.*

Aloud he went on genially: "Mr. Trebuchet is ready to go and anything you get in the way of the parts—like your hand, for instance—is going to go with it."

He waggled the steel hook at them and grinned. The squad of young Bearkillers and ranchers' kids nodded back at him eagerly, looking up at the great machine. None of them seemed to notice the late-afternoon chill or overcast that made his bones ache a little, and the stump where his left wrist used to be ache a lot. Their enthusiasm did make him feel better . . . and the trebuchet was something to be proud of, as well.

It was basically an application of the lever principle; a long beam between two tall A-frames, pivoted about a third of the way down its length. Swinging from the end of the shorter arm was a huge basket of welded steel rods full of rocks; fastened to the other end was a sling of chains and flexible metal mesh. You hauled down that, fastened it to the release mechanism, and loaded a rock or whatever else you wanted to throw into the sling—dead horses or plague victims pitched over a city wall had been a medieval favorite.

Then you hit the trigger, and the huge weight of the basket full of rocks swung that end of the lever down, *hard.*

The longer section on the other side of the pivot went up, and turned that force into speed, with the sling adding more leverage. Your projectile went hurtling downrange, as far and fast as anything before cannon. Or after cannon stopped working. It was that simple.

*Simple. Simple until you get down to the details,* Larsson thought.

He was quite proud of his version. The basic idea was seven centuries old; like so much else, it originally came from China. But he'd thought of improvements—from the base resting on wheel bogies from heavy trucks, to the geared winches that hauled the weight up, to the neat grapnel mechanism that gripped the lever. The medieval models had been built by rule of thumb; precise calculation of mechanical advantage and stronger, lighter materials made this one considerably more efficient.

And now it was ready. . . .

"Stand back, kiddies," Larsson said, remembering Fourth of July celebrations past. Fireworks didn't work, not anymore, but . . .

"Daddy's going to give the Protector a boot in the ass!"

They cheered, but obeyed. Larsson squinted at the outline of the Protector's Echo Creek castle—at least the sky was cloudy, so he wasn't looking into the sun—ran his hook through the loop at the end of the lanyard cord, and gave a sharp tug.

Chang-*whack!*

The claws holding the beam snapped back. Cable unspooled with a rumbling whirr. The great basket of rock seemed to drop slowly at first, then faster and faster, and the steel beam of the throwing arm whirred upward so swiftly that inertia bent it like a bow.

*Sss-crack!*

At the very top of its arc the chain-and-mesh sling swung upward as well. Another hook was cunningly shaped to let the upper chain of the sling go free at precisely the right moment, and the big boulder flew westward—tumbling as it went, slowing as it reached the height of its arc and then dropping down towards the fort like an anvil from orbit. Dust puffed up around the trebuchet, from under its wheels and the four screw jacks that stabilized it for firing.

"Hit!" shouted a Bearkiller trooper, looking through a pair of heavy tripod-mounted binoculars they'd reclaimed from a tourist lookout point. "Hit!"

Larsson had his own monocular out and put to his good eye—the castle was about half a mile away, and he wanted to know just how his baby functioned. He could see where the quarter-ton rock had struck; in the middle of the earth wall of the fort, halfway between ditch and the palisade. A cloud of dirt drifted away, and he saw the boulder three-quarters buried in the heaped soil.

*Well, so far we're just helping build the castle wall,* Larsson thought. *No damage except to the barbed wire. But next time . . .*

"Incoming!" the woman at the binoculars shouted. Then: "Short!"

Larsson looked, tensed to dive for the slit trench. A rock rose over the gate of the castle, arching up—in a reverse of his own shot, it seemed to get faster and faster as it approached.

*Thud.*

It landed in the roadway, cracking and cratering the asphalt, then rolling along until it came to a halt about a hundred yards in front of his own trebuchet. More than enough to hammer anything trying to sneak by the castle on either side, but less range than his, with a lighter load. Probably mounted on some sort of turntable.

"You shouldn't have thought you'd be the only one to come up with this idea, Professor," Larsson said with an evil chuckle. To the crew: "All right, winch her down!"

The crew sprang to work, pumping at the cranks on either side of the frame's rear. There was a quick ratcheting clatter as they took up the slack on the two woven-wire cables that ran up to the peak of the throwing arm and out through block-and-tackle at the middle of the rear brace. That slowed as the weight came on the cables and they had to work at it, but the gearing made the effort steady rather than hard. At last the arm was down, and Larsson threw the lever that brought the jaws of the clamp home on it and slipped home the safety pin—a steel rod the thickness of his thumb and as long as his forearm.

"We need something a little lighter, if we want to hit the palisade or the interior," he said, looking down the row of boulders. Each had its weight chalked on the surface, along with a serial number.

"Number thirty-two!"

The loading crew had two-man pincers for carrying stones, with turned-in sections at the tips, and stout horizontal wooden handles like spades. Four men went after boulder thirty-two, each pair clamping their pincers on it and walking it over to the sling. Larsson carefully raised the chain and loop and dropped them over the hook, removed the pin . . .

"Incoming!"

This time the yell was much louder, and the sound from the castle was different, a long vibrating *tunnngg!* from the motte tower.

"Cover!" Larsson said, and jumped into a slit trench; Havel had smiled that crooked smile when he told them those should go in *first.*

*I'm not doing bad for an old man,* he thought, puffing and keeping his head down. *So I may not be good at waving swords . . .*

Something went over his head with a loud *whhht.* A fractional second later there was a sharp *crack* from behind him. He turned and raised his head. There was a row of mantlets about ten yards behind the rock-thrower—heavy shields on bicycle wheels, for archers and crossbowmen to push towards hostile walls. One had been hit.

*Not just hit,* he thought, whistling softly to himself.

The missile was a four-foot, spear-sized arrow with plastic vanes and a pile-shaped head. It had punched right through the metal facing and double thickness of plywood, and buried itself in the rib cage of a rancher's man who'd been leading a horse behind. The man went down, screaming like a rabbit in a trap and flailing with his arms, but the legs stayed immobile. More people scattered eastward, running from the sudden danger; a few ran three or four steps, then turned and dashed back to drag the injured man to safety. He screamed even louder at that, and was undoubtedly going to die anyway—a pre-Change trauma unit probably couldn't have saved him, but . . .

*That was well done,* Larsson thought, wincing slightly. *Still . . . ouch.*

He'd gotten case-hardened since the Change—his mind

suppressed memories of the night of blood and screams in the ranger cabin with an effort so habitual that he didn't even have to think about it.

*But this isn't just a game of engineers, the way business was a game with money for counters. Or if it is, it's a game with human beings as pieces.*

On the heels of the thought came more distant sounds from the castle: six together this time, *tunng-tunng-tunng-tunng-tunng-tunng.*

"The first one was a ranging shot!" Larsson shouted. "Heads down, everyone!"

More black dots came floating out from the castle, from the tower and along the wall. Deceptively slow-looking at first, then gathering speed. Larsson dropped to the bottom of his hole and looked upward. Something went overhead in a blur, and there was a hard *whack!* sound of metal on metal, duller chunks as steel spearheads buried themselves in wet dirt. There were shouts, but no screams.

Larsson shouted himself: "Everyone stay in their holes until I say you can come out!"

There was no quaver in his voice; he was proud of that. He *knew* the javelins probably couldn't hurt him ... but his gut and scrotum didn't seem to know that, and they were sending very unpleasant messages up to his hindbrain. When he thought about what he was going to do next, his sphincter got into the action.

*And I can come out myself whenever I want. I don't want to, but I'm going to do it anyway.*

He launched himself out of the trench. The loop at the end of the firing lanyard was about a dozen yards away; the point of his hook sank into the dirt in the middle of it, and he let his backward slither pull it taut.

Chang-*whack!*

The boulder arched out towards the Protector's castle; before it was halfway the multiple, musical *tunnng* of the dart-throwers sounded.

"Now I understand why they had so many sieges in the Middle Ages, and why everyone hated them," he muttered to himself as he tumbled back into the protective embrace of his foxhole.

"Hit!" someone shouted, after the javelins struck. "Broke off a section of the palisade this time!"

He could hear the crew cheering from their trenches and felt like shouting himself . . . until he realized that he'd just probably pulped several men into hamburger with a three-hundred-pound boulder, and equally probably mutilated and crippled several more.

"But I'm not going to get bent out of shape about it, as Mike says," he murmured to himself, his lips thinning. "So many dead, and you cretins are *adding* to the total, when you could be *helping*. If your Protector had organized to get people *out* of Portland—"

He yelped involuntarily as one of the man-length darts plowed into the dirt near him; it sank a third of its length into the hard-packed rocky soil and quivered with a harsh whining sound that played along his nerves like a saw-edged bow on a violin. Three more banged off the steel framework of his rock-thrower.

*And we are* not *going to stand around cranking Mr. Trebuchet down again,* he thought, swallowing an uneasy mix of terror and exhilaration. *Hmmm . . . next time, really big, thick movable shields to protect the crew?*

"All right!" he called out aloud. "Next flight of javelins, one of us runs back—you, Jackson, the minute they hit you get out of your hole. We've given the Protector's men the kick in the ass we promised 'em!"

The crew cheered again. Larsson nodded, looking at the luminescent dial of the mechanical watch he'd found. Just before sunset—though with this overcast, it was hard to tell; it was definitely getting dark, though.

He looked towards the castle—and saw only mud, because he certainly wasn't going to risk his life for a gesture.

"When you want to set a man up for a punch in the face, get someone to kick him in the ass," he muttered to the dirt.

*Thanks for getting Astrid off to that bunch of Wiccans, Mike,* he thought, not caring to share the thought even with the wall of his trench. *Just the thing to keep her fascinated.*

With a wrench like a hand reaching into his chest and clutching:

*And take care of Pam and my kids, you hear? My strong and beautiful kids. Christ, why did it take a disaster to realize how great they are?*

The trail was doubly dark, with the overcast night and the

branches overhead. It smelled cold, and wet as well—it hadn't started raining yet, but the wind from the west had a raw dampness to it, a hint of storms to come. They were nearly a thousand feet above the castle at Echo Creek, and the air was colder here, closer to the approaching winter.

Mike Havel grinned to himself in the darkness, an expression that had little mirth in it, placing each foot carefully on rock and damp earth.

*Which means we better get this done soon, if it's to be done at all, or we winter at Pendleton. Which would be goddamned chancy for half a dozen reasons.*

He walked slowly but quietly, listening to the quick panting of the burdened men ahead—locals from the CORA force, hunters who knew the deer-tracks over these hills as well as their home-acres. He didn't, and neither did Sam Aylward, but they moved almost as easily, instinct and the faint reflected light and the whispering of air through trees and around rocks giving them clues enough. Both were dressed alike, in loose dark clothes and boots and knit caps and dark leather gloves; Havel had his sword across his back with the hilt ready over his left shoulder, and his bow case and quiver slanting to the right.

Aylward had a take-down longbow resting in two pieces beside his arrows, all muffled so that they wouldn't rattle and under a buckled cap. Neither bore armor, besides buckler or targe.

"Wish we could have practiced this more," the Englishman grumbled softly.

They didn't need to keep absolute silence, but quietness was a habit in circumstances like this.

"Too much chance they'd have heard about it," Havel answered in the same tone—not a whisper, which actually traveled further than a soft conversational voice. "That camp leaks like a sieve. Hell, I didn't tell *you* what I had in mind, until I learned you'd done a lot of hang gliding, did I?"

A soft chuckle. "Run me down on the others," he said. "I presume they're the best—or I bloody well hope so."

"They're the best who happened to have the necessary experience; it's not a sport your ordinary Idaho plowboy takes up," Havel said. "Pam's cold death with a sword, and she's learned the rest of the business very fast. Eric and Signe are pretty good, they've had seven months hard practice and they're natural athletes, and I've seen them both in real action. Good nerves and good *muga,* both of them, and coming along fast."

Aylward nodded, unseen in the darkness. *Muga* was a term they were both familiar with from unarmed-combat training; it meant being aware of everything around you as a single interacting whole.

*And I wish to hell Signe was knocked up and off the A-list for now; we're going to be* married *soon, for Christ's sake,* he thought, then pushed it away with a swift mental effort.

*Can't afford to get worked up about that, or I'll make mistakes and get us killed. Christ Jesus, that's likely enough anyhow!*

There was a little amusement in the Englishman's voice: "And this is probably the last chance you'll get to go off on your own, away from the paperwork and the all those cloudy decisions, eh? Corporal to general—and if you knew how hard I'd fought to keep the same bloody thing from happening . . ."

Mike shrugged. "Maybe not. Things are different now. No Pentagon, no brass."

*And how. There's probably nothing but bands of Eaters haunting the Pentagon,* he thought. *Sort of . . . what did Greenberg call it? A literalized metaphor?*

He'd loathed the place and the city it was located in at long distance every day of both hitches.

Idly: *I wonder what happened to the President?* He'd never liked the man much. *Probably the Secret Service got him out, and he's still running things . . . in about a hundred square miles around Camp David, maybe.*

He went on aloud: "Hell, what was that Greek king, the one who got all the way to India—"

"Alexander the Great?"

"Yeah. Always the first one in . . . here we are."

The hunters had brought them to the clearing on the crest of Echo Mountain, and carried the hang gliders as well, bearing them lengthwise up the narrow trail. Aylward went forward to check them over, using a tiny metal lantern with a candle within and a moveable shutter. Havel did his own examination, and then went the other way, up the sloping surface of the open space until he reached the steep up-curled lip facing southeast.

That made a natural slope to lie on with only his head above it, until all the others had gathered behind him. He used the time to see what could be seen of the castle, matching it to the detailed maps he'd memorized.

There was more light over there than you'd expect; he hadn't seen anything like the actinic glare of the searchlight since before the change. The beam flicked out, traversing slowly back and forth along the parapet.

"Puts them in the limelight, doesn't it?" Signe said from his left.

Havel grinned in the darkness. *Literally* in the limelight; lime burning in a stream of compressed air, with a big curved mirror behind it. That was what they'd used in theaters to light the stage, before electricity. His father-in-law's education was coming in *really* useful.

"Don't look at it," he said, turning to repeat the order on the other side. "It's supposed to blind them, not us. All right, now take a *good* look at that tower. Match what you're seeing to the maps you studied."

He did himself. The enemy had obligingly put torches all along the palisade of their motte-and-bailey castle, which would give them a better view of the first ten yards and kill their chances of seeing anything beyond that, even without the searchlight stabbing into their eyes.

"Amateurs," Aylward muttered.

Havel nodded; the best way to see in the dark, barring night-sight goggles, was to get out *in* the dark, well away from any source of light. It was a lot easier to see into an illuminated area than out of it. If he'd been in charge of that fort, he'd have killed every light, and had a mesh of scouts lying out in the darkness and damn the cost. The CORA men hadn't been able to threaten the fort, or get much past it . . . but they *had* been able to discourage the garrison from walking around after sunset.

The torches outlined a round-shouldered rectangle with Highway 20 running through it from east to west. There were buildings on either side of the roadway, and the circular cone of the motte halfway between the corner and the gatehouse. Obligingly, the Protector's men had a big iron basket full of pinewood burning on top of the tower.

"Everybody satisfied they know where they're going?" Mike said, waiting for the nods.

Aylward's had an edge in it: *We should have practiced this more, chum.*

Havel's reply: *We should have, but we couldn't. Pray hard.*

"There's a nice updraft over the lip of this cliff and we've got better than fifteen hundred feet of height on the target, so there's not going to be any problem with that. Come at the tower from the west, with a bit of height to spare. If you miss, just keep going—we've got people out there in the ground between our lines and the creek. And do not—I say this twice—do *not* launch until I'm down and give the signal."

He caught Pamela's eye, and Aylward's; they could be counted on to restrain any adolescent foolishness. Eric was grinning, despite all that had happened since the Change . . .

*I told him he'd be a dangerous man once he got some experience, and Christ Jesus, I was right!* Havel thought.

It wasn't that his brother-in-law had a taste for blood, but he *did* like to fight.

Signe and Pam were ready, both looking tautly calm. *Good. They both know this is serious business.* Aylward's calm was relaxed; for a moment Havel felt a bitter envy of Juniper Mackenzie. *God, I'd give a couple of fingers for someone with his skills* and *no ambition to be numero uno!*

It was time.

# CHAPTER THIRTY-ONE

Two of the ranchers brought Michael Havel his wing. They helped him into the special quick-release harness as well; nobody could have made it before the Change, for fear of lawsuits.

*Well, the world may have collapsed into death and darkness, but at least we don't have lawyers and nervous Nellies trying to encase us in bubble-wrap,* he thought. *Hurrah, not.*

He gave a slight chuckle at the thought, and found them staring at him in awe as he tested his grip on the steering bar of the hang glider and the bundle of rope lashed to the frame above his head.

*It's not courage, boys, just realism,* he thought sardonically. *It's a little late for the 'Christ Jesus, this is crazy, run away, run away!' reaction.*

One of them handed him a pair of goggles, and he slipped them down over his eyes.

Then: "Remember the guide-lights. See y'all soon!"

Four steps forward and *leap* . . .

Wind pouring up the slope caught the black Dacron above him and jerked him skyward; the lights below dwindled, and the air grew yet more chill, making his cheeks burn as his body swung level in the harness. A great exultation flowed through him: *Flying again, by God!*

In a way, this was even more fun than piloting light aircraft. Less power, but you were one with the air and its currents, like a fish in water. Pull back on the control bar and tilt yourself to the right; the nose came down, the right wingtip tilted up, and you went swooping across the night like an owl. You weren't operating a machine; you were *flying,* as close to being a bird as a human being could get, barring magic. Once you'd learned how, you didn't have to think of controlling the wing any more than you did of directing your feet.

You just went where you wanted to go, down the mountainside and over the tall pines, out into the valley . . .

*There.*

The oval of the castle lay eastward, with the great beacon fire atop the tower on the motte. He banked, leaning and pushing leftward, inertia pressing him against the harness as the hang-glider swerved. And beyond it, beyond Echo Creek, six more big fires; set by Ken Larsson, in a line that gave a precise bearing if you kept them strung like beads behind the beacon.

*And don't forget altitude,* he told himself, lips peeling back from teeth despite the cold wind in his face.

Too high, and you overshoot and the mission fails. Too low, and you bugsplat on the side of the tower or land right in the middle of the bailey.

Wind cuffed at him, pushing him away from the line of lights. The darkness rushed past . . . he imagined a line through the night, a line drawn straight towards the beacon fire and tried to keep to it; like a landing approach at night, but without instruments.

Suddenly it was *close.* The beacon fire wasn't a flickering point of light in the darkness any more; it was a pool of light, then a mass of flames spitting sparks upward, with the black lines of the basket outlined against the ruddy embers . . . and slightly too low. He was headed for the side of the tower, the rows of narrow arrowslits.

*Up.* Push at the bar, bring the nose of the triangular wing up . . . just a little, just a little, feel how she turned speed into height but don't slow down too much, or you'll stall and *drop* . . .

There was a checkerboard of machicolations around the top of the tower, unpleasantly like a gap-toothed grin with square teeth. They loomed up at him as he approached, swelling faster and faster.

Mind empty, he felt for the currents of air. They turned rough and choppy—heat rising from torches and fires and hearths bouncing him up and down as he sliced the air over the castle; it made things a lot harder, since he couldn't judge his angle of attack as well. Fabric cracked and thuttered along the rear edge of the hang glider.

*Nobody looking up,* he thought, with some corner of his consciousness that wasn't in use processing the information that flowed in through balance and the skin on the palms of his hands. *No point in looking up, not anymore . . .*

And the moment was *now.*

A sentry turned at the last moment; he could see the man's mouth and eyes turn to great Os of horrified surprise. Havel pushed forward on the control bar with all his strength as the edge of the crenellations passed beneath him. Now he *did* want the wing to flare nose-up and stall, turning from a lifting surface into a giant air-brake catching at the wind.

It jerked Havel's body forward with savage force as it stopped in midair, as if he'd run into a solid wall. He let that force pivot him in the harness, booted feet snapping forward as he swung like a trapeze artist. Both heels struck the guard in the face with an impact that knocked Havel's teeth together so hard that he tasted blood despite the tight clench of his jaw. Stars exploded before his eyes; pain lanced through his body at the contact, and then again when he fell to the rough timbers buttocks first and four feet straight down.

The guard flew backward and landed with his head folded back between his shoulders, so freshly dead that his heels drummed on the wood in a series of galvanic twitches. Havel scrabbled at the release of the harness and flipped himself to his feet while he took an instantaneous inventory; bruises, but nothing torn or broken or too badly wrenched, and the joints worked. The wing fell back behind him, tenting up on the central pole that held the bracing wires.

*Someday I'm going to pay for all this . . .*

The other guard turned at the sound of boots meeting face and the jangling thump of an armored body falling limp as death. He stood goggling at the black-clad man from nowhere for a crucial three seconds, then brought his shield up and drew his spear back for a thrust.

Havel drew the *puukko* from its sheath in a backhand grip with his thumb on the pommel, the thick reverse of the blade lying along his forearm. By then he was charging in a swift silent rush, and the spearhead jabbed out to meet him. He ducked under it with a motion as precise as a matador's, and the edged steel hissed past his left ear; he felt something cold touch him there, too thin and sharp to be pain, and a hot trickle down his neck.

Then he was in past the point, the spear useless. His left hand clamped on the edge of the kite-shaped shield, down below the curve, and he wrenched with all his strength—pushing up and to his right, drawing the man's left arm across his body. In the same fluid motion Havel's right hand punched to the left, and the blade of the *puukko* snapped out from his fist, shaving-sharp and with all the force of arm and shoulder behind the cut.

The spearman had been about to shout, mouth wide. Now nothing came out of it but the sound of a loud cough, with a fine spray of blood. Havel threw an arm around him and dragged his body to the wall, taking care to prop him over the crenellations—his throat was sliced through the windpipe, and there was a *lot* of blood in a human body. He didn't want a huge pool making things slippery, and perhaps dripping through to the guardroom below. Nobody would notice it running down the timbers of the motte tower.

*Probably. Not in time to make any difference.*

For a moment he stood, panting; sweat soaked his clothes despite the night chill, running down his flanks and dripping from his chin mixed with blood. Then he shed his goggles, dragged an arm across his face and let out a long breath. The brief burst of violent effort had taken as much out of him as half a day's marching, and he suppressed a bubble of half-hysterical laughter.

*I threw sixes again and it's got to stop sometime! But not right now, please.*

Instead he wiped the knife on the dead man's sleeve and re-sheathed it, and unslung the targe from his back. The night was quiet; the crackle of the fire was the loudest sound, and underneath it ran the soughing of the wind, and an occasional challenge-and-response from sentries on the walls.

*Christ Jesus but I'd rather be back in my tent, making out. I discover the delights of soon-to-be-married life, and what do I get? Sent back to doing goddamned Black Side ops! And right now I'm remembering very vividly why I didn't reenlist.*

A whistle sounded from the rear left—southwestern—corner of the tower top; a wooden stand there held a section of three-inch pipe, with a cone to listen or speak into—an old-fashioned speaking tube, the sort they'd used on ships before telephones. Havel trotted over, pulled out the rubber cork at the base of the cone and whistled back. A voice floated up, tinny and distorted but understandable enough.

"Dinkerman, what the fuck are you two lazy SOBs doing up there? Dancing?"

"We're doing zip, Sergeant Harvey," Havel called back.

He kept his mouth away from the opening, and blessed the patriotic hooker who'd flatbacked her way into a thorough knowledge of the fort's routine. Men heard what they expected to hear, and saw that way too. If you were sitting on the only way up a tower most of a year after the day the aircraft fell, you didn't expect to have someone drop in from the sky and replace your sentries . . .

"Except we're fighting off enemy paratroopers," he went on. "That keeps us awake."

"Ha fucking ha ha, Dinkerman. You'd fucking *better* keep awake," the voice warned. "It's seventy-five strokes with the blacksnake if I catch you napping."

Really *vigorous zero-tolerance policy,* Havel thought. *I was always in favor of discipline, but flogging? This is ridiculous.*

The round target let him signal, by waving it in front of the fire; it would be visible to the others back on the mountainside, and to the men hidden out on the flat prairie behind the creek too. Then he examined the basket that held the fire; it had a solid concave bottom, hinged on one side and with a release catch on the other, presumably for cleaning and removing ash in the daytime.

*One more cheer for you, Ellie Strang,* he thought. *I'm going to see you get a retirement fund out of this, God damn me if I don't.*

The rest of the tower top was a flat square thirty feet by thirty, bare save for a keg of water, a slop bucket, and racks of javelins and piles of stones just right for throwing down on anyone trying to get up. The only equipment was a little portable crane, probably used for hauling up firewood; that was on the eastern side. The floor felt solid beneath his boots; the intel was that it was two sets of twelve-by-twelve timbers laid at right angles to each other with a couple of inches of asphalt and roofing shingle in between, the whole held together with massive bolts. The trapdoor was in the center, a slab of the same square timbers, strapped with sheet metal on top and bottom.

There were strong steel bars that slid across it into loops set in the equally massive floor. Havel grinned in the fire-lit night as he pulled them through and dropped in the locking pins. The tower had been designed for defense from the bottom *up,* each floor a fortress on its own if the one below was taken. Hence the hinges were on this side, and the trapdoor opened upward; or didn't open, with the bars locked home. The story below was only ten feet from floor to ceiling, and *its* trapdoor wasn't in line with this one.

*Good luck to you trying to batter it open when you twig to what's happened,* he thought. *You'd have to use drills and cutting tools, it'd take hours.*

The hang glider came apart easily; he bundled it off to one side. Then there was nothing to do but check the layout; so far their informants had been right all down the line. He looked over the outer, eastern side. The tower face was sheer to the ground; its walls were yard-thick interlocking timbers, smoothly covered with quarter-inch sheet metal in ten-by-ten squares spiked to the wood and then welded at the edges to make a homogenous slab.

*Well, Ken was right. Throwing incendiaries at the surface wouldn't work, even if we could get within range. But . . .*

The mound the tower stood on was narrow and steep, sloping right down into a dry moat filled with barbed wire; a staircase went down the inner side to the bailey. Eastward a raised walkway connected the tower with the fighting platform behind the outer palisade; to the right that ran right to the gatehouse.

*Not too many men on the wall.*

No point; if the Protector's CO here had them well drilled, they could turn out of their barracks and pack it full in far less time than an assault force would need to get going.

*But . . .*

His ears caught a flutter of cloven air. He turned, back against the crenellations, mouth firmed to a thin line. Signe was scheduled to come in next. She was also supposed to be a better hang glider than he was; that might be true, but he was certain she hadn't had as much time in the air ... or experience at judging distances in the dark, with life for a forfeit if you were wrong. He pulled out one more piece of equipment; a Ping-Pong paddle with one side painted luminescent white.

His heart tried to hammer as he waved it back and forth with the bright side westward, but he seized control by forcing his breath into regularity—slow, steady and deep. Tension unlocked, and he waited with his hands ready, knees bent and weight forward on the balls of his feet. His eyes were dazzled by looking at the fire, and the torches below; the black wing and black-clad flier were invisible until the last moment ...

*"Too high!"* he barked, throwing out his hands and waving the paddle downward. *"Too high, damnit, Christ Jesus, girl, too high!"*

The wing cut across the stars overhead, a wedge of deeper blackness. Signe seemed to realize her mistake at the last moment, and did what Havel had done: flared the nose upright to let the wing brake itself against the air. She'd cut it far too close, though: it was above him—and the eastern edge of the tower—when it jerked to a near-halt against the air and started to slide downward.

Havel hopped backward, onto the top of one of the crenellations, one foot braced on the arm of the cargo crane. His hand caught something, clamped hard on a guy wire; it would have cut his hand to the bone, like piano wire through a cheese, save for the tough leather of his glove. The weight tried to snatch him forward off the wall, would have if he hadn't had the crane under his foot for leverage. He threw himself backward instead, and it pivoted inward like a weight on the end of a rope. The half-seen length of Signe's body came down half on and half off the wall, with a startled *ooff!* as the edge drove the wind out of her.

Havel released the wingtip, and she started to slide backward; he leapt and grabbed, a black blur in the darkness, and his hands slapped down on the control bar. He heaved again, feeling the muscles of his shoulders crackle with the grunting strain, heedless of the way she knocked against the parapet; the alternative was falling sixty feet straight down into a moat full of sharp angle iron and barbed wire.

"You all right?" he asked.

"No," she wheezed, one hand on her stomach and the other rubbing her knee. "But I'll do."

"That you will," he said, grinning relief, and helped her out of her harness, stripping her section of rope loose from the frame.

By then it was time; after they saw his signal from the tower top the others were supposed to launch at four-minute intervals. He and Signe spread out to the eastern corners of the tower, waving their paddles with the light side westward. This time it was Aylward, and he flared his wing neatly right in the middle of the flat space. He shed his equipment with businesslike speed, then pulled out his longbow and snapped the halves together; the bottom half of the riser was a metal-lined hollow, and the top its mirror image.

"Next," Havel muttered, as the Englishman strung his weapon.

That was Pamela; she came in so low that for a heart-stopping instant he thought she was going to ram the tower's western wall.

"Not *quite!*" Signe said beside him, with a gasp of relief.

Instead she skimmed it, so close that a corner of the control bar tapped against the corner of a crenellation; the wing went pinwheeling across the surface of the tower, while she threw her hands in front of her face. Despite that there was a bleeding graze across cheek and nose when she rose.

Havel gave her a nod as she came to her feet and collapsed the wing, hauling it aside to clear the landing area.

"One more and we're safe .... on top of the tower of an enemy castle," she said.

"Yeah," he replied dryly.

He did a quick check; they all had their tools ready, and a bandolier of rope over a shoulder. The speaking-tube whistled again. Havel pulled out the plug.

"Dinkerman, why the hell have you locked the trap-door?" Sergeant Harvey barked. "Get it open, *now!*"

"Can't do that, sergeant," Havel said regretfully. "The enemy paratroopers are landing more men."

"*You make me look bad in front of the baron and I'll have your fucking balls for this, Dinkerman!*" Harvey shrieked. "*And that's a goddamned promise!*"

*Ooops,* Havel thought, replacing the plug in midtirade. *Surprise inspection coming. Well, unless I misread the Protector's little toy army completely, Sergeant Harvey is going to do everything he can to get that hatch open* before *he pushes it up the chain of command—probably afraid of ol' Blacksnake himself.*

He grinned like a shark. That was the problem with a zero-fault policy; people got desperate to cover their asses, rather than get the job done. The Protector was just the type to assume warriors could only be disciplined by terror, too.

*But what, O Protector, do you call men who can be easily controlled by fear?* he asked sardonically.

Signe's shout of alarm brought him wheeling around. Eric's hang glider was coming in . . .

"Too high!" someone shouted.

This time it was *really* too high; fifteen or twenty feet too high, even with the steep dive he'd started when he realized the mistake.

"Wave him on!" Havel said.

They did, with blasphemous additions from Havel and Aylward; the glider was still at least ten feet above the level of the crenellations when it crossed the eastern side of the tower. Havel caught a glimpse of Eric's face, wide-eyed and teeth bared.

"No, no, just pass on and clear the wall!" Havel shouted, knowing exactly what was going through that adrenaline-saturated teenage-male mind.

The shout was probably futile and possibly dangerous, if Sergeant Harvey was listening at one of the arrow slits below. Eric tried to bank and turn instead, and for that he was too *low*. Any turn loose enough not to stall would bring him around below the level of the tower's top; he saw that, and tried to turn more tightly instead—more tightly than the hang glider's speed and lift could take. For a long instant the black shape hung with its left wingpoint down; then it fell off and fluttered groundward like a huge leaf falling in autumn. Then it struck, vanishing in the blackness to the left of the bridge that spanned the motte's protective ditch.

Signe stifled a scream as she watched her brother fall. Havel nodded respect as she choked it back, and again as Eric augured in silently.

"That's torn it," he said grimly. "Let's go—get that cable down!"

A heave and a kick sent the piled firewood toppling; it was mostly pine, and nicely dry. With the tip of his sword he flicked at the release catch on the fire basket, skipping backward as a torrent of ash and embers and burning wood came flooding out.

*Stay warm, Sergeant Harvey,* he thought.

Behind him he could hear a *chunk* sound, then a whirr as the cable on the crane paid out and down. As he turned, Aylward had swung the crane out—that put the cable six feet out from the wall—and taken stance beside it, one foot up on a crenellation, an arrow nocked, his quiver over his shoulder with the cap open, and the spare bundle of arrows leaning against the parapet ready to his hand.

"Go!" Havel said.

Pam nodded, leaned out, grabbed the cable and went down it with her shins and boots locked around it in good rappelling form—all that rock climbing hadn't gone to waste. He followed, stepping off into space, grabbing the cable and locking it between hands and feet. It was smooth woven wire, three-quarter-inch, capable of bearing a dozen tons and well greased. He clamped hard, felt heat on the insteps of his feet and palms of his hands as friction heated boots and gloves. As he slid-fell through the darkness, there was one wash of light after another. Narrow slivers of light—lanterns coming on behind the firing slits of the tower. Then he let go and fell the last eight feet, landing crouched and drawing his sword with a hiss of metal on leather.

Pam's sword was already out. The walkway they'd landed on was twelve feet across, and the door into the tower was about the same width and height. It had already swung partly open—outwards—and he squinted against the wash of lantern light from within. Men crowded forward, half-armed, confused.

The Bearkillers' swordmistress danced. Her targe beat aside a spearhead, and then the backsword flicked out in a blurring thrust. There was a gurgling scream, a moment of whirling chaos as a man staggered with blood spurting from a severed jugular; a louder scream as she pierced a thigh beneath a scale-mail shirt, ripping the point free with a twist. Havel stepped in, swerved aside from a clumsy spear thrust, grabbed the wood behind the metal and jerked forward. The wielder came with the weapon, running face-first into the punching brass guard of Havel's sword with a wet crunch that jarred up his arm and back with a gruesome finality. The impact kicked the man's body back into the arms of his comrades.

That left three dying men in the entrance, blocking the others with their thrashing and spreading confusion with their screams. Havel and Pamela set their shoulders to the door and ran it closed in stamping unison, like football forwards at a training bar, desperate with haste. Someone would think to get a crossbow eventually. . . .

*Booom,* as it rammed home.

Pamela was already down on one knee, knocking home three wedges with a wooden mallet and then sticking the handle through loops at their rear to give them each six twists—Ken Larsson had designed them to screw open and lock rear-facing tines into the wood, and Springs had a functioning machine-shop running off horse-cranked belts.

Havel was faintly conscious of boots hitting the walkway behind him, a shout, the clash of steel.

There were two firing slits on either side of the doorway, and only one of him. He'd just have to be quick. . . .

His sword went point-down in the wood beneath his feet. The aerosol can came out instead, and his lighter in his left hand. A savage smile, despite the need of the moment: he'd gotten in trouble for doing this at school, too, but it had impressed Shirley to no end.

This can was much larger and its contents a lot more volatile.

The mist sprayed across the flame, and turned to flame itself—a four-foot gout of it, through the slit and into the eyes and face of the crossbowman within, then two more to set the edges aflame. A bolt whipped out from the other slit; he leapt across, repeated the trick, heard a scream within just as the can hissed dry.

"Eric's alive!" Signe called, as Pamela and he whirled and snatched up their blades.

Havel spared a glance that way. There was more light—the fire on the tower top was brighter as the timbers of the platform caught, lanterns from the upper stories were being brought to the firing slits, and there was a growing blaze around the ground-level slits he'd torched.

That made the black shape of the hang glider in the moat clear enough, and the form writhing out from beneath it. Two of the sharp-pointed angle irons that braced the wire filling the moat pierced the cloth, but none had speared into Eric Larsson. The face raised to the light was still a mask of blood; it had gone into the barbed wire at speed with only his arms and hands to shelter it . . . though the goggles had probably saved his eyes.

*But the wire saved his life, too,* Havel knew—the springy mass of it had acted like a pile of mattresses to cushion the impact.

"Get him out," he said. "Don't get caught up in that stuff!"

Signe nodded, lifted the coil of rope from her shoulder and hooked the grapnel over the railing of the walkway. Then she went over it backward, rappelling down as they had on the cable.

"Slight glitch in the plan," Havel said.

Pamela and he exchanged a glance, then stepped past the grapnel. There was another ten yards of walkway beyond that, then the broad, well-braced fighting platform inside the castle's palisade. Just across from that joining was one of the throwing engines, a metal shape hulking under its tarpaulin; the platform extended into a circle around it, and their intel said it could be quickly traversed three-hundred-sixty degrees.

And running towards them were a dozen men—spearmen with shields, and crossbows following. More men shouted and milled around along the wall, but they'd be getting things in gear soon enough.

"Horatius on the fucking bridge," Havel snarled.

"Except that the Etruscans were too idiotic to stand back and shoot arrows," Pamela said tightly. "You know, this isn't what I had in mind when I went to veterinary college."

Noise was mounting too; shouts, the thud of boots on timber, and the growing crackle of the fire on the top of the tower. The *snap* of bowstring on bracer was lost in it, and the wet meaty thunk of an arrowhead striking flesh at two hundred feet per second. One of the rearmost cross-bowmen stopped and raised his weapon, then buckled at the knees and collapsed forward. Havel *saw* the arrow strike the next man, even before the first dropped face-down. An armor scale sparked as the bodkin point struck. And another, and another, working forward from the rear—

The tower top was forty yards away. The ripple of fire would have done credit to a bolt-action sniper rifle in an expert's hands.

"Angel on our shoulder," Havel said, and then: "*Haakkaa paalle!*"

Three men survived, the first three in the enemy group, too close to the Bearkillers for even a marksman of Aylward's quality to shoot at safely; he'd transferred his attention to the walkway, sweeping it to left and right. All the attackers were in full-length hauberks, with the big kite-shaped shield of the Protector's forces. Havel was acutely aware that he had a lot more target area to cover, with only his sword and targe to protect himself.

*Not to mention Signe and her damned fool of a brother,* he thought. *You know, things are going to get a lot tougher when people who really know how to shoot bows and use swords get more common.*

Then there was no time for thinking. Pamela struck first with that smooth economical motion he envied, utterly without wasted effort; she wasn't faster than he was—he'd never met anyone who was—but she did have a lot more experience with sword work.

And a nasty trick of doing the unexpected. Her long lunge started out as a thrust to the face of the man on the left. He threw up his shield, glaring over the edge and drawing back his double-edged sword for a counterattack. But Pam's right knee bent farther, and her arm darted down and to the right, towards the man in the middle, a little behind his comrades.

Into the top of his foot, carelessly advanced beyond the protection of his shield. Pamela's strike was at the end of the foot-arm-blade extension, and the boot was tough leather; there was a crisp popping sound as the point struck. But two inches of sharp steel punched into a man's instep were more than enough, considering the tendons and small bones and veins, not to mention the nerves. She recovered as if driven by coil springs. The injured man shrieked in a high falsetto and spun in a circle, shedding shield and spear and then toppling to the boards with a clash of armor scales, clutching his crippled foot.

The man facing Havel stumbled backward and threw his spear. The weapon wasn't designed for it, but surprise nearly made it work; Havel felt the edge sting his skin right above the kidney as he dodged. The spearman fumbled for his sword and got it out, staring wide-eyed past a shock of black hair—he'd forgotten or lost his helmet. Havel feinted low to draw shield and attention, then attacked with a running step, backsword flashing in a looping circle.

"*Haakkaa paalle!*" he screamed, as foot and arm and blade moved together.

Underneath it came a sickening *crack* of cloven bone that jarred back into his arm and shoulder, like the feeling of hitting a post at practice, except that this time the blade went right on in a broad follow-through. The Protector's trooper stumbled backward with a giant slice taken out of the top and side of his skull; brain and membrane glistened pink-white and bloody in the firelight. Weirdly, the man didn't fall at once; instead he turned and took three weaving steps, shrieking like a machine in torment with each one, before he went over the side of the walkway and into the barbed wire of the moat.

*Well, shit,* Havel thought. *Ouch.*

His eyes were darting about. Aylward came sliding down the cable; he'd probably fired off all eighty shafts, and the tower top showed another reason. The fire up there had spread to the bone-dry pine timbers; melted asphalt was probably dripping down into Sergeant Harvey's ready room . . . or catching fire and falling as little burning drops. The tower looked like a candle now, with a broad teardrop of fire reaching into the night.

"You two take the ballista," Havel snapped. "Move!"

They ran past him. Havel ran as well, to the spot where Signe's grapnel stood in the wood of the walkway. When he looked down, she waved up at him; the loop at the other end of the rope was under Eric's armpits.

*Guts,* he thought, as she signaled. *She's been wading in barbed wire; has to feel like a pincushion.*

Havel heard a sullen *boom* as he braced a foot against the railing and started to haul hand over hand, slow and steady. Someone inside the tower was trying to break down the door out onto the walkway; they should be able to do that eventually, smashing the hinges if nothing else. The growing bellow of the fire over their heads would add motivation; the only other exit was the staircase down into the courtyard of the castle's bailey.

*And I wouldn't want to try to run away while the command structure here is intact.*

Ken and Pamela and Aaron Rothman had given him a rundown on various tyrants of history while they discussed Arminger.

Stalin had put it very succinctly: *It takes a brave man* not *to be a hero in my army.*

Weight came on the rope—Eric weighed in at around two hundred pounds. Havel couldn't haul quickly; Signe had to free her brother barb by barb as he came clear. She'd already snaggled away hanks of Eric's longish hair that had caught in the dense tangle of wire. Havel had to keep a steady tension so Eric wouldn't drop back into the embrace of the barbs.

After a while Eric could help her, but it still took minutes that stretched like days, and the *boom . . . boom . . .* of the ram beating to free the tower door was like the thudding of some great beast's heart. Seconds ticked by, counting out the balance of life and death, but you didn't save time by rushing.

"*Got* it," Havel snarled, as the younger man's boots cleared the wire.

"Sorry—" Eric began, as his bloody face came over the railing; blood leaked out from beneath his gloves as well, but he chinned himself and rolled over to the walkway planking.

"*Shut* up," Havel said. "Let's get her out."

Signe waved as Havel came to the edge of the walkway; she'd managed to crawl onto the surface of the wing, but that didn't help as much as it would have if the hang glider had landed closer to the walkway. They couldn't just snatch her up; there was too much lateral distance.

*Boom*-crack!

This time a crunching sound ran under the battering; the men in the tower were going to knock the door free soon.

Havel and Eric couldn't wait for her to unhook each barb when she hit the wire, either. They'd have to rip her free by main strength and hope that most of what tore was cloth rather than flesh.

"Get ready!" Havel called, tossing the rope. "We can't take this slow!"

Signe rigged the loop under her arms and crouched on the fabric of the hang glider's wing.

*"Now!"*

She leapt as the rope came taut and pulled up her legs in a tight tuck, and the two men hauled the line in hand over hand as fast as they could.

The lower half of her body still sagged into the barbs. Both of them heaved at the rope again, pulling her free despite the half-stifled scream as the metal hooks had their way with cloth and flesh. Once more, and she was right beneath the walkway, and from there it was a straight lift. He let Eric take the weight on the rope and leaned down, caught her by the back of her harness and heaved her straight over the railing with six inches to spare.

*"Mike!"* Eric cried.

The rending crash of breaking timber came a second before a flood of lantern light. And from behind him, Aylward's cry of:

*"Down!"*

Havel launched himself forward with Signe still in one arm, taking her twin behind the knees with the other; neither of the Larsson twins had his conditioned reflexes—they'd seen a lot of fighting these past eight months, but none of it was *that* sort. All three of them thumped down on the timbers; Eric screamed a curse as his abused flesh struck, and Signe moaned.

Ahead of them the Protector's men were in the doorway. Ready this time, conical helmets and mailcoats and big kite-shaped shields up, the first rank had their swords out, and the one behind spears ready, hefted to stab overhand.

*Chance of us surviving more than thirty seconds in contact with them, somewhere between zip and fucking zero . . .*

Behind the three Bearkillers, something mechanical sounded, a clicking, ratcheting sound. Then:

*Tunnngg.*

The shot from the ballista went overhead in a rush of flame, with a sound like wind whipping through burning pines and a stench of burning fuel; it was a glass fisherman's float filled with a mixture of gasoline, soap flakes and benzene, and wrapped in gas-soaked cloth.

*Score another one for Ms. Strang,* he thought. *They can throw weights as well as javelins.*

The missile struck the line of shields hard enough to knock a man over backward, and the one behind him too. It also shattered; gobbets flew, caught fire from the coating of burning cloth, clung and burned. Men screamed as the liquid flame splashed into their faces or ran beneath their armor; their formation broke apart like the glass of the missile.

*Tunnngg.*

Another globe of fire flew overhead. This one went directly into the garrison hall and armory that occupied the bottom story of the tower, shattering on the floor and spattering across bedding, furniture and support timbers.

"Start crawling!" Havel said, and did so.

Aylward had the ballista pivoted at right angles to the wall now, and he was lobbing incendiary missiles at the main gatehouse.

*And just maybe we can make something out of this cluster-fuck.*

It was then that the crossbowmen in the second level of the tower started firing down at the three black-clad figures crawling away from them along the walkway. A bolt slammed into the thick planks before Havel's face, the heavy dart quivering for an instant like a malignant wasp stinger. More were shooting from the walkway on either side of the ballista, their shafts going overhead with vicious *whickt* sounds.

If you surprised someone and knocked them back on their heels, got them running in circles, you could use their confusion as a force multiplier. The trouble was that when they got their shit together, numbers started counting again. In a plain stand-up fight, they counted for a great deal.

Another crossbow bolt struck in the wood ahead of him, this time a bare inch from his outstretched fingers.

*"Crawl faster!"*

# CHAPTER THIRTY-TWO

Juniper Mackenzie had lived in the Willamette all her life. Autumn was her favorite season there, and it was a relief to find that the Change at least hadn't changed that. Winter she liked hardly less, and the two seasons were in balance as she led the war levy of the Mackenzies northward.

The greens were still more vivid once the rains started, and the leaves still turned bronze and old gold against the darker, unchanging firs, streaking the lower parts of the hills until they flew away like coins, or wishes fading into memory. Fallen leaves still gave their damp musty smell, and the air had a wet coolness that would endure the long months to come, when the gray clouds marched in from the sea and rain would drizzle down day after day.

Today the sky was bright, dazzling afternoon light slanting through white foaming canyons of cloud, gilding stubblefields and bringing out the different shades of green in firs and grass, of brown in turned earth and bare-limbed fruit trees.

*Mind you, some things* are *different,* she thought wryly.

Forty on horseback followed on either side of the road, the yellow yew staves of their longbows slanted over their shoulders, and the baggage wagons and ambulance were on the pavement behind her. Wheels hissed on wet asphalt; hooves clattered or made a duller rumbling crunch on the graveled verges. This stretch had been cleared of dead cars and trucks some time ago, but it was best to keep hoof off hard pavement as much as you could. She waved to a party working the fields as the buggy trotted northeastward towards the beginning of the hills.

The face of the man behind the handles of the lead plow

in the field to her left was calm and intent, with the slight frown of someone concentrating on his work. The plowman jerked in surprise, startled as he broke the focus of his effort and looked up, leaning back to halt his team with the reins knotted around his waist and a long *whoa.* Two more teams followed him, and the furrows lay neatly parallel, stretching off towards the distant fence and line of trees. The dark brown earth curled up behind the moldboards, moist and soft; the green clover sod went under amid a sweet scent of cut roots.

The other plows kept going for a moment more, making more acres ready to be planted with wheat.

*Doing a lot better than we managed this spring,* she thought, as all of the plowmen halted to shout greetings. *And we need to; it's those fields we'll harvest by next Lughnassadh. The Wheel of the Year, and the wheel of worries!*

Every day since the Change had reminded her why her ancestors had so celebrated getting a season's work done successfully.

"The bicycle corps is half a day ahead of you," one of them called, and added a little awkwardly—he was still in jeans, not a kilt—"Blessed be! Goddess with you, Lady Juniper!"

"Blessed be, and She's with us all!" she called back. "And She is, you know! Merry meet, merry part, merry meet again!"

Beside the buggy Eilir and Astrid were deep in conversation:

"—we're finishing off late because we sent a lot of teams to get you guys' land plowed and seeded over at Larsdalen, us and the University Council people—"

Which had been the essence of the deal; the Bearkillers' military services, and grain stored over winter in Bend and Madras to be paid next spring, in return for the plowing and planting they'd been too late to do this year themselves.

"Not to mention we and Corvallis acknowledge that Lord Bear owns a great whacking chunk of the valley west of Salem and rules all those on it," she murmured to herself, too softly to be heard.

That sort of conversation could help you organize your

thoughts, and it was a habit she'd fallen into through long years mostly alone or with Eilir.

"Not that Mike isn't the charming lad"—she smiled reminiscently and laid a hand on her stomach—"and not that we don't need him to help against the Protector, for he's a very Lugh of the Long Spear come again in splendor and in terror, but still, the precedent of the thing. . . ."

"Talking strategy to yourself?" Chuck Barstow said.

He was riding close by her right hand; looking nervous, too, if you knew him very well.

"Who better?" she replied. "We're none of us professionals at it, Chuck."

"I wish Sam Aylward were here," he said, looking to check that the scouts were busy, out on the edge of sight and beyond. "It takes more than nine months to learn all I need to do *his* job."

"Well, the man's neither a god nor an electron, to be in two places at once," Juniper said. "And with luck, we'll but have to look imposing; over the mountains, they have to fight for certain-sure."

"You ever play poker, Juney?"

"No. Bridge, a little . . . Why?"

"I do play poker, and I *hate* bluffing."

Juniper's mouth firmed into a pale line. "But we're not, Chuck. And that's the best sort of bluff there is. I'm not going to have that gang of bandits a half day's travel from my home and kids and clan, or controlling our access over the mountains."

He nodded. "That's why I wish we had Aylward with us."

The road wound northeast up into forested hills as the day wore on; occasionally they came in sight of the main Mackenzie war party on their bicycles, but the horses had to rest more often than the humans. About noon they halted for an hour; horses bent their heads over oats and pellets of clover hay, and the Mackenzies ate bread and cheese, smoked sausage and dried fruit. The bread was still soft and crumbly-fresh; tomorrow they'd be down to twice-baked crackerlike waybread—what they'd called hardtack in seafaring days.

A challenge-and-response came from the sentries up the winding road, and then Dennis, puffing as he pushed his bicycle up to them; it was downhill from here to Sweet

Home. He'd acquired a length of the sausage from someone and was munching on it as he came up. What with kilt, jack, bearded ax and longbow, bicycle and helmet pushed back he looked like . . .

*Like nothing from the twentieth century or any other!* she thought. *But it's good to see him, nonetheless.*

He looked at her as she chomped her way through her share, and grinned. "God, Sally would howl and throw things if she could see us stuffing ourselves like this!"

Juniper snorted: Sally was about as enormous as she was, but unlike the original Mackenzie, she'd had so-called morning sickness at unpredictable and frequent intervals since her second month. She was also safely back behind the palisade at Dun Juniper, and the Chief of the Mackenzies frankly envied her.

"What do you know about these mysteries of the Goddess, male one?" she said.

"As much as you, iron-gutted female one," Dennis pointed out with irritating calm. "More. I was holding the bucket for her all these months." Then he sighed.

"The news isn't bad, I take it?" Juniper said.

"No. Met the Corvallis guys outside Lebanon, and the Protector's men did just what the Bearkillers said they would—bugged out fast."

She relaxed with a sigh of her own. "That's what the Bearkillers *hoped* they'd do," she said. "They're relying on those castles further east on Route 20. Those have Route 22 to link them to Portland. There's no point trying to hold the towns; besides which, we outnumbered them fifteen to one."

Dennis frowned. "Why bother to put men in Lebanon or Sweet Home at all, then?" he said.

"The Protector's greedy, and he was expecting us to sit and wait until *he* was ready," she said. A deep breath. "Let's hope it's an omen."

Dennis hesitated. "There are still a couple of hundred civilians there. . . . They're in pretty bad shape, Juney."

*But for once we can do something for them without worrying,* she thought. *With the grain we'll be getting from the Bearkillers. That* was *clever of Mike, to realize we could still use the railroads, for a few years at least, until there are too many washouts.*

"Let's be about the work of the day, then," she said, and nodded to Chuck. "There's no point in just chasing the rest back to Portland; we'd just have them back at us again next year."

*"Crawl faster!"* Mike Havel shouted again.

Another fireball rippled overhead. Then Signe screamed.

"Christ Jesus!" Havel hissed.

The crossbow bolt had hit her high on the left shoulder, slanting right down through the meat and leaving the head sticking out the other side. She screamed again when Eric grabbed her under that arm; Havel took the other, and they ran crouching to the shelter of the catapult. Aylward hit the release toggle one more time, then snatched the arrows out of Signe's quiver.

"We're cutting it too bloody tight," he said, turning and shooting. "You two take the north approach; we'll cover the blockhouse."

Havel grunted agreement, taking the remaining loops of rope from Eric and Signe and fastening them to the bailey's outer palisade, dropping the long knotted cords down the wall and into the moat. Pamela bent over Signe, then pulled out a hypodermic, stripped it with her teeth and stabbed it dagger fashion into the back of the younger woman's thigh. The morphine brought a long hissing sigh, and relaxation.

"I don't know how much damage there is inside, but she's not in immediate danger," the veterinarian-swordswoman said.

"Oh, yes she is," Havel snarled, crouching behind the throwing engine's cover. "We all are."

The ballista was in a horseshoe-shaped embayment in the castle wall, and it was mounted on a turntable about six feet across. There was a sloping steel shield with a slot for the throwing trough; that was pointed towards the burning tower right now. Crossbow bolts were pattering off it at about one a second, each one with a nerve-wracking *ptinnng* sound and a spark as the points hit the quarter-inch sheet plate and the bolts pinwheeled off into the night.

It was crowded, too; they had to get right up against the

shield because the upper floors of the tower overlooked them and the crossbowmen there could shoot down . . . at least until the fire got that far. The tower's own moat and the bellowing fire in the main gateway meant they were cut off from the tower otherwise, though; its garrison could shoot—until the fire drove them out—but they couldn't come out on foot. The heat of the burning tower was enough to dry the sweat it brought out on Havel's face.

Unfortunately, there was no cover at all on either side, where the fighting platform of the eastern wall ran, and everyone else *could* get at them that way.

"Get here fast, stalwart ranchers," Mike snarled to himself, and slid the recurve bow free from its case over his shoulder. "Real fast. Eric, you fit to fight?"

A drift of wind down from the mountains and the pass blew smoke over them, thick and dense and sooty-hot.

Eric coughed. "I'll manage," he said.

"Good," Havel snapped. "Shoot when I do."

By the increasing light of the tower's fire he could see more of the Protector's men dashing across the open ground from the barracks and up ramp-ladders to the palisade. A few of them were already trotting towards the ballista; Havel coughed again as he saw their heads weaving.

*Trying to figure out what's going on,* he thought, carefully not thinking of the probability that he'd be dead in a few minutes. *Got to get closer before the impossible becomes visible.*

At about fifteen yards they goggled and halted. Havel came up to one knee and drew, the familiar push-pull effort.

*Snap.* An instant later, the crack of a bodkin point on sheet metal as the arrow punched into a black-painted shield.

A soldier yelled and danced, shaking his shield and screaming—four inches of arrowshaft had pinned his forearm to the plywood. Havel ducked back as another crossbow bolt went by with an eerie *whuppt* of cloven air, close enough that he felt the wind of it on the sweat-wet skin of his face.

Movement brought his head around, with the bow rising behind it. He lowered it again as he saw the CORA fighter lever himself over the palisade.

"Get down, you fool!" Havel shouted, crouched back under the ballista's shield.

The rancher's man looked at him, then jerked and grunted as two bolts hammered into his chest. He toppled backward, but three more heads followed, and then hands held up a pair of thick shields. . . .

Eric shot once more and then slowly toppled over backward in a dead faint.

"I am getting too old for this shit," Havel wheezed, suddenly exhausted beyond bearing. Then he shouted:

"Corpsman! Stretcher party, here!"

"I'll look like a football!" Signe said. "All over stiches!"

"Actually, you look more beautiful than a sunset," Havel said. "See? I'm learning!"

She smiled back at him from the cot, then winced as motion pulled at the shoulder wound. She drifted back off to sleep.

Aaron Rothman sighed. "Thank God for morphine," he said. "I really, really hope someone is planting opium poppies!"

The big hospital tents were crowded; mostly CORA ranchers and their men, but more Bearkillers than he liked—it would have been politically dicey to hold them all back. There was a smell of disinfectant and blood, faces waxy and pale under the light of the Coleman lanterns. Gasoline stoves kept it fairly warm, but the air was close and stuffy as well.

"Her brother was just faint from loss of blood," Rothman said. "I gave him some plasma and a painkiller; he'll be sore with all those superficial cuts and punctures, but he had his tetanus shots, thank *God.*"

"What about Signe?" Havel asked, his face impassive.

"I used the pin test," Rothman said, holding one up. "She's got feeling and movement in all the fingers and no numb spots on the arm, so there isn't any nerve damage to speak of. The clavicle's cracked, though, and the cut muscles will take some time to heal. Full function, or nearly, but not for a while, and she'll need physical therapy."

Havel gusted a sigh. "Could have been a lot worse," he said.

Then he went down the rows of cots; for many of them

it *had* been a lot worse. He talked with those who could use it, gave a nod and a touch to others.

"Thanks!" a young Bearkiller they'd picked up in Grangeville said, with a smile despite the broken leg.

"Been there, done that," Havel said, grinning back.

The grin died as he ducked out of the tent's entrance, pulling on his armored gauntlets and settling his helmet; for one thing, the blanket-wrapped bodies of the dead weren't far away, waiting for friends and relatives to take them away, or for time to free up for burial details. For another, out here the smoke of the burning castle still lay thick, in the cold gray light just before dawn. The tower had fallen in a torrent of flame and sparks hours ago, and most of the rest of the palisade still smoldered.

Also present were the prisoners taken, two score of them; all the guards were Bearkillers or Mackenzies, most of them lightly wounded.

The CORA fighters and camp followers gathered glaring in the dark chill of morning, bundled up in down jackets and muffled in wool scarves. Breath steamed. Enough could be seen of their faces to know their mood, though; some were bandaged, and all had lost friends or family in the swarming, confused fight through the Protector's burning fort.

"*String the bastards up!*" sounded again; the Bearkillers turned their horses' heads outward, and a few of the kilted clansfolk reached over their shoulders for arrows.

Havel opened his mouth. Before he could speak, another voice sounded—John Brown, the CORA delegate.

"Go on!" he shouted, waving his hands. "These folks fought for us—do you want to start a battle with them, too? Go on—go on back to your tents. We're civilized people here, by God; we're Americans, not a lynch mob. Git!"

Then the leathery bearded rancher turned to Havel. "Sorry about that."

"No problem, but we'd better get under way," Havel said. *Everyone's gotten a bit rougher-edged since the Change.*

"Well, we've got the roadway through the fort cleared and the bridge is ready," Brown said. "Pretty hot and smoky, though."

Havel shrugged. "Well over half of them got out of the

castle. We need to make sure of them before they get west to their other fort."

Josh Sanders came up, leading Havel's horse. Havel swung into the saddle with a clink and rustle of chainmail; the horse was a strawberry roan mare, not quite as well-trained as Gustav. He quieted it and stroked a gloved hand down its neck.

"No sign of a rear guard?"

The Hoosier grinned. "Boss, once they bugged out of the castle, that bunch straggled so bad I'm surprised they managed to get *anyone* together. But they're closed up into one group now, more or less, and less the wounded they've been leaving behind. Stopped about two hours ago, but not for long is my guess. They remembered to take their bicycles, at least."

"Good work, Josh," he said. "Aylward's people are in position?"

"Got into place about the time the fight was over here. That Brit's pretty damn good in the woods."

Will Hutton was ready at the head of the Bearkiller column, a hundred armored riders with Sanders's scouts in a clump before, and their supply echelon on wagons and packhorses behind. Havel trotted down the column of fours and into position at the front beside Luanne Larsson, where she rode with the outfit's flag drooping from her lance in the still, cold air.

A sudden gust snapped it out, brown and red in the soot-laden breeze; humans coughed, and horses stamped and snorted, tossing their heads in a jingle of bridles.

Ahead was the column of smoke from the castle, bending towards them like a reaching hand. On either side the mountains reared steep and rugged; to the north the dawn sun gilded the snowpeaks, leaving the blue slopes below in shadow.

"This part ought to work fairly well," he said.

Will Hutton nodded and spat thoughtfully aside. "Whole strategy feels sort of . . . odd, Mike."

"Lady Juniper *is* odd." Havel grinned. "And it's her idea. Yeah, it's not my own first impulse—I was always the kill-'em-all-let-God-sort-'em-out type by natural inclination, and God knows life is cheap these days—but I can see her point, long-term. And she put this whole deal together."

He raised his arm and chopped it westward. With the sun at their backs, the long shapes of horse and rider lay before them, and the hooves trod the shadows down as the Bear-killers advanced. The honed edges of the lanceheads above caught the dawn light with a rippling sparkle like stars on the sea.

"Here," Sam Aylward said.

West of Santiam Pass, Route 20 wound between forested hills that crowded close to the roadway. Eventually it swung north and east for a while before turning west and then south again, like a long U around an outthrust ridge of the mountains that reared ever higher to Three Fingered Jack on the north and Mount Washington to the south.

Creeks brawled down from the steep slopes on either hand; they were west of the Cascade crest here, and the extra moisture showed—more Douglas fir and western hemlock, less lodgepole pine. The forest was dense, dark green, seeming to wait eagerly for the heavy snows to come, breathing a cold clear scent of pine and moist earth.

*Speaking of moisture . . . hope Lady Juniper's magic actually works. A blizzard would bugger things for fair.*

The Englishman cocked an eye at the sky; about noon, not quite time for the party to begin, but getting there, and he didn't like the look of the clouds. It was chilly enough to make him think that might mean snow, too—they were four thousand feet up here, with wet air sliding in from the Pacific, and it was December, albeit only just.

*Just enough to make me doubt me sanity, wearing this Jock skirt,* he thought wryly.

In fact, the kilt wasn't all that uncomfortable—the Jocks *had* worn them in all seasons in the Scottish Highlands, after all, with a climate that made western Oregon look like Barbados. The colors were good camouflage, and the boost to morale was more than worth it. Few of these people had been fighters before the Change, any more than they'd been farmers; wearing strange clothing helped them adjust to doing things strange to them.

There was a clatter and rustle as the Mackenzies moved into position; a lot of them were puffing from the night march in full gear, but nobody had fallen out. He grinned slightly to himself at the thought; after the past eight months, most of them were stronger and fitter than they'd ever been in their lives—Yanks had tended to lard before the Change, but he hadn't seen a fat one for months now.

*Now if only they were better shots,* he thought.

About a dozen out of fifty were what he'd call passable archers, and as for the rest . . .

*Well, they can hit a massed target at close range. Most of the time. And we've got plenty of shafts along.*

He looked up and down the stretch of road. There were four abandoned vehicles in sight, all shoved off the road—courtesy of the Protector's men when they moved in on Route 20—but one was impossible, a heavy truck. The other three included two ordinary four-doors and a Ford Windstar van, and should do nicely.

"That one, that one, that one, and put them there. Move your arses, Mackenzies!"

A platoon's-worth flung themselves on the vehicles. They weren't easy to move, with months for the transmission fluid to solidify, and resting on the rims of the flat wheels, but enough musclepower served. Once the cars were in place, more hands rocked them until they went over on their sides, spanning the whole width of the road and its verges, presenting their undersides to the enemy. Those would stop a crossbow bolt well enough, and they were too high to easily climb over. Of course, that meant they were also too high for defenders to shoot or stab over the top.

"Right, get rocks and dirt and logs; get a fighting platform in behind them," Aylward went on. "Move it!"

The section leaders gathered around him, shaggy in their war cloaks, leaves and twigs pushed into the netting of the hoods drawn up over their bowl helmets.

"Look up there," Aylward said, pointing northwest up the road. "We're a good five hundred yards down from that curve. I want two sections"—eighteen archers—"behind the barricade. The rest of you, get your people up on the slopes either side—no more than fifty yards total, but I want each and every one to have a good tree to hide behind and a clear field of fire. Go do it!"

Everyone did. Aylward watched, which made him itch; circumstances and the growth of the Mackenzies had pushed him into an officer's boots, much against his will.

He comforted himself by walking back up the road and looking to either side. You *couldn't* see far; the verges at the edge of the road's cleared swath were thick with Pacific rhododendron, vine maple and bear grass. *His* eye could trace the Mackenzies settling in, but once they were motionless, only knowing where they were let him see them.

"Good enough," he muttered to himself. "In a couple of years, they'll be *bloody* good, if I do say so myself."

A check behind the barricade showed that everyone there had a good step, high enough to shoot over the metal, but convenient for ducking down. They also all had a spear to hand, if things got close and personal; he'd picked two sections with people who'd fought the Protector's men back before Lughnassadh....

"Christ, they've got me doing it," he muttered to himself again, as he climbed up into the woods. "It didn't even occur to me to think *August.*"

There was a little more work for him here. The archers were spaced about three paces apart, with a tree or bush to conceal each—and with the hoods of their cloaks pulled up over their helmets and shadowing their faces, they were *hard* to see. A few had picked spots that would block their fields of fire, though. He patiently corrected those, with a quick explanation why and how to check—he wanted them to do better next time—and made sure that each had two bundles of extra arrows from the packhorses, which made a hundred and twenty arrows altogether, counting those in the quivers. Most of the archers had a dozen or so pushed point-down into the dirt or a convenient fallen log, which was a good trick—faster than reaching back over your shoulder.

"Listen for the horn calls, lad," he repeated again and again, or variations, with the odd slap on the shoulder. "Just do what you've practiced, and it'll all come right."

*And if things go wrong, the order will be to scarper upslope, right quick; we can climb the hillsides faster than the Protector's men; their armor is heavier and they're going to be a lot more tired.*

All done, he settled down to wait behind a hundred-foot-tall lodgepole pine on the west side of the road, taking out a hardtack and gnawing quietly at it, his bow across his knees. It took him half an hour to eat it—if you went too fast, you risked damage to your teeth, which since the Change was no joke. It was about two o'clock when the scout stationed at the northward curve of the road stepped out onto the pavement, waved her bow overhead, then vanished back into the undergrowth.

"That's that, then," Aylward said, standing and dusting a few crumbs off the front of his jack.

"How many's that?" Havel asked, as they stopped to pick up a wounded straggler.

"Twenty," Luanne said. "Not counting the three deaders."

Havel made a *tsk* sound as he looked at the steep slopes on either side. In theory the Protector's men could have set an ambush; Josh's scouts were only a couple of hundred yards ahead, and the only way to get a horse into the forest would be to dismount and lead it. The enemy still had half again his numbers. In practice . . .

"The Protector thought he had a real army because they had weapons and ranks," he said to her father. "Big mistake."

Will Hutton nodded; he had his helmet pushed back, and now he pulled it back down by the nasal bar.

"Sure was," he said, looking as a Bearkiller stretcher party carried the wounded prisoner back towards the ambulance wagons. An abandoned bicycle lay tumbled not far away.

"What was that you said about these here?"

"Low unit cohesion," Havel said with a grin. "Aka, bugging out on your buddies. Gunney Winters would have been livid. Still, they may improve with time, if we let them."

He looked around, matching the terrain to the maps. "All right, people!" he said, louder. "Dismount by squads, water and feed the horses, and final equipment check. We're going to be caught up to them pretty soon."

"Timing's going to be tricky," Hutton said. "Don't want too much of a battle goin' before we get there."

Havel shrugged. "Well, that wasn't Lady Juniper's plan," he said. "We'll see what happens."

Aylward made a sound of disgust between his teeth. "Straight into it," he said contemptuously.

"You'd rather they were alert?" someone muttered.

He snorted; the Mackenzies had learned to do what the one in charge told them when a fight was brewing, but they weren't long on deference. And they *did* love to talk; probably picked it up from Juniper and her original crew.

The column of Protectorate troops halted and milled around when they saw the barricade; through binoculars he could see some of them looking over their shoulders.

There was shouting and shoving before they all got off their bicycles; eventually a banner eddied forward, black with the lidless eye in red, hanging from a crossbar on the pole. The enemy opened out into a deep formation, sixteen across and eight or nine deep, and began to trot forward; the man beside the flag had a plumed helmet, and was almost certainly the leader—the baron, in Protector Arminger's terminology. Besides the plume and the position, he was wearing a chain mail hauberk, and that was officer's garb in the Portland Protective Association's forces.

*Probably has to lead from the front this time,* Aylward thought. *Or the others won't follow at all.*

Lady Juniper's plan depended on demoralization. It was time to help that along. . . .

He rose, throwing a wisp of dried grass in the air to gauge the wind direction, and looking at the extremely helpful banner to do the same for the target area. Seventy-five yards, give or take a foot; not too far . . .

"Now," he said, throwing off his cloak and plucking an arrow out of the ground to set it on the string of his war bow.

A signaler put his cowhorn bugle to his lips and blew. *Huuu-huuu-huuuu,* the weird dunting bellow echoed back from the hills. A banshee squeal answered it; this time they had *four* bagpipers. They stayed hidden, but all along the hillsides on both sides of the road Mackenzie archers shed their war cloaks and stepped forward, bows in their hands.

The sudden appearance and rustle of movement combined with the eerie keening of the pipes to make them appear more numerous than they were; imagination painted scores more behind them in the trees. Aylward watched as the ranks eddied and milled, heads twisting this way and that—and behind them again. The baron beside the banner of the Lidless Eye drew his sword.

*Well, I can read your bloody mind, mate. Neck or nothing, a charge is the only way you're getting out. Got to put a stop to that.*

Swift as a thought, he drew the string to the angle of his jaw, the heavy muscle bunching in his right arm, then let the string fall off the balls of his fingers. The cord went *snap* against his bracer; before the sensation faded the next was drawn, and the next, and the next. Pale and gray and directionless, the light was still good for shooting; he could see the slight glint as the arrow hit the top of its arc, and anticipate the sweet smooth feeling you got when you knew it was going to hit. . . .

The bagpipes and the rustling and clanking of his own men must have masked the whistle of cloven air. The first arrow smashed into the face of the Protector's baron beside the nose. The steel point and six inches of the shaft came through just behind the hinge of his jaw, sending him turning in place with a high muffled shriek. The second hit him in the upper chest, made a metallic *tink!* sound as it broke two metal rings and sank almost to the feathers. The third struck between his shoulder blades as he continued the turn; that ended with his knees buckling and the armor-clad body falling limp with a thud and last galvanic drum of feet on the pavement. The conical helmet rolled away, its strap burst by the force of impact.

Aylward flung up his bow. The bagpipers fell silent, and the Mackenzie archers stood motionless, their bows up, the pointed-chisel bodkin heads of the arrows aimed down at the dense mass of men on the road. The silence was so profound for an instant that he could hear the sheet metal of the helm ring on the asphalt of the roadway.

His own mind could paint what came next; the whistling of the arrow-storm, the hundreds of shafts arching out and down, the punching impact on armor and flesh and bone, the screams of the wounded and dying . . .

*And those laddies don't know that most of us can't shoot as well as I, or draw a hundred-pound stave. So their imaginings will be still more vivid and unpleasant.*

A Mackenzie beside him raised a white cloth on the butt-end of a spear and walked forward, gulping a little as crossbows were leveled. He got to within talking distance of the men grouped around Arminger's standard, but when he spoke he pitched his voice to carry to the whole group:

"You'd better surrender," he said, keeping his voice neutral—getting their hackles up was the last thing he wanted. "I'm authorized to offer you your lives, food for the winter and homes for you and any families you had back at the fort—for everyone not guilty of war crimes."

The second-in-command swallowed and looked up from where he'd been staring, at the leaking corpse of the baron. Blood pooled under the slack arrow-transfixed face and spread; there was an astonishing lot in a human body, and it looked worse when it spread on a watertight surface like this. The fecal smell of violent death was muted by the chill of the air, but nonetheless final and unpleasant for that.

A bugle sounded from the northeast, and the clopping roar of hundreds of hooves on pavement. Every face in the Protector's force turned over their shoulder as the Bear-killers came in sight. They pulled up four hundred yards away, their armored bulk and their horses filling the roadway from verge to verge; heads swiveled back to the silent longbowmen on either side, ready to shoot.

Aylward hid his grin. The expression felt far too carnivorous to let into the negotiations.

"You can see we've treated our prisoners well," Juniper Mackenzie said. "And you can see that you can't fight us all—we're on both sides of you."

She was close enough to the western wall of the castle at Upper Soda for the troops who lined the gatehouse and ramparts to hear her plainly. The air was still and cold in the bright day, and her voice had always been bigger than you'd think to look at her. They stirred and murmured along the fighting platform behind the sharpened logs; she could hear the buzz of their voices in the intervals between her sentences, and see the twinkle of sunlight on edged metal. She was *almost* close enough to see expressions.

Unfortunately that put her well within crossbow range, not to mention that of the great dart-casters and ballistae. The men beside and in front of her—unarmed prisoners from the eastern castle, at once witnesses and shield— knew that too. Their sweat stank of fear, and her stomach turned a little at the smell. Then the baby kicked, and she gave a little *whoosh* of effort as she kept herself erect and forced her hands away from the gravid curve of her stomach.

Yet it heartened her. "Just look!" she said.

Memory filled in what lay behind. The University militia had come tramping in step; it was even more impressive when they fanned out across the grassland to either side of the road. Three hundred long pikes, moving in bristling unison like the hair on some steel-spined porcupine's back; as many crossbowmen to either side; flanking those her own clan's archers, moving to the wild skirl of the pipes and the hammering of the Lamberg drums, shaggy in war cloak and kilt and plaid, voices roaring out:

> *"From the hag and the hungry goblin*
> *That into rags would rend ye;*
> *All the sprites that stand by the Horned Man*
> *In the Book of Moons defend ye—"*

"And to be sure," she murmured softly to herself, "the trebuchets and catapults are impressive, too, in their own way. And Mike and Aylward on the other side with their merry bands."

She took another breath; beneath her plaid her hand moved in a certain sign, and her will poured into the words:

"All the world is full of dying," she went on. "Why add more? We've food enough for all of you and your families"—the reports said about half did have their womenfolk and children along—"for the winter, and there's land and work in plenty, or we'll help you go anywhere else you will. We know the most of you did what you had to do to live; it's only your leaders who are evil. But don't you want to live like free men again? Don't you want to live without hurting anyone, live honestly without being surrounded by hate and fear? And to show we're honest, here are ten men who're your friends to tell you how we've treated them. Don't let the men who use you and abuse you silence them!

"Go," she added in a normal conversational voice.

Ten of the prisoners trotted forward towards the gate of the castle. They'd volunteered—they must be brave men, and none of them seemed to be very fond of the Protector right now, or his barons. And she *didn't* think the baron of Upper Soda would dare order them shot down, or thrown into prison.

*It's a cleft stick he's in, and nobody to blame but himself,* she thought. Bionn an fhirinne searbh an bhfeallaire: *The truth is bitter to the betrayer!*

Actions had consequences. You didn't have to be in the Craft for the Threefold Rule to apply.

"You have until tomorrow morning," she called aloud. "Be wise and make peace, and you'll see tomorrow's sun set."

She turned and walked away . . . or waddled, as Judy would have put it. The rest of the prisoners crowded along behind her, until she spread her arms to remind them to hang back a little. Still, the distance to her buggy seemed eternal, the climb into it hard—even with Eilir and Astrid to assist, and as well try to catch the moon with a spoon as keep them back! The whole party walked back to the safety of the allied armies. . . .

*Armies!* She thought. *And aren't we getting grand! That Astrid has a talent for the grandiloquent, that she does!*

Luther Finney waited with the others; he was the University Committee's man here, though not in command of their militia.

"Juney, you've got more guts than sense!" he scolded. "You shouldn't be doing that sort of thing in your condition!"

Juniper smiled at him. "Well, why not, Luther? I'm doing it for *him,* too."

She laid her hand on her stomach and looked at Mike Havel. "What better reason?"

He nodded soberly. "And that was quite a speech, too," he said. "I think—"

Everyone froze as her expression altered. "Oh, my," she said, both hands on her stomach this time. "Oh, *my.*"

Dennis and Chuck were at her side as if by magic, supporting her elbows.

"I think someone should fetch Judy," Juniper said. "This feeling's all too familiar."

Exhausted, Juniper lay back against the pillows and looked down at the tiny crumpled face in the crook of her arm; amazed blue eyes looked back at her from beneath a faint fuzz of wispy red-gold hair. For once she didn't feel guilty about having a fair-sized tent all to herself; the baby needed warmth, and the Coleman stove and air mattress made it fairly comfortable.

"And my own battered, stretched, sore-isn't-the-word self can use a little comfort," she muttered to herself.

*Thank You,* she added to the image of the Mother-of-All on the portable altar in one corner of the tent. Incense burned there, sweet amid the canvas-and-earth scents and the underlying tang of sweat and blood.

Judy came back in, buttoning the sleeves of her shirt and yawning; she'd taken out the last of the soiled linen, and the birthing stool.

"Half the camp is still up," she said. "The other half is getting up and asking for the news. You'd think nobody had ever had a baby before."

"Born on a battlefield, poor mite," Juniper said. "My little Rudi, my warmth in a darkling time."

A voice coughed outside. Juniper sighed, weary but not ready to sleep just yet.

"Yes, yes," she said.

Four men crowded in; Dennis, Aylward, Luther Finney . . . and Mike Havel. He was out of his armor and padding, looking younger and less strange—more as a man might have before the Change.

He was also carrying a tray; porridge cooked with dried apples and cherries, cream, scrambled eggs. Juniper's nose twitched, and she was suddenly conscious of a bottomless hunger, deeper than anything since the harvest.

Judy took the well-wrapped baby and handed him to Luther; the elderly farmer took the tiny bundle with the calm ease of experience as father and grandfather and great-grandfather.

As she helped Juniper sit up and fluffed the pillows, Judy launched a preemptive strike:

"Easy ten-hour delivery, nice bouncing six pounds, eight ounces baby boy, with all the limbs and facilities—including good hearing, by the way."

The women's eyes met: *And you'd scarcely know he's nearly a month early.*

"And a good set of lungs, as you may have heard earlier. He's eaten; the mother should now."

The other men awkwardly admired the baby. The flap of

the tent opened again as Eilir darted in with Astrid on her heels.

*Mom!* she signed, her gestures broad with excitement. *Mom! Someone inside hit the baron on the head with an ax, and they're fighting each other—the ones who want to surrender have opened the gate! Chuck's going there now!*

Luther Finney put the infant back on Juniper's stomach, careful even in his haste. Her arms took it, but her eyes held Mike Havel for an instant.

"Mike . . . keep my word for me," she said quietly.

A silent nod, and he was gone. She sighed and lay back; a wail, and she put the baby to her breast.

"It's not the quietest of worlds, my sweetling," she murmured, stroking his cheek. "But I'll try to make it the best I can for you."

# CHAPTER THIRTY-THREE

"Yeah, she's calling him Rudi—after her husband; he didn't make it through the day of the Change," Mike Havel said.

They were all standing and watching with satisfaction as the long wagon train trundled west through the little town of Sisters and up Route 20. The wagons—everything from old buckboards from rodeo shows to post-Change made-from-anything makeshifts—were loaded high with the Bearkillers' gear, but all of it was on a solid foundation of plump grain sacks, usually two or three deep. It was eerily appropriate that Cascade Street was lined with false-front stores like something out of a Western movie; pre-Change pretense and makeshifts done after the Change in desperate earnest.

The horses' breath puffed out in the chill as they bent to the traces, but the road was smooth and still dry. . . .

*At least here,* Havel thought, looking westward at the clouds that hid the mountains. *I hope to hell we don't get any more snow—we've had to shovel more than I like already. And this is definitely the last load until spring!*

Signe was walking well now if she was careful, but her left arm was in a sling and immobilizing elastic bandage. Every once in a while she'd reach over and, very very cautiously, scratch. Right now she was obviously counting back nine months, reaching a conclusion that pleased her, and smiling.

"I sort of envy her," she said wistfully. "So much death . . . it makes you feel better, new lives starting."

"Well, when you're feeling better—" Mike grinned and dodged as she cuffed at him with her good arm.

"Are you sure it's all right for us to drop in on them?" Signe said. "I'd love to, but—"

"We're just taking the headquarters group," Havel said. "Bearkillers are still the blue-eyed boys with our allies; they want to give us a feed before we settle in."

"We're going to be busy this winter," her father said, only half paying attention to the discussion. "How many did you say were living in the area we've been handed?"

"About two thousand, including the ex-POWs who want to settle on our land," Havel said. "Which puts our total numbers up by eight times overnight! Mostly it's people who managed to survive hiding out in the hills; families and little groups. Surprising so many came through, so close to Salem . . . but human beings are *tough.*"

He thought for a moment. "A lot of them are at the end of their tethers, wouldn't make it through the winter. How much land would you say it would take to support a family?"

Ken Larsson began to scratch his head, then stopped when he realized he was about to use his steel hook.

"In the Willamette? Well, real intensive gardening style . . . say five acres. It's *good* land and the weather's reliable."

Havel nodded, feeling things slip into place in his head.

"OK, let's kill a lot of birds with a few stones. Look, we've got a hundred and twenty A-lister fighters to support. An armored lancer takes a lot of supporting; it's not just the gear and horses, though those're no joke. He—"

Pamela stood with her hand on Ken's shoulder; she cleared her throat ostentatiously.

"—or she, in some cases . . . anyway, they need time to practice. So they can't be farming all the time. And we can't have them all camping on the front lawn and hand them a peck of meal and a side of bacon every week, either. Christ Jesus, it's inconvenient, not having any money! Swapping's so damned slow and clumsy. So, we've got a lot of vacant land, a lot of people with no seed, stock or tools, and an army to support—an army we're definitely going to need for the foreseeable future. Let's put 'em together."

He tapped the back of one hand against the palm of the other. "See, we give each Bearkiller family a square mile, we jigger it so they've got a good mix of plowland, pasture, woods and such."

"That's a lot of land," Hutton said. "Even if we get some reapers and horse-drawn gear together."

"Yeah, but we don't just give them a farm," Havel said. "We need those A-listers for fighting. They'll be the local Justice of the Peace and they'll train and command the militia, and look after the roads and local school."

Josh Sanders nodded. "Sort of decentralized. I like it. How do we handle the fightin' side, though?"

"They have to equip and bring . . . oh, say three or four lancers and an apprentice for each when there's a call-up, and we make arrangements to check training and so forth, and muster like the National Guard did back before the Change in peacetime."

"That'll be a heap of work," Hutton said. He shrugged his shoulders. "Still, what's life for, if you don't have a job worth doin'? Most of our A-listers, they've got some farmin' background, too. The ones who don't can learn fast."

Havel nodded. "Some of these people we're taking in, the clueless ones, they can work for the Bearkiller family— help work the farm, get paid in food and clothes, and a house and a big garden, too. The rest, say ten or twelve families, they each get thirty acres and a yoke of oxen and tools we make or trade for, and they help the Bearkiller with his . . . OK, Pam, her . . . *their,* goddamnit . . . farm. More land for troop and squadron commanders, of course, but they'll get more responsibilities, too. We at Larsdalen sort of supervise the whole setup and collect a reasonable tax through the JPs, and keep a chunk of land around the house for ourselves; your original spread, Ken, and a bit more."

He beamed at the others. Will Hutton was nodding and rubbing thoughtfully at his jaw.

"Sounds sensible enough, Mike," he said. Brightening: "Even without money, we could arrange the taxes pretty fair—you know, every tenth calf or sheaf or something, or work with their plow teams; the A-listers collect it, and pass on a share. And heck, we'll need our own infantry, too, pikes 'n' bows for the farmers. Hmmm, and mebbe these apprentices, they could sort of spend some time at Larsdalen, learning?"

"Sounds *good*," Josh Sanders said. "I was wondering how we were going to keep our edge once we settled down.

With farms that size, we could get all the, ah, the renters, to clump together, too. I could help the A-listers run up some sort of berm and so forth, so people could duck in if there's an attack, while we pass the word and mobilize."

They turned to the others, their smiles fading a little when they saw the raised eyebrows on Ken Larsson and Pamela and Aaron Rothman.

Ken cleared his throat. "You could call the square mile grants *fiefs,* for starters," he said. "That was the traditional term. Or a *knight's fee.* And you could call the apprentices *pages* and then *squires.* . . ."

Havel frowned. "Well, so much for my brilliant originality. Someone's come up with this before?" he said. "I was thinking of *strategic hamlet* for the A-lister grants, actually."

Pamela coughed into her hand, and Rothman giggled. The swordmistress spoke: "Ah . . . yeah, Boss. Something a little *like* it has happened before. You might want to make a few modifications. . . ."

"Welcome to Dun Juniper, Lord Bear, you and yours," Dennis Martin Mackenzie said formally.

He was heading up the ceremonial guard of archers and spearmen, down at the base of the plateau that held the Hall. Juniper could just barely hear him up here on the flat roof of the gatehouse tower; there was a murmur from the crowd waiting inside the gate, and it was a fair distance—they'd run the new approach road up the side of the slope below the palisade, so that you had to come up with your right hand towards the wall and your shield arm uselessly away.

She could see the Bearkillers all look up for a moment, and grinned to herself. The little plateau looked a lot more imposing now that the palisade was all in place; twenty-five feet of steep hillside, and then the thirty-foot rampart of thick logs, sharpened on top. Sunset light sparkled on the spearheads of the guards on the fighting platform behind the parapet, and hearth smoke drifted up in near-perfect pillars; it was a still, chilly early-winter evening. Snow had fallen last night; it wouldn't last long, and things would be dismally muddy when it went, but for now the thick blanket gave field and branch and roof a fairyland splendor.

While they talked with Dennis, she hurried down the interior stairway, arriving in time to be composed and dignified as they walked up the roadway, leading their mounts.

They'd come unarmored; all wore broad-brimmed dark hats with silver medallions on their bands, and they were all dressed alike in what wasn't quite a uniform. Boots, loose dark trousers and lapover jackets secured by sashes and broad leather belts, with a bear's head embroidered in red over the left breast . . .

She felt something of that first shock again, like an echo from distant cliffs. Her body remembered the way he moved, light and quick and easy, with a relaxed alertness. . . .

*Mom,* Eilir signed discreetly. *Stop it with the lascivious drooling! You're practically ripping his clothes off with your eyes!*

*I am not!* she signed, and then thought silently to herself: *Not quite. Still, if this one were a movie star in the old days . . . as the saying goes, there wouldn't have been a dry seat in the house.*

The tall young woman beside him . . . *Her* looks were Nordic perfection, in an outdoorsy way, down to the long butter-blond braids that framed her face. Except for a small scar across the bridge of her nose, almost a nick, leaving a slight dent, and a continuation on one cheek; her coat hung loose, and her left arm was in a sling. That didn't seem to dampen her spirits, though; she smiled as she walked, curving in instinctively towards the Bearkiller leader.

*Ah, well,* Juniper thought wistfully. *I have my Rudi . . . and the best of the bargain, perhaps. Lord Bear's luck is hard on those close to him, I think.*

As the Bearkillers walked up the roadway, Dorothy cut loose with her pipes, pacing formally back and forth along the battlement of the gatehouse. That was three stories of squared logs up, but it was still loud. Juniper and her Advisors—it was becoming a title, somehow—stood to meet the Bearkiller leaders. She was in full fig; jacket, ruffled shirt, kilt, plaid fastened over her shoulder with a brooch, down to the flat Scots bonnet with antlers-and-moon clasp and raven feather and the little sgian dhu knife tucked into her right stocking. Most of the others were in kilts as well, and as much of the rest as could be hastily cobbled up—some of it had served as costumes, at Samhain.

The blond woman leaned closer to Lord Bear. Juniper had a great deal of experience at picking voices out from background noise; it went with being a musician. She fought to keep her lips from quirking upward as she heard:

"Help, Mike! I've fallen into Brigadoon and I can't get out!"

"It's like . . . it's like Edoras, and the Golden Hall of Medusel!" Astrid said, waving an arm through the open gates at the carved and painted wood of the Hall. "Didn't I say so?"

"Oh, great, Hobbiton-in-the-Cascades," Eric grumbled.

*He* had new scars since she'd seen him that spring; long white ones on the backs of his hands, and several the same on his face; he'd also shaved his head, save for a yellow scalp lock on top. It all made him look older and grimmer, and there was a hard light in his eyes now, but his grin was still charming and reminded her of the boy he'd been.

The Bearkiller leader made a slight shushing sound, and his eyes met Juniper's. That gave her a slight jolt; it also made her sure as they narrowed slightly that he knew she'd overheard the remark, and met her suppressed grin with an equally discrete one of his own.

*I like this man,* she thought, and went on aloud:

"Lord Bear."

She glanced down the laneway; that was where they'd set their rampant-bear flag with with the polished bear skull on the top of its pole.

"Point taken," he said, acknowledging the flamboyant standard and his own title. Then he did grin. "My fiancée, Signe Larsson."

"I'm Juniper Mackenzie, chief of Clan Mackenzie," Juniper said, shaking hands and smiling. "And a musician before the Change. I'll play at your wedding, I hope!"

He went on with introductions for the rest of his party: "Angelica Hutton; our camp boss and quartermaster. My prospective brother-in-law, you've met. Only since then he's become Taras Bulba."

Eric snorted as he shook her hand; a strikingly pretty dark-skinned girl stood next to him. "Glad to see you again, Lady Juniper. And Mike has no sense of style. Besides which, I nearly got killed when my hair was caught in some barbed wire. My wife, Luanne. Née Hutton."

Lord Bear—*Mike Havel, let's not keep the show going* all *the time,* she thought—took up the thread smoothly:

"My father-in-law to be, Kenneth Larsson, engineer."

He looked to be nearly sixty, though fit: with another small shock Juniper realized he was the oldest person she'd seen in weeks; the first year of the Change hadn't been easy on the elderly. It took an instant before she realized that his left forearm ended at a cup and steel hook where his wrist and hand should be.

The woman beside him was in her thirties, tall and wire-slender, olive-skinned, with a narrow hawk-nosed face and russet-brown hair.

"Pamela Arnstein, our swordmistress—fencing instructor—and historian."

"Also the vet and horse doctor," she said. Her accent was Californian, like Dennis's.

Juniper let herself smile as she introduced her people in turn.

"This way," she said when the introductions were done. "Doubtless you've seen our wall—"

"Very impressive," Havel said, sounding like he meant it.

She nodded, proud, and even more proud of the cabins built against its inner surface; that meant every family living here had its own hearth at last. The rest of the four-acre plateau held the two-story Hall, flanked by two near-identical structures, an armory on one side and a school-library-guesthouse on the other. And sheds, workshops and storehouses, log-built on stone foundations.

It all looked a lot neater now that they'd had time to clean up the litter and lay flagstone paths to connect the buildings. Open space lay at the rear of the U, used for everything from soccer matches to public meetings, with another blockhouse tower to watch over the gully that separated the plateau from the hillside behind.

"This is where we started," she said. "There was nothing here but my cabin and some sheds, back before the Change."

Havel's brows rose; she could see that he was impressed again. "Log construction goes fast, but that's a hell of a lot of timber to cut, considering everything else you had to do."

Dennis cut in: "Lady Juniper's luck—Cascade Timber Inc. felled a couple of thousand trees before the Change, and hadn't gotten around to hauling the timber out. We just dragged it out and set it up."

Juniper nodded. "We've got other sites fortified pretty much like this, except that they're down in the flats," she said. "Dun Carson, Dun McFarlane and Dun Laughton—where the other septs of the clan are based."

Signe Larsson chuckled. When Juniper looked over at her, the younger woman said:

"It reminds me of a story I heard once, about some Scottish pirates who retired and settled down. They built three towns—Dunrobbin', Dunrovin', Dunleavin'."

"God, Mike, they have a *salad bar!*" Signe Larsson said, licking her lips. "Come *on,* Pam, give me a hand! That'll make three between us."

"Get me some too, would you, *askling?*" Havel said. "I won't say I'd kill for a green salad, but I'd certainly *maim.*"

She bounced up eagerly. "And this is the man who said a Finnish salad started with a dozen sausages," she cast over her shoulder.

"Impressive spread," Havel went on to his hostess.

Juniper nodded with what she thought was a pardonable smile of pride at the setting as well as the meal. During the rebuilding they'd taken all the interior partitions out of the first floor of her old cabin, save for the cubicle around the bathrooms; the kitchens were gone too, replaced by a long lean-to structure along the rear of the building with salvaged woodstoves and clan-built brick hearths.

That made it easier to use the ground floor of the Hall for public occasions; tonight tables along the rear wall held the food, and clansfolk and guests sat along the outer perimeter elsewhere; the old fireplace was freestanding now, crackling and adding a reddish glow to the butter-yellow of the kerosene lamps. Holly and ivy festooned the walls, to invite the Good Folk in and bring luck; there were baskets of apples and hazelnuts laid in evergreen boughs, twined with wheat stalks and dusted with flour. Above the hearth where the huge Yule log burned were candles: red, green, white for the season;

green and gold and black for the Sun God; and white, red and black for the Great Goddess.

And a big barrel had been set up, full of water and thick with apples.

"Bobbing for apples?" Havel said.

Juniper grinned. "Symbolizing the apples of eternal life," she said. More gravely: "After the past year, we need reminders."

Two roast wild pigs and a haunch of venison held pride of place on either side of it, and roast chicken and barons of beef. But there were heaps of greens as well, the last of the winter gardens: tomatoes, onions, peppers, steamed cauliflower and broccoli, boiled carrots, mashed turnips, potato salad with scallions and homemade mayonnaise, and potatoes grilled with pepper and garlic, mashed and whipped . . .

For dessert there were fresh fruit and dozens of pies, apple and blueberry and strawberry with rhubarb—honey sweetener instead of sugar, although next year they might be able to cultivate some sugar beets. There was even whipped cream, now that they had a decent dairy herd.

Dennis had the product of his brewery—it was getting a bit large to call it a micro—set up in barrels, along with the mead and wine and applejack.

Juniper waved a hand. "Yule is a major holiday, of course, and . . . well, right after the Change, we—my original bunch—just planted every garden seed we could get, regardless. So did most of the people around here, the ones who joined us later. Things were very tight until about June, and we're storing all we can, but you can't keep lettuce or green peppers, and we might as well eat the last of them while they're here. Things will be a lot more monotonous again come January and February."

*Monotonous, but ample,* she thought with profound satisfaction.

The thought of the storehouses and cellars full of wheat and barley and oats, of potatoes and cabbages and dried tomatoes and dried fruit and onions and parsnips and turnips and beets, of the herds and flocks in paddock and byre and pigpen, the full chicken coops, gave her a warm glow she'd never known before the Change. She'd never cared much about money, but hunger and hard work had taught her what real wealth was; it was being full and knowing you could eat well every coming day to next harvest—and that the seed for that harvest was safely in the ground.

Havel nodded. "You're certainly doing very well," he said.

The buzz of conversation rose to a happy roar as people filled their plates and made their way back to the seats. There were a hundred adults here, and many of the older children—the youngsters were over in the schoolhouse building, having their own dinner.

Dorothy Rose, their piper, strode up and down the open space within the tables, making what the charitable or extremely Scottish would consider music.

"You know why pipers walk up and down like that while they play?" Juniper asked.

Havel shook his head; so did Signe, back with a heaped plate, followed by Pam with two more.

"To get away from the music, of course," Juniper said.

They both laughed, although that didn't slow down their eating; roast pork with applesauce, she noticed, as well as the salads and steamed vegetables. She'd scattered the other Bearkillers among the people at the high table; Astrid was deep in conversation with Eilir again, catching up on all they'd missed in two weeks' separation.

When the plates were cleared, the children filed out.

"This is our . . . well, sort of a school play," she said.

The leads were Mary, Sanjay and Daniel. Mary got to play the Goddess with tinsel woven into her mahogany hair, as the Crone, while Sanjay was the Holly King, slain by the Oak King in a dramatic duel with wooden swords; the Goddess held a wand out over them during it, then made a speech about the Wheel of the Year. A chorus sang in the background, skipping around each other in a dance that looked quite pretty between the collisions.

It gave the kids a chance to show off what they learned in Moon School, and it didn't have to compete against TV.

"Errr . . . you're *all* pagans here now?" Havel said. "Not that I object—I'm a lapsed Lutheran myself—"

Juniper nodded: "Well, we call ourselves Witches. To be technical, we're rather old-fashioned Wiccans, at least my original group were, and something like two-thirds of those who've joined us since have signed up—as fast as we can run the Training Circle, with some corners cut. It's a new situation for us, having actual congregations!"

A little way down the table, Ken Larsson leaned forward to talk to her:

"Founder effect," he said. "First bunch in a community tend to have a disproportionate influence on what comes after."

He waved around the room with his fork. "I suspect this is happening all over the world—some leader or small group is lucky and smart and attracts individuals to join, and then they take on the same coloration, grabbing at anything that seems to work in a world of death. It certainly happened with us. I bet there will be some pretty weird results in a couple of generations."

Havel nodded. "Although—" He cut himself off and nodded again.

Juniper grinned. "Although we don't remind you much of pagans you met before the Change?" she said helpfully. "Although you might think the obsession with dressing up in costumes has survived?"

Havel coughed into his hand, then looked around as if he was contemplating something on the order of: *My, aren't the walls vertical today?*

Signe smiled slyly and nudged him with an elbow. "Gotcha, Lord Bear. Roll over and show your tummy, boy! You're whipped! I told you to leave all the diplomatic stuff to Dad."

Juniper took pity on him: "Types like that did get lot of attention before the Change," she said. "They weren't the whole story even then." She smiled. "Do I believe magic works since the Change? Of course! But I believe it worked before the Change, too, remember, and I never took"—she gestured at the decorations— "'My other car is a broomstick' bumper stickers literally."

"Err . . . thanks," he said. "It's nice to know we'll have sensible neighbors."

"Good save," Signe muttered in a stage whisper.

"If only we didn't have the *Protector* as a neighbor," Juniper said. "We've been fighting him most of the year. . . ."

"Us too," Havel said, and smiled grimly. "Oh, yes, the castles on Route 20 weren't our first encounter."

She frowned. "I think you mentioned . . . well, tale-telling is a Yule tradition too. We'd be very interested to hear it. If you wouldn't mind?"

"Not at all."

Juniper smiled and nodded. Havel looked as if he'd rather gouge out his own liver than talk in public, so . . .

She caught Signe Larsson's eye, and got a wink.

"In fact . . ."

She used a fork to ring a small iron triangle before her, tapping out a simple tune. The pleasant buzz of conversation died away.

"Our guest, Lord of the Bearkillers, has a tale to relate."

The buzz warmed up again for a second; hearing a story like that was entertainment now, and of high practical value as well. Everyone was eager for news from outside their strait local horizon.

"He and his had to fight earlier in the year—even before the Protector's men attacked Sutterdown. He'd like to tell us about it."

Havel gave her a stricken look. Signe gave him a nudge in the ribs, and he sighed and cleared his throat.

"We were around Craigswood, in Idaho," he said. "A bunch of bandits—they called themselves the Devil Dogs; a lot of them were in a biker gang before the Change—were trying to—"

Juniper leaned back with a cup of the mead and listened, smiling slightly to herself. Havel gave the story baldly, in what she imagined was the style of a military report.

The Chief of the Mackenzies let her storyteller's mind take them and weave in scent and sound and the thoughts of humankind; she could feel the beginnings of a song stirring and that felt very good indeed. Her fingers moved, unconsciously strumming—Mike Havel's theme, sharp as knife steel, but with hidden depths like rushing water, and a cold clear tang of danger. . . .

It had been too long a time since she'd done much composing, and she'd never had quite this sort of subject.

# CHAPTER THIRTY-FOUR

"So that's Larsdalen," Juniper Mackenzie said.

Her clansfolk—the score or so who'd come along to escort their allies home—clustered behind her, their horses stamping and snorting breath-plumes into the crisp evening air. The clouds had parted for a while, and the sun gilded every grass blade and spiderweb with diamonds. The noise and bustle of the Bearkiller caravan and their herds were behind for now, though she could hear the lowing of cattle in the distance.

Ahead the broad valley narrowed, rising to low forested heights north and west, shaggy with Douglas fir and yellow-leaved oak, silhouetted against the setting sun. Below the rolling lands were silent, grass waist-high in the pastures, the blocks of orchard and vineyard gone shaggy with a year's neglect and sere with winter—save that not one bunch of grapes hung withered into raisins. Willows dropped their tresses into ponds, and ducks swam. The big house on its hill was yellowish-red brick, mellow, bowered in its trees—from this distance the broken windows and doors swinging free couldn't be seen.

No smoke came from its chimneys, but you could imagine it, and a bustle of life among the barns and cottages and outbuildings, under the musty damp-leaf smell of the dying year.

Havel and his Signe walked past them, leading their horses. Hooves and feet crunched on the gravel of the drive. The Bear Lord stopped, handed her his helmet with its snarling namesake crest. His people gathered around him, mostly afoot; from the saddle Juniper could still see him over their heads.

"I've run far enough, come far enough. This earth is *mine*."

Signe whispered in his ear, and he nodded before he went on, a little louder: "None of its folk will want for bread or justice or a strong arm."

His eyes met Juniper's for an instant, wholly serious. He went to one knee, cut a section of turf loose, and plunged his hand into the moist dark dirt below. For a moment he looked at it, brought it to his lips for an instant.

Then he stood, his voice powerful, harder somehow than usual:

"And I shall be father to this land and all its people. So witness all of you here."

"So witness Earth—" He held out the handful of soil. His fist rose heavenward, clenching on the dirt:

"So witness Sky."

Juniper felt a sudden chill as the Bearkillers broke into cheers and waved their blades aloft; not fear or anger or alarm, but a whistling like great winds blowing through her soul. With an effort, she shrugged it aside and rode her own horse forward, Eilir at her side.

"Lord Bear," she said.

He turned, and something seemed to pass from his face; the crooked smile came back.

"You're still welcome to stay the night," he said. "We owe you Mackenzies, and it's a long ride back to your land."

Juniper laughed. "I'll take you up on that, and many of mine, often. But right now you'll have plenty to do settling in."

"God knows we do," he said, reaching up and shaking her hand. Then: "Sorry."

Juniper looked down and saw that the soil had rubbed off on her fingers as well.

"Not a problem," she said. "It's our Mother's earth, after all. Good luck—and blessed be. Merry met, and merry parting, and merry meet again!"

She nodded to Signe and turned her mount. They rode beside the graveled road, then cut across a pasture to let the great caravan pass, waving to faces they knew. Eilir turned in her saddle to exchange an exuberant two-armed wave to Astrid Larsson, before the youngster lifted her horse over a fence and rode whooping up the valley to her home.

*Astrid is* very *cool,* Eilir signed. *I am most definitely going to visit my anamchara a lot.*

Juniper nodded absently. Her daughter cocked an eye. *What's with, excessively spooky High Priestess Mom? You've got that the-Otherworld-is-talking-to-me look again.*

The Chief of the Mackenzies made herself shrug and laugh. "Nothing, my heart," she said.

*Oh, sure.*

"It's just . . . the King is Bridegroom to the land, and the Goddess . . ."

Eilir looked at her. *What is* that *supposed to mean?*

"I don't know," Juniper said.

Suddenly she wanted to be home, very badly. She legged her horse up to a trot, and the clansfolk settled their long-bows over their shoulders and followed, their plaids fluttering in the wind of their passage.

*I don't know,* she thought to herself, and made the Invoking sign. *But perhaps You will be telling me, eh?*

# Epilogue

A Wiccanning was a merry sort of ritual, introducing the newborn or new-come children to the Lady and the Lord; it was usually done during the day. Today was cold, but there had been a break in the clouds, and the great snow-peaks towered over them like citadels, the firs deep green and secret. Her people sang as they trod the path up to the sacred wood, carrying the bundled little ones and leading those a little older by the hand, and there was to be a party day afterwards, with roast spiced apples and games.

> "... *Come away, human child*
> *To the woods and waters wild;*
> *With a faerie, hand in hand ...*"

The oaks were leafless, and the spring burbled over rocks flecked with ice, but the last of the snow had melted; the grass within the trees was a soft muted frost-kissed green. The air smelled of earth and cold, a smell like deep sleep, and the chill freshness of the conifers. Eilir carried her brother—with the High Priestess and the High Priest both having children of their own to be welcomed, there would be a bit of juggling back and forth.

Outside the Circle they all stood silent for a moment, listening to the world. A crow cried somewhere, *gruk-gruk-gruk*, loud beneath the creaking of wood and the fall of water. Dennis sighed as he opened his eyes and looked down on the face of his daughter; Terry stood beside his mother and watched his newborn sister with something of the same wonder.

Sometimes casting the Circle was a thing that made the

hair bristle along Juniper's spine with awe. Today it was as if a hand was laid gently on her head, bringing spring's promise, dancing in a meadow starred with flowers. Sword and censer, water and salt went about the ring.

Chuck's face was smiling behind the elk mask as he spoke:

*"Now do I call you to this our Circle, great Lord of all, by Your many names; Green Man, Horned One, Trickster, Brother, Lover; mighty Warrior, strong Defender, wise Sage—"*

Her own voice was soft: *"I call You as Mother-of-All. Triple Moon, Ever-changing One, I invoke and call upon Thee."*

The words and gestures flowed, as each child was presented to the Quarters. For Chuck and Judy, things were a little different as they brought Mary and Sanjay and Daniel to the altar in turn, lighting a candle for each; the ritual changed a bit for an adoption:

*"We chose this child above all others. We freely bring Mary to the altar to thank the Lady and the Lord for joining her with us . . ."*

But for the solemnity of the moment she would have laughed with joy as the girl sipped gravely from the consecrated chalice and tasted the biscuit, face brimming with the moment, as the voices rose in the cry of *Blessed be*.

Then it was her own turn. Little Rudi had been quiet all through the rite, and he was now, as she took him from his sister's arms—still and wide-eyed even when she raised him to the Quarters, a small bundle of infinite possibilities.

She dipped her fingers into the chalice, and gently touched her son's forehead:

*"We bless you with Water and Earth. I name you—"*

Her tongue stumbled. Chuck looked at her curiously; that wasn't expected.

*"—in the Craft, I name you Artos,"* she said very softly.

The High Priest's eyes widened, and so did the Maiden's—Judy was close enough to hear as well. Chuck passed the candle over her son.

*"We bless you with Fire."* He waved incense smoke towards the baby. *"We bless you with Earth, Air, Fire and Water; Four do we give. The fifth is Spirit, and that lies in the gift of the Lady and the Lord."*

The rite flowed on; she touched the infant's lips with a drop of the wine, a crumb from the plate; then she reached into the cauldron for the piece of jewelry. Normally she'd hand that to the parents; here she would pin it on his blanket herself.

Her foot turned on the damp earth as she reached across the wide top of the hewn boulder that made the altar. With a gasp she righted herself, but for an instant Rudi-Artos slid as she struggled for balance. Then she had him in both hands . . .

. . . but not before his own had reached out in instinctive reflex. The perfectly formed pink fingers waved, then clamped down with the surprising grip-strength of newborns.

On the hilt of the ritual sword that rested across the altar in its rack; the long steel blade quivered and turned as the baby groped at the rawhide-wound grip.

Time stretched. There was a long-drawn *aaaaah* from those within the Circle, awe and a little fear and wonder, too.

Then she knew what she must do; or better, knew that she must step aside and let Another do through her. Of themselves, her hands rose, lifting Artos upward—presenting him not to the Quarters, but to the altar itself, and the Ones who presided over it. With that, she turned, her son still raised over her head, feet and arms making the double-V of power:

The voice that sounded out in tones as perfect as cut crystal was hers, but the words . . .

> *"Sad Winter's child, in this leafless shaw—*
> *Yet be Son, and Lover, and Horned Lord!*
> *Guardian of My sacred Wood, and Law—*
> *His people's strength—and the Lady's sword!"*

NEW IN HARDCOVER FROM ROC

# S. M. STIRLING

NATIONAL BESTSELLING AUTHOR OF *DIES THE FIRE*

## THE PROTECTOR'S WAR

"S. M. Stirling gives himself a broad canvas on which to display his talent for action, extrapolation, and depiction of the brutal realities of life in the absence of civilized norms."
—David Drake, Author of *The Far Side of the Stars*

0-451-46046-4